Kaoto

NORMAN D. MESSENGER

ISBN: 0-9674766-8-2

First Production: July, 2000

Kokopelli Publishing, L.L.C.
Colorado Springs, CO
www.kokopellipublishing.com

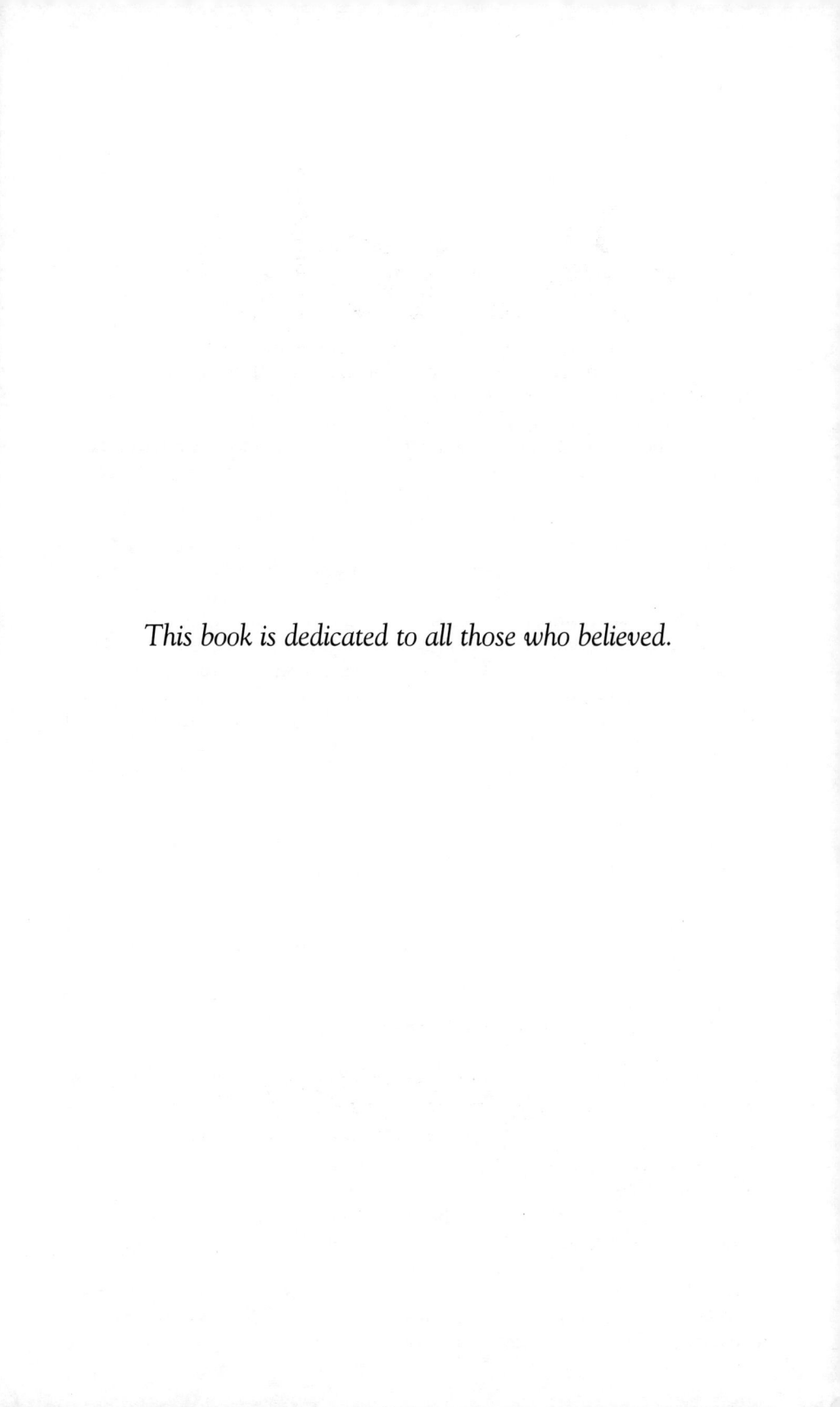

This book is dedicated to all those who believed.

Prologue

For this story I have used names that the Spanish and Native Americans have given to many pueblos or ruins of the Anasazi villages. It is easier for the reader to locate and identify them. Of course we have no indication of what the Anasazi themselves might have called these places, if indeed they had any names for them. They didn't leave us any written records to go by, and even later Indians didn't have real names for them or their homes.

The name "Anasazi" itself is a pseudonym. It is a Navajo word that was originally translated from the words Anaa' s' z. Anaa', meaning 'alien', s', meaning 'ruins' and z, indicating a state of being or condition of, as well as applying to humans. The Navajo People came upon Pueblo ruins not knowing who occupied them, and called them Anaa' s'. Alien ruins. As time went by, the phrase Anaa' s' z was coined to mean "people of ancient beings." The words Anaa' s' z were combined and anglicized to "Anasazi, The Ancient Ones," and it is the name we will always remember them by. Everything about the Anasazi is a mystery. We do not know where they came from or where they might have gone. We don't even know if they left of their own accord or were driven off by an enemy, by droughts or simply died. The question is still, why did they leave?

All we know about these people is what we can determine from their building sites, artifacts and graves. We know they were of small stature and that they were a highly skilled people. This is evident from the pottery, baskets and clothing we have recovered in their ruins. Their buildings speak for themselves. Although they were an uneducated people by modern standards, they were able to build round and square structures that were pleasing to look on. They were evidently very durable since there are many of them still standing today, several hundred years later.

We are sure they were an agricultural people who grew a wide range of crops and domesticated some animals. They were not the ignorant savages I was lead to believe when I was a youngster in school.

Their sturdy, long lasting buildings are works of art and show long range planning. At the Aztec, New Mexico ruins, there is a long line of green stone incorporated into one wall that had to be intentional, not accidental. All the walls that were to support several stories are wider at the base and taper to the top. This means they were planned in advance. Some buildings were evidently as much as five tiers high. Their perfectly round kivas and towers, combined with the squared corners and straight walls, make one suspect they might have been a higher civilization on the wane rather than a lower form moving up.

They left many puzzles for us to ponder. For example: In the Cortez, Colorado region, a skeleton of a man who would have been well over six-foot, has been recovered. He would have been a giant among these little people. In the same general area, the skeletal remains of several macaws, birds not indigenous to this climate, have been found. They would have to have been brought up on trade routes that led into Mexico or even Central America. On the top of a ridge behind Chimney Rock, near Pagosa Springs, Colorado, is the remains of a village that shows no signs of women ever living there, only men. At the upper end of Navajo Lake in a museum, is a folding flint knife with wooden handles. A pocketknife. They were able to make cotton clothing and grew a wide variety of crops. Seashells and copper bells were also brought in from some distant point. It is possible the Anasazi had trade routes in all directions and may have even been in contact with the mound builders of the Midwest.

In Chaco Canyon a discovery, not to long ago, brought to light a sealed room in which were found a number of straight-sided pieces of pottery unlike the normal Anasazi pottery. With them was a collection of slender straight sticks. No explanation has been given for them.

With the advent of sophisticated equipment used in mineral exploration, roadways have been discovered that run in straight lines from one settlement to another. There are even indications they ran as far north as the Medicine Wheel in Wyoming. Some of these roads were thirty feet wide and had an eight-inch curb on them. There are signs of bridge abutments. Their paths up cliffs were not inclined because they did not have the wheel. They simply carved steps up the face of the sandstone and continued on. It has been suggested that since they did not have draft animals they did not need to invent the wheel.

The Anasazi left us paintings and etchings on the sandstone cliffs all over the southwest region, and while they are similar to each other, there is little in them to give us a clue about what they might mean. There are only educated guesses. The Hopi Indians may know the most about these people. They are probably descendants of the Anasazi.

There are those who will tell you the Anasazi did not cover as much of the country as those in this story. But the same type of people built the same kind of dwellings and drew the same kinds of pictures over a tremendous area of the four states induced here. The ruins at Camp Verde, Arizona bear a striking resemblance to those of Mesa Verde, Colorado. Similar houses and drawings can be seen on the walls of the Colorado River if you follow the road from Moab, Utah, down stream to Potash, Utah. And scattered all over the Four Corners area you will find little clusters of the cliff dwellers and evidence of small pueblos. Hundreds of people drive through Kayenta, Arizona, going west. They pass through a narrow section of extremely rocky terrain and never see the tiny dwellings nestled in among the cracks and crags. All of them were part of "The People" whether or not they were of the "Basket Weavers."

So much of their life is still a mystery. I don't claim to have all the answers to the questions, but I offer my guess as to what might have happened. I try to present a possible reason for their sudden departure, leaving their homes with food in the bowls and weapons leaning inside the doorways as if they intended to come back soon. But they never did. My guess might be as good as the next, maybe better, because I had one advantage. My characters came to me and told me this story. I did not invent it or make it up. I simply wrote down what they told me about their life during the last fifty years before they disappeared.

I don't claim to be a psychic, but I am sure I received some sort of influential instructions during the writing of this story. Whether or not you choose to believe it, this is the way it was told to me, and the characters seemed to be content when I had written it all down.

Norman D. Messenger

Chapter One

The year of the Christian calendar was 1225 A.D. To the People, it was the summer of the birth of the great child, remembered in legend and tales for all the summers to come.

Maata was happy as he worked on the shelter in a tiny recess on the canyon wall. He was building a place for his wife Keenwah to give birth to their child. The place he had chosen had been carefully selected. It was far enough from the village that it would not be a bother to anyone, yet close enough so that Keenwah would not have far to travel when it was her time.

Maata was happy as he worked because this was the first time out of four previous attempts that Keenwah was carrying her child to nearly full term. The other four children had been born much too soon and had not lived. They had come so soon that Maata had not even prepared a shelter for their birth, but this time was different. This time Keenwah was proud to walk about with her little stomach protruding far out, much larger than any other woman in their tribe had ever carried a child. She was constantly reminded from within of this presence by the healthy kicks. The entire village was in a state of blissful contentment for her. Not a day passed that someone did not lay their hand on her stomach to feel the strong youngster concealed inside her proclaiming its desire to be free. She was told repeatedly. "Keenwah has swallowed the seed of a pumpkin." This was a common saying when a woman was late in time and was extremely large. It pleased her to be the center of attention. Before, she had had to endure the sorrow and the comfort offered by her neighbors, but this time it would be different. She had known from the very first moment of conception that this time her child would live. This time she could celebrate with them when her child was born. No longer would she and Maata have to be content with patting the head of someone else's child. They would have a child of their own to love and share with the village.

Keenwah hoped for a man-child, it would please Maata so much, and after all he deserved a man-child because he had been forced to wait so long. She had asked the Great Spirit Watcher, the one who lived in the sun, to make this child a man-child. She did not fear the Spirit Watcher; after all, who should know better that Maata was a good man, a good provider, and a good husband? Who was there better than him? The Spirit Watcher knew Maata deserved a son, although if it did turn out to be a woman child, it would be just as honored and revered, and even Maata would be happy. He would not complain, or blame her for having a woman child like some men did. But a man-child would make him even happier.

Maata had picked a small overhang up near the rim of the canyon. From this place he could easily climb to the rim. In fact, this was the way he intended for Keenwah to get to the shelter, yet he could descend to the bottom of the canyon, although not as easily. Keenwah had nothing to fear here, no warring neighbors, only an occasional wild animal, such as a bear or a cougar. She would not have to worry about them because he, Maata, would be seated right outside her doorway, and nothing in this world they knew of could get past him to her and their child. It was a small space, hardly big enough for a storage room, but it would be big enough for Keenwah. She was not very big either; even among this small race of people she would have to be called tiny. A slight bit over four feet tall and so small around the waist, Maata did not see how she could possibly carry a child of any size, let alone one so big as this one must be.

Maata was of average height for his people, about five-foot, but he was stockier than most, and he was stronger. He had been known to bring down a full-grown buffalo with one mighty swing of his rock-crested club. He could throw a spear farther than any man in their district.

Maata was fair skinned, as were all the People. They tanned in the eternal sun until they appeared quite dark, but they were not the true copper-hue of the Plains Indians. Maata's hair was dark brown and his eyes were nearly the same shade as his hair. Some of his people had darker or lighter hair, but they all shared the same color of eyes, with a very few exceptions. They were not of the same stock as the rest of the Indians. They had migrated up from some place far to the south. It had happened so far back in their history that even their official rememberer could not be sure where or when.

Maata had cleaned the shelf with a bough from a pine tree, one with the long needles. He saw to it that there was no loose sand left on the walls to fall down and bother Keenwah or the child. There would be no loose sand in her drinking water or the water she used to clean herself and the child with after the birth. There would be no sand falling in the eyes of his first child.

After he was satisfied with his cleaning work, he had crushed the needles of the pine and rubbed them into the walls to permeate them with the pungent smell of the evergreen tree. It was fitting to use the tree of everlasting life for this chore. Maybe it would grant long life to his child. Maata was careful never to call the child "he." It might make the Spirit Watcher angry with him. If this happened the Spirit Watcher might take the child away from them as it had before. No, Maata would not risk making the Spirit Watcher angry with him for any reason.

When he had completed this task, he began to build a wall at the outside edge of the shelf, bringing it up until it was level with the sloping back edge of the shelf. Before he went any further he carried in baskets of fresh, new earth and jugs of water. Mixing the two together, he had filled in the floor until it was level. The fine red earth when mixed with water formed a smooth, almost a polished surface to the floor. Over this he would place a mat woven from the fibers of the yucca plant. He himself had woven it and it was long enough to not only cover the floor, but it would be pegged up on the walls and ceiling. This was just another of the thoughtful actions of Maata to keep the sand and dirt from his beloved wife and their new infant for the ten short days they would live there.

Ever since Maata had started work on this shelter, his friends and neighbors had come by one at a time. Each had sat for a short visit; they had not offered to help, and Maata would have refused if they had. It was understood that this was the job of the father, the husband. For anyone else to work on the project would have defiled it and it would never have been a proper place for a birth. The only exception was for an unmated girl, and her first child; then a father could perform this ceremony for her and thus honor the child and recognize its existence.

Although Maata's friends could not help with the actual building, they could help in other ways. They all knew how much time and effort went into building such a wall. The actual building was not the time consuming part of the work. It was the selecting and dressing of the stones that took the most time. So while they could not build the wall, they could carry up baskets of sandstone, each stone selected with care in respect to size and to shape. These could be used in the construction of the walls.

The stones were gathered during the day either in the fields or along the paths, or from a special place along the cliffs where they could be found in abundance. During the hot part of the day, the men would retire to shady places or to one of the many kivas. Here, away from the heat and the torment of the flies, they would dress these stones. They would rub them together to form a smooth, flat surface. Without the use of gauges, or any measurements, they would all produce stones of nearly the same dimension. When they had completed a basketful, they would carry them up to the rim of the canyon and deposit them in a neat stack where Maata could easily reach them. No words were spoken about the stones. The men could visit about anything else, but no one mentioned the stones, no one took credit for them. It was just fortunate for Maata to find so many usable stones within reach.

As long as no one talked about them, they would not defile the structure and in turn they gave each man, and his family, a claim to the new child. Through their actions they announced their recognition of a new member to the tribal family. They were signifying their acceptance to the new member and the infant would be surrounded with real, and honorary, aunts and uncles and grandparents.

The women had their own customs. They too were making their recognition ritual by contributing bits of clothing and sleepwear for the new arrival. Keenwah accepted each offering with reverence and cried out to all that she was indeed the most fortunate woman to ever live in this tiny village, to be surrounded by such generous friends and relatives. All in all, everyone was happy and looked forward to the great event with much pleasure. This was the only way they became more powerful in their world. They were not a war faring people, and they lived in peace with the adjourning villages. The larger the village, the more respect its people could command, and the more food they could produce. It was well known that one person could furnish enough food for at least two people and often many more. So a new child, man or woman child, was an addition to their prestige.

Maata laid the stones with great care; selecting each stone for the exact spot it would fit the best. He was careful to take one stone from each stack, in turn, so no one would be contributing more or less than his neighbor. So no one would be slighted. He cemented them together with more of the fine red earth mixed with water to form a paste. As the wall grew upward, he left a narrow opening. About a third of the way up he spread this opening wider on each side until he reached the desired height of the doorway. Over the top of the doorway he placed a carefully selected timber, one that had been carved square. Each end would extend out over the wall for support and these ends had been rubbed on a large coarse stone until they were squared and straight. Maata did not know why it must be done this way, he only knew it was the way it had always been done.

The walls continued up until they merged with the overhanging cliff ceiling. The ends of the walls had been sealed up tightly with only a small, square hole the size of Maata's two hands, in the end opposite the doorway. This would allow for air circulation when there was too much heat generated by their God, the Spirit Watcher. The narrow bottom part of the doorway could be closed off with a thin stone chosen for this opening. With it in place, the smaller animals and reptiles would be kept out, while the larger, upper part of the opening would permit air to enter and keep the place fresh and clean.

He felt he was fortunate to find a spot where he could build the shelter so it would catch the first rays of the morning sun. The Spirit Watcher would be the first one to come into his infant's room. His first visitor would be the sun every morning of his short stay there.

When the walls were up, Maata slowly and lovingly covered them, both inside and out, with a plaster of fine red earth. On the inner wall he would paint happy designs. He would paint pictures to remind Keenwah of their happy times together. He would paint pictures of animals, those they depended on for food and clothing. Opposite them he would paint pictures of those they must fear. They also would have to be recognized by the new member of the tribe. Keenwah would point them out to the infant so it would know from its first breath, which animals could be trusted and which must be feared.

It was a fine shelter, and now all it needed was Keenwah to announce her time. Each evening Keenwah would ask Maata if the shelter was ready yet, and each time he would reply, "Not yet, but it will soon be done."

"You had better hurry, I cannot make this wild youngster wait forever while his father sits and visits with all the worthless men of our village and anyone else who passes by." Keenwah would say.

It was their own private joke. Both were so proud that this time they were going to be able to have a child and nothing could spoil it for them. When Maata had done all he could, when he had fussed and worked on every detail until he could find nothing more to do, only then did he tell Keenwah it was ready and waiting for her.

"You have nagged me all the time, now it is ready and you are not. What is the matter with you, woman? Do you not know what to do? Maybe the men should have the babies. Then we would not have to wait so long. You women can never make up your minds."

"Maata would make a very funny looking mother. So big and stern, the child would take one look at you and be so frightened it would never come out." Keenwah said.

At the approach of the new moon, Keenwah came to the door of their portion of the pueblo and motioned to Maata, who was seated a few doors down, visiting with one of his friends.

"I think it is time Maata, I think I should go to the shelter tonight." She rubbed her extended stomach and said, "Yesterday the child would not lay still, today it has slept all day and not moved. It is resting for its journey to the light. I think it will be tonight."

"Well, it is ready. Come. What are you waiting for?"

Keenwah smiled at the other women who had come to listen when she had called Maata. They were all amused at Maata's effort to be unconcerned. He was failing miserably. He had forgotten everything in his haste to get her to the shelter.

"I was waiting for some strong man to help me carry my bundle and maybe even a little help with one of the water jars," she said innocently. "But maybe I can get Tupla to help me."

Tupla was the oldest man in the village. He could hardly hobble around with the use of a stick. He was almost blind and would not be with them long; in fact, if it had not been for his daughter and her mate, he would long since have died. All the women joined in to laugh at Maata. Even Tupla rose to the occasion as he tried to get up and offer his help.

"Maybe I should help. After all, I'm not so sure I'm not the father anyway," Tupla shouted for all to hear.

"Sit, ancient one. Rest your weary bones and wandering mind. You are so ancient you do not even remember what causes babies," Maata shouted at him as he hurried back to gather up everything Keenwah had set outside of their door. He was still laughing with them; nothing would mar his happiness this evening.

"Ho, ho, Maata. You will never get that old," replied Tupla as he settled back against the warm stones of his doorstep.

The village of Keenwah and Maata sat on the top of a ridge only a long walk from the Chaco Canyon. The edge of this canyon rim was only an arm of the Chaco Canyon proper. It was a small village, with one small pueblo housing about twenty people, counting the children. The shelter Maata had built was just over the edge and he had made sure the trail down to it was clear and easy to traverse so Keenwah would not trip and fall down the side of the cliff.

The new moon was just clear of the earth when they arrived at the shelter. It was the first time Keenwah had seen it. In the mellow light of the moon, Keenwah could see the shelter that was to house her and her infant for the first ten days, until they were sure the child and she would both live. It was beautiful; the new moon shed its soft glow over it and made its lines even more smooth and perfect.

"Will it do?" Maata asked. It was the custom that the woman must approve before she would enter. Sometimes a woman would be contrary and the man would have to beg, or even make changes in the shelter before she would accept it. Keenwah was not one of those women. She was proud of her mate; he had done very well.

"It is the most beautiful place in the valley, I think I will not go back to the village. I think when the child is born I will move here forever." This was the highest praise she could give Maata and he was grateful to her.

"It is nothing. I only spent a little time on it in the afternoon. I could have done much better if I had wanted to."

The customs observed, Keenwah went inside and arranged her belongings along the wall. Even in the dark she could see some of the paintings where the light of the moon shone through the doorway. Her heart felt warm for her mate. No other man could have done better; no other man was a better provider than her Maata.

When she had settled everything to her satisfaction, she returned to the doorway and sat to enjoy the view down the canyon. Maata was seated nearby, his club and spear nestled in his arms.

All they could do was wait, wait until the child wished to be born. It was out of their hands now. They had done all they could. It was up to the child and the Spirit Watcher now.

Chapter Two

The new moon had set and the sun, carrying the Spirit Watcher, was tinting the eastern sky, painting the shelter in a soft pink glow. Maata had heard the first signs of Keenwah's struggle to give birth. Keenwah, like all women of her nation, tried hard to control herself and make no outcry. If the mother cried, then so the child would also. The mother must set the example by not making any sound during her pain. The sound a child should hear first should not be a mother's cry of pain.

Keenwah did not cry out, but Maata could hear her labored breathing and the movement of her tortured body as she tried to deliver the child. Just as the first rays of the sun struck the rim of the canyon, Maata heard the strangled and disapproving utterance of his first child. The voice was hearty and full toned. Maata smiled; it was a lusty child. He longed to call out and ask Keenwah if all was well, but this was forbidden. He must wait until she either called him, or as sometimes happened, there would be no sound and he would know they were both dead. In such a case, the delivery room would be sealed up and left in peace.

He feared for his mate. She had carried a very large child, and while everyone teased and joked about it, Maata had worried because she was such a small woman. He could hear the child very well but could only assume Keenwah was all right.

Was it a man-child or a woman child? He hoped it would be a man-child, although the old women claimed that woman babies were always the largest at birth. Surely such a large child could not be a woman child. It would have to be a man-child, but he would be happy with either as long as Keenwah lived. Why did she not call for him? What could be wrong? It should not take this long for her to call him.

Inside the shelter Keenwah was busy. She was also happy. While her labor had been long and hard, the child she held in her arms was worth the trouble. She held a strong, defiant, man-child to her swollen breasts and smiled as it greedily began to nurse. This was a very good sign. To nurse as soon as it was born was sure proof that the baby would live and grow strong.

She knew Maata was becoming impatient. She could hear him moving about outside, but first she must let this baby nurse. Then she must clean herself and the child, and also the shelter. All this must be done before she could call her mate and let him know what kind of son he had. The wait would not kill him. Had she herself not waited through nine changes of the moon for this event? After what seemed an eternity, Keenwah called to Maata.

"If you are not asleep, my lazy man, you could come and look at your son."

Maata leaped to the doorway. He would not enter, nor would he touch the child, but he could look. Keenwah brought the infant to the doorway so

Maata could see him clearly. As she held him up for Maata to see, the sun reached out its first full rays and entered the doorway before Maata. It was just as Maata had hoped. The first visitor his infant son had was the Spirit Watcher. Well, let him see the fine son of Maata and Keenwah. He looked longingly at the squirming, red-faced baby beside Keenwah, who was so pale and drawn from the difficult birth. The baby looked strikingly dark. His head was covered with a heavy mantle of hair and his fist was clenched as if he would do battle with anyone who would dare to intrude on him and his mother.

"He will do," Maata said with feigned indifference.

"Indeed he will do. He is the greatest man child ever to be born," Keenwah said defending her charge.

A mother could brag about her child, but a father must never pretend it was important, or worthy of praise or notice. Keenwah could see that Maata was so proud he would be lucky not to burst. She could already hear him telling his friends about the man-child. He would not boast, he would make so little of him that his friends would understand just how special he really was, and they would be most anxious to see this child that Maata tried so hard to belittle. She understood he must do this so the Spirit Watcher would not become jealous and come to claim this precious gift from them.

As the sunlight played on her son's face, Keenwah had a swift twinge of foreboding that passed almost before she knew it was there. She frowned slightly and pulled the child back inside the security of the shelter built by the child's father. Nothing could harm them here.

Each day, for ten days, the women of the village would come by the shelter, one or two at a time. They would bring food and water for Keenwah. In this way they could all have a chance to see this great new son of the village. All day Maata would scornfully avoid the shelter and the women. He would go about his business of hunting, farming, or whatever he chose to do. He would visit with his friends and sit in the kiva to avoid the heat. He would not even glance in the direction of the canyon where the shelter held his mate and their son. His wanderings still brought him to the canyon just before dark, after all the women had thoughtfully disappeared. He would pause by the doorway and let his eyes feast on the proud new person. Then, with spear and club, he would post himself before the doorway to make sure his family was not molested during the night.

At the end of the ten-day waiting period, Maata and Keenwah gathered up their belongings and carried their new son back to the village. He would live and so would she, at least for a time. The first ten days were the critical time, a time when many newborn babies died as well as their mothers. If they lived their first ten days, it was reasonable to expect they had a chance to live longer, but even yet it was not a certain thing. Many children did not live to maturity, so the new baby would not have a name. He would be called "baby" for the next few summers, more specifically, he would be called "Keenwah's baby." If he still lived at five summers, he would be given a pet name. By this name he would be known until his twelfth summer. Then, if he passed his manhood rites, he would be given his man's name to be his for the rest of his life.

There was a reason for this prolonged delay in naming a child. The mortality rate among these people was very high, and it was not every child who would reach the age of manhood rites. If the child did not have a name, it was as though it had never existed. It was easier to forget, easier to start a new life with a new child to replace the one that had never been. It was thought that since a child did not have a name, it was less likely to attract attention to the Gods who were responsible for taking young lives to themselves. While it might be an honor to have the Spirit Watcher claim a child, all parents were content not to be so honored.

Back in the village, the new child drew much attention because of his unusual size. Already he was an armful for his mother to carry. He was larger than many babies after their first summer. Everyone commented on the length of his arms and legs. They were less inclined to mention his facial features, although he did have a long nose. The fact that his body was covered with a downy soft covering of silky, brown hair that shone like gold in the light of the Spirit Watcher was also noticed but seldom mentioned until Keenwah herself spoke of it.

After this the women of the village teased Keenwah, saying she must have lain with a bear to produce such a big hairy son. Keenwah only smiled and told them they did not know Maata after dark, that he was a bear, to which they all laughed and made more jokes about his prowess and abilities as a man and a mate. It was assumed that the father was responsible for all the child's attributes. The mother was only the vessel that carried the seed until harvest.

News of this new baby who was so large and unusual spread among the various villages until word of his being was carried even to the main part of the canyon of Chaco, where the leader of the district resided.

Matuga was the name of this leader. He was chosen for his wisdom and courage. He did not rule with fear of threats; he ruled as a benevolent man, with compassion and good will for all his people. There was always some small dispute over land rights, or the kidnapping of someone's daughter for a mate. Matuga's judgment would be respected by all without serious argument.

Matuga had heard several references of the new child born in one of his outlying villages. He had been told that this new child, who at one summer was already as big as a child of several summers. Matuga made it a point to stop at the village on one of his periodic trips. Keenwah and Maata were honored to receive the ruler of all the People into their humble home. Of course, Matuga was not the ruler of all the People, but to them he was the ruler of all their immediate People.

Matuga was impressed with the youngster. He was indeed a large child. It was hard to believe he was only one summer of age. Matuga made a mental note to keep track of this child. The future might hold a place for him.

Once again Keenwah felt a keen stab of uneasiness when her child drew so much attention from Matuga. She wished he would leave them alone, would stay away. He had never visited this little village so often before. Why now?

Baby learned to walk before his first summer was over and once he had mastered the art, he was never content to be still unless he was eating or sleeping, and he did much of both. Early in his life Keenwah had found he could not get enough nourishment at her breasts and she had started feeding him gruel made of maize and broth with tender shreds of meat in it. Soon this was not enough and she had to cook more meat until he ate almost as much as an adult.

Shortly after he began to walk, he had a good start on a set of teeth and nothing was safe from him. If it could be eaten and could not outrun him, he considered it fair game.

Baby learned from his mother not to cry out at pain, and so was a good baby. He fell often, but did not cry or come to his mother for sympathy. Instead he got up and went on about his adventures.

Baby was a healthy and fast growing young lad at the end of five summers. He was head and shoulders taller than any of the other children his age or even several summers older. His face was longer and sharper than theirs, his nose, always large, was long and pointed instead of the short pug of his people, and his forehead was higher than most. His hair, while the same general color as the rest of the people, was unyielding and refused to lay back. It lay forward with a tuft of particular unruly hair sticking erect like a crest.

Being large for his age made it difficult for him to have friends. The children his age were so much smaller that it was unfair to compete with them. The children of his size were older and more advanced in their thinking, so there was a gap between them also. At eight summers they were already starting to think seriously about their manhood rites and were training for it, although the rites were still four summers away.

Baby was too developed to be called baby anymore, so a pet name was given to him. At birth he had been covered with a silky down. As he grew, the downy hair covering his body did not go away. The soft hair was lighter than the hair on his head. In the sunshine it gave off a faint golden glow. Because of his size and the downy hair, they called him Sun Bear.

Being lonely and without friends, Sun Bear was forced to find his own entertainment. He would follow his father most of the time, traveling at a trot. Sun Bear was soon able to keep up with Maata, if he did not run too fast for too long. This led to the discovery that he could run well. With practice he was able to run farther each day, and soon he was running up and down the trails with wild abandon. Keeping up with Maata was no longer difficult. By his eighth summer he could easily outdistance his father, not only for a short distance, but all day if necessary.

All of the people were runners; there was no other way to travel. There were no horses or other beasts of burden. All travel was on foot and running was a natural way to go. They ran everywhere and racing was as common as gossip with them. The best runners were often chosen by the district leader to be his personal messengers, to carry word from one village to another. It was an honor sought by nearly every young man in the nation. Sun Bear thought of this often as he ran.

He would keep his eyes open for a runner on the trail near his village and would pace them for a great distance before he would break off and run home again. The runners were helpful to him, and gave him many pointers in the proper way to run and how to pace himself for a long day's run. Word of the new runner spread with the messengers themselves as they went their rounds over the country, and often when they were going out of Matuga's district to contact rulers in the next district. Stories of Sun Bear's running ability and his increasing height, spread from district to district until everyone knew of this strange new man child.

Those who knew him often described him as one of the birds that live in the southwest. Now known by its formal name of Geococcyx Californianus, sometimes called the Chaparral Cock, it is most commonly known as the Road-runner. To the People the bird was De-Kae-Oto-Nye-Paz, or the bird who runs with the wind.

Matuga continued to pay periodic visits to the village of Maata and Keenwah. He always had some official reason for his visits, but made it a point to inquire about Sun Bear.

"How is the little giant," he would ask, or "How can you possibly feed such a person as this?"

"It is no problem," Maata would say "I can provide for ten like him. Besides, he does not spend all of his time running and playing. He does his share in our fields, just as every other boy must do."

"Oh, I do not doubt that. It is well known that he does more than his share, but I was just thinking, he must be a burden to feed and even keep in sandals."

Maata remained silent. He knew Matuga was not just talking to make conversation, or to hear his own voice. He was not vain. No, Maata knew that Matuga had something specific on his mind, and in his own time would tell them what it was.

On one such visit Matuga asked Maata if he had ever considered moving to another pueblo, maybe in closer to the hub, perhaps somewhere in the Chaco Canyon itself, or even into Bonito, where Matuga lived.

"I have never had any desire to move from this village. I know everyone here, I was born here, they all know me here, and we have many friends and relatives here. Why would I want to move? I would have to give up my land and settle for the leavings of another village." Maata fidgeted. He knew this was a long way around but it was not a question. Matuga was giving a command, but phrasing it so he could accept it gracefully without losing the respect of the People. Why did Matuga want them to move?

"The father and mother of Sun Bear will be known wherever they live and will not want for friends. As for land, I have several fields that are close in. In fact, I have more than I can easily take care of. I would gladly let the father of Sun Bear have his pick of these fields." He paused to let Maata think over his offer.

"It is no chore to take care of this child, and I have no need of another field," Maata answered stubbornly. He was afraid for one of the few times in his life. He wished Matuga would go away and leave him and his family alone. For the first time since the birth of his son, Maata wished his child were not so unusual, not so tall, not so fast a runner, nothing to catch the attention of the ruler.

Matuga knew he was in danger of offending Maata's pride. He did not want to insult such a proud and stable man. He decided to use the direct approach and hoped Maata would understand him.

"As you must know Maata, as ruler I can adopt anyone I wish as a member of my family. It is done occasionally, and such a person is entitled to certain privileges. Among them is the right to food and lodging any place in the country, even among rulers of other districts."

"I know of this custom. What has it to do with us? We do not lack for anything; we have no need of Matuga's bounty. I have already told you I can easily provide for us all," Maata answered while Keenwah held her breath in fear. It was considered an honor to have a child singled out this way by the ruler. Many parents would have been eager to accept the attention of Matuga, but she could see no honor in losing her only child, the one she had labored so long and so hard to produce.

"I know you and your mate are a hard-working people, who have never come begging to anyone at any time. I also know you are a proud man. I would not want to offend you by taking your son from you, although it is my right. I would not want to adopt him until after his manhood rights. At this time the adoption is only a formality and would not take him from your home. It is just that I think I recognize something in this boy that will be beyond the normal, not just in size. He is already beyond normal in that respect, but something even more, perhaps more than just a great runner, for surely he will be that." Matuga stopped and looked far off over the horizon as if he could see a vision of the future that no one else was able to share with him.

"I would like to have a part in raising such a person as this. I thought that if you moved closer to my home, I could see Sun Bear more often and could contribute to his well being and support without taking him from his parents. Maata is the only man fit to be the father and raise such a man child and Keenwah has already proven her worth as his mother by giving birth to him."

Keenwah and Maata bowed their heads in acceptance of his compliment, knowing that Matuga did not have to ask their permission, nor did he have to offer them any consolation. He was truly being gracious to them with his praise and his offer.

"It has come to my attention that Sun Bear has no friends here. He is considered too big for those his own age and too young for those of his size. If he lived close to me and wore my token, he would be respected by all. None would question his rights. Also, he could have the benefit of being associated with my best runners; this would not be a bad thing. Think on it."

Maata and Keenwah thought on it. They thought it was better to move and keep their son a little longer than to refuse and take the chance of losing him now. So when Sun Bear was in his eighth summer, he and his parents said goodbye to their village, their friends and their relatives to move into the section of the Chaco Canyon where the pueblo called Bonito was located.

Maata took his choice from several good fields and a home in the lower section of the pueblo. True to Matuga's word, they were well received by the people of this pueblo and Sun Bear was treated with respect by all the adults. But the children still did not accept him. He was even more lonely here. He spent more of his time alone, except when he ran with the runners of the village. This was an activity that knew neither age nor size, only endurance and skill.

There was more to learn about being a runner than just speed and distance covered, and he had the best teachers in the nation. Probably due to this, Sun Bear matured faster than his counterparts. In many ways his manhood rites were forced on him before the ritual was ever undertaken. Speaking and working with men gave him insight into adult life that was not offered to the other boys growing up.

Sun Bear accepted his new role, just as he had before in his old home. Wise enough to know he could not change matters, he made the best of things without complaint, so no one noticed his lonely life. No one but his mother and a certain old woman who everyone respected and feared. But Sun Bear was too busy running and learning to take any notice of her.

Chapter Three

In front of every village was found the place where all the left over and discarded bits of clothing, skins, and broken pottery were thrown. It was located in front of the village to make a natural barrier between the People and the scavengers that hung around every village. Over a period of many summers, this pile became quite large and contained a diverse collection of materials.

It was also the foraging place for the disabled, or those too old to look after themselves, those with no family left to care for them. Here they could sort through the cast off garments and scraps of food and were able to live on a few more months, especially during the summer. The winters usually took a heavy toll on those who were left.

People who were totally disabled were carried out and placed here, just as any other broken or useless piece of equipment would be. Those who could walk had a slight chance to live; those who could not had to either depend on others or die. When they died, they were usually buried in the dump heap without any ceremony or even recognition. When they were retired to the dump, they ceased to exist in the eyes of the People. They no longer had a name or a face. No one looked at them, no one saw them, no one knew them, no one cared, and no one talked to them. It was not considered cruel or heartless, it was just the way it was done. To recognize them, to speak to them, or to see them at all was to bring shame on the memory of the people they use to be. To ignore them was considered to be a kindness, to let them retain what dignity they had earned in the better times of their lives.

Not all the old or disabled were placed here, only those who had no family left to provide for them, or to bury them when they died. If they had nothing to contribute to the community, they were discarded and left for the Spirit Watcher to decide their fate.

At eight summers, Sun Bear began to seriously think about his manhood rites. Even though he was bigger and more skilled in many things, he was still as nervous as every other boy about this event. It was still several summers away, but they must all train for it to be able to pass into adulthood.

He was determined to excel in everything that was required of him. He would train until he was better than any other boy in the village, any boy in the nation. He would show them. He could run faster than any of them, and no one wanted to wrestle with him. He could hurl the short spear nearly as far as his father could, and he was very skillful with the bow and arrow. Now he would practice with the new bow his father had made for him. It was a long bow; no one else had such a bow. In fact, not many could pull this large bow. Most men considered it too large and clumsy for practical use, but Maata, knew his son would soon outgrow the smaller bows they used.

Maata had searched for the right wood and had been carving and curing it for several summers. He had tested its strength, and when Sun Bear struggled to pull it back, he told him that practice would make it pull easier. The bow was slightly taller than the boy, but already Maata was preparing another longer bow for his son when he reached manhood. The arrows were also much longer and the points heavier. Men of the village teased Maata about his spear thrower because the arrows looked more like slender spears than they did the short arrows most of them used.

Testing the strength of the new bow, Sun Bear knew he must get use to it. He was at the dumpsite getting some practice with it. The new long arrows were too precious to lose while practicing, and at the dumpsite he could retrieve them easily. There were very few of the nameless people at the dump, so he did not have to hunt for a place to shoot without endangering some of them.

He had shot all of his arrows, one for each of his ten fingers, at a piece of matting lying at the edge of the dump. He swaggered up to retrieve them from the tight cluster they made, all grouped inside a small area of the discarded piece of rug. As he pulled them out one at a time and wiped them clean with a piece of deerskin, he noticed a small lump of rags perched nearby, watching him. He looked closer at this piece of human garbage and was shocked to see two piercing eyes observing him from the bundle of skins, eyes that peered through tangled and matted hair. What surprised him the most were the eyes. One was brown as it should be, but the other was yellow, like the wild cats.

"What are you looking at?" He asked, indignantly. He was sure no one on the dumpsite had the right to even look at him.

"I was watching the mighty hunter," came the reply, from a nearly tooth-less mouth.

Sun Bear thought he had never seen anything so hideous. Not only did the eyes not match, but the rest of the tiny person was covered with filth and running sores. Flies crawled about it undisturbed. The hair was long and straggled, uncombed for many days. The head was too large for the rest of the tiny body; it looked like the head of a frog or a lizard. The back of the head sloped away so the creature did not have a forehead, and the two colored eyes were large and seemed to bulge from the creature's face. Looking down, he could see the creature's legs were twisted and crooked, making it almost impossible for it to walk.

"Well," he boasted. "You have seen the best." He was sure of his boast, but something about those two colored eyes held his attention. "Do not stare at me!" he shouted more than a little disturbed.

"The Sun Bear is grouchy this morning, is he not?" the creature asked. The voice coming from the gaping mouth was surprisingly soft and mellow, with only a hint of a lisp caused by the missing teeth. The large, two colored eyes searched his face as if they were looking for a sign.

"I am not grouchy," he mumbled. "I am just not use to being stared at while I practice."

"You should try living here, then. People can look at you and never even see you. No one stares at you, no one even sees you. I have been here for quite some time. Have you ever seen me before?" The mellow voice belied the tortured, twisted body and face.

"Ugh. I would never live here, I would die first."

The creature looked at him almost with pity. "That would be very nice, but even dying is not simple. The body will not give up as easily as the mind."

Sun Bear was becoming uneasy. He knew he was not supposed to talk to this kind of creature. He wished he could turn and run, but he could not very well claim to be a man if he was afraid of a creature that lived in the dump heap. He engaged himself with cleaning his arrows, making a big show of cleaning each arrow until it fairly shone in the sunlight. The creature was silent but still continued to watch his every move.

"Do you not have anything else to do besides watch me?" he asked defiantly.

"No. What else can I do? Do not begrudge me what little joy I get from life. Surely I cannot harm the great Sun Bear just by watching him, but if I offend you, I will move." Painfully the creature started to pull itself away from the small burrow it was perched in. Looking back at him, it said, "Although I was here first, you know."

Sun Bear could see that even this simple movement was both painful and slow. He could also see the creature was right, it had been here first, probably this burrow represented its home. He did not have right to make it leave its home just to please him. Besides, he could move so much more readily than it could.

"No. Wait. I can move easier than you, and as you said, you were here first." He took his arrows and prepared to leave.

"I like to watch you shoot. You do not have to go. Surely you must be the best shot in the whole village," the creature said in the same melodious voice.

"Oh, no, there are many men better than me, but I will keep shooting until I am the best." Modesty forced him to admit he was not as good as the creature claimed, but it was pleasing to have someone notice and praise him while he practiced, even if it was this horrible little lump of human refuse.

He had no friends he could compete with; the rest of the boys considered it unfair because of his size and strength, even though neither had anything to do with accuracy. There was no one to talk to, no one to brag to about his skills, no one to appreciate how well he was doing. He decided he would stay for a while; after all, if it gave the creature pleasure, it surely would not harm him. Just as long as he did not get too close to the smell and the dirt, along with the crawling things that lived with it.

"You can watch. But do not get too close. After all, I do miss sometimes."

Sun Bear practiced long this day, until his arms ached and his fingers were sore, but the creature was ready with praise after each session. It even made excuses for him when he missed. It was not really so unpleasant, if you could get used to the smell.

Sun Bear found himself returning each day to the same spot for a session of practice, and the creature was always there, in the very same place. As the days went by, they talked more and as they talked, Sun Bear began to get used to the smell and the flies. He even became used to the appearance of the strange creature. It did not seem quite so repulsive as it had at first.

"What is your name?" he asked one day as he cleaned his arrows.

"I have no name," was the solemn reply.

"Oh, come on. Everyone has some sort of a name."

"I have never had a name."

"How long have you been here?" Sun Bear asked.

"I do not know. It seems like forever, at least five summers," the creature told him.

"Five summers! You are not big enough to have five summers yet." Sun Bear stared at the creature, trying to decide if it was lying to him or not.

"I was very small when they threw me here. That was before you moved to this village, because I remember when you and your family came. I thought you were such a funny looking boy, so tall, and with you hair sticking up." What could pass as a smile played over the creature's horrid features?

"I guess I am funny looking compared to the rest of the boys, but I cannot help how I look," Sun Bear offered.

"Nor I," the creature answered. "And living here does not do much to make one grow larger or more beautiful."

For the first time Sun Bear felt ashamed, ashamed of his words and actions over the past several days. He knew what happened to deformed or retarded children, especially when both parents died. No one wanted the responsibility of raising them, so they were thrown on the dumpsite to live or die as the Spirit Watcher saw fit. It was unusual for anyone to live so long, and it was unbelievable that a misshapen, crippled child such as this one could live for five summers here unassisted. Perhaps the creature's mind was also crippled and it could not remember how long it had been here and had made that part up.

The creature was a dwarf with an oversized head and a stunted body. This, coupled with neglect and lack of nourishing food, along with exposure, made it truly repulsive.

"Do you not even have a pet name?" Sun Bear asked in awe.

"I told you, I have never had a name, or if I did I have never heard it."

"Then what am I to call you? Creature?" He asked.

"I guess it does not matter. Creature will be fine." The creature was evidently pleased with so much attention. It never occurred to Sun Bear that the poor creature could be even more lonely than he was.

"I do not even know if you are a man creature or a woman creature," he said hesitantly.

Again what could pass for a smile played over the creatures face, and the two colored eyes sparkled for just a moment. It was plain the creature was studying about its answer and had decided to tell the truth.

"I am a woman creature, Sun Bear, but please do not leave just because I am a girl. I will never tell anyone else and they will never know." She pleaded with him.

"I do not care what others think. They do not like me anyway, besides they do not pay any attention to what I do or whom I am with. Still, I think you should have a name, a pet name at least. Let me think." He furrowed his brow as he puzzled over this problem. He had never given anyone a name before.

"I know!" he said suddenly. "I will call you Little Frog." This was a common name for little children, especially if they liked the water. In this case it seemed to fit because to him, the creature looked more like a frog than anything else he could think of. He would not have been surprised to see her lick out her tongue to catch the ever-present flies.

"If it pleases you, then you can call me that," she replied. Any name was preferable to no name. A non-person had no name, but if she had a name, even this name, then she was someone.

As the days and weeks passed, Sun Bear and Little Frog began to accept each other and each was glad for the other's company. One afternoon, as he was shooting, a quick shower began, as it often happened in the late summer. Not enough to really do any good, just enough to make a mess of the dust around the village. Sun Bear scampered quickly to the shelter of his portion of the pueblo and watched the rain pouring off the building tops, forming little streams, which were led into a cistern in the corner of the plaza. After the storm had passed over and the sun came back out again, Sun Bear crawled up to a favored spot on the roof and waited for the sun and wind to dry up the mud before he returned to his practice. From this elevated position he could look down on the dump. He was surprised to see Little Frog still sitting just where he had left her. In her soaked clothing, she looked even more sodden and bedraggled. It suddenly dawned on him that Little Frog had no place to go, and even if she had, she would not have been able to move fast enough to escape the sudden shower. As he watched her, he saw her take up a broken piece of gourd and drink the rainwater collected in it, then carefully set it back down again so it might catch more the next time it rained.

Sun Bear became engrossed in his first long and difficult train of thought. One question led to another and another until he was overwhelmed with what he had started.

How did she find enough to drink when it did not rain? What did she do for food? What did she do in the winters when it snowed and became very cold at night? All these questions bothered the young giant and he was determined to do something about it, although he was not sure what. But for now, he would do what he could.

Keenwah did not think anything about her son taking an older bowl with a little corn mush and a few scraps of meat from the cook fire. Most boys had a dog or a puppy they fed from time to time. She did think it was strange when he took a small gourd full of water. She would have to speak to him about that. Water was precious; it had to be carried from the stream, when there was enough to run. Too many times it was either dry or stood in little stagnate pools. Much of the time they had to store their water in huge jugs that were buried in the ground with only the clay stopper showing. The water in the cisterns was for emergency use only, such as a real drought. A dog could hunt for his own water just as they did and not use the water she carried from the stream. But for now, she did not say anything. She knew he was a lonely boy.

Sun Bear carried the bowl of mush and meat scraps in one hand and the gourd balanced on top of his head, so he still had one hand free to carry his bow and arrows. He circled the dumpsite until he came to Little Frog sitting in her burrow. He placed the bowl of food and the gourd of water in front of her.

"Is this for me?" she asked in surprise. No one threw away perfectly good food or a sound gourd filled with water.

"Yes. I took more than I could eat. My mother was cleaning out the cooking pot and did not want me to put it back, so I thought maybe you could eat it," he stammered. Lying was new to him and he was not very good at it.

Little Frog looked longingly at the bowl. Sun Bear expected her to dig in with both hands and cram it into her toothless mouth. Instead she picked up the gourd and sipped a little water sparingly, then she tucked it into the front of her bundle of rags and skins. She picked up the bowl of food with one hand and used the other hand to help scoot herself along the edge of the dump. Sun Bear was conscious of how painful her movements were, but he did not know how to help her. He was not ready yet to touch her.

Near the end of the dumpsite she approached a wizened, emaciated, old man lying at the very edge of the heap. Sun Bear became angry with Little Frog when he saw she intended to feed the mush to this old non-person man. Dipping her fingers into the mush, she scooped it into the old one's mouth. His tongue and gums worked desperately to get it down his throat. Each time he swallowed she was ready with more.

"Hey! I brought that for you, not some old pile of bones. Let him find his own food," Sun Bear cried indignantly.

Little Frog looked up apprehensively at Sun Bear and she clutched the bowl to her to protect it, but did not stop scooping more into the old man's maw.

"It is true you gave the food to me. Did you not?" she asked.

"Yes, of course I gave the food to you, but I did not mean for you to give it to someone else. I meant for you to eat it."

"If you gave it to me, it is mine, is it not?"

"Yes. I already told you that."

"Then if it is mine, I can do with it whatever I please, can I not?" she asked again.

"I suppose so, but why waste it on him?' Sun Bear was still perplexed by her action.

"He cannot move at all, he cannot get food without help. I share whatever I find with him. Who else is there to help him?" To Little Frog, this seemed only natural.

"I do not know. But it seems like such a waste," Sun Bear complained.

"Before you came, we only had each other. We are the only family we have," Little Frog tried to explain to Sun Bear.

"It still seems like a waste to me. He is nearly dead anyway and to feed him does not seem like it would do any good."

"Yes, he is nearly dead. But he should not have to die with an empty stomach when I have more than I can eat."

"What you did not eat now you could have saved for tomorrow, could you not?" he asked.

"Tomorrow? Who knows about tomorrow? Neither of us may be alive tomorrow." Little Frog never stopped dipping in her fingers and passing it to the old man until he made a feeble motion with his hand to indicate he was through. Sun Bear could not help but notice that even when he was through he had taken very little from the bowl. There was still enough for her, no bigger than she was. She ate a little of the mush and sucked noisily on one of the meat scraps. She poured a little water down the old man's throat and watched to see that he swallowed.

When she was sure the old man had all he wanted and she had taken what she wanted, which was precious little, she carefully hid the rest in the trash heap near by. Then she asked Sun Bear, "Did you want the gourd back?"

"No, you can keep it and the bowl. When they are empty, I will see if my mother has some more scraps left over. I can fill the gourd for you down at the stream, if you like." It seemed like a small thing for a healthy young boy to do.

"Oh, Sun Bear, you are truly a great man, or you will be when you grow up." The huge, two-colored eyes were spilling tears down her cheeks, leaving a clean streak in their path.

"Ah, it is not much." He meant it; to him it was nothing. They threw more food than this away many times.

"Maybe to you it is nothing, but to me it is everything. It is the difference between life and death. For me to go down to get water would be like you trying to run to catch Sister Moon."

Sun Bear turned hastily and nearly tripped as he left. He was very troubled. This was not the way for a boy approaching manhood to feel. After all, the men of the village, including his father, passed this way every day on their way to the fields and it did not bother them. The women brought out the garbage daily and it did not seem to bother them. He supposed it was a weakness, something to be ashamed of, to bring food and water to a non-person, but he did not feel weak or ashamed. Instead, he felt warm inside. He felt good about what he had done.

Every day Sun Bear took a bowl of mush and whatever meat scraps he thought he could get away with. Keenwah assumed it was for the dog, and since he took no more of her water, she was content to let it go. She did not say anything, letting him enjoy some of the things a young boy was supposed to enjoy.

So it was that Sun Bear made his first friend, a creature from the dumpsite. The ugly, deformed little dwarf girl he had named Little Frog. Neither of them knew she would play an important part in his life for as long as he lived. It was enough for them that they filled a need for each other and they gave no thought to the future.

Chapter Four

Sun Bear's eighth summer had drawn to a close. He had spent as much time each day as he could with Little Frog, but being an active boy, he had to keep moving a good share of the day. He also had to spend a share of his time in the fields. During the day they must pull the ever-present weeds and drive off the birds. At night it was the responsibility of the younger members of the village to take turns guarding the crops against the rodents and other animals. The biggest threat to the corn was the masked bandits, the raccoons, who were more wary because they often would be the next day's meal if they were caught.

In spite of these other activities, he always found time to check on the water gourd and bring out a small bowl of food. It seemed like such a tiny amount to him but to Little Frog, this much regularly each day was like a feast to her who had gone for so long living on so little.

She appreciated his kindness and knew that he was running the risk of his parent's anger if they should discover he was feeding her. That he was recognizing her was enough to bring shame on the whole village. Still, she was glad he did. It was the only light in her otherwise dark and gloomy life.

As fall drew to an end, and the encroaching winter crept up their valley, Little Frog struggled to dig herself a shelter in the south end of the heap. This was the way she had managed to survive the previous winters. The rotting and decaying matter in the heap created a small amount of heat that made it possible for her to stand the cold nights and blustery days.

Her only fear was for the old man. He was unable to move on his own and she could not move him without help. Although she was sure he would not last much longer, she decided to ask Sun Bear to help her with him. She was spared this when she awoke one morning to find he had expired during the night. He was buried in a shallow trench at the edge of the dumpsite. In a few summers the heap would expand out over his body and there would be no stone to mark his final resting-place.

Little Frog's days became longer and even more lonely now that she did not have the old one to look after. The brief visits from Sun Bear only heightened her loneliness. Before he had come into her life, she had resigned herself to this stoic existence, but now Sun Bear had aroused feelings, which she had thought, were long dead and buried in her miserable past.

Sun Bear knew nothing of these feelings, but he was aware of Little Frog's plight. He worried about her, and wondered how she could possibly live out the winter in the heap without more protection. His gifts of food, water, and whatever rags and skins he could find were not enough. He knew it would be miserably cold without a fire; still, there was no way he could help her. A fire in the dump, besides being dangerous, would call attention to her and then he would no longer be able to take her food and water. The best he could do was to find her more coverings and help her dig deeper into the heap. To this end, he helped her fashion a rude but sturdy little burrow on the south end of the dumpsite. At least she would have some protection against the worst of the storms.

Keenwah had noticed he was still taking food and wondered how long he would have to feed his dog. A pup sometimes needed a little help but soon learned to shift for itself. Food scraps were not that hard to find around a village of this size. She also wondered why she had never seen the dog with her son. Most times a dog and a boy became inseparable, but she never caught even a hint of his dog.

Sun Bear was becoming more careless as time went by, so when Keenwah saw him take a cloak of old, but still usable skins, and head for the dump, she was naturally curious, and followed after him. She stayed far enough back not to attract his attention but close enough to see what he planned to do with the cloak. In the back of her mind she was telling herself he was making a bed for the animal, and a usable cloak was going too far for even his dog.

Rounding the end of the dump she was in time to see him pass the cloak to a horrible looking figure half buried in the heap. She watched as he took a gourd and ran to the stream and returned with it filled with water. This too he passed to the creature in the dump. Keenwah was perplexed. She did not know what to make of this. She would talk to Maata and ask his advice.

Normally children were the responsibility of their mother until their manhood rites. The father would help in their training, but would never interfere with any chastisement dealt out by their mothers. This was one of the times Keenwah was ready to ask for help. She had never encountered this sort of an obstacle, and as far as she knew, neither had any mother in the village.

Maata listened to her recital without comment, thinking about what she had told him of their son's actions. He too was puzzled and would have liked to ask someone for advice, but there was no one to talk to about a matter such as this. He told Keenwah he would think about it for a few days and they would talk again.

Maata made it a point to investigate the creature for himself. Like all the people of the village, he knew there were those on the heap from time to time. They usually did not last long. He had helped bury an old man only a short time earlier, but he had never looked at them; they did not really exist as long as you did not recognize them. They were something to be tolerated, but no one had to accept them.

Seeing Little Frog in all of her ugliness, he wondered how his son could have ever become involved with someone like that. She might have put a spell on his son, but he had his doubts about that. If she had power for a spell, it stood to reason she would use it to do better for herself than a small bowl of mush and a gourd filled with water. Still, he could see no real harm in what Sun Bear was doing. He thought long about it before he brought the subject up again with Keenwah.

"When you thought he was feeding a pup, it did not worry you about the food, did it?"

"No. Of course not. Every boy has an animal he takes care of," she answered, trying to follow his line of thought.

"He does not take much food, does he? I mean, even a puppy would eat more than he takes, is this not true?"

"Yes. He takes very little and nothing of value. Why do you ask such questions? What have they to do with what he is doing? We know now that he is not feeding a dog, he is feeding that creature on the dump." Keenwah was upset by her man's talk. What was he trying to get at?

"It seems to me that if you did not begrudge the food when you thought he was feeding an animal, then you should not feel any differently when you find he is feeding that creature." Maata had given this a lot of thought, and while he did not know the right and wrong of it from the social stand point, he knew in his heart that it was not wrong to share with someone less fortunate, especially if they were unable to look after themselves. This poor creature obviously could not.

"This is different. The creature is not a dog, it is a non-person and certainly not a fit companion for our son," she said angrily, raising her voice at her mate for the first time in their life together.

"Our son has no other companions. His size has excluded him from the joys of normal boyhood. I too would have rather he had taken a dog for a friend, but he has not, he has taken time to be kind to a poor, unfortunate creature. But I do not see where we should interfere with him. I suggest we ignore or even offer to help him. Our son grows toward manhood rapidly and soon will have to make his own decisions. We should encourage him to make wise decisions when we can, and support him even when we think he might be wrong. Is not this the duty of his mother and father?"

Keenwah let this go without a comment but she was far from being satisfied with Maata's answer. She did not know what she expected exactly, but she had hoped for something better than what he had to offer. She decided to take the matter to the old wise woman who lived on the lip of the canyon west of the village. She was reputed to be the oldest and wisest person in the People's world. She could be trusted not to say anything indiscreet nor would she do anything to cause harm to come to Sun Bear. Maybe she would know how to deal with this situation.

When Keenwah returned from her visit with the old Wise One, she was still much troubled, but infinitely relieved. The wise woman, Paataga, had told her not to worry. She had not bothered to explain why, but she had given instructions on what to do to assist Sun Bear without recognizing his actions or interfering in any way. Keenwah was still not sure this was the right thing to do, but she felt if she was helping her son, then she could accept part of the blame if the Spirit Watcher became angry with him. She did not fear the Spirit Watcher, but she did respect him.

Following Paataga's instructions, Keenwah called her son to her and told him it was time for him to learn more of the skills of the People. All men were able to weave baskets and mats, as well as blankets and cloaks. The women did most of this work, but it was considered necessary for the men to know how. It was going to be part of his manhood rites, anyway, and he might as well start learning now. Maata would teach him all the things about the hunt and the raising of crops, but it was Keenwah's job to teach him the weaving and pot making skills he would need.

First Sun Bear must capture as many rabbits as he could for the skins. He was to use the snare his father had taught him how to spin and set. The snare did not destroy the skins like the arrows and spears, or even skillfully thrown rocks. When he brought a rabbit to Keenwah, she had him skin it and place it fur-side down on a log in front of the pueblo. With the razor sharp edge of a flint knife, she taught him how to cut it in one long, continuous, narrow strip, going in a circular motion around the skin and ending in the center. This way, only the legs and the ears were trimmed off. While the skin was still wet or "green," he tied one end to a pole sticking out of the ceiling. The other end was tied to a small stone with a hole in it. The stone had been selected for just this purpose. It was heavy enough to stretch the skin out straight, but not heavy enough to tear the delicate rabbit skin. As the sun and wind dried the skins, they were taken down and stored inside until the time when there would be enough to make a blanket or robe from them.

During this time Keenwah also kept Sun Bear collecting shoots of yucca plants, and together they pounded them to separate the long, stringy fibers from the pulp. These fibers were spun into ropes or cords. As they spun the smaller strands, she taught him how to entwine turkey feathers into them to make a strand of insulated material for warm cloaks and robes.

Gathering of turkey feathers was a job for everyone. Turkeys had been domesticated and now roamed the pueblo and the surrounding area freely. Their feathers were constantly being dropped about the place and were gathered up and put in large baskets, where they became common property. Of course little children and girls were expected to do most of this.

As they practiced the art of spinning, Keenwah made sure that Sun Bear still had time to visit his friend at the dump and that he had enough food. Keenwah even insisted on giving him more choice pieces of meat, just as Paataga had instructed her to do.

Sun Bear's first attempt at a robe for himself turned out to be much too short and narrow for his body, although he thought he had followed his mother's plans very carefully. The robe she had made for his father had turned out beautifully, while his was useless as far as he could see.

"Oh, my. What a mess we made out of that robe," Keenwah laughed. "I wonder what I did wrong." she continued, taking the blame on herself. He was prepared to take it apart and save the strips as best he could to try to make it over, but Keenwah, still laughing, told him. "No, Sun Bear. Why do we not throw it away? We have plenty of skins to work with. Besides, you can always find more rabbits if we need them."

Sun Bear looked at his mother inquiringly. Did she know about Little Frog, or was it just by chance that this new robe would come close to fitting her? Maybe she had seen the creature and was thinking about her. Whatever the reason, Sun Bear was glad to oblige his mother and discard the robe. To think, Little Frog would have her very first new garment, one without holes or rips, one that was not splattered with grease from the cook fires.

When he presented it to her, Little Frog's joy left her speechless. Finally Sun Bear backed away and left her by herself. He did not pretend to understand everything but he though he knew how she must feel and he was an intruder.

During the winter, Keenwah continued to guide and instruct her son in the making of many useful items. The results of many of his toils ended up on the heap, but they were never wasted. There was nothing that she had him throw away that would not benefit Little Frog in some way. It was always useful, protective and gratefully received by the creature.

Of course, Sun Bear became more suspicious of his mother and her motives, but he refrained from asking any questions. He was satisfied to be able to provide for his little friend in any manner that he could, without having to steal from his family to do it.

When Little Frog questioned his gifts and how he happened to be able to bring her so much, Sun Bear assured her that all he brought was willingly thrown away by his parents, and that she was not to worry. He was not stealing. He was not taking any chance of bringing shame on himself or anyone else.

"Your parents must be very rich to be able to throw away new material," Little Frog commented.

"No. It's just that my father is a good provider and my mother wants me to make things right, so she will not let me keep anything that is not right, or does not fit me. She says to keep a failure around is a bad thing. It just reminds me that I failed and the best thing to do is get rid of it and start fresh."

With help from Sun Bear's strong and capable hands, Little Frog burrowed deeper into the heap. Sun Bear piled anything he could find to make walls, and even constructed a rude doorway and covered it with a piece of matting to keep the wind out and a little warmth in.

The Spirit Watcher must have approved of them because he shed his light on them nearly every day for the next three winters, leaving the Chaco Valley basking in his warmth. This made it easier for Little Frog to survive. Sun Bear and Little Frog were happy together, and they were thankful for the Spirit Watcher's aid. The adults, on the other hand, were not so thankful. They knew little and cared less about the creature in the dump. They looked at the dry, bare ground and knew there would be less water for them next summer. They knew the summers would be even hotter and drier than the last. The older members of the village swore that each summer was drier than any they could ever remember, even when they were children, and they were right.

Sun Bear continued to grow. He was taller than his father, and while not as wide or as heavy, he showed every promise of growing much taller. His arms and legs were long and sinewy and his torso developed into near perfect form as he ran the roads leading out from the hub of his world.

Every day runners came and went, and the people from far and near came to sit in the Great Kiva and watch plays performed there. Singing and dancing went on from early spring to late fall, and often into the mild winters when it was still warm enough to be comfortable.

Sun Bear and Little Frog did not get to see the plays in the kiva. Little Frog would have been forbidden entrance because she was a woman child. Sun Bear still had not had his manhood rites, so he was not qualified to attend either, but they could still hear the songs, and sometimes they could see the dancers practicing outside of the kiva.

Sun Bear often wondered why no one teased him about his association with Little Frog. He was sure they all knew about her by now. The boys of the village gave him a wide berth and said nothing to him at all, and the adults were as kind and courteous as ever. It never occurred to him that his size alone was enough to preclude him from their torment. Nor did he know that Paataga had quietly passed an edict to the adults, telling them in no uncertain terms, to mind their own business and leave the business of Sun Bear to her and the Spirit Watcher.

As he approached the twelfth summer of his life, Sun Bear was well prepared for his manhood rites. He would become a man. Little Frog was elated for him, but could not help but wonder how it would affect her. How could he still care for her as he became a man and took his place with the men? Soon he would be picking a mate of his own and have a home of his own. She was sure his mate would not want to share him with her as Keenwah had done. Little Frog's heart grew heavy with mixed emotions as the day of his manhood rites drew near.

Chapter Five

The manhood rites for the boys of twelve summers were always held at the same time each summer. It was after the corn was tall and the grain was well established but, before the harvest time. It came after the celebration, which marked the longest day of summer. With the official passing of the long day of summer came the marking of a person's summers. Any boy born after this time was considered not old enough to participate in the manhood rites. Sun Bear had been born in the spring, so he was well past his twelfth summer and would be taking his rites with the rest of the boys his age.

There were many preliminary tests to determine if they were ready for manhood. The complete ritual took nearly one full turn of Sister Moon. In the late summer and early fall, the weather was agreeable and everyone had time to watch the contestants in their various events.

First there were tests with their weapons. They must display their accuracy and speed with bows and arrows. Then they must hurl the short spear and be judged for both distance and penetration, as well as marksmanship. It was seldom that anyone was disqualified in these early trials. Next came the common skills, much of which they had learned from their mothers. Some things might be considered women's work, but all of the People were expected to know the rudiments of establishing a home. Each lad was asked to perform specific tasks. Some were asked to display their talents in pottery making. Not just common pottery, but finely finished hand painted pots. Others were expected to weave baskets or rugs, and again it was to be their finest work. Still others were required to knap stones for points or tools. Every boy had been watched and coached by the elders in the village and they were asked to do what they were most proficient in. This was not really a test, but more of a chance for them to show off their best skills so the parents could take pride in their pupils.

More demanding tests consisted of making a long rope from any material they desired. This rope had to be long enough and strong enough to allow them to descend from a designated cliff or rock formation. If the rope was not long enough, they had two choices. They could either climb back up in shame, or drop the remaining distance. If the rope broke, they had only one choice, to land as well as they could. Beginning with this event, some lads could be disqualified, though seldom were any careless enough to allow this to happen.

They were also expected to gather and dress stones for building purposes. Here they were judged on their ability to pick suitable stones and to come up with a uniform size without measurements. The elders would choose one stone from each lad and dress it, and this was used as a measure of the boy's efforts. Certain latitude was allowed, but the overall results must be close. Each summer's collection of these stones was added to an already standing wall in the courtyard, and old men would come and point to the stone they had chosen many summers ago.

The test of strength was one many of the boys dreaded the most. They must carry rocks; not just one, but quite a number of them. The rocks were of various sizes and weight, usually increasing as they went along. Each had to be carried a prescribed distance, and as the rocks became heavier, the distances became longer. It was a real test of strength and endurance. The rocks were the same rocks that had been used for ages. They had been carried up and down the valley by countless generations of boys. The lads had known of the rocks all their lives. They had played around them, but had never been allowed to test them for weight. There would be a few surprises here and a few more boys would be disqualified.

Up until now all the events were considered simple, but the main tests were saved for the last. Second to last was the survival trial; where the boys were taken out into the wilderness and stripped of every possession, even their last shred of clothing. The sites were selected in advance, and like the rocks, had been used for many summers. The site must have all the necessary items for survival. Necessities included at least a small amount of water, even if a small jug had to be placed there, suitable rocks for knapping knives and spear points, and wood for handles of spears and a club. There had to be sufficient game to provide what was required. The yucca plant, too, was considered a necessary item.

For ten days a boy must survive, but he could not just sit and suffer it out. He was given a list of things expected of him during these ten days. He had to capture and gather food, make a fire bow, and make a fire. He must make at least one pot, just a plain, serviceable cooking pot. He did not have to make bows or arrows. These items took longer and the boys had already demonstrated their ability with their bows for the earlier events. However, he did have to make a short, heavy spear with a large point. With this he would kill larger game. To do any of these things he first had to make a simple knife. All of these skills had been taught to the boys by their parents and elders of the village, so their abilities would reflect on not only themselves, but on the whole village. It was seldom that a boy did not complete this survival test with honor.

When the boys returned to the village in ten days, they must be armed with the short spear and carry a club. They must have the skins of several animals, one of which had to be from a larger animal such as a deer or an antelope. He must have a coil of all-purpose rope made from the yucca plant. He could wear skins for clothing and any type of footwear he could devise. The last, and most important, item he must bring with him out of the wilderness was his cooking pot, and in it he should have live coals from his fire. These items proved he would be able to provide for himself and his family, and were necessary to be called a man. But there was still one test left, and while it had nothing to do with a man's ability to provide, it was still considered most important.

With the conclusion of the last test, the boy could claim to be a man and demand the rights of a man. While he would always respect his mother, she would no longer have any voice in his life, nor could she punish or scold him.

The ruler or the elders would dispense any chastisement he might receive after this. His father could still counsel him, but as a friend, not as a parent. If the boy succeeded he would be able to start courting for a mate, and in a few summers would be settled down in his own home, with his own fields and children. Life expectancy among the People was quite short, usually not over four hand spans or forty summers, so adult life began early.

Sun Bear had completed each test successfully and in record time. Even in events where his size was no advantage, he still excelled because of his determination. The elders were satisfied he had accomplished all that was required, but there was some grumbling among the other contestants that it was not fair for them to have to compete with someone like him. Matuga heard the complaints but made no move to change the course of events. He knew there was another test going on here that was not in their normal schedule and he waited anxiously to see how it would turn out.

The last event concerned even Sun Bear because he knew of the complaints and knew they were founded in this particular event. The last test required endurance and strength and determination. It was a foot race, a long race for a boy, if not for a man.

There was a course laid out from the Pueblo Bonito circling out though several smaller villages to make a loop and come back to the valley. Everyone would leave at the same time and run their best, according to their ability and strategy. The qualifications were determined by the first runner to come in. He must run up to where Matuga sat and pull the stopper from a gourd hanging near by. The gourd was filled with sand that began to trickle out when the stopper was removed. When the last grain of sand had fallen, the race was announced to be over and anyone who had not come in by this time was disqualified and must wait another summer before they could try again. They would not have to complete the other tests again, just this last one.

Sun Bear, like all the other boys, had made the run several times. The course was no secret and they were allowed to practice on it the last summer before the final race. He had timed himself with a similar sized gourd and with the help of Little Frog. He had also timed some of the fastest runners among the other boys. He knew he could finish in record time, but he also knew he would disqualify every other boy in the race. There were none that could come close to him. He did not owe them any debt of friendship, because none had offered him friendship. Still, he knew in all fairness he could not do this to them. He had thought of pacing himself with the leading runner, but this would only shame them more and everyone would know what he was doing. It looked to him that no matter how he ran the race, it would be no contest to either the others or himself.

After a talk with Little Frog, who could also see there was nothing fair in this race, he came up with what he hoped would be a fair alternative. He went before Matuga on the day before the race and presented his request.

"I cannot run in this race with the other boys. It would not be fair to them, or to me."

"How so, Sun Bear?" Matuga asked innocently, as though he did not see any difference in the runners. This was what he had been watching and waiting for. He knew it was an unfair race, but he wanted to see who would be the first to call his attention to it. The other boys had been complaining but none of them had come forth to speak to him about it.

"I have timed myself and some of the others in this race and I can disqualify them all, but this would not mean they were not good runners. They cannot be blamed for not having my long legs, and I do not think it would be right for me to lag back and not run my best."

"So, what do you propose we do about it? I cannot qualify you without letting you prove you can run this race, even though we all know you can. Still, it must be done."

"I know this, also." The lad kept his head erect, carefully looking just over the ruler's head to show respect without being arrogant.

"Do you have another suggestion?" Matuga asked, for he was sure Sun Bear had something in mind and was curious to see just what he might have come up with. If it was a reasonable request, he was sure they could grant it, as long as it satisfied the conditions of the race.

"Yes, sir, I have. I propose they run their normal race and that I run a race of my own, separate from them."

"And who would you run against? There is no one here who can run with you, not even my own runners. Who then would you compete with? There has to be competition or it is not a race, only a run."

"There would be competition. I would race against my own best time. I would race against time itself."

"And how could you do this, Sun Bear, so it would be fair to all, including yourself?"

Sun Bear took a long breath and released it slowly. Then he spoke before his courage deserted him. "I would run to Aztec and back." There. He had said it. If Matuga accepted his challenge, he would be forced to try an impossible run, but he would not back out of it now.

Matuga did not seem surprised by this request. It was similar to what he himself had been thinking.

"And what time would you set on yourself for such a feat? To make such a run at all is quite a task for a boy, even such a big boy as you are. How long do you think it would take you? Two days? Three, maybe?" Matuga asked. It seemed like a fair time to him.

"No, sir. I would make it in one continuous run. I would leave when the rest of them do, and if I am not back before the last grain of sand has fallen, I will be disqualified just as any other boy."

Matuga's face registered his surprise. This was far more than he had expected. He looked at the tall, thin lad standing in front of him. Was this just an idle boast? He did not think so. He had watched this boy grow up. He had never seen anything false about him, no bravado. He knew him to be a simple, kind-hearted boy who had never caused anyone any trouble.

"But Sun Bear, do you realize what you are saying? The course you have chosen is at least twice as long as the one they will be running. I think it is noble of you to make such an offer but, well, let's be reasonable, son. No boy could make such a run in that length of time. To set yourself an impossible race is not fair either."

Maata had stood silent as his son had made his request. He was also surprised, although he knew he should not have been. Sun Bear had not mentioned this to him, but he had known his son was troubled by the upcoming race. He felt he must speak in his son's behalf, so he stepped forward and asked permission to speak his own counsel on the matter.

"My son can make the run. I know. I have run with him and I know what he can do. I do not know, however, if he can do it in the length of time he has set for himself, but it is a competition, a race, and surely this would satisfy all the conditions of the elders. I say let him try. If he does not make it, it will not bring shame on the village and he can always try again next summer."

Matuga consulted with his elders and, after much head shaking and disagreement between them, it was finally decided to allow Sun Bear to make the run since no one had a better suggestion. It was agreed that he could, in all likelihood, make the race, but none of them thought he had a chance of returning in the required time.

Once this change became known, there was noticeable relief among the other boys and their parents. The whole village looked on this strange lad with a new respect. He was doing something they were not sure they would have done in his place. They did not know if he was just foolish or bragging, or if he was actually trying to be fair to them. Whatever the reason, they all had a chance now, all but Sun Bear. They knew that none of them could have competed against him in the regular race. Now they felt a strong hope that he would succeed in his race. At least they hoped he could finish it, and then maybe next summer he would be in better shape for it and they would all be men and not have to worry about him again.

The race had to be postponed for a couple days to make the necessary arrangements for Sun Bear. Toolke, the ruler of the Aztec district, had to be notified of the event so he would be prepared for Sun Bear's arrival. To meet the requirements, Toolke would have to verify that Sun Bear had actually been there. Matuga would send a small gift with the runner, who would present it to Toolke, who in return would send back a token for Matuga. This would be proof that Sun Bear had completed the race.

"What shall I send as a fitting gift?" Matuga asked of his elders, while Sun Bear was still before him.

The elders were quick to catch Matuga's meaning and they began to shower him with suggestions.

"We could send him a jug of our water. It is well known they do not have as good water as we do down here."

"No. That might spill and be wasted. Besides, Sun Bear might be tempted to drink it all before he got there."

"How about a basket of corn?" called another.

As they named different items, Sun Bear became alarmed. All the gifts these men were suggesting were heavy and bulky, and the extra weight could make a difference in a race like this. He had hoped for something little and light.

From the corner of his eye, Matuga was watching the lad. He was enjoying his little joke, but he did not want to carry it too far. So his next comments were aimed at relieving the boy.

"I was thinking of something worthless but still representative of our esteem for the distinguished ruler in the north."

"Ho! Ho! Matuga, are you going to send him your wife?" one of the elders jeered, to the laughter of everyone. They all knew of the devotion Matuga had for his mate of many summers.

"No, not that worthless. I had in mind to send him my turquoise pendant. Sun Bear could wear it around his neck on the run and it would not hold him back too much."

Sun Bear realized he was the victim of their prank; and they were just having fun at his expense. They were not seriously considering weighing him down. He should have known they were all on his side, and that they wanted him to succeed. It was not only for himself he ran, but for the honor of the village. It was something he had not considered when he made the offer. He must make the run and he must make it in time; to fail would bring shame to his village. He had a new admiration for the elders who had agreed to let him try the run, knowing his chances of success were less than great.

The original run was considered to be a long day's run at best. It usually started around the middle of the night with Sister Moon's light to help them. With any luck they would all be back in late afternoon. For Sun Bear to make his run he knew he would have to push as hard as he dared all through the night and early morning before the heat became too intense. After that he would need to watch his pace for the rest of the day. The hardest part would be in the afternoon, when the sun was hot and the thirst would be on him. He would be tired and want to rest, but he must not. He could not afford even a short rest for two reasons. First, he would not have the time to spare, and second, if he stopped after a long hard run, it would be almost impossible to start running again and he could never keep up the pace.

Several of Matuga's personal runners came to coach him. They had all seen him run, and this young giant had paced many of them for the past few summers. They gave him landmarks to look for since he had never been very far along this trail. By watching the stars and the landmarks, he could gauge his distance and pace. They told him where he needed to be by sunrise to be of good time. One of them handed him three small pebbles taken from the streambed of a river far north.

"Place these in your mouth when you become thirsty but know you cannot drink more. They will help drive the madness from your mind by making your body think it is receiving a drink."

His father drew him aside and gave him advice on how to handle a long run. It was evident that all were trying to help him; all of them wanted him to succeed, not just for the village, but for himself. If he finished in time, everyone could share in his achievement

"You must drink a little water at regular intervals so your body will not dry out. You cannot carry very much water, but it will be twice the normal boy's ration. This is only fair since you are bigger and are going twice the distance. You will cross two streams, but to drink from them would be cheating. No one but you will know about this. Also, the cold water might give you cramps and deprive you of your chance to win."

Sun Bear appreciated his father's confidence. He talked as if he really expected him to return on time. This was more evident with his next piece of advice.

"Remember, son, it is not so important that you should win the race, although I am sure you will. What is most important is to complete it. When you come back, for you shall come back, and if you are making better time than you thought, there will be a temptation to call out as you come over the cliff. I know you will want to cry out to announce your return so everyone will hear and rejoice with you. But you must not. This would be boasting, and it is not right for a man to boast of his deeds. I would go up there myself but it is not right for a father to boast of a son. Others may boast if they feel you deserve it, but you and I must not do anything to call attention to you, lest the Spirit Watcher becomes angry with you and strikes you down as punishment as you come down the steps on the cliff."

"I will not make a sound, Father, unless it is the pounding of my heart and the wheezing of my breathing," he promised.

As they talked, they were close to the dump and Little Frog heard their words. She heard Maata say it was all right for someone else to brag about him. She made up her mind she would brag as loud as she could, even if no one heard her or recognized her.

Two days later it was announced that all was in readiness. Runners had been sent out ahead to let Toolke know of Sun Bear's coming and the purpose of his run, so he would be prepared to receive him and have a gift ready for his return. There was a festive air in the village as many people came to wish him well, people who had never spoken to him before.

Keenwah prepared a special meal for him the day before his run. It was high in protein. She did not have the advantage of advanced technology, but summers of experience in the ways of the People had taught them what was best for runners. She had prepared a casing from deer intestines filled with pounded dry meat and mixed with sweet red berries. He would be allowed to carry this ration with him on his run. It had been agreed that he should carry the same rations as the other runners, only in double proportion.

He knew he should take a long rest while he had the chance, but he was unable to lie down because of the excitement. Finally Maata came to him with some last bits of advice.

"As a man, you must learn to control you body and your mind as well. You cannot let them control you. Any boy can grow to be old, but he cannot be a real man until he can make his body and mind work together and obey him. Now lie down and force every muscle in your body to relax. I do not say you must sleep, but you can rest and build up your strength for the race. You will need all of it."

Sun Bear obeyed his father. He lay down on the rooftop and tried to make his body relax. At first he did not have much luck, until he thought of Little Frog. She had to spend every day in one place; she could not move around much without a lot of discomfort. Surely she must have learned control over her twisted body. If a little, deformed non-person girl could do this, then so could he. Just thinking about Little Frog took his mind off himself and his body began to relax. Soon he was asleep, and his mind took care of itself and his body.

When Maata came to tell him it was time to prepare for the race, he found his son soundly sleeping with a smile on his face. Maata knew this was a good sign. Sun Bear was no longer troubled and he had rested well.

"Come, my son. It is almost time for the race to begin. You must come down and warm up so you will be in shape for the run."

In the light of Sister Moon and the pale stars, the boys were all jogging around, flexing their arms and legs, and breathing deeply to fill their lungs to the limit. When the word was passed they all came to the starting line to determine their right to be called a man.

One of them first, and then by twos and threes, they came to Sun Bear and wished him well. It was their way of thanking him for giving them a chance. It was the first time for most of them to speak to him, and it was awkward for all of them, including Sun Bear, who did not know what to say in response to their good wishes.

"I can only hope the first of you to come in will stumble a little before he reaches the gourd. I will need all the time I can get." It was taken as the joke he intended, but gave them all a pause for thought.

When the signal was given, each one took off at top speed, giving a burst in the moonlight. The boys heading east left in a group with no one giving ground. They would hold this speed until they were out of sight. Then they would settle down to an easier pace, each setting his own pace and stride in accordance with what he knew he could do. Sun Bear faced to the north, a few seasoned runners beside him to pace him for a short distance. He too put on a burst of speed, but he knew he must hold his pace faster all the way. He could not afford the slower pace of the pack. They would have each other to gauge their time and speed. He would have nothing but what the runners had told him. Every heartbeat had to count; he could not tarry, nor could he run too fast,

lest he should burn himself out before he completed the race and end by walking back slowly and in great shame.

As he passed the dump, he was surprised to hear Little Frog call to him,
"Run, Sun Bear. Run with the wind. May the Spirit Watcher smile on your good
deed."

"Watch for me, Little Frog, you will see me before the sun goes down."

He hoped it was not an empty promise. He had never made such a run
as this before. He only hoped he had not set a goal he could not obtain.

As he neared the steps cut up the cliff the other runners fell back and
shouted last bits of advice and encouragement to him. He waved to them but
did not waste his breath as he sprinted up the steps. He made a mental note to
be careful on his return. His legs would be weak and he could stumble to his
death instead of glory.

At the top of the cliff the road led straight toward the distant village of
Aztec. The runners had told him his pace was faster than they would set for the
run, but he knew he had to push, he could not relent. Over the past summers he
had developed a pace that he knew he could maintain for long periods of time.
He had never had to keep it up for this long, but he struck it now and intended
to keep it up as long as his body would allow.

He started watching for the first landmark. It was one he knew well
because he had run this way before, not very far but far enough to recognize it.
This time it had special significance to him. This time it was the first marker on
a long, long trip.

Chapter Six

Sun Bear was glistening with sweat and his breath was coming with a little difficulty already. He knew he was pushing too hard, but until he could see the first landmark, he would not slacken his pace. In the silvery light of the moon, he caught sight of his first goal: a strip of bare rock sloping off to the side of the road. It was pale colored and in the moonlight it appeared almost white, like bleached bones of a long dead monster. As he drew along side of the naked stone, he checked the position of the stars in the north. If the runners were right, he was well ahead of his schedule. He slowed his pace; he could afford to take a breather. Not that he would stop; he would only trot at a slower pace for a little while until he could catch his breath. The second wind, as every runner knew, was the savior of the runner. Without this second wind, no one could ever accomplish any of the great runs.

The cool of night felt refreshing to his warm body, the air moving by as he ran created enough draft to evaporate the perspiration streaking his body. As he trotted on, he began to feel more confident. His breathing was smooth and regular; his body was warm but not feverish. For a short period of time a pain bothered him in his left side. This was common among runners, not serious, just unpleasant. It came and it went, as he knew it would, never staying long enough to seriously hamper him. Once he felt the tremors of a cramp in his lower leg. He ran stiff legged for a space until it relinquished its hold on him.

By the time the Spirit Watcher made his first appearance, Sun Bear was in full stride and running comfortably. His home in Chaco Canyon was far behind him and receding with each long stride he took. He was farther north than he had ever been before and everything was new to him. He watched for the landmarks the runners had described for him, checking against the time. He was less sure of his schedule now, but felt he was doing the best speed he could hope to maintain.

The pine trees had thinned out until only here and there, in the far valleys, they could still be seen. The stunted junipers and the nut pines grew widely spaced. In between, the straggly sage bushes grew.

Coming over the crest of a long rise, he could see the distant mountains far to the north, their peaks still harboring small strips of dirty snow. Sun Bear speculated on these formidable mountains. He had seen them before from an even longer distance. Every time he saw them he wished he could go to them. He would love to explore them. He had heard tales from some of the runners who had actually been there. They told him how the air was crisp and clean, a little hard to breathe for a low land runner. They told of streams of water so cold that you could not stay in them, of valleys filled with green grass that stayed green all summer. Game was so plentiful there that no one ever need go hungry. They also told him of the snow that sometimes got so deep in the winter that a man could not walk through it, but must make special shoes to walk on top of it.

It all seemed so strange and wonderful to Sun Bear. Someday maybe he would make a trip to see all these marvelous things.

One landmark after another dropped behind him. He was amazed at his own strength and endurance. He was far ahead of the schedule the runners had suggested and yet he was not tired. Nor was he out of breath; he was running his usual gait, which he had used ever since he had started following his father and the other runners.

According to his estimation, he would be in Aztec early in the morning. Another slight rise ahead of him shielded his view. When he topped the rise, he could see the sharp peak off to his right. The peak did not rise high above the plains. Instead, the ground dropped away from it, leaving it setting by itself out in the barren valley. It was another of his landmarks. Just ahead he could see the first of the two rivers he must cross. From here the road ran mostly downhill to the first river. Across it, he had only one more series of hills to climb before he came down to the second and last river, where Aztec stood. He had never been to Aztec, but the runners had told him what to look for. The road ran directly to the village on the other side of the river. There were other villages nearby, but he would not stop at any of them.

Splashing through the first river, he was reminded of what he had been told of the rivers in the mountains. If the water in them were much colder than this, it would surely take a man's breath away. This water was so chilling, it made him hurry to get to the other side. Even as hot as he was, the cold water made the Spirit Watcher's beams feel good on his bare, wet skin.

Ahead the road ran through the willows and bushes before it began the steep climb up the hill. In this lower ground, hordes of hungry mosquitoes tried to keep up with him. He could hear the angry roar of the millions of wings all moving at once. Looking up he could see them forming a dark cloud over his head. Never had he seen so many in one place. He was sure they could suck all the blood from a man in a very short time if they had the chance. He was glad when the road climbed the hill and the morning breeze swept them away from him.

If possible, the second river was even colder than the first. Sun Bear did not know that this river had only a short distance to travel since it had left the snow fields of its birth, while the other had traveled several days in the sun before the crossing place. The second river was not as wide as the first, but it was more swift and deeper than the other. He became frightened for his life when he was nearly swept from his feet in mid-stream. If he had not been warned in advance, he did not think he would have made it.

The runners had told him to pick up a rock as large as he could carry before he entered the river. The stone would hold him down in the swift water and help him keep his footing. Even so it was all he could do to hang on to the rock. He wanted very much to drop it and try to lunge for the far shore. If he had, he thought, he would have been swept away. He was glad there was no one watching him to see his shame. He remembered his father's warning about letting the mind and body take control. Now he must remain in control of them. It was the only thing that saved his life. He dropped the stone with a sigh of relief as he came up the opposite side of the river only a short way from the village of Aztec.

It was a large village and its neat square design made it a pleasant sight nestled in the trees and dappled with sunlight. The People of Aztec did not see Sun Bear until he was almost in their courtyard. He was not expected until midday at the earliest. The first person to spot him and recognize him for who he was let out a series of high pitched, shrill cries which alerted everyone of his approach.

The ruler, Toolke, an old man by the People's standards, bustled out looking important. He was ready to argue with anyone who would try to tell him that the one called Sun Bear was already here. One of the runners sent up to announce his coming stepped forward and identified him as the lad they were expecting.

Once his identity was established, there came rounds of questions about when he had left. They were sure he had slipped out last night and gotten an early start on the others. There was no question of honor or ethics; it would have been considered a wise move on his part. When he tried to assure them he had not left early but at the same time as the rest of the boys, they were once more suspicious of him. The same runner who had identified him earlier stepped forward to speak again.

"I have seen the Sun Bear run; indeed, he has run beside me many times, often turning back when another runner came from the opposite direction. I know he can run. I also know him to be an honest boy. I have never heard anyone question his integrity, or that of his parents who are most honored in Bonito as the friend of Matuga. If Sun Bear says he did not leave early, then I believe him. He has the spirit of a true runner."

This was a high complement to the lad, and Toolke considered the word of the runner as the truth. Runners were the most trusted men in the nation. There was no written word, and everything the runner carried, he carried in his mind. He had to memorize and be able to recite what he had been told. He was not allowed to make mistakes. If this runner spoke these words, then they must be true.

"I guess I owe you an apology, son. Come, sit, and we will have a meal prepared for you," Toolke offered.

"No thank you, sir," Sun Bear said as he continued to trot around the group in slow easy steps. "I would not dare eat a meal and I have to return before darkness sets in."

"Do not tell me the Sun Bear is afraid of the dark?"

"No sir. I am not afraid of the dark, I am afraid of not returning before the sand runs out of the gourd," Sun bear said, still keeping his pace.

"Come now. Stop. You are making me dizzy, running around like a lizard in the sun. Stop. Stop and sit, and at least take a drink of cool water."

Sun Bear never stopped or slowed his pace as he explained to Toolke about the danger of cramps if he drank cool water or let his steaming body cool down too fast. The other runners backed up his words with their own.

"If you do not mind, sir? I will turn this pendant over to you and be on my way."

"What? Why? Well, that is impossible. What is the matter with Matuga? He should know better than to send a runner on an impossible run like this, no, indeed. You cool off and rest. You can go back tomorrow morning. I will send one of my runners with you to explain to Matuga the reason you were held up."

"Oh, no, sir. Matuga did not send me on an impossible run, I sent myself and I cannot stay. I must return tonight, before the sand runs out or I will have failed my manhood rites," Sun Bear pleaded.

Toolke's young wife had been listening to the exchange of words, and took this occasion to speak to her husband, who was many summers her senior.

"Toolke. Stop teasing the boy. Can you not see it is not a joke to him? He is serious and every bit of time you rob him of makes his return run more difficult. Now take the gift offered and give him yours so he can be on his way."

Sun Bear gave her a thankful glance and again held out the pendant for Toolke to take. In return he was handed four eagle feathers.

"These were to be for Matuga, but I have changed my mind. Two are for Matuga, one is for your father, and the other is to be for you."

Sun Bear stopped running. He was awe struck; an eagle feather, for him? This was unheard of.

"Truly sir? For me?" he stammered.

"Ah. Yes. That is of course only if you complete your run. That is in time so you are recognized as a man. A boy could not wear a feather. However; even if you do not make it back in time, which I do not see how you can, you may still keep the feather until the day when you can wear it as a man." Toolke was rather proud of himself. This would show Matuga what Toolke thought of a man letting a boy attempt such a run as this, just to prove himself a man. No man had ever done this, let alone a boy.

Toolke's wife wanted to do her part in sending Sun Bear on his way. She knew how important this race was to the lad and to his family. She took her headband from her hair and handed it to him. It was heavily worked with shells, stones, quills and beads. It was a thing of beauty and far from worthless.

"Sun Bear, take this to your mother. If you return in time, she may wear it with pride, and tell her that the wife of Toolke is honored to have met her son. If she ever is in our village, she must be my guest for as long as she wants to stay."

"The son of Keenwah thanks you for her and by the same token, if you are ever in Bonito, my mother and father would be honored to have you as their guest." Sun Bear had started to trot again and was anxious to be on his way.

"Go, Sun Bear, and may the Spirit Watcher watch over you on your return trip," Toolke told him. Somewhere in his memory he could recollect his own boyhood and knew the importance of this day and its events to a youngster.

Sun Bear bid them farewell and started back over the return trail. He had one advantage; he knew the road all the way back now. He had a very good memory for any place that he had seen once. In his mind's eye he could recall every hill and valley along the return trip. He was well ahead of schedule and could not help but wonder how the other boys were doing by now. Would there be one boy who ran faster than the others on this day? He had never noticed any one boy being much faster, but then he had never run with them either, and in this keen competition one could never tell for sure how others might react. He hoped they all ran well, but he could not help but hope none of them were running too fast. He had already run as far as their entire course. A good runner would not be too far behind him. He tried not to think of how far he still had to run. Instead, he tried to imagine how far he could run once the stopper was pulled from the gourd. It ran slowly, but it was definitely a time limit and he would have no way of knowing when the stopper might be pulled to start the sand running to announce the last stage of the race.

"Control yourself," he cautioned. "You know that the best runner could not match you. He would not be much more than halfway by now. He might just now be turning and heading back, just as you are. He will be tired also; he will know that he is in the lead and that not even the mighty Sun Bear can offer him any challenge. He will not stretch himself and risk a burn out. He will look back over his shoulder and keep his eye on his nearest competitor and pace himself accordingly. It is what he would do, was it not? The object of the run was not to eliminate the other runners, only to complete the run."

Feeling better, he settled down to the swinging, easy lope, which had carried him up here in record time. He was feeling great; he knew that his body must be feeling the stress and wear, but it was not registering in his mind. He nibbled on his rations and could not resist the temptation to scoop up a handful of water from the second river. He had already crossed the first and had followed his father's advice to resist the temptation to taste the icy water. The second river was cold enough to cause him trouble if he drank very much, but he must taste this water from the mountains. First he only wet his lips and let a tiny trickle run down his throat. Then he held a mouthful until it warmed before he grudgingly let it slip, one drop at a time, down his throat. He shook his water gourd tied at his side. There was still more than half of it left, more than enough to complete his run. His father had told him it was all right to boast by being able to pour out some of your water ration at the end of the race to show that you had not needed it all. So he ran smoothly as the Spirit Watcher toured overhead, keeping watch over this son of man who dared the impossible.

With his legs quivering and his motions mechanical, without any attention from his brain, he suddenly became aware of an approaching landmark. It was the naked strip of bare rock just north of the canyon. Where had the time and distance gone? Could he be mistaken? Was there another strip of rock like this? Not on the trail he had followed. Had he gotten lost? No, everything was in the right place, he knew where he was, he had run out this way many times.

Ahead he could see the valley opening up. He could almost see the villages in the valley. Checking the sun's position he decided he still had time to make it before dark. Again his mind turned to the other runners. Surely they must all be in by now, but for how long? Could he still complete the race in time? It did not seem possible. He did not dare risk increasing his pace now; he was committed, and any change of pace would prove disastrous. If he was lucky he could hold his pace a little longer, possibly long enough that he would not have to walk the last part of the way in shame.

He drew near the lip of the canyon where the steps were cut down to the lower level. He thought he could hear some one calling encouragement to him. Then the voice became loud and clear and there was no mistaking who it was or what she was saying.

"He comes! He comes!" Little Frog sat on the edge of the cliff by the steps, shouting at the top of her little lungs. "He comes! He comes! He runs like the wind. There is no one who can run like him. He runs like Kaoto. Ayiee! See him run like the Kaoto. Run Kaoto. Run. There is still sand in the gourd." Trying to jump on her crippled, twisted legs, Little Frog continued to shout for him although she nearly toppled over the edge of the cliff.

"Everyone! Look! He comes; like the Kaoto, like the bird who runs with the wind. Run Kaoto. Run."

Sun Bear felt his spirits lifting. She said he still had time. She could see the village below and knew when the other runners had come in. She had timed him many times and she should know. She knew how far he could run while the sand was running out. His legs became stronger, his mind cleared and his breath was coming easier again. He was not even tired; he could run like this forever. "Ayiee!" It was a silent shout; it would not offend the Spirit Watcher. He was like the Kaoto; the little bird that could run so fast.

As he approached the place where Little Frog sat he could see her face. It shone in the late evening sunlight. Why had he ever thought it ugly? She was not ugly; she was just different, but definitely not ugly. Her large gaping mouth was spread in a horrible smile, but it was a smile of victory for him, so how could it be ugly? Then it came to him what an effort it must have been for her to reach this spot. She must have crawled here by herself. No one would have carried her. How long would it take her to get back?

When he was beside her he stooped and lifted her up without slowing down or missing a step. Depositing her on his shoulders, he ran down the steps with dizzying speed, never giving the danger a thought. There was no danger as far as he was concerned. He was invincible. He was the greatest runner ever.

He could see Little Frog's knees on either side of his head as he carried her along. They were scraped and crusted with blood. They were raw, without skin. How the poor soul must have suffered to make this climb just so that she could shout for him. Then he remembered how he had treated her. He had helped her, but he had never spoken out for her, never talked to her in front of others. He had been ashamed, afraid someone might know that he fed her and talked to her. He was determined he would make amends somehow.

She was so light, like an owl, all feathers and skin with only bones beneath. She was so light he could hardly feel her weight on his shoulders.

He could see the village and all those who were out waiting for him as he ran the last distance. His father was standing with his arms folded across his chest. He was silent, he would not say anything, but Sun Bear could see the pride in his eyes and the eyes of his mother.

Some of the elders were calling to him, but he could not understand what they were saying. There seemed to be a ringing in his ears that drowned out their voices. He could only assume they were telling him to hurry, so he gave one more attempt at a burst of speed as he fumbled for his water gourd. He wanted them to know he still had water left. The speed seemed to come. He could almost feel his body flying through the air. It did not seem like his feet were even touching the ground.

When he was close enough to see the gourd. He tried to see if there was still sand running from it. No one else was looking at the gourd, only at him, so he was the only one to see Matuga dusting sand from his hand as it dropped into the top of the gourd.

Chapter Seven

For the last few strides Sun bear was sure he was flying. He could no longer feel his legs touching the ground. There was no jarring of his feet hitting as he ran, only a floating sensation as he flew up into the plaza where Matuga was seated in the shade of an ancient willow tree close to the courtyard wall. When he did come to a stop, he was surprised to see the ground come rushing up to hit him in the face. He tried to put out his hand but the thong on the water gourd was caught on something and he could not get his hand free in time, so he fell unprotected to the dusty earth at the old man's feet. He thought about it as he lay there and came to the conclusion that of course he would fall. He had been flying and he had forgotten to put his feet back down. Even little birds knew enough to do that the first time they flew. He tried to laugh, but no sound came from his dry throat.

As he hit the ground, Little Frog rolled free and would have scurried back to the safety of the dump if she could have. The People waiting in the courtyard had closed in around the fallen pair and made a half circle around them. Their legs made a prison for Little Frog on one side and the low wall was a barrier on the other. Frightened, she crouched in a tiny ball at Sun Bear's side. Would they blame her? Was her extra weight the reason he had fallen? Why did he not get up now that the run was over?

There was complete silence in the courtyard. No one moved or spoke. Even the ever-present magpies seemed to sense the importance of the event unfolding below them, and refrained from screaming their outrage, as they normally would have.

Maata ached to go to his son but he must not. Even Keenwah remained motionless. She could do nothing for him either. Their son hovered between boyhood and manhood. No one could assist him. He must either get up on his own and stand like a man or he would lie there helpless as a boy.

Matuga watched the last bit of sand trickle from the gourd. He had done as much as he could when he had scooped up the handful of sand from the pile and put it back in the gourd. It was up to Sun Bear and the Spirit Watcher now.

Everyone waited, holding their breath. Each one of them was willing him to rise; every muscle was tense, trying to help him up. They were proud of this man-boy who had made such a magnificent run. If he rose and stood unaided, he would be the center theme of next summer's plays and songs, which would be held in the Great Kivas all over the nation. The name of their village would be on everyone's lips.

The long, gangly lad lay very still. Only his heaving chest moved in ragged gasps as his lungs tried to pull in air. He was unaware of the tense expectancy surrounding him. He was on the verge of unconsciousness. A small puddle of water seeped away from the broken gourd near his hand. The significance of his remaining water was not lost on any one present.

From one side of the half circle came a disturbance as someone forced her way through the tightly packed people. They drew back in both fear and respect from the ancient crone who was pushing her way amongst them. Wielding her walking stick right and left, without regard to whom she struck, she cleared a path before her until she stood beside the figure in the dust.

Matuga looked at her and then quickly dropped his eyes. He could not meet her withering gaze. Matuga was the ruler of the People but even he had no power over this old woman. In fact he had to answer to her just as anyone else did because she recognized no ruler. She was the oldest person in the nation. No one could say just how old but she claimed more summers than any two of the men could. Counting all her fingers and toes twice over, she claimed at least eighty summers. An age beyond belief, but no one disputed her on this claim.

Paataga was the Wise One of the people. The Wise One was sometimes a man and sometimes a woman. Paataga's teacher had been a man, who like herself had lived to a venerable age before he had passed on his office and its powers to her.

"Well Matuga, what are you going to do? Let him lie there and die?" she snapped at him, much as a mother to a naughty child, which is how Matuga always felt in her presence.

"What can I do? If I pick him up, he will have failed his manhood rites. I have to let him have his chance, do I not?"

"Fool! What manhood rites? Has he not already done more than any man is capable of? What more does he have to prove to you? Must he now crawl all the rest of his days on crippled legs because none of you had the sense to take care of him?" she asked in a wondering tone. The answer seemed clear to her. If Sun Bear was not helped soon, he was in grave danger of permanent damage to the muscles of his legs, not to mention the agony of cramps that would lead to his destruction.

"Look at his legs, man! Can you not see they are already knotting up like the limbs of the oak tree? If you leave him lay, he may never run again. He will only be fit for the dumpsite. A fitting tribute to the only person to make such a run and bring such an honor to his home village and its leader." She looked around her in disgust. "Would you treat any other of your runners in this manner?"

Matuga was deeply troubled. He knew what she said was true but he had never encountered such a circumstance before. There was no precedent to guide him. He held out his hands to show his helplessness in this situation.

"No. Of course I would not treat any runner this way, but he is not yet one of my runners. He has not completed the run yet. You know he must give me the gift of Toolke to prove he has completed his run. What can I do? I am just a man who has been chosen to uphold the rules. I have no power to make new ones. You are called the Wise One, tell me, what can I do?"

"Nothing," she agreed reluctantly. "As you say, you are only a man, and not a very smart one. Nor are any of the rest of you." The crowd around her drew back and began to fidget nervously. "You have to have some set of rules before you can make a decision. None of you are smart enough to make a decision on your own. You will let him lie here and suffer, maybe even die, but you will not bend or break your precious rules to save his life. He must prove himself a man to you by your rules, not by the deed he has already done."

She paused and looked around at the People. They were waiting for her to make a decision, waiting for her to solve the problem for them. Shaking her head, she continued.

"Yet, I know rules are necessary. No People can live together in harmony without them. So you are helpless, trapped in your own rules and customs. I suppose there is nothing you can do to help him without robbing him of his so-called manhood." She never took her eyes from the lad, and noted the quivering of his legs and the shuddering of his whole body.

"But!" she shouted as if inspired. "I can do something. I can do anything I want to. I can make my own rules, or break them, and there is nothing any of you can do or say about it. Who will dare to argue with me?" She cast a baleful eye around; well knowing no one would meet her gaze, let alone challenge her.

She beckoned to several runners who were standing nearby. They were also helplessly watching a great runner in danger. They were sworn to help any runner, but even they could not see a way out of this dilemma.

"You two, do not just stand there like turkeys. Come tend to him. Take him as you would one of your own. Minister to him. Do not just stand there gawking, do as I say." She dashed her stick to the ground several times to emphasize her command.

This was something they could understand. No one had the right to question the orders of the Wise One. They sprang forward and lifted him up. Paataga's word was law; whatever would be would be as she ordained. They could help a runner and not worry about the consequences.

With a man on either side, they lifted the youth up and wrapped his arms over their shoulders, thus supporting his weight between them. Without a backward glance, they trotted slowly down the lane and out into the roadway. They spoke to him, low and for his ears only, although they doubted he heard them. They were giving him helpful instructions, instructions to help him help himself. One of them continued to talk to him while the second began a spaced cadence chant each time their feet struck the ground.

At first Sun Bear's feet only dragged along the ground and did not move of their own volition. The runners hitched him up as high as they could so his feet began to swing as they moved him along. Slowly they could feel his legs making a desperate effort to move of their own accord. Painfully, he tried to pick up his pace to match theirs. At first only a few feeble steps and then he would lag but shortly he would make another attempt. Each time was a little longer and stronger. Then he was keeping time with them and they were only supporting him, not carrying his full weight. Gradually they increased their speed until they were running at an easy but brisk pace known to all runners.

Sun Bear became conscious of the pain in his legs, and then in his entire body. Shaking his head, he opened his eyes and was surprised to see the two men half-carrying, half dragging him down the road away from the pueblo.

"Where are we going?" he asked.

"Save you breath, runner," one of them told him. "Let us carry most of your weight, but keep your legs moving. I know of the pain. I too ran such a run once, not as long as this one, but long enough for me. It was very painful at first but it is necessary to keep moving until you cool down. We will run with you until you are able to stand by yourself."

"What of the time? I do not have much time left, do I?"

"You have all the time in the world, Sun Bear. The Wise One has given you all the time you need." they tried to reassure him. Although he did not understand, he did not waste breath on more questions. He tried to concentrate on his legs and to make them move in rhythm with the men on either side of him. Slowly his legs began to make their presence known to him by the shooting pains that ran up them every time his feet struck the ground.

The runners took him down the road and then circled back, passing the watching villagers. They went up the road and once more and circled back again. They made this trip twice, and on the last swing by the village, Sun Bear was able to remove his arms from the men's shoulders. He supported his own weight. The runners stayed close beside him to catch him if he faltered or fell as he turned toward Matuga.

He did not fall. He was weak and dizzy but his head was clear, and he found he could stand even though the pain was intense. Sun Bear was once more in command of his body.

During the confusion, Little Frog had tried to slip away back to the security of the dump. The people were all ignoring her, but still formed a barricade she could not navigate through. Several times she was stepped on cruelly, not out of malice but by feet of careless owners who did not see the tiny misshapen creature on the ground. Huddling in a pathetic lump, she was resigned to any fate dealt to her, when a pair of strong hands suddenly lifted her up. She was placed on top of the low wall out of harm's way. Keeping her head down, she peered out of the corner of her eye to see who had picked her up and what was to happen to her next. She was just as helpless up here on the wall, but at least she would not be trampled.

She wondered if she was being saved so she could face some sort of punishment. She had seen Paataga. Was the Wise One angry with her? What would they do to her for causing the Sun Bear to fall and be shamed like he was?

The man who had picked her up was a sturdy, wide faced man. She recognized him as Sun Bear's father. His stern features did nothing to reassure her or alleviate her fears of retaliation.

"Sit still, little one," he commanded her. Then, sensing her fear, he added, "Have no fear, little one. No harm will come to you here. I am Maata, father of Sun Bear. You have done a great thing for him today. I could hear you shouting for him up on the cliff. Surely I can do no less than to keep you from being trampled until he can come back and thank you himself."

Little Frog swooned and would have fallen from the wall if Maata's strong arms had not supported her. He had spoken to her, a non-person. He had said she had done a great thing for his son. What great thing had she done? All she had done was climb the cliff and shout for him on his return. This was no great thing, many of the People had shouted for the other boys as they had returned. Anyone could have done it, although they had not. Little Frog did not understand that the reason they had not was because they had feared he would not return in time and they did not want to add to his shame.

Oh well, Sun Bear's father had said no harm would come to her and soon they might forget about her and she would make her way back to the dump, and safety. Her heart was near to bursting with pride for her friend. Her body might be small and twisted, but her heart was as big and faithful as anyone's.

As Sun Bear came up the path, he was weak and dizzy. He wavered but he was able to stand alone before Matuga, who had remained silently seated. Sun Bear dropped shakily to one knee, and from a small pouch at his waist he produced the four eagle feathers, no worse for the days running. He presented them all to Matuga as he said, "Toolke instructed me to say that two feathers are for you."

Matuga took the feathers and replied, "Toolke does me much honor." He separated two of the feathers and held out the two remaining ones. "And what of these two?" he asked.

"Sir, he instructed me to tell you one of these is for my father." Maata came forward and accepted the feather Matuga held out to him and repeated Matuga's words.

"Toolke does me much honor. I accept them in the spirit they were given, and will keep them with much pride." He stepped back and took his place beside his mate.

"Toolke's wife bid me present her head band to my mother and ask Keenwah to pay her a visit sometime." Sun Bear was weak and weary, but he could feel the strength being pumped back into his body as his mother stepped forward and accepted the headband without a word. Women did not speak in matters concerning men. She did, however, place the headband on her own hair to signify her delight in being so honored. She searched the crowd for Paataga, but already the lonely figure could be seen retreating to her home on the opposite side of the canyon.

The two runners still stood just behind and off to one side of Sun Bear. Their arms were crossed over their chests, but they were close enough to catch Sun Bear if he should fall.

"And what of the last feather? Who is if for?" Matuga was watching Sun Bear closely. He was sure he already knew for whom Toolke intended it. He was therefore taken by surprise by the lad's answer.

Searching the crowd, Sun Bear saw Little Frog perched alone and ignored on the wall where his father had left her.

"This last feather is for the most brave and courageous person in this village." His voice was firm, although his mind was filled with doubts and misgivings over his decision.

"And who is this paragon of bravery and courage?" Matuga asked. He was much in doubt that Toolke would have said these words, and even if he had he did not think it proper for Sun Bear to repeat them to his own glory.

Stepping across to Little Frog's side, Sun Bear placed the honored feather in her hand. She looked at him in wonderment. She could not understand what he was saying or doing. No one recognized a non-person, and most surely not the ruler of some other district. He would not have even known she existed, let alone have offered her honor for things she did not do.

"Little Frog has shown more courage and bravery today than anyone else in this village. She climbed the cliff. To you and me this is nothing, but look at her legs. Look at her knees. This journey she made today, just to shout encouragement for me, took more courage than any of us who ran today. The feather must surely be for her?" The last sentence was more of a request than a statement, a plea to Matuga to let her keep the feather.

Matuga called Sun Bear to his side and in a low voice he said, "I do not believe Toolke said these words."

"No, sir. He did not. They are my own words." Sun Bear remained resolute.

"I also believe, knowing Toolke as I do, that he intended this last feather to be yours, if and when you completed your race. Is this not true?"

"Yes, sir. He said I could wear it if I finished the race in time, but even if I did not it was to be mine."

"Well? You did finish the run and an eagle feather is not only of great value, it is also given as an honor. To be so honored by the ruler of another village is a privilege few young men earn. Do you think it is wise to give his gift away? And especially to some creature from the dumpsite?" Matuga was still keeping his voice low, and although those closest to them strained their ears, they could not hear the words spoken between them.

"Toolke gave the feather to me. Then it is mine, is it not?"

"Yes. There is no doubt about that." Matuga answered him.

"Then if it is mine, I can do as I wish with it. Can I not?" the youth persisted.

Matuga sighed deeply. "Yes. That is also true. But are you sure this is what you wish to do? Many young men would do almost anything to posses such a gift, and coming from another ruler is a special honor, not to be taken lightly, not something to be cast aside carelessly on such a worthless creature. If you wish to give it to your father or mother, yes, but this creature?"

"She is not unworthy, sir. I know her and what I have said about her is true. She did a far greater deed today than I have done. She is the only person to speak for me today. Can I do less for her?" Sun Bear remained firm although his knees were shaking for other reasons than exhaustion.

Matuga sat silent. He too wished Paataga was still around to consult, but she was gone. This was for him to decide. He thought on it until he had an answer.

"No. I guess not. But she cannot wear it. This feather is reserved for rulers and their favored ones."

"Yes, sir. I know that. But at least let her keep it as a sign of her value to me, if not to anyone else." Again there was a note of pleading in his voice and Matuga knew it was the lad's sincere wish.

"So be it. Little Frog, you may keep this feather." Matuga had raised his voice so all could hear him. He paused for a moment and decided he could do no less than this man-boy before him. "Let it be known to all my people. I, Matuga, ruler of these people, do now adopt the one known as Little Frog."

There was an audible gasp that ran through the gathering. This was something new, something to talk about. They all had known of the strange attachment of the hairy young giant and the deformed creature from the dump, but now all could recognize it. They grew quiet as Matuga spoke again.

"She is entitled to my protection. From now on she will have a place in the pueblo and the right to my food and clothing and anything else she desires. Furthermore, as my charge, she is allowed to wear the feather. Of course, it must be worn inverted."

People adopted by the ruler were entitled to wear feathers in their headbands, but it must not stick up if the person was a woman. Women could wear them inverted so that they hung down over either cheek. Matuga was satisfied, it would be a sign for all to see and know. Now that this was done, he could get on with the final part of the ceremony. Holding out the two feathers sent to him by Toolke, he said. "These two feathers are for you. One is from Toolke, the other is from me."

"Oh, no, sir. I could never take your feathers. They are, as you told me, very valuable and not fit for a boy."

"And as you have just said to me, they were given to me. Were they not?" Matuga's crafty face broke slightly into a smile.

"Yes, sir. There is no doubt about that. I personally heard Toolke say that two feathers were for you," Sun Bear answered.

"Then if they are mine, I can do with them as I wish. Can I not? If they are mine, I can give them to you, not as a boy, but as a man. Please accept them as an honor from both of us."

Sun Bear, with a huge lump in his throat, accepted the feathers from Matuga's hand. He accepted them with a humble pride, the type of pride that is held inside and not shown to the world. He felt unworthy of the honor and this made it even more of an honor. To know that even as unworthy as he thought himself to be, Matuga still wanted him to have them.

"I have another announcement to make." Matuga's voice rang out in his official tone. "I have watched this young man grow from a baby to a man, and have long desired to adopt him as my own son. Only my deep respect for his father and mother has stopped me. Now he is a man, he will no longer be living in this father's house, so now I can adopt him without offending his parents. With the presentation of these two feathers, I officially adopt him. He shall be one of my runners, and as such be entitled to both the honor of a runner and the son of Matuga. It is fitting that my new son should have a new name, a man's name."

The gathering became very still. A new development was taking place. When had so many important things happened and all in one day? They waited to hear the new man's name to be given to the hairy young giant.

"I have been thinking on this for many summers now. I have tried to find a name that would be fitting, something that would describe both his size and his actions. None has made itself known to me. Now it seems the one called Little Frog has found the name for me. She called him Kaoto, the little bird who would rather run than fly, the bird that runs with the wind. He did indeed run with the wind today. There are times when he does look much like this bird. With his hair sticking up like a crest and his long nose sticking out in front of him like a beak, he resembles this little bird in many ways. I can think of no name more appropriate than Kaoto."

Sun Bear hung his head in embarrassment from the comparison. He had always known he looked different, but had never thought of himself as looking like a bird. He had always been shy of his looks and had longed to look more like his father so he would not attract so much attention. Being bigger was bad enough, but being so much different in appearance was doubly embarrassing.

"Is this name is acceptable to Maata and Keenwah?" They both nodded their heads in agreement to the name. "Then so it shall be."

Looking again at the young man before him he said, "Kaoto. Do you accept the position as my son and as my runner?"

The man-boy looked to his mother, who nodded, and then quickly turned her head to remind him that a man does not ask for his mother's permission. Maata starred straight ahead but did not give a negative sign.

"I accept the honor Matuga gives to me, although I do not deserve it. I will gladly be your runner; every boy dreams of this. I will be your son but only in name. I shall never forget those who have raised me." He spoke firmly, with a new confidence in his manhood.

"If you should ever forget your parents, you could never be a son to me," Matuga told him seriously. "Now there is only one more piece of business to attend to before you go to a well-earned rest. As a son and a runner, you are entitled not only to a room in my house, but you also may have your pick of the young maidens. She will not be your mate yet but she will look after your room and your body until you decide to mate for life. Most runners do not mate until they give up running. It makes for a happier life that way."

The new man took a deep breath as he prepared to answer his new father. He had to speak quickly before his courage deserted him. He had already gone far beyond what propriety allowed, and what he proposed to ask next was even bolder.

"I have no need to look them over, sir. I am prepared to make my choice right now." This caused a stir among the young maidens of the village. They did not really know this young man. He had never entered into their games or swam with them in the stream. He had always remained aloft and alone. Surely then, it must be someone from another village. Who could it be? Did any of them know her? Most of them were hoping it would not be them. A few had mixed feelings about him. He was so tall, and covered with hair. What would it be like to sleep and mate with someone like him?

"Oh. So you have already been looking them over, huh?"

"No, sir. I have not looked them over. I do not know them and they do not know me. Besides, it is not one of them I ask for."

"I see. So it is some little girl from another village. Very well, tell me who her father is and I will negotiate with him for her, providing she is old enough, of course." Matuga smiled. He was already enjoying his new son. So sure of himself, so certain of his rights, he was truly a man. He liked that in the lad.

"There is no need for that either, sir. She is here and her father can speak for her right now."

"All right then." Matuga was puzzled. "Who is the lucky young maiden? Let her father dare to refuse me."

The tense young lad's voice broke as he spoke. Even so, he tried to speak bravely. "She is your daughter, sir."

"My daughter? But son, my daughters are already old and mated. They are much too old for you anyway. What are you thinking?"

"No, sir. Not all of them. I refer to your youngest daughter. The one you just adopted a few moments ago. I guess she would be my sister by custom but not by blood, so I choose her."

"Little Frog? You want this creature for your mate?" Matuga asked incredulously.

"I want to be able to look after her just as I have in the past. I am not ready to mate, but even though you have agreed to adopt her, she still needs someone to look after her. We need each other, sir. We are the only friends we have. If you will permit it, sir, it is my wish."

Matuga shook his head. He was puzzled by the lad's request. But he was asking as a man now, with a man's rights. What should he do? He thought of speaking to his elders but decided against this action. He knew they would object; find some obstacle or rule by which they could block the lad's request. He did not want to turn down his new son's first request. He looked across the valley to Paataga's tiny home on the side of the canyon wall. Somehow he knew what her advice would be if she were here to advise him. The very fact that she was not here only confirmed her approval.

Nodding his head and thrusting out his jaw in a gesture of stubbornness, which denied any protest, he said, "So be it. There will be no more discussion." He looked each of his elders directly in the eye until they all dropped their gaze in deference to his wishes.

Chapter Eight

The newly accepted men of the village were taken to their respective homes and cared for by their families in the best manner of their time. Kaoto was given extra treatment by the runners. They assisted him in limbering up his muscles, and in general, relieving his distressed body. Ointments, brought up from the south by traders, were rubbed liberally on his legs and back. The stinging ointments soothed and relaxed his overtaxed muscles. Hot packs were applied and warm stones from the hearth fire were place around his body. Heavy coverings were piled over him to hold in the heat. Exhaustion, plus the warmth inside and out took over and Kaoto slept like death. He was oblivious to the coming and going of his parents and the runners. He never knew of Matuga's inquiry from time to time about his health. He thought he awoke once to find the Wise One seated beside his bed. He started to get up, but she put her hand on his shoulder and gently pushed him back down. She had tucked the covers tightly around him and left. Later Kaoto could not be sure if it were true or only a dream. It must have been a dream. Why would the Wise One be concerned with someone like him?

Young bodies quickly rebound, and the next day, other than a few blisters and aches all the young men were able to attend the celebration marking their manhood.

Kaoto was received with respect and held in awe by his fellow members, but he was still not accepted as a friend. They were grateful for what he had done to insure them all of a chance in the run. If this had been all that had happened, it is possible it might have made a difference in their feelings. But this was not all that had happened. Even the adoption by Matuga was understandable, but the intervention of the Wise One was something else. When this powerful woman came to stand by his side and took issue with the ruler of the nation over the standings of their rites, it only seemed to widen the gap between them. They could respect him, admire him, even feel some sympathy for him, but they could not feel comfortable in his presence. In some way it was as if the essence of the Wise One had rubbed off on this tall, hairy giant, and they felt some of the same uneasiness with him as they did with her.

Kaoto did not miss their companionship. He had never had it in the first place. Besides, now he had the fraternity of the runner's brotherhood. While all were several summers his senior, they still treated him as an equal. In truth, they all admitted that as a runner he had already proven himself superior to any man in the nation.

Kaoto began his training as a runner almost immediately. He did not have the gentle transition period granted the other young men. They would spend the next three summers adjusting to the cloak of manhood. During this time they would still have to spend their allotted time in the fields, but now they would be allowed to enter the Great Kivas. They would start courtship with the maidens of their choice. This was a long dalliance much looked forward to by both parties. By the time they had attained fifteen summers, most of them would be settled down to domestic life and have started a family of their own.

Not so for Kaoto. He had already taken on the responsibility for Little Frog. Not that this was a real burden to him; rather, it was in some ways a relief. He could draw on the supplies of Matuga for both himself and Little Frog, and her privilege, as Matuga's daughter would open new doors for them both. However, the life of a runner restricted him from participating in the games and frolics of the other young men. He would not have taken part in them anyway. He was dedicated to perfecting his skills. He would become the best runner in the nation.

Runners were unique persons in the nation of the People. They held a rank nearly equal to the ruler they served. They owed allegiance only to the ruler of the district they were assigned to. They answered to no other person, with the exception of Paataga, who seldom even spoke to them.

As runners they had to meet several qualifications. The least of these was their ability to run. Everyone in the nation could run, even the women and children were superior runners. It was their natural way of life. When they learned to walk, they began to run. Visiting women would run back and forth from one village to another with the little children running beside them. So this was not even considered a qualification, although a faster runner, or even one with more endurance, certainly would receive more attention.

What was really important was their memory, not just short term, but their ability to retain information over a long period of time. They must be able to listen to a message, usually only once, and then be able to repeat it as often as required for the next several days, sometimes as long as a full turn of Sister Moon. Not just repeat the words but to be able to mimic the speaker's actions and tones, so as to render the message as authentic as a visual record. They were actually the living words of the man who sent them.

Another important qualification was their dependability. They must have an impeccable reputation. No one ever caught in a lie could be used as a runner. Many command decisions would be based on their memory and integrity. The People could not chance using a man who might lie, or make up what he forgot. To forget was a disgrace but to lie was unforgivable.

The other equally important factor was their wisdom, and their ability to understand the message they were transmitting. They had to know the mind of the man they represented well enough to make a decision in case an alternate plan was necessary. They must know what the man for whom they spoke would do or say if he were present. The responsibilities of the runner were a great and often heavy burden, a burden they must be willing to accept and carry without complaint.

Kaoto possessed all these traits. He had already discovered his remarkable memory, and learning to think like Matuga would not be that difficult. Matuga was basically a simple man who dealt only in truth and had genuine desire to serve his people to the best of his ability. Common sense was all that was required to represent him. Of course, Kaoto would not be sent into a situation where he would have to tax his talents until he had more time to know all of the running business and had a chance to get to know Matuga even better. At first he would make only short runs, with messages that were easy to deal with and did not demand any significant decisions. Gradually his runs would become longer and the messages more difficult. As the distance increased, so would his responsibilities.

It was an ideal life for one such as Kaoto. He needed no one to keep him company. He had no friends to leave behind, with the exception of Little Frog. At least now he knew she would be cared for and would no longer have to sit at the dumpsite and wait for handouts.

Three days after his return from the notorious run, he was established in a room of his choice. He chose a room on the ground floor, one with a doorway opening to the south to face the Spirit Watcher. Little Frog never seemed to get enough sunshine, and even on the warmest day could be found sitting in the brightest rays just outside their door.

All provisions were brought to her so she did not have to forage for food or water. Maata had seen to it that she had a cook fire whenever she needed it. When Kaoto was present, he cared for her, and in return she attempted to cook for him. During his absences she seldom prepared a meal and chose to live on parched corn and water.

Kaoto was soon getting more long runs and was often gone for several days. During one of these absences, Keenwah received a visit from Paataga and the two of them converged on the room of Little Frog. Without explanation, they picked her up and carried her down to the stream, to a pool formed by a stone dam. At first she was terrified. She was sure they were going to drown her so she would no longer be a burden to Kaoto. She was resigned to this fate until she found they only intended to bathe her. This in itself was a little frightening, but Keenwah's strong hand held her safely in the water.

She reveled in this new experience. She had never had the luxury and balm of this much water, water to be wasted on washing instead of drinking. Many summers of encrusted dirt were soaked loose and washed away. Using the roots of the yucca plant for soap and the bark of the cedar for a scrub brush, they dissolved the dark stains of time and left her a glowing pink. Keenwah cut her hair short enough so that with soaking it could be combed out. The entire morning was devoted to this chore and at mid-day they shielded her from curious eyes with a blanket while the Spirit Watcher dried her off. She was then rubbed down with crushed pine needles to give her a pleasant scent and, as Paataga informed her, "it would help control the uninvited little critters that were a constant nuisance to them all."

A simple leather strap held her hair back, although given the odd shape of her head it was hard to keep in place. When she was dry, they wrapped the blankets around her and carried her back to the plaza, where Keenwah helped her make a dress from a piece of doeskin. Little Frog was overjoyed at this. She had never had a mother to show her how to cut and sew properly, let alone a new piece of skin to work with. Keenwah worked in some porcupine quills on the front and Paataga furnished some hard to find dyes to paint designs. The best they could do was not enough to make her pleasing to look upon, but at least she was clean, fresh, and fragrant.

While Keenwah helped her sew, Paataga gave her the benefit of her tutelage. She taught her of the inner person and how to deal with life even when you were alone and discarded. The rest of the reclamation came from within her. For the first time in her life she felt like a person. After so many summers of being a non-person she was uncertain of how to act, but Paataga's quiet assurance gave her hope.

"What has happened to you?" Kaoto asked on his return. He could see all the obvious changes but there was a newness about her person, a glow of happiness that he had never seen before.

"Oh Kaoto! It is the most wonderful day of my life. I am a person! I know I am still an ugly and deformed person, but your mother and the Wise One have made me feel beautiful, on the inside at least." Her two colored eyes were misty with another new sensation, tears of joy.

"How many times must I tell you? You are not ugly; you are just different, just as I am different. That is all. Different. We are both different from the rest of the People, but that does not make us useless or ugly," Kaoto explained patiently, as he had many times before.

"Kaoto, I have been to the water today. I have seen the reflection of my twisted and ugly body and face for the first time. I have always known I was ugly, but I never knew how disgusting I looked. It was a terrible shock to me. I do not know how you can stand to be around me. But somehow, I do not know just how, they made me feel beautiful inside. Paataga told me about the other person who lives inside me. This person feels as tall and as beautiful as anyone else. I know the bath and the new clothing do not really improve my outward appearance much, but they make me feel clean and wonderful." She sat in the sunlight with her new dress and her hair cropped back and held out of her eyes by the headband. She had even brought out the eagle feather and tucked it up under the band so it fell down across one cheek.

"I can only thank you for allowing me to stay with you. I want you to know that you do not have to look at me. I will understand now. But I do promise to keep myself clean for you and freshly scented. How can I ever repay you for all you have done for me?" Her voice, which had always been mellow, was even more subdued and muffled as she spoke from her new body.

Kaoto gave up for the time being. He was never able to convince her that he no longer saw her ugliness. Her deed of climbing the cliff, to shout for him, had erased any trace of her ugliness from his eyes. He was glad that his mother had come to help her, but he was puzzled by the visit of the Wise One. Why had Paataga taken an interest in them? Oh well, who knew what the Wise

One might want?

No one really knew Paataga. They all knew of her because she was the oldest and most wise person in their entire world, but no one could honestly say they were friends. She was a person set apart from the People and she seemed to prefer it this way. She lived in a small shelter up near the lip of the canyon. Her food and firewood were delivered daily but she seldom appeared at her door, and if she did, she never spoke. She was the most powerful person in their world. Even Matuga must answer to her and bend to her will. If she made a demand it must be accepted; however, she almost never interceded for anyone. Kaoto had been the one exception. He had seen her many times from a distance, as had everyone else. It was her custom to walk alone in the early mornings or evenings. She would climb to the top of the canyon wall and walk slowly along, looking down on the valley and presumably the People who lived there. Everyone made it a point to stay far away from her path at all times. From her vantage-point she could see the Great Kiva and most of the villages in the valley, as well as many of those located on the plateau on both sides of the canyon. The People did not realize that she was just a lonely old woman waiting for certain events to take place so she could go to her rest in peace, knowing she had fulfilled her obligation to the People who trusted her.

She bore no malice towards anyone and occasionally she took an interest in someone she felt was in need; someone who was not being properly treated by the rest of the People. There was very little she could actually do for them other than offer them her help and influence. If they chose to call this being wise, she did not object. If being old made one wise, then she surely qualified twice over for this distinction.

Over the next three summers Kaoto forgot about Paataga. She had not concerned herself further with either him or Little Frog. He was always busy with his errands as a runner. Matuga had given him more and more responsibilities, sending him on longer trips, with the power to make decisions for him. The name of Kaoto became familiar in many villages across the land. Every time he entered a strange kiva he would be greeted by men who had never seen him before but they knew his name and of his size and his great run. Who could mistake a young man who stood head and shoulders above all of them? A man who was covered with golden hair and could run faster and farther than any one of them? Yet he was not greeted as a friend, only with respect due a runner and also a little fear.

Early in his running days he had told Little Frog of his regret that she was not able to go with him and see the wonderful sights he saw and meet the people he did.

"I know I shall never be able to walk with you, let alone run at your side, but I am happy for you just the same. It has occurred to me that you could bring some of these things home to me."

"How can I do that, little sister? Can I bring each person I see by here for you to see? Shall I carry each rock and tree? Come little sister, tell me how I can do this."

She knew he was teasing her. Lately he had started calling her little sister. It pleased them both, for this was truly how he felt about her now.

"You are big enough you probably could, or I could ride on you shoulders like I did once before and you could show me all the sights." Humor was something new to her and she liked to use it when the mood was right. "Seriously, you could remember everything you see and hear; then when you come back to me you could tell me all about it. I know you have to remember the words and I know you can mimic many men. You can describe them to me so I can make my mind see them. This way, I too can see and hear them just as you do."

"That should be easy enough. After all, I must remember what is said and I have a picture in my mind of what the trail looks like after being over it only once. I never forget a person's face. I do not know how good I am at recreating moods and voices, but I will try to do my best."

He became excited with her idea. "It will be great training for me." He began to relate his last trip to her. He described the land he had passed through and the people he had met. She questioned him occasionally until she discovered he had total recall. Later, on the trail again, he found himself studying each detail with new eyes. He was trying to see everything through her eyes, eyes that had seen so little in her short life. What was common to him would be new and wonderful to her.

He listened even more, not just to the message and replies but to all the talk of the People in each village he went to. He was surprised to find that listening was an art, just as running was, or repeating a message with precision. Unknown to himself, he was gaining a vast storehouse of knowledge about the People and the problems faced by different groups in outlying districts. This was a trait that would become essential to him in the many summers ahead. He was ready now for all of Little Frog's questions. Some of them amused him, but he found most of her questions had merit.

"Where do you take your meals when you are out on a run?" she asked him during one of their meals together.

"When I am running I seldom eat on the trail. People always prepare a meal for me when I reach my destination. It is one of the privileges of being a runner," he told her.

"Yes, I know that," she replied. "But where do you eat the meal? With the ruler? Or do families take turns feeding you? Or do you have a special place reserved just for runners?"

"Most often, if the weather permits, I eat outside in the courtyard. If it is too wet or cold I can go to the kiva or to anyone's home. I guess I spend so much time outside that I just prefer it to being inside. Why do you ask?"

"I just wondered. I miss you when you are gone, but I miss you most at meal times. It was the time when I could always count on you being there when I was on the dump." Seeing Kaoto frown, she hurried on. "I know those days are gone and I do try not to remember them, but I cannot forget them so easily. They were the only life I knew until now."

Kaoto shook his head but did not argue with her about it. He knew it would be impossible for her to ever forget those days, but he did not like to recall them.

"I was wondering?" she went on. "If it would not be too much trouble, if you could do something for me?"

"Nothing is too much trouble for me to do for you. Ask anything, little sister."

"Well, when you take your meal, could you set aside a little for me, just like you used to do?"

"I can do that, no problem there. Do you want me to bring it back to you? It does not vary much from one place to another," he explained.

"Oh, no. I did not mean for you to bring it back to me. I just thought if you set some aside, it would be like we were together again, like we used to be. I know I cannot share all your meals, but . . . well . . . this might seem like too much to ask, and if you refuse I can understand." She paused. It had seemed easy enough to say when she was alone and had first thought about it. Now she was not so sure she should have even brought it up.

Kaoto knew her well enough to know she had something on her mind and he encouraged her to speak on.

"Are there non persons on the dumpsites at the other villages, just I was here?" she asked timidly.

"Yes, in some places. Not every place has them, or not all the time. You know most do not live long on the dump." He was very puzzled as to what she was trying to ask of him.

"When you take your meal, could you set aside a small bowl like you did for me? Then could you, I mean I do not want to cause you any trouble, but could you maybe see that it got to those on the dump?" She rushed forward before her courage deserted her. "I mean, if you could share it with them the way you used to do with me, it would be like we were really together. I would know this and I would feel it here." She touched her breast with one tiny, knotted hand. "This would truly be sharing, would it not?" She raised her eyes to see his reaction to her request.

"I can do that. It is no trouble and it is within my power to do almost anything I want, so long as it does not harm anyone else. I will do it and I will tell them it is in the name of my little sister, Little Frog," he said, glad he could do this much for her.

"Could you not just say you do this in the name of your little sister? If anyone asks, you could just say she has no other name," she said shyly, afraid of angering him.

"If you wish it so. But why no other name? Are you not happy with the name I have given you? We could always change it now that you are here with me. Matuga would give you a new name if you like."

"I am very happy with my name because it is the name you gave me. It is the only name I have ever had and the only name I shall ever want. But the rest of the nation does not think of me as you do and I am sure they would not feel the same. I just think it would be better this way."

Kaoto agreed, rather than argue with her, and started the custom everywhere he went. It became a habit he would never forget. Soon this custom was picked up by some of the runners who did not know why the custom was observed but followed it anyway. They even repeated the phrase, "It is in the name of little sister who has no other name." As a result the poor creatures at the dumpsites began to get a few decent meals and were always the first to spot the runners and greet them.

At the end of his fifteenth summer, when the days were starting to grow shorter, Kaoto was surprised to receive a summons from Paataga. The Wise One requested his presence at her home on the side of the canyon. He had never been near the place but like everyone else he knew where it was, and like everyone else he did not relish the idea of going there.

With apprehension he made the trip to her doorway to find what she wanted of him. Maybe she had an important message to be delivered and wanted the best and fastest runner to deliver it. He did not know what to expect from her, but when she greeted him he was completely unprepared for what she had to say.

"Kaoto, I have watched you for many summers now. I think you are the one I have been searching for."

"I am honored the Wise One has noticed me," he said stiffly.

"Of course you are. But I admire your quick thinking anyway," Paataga told him, with what might have been a twinkle in her shrunken eyes.

"What have I done to attract your attention?" Kaoto asked; his curiosity piqued by her interest.

"Not so much by what you have done, but more by who you are," she replied.

"And who am I, Wise One?"

"That we shall find out soon enough." Paataga indicated an ancient log near her fire pit. "Sit."

When he said he preferred to stand, she scowled at him and struck the log with her stick. "Sit! I am too old to stand here and get a stiff neck looking up at you, young man. I want to be able to look you in the eye. So sit!"

He hastily took a seat on the log and noticed that his head was still above hers as she took a position in front of him and gazed intently into his eyes. He returned her stare unflinchingly until she seemed to be satisfied.

"Great herds of buffalo. Even seated you are still taller than I am and I still have to look up at you. What were they thinking to pile so much body on one person?" she asked of no one in particular. "Sit on the ground and I will sit on the log. That is not much better, but at least it is more comfortable."

Paataga began asking him questions about his life, his running, his family and friends.

"I have no friends, other than Little Frog, of course," he told her.

"Are you not well treated everywhere you go?"

"I am. But not as a friend, only as a runner should be."

"Are you not the adopted son of Matuga? Does this not get you special attention? Does this not make friendship easy and natural?"

"No. Respect I am given, special treatment also, but friendship? No. I think everyone is a little afraid of me. I guess it is because I am so tall and I have all this hair."

Paataga was thoughtful for a moment as she placed a piece of meat in a pot of stew along with some fresh roots. When she spoke again, it was on a different subject, once more catching him off guard. It was part of her strategy.

"Do you ever dream Kaoto?"

"Yes." he replied, startled. "Does not everyone have dreams?"

"I suppose so, but I was referring to a special dream, not just the ordinary everyday dreams. Do you have dreams that happen often, more than once?" She pierced him with a penetrating, unblinking stare. "Do you have one dream that is different from all others, one that you have told no one about because you were afraid of it?"

Kaoto returned her look, never blinking, held rapt as if under a spell. After what seemed a long time, he answered her.

"Yes. Yes. But do you know of this dream? Truly. You are the Wise One. Can you tell me what it means? They do frighten me." Kaoto searched her wrinkled face intently, hoping she had an answer for him about something that had been troubling him for some time now. He had not told anyone, not even Little Frog. It was something he kept a secret because he did not know what to do about it. Now he hoped the Wise One would help him.

"You say they frighten you? How do they frighten you? Such a big person as you should not be easily frightened by anything."

"They have nothing to do with my size. There is nothing I can fight back against. They come often, more often of late. It seems as though someone is asking me for help, but I do not know who they are or what they want me to do. It is so confusing, and when I wake up I can only partially recall the dream, but it disturbs me greatly. Can you help me? Can you tell me what it means? Wise One, please."

"Tell me about it, all you can remember. I will see if I can help you. Maybe between us we will be able to understand it. No, this is not wisdom; this is just many summers of living. Believe me, there is a great difference between the two, as you will find out soon." Paataga shifted her weight on the log, leaning more on her walking stick and leaning slightly toward him. "Come. Tell me all you can about this dream and we will see what we can do."

Paataga waited patiently as Kaoto searched his mind for all the details of this dream that so often bothered him. He felt no hesitation in telling it to the old woman seated before him on the log. It seemed natural to him to confide in her, as if she was the one person in the nation who might understand and thus help him.

Chapter Nine

Kaoto began to tell the old woman about his dream. Like all young men, he had many dreams, but only one that bothered him. Only one dream that insisted on returning night after night until he knew every step of it from start to finish.

Up until he had made his run and celebrated his manhood rites, his dreams had been the simple dreams of any boy and while some of them were frightening, none of them had returned to bother him as this particular dream did. After his great run this dream had come to haunt him. He could not remember how many times he had it but knew it was much too often to be ignored.

"You must tell me everything about this dream, leave out nothing. It might be that I could help you. I have had some experience with dreams. I have had some of my own, although I have not had a dream now for many summers. Do not look at me that way, I was young once." Her gaze drifted off over the valley. "So very long ago. But back to your dream, tell me about it."

"My dream always starts the same way. I am up on a high place. It is not like a hill, it is more like I am on the back of an eagle, no, not really. I know this sounds stupid bit it is like I am in a portion of a giant bowl, or more like a ladle cut from a great gourd. I think I must feel like the Spirit Watcher." He cast a quick glance towards the sky but continued.

"From here I can look down and see the whole earth spread out before me. It is like I can see into the past and the future all at one time. I can see all the People and how they have lived in peace and happiness for many summers. But there is something in the future that troubles me." He paused to see if the Wise One would laugh at him and his dream but she was listening to him indeed she was hanging on his every word as if they were her own.

"It seems they can see me and hear me. I am telling them they must leave their homes, that they must leave the land. There is something dark and sinister looming around the edge of my vision, something threatening all the People. They begin to moan and cry out to me that they do not want to leave the land, and they do not want to leave their homes. But I keep insisting that they must."

"Where do you want them to go?" Paataga asked.

"I am not sure. I can hear myself telling them they must go back to the land of little earth. It seems right to me in my dream but when I wake up it sounds strange. It does not seem to make any sense when I am awake and think back over it. I do not know of any such places. Have you ever heard of the land of little earth?"

Paataga shook her head slowly. "I might know what you are talking about. There is something similar in the history of the People, but I do not know where it might be. There is more, is there not?" She gently probed him back to his memory.

"It all seems so real to me. It is like I am standing beside myself, watching myself, seeing myself do and say these things, like I was two different people at one time. It is so confusing, I do not know what to believe." He stopped and seemed to be looking far out over the valley to some far distant, invisible place only he could see.

"Please go on, Kaoto. Do not worry about how strange or odd it may sound. Dreams are often very confusing. They sometimes get all mixed up. But please go on, tell me everything."

"I can see a place, far to the south, so far that I cannot count the day's runs it would take to reach it. It is a place where there is much rain and everything is green with strange plants and trees. I can see bright colored birds, and fruit in the trees. It is warm there all the time; there is no difference between summer and winter. I can see the land, and it is very narrow. There is water on both sides of it. Big waters, so big I cannot see the other side and the land twists and turns like a snake swimming through these waters."

Paataga continued to nod her head but she did not add anything to what he said; she only asked him if there was more to his dream.

"Much more and even more strange, if that is possible. It is like I am looking into the future and I see the People standing in a desert. The sun is hot and the wind is blowing all the time from all directions at once. I see the People start to dry up, like corn stalks, until they are only bones with no skin or flesh. But they are not dead; they are like the oak trees in the winter when their leaves are gone. They do not fall down, they just stand there as if they were waiting for something to happen to them."

"And does something happen to them?" Paataga prompted him.

"Suddenly from all sides, big savage men, strange men, not like the People, come running at them with clubs and spears. They hit the People. The People do nothing. They just stand there. I try to call out to them but somehow I know it is too late and I must watch them be destroyed. When they are hit, their bones fly apart and are scattered all over the sand. The sand is white and their bones become white like the sand. Then the savage men leave and the winds blow the sand until it covers the bones and nothing remains to show they were ever there."

"Is that all? Is there not more to your dreams?" Paataga asked.

"After that it becomes hazy and I have trouble making out what is happening."

"Try hard. I must know everything before I can help you."

"Well—after the sand covers the bones it becomes very dark. There is no sun or stars or moon for a long time. I do not know how I know it is a long time, but I do. It is dark and silent. There is no sound to be heard, not even the sound of the wind blowing. Then the sun comes out and it is bright and clear, like after a rainstorm. The wind has stopped blowing and from all over the sand I can see the bones again. They are working their way up out of the sand. The bones come together in front of me." Kaoto stopped and a puzzled look crossed his face as if he was seeing his dream for the first time himself.

"I am no longer high up, I am down on the ground. Not really on the ground but very near it, as though I am standing just above the sand. The bones begin to attach themselves together until they are two complete skeletons. As though all the bones of all the People are combined into just two skeletons. As I look at them, they begin to take on flesh and skin and are alive once again."

"Yes, and then what?" Paataga could hardly contain her excitement.

"That is about all. I do not know who they are. They are strangers to me. One is not unlike myself except his clothing is different from anything I have ever seen before. The other is a woman but she is not like the People. Her hair is like the Spirit Watcher's glow. It is long and straight and hangs down to her waist. But even though they are strangers to me, it seems that I should know them, I should know who they are. They seem to know who I am. They look at me and smile, but they seem to be asking me something. I cannot hear what it is they are saying, but before I can ask them to repeat their question, they just fade away until I can see the sand right through their bodies and then they are gone. The dream is over and I wake up. When I wake up, I feel very sad but I do not know why. It is a mystery to me." He looked longingly at the old woman, searching her face for a clue.

"What can it mean Wise One? In your wisdom can you tell me what it could be about? What is it they want of me? What am I supposed to do?"

"Perhaps I may be able to help you find the meaning of it. I have had a similar dream in my youth, many summers in the past. It has been so long that I had nearly forgotten it until just recently." Paataga poked at the remains of the fire absently with her walking stick, turning over a glowing coal and spreading the ashes.

"But what does it mean?"

"Patience, Kaoto. The Spirit Watcher does not reveal everything at once. We must learn to look for our own answers."

"We?"

"Yes, we. It is time for you to come and join me. There is so much you must learn, and I fear, so little time left for me to teach you."

"You will teach me? What is it that you will teach me? And when will I find time to learn? I spend so much of my time running that I do not have time to be taught."

"I will speak to Matuga. Your running days for him are coming to an end. From now on you will live here with me so I can teach you all the waking time of your days."

This troubled Kaoto. He enjoyed his life as a runner. He knew, of course, that some day another young man would replace him, but until that day he had planned to remain a runner. There was also Little Frog to think about; he did not want to bring her up here so far from everyone and Matuga's bounty and protection.

"What of my little sister?" he asked. "You did not say anything about bringing her with me, did you?"

"She will be taken care of. You do not have to worry about her any-more." Paataga told him.

"I am the only one who has cared for her. I do not think she would be happy without me being near her."

"Trust me, Kaoto. She will be happy, happier than she has ever been before."

Kaoto was still doubtful. "I will not leave her until I see who takes care of her and that she is truly happy," he said with his jaw thrust out stubbornly.

"So be it. I admire your loyalty to your little friend, but you will be here, at my home, in ten days. No longer can I wait. I do not have all the time of a youth. I am old and I grow weary." Paataga got up and dismissed Kaoto. As she left him and entered her rooms, she seemed spry and quick of step to Kaoto. She did not appear to be a tired and weary old person as she said she was.

Kaoto returned to the pueblo and the room he shared with Little Frog. He said nothing about his visit to the Wise One and Little Frog refrained from questioning him. She felt that Kaoto would tell her when he was ready for her to know.

Eight days passed and Matuga did not send him on any more runs. This was the longest he had ever been off the trail. When he tried to find Matuga to ask him why, the old man was always too busy or could not be found. He saw other runners coming and going and knew that it was not because there was no need for him as a runner. He became restless and testy, speaking very little. Little Frog noticed but waited patiently for him to tell her what was wrong. The summers at the dumpsite had taught her patience. Even her attempts at humor failed to rouse him and this had always worked in the past. At last she decided to bring up the subject.

"What is wrong, Kaoto? Why are you not running any more?"

He shrugged his shoulders but still did not speak.

"Why do you sit around all day looking like a storm cloud? Is it some-thing I have said or done? Have I forgotten to clean or cook enough? Have I become careless and more ugly? What is it? Can you not tell me?"

Kaoto jumped up and ran from the room without a word. He could not answer her because he did not know himself what the problem was. He felt an impending doom overshadowing them, but he was not clear as to what the threat was. In some ways it was not unlike his dream.

He took a brisk run down the valley. Running had always been best time for him to think. His body was active and restless, but it did not need the attention of his mind when it ran. He loped easily up a side canyon that would come out on top of the plateau. On reaching the open land on top, he ran in his long, easy stride, one he had learned to use early in his running days. The can-yon fell far behind him and he circled wide, combing back without any destina-tion in mind. He let his head sort through the past few days, beginning with his visit to Paataga and the talk of dreams. He began reviewing his dream once more and did not realize where he was until he came to a stop in front of Paataga's lodging place. The shriveled old woman sat on the log by her fire pits as if she had been waiting for him.

"Are you ready to come to me now?" she asked of him.

"I told you I would not leave Little Frog," he said, with his back stiff and his hands clenched into a fist.

"And I said she would be taken care of. Do you not trust me?"

"I have seen no one offer to aid her. I have heard of no one who wishes to look after her. Even Matuga has ignored us, thanks to you I suppose. I will not leave her as long as she has need of me." He was defiant and determined she would not change his mind.

"Go back to her. But in two more days you will come to me."

He left the home of the Wise One feeling even worse than before. He once more tried to run off his feelings and clear his head. Although he ran most of the rest of day, he could not get over the feeling of depression that had settled down over him. He had never had such a feeling before in all his short life. Finally he stopped running and began to walk; something he almost never did.

Kaoto was dejected as he walked down the trail. No one had the right to refuse the Wise One. The Wise One was more powerful than all the rulers put together. He knew he was in the wrong when he said he would not leave Little Frog, but what could he do? Perhaps he could take Little Frog and run away to some place unknown to anyone. Maybe they could hide from the Wise One. But if she communicated with the Spirit Watcher, there was no place safe for them to hide.

When he returned to the room he shared with Little Frog, he noticed a change; something was different about her. He could not quite place the difference; it was not something obvious, not something he could see, only something he could sense. Something had happened while he was gone. He waited for her to speak of it, but she was strangely silent.

"What is wrong, little sister? Why do you not talk to me? Are you angry because I ran out on you today?"

"No, I am not angry with you. Why should I be? You have not done anything to make me angry. If I am not talking, it is because I have something to tell you, something very important to us. But I am afraid to tell you," she said so softly it was almost a whisper.

"Afraid of me? What have I ever done to make you afraid of me? All the rest of the People are afraid of me, but I never thought you would be."

"I am not afraid of you but of how you will take what I have to say. I am afraid you will not understand, and then you will be angry with me. It is something you will not like to hear, but I must say it." She gave him a pleading look; her hideous little face seemed to almost glowing in the near darkness. "Promise me you will let me tell it all and not stop me until I have finished."

"So be it. Talk. Say something. Anything is better than your silence."

"I had a visit from Paataga a few days ago."

"When? She was here? But she has not been here since I stopped running."

"No. It was before you went up to see her."

"Why did you not say so earlier? What did she want, anyway?" Kaoto was mildly curious as to why the Wise One had come to see his companion instead of him.

"She came to help me with a dream I had. I did not know what to make of it, it was so different from anything I had ever dreamed before."

"Dreams? It seems that everybody is having dreams. What are yours about?"

"Quiet. You promised not to interrupt me until I was through talking." She waited to see if he had more to say. When he sat silent, she went on with her story.

"I dreamed I was in a different place than I have ever seen before. Of course, I have only seen this place, but it was beautiful there and I loved it. Paataga told me I would be making a trip to this beautiful land."

"Wonderful. I have had the same thought. Where is the land?"

"Shhh. Remember, you promised. I do not know where it is or how I will get there. That is not the important part. I only know that when I do get there, everything will be beautiful. I could see it in my dream. And even more important, I was walking in the flowers, yes, walking, on long straight, wonderful legs. When I came to a pool of water, I could see my reflection and I was no longer ugly and deformed. I was straight and whole. I was beautiful, too," Little Frog told him wistfully.

With a long sigh Kaoto told her once again, "You are not ugly, little sister. I have told you this many times, but I am so relieved. I have wanted to take you away from here. Paataga wants me to come and study with her. That is why she wanted to see me. I told her I would never leave you as long as you needed me. I thought she was angry with me but I guess I was wrong." He was crouched in the little room that always seemed to shrink even smaller whenever he was inside. "I see now that she is going to help us both. Maybe it has something to do with my dream, although I cannot see how." Scooting out the door, he said, "I will go back and see Paataga and find out where we are going."

Little Frog called him back as she shook her head sadly. "This is the part I did not want to tell you, Kaoto. We are not going. You cannot go with me. Paataga says I am going by myself. This frightened me, but Paataga said I did not have to be afraid. She said I would be strong enough to make the trip by myself and I would not need anyone to look after me. She said that you must stay here, that you were needed here more than I would need you. Forgive me, Kaoto, I did not want to go without you, but she says I must. Please do not be angry with me, Kaoto, and promise never to forget me."

"I could never be angry with you, little sister, nor could I ever forget you, even if I tried."

"Then listen to me now while I still have time to talk. I am not as much of a little sister as you think, Kaoto. I am as old as you are. Oh, I know, you always think of me as being younger because I am so small, but I was over five summers when I was put on the dump and I had been there at least three summers before you started helping me. So you see, I am just as old, if not older than you. I must also confess that I have not always felt as your sister should. Deep down in my heart I have loved you, as any young maiden would have. I have tried to keep it a secret because I have nothing to offer you. It seemed better to try and stay your little sister. This way no one was hurt."

Kaoto stood in silence. She had loved him, as a young maiden would have. He had never guessed this. He had never even given this a thought until she mentioned it. But of course, she was a real person inside; he of all persons should know this. And she would have real thoughts and real feelings and love was one of those feelings. He wanted to say something to reassure her, but the words did not come.

"After I have left on my trip I hope you will still remember to set aside a bowl for me wherever you are. That way we will never be separated."

"It is an easy promise to make, little sister," he told her, but his mind was on something else. He was determined he would discover where she was going and he would go there with her. He would make sure she was all right without him. He was sure now that Paataga intended to help them, and if everything turned out the way it was supposed to, then he could come back and study with Paataga. This way he could still go and see Little Frog occasionally. He was still feeling guilty about not responding to her words of love.

They sat quietly in the moonlight for a long time before she told him she was very tired and would like to sleep now. He gathered her up and again was amazed at how little she was. Her weight was as nothing to him. He could have carried her in one hand. As he tucked the blankets around her in the pale light of sister moon, he whispered "I love you too, little one." Little Frog stirred and smiled, but he never knew if she heard him or not. He lay down on the opposite side of the door and spent a long and nearly sleepless night.

Early the next morning he slipped out without waking his companion and ran lightly up to Paataga's home. Even though it was early, Paataga was up and around with her cook fire going.

"You are a day early, Kaoto. Why have you come today?"

"I have come to find out where you are sending Little Frog. She has told me all about your visit; we do not have secrets from each other."

"Oh, do you not? You have told her all about your dream, then?"

"No. But she has told me about hers. I only want to go with her long enough to satisfy myself she is all right."

"You cannot go with her. Did she not tell you that? If you should go, you would not return," Paataga explained patiently.

"Yes I will. If everything is as you say and she does not need me, then I promise I will return."

"You make a promise you could not keep. One must be very careful about making promises when you do not know all the facts. I told you she would be taken care of, did I not? Then why do you still doubt me?"

"And I told you I would see for myself how she was being taken care of before I would leave her." He was trembling but he would not let this old woman back him down or bluff him.

"Then go. See for yourself. Do not trust an old woman. Go." She almost shouted the last as he backed away from her, nearly tripping in his haste to get away from her.

As he jogged back to the pueblo, he puzzled over Paataga's reaction to him. She had seemingly given up to his demands, but still she acted as if she were disappointed in him. He had thought she meant to help them, but now he was not so sure of what she wanted of him.

When he approached the courtyard, he saw his parents standing at his doorway. Calling to them, he hurried across to meet them.

"Have you come to take care of Little Frog?" he called.

"Yes, my son," Maata replied.

"Good. But why did Paataga make such a mystery of it? Why did she not just tell me that you were the ones? I could have understood that and saved us all a lot of problems." He was greatly relieved. This would make it much easier to go back to Paataga, now that he truly knew Little Frog was in good hands.

Keenwah stood silent, watching her son as he walked towards them. She held out her hand for him to stop. His parents puzzled him. They did not seem very happy with this new arrangement. As he stood watching, he saw several women of the village enter his room carrying blankets and matting. Soon several more arrived and also entered the room he shared with Little Frog. He could not see any sign of her.

"Where is Little Frog? What are all those women doing in our room?" he demanded of his parents. "Do not tell me she has already left without me."

"Yes, my son, she has left, but surely you must have known that already. You were with her all night, were you not? Did not you know? Surely you must have known? Oh no. You do not know, do you?"

"Yes, I was here all night. We sat up late and talked much. She told me she was going on a trip to a beautiful land. She had a dream in which she was strong, tall and beautiful. She told me she would not need me to look after her anymore and Paataga had told her that I could not go with her. I got up early this morning without waking her and went to see Paataga to ask if she would help me. She told me to come back and see for myself how she was being taken care of. But how can I if she has already left? I thought you were going take care of her."

Maata stood to one side and motioned for his son to enter.

"Then go see for yourself, my son. See how she is being taken care of," Maata told him.

Kaoto stooped to enter the door. Inside he could see the women kneeling on the floor. In between them was a tiny bundle wrapped in the blankets they had brought. They were carefully wrapping this bundle in the matting. Only then did he understand what they were doing.

Little Frog was on her long trip without him and he could not go with her, he could not follow. Little Frog was dead. This was what she had been trying to tell him last night. But he had been so busy with his own plans that he had not listened to her. Now it was too late for him to listen to her. Now she was gone.

Men did not cry. Kaoto ran.

Chapter Ten

It was with a heavy heart that Kaoto left his home, and with his few belongings, went to live with Paataga on the canyon wall. He was sure he could never learn anything from the old woman even if she was the Wise One. He did not even know what it was she wanted to teach him. He was so entangled with his own thoughts of Little Frog that he could not possibly concentrate on the words of the old crone.

Paataga did not try to force him to learn anything at first. Wisely she let him brood and mourn the loss of his friend for the first day, not even disturbing him for the noon meal. When evening came she set a bowl of corn at his side and a piece of meat on top of it. Next to this large bowl she sat a small empty bowl.

Kaoto watched her. How had she known of the empty bowl? Was she indeed as wise as everyone said she was? He picked at his food until he could go on no longer. The small bowl sat at his side. Out of habit he had placed a little food in it but the untouched food only made it harder for him.

"There is no one here to share this with," he said defiantly.

Paataga had ignored him until he spoke; then she looked at him as if surprised to find him still there. Bustling about in and out of her small home, she spoke to him without looking up.

"Why do you not set the bowl over on the rock, the one by the little bush? There might be someone who would share your food if you offered it to them."

Kaoto looked at the bush. There was no one there; there was no one within calling distance of them. What was her meaning? Was she so old that she was crazy?

"Well? Are you going to share or are you going to sit there and let it spoil? Is that what your little friend would expect of you?"

"Little Frog is dead. She can no longer eat the food I would share with her and there is no other creature from the dump here to share it with, either."

"What do you know of death? Nothing; that is what you know. Did not your little friend ask you to remember her after she was gone? Did she not ask you to still take a small amount of food and set it aside for her, in her name? Is your memory so short? Is your friendship dead also? You did not deserve such a friend if you do not intend to keep your promise to her. Remember? I warned you before about making promises you could not or would not keep."

"All right!" Kaoto shouted as he thrust the bowl from him and placed it on the flat rock under a bush hanging to the side of the cliff. "Now are you satisfied?"

"You are a very rude young man, and noisy also. Who would want to come share a meal with you when you are so rude? Is this the way you were summoned to your meals? I think not. I know your mother and I knew Little

Frog. You were called with love, not anger."

Kaoto did not reply. Why did she not leave him alone? Could she not see how much he was suffering? Did she not know how much he missed Little Frog? Could she not tell he did not want to be bothered?

In the silence that followed he heard a slight rustling sound, and then on the rock beside the bowl, a tiny furry animal appeared. A chipmunk that was used to being fed by Paataga sat surveying the bowl and the huge angry young man. Timidly at first, because of the stranger, it cautiously watched him before it picked up a piece of corn, and in a wink it had vanished. In a little while it was back to get another piece. Kaoto remained motionless and quiet. Each time the chipmunk returned it stayed a little longer and was not as frightened. After several trips it became brave enough to perch on the edge of the bowl and stuff its cheeks full before it left. Paataga had watched quietly and now she spoke.

"What do we know of the little People? Some say they are the spirits of our departed loved ones. Can you tell me they are not? Either way you are sharing your meal with someone who has a need. Is not that what Little Frog asked you to do?"

Kaoto nodded his head. He did not want to speak for fear of scaring the little creature away. They were not strangers to him. He had seen them all his life, but he had never paid them any attention. Now he was looking with a different perspective.

The next morning Kaoto was still quiet but he was much more attentive. He placed the small bowl on the rock and again the chipmunk came and ate with him. When Paataga came out and watched them, Kaoto drew back slowly so as not to frighten his visitor away. He spoke in a hushed voice to her.

"Is it true? What you said about the animals being the spirit of People?"

Paataga mumbled as she brought out her bedding to hang in the sun and wind, going in and out several times before she answered him.

"Who are we to say? We know nothing of death; we know nothing about the spirits that live in the little ones. But surely they must have a spirit. It is a pleasant thought, do you not think?"

"But if that is true, then every animal might be someone we knew or loved."

"So?"

"But what of the animals we kill for food? Could they not be our ancestors?"

"It is possible."

Kaoto looked at the piece of venison he had been chewing on. "Then how could we kill them? It would be like killing our mother or father, would it not?"

Paataga smiled. She was pleased to have this deep reasoning in her pupil. This line of questioning did not disturb her. Questions were to be answered. Questions indicated the measure of the person who asked them, and often the one who asked a question would supply his own answers. With a little guidance in the right direction, the answers he derived would be correct.

"Kaoto, you are a man now, not a full-grown man in summers but a man just the same. Your father still loves you, does he not?"

"I am sure of it. He has always been kind to me and still is to this day."

"If you were hungry and went to his fire, would he feed you?"

"Of course. He would give me the last food he had rather than see me go hungry."

"We must have some meat to live. The deer and the antelope are the best source of food when we cannot find the buffalo."

"Yes, this is true." Kaoto wondered where this line of talk was leading. He saw no connection between this and what he had asked her.

If your father was dead and his spirit lived in the body of a deer and if you were hungry, would he not still want to feed you?"

"With his life?" Kaoto asked incredulously.

"Not his life. I did not say his life was the life of the deer. I said his spirit might live there. There is a difference. Do you see? Do you not think his spirit would want you to eat?"

"It would be a puzzle. I would have to think long about it. All I know is it will be hard for me to kill any animal from now on. It will be even worse after my parents are dead."

"We must never kill for entertainment, only for food."

Kaoto did not realize it yet but his training had already begun. Paataga was indeed a Wise One. Her many summers had helped, but even without her age she knew instinctively how to use everything available to work for her goal. Kaoto would not be hard to teach. He already had the seeds of wisdom. Wisdom was not something one learned, it was something one had before they were born. It could be pushed and made to grow and Paataga intended to do just that. She would prod and push until he developed to his full potential. She would make him think and when he thought she would be ready to help him, not by making decisions for him but by placing obstacles in his path so that he must work his way around them to come to his own conclusions. She would be there to make sure they were the right decisions. If he faltered or wavered she would be there to challenge and test him.

Yes, Paataga was pleased. She had made the right choice. Already she had discovered a depth in Kaoto she had only dared to dream about before. He displayed a quest for answers. What could be more important than this?

For now she was content to go slowly and let him work out his personal problems first. She would not push him too fast; she would let him have time to get used to her and her way of thinking. When he came with a question, she would have a little help ready for him. Not a lot, just a little.

When he asked, as she was sure he would, why Little Frog had to die she was ready with more questions to make him understand not only himself but others as well.

"You have asked why your little friend had to die. I ask you why did she ever live? What was the purpose of her life? Can you tell me that?"

"I have never thought about that. Why does anyone live?"

"We all have a reason for living. Some are more useful than others. Some are just to ensure the population will grow, others are here to instruct and aid those who are weak, or those who must prepare for a difficult task."

"Do you think she was here to help me, to prepare me for some difficult task? I always thought it was the other way around. I thought my purpose was to help her. I did do that, did I not?"

"Hmmmm, perhaps. But who received the most help? Who benefited most from your relationship? True, you probably kept her alive for a few more summers, but was this a pleasant time for her? And did it not make you feel good to help her almost like a parent taking care of a child? In turn the trust and dependence she had for you were also pleasant for you, were they not? Her life was short; you made it a little longer, but now her life is over. Your life on the other hand, has just begun. I think you will benefit from knowing her all your life. So it is hard to say who gained the most."

"I believe it would be easier to accept her death if I could believe the Spirit Watcher put her here to help me."

"And what makes you think the Spirit Watcher is interested in you? Does he not have more important things to do than put a little crippled girl in your path to help you?" Paataga could see she had shot her arrow deep into his ego. Good. It was not good for him to become puffed up, like the grouse, with his own importance.

"Let me tell you something about the Spirit Watcher. We are old friends, he and I. I have established a very comfortable relationship with him."

"I would like to hear about the Spirit Watcher. I have been wondering about something ever since I came up here to talk to you the other day."

"Ask. If I know, I will tell you." Paataga was prepared for whatever he wanted to talk about.

"When I told you of my dream, I said I felt almost like the Spirit Watcher."

"Yes?"

"Why did you not act surprised? Why did you not tell me this was wrong? No one should think they are like the Spirit Watcher."

"Oh. Is that so?" Paataga acted as if she really did not know this.

"Yes, and when I said I was telling the People they must leave their homes and go to a strange place, why did you not tell me this was also wrong?"

"And how is it wrong?"

"I should not tell anyone what to do. I am not a ruler, a teacher, a leader, I am only a young man who has no friends and does not know much about anything except running. I would have no right to tell People to leave their homes."

"Who says this?"

"Everybody."

"Everybody? I do not know this, so it cannot be everybody. My, you are a conceited young man to think everybody would be concerned with what you think or what you do, especially the Spirit Watcher. I bet he is laughing at you right now, saying what a swelled head this boy has to think I care one way or the other about him or what he or the old woman thinks."

Kaoto looked at the old woman in wonder and awe. She was making a joke about the most powerful deity in their world and she did not even seem to be afraid of his wrath.

"Are you not afraid to talk about him that way? I was taught one did not talk about the Spirit Watcher for fear of attracting his attention and making him angry with us."

Paataga looked up at Kaoto in indignation, as if he had asked the most stupid question in the world.

"Hmmmm!" She snorted. "Angry with me? Indeed." She shook her head as if in disbelief of this unheard of suggestion.

"Oh, I can understand your fear. You cannot help it. It is the way most of the People are taught." She waved her hand in the air as if resigned to dealing with total ignorance.

"Let me start back at the beginning. When I was young, oh yes, I was young once, and strong, and full of questions and doubts and fears. I too had been taught, just as you have been taught, that one must not take a chance of attracting attention to oneself. But over the many summers of my life I have learned that we are not nearly as important as we would like to think we are. We do not attract the attention of the Spirit Watcher or any other spirits. The Spirit Watcher sees what we do, and us, do not misunderstand me. That is why we call him the Spirit Watcher, but he is not that concerned with what we do." She was warming to her subject now and was content to expand on it.

"When you are running down a path, how many ants do you suppose you might have stepped on?"

"No one could answer that. There are so many ants that no one could count them all. A runner could never run if he stopped to count them all."

"Very true. Yet you must admit that you have stepped on and killed some everyday." Kaoto nodded his head in agreement to this statement.

"Did you ever hear an ant calling to you, asking you not to step on him?"

"No, of course not."

"Did you ever think to yourself, I will swing my foot right or left so this ant will live and that ant will die?"

"What are you trying to say? I have never heard an ant speak. They cannot talk."

"You do not think so? Have you ever wondered how they know where to go, or how they can tell when their hill is disturbed, even though they are deep under the ground? I think they talk to each other in some way but maybe not in the same language as the People. Animals make different sounds than we do, and though we do not understand them, they seem to understand each other."

"If they talk I cannot hear them and if I did I would not understand them."

"Well, just suppose you did hear them and you could understand them. What would your answer be to an ant that asks why you killed his family? Why did you pick them instead of someone else? Why did you break his leg and leave him crippled to die? Well? What would you tell him?"

"Again I say if I stopped to talk to every ant I would be so busy that I would not be able to get anything done. This is stupid."

"Stupid? No quest for an answer is stupid. Some may be better than others, but none of them are stupid." She let him have a moment to think.

"It is true. You would not have time to take care of your own life, would you?" Kaoto was thinking now. He was beginning to understand her point and the way she worked.

"So you think that maybe we are like ants to the Spirit Watcher? You think he is too busy with his own affairs to pay much attention to us? And he does not pick who lives and who dies, sometimes it is just an accident? We just get in the way?"

"It is a thought. We do not go out looking for ants to crush. Have you ever said, there goes a wicked ant, I have been watching him for a long time now and I do not like him, I will punish him, and then go kill him?"

"No, but if one of them bothered me too much, crawls in my food or bed, then I might kill him. But if he does not bother me, then I would not bother him."

Paataga smiled. Her wizened face was wrinkled from many summers of squinting from the sun light, wind and sand, and it was hard to tell whether she was smiling or not. Only the twinkle in her eyes gave a clue. Kaoto realized she was smiling at him, that she was pleased with their conversation so far.

"You are telling me that the Spirit Watcher is not concerned with us either, are you not? That the only time he deliberately harms us is when we bother him. Yes. I can see how that could be true and it makes sense when you stop to think about it. Does it not?" Kaoto was pleased with himself, and rightfully so.

"Let us say we are just another animal to him, no more important than any other animal," Paataga suggested.

"And there are so many of us, all animals included, that the death of one of us, any one of us, is nothing to him." Kaoto was beginning to understand now. "If we are in the way when he walks, we might get crushed just as we crush an ant, not to punish us, but just because we were in the way. He probably never hears us if we complain."

"It may not be quite that simple. If we believe that, then there would be no need for us to revere him and by all means we must respect him and pay him his dues. What I am telling you is that he does not come hunting you for talking about him, or when you brag a little. I do not feel you should blame him for your friend's death. Many ants die every day from other causes. You do not kill every ant that dies. Of the many ants there must be in this world, the few we kill would be as nothing to us. So why should they hold us accountable for all their deaths?"

Kaoto studied the idea. It was truly something new to him. He had never been taught to think about such things. In fact, he had been taught just the opposite. He had been taught to never think about the Spirit Watcher at all for fear of bringing down his wrath.

"This presents a problem within a problem, and each one opens up another set of problems. To answer one you must answer them all. This, of course, would be impossible. So, maybe we would be better off not to know anything, like the animals; then we would all be happy," Kaoto pondered.

Again Paataga was smiling and he smiled back, the first smile to crease his face since Little Frog had left him to make her solitary journey into the next world.

"That would be too simple," she told him. "We can never answer all of the problems, this is true. But to satisfy ourselves, we must answer all that we can. We can continue to think about the ones we cannot answer. That is the reason we are different from the other animals." She turned and gave Kaoto a steady stare. Her eyes were not smiling now, nor did they show anger. Kaoto understood that she was trying to convey something very important to him. Something she wanted to be sure he understood.

"Some of us must be able to help others. Sometimes we can help them find the answers when they are misled or stray from the truth. I have chosen you, Kaoto, because you will not be content to let things go unanswered if it is within your power to find the truth. By doing this you will be in a position to help others." The old woman sat silent for a short space of time, letting her pupil digest her words before she continued.

"Over these many summers I have found that the People are the happiest when they can do something for themselves. That is why you must never try to tell them everything." Another long pause ensued, but Kaoto did not interrupt. He sat thinking and waiting, his mind working on a new line. This was a challenging new way of thinking and he found he liked it.

"You must be patient with them and understand their doubts and fears. You must be prepared to offer them comfort when they need it, guidance when you can, and make decisions for them only when it is the last resort. I think you will find it is best to let them find their own answers, even if you have to guide them without their knowing."

Kaoto lifted his eyes and looked long at the ancient crone. He no longer had any doubts about her wisdom; she was indeed entitled to be called the Wise One.

"Like you are guiding me now, Paataga, wisest of the wise?"

Chapter Eleven

Life with Paataga soon settled into a routine, with the wise old woman usually taking the lead to open a subject. It did not matter so much what the subject was as long as it got her pupil to ask questions. Each time he asked a question, she would turn it back on him until he was able to find an answer they were both satisfied with. Some subjects were simple, taking only a little time to solve. He soon discovered they were the building blocks of later discussions.

Others were more complicated and the discussion would continue for a longer time, often days. Sometimes they would set a problem aside to return to it later.

Kaoto was pleased to discover he had someone he could talk to, someone who would listen and not tell him he should not think, or talk, about such things. He was surprised to discover that his judgement was accepted. He was accustomed to the older People always assuming that young men lacked sense and that most of their ideas were to be laughed at, not listened to. He soon found he could talk things out and explore all aspects of a subject, even to how they were affected by the Spirit Watcher, without the customary words of caution being heaped on him. There were no forbidden subjects as far as his teacher was concerned. There was nothing prohibited by Paataga. If it interested her pupil, it was worthy of questioning. Whatever happened or whatever was done was open for debate and speculation. He became very adept at ferreting out the truth and finding the seeds of knowledge in a pile of rubbish.

Paataga could see that it would not be long before he passed her by and went beyond what she was able to teach. She was also sure that when that day arrived, her pupil would be well equipped to travel those roads alone. This pleased her because it only confirmed to her that she had made a wise choice in this outcast giant youth.

He showed an almost reverent feeling for others, so much so that Paataga worried for him. In his future he would come in contact with so many of the People and so many problems that his concern for them could be dangerous to him. Too much compassion could rob him of his own peace of mind and thus undermine his well being and his efficiency in the life she knew he was destined to lead. Unfortunately, there was nothing she could do to forestall this occupational hazard. All she could do was arm him with all the knowledge and truth that she had accumulated in her long life span. And hope it would be enough to carry him through until he had established his own beliefs and convictions; until he had the perspicacity he needed to see him through the demanding days ahead of him in the life she had chosen for him.

He enjoyed discussing the problems of the People with her and was soon able to make sound suggestions of his own on how to solve some of these problems. She knew that one day she would turn her office over to him and he would have to face more demanding issues than these small matters that were brought to her. This is what she was training him for. She needed someone to pass on her duties to, someone to take over her responsibilities.

Paataga was beyond being old by the Peoples' standards. Her time was limited. In fact, she was surprised to still be living. There was yet another reason. The future called for someone capable of moving about the nation, something she could no longer do. She could see there would be a crisis arising that would require much travel and much time. She could not travel, and the People could not and would not come to her. Even if they did, she did not think she would live long enough to see them all.

Yes. She had made a good choice. Kaoto not only had the wisdom and compassion needed for this assignment, he also had the necessary stamina of a young man, more than most, to travel whenever the time was right. His natural curiosity, coupled with his concern for the welfare of the People, made him the best possible person for this task. Her only regret was having to dump so much responsibility on him that he would never have a chance to lead a normal life. However, from what she had observed so far, he would never know a normal life anyway.

He was ready to assume the responsibility, although he was not aware of just how great it would be or what the conditions of her office would mean to him in the long summers ahead. No one ever was. She surely had never suspected what she was getting into when she had accepted it. She was convinced there was no vanity in Kaoto. The prestige of the office of the Wise One meant nothing to him other than a chance to serve those who would need help. She almost envied him this innocence. It was one of the factors that made her sure he would succeed.

Although she had not told him what she expected of him or what she planned for him to do, she was sure he was ahead of her already and knew instinctively that this was to be his fate and was willing, even anxious, to start.

Daily there was a pilgrimage of more than the usual number of people with minor problems coming to Paataga for her help. She knew this was mainly because of her new student. She dispensed wisdom as easily as a stream of flowing water. Soon she was not only including Kaoto in these discussions; she was asking his opinion. His opinions were welcome, and they were more and more often accepted.

Kaoto never left Paataga's home except for a long run in the morning and again in the evening. She knew that he must not only stay in shape but must have some diversion from the rigorous mental training she was putting him though.

He did not know that his name, already known far and wide as that of an outstanding runner, was now being used in connection with the Wise One. He was establishing a reputation for mercy and compassion, along with sound, practical judgment.

They talked of his dream, which strangely enough had stopped since he had taken up the training of the Wise One. Paataga told him of her own dream, which was very similar to his. She told him that she had never felt she was actually there in the dream or was a part of it. She had never heard him tell the People they must leave their homes and return to the land of little earth. She had seen some other things that he had not.

"I have seen the dark, threatening shadows on the outside edge of my vision. I could never see what was in the shadow, but I knew it was a threat. I could see one little speck of light, which grew until it was a man standing before the People. That man was you, Kaoto. He looked as you look, or will look in a few more summers. He had the same nose, the same crest of unruly hair, and he wore his eagle feather as you wear yours." Kaoto absently reached up and stroked the two feathers in his headband.

"Many men wear two eagle feathers, Wise One. It could be another man."

"No one in our land wears them as you do. Most men wear theirs proudly, sticking up like the ears of a rabbit. But you wear yours laid back on either side of your head like a deer creeping through the brush. Do you mind telling me why you wear them in this manner? You are proud of them, are you not?"

"I am very proud of them, but it did not seem right for me to parade them when I won them so easily. Most men have to work hard to deserve the right to wear even one feather. They have the right to wear them proudly, to display them with honor for everyone to see. As for me, well, I am happy to have Matuga honor me so, but it just does not seem right to brag about them and make a display of them to make other better men feel jealous. They do not like me the way it is, so why make them hate me? Besides, at my height, they are always catching on things, and with them laid back they clear almost anything my head does."

Paataga did not comment on his answer. She did not agree with his opinion on this manner, but she could respect his feelings.

"What of the feather you gave to Little Frog? Did she wear it to the new land?"

"Yes. I made sure the women left it in her headband with it lying over one cheek, just as she always wore it. I wanted her to have it in the next world, where she would be strong and tall. I thought the feather might have a value there also, and those who welcomed her would know she was a person of importance and thus treat her with proper respect. It made her happy to own it." He hung his head humbly as he talked. Even though he accepted her death, it still made him sad to talk about her. "I also thought it might help her to remember me in the next world. I did not want her to ever forget me, as I will never forget her."

"Hmmmm. Many People would have been tempted to keep it for themselves. They would have argued that their loved one would want them to keep it rather than to have it buried where no one could ever see it again."

"I am sure she would have been glad to have me keep it, but what need have I for another? I have two already. Besides, we always shared the things we enjoyed."

Paataga was impressed with these words and did not doubt his sincerity. It seemed to her that Kaoto could not and would not deceive anyone. All his ideas or thoughts were genuine and straightforward.

"The reason I ask is because in my dreams the man, who appears to be you, wore two feathers as you did, but he also carried a third feather in his hand. I just thought perhaps you should have kept it to fulfill the accuracy of our vision."

"No. If the time comes and I have a need of another I will go out and earn it, but what of the rest of the dream? The part where the bones are knocked apart and spread over the sand? Where was this man? I do not remember seeing him, or for that matter anyone else but the People."

"No, of course not. You could not see yourself. In my dream you do not go out in the desert with them. You are not one of them. You fade away just as you appeared, without leaving a trace. I do not know where you went, I only know there is this tiny speck of light like a distant star, which remains after you leave." Paataga took a twig and stirred the dying coals in preparation of starting a new cook fire for the evening meal.

"After that," she said as she placed some small pieces of dry wood on the coals, "I dream no more. I did not see the bones come together to reassemble and become living People again. That part is beyond me; the rest I can only guess at."

"Will you tell me what you think it means?" Kaoto asked her.

"Soon. Soon. First I will tell you all that has been told to me. There is much I do not understand. It makes no sense to me; maybe it will mean something to you." Paataga eyed her pupil intently, once more confirming the wisdom of her choice.

"The important thing is for each of us, in our turn, to remember exactly what we have been told and then to pass it on to our successor. I of course will add on what has occurred in my lifetime so each new person is kept up to date. After I have told you all of it, I think you will know more about your dreams without my help."

"Still making me find my own answers?" He smiled at the old woman.

"I have found that the answers we find for ourselves are the only ones we can truly trust," she replied, returning his smile.

While she had been talking, Paataga had produced a necklace from under her loose fitting, shapeless robe. It was made of finely polished bits of alternating stones, bones and fossil shells. There were twenty-four flat chips, each alike, yet distinctly different from each other. Several of them could lie in the palm of his hand without touching each other. They were so thin they remained light enough to wear and yet strong enough to endure the many summers that were required of them. As she showed them to Kaoto, he could see that each one had been carved in its own peculiar fashion. They carried designs made of straight lines, swirls, and spirals, accented with dots and crosses or slashes either to right or left. These bits of stone, bone and shells retained the history of the People.

As Paataga began to recite the history, her fingers would trace the almost invisible pattern on one side and then the other of each piece. They were kept in their proper order by their position on the string. Each tiny groove or raised area could represent a segment of time in the past back to the beginning of time. They served as a perpetual reminder to her of how the story should go.

Her voice droned along in a monotone cadence. Kaoto could tell that she did not understand all of what she said, but was only repeating what she had been taught and told she must remember, word for word. She must be able to repeat this at any time and eventually she would be required to pass it on to someone else, someone younger, who would relieve her of her burden.

Kaoto was fascinated by the story and equally fascinated that it should continue for several days, with short breaks occasionally for food or drink, or just a rest. He knew that even his supreme memory would be put to a test amassing and retaining this history, and then being able to recall it and deliver it when called upon to do so. He would have to begin to gather material to make his own necklace and devise his own brand of shorthand to record it. The story went like this:

"In the beginning the Spirit Watcher was asleep. He did not travel the sky each day and then go to sleep each night as he does today. He was so soundly asleep that nothing seemed to be able to wake him. The world was dark and there was nothing living on the face of the earth. The People existed but they were afraid of the darkness, so they all lived deep in the ground where the darkness could not reach them.

"Then something happened to the earth. Some sleeping giant shook it. The ground was torn open in places, leaving the People exposed like ants on a disturbed anthill. They were exposed to the darkness that they so much feared. The noise of the earth breaking and shaking was so great that it woke the Spirit Watcher from his long sleep. He looked down and he saw the People and saw they were afraid of the darkness. He took pity on them and sent them his light. He began his daily ride across the sky to patrol the earth and protect the People. As long as he was in his great shining bowl in the sky, the People would walk about and were not afraid. But as soon as he went down to his bed to sleep, the People became frightened of the darkness and would dig into the earth to hide. In the morning when he arose they would come out of their holes and walk about again.

"This went on for a long time until the Spirit of Storms flung down one of his bolts of light and struck a tree to make a fire. Men were afraid of the fire at first, but discovered that they could use the fire to hold back the darkness after the Spirit Watcher had gone to sleep. They learned to use the fire for other things such as warmth and cooking, and then they learned how to make fire without waiting for the Spirit of Storms to bring it down to them.

"Now the People were no longer afraid of the night, but they still lived in holes in the ground and did not walk about in the darkness. They only felt safe in the circle of their fire. They were always glad to see the Spirit Watcher in the mornings. They were so happy that they made up songs to sing to greet him. They would beat on hollow logs with sticks to imitate the sound of the earth breaking. When he awoke, they would sing their songs of gladness to him.

"The Spirit Watcher became weary of all the noise they made so he ask his Sister, the Moon, to come and make light at night for them so they would leave him alone. Sister Moon was lazy and indifferent to the People because they never sang songs to her. She would not come out every night and never at the same time. Sometimes she would forget to look toward them; they could see her, but her light was not on them. Still, it made some of the People more brave and when she did send light, they began to stay up at night with her.

"This is when evil comes. Everyone knows that evil lurks in darkness and gloom and cannot stand the light of day. It awaits the unwary and lures them into destruction. The People discovered evil things and some of them grew to like evil things."

Up until this point, Kaoto thought he could at least partially follow the meaning of the history. But soon after this it became as much a mystery to him as it was to Paataga. She was caught up in a trance-like state. She spoke words she did not know the meanings of and told of events he could not fathom.

"All the People worked together to make marvelous machines." Paataga did not know the word for machines so she could only call them things.

"The Things made life so easy for People that they became lazy, as lazy as the Spirit Watcher's Sister. The People became greedy and wicked. They stole from one another, they killed the animals for fun, more than they needed for food, and the bodies of the beasts rotted on the ground. They were not satisfied with just killing animals and began to kill one another for no reason other than greed and boredom.

"They became more dependent on the Things. They would not grow their own food. They wanted the Things to feed them, to make their clothes for them and to build their homes. They wanted the Things to do everything for them and the Things did. One day the Things became so powerful they found they did not need the People anymore. They became annoyed with the People and all their demands on the Things. So the Things banded together and drove the People out of the lovely land they lived in.

"The People had to move. They crossed the land and came to a great water. They could not cross the water but the Things did not want them to stay even here, so the Things built them strange bowls. These bowls were large enough that many People could be seated in them. The Things pushed the bowls out in the water and left them to look out for themselves. They drifted many days in the water. They could do nothing to help themselves; they did not know how. After a time they were all near to death.

"The Spirit Watcher had seen what the Things had done to his People, and even though he knew the People had done evil, he was still very angry with the Things for mistreating the People. He caused the land where the Things lived to sink into the water and leave them buried deep in the water where they could not work anymore, nor could they help or hurt the People ever again. The death of the Things poisoned the water so it was never fit to drink again.

"There was no land for the People to go back to, so the Spirit Watcher called on the Spirit of the Wind to come and blow them to a new land. All the People did not come to the same land. Some were blown in different directions and scattered all over the earth. Only the People of the Anasazi came to this land. This was the land of the Anasazi but it was not in this valley, it was far to the south.

"The new land was lush and green, similar to the old land they had left. There were many new trees with new fruit, birds they had never seen before and different animals, all of which provided food for the People. No one went hungry; there was plenty for all.

"Slowly the People began to fill up the land until they became too crowded and were forced to move inland, farther from the water. Soon they could only see the water from high mountains. They liked the mountains, but all could not live on them. It was easier to raise and gather food in the lower valleys. Still, they longed to see the water, so they built their own mountains wherever they went. Their living was so easy that they had plenty of time to build the mountains, and every summer they added a little more to them, making them bigger each time.

"The People multiplied quickly in this friendly land. They grew so close together that they had to spread out, some to the south and some to the north. The strongest, oldest and laziest stayed and forced the others to move on. They spread farther and farther each summer until they no longer could remember the land where they had lived.

"For many summers the People multiplied and moved north until the land became wider and wider; until it became so wide a runner could no longer find the water to the east and it was many days' run to the west. They could no longer build mountains high enough to see the water. So this custom died. Eventually they came to this land, the land of the Chaco, and spread as far north as the weather permitted and as far east and west as the terrain permitted, stopping only at deep canyons or open, hostile plains.

"Here the land was not so lush and green. There was enough water for them to raise their crops but they had to spend more time working. After they had planted their crops they built their homes, but they no longer built the mountains because no one remembered why they built them in the first place.

"It was a big land and there were no other people here. The animals were plentiful. There were great herds of buffalo, deer and antelope, enough for anyone willing to hunt. The streams ran deep with cold water all the time and there were big fish in these streams. Some fish were so big that one of them would feed two families for many days."

From here on the story became more understandable. Paataga was now on the last chip of her necklace. This chip was not fully covered with markings. There was room for more history on it but Paataga knew she would make no more records on her necklace. This would be Kaoto's job from now on.

"The People prospered and lived a good life. They never tried to make Things again. They had forgotten how; many did not believe they had ever existed in the first place. Because of this the Spirit Watcher loved them and he wanted to spend more of his time with them, too much time. He became jealous of the Spirit of Storms and drove him away so the clouds did not block his view. The land began to dry up. Each summer the streams were smaller, and the fish had to leave them. The grass did not grow as tall so the buffalo had to spread out to look for new pastures. There was still enough to feed the People, but the hunt was harder.

"The People built dams to hold back the water in the spring so they could use it in the summer. They dug ditches to carry the water to the fields, to ensure the crops. The People began to worry. Then a new threat appeared in the distance. She did not know what it was but was sure it was real."

Paataga ended her story. This was all the history to this moment. This was today and Kaoto recognized it.

Chapter Twelve

Now that Paataga's long recitation was completed, Kaoto returned to question both their dreams. They could associate his dream about the little earth with the land to the south. According to the history, the land narrowed and there was a great water on both sides of the land. This must be what was meant by the 'land of little earth'. But how had he known this? He had never heard the history before and had never known of anyone who had traveled that far. Why must the People return to the land of their forefathers? Was the danger so close? Was the time so near? Were they to be surrounded by darkness? It was a puzzle within a puzzle and together they tried to untangle the twisted skeins of dreams and history. They were trying to make sense of it all.

Kaoto began to search for material to make his own necklace. Each day as he ran, he would look for small chips that he could possibly use. Over time he chose and rejected many pieces until, one by one, he was satisfied with them and added them to his final collection. He polished them until they were smooth and then he used a flake of flint embedded in a small stick to make his own grooves and swirls to remind him of the history as told to him over and over by Paataga. They were to become an intrinsic part of his life.

Paataga was not surprised at his ability to learn and retain facts so quickly and so accurately. This part of his runners' training manifested itself in a very short time. Many passages he could repeat after hearing them the first time. None took more than a few recitations before he had them mastered. The hardest part was keeping each segment in its proper sequence. This is where the stones, bones, and shells were of value. He was able to use them to prompt his memory and keep everything straight. Yes, Paataga was satisfied with his memory. She was afraid she might have waited too long to begin teaching someone to take her place. But what else could she have done? There had been no one she could trust before Kaoto.

It soon became apparent that Kaoto was no ordinary pupil. He had the capacity of a great rememberer. Once he had gathered and made all of his chips, he became proficient in their use. He could not only recite each part of the history from the chips, he could do something she had never been able to do in all her long life. Kaoto could pick up any chip and start to recite from it going either forward or backward without the chips on either side of it. Paataga had always had to start in the beginning and work steadily through to the finish. She had been able to stop and pick up the skein of the history the next day. But she had never been able to pick up a chip at random and start from there. Kaoto could even take the chips from his necklace and mix them up and then sort them instantly and without error. Further, the more times he went over the history, the more he seemed to grasp its meaning.

For three summers he lived with the old woman, studying at her feet, reciting the history at every opportunity until she was satisfied that it was forever engraved on his mind as it was on the chips. She warned him to constantly keep it fresh in his mind, by reciting it as often as he could, even if only to himself when he was on a lonely trail and no one was present to hear him.

With each passing day she let him handle more of the problems that were brought to her. She was satisfied with the way he handled these problems, although at times she was perplexed by his methods until the end results became evident. Other times she had trouble containing her mirth, like the time two men came up the trail carrying a huge pumpkin. They were angry men, both of them. The grounds for their anger were soon disclosed.

They shared a field, which was a common practice where geography did not recognize dimensions or proportions of the fields. In this field had grown the huge pumpkin, larger than anyone had ever seen before. Both men tended the field and worked the land together. But when it came time to harvest, they had divided the field in the usual manner and each man was to harvest his portion of the field. This was a fair way that most men used to divide up the crops, and there was seldom any dispute. In this case all the crops had been brought in with equal results in corn, squash and pumpkins, with the exception of this one huge pumpkin, which straddled the dividing line. It was by far the largest pumpkin in anyone's memory. Both men claimed it and they were reluctant to cut it in half so they could share it. First they had taken it to Matuga. All he could suggest was dividing equally between them. This did not satisfy either of them. Now they had carried it across the valley and up the side of the canyon to the home of the renowned Wise One and her pupil.

Kaoto walked around the offending specimen. It was truly something to take pride in. This would be a difficult situation. How could he make both men happy without cutting it in half? How could he expect either of them to give up their interest in something as unique as this? He looked at Paataga to divine what she might think on this subject. He did not ask her for her opinion, only a mental picture of what she thought. She shrugged her shoulder as if to say, "Why fight over a stupid pumpkin?"

"I suppose we could have a game of chance and the winner could claim it," he said, knowing this would not satisfy them even as he spoke.

"Why should I take a chance of losing what is already mine by rights?" asked the first of the two men.

"Yours? What makes you think it is yours? It is plainly mine, everyone but you knows that," the second man retorted in anger.

"Yes," Kaoto said as he continued to inspect the source of the problem. "I must think on it more. The problem seems to be as large as the pumpkin itself." He continued to walk around in a circle, glancing secretly at Paataga, who was amused to see the perplexed expression on the young man's face.

This was only a minor dispute but it might prove to be a very difficult one. She knew he was putting himself in the place of the two men and trying to see with their eyes and think with their minds. Kaoto stopped and searched each man's face long and studiously, as if the answer might lie hidden under the masks of their faces. This would be a measure of a Wise One and would forecast his future ability.

"Let me make this suggestion. One of you must be the richer of the two of you. So let the one who is the richest, the better farmer, who can claim the best mate, let him give his share to the less fortunate of you."

Paataga looked wonderingly at him but she could see he was serious. He was actually making this proposal with the intention of settling the dispute. Then she started to smile. Turn the question back on the person who asked it. Is that not what she had done to him and did he not learn fast? But even she had never gone this far and she did not know if she would have dared to try, even if she had thought of it. She waited to see what they would do. She was sure neither would accede to these terms.

Both men fidgeted and stared at each other. It was impossible. Both could admit to being the best but neither could admit to being poorer and accept under these terms. With one voice they said, "You have tricked us. This is not wise. You know that neither of us will claim to be more poor or unlucky than the other. Is it your intention to keep it for yourself? Or do you think we should let it lie and rot? That is not a way to solve a problem, is it?" they asked, even more angry than before.

Kaoto turned his back on them as if dismissing them and the offending fruit of the vine. He continued to ignore them and their questions as he spoke to Paataga. "Are we not scheduled to have a feast in a few days, a feast to honor the new ruler from the south of us? I'm sure he has never seen such a pumpkin as this. Would Matuga not be proud if he could show it to him and let him see what our men are capable of? Too bad no one can claim it so they could offer it to him. I am sure Matuga would honor, before all men, the owner of such a pumpkin as this."

"I see your meaning, Kaoto, but as you say, there is no one to claim it. As you can see, both of these men are too proud to admit they are not as rich as their neighbor or that they have inferior mates. They are not smart enough to figure it out for themselves. Oh, no. They have to come up to us like a couple of children fighting over a cornhusk doll. And as long as they fight, no one can have it. I guess they are right, it will just have to lie here and rot, for neither of them can, or will, claim it."

Kaoto and his teacher continued to talk and ignore the two men who were at first bewildered, and at last, ashamed of themselves. Without waiting for further instructions, they picked up the pride of their field and went back down the trail to present it to Matuga. When he offered them a reward, they insisted the whole village should share the credit for it. They suggested Matuga tell the visiting ruler that it was one of the smaller ones of this summer's crop. It was a good joke and the entire village laughed, not only at the joke but also at the two men who had bothered the Wise Ones with such a trivial matter.

The visiting ruler also enjoyed the joke and replied with humor of his own. "I must learn your secret," he told Matuga. "I would like to take this knowledge home to my People so they too can raise these tiny pumpkins. The ones we raise are so large they have to be eaten in the field. Sometimes a family will just move into one until it is all eaten." The story was told and retold for many summers thereafter. Also they mentioned the young Wise One who was able to solve this problem by turning a dispute into something to laugh about.

Kaoto had reached the end of his eighteenth summer when Paataga came to him one morning after his usual run. She studied him as if for the first time. Finally she nodded her head as if satisfied. "I have taught you all I know. I can add no more to your wide range of knowledge. Already you have surpassed me in most matters. What you learn from now on, you will have to learn from going among the People, talking to them and settling their problems first hand."

She knew that he had the history of the People committed to memory for the rest of his life. He had taken care of many of their problems without causing anyone to be hurt. He always found a way so everyone felt they had won, just as he had with the large pumpkin.

"I made this decision some time back and plan to take advantage of the fall festival to make the announcement to the People. Matuga has long since sent out runners to spread the word as far as it can reasonably be sent. This way it will be possible for many of the other rulers to be present to witness the changing of office."

The actual ceremony would take place in the Great Kiva, located between her home and the Pueblo Bonito. Women were not allowed in the Great Kiva as spectators. They could come as dancers or singers, but they must enter and leave by the hidden tunnel and they must never leave the stage while they were inside. Under no circumstances could they enter or leave by the main entrance. Even though Paataga was a woman, her position of Wise One was beyond consideration of gender. So she would enter through the main entrance, but after she had passed her office to Kaoto she would no longer be the Wise One and would have to leave by the tunnel as another performer. She would just be a tired old woman who was no longer of any use to the People.

Kaoto did not make any protest or pretense about his ability. He knew he was as ready as he would ever be to take the position she had trained him for. He knew that the moment she transferred her office to him, he would be in position to make his own decisions and ask for the concessions he felt necessary. With this in mind, he made some plans of his own without consulting his teacher or the ruler and his People.

One portion of his plan he did reveal to Paataga. He insisted on having his mother present as well as his father. Paataga agreed that Keenwah could enter through the secret tunnel to stand at his side when the time was right. Later, she and Paataga would exit together out the same tunnel. His father would of course be there as a father, with a man's right and would take his place beside his son during the ceremony. Keenwah had given only a mild protest but was easily persuaded to be there at his side. Her pride in her son won over any feelings she might have had about being inside the kiva. It would be the only time in her life that she would see the inside of the Great Kiva.

Ten days before the ceremony was to take place the surrounding pueblos took on the appearance of anthills on the first sunny day after a rain. There were many distinguished visitors coming and the runners were on the road in all directions day and night. Extra shelters were set up to accommodate the extra guests. Huge piles of foodstuffs were gathered and laid out. A herd of buffalo was located and driven to within easy hunting distance. The younger members of the tribe held the herd in the general area. There were not as many of these majestic beasts left as in the earlier days, but there would be plenty to feed all who came to see the new Wise One. Chaco was in its finest age and Matuga basked in its glory.

In the meantime, Keenwah was busy putting the finishing touches on a special cloak she had made for her son. She had consulted Paataga on this matter, as it was not proper for a mother to make the clothes of her son after he had reached manhood. She did not know if it would be proper for her to do this. Paataga solved this problem just as she had all the other problems brought to her over the many summers.

"True. It is not proper for you to make a cloak for your son now that he is a man. But it is perfectly fitting for you to give a present to the new Wise One when he takes his office. None can fault you for this. Just let anyone dare." Her mouth was drawn down into a hard firm line, and Keenwah was certain that she would not want to earn her displeasure. She was equally certain no one else would, either.

She had been working on the cloak for most of the summer. A lot of work had gone into it. She had a secret place to work where Kaoto would never stumble in on her. It was the room he had shared with Little Frog. The room had remained empty ever since her death. The room was still officially Kaoto's, but he could never bring himself to go there.

"It is the home of many pleasant memories and that is the way I would like to keep it. If I should enter it and see it is just an empty, bare room, I would destroy all the memories I have of it. As long as I never go back there, it will always remain the same to me," he had explained to his mother the one time that she brought it up.

Her neighbors had contributed materials for the cloak, but the work was all Keenwah's. For a pattern, she had made Maata stand on a rock to get the right length. It must be long enough to come within a hand span of the ground, but it must not be long enough to drag. It would be ready in time for the new Wise One when he took his office.

In the last few days before the ceremony, Paataga had told Kaoto the story of her younger days. This was partly to help pass the time and partly because there was little else to speak of. She had never told anyone else of her past life and there was no one left old enough to remember. She wanted Kaoto to understand that she was no special, gifted person. She was just a normal mortal who had taken on the mantle of the Wise One when it had been passed to her. If she could succeed, then she knew he could.

"Were you ever mated, Paataga? I have never heard you speak of a mate or of children."

"I was mated once, many, many summers ago. It soon became evident that I was barren and would never have children of my own. My mate was a good man, much like your father, strong, brave and kind. We were happy for a few summers. Then he was killed during a buffalo hunt. It seems he had been caught in the path of a wounded bull who gored him before he could bring it down." She sat staring off into the distance as the long dead memory came back to her.

"Why did you not find another mate? Was your bond so strong with him that you could take no other?" Kaoto asked.

"No. I could have broken the bond. In fact, time has a way of doing that for you. But since I was known to be barren, I could not find another man who would have me. So the only way I could live was to take to the road."

The People had long maintained a road system for trade with all the outlying districts. Over time they had expanded and improved these roads until they were arrow straight and often as wide as the Great Kiva. The Chaco Canyon was at the center of these roads. To maintain and keep the roads free from weeds, trees and wind blown sand, the People had let the elderly, the widows, and the orphans who were capable take a section of the road and work it to keep it in shape and clean.

The local ruler would contribute a small amount to support these people, but their main source of living was derived from charging a small fee for anyone using the road; anyone but the runners, of course, who were covered by the ruler's fee. It was a tradition known far and wide, so every trader who traveled these roads would carry an extra supply of dried foods to pay his way through their territory. This consisted of meat, corn, and beans. Once in a great while there would be a fee of fresh meat or vegetables. This seldom happened and was always considered a luxury.

"I was working a section of the road south and east of here when I met the Wise One of my day," Paataga continued. "He was old, sick, and weary when he came by my part of the road. I felt sorry for him. Of course, I did not know he was the Wise One. To me he was just a person in need. I took him to my little house of sticks and mud and fed him and nursed him back to health. His recovery was slow, so he spent a lot of time with me there. After many days he told me who he was, but I did not believe him. I thought he was just wandering in his mind. One day he was strong enough to walk out to the road. He stopped the first runner to come by. Well, you can imagine my surprise and shame when the runner paid homage to him." She chuckled as she remembered how she felt that day, so in awe of a man of such power. Now she held that power and felt no reverence for it.

"He had the runners spread the word as to where he was, and soon we had more provisions than I knew what to do with." The old woman smiled in recollection of those days, when food was her main problem.

"Now I always have more than I need. Anyway, the old Wise One seemed content to rest and stay with me for a longer time. In the course of our conversations, I told him about my dream. It was coming to me often in those days. He was very interested in my dream, just as I was in yours. The difference is that he had no dreams but still he seemed to recognize mine and placed some significance on it. He asked me many questions about my dream and from that day he began to train me, just as I have trained you. Now you can see where my time on the road was helpful to me. I met so many of the People and knew so many different types that it was as if I had really traveled. I listened to everything they talked about and asked questions until they became quite weary of me. It was a good training ground for me. Since I have never traveled and have spent most of my days right here, this experience allowed me to know much that I would have otherwise been ignorant of."

"This explains how you can know so much without ever having left here."

"Yes. I learned to listen. One must not be in a hurry to do all the talking, as I am doing now. But it is your turn to listen anyway. Being wise does not mean you have to tell people everything. Sometimes just listening to people, asking a few questions, makes them think you are wiser than you really are. Just being in the presence of the Wise One often brings out wisdom in the person who came to you for advice. You just have to know when to talk and when to listen. Most of the time, you must listen."

"You have done that with me, have you not? You have used me to get more knowledge and make me find my own wisdom." He reached across the gap between them and patted her withered hands. "You are truly a Wise One. I will never be equal to you, not even if I lived to have as many summers."

"Yes. I used you. But you have been a good pupil and have learned to listen. You have much more patience and love for the People than I have. It will be an exacting ordeal for you but the People will learn to love you for your wisdom. That is something I have never had from them. They respect me, fear me, some even hate me, but none have ever loved me as I believe they will love you."

"It is too bad. There is much about you to love, old mother."

Paataga got up and kicked the coals as she tended her cook fire. While her back was turned she hastily made a swipe at her eyes.

"Smoke," she snorted. "Always follows you and gets in your eyes no matter which side of the fire you are on." Kaoto smiled; he was listening.

The day of the ceremony finally arrived. Early in the morning the People came drifting in towards the Great Kiva. There would not be room for them all; only a select group would actually get to see the change of office. The rooms surrounding the kiva were reserved for the rulers and their elders. When the ceremony was over the People would get to see the new Wise One and pay homage to him when he came out.

In spite of the momentous occasion, it only took a short time to accomplish. Paataga walked through the main entrance of the kiva with Kaoto following behind her. The contrast in their height would have been greeted with a burst of mirth at any other time, but now it was not noted. They were both great persons in their own rights.

On the stage he took a position beside her. She introduced Kaoto to the assemblage and gave a brief history of his life. All of them knew of him and some knew him personally. Most had heard of his great run, so telling the story was more of a formality than a need. Kaoto then gave his pledge to the assembled leaders and their elders or advisors. He pledged to serve the People to the best of his ability. He gave his thanks to his mentor, whom they already knew. When this had been done, Paataga spoke again.

"Hear me, my People. I have held this office for longer than any of you can remember. I have done my best and I know that it was not enough. Forgive me for my failures. They were due to weakness of body, not lack of desire. Now you have one who surpasses me in all things - strength, knowledge, and ability. Let him serve you." She backed away and prepared to step down into the tunnel that would lead her out under the floor of the kiva, out to a lonely life of oblivion.

"Paataga." The note of command in Kaoto's voice was something new to the old woman. She had never heard him use such a strong, forceful voice before. She stopped and turned to see what he wished of her. "You, who have served the People so long and so well, I will not allow you to slink out of here like an unclaimed pup. I have a request of you."

Paataga looked at him mutely, not knowing what to think. What could he want of her? He had made no mention of a request in the days before the ceremony. That would have been the time to ask, not now.

"What does the Wise One ask of me?"

"I would ask you to do me the honor of staying here and serving in my office just as you have been doing. I will be traveling all over the land, as we have talked about; you know my mission. I will need someone to stay here and answer questions in my absence. Who better than you?" She started to shake her head in the negative, but he went on quickly before she could speak or refuse him. "I ask you to do this, not for the People, but for me."

Trembling with emotion, the old woman stepped back to his side where she looked up with a new admiration and respect for this strange young man who she thought she had known so well.

"I would be honored to do what I can for you," she answered humbly. "But my time is short and I cannot carry on much longer alone."

"You will no longer be alone. Everywhere I travel, I will search for those who show great wisdom and mental strength. I know I will find this among some of our women. I will select healthy young women with strong mates and children. These I will send to you. They will become your pupils and their husbands will be here to support them so that there will be no extra burden for Matuga. These strong young women will help hold you up if you stumble, and the children will make your home a noisy chamber, more noise than you may care for at times, but you will no longer be lonely."

He ignored the stunned People and, kneeling down, he looked the old mother in her eyes. "Will you do this for me?" His voice was almost a whisper. Paataga stood with her head down. There was no smoke to disguise her tears and she let them run unhampered and unashamed down her parched cheeks. She swallowed many times before she could return his whisper.

"For you, my son, I will do all that you would ask of me."

Kaoto's word came loud and clear again, and although they were meant for all to hear, they were still addressed to her. But each man felt they were addressed to him also. "Paataga, great mother of our nation, for three summers I have studied at your feet. I have studied more than just your lessons. I have studied you. I know you to be a lonely old crone who loves her People but has been unable to show this love. You were afraid it would be considered a weakness, a weakness you felt you could not afford."

He placed his arms around her tenderly, as if she were a child. He did not attempt to draw her to him, but simply encircled her as if to ward off anything that might threaten her. "I will not let you go to live alone, to die alone, unloved. Your home will ring with the happiness of children, the children you could never have. These children will come to think of you as their Great Mother, just as I do. You will teach their mothers to handle many problems, to use their own wisdom, just as you have taught me to do. Teach them a short version of the history, each according to her ability to learn and comprehend so it can be known by all."

He swung his eyes around the kiva to see if anyone would oppose him. No one did. In the silence that held at this moment, Keenwah stepped timidly forward and draped the cloak around his shoulders. He rose and the cloak fell gracefully to sweep just short of the floor. Keenwah's eyes were also misty, and while she did not speak, all could plainly see the pride she had for her son, the Wise One, who now belonged not to her but to all the People.

Chapter Thirteen

When Kaoto emerged from the kiva a great throng of the People greeted him. Women held up their babies so they might see and be seen by the Wise One. It was a day to remember, almost as important as seeing the new Wise One was seeing the new cloak he wore. Everyone from the immediate area known that Keenwah was making something special; they did not know what but they knew she used more feathers than anyone ever had before. Knowing all this did not prepare them for what they saw.

Keenwah had always been skilled in weaving and had been often sought after for help and advice, however, she had outdone herself on this single garment.

The People had known and used cotton for as long as anyone could remember. It was warm and soft and easy to work with. The only disadvantage was that it did not last as long as some of the tougher fabrics. The fibers of the yucca, for instance, were much stronger and more durable, but were also harder to work. They were most commonly used for rope making and sandal construction. Keenwah had found a way to tame these stubborn fibers and make them suitable for her purpose.

She had pounded the plant longer and harder until the single fibers were separated and were nearly as fine as spider web. By experimenting with several ingredients she found that cooking the fibers in bear grease made them pliable. It also made the fibers resistant to moisture. She was sure they would last much longer.

Once she had mastered this art she had spun them into thin, even threads which she rolled on sticks for storage. With the help of Maata she had constructed a framework much like a large table. This allowed her to spread the fibers out in the shape she desired. Each thread was tied down at intervals to hold it in place while she worked. Starting at what was to be the bottom, she had worked her way up the full length of the threads with a second strand of threads. These were interwoven in much the same manner as a loose basket weave. At each intersection she had tied the threads together with a single strand of hair.

Once the dimensions were established, she began again at the bottom and sewed feathers over the fabric. Single strands of hair were once more employed and Keenwah had to ask all the women to contribute to her project.

Most of the feathers were from the backs of the turkeys. She overlapped them in such a manner that they resembled their original pattern. This way they would shed both wind and rain but not be a heavy burden. Slowly the cloak began to take shape.

When she reached the shoulder area she stopped using turkey feathers and switched to those of the snow colored owl. These were more scarce and harder to obtain. It took the combined efforts of several men to produce enough to cover this portion. Above this she used the feathers of the blue jay, which were easier to find, but were much smaller and were tedious to work with. Still, the blue mantle above the white shoulder was worth the extra effort.

For the last touch she had called on the runners. She desired the feathers from the little bird her son was named after. To make it more difficult, she had insisted the feathers must be picked up from the ground. Under no circumstances was anyone to kill one of these birds for their feathers. If one was found dead it could be used.

It had taken all summer to collect enough to cover the hood of the cape. The finished product was a unique cloak, never seen before in this land. When she was asked where she got the idea, she would only smile and say, "From my head."

This was true. Keenwah had never seen such a cape, but somewhere in the back of her memory, passed on to her for many generations, was the knowledge that such a cape could be made and had been made before. She had no way of knowing that in the land to the far south, men of power and prestige were still wearing such cloaks as a sign of their rank. All she knew was that her son, the Wise One, should have such a cloak to proclaim his office to the world.

Aside from all that, it was very practical. It was so light a child could carry it, yet it was warm and comfortable to wear. It would turn away wind and rain without becoming sodden and heavy. She did not know how long it would last. No one could make clothes to last forever, but hers came close.

With the ceremony over and his days as a pupil behind him, Kaoto became restless. He felt he should be on the move. He felt an urgency, a desire, to be about his business, the business he had been trained for. He did not know for sure just what he should be doing, but he knew he could not stay here any longer. There was so much he did not know about the People that he was to serve. He must travel and get to know them better. While he had covered much of the surrounding land as a runner, he had never gone to the far corners of the nation. He had only seen and known a very small part of it.

He had made a point of visiting with every ruler present at the ceremony. He had talked little and listened much. From them he had learned there was a great difference in the other parts of the land. Farther south and west, the land was drier and warmer than here. To the north it was colder and more moist. All the People were farmers but the different locales made for different crops and sometimes this led to a different culture. All the buildings were similar in shape but the materials for building them varied greatly.

He was invited to come and spend as much time with each of them as he desired. They would be only too happy to host the Wise One in their villages. It would be an honor to them and their People to receive him. They had never had a Wise One come to them. Nothing in their legends recorded a visit from the Wise One in the past.

Kaoto made a promise to visit each and every one of them during his term as Wise One. It was another promise made without knowing all the facts. Kaoto had no idea how large the nation was, nor how many villages there were spread throughout the land.

He had a recurrence of his dream, the first in over three summers. He had forgotten the urgency it brought with it. He knew he must be on his way to find the threatening shadows and determine what they had to do with his People. If he were to ask the People to pick up and leave, he would have to have more than just his dream or his word. He would have to have proof of some kind. Something they could see and feel.

So he came to his first and possibly his hardest test. He must say farewell to his old teacher. They both knew it was very likely they would never meet again in this life.

"Paataga, Great Mother of Kaoto, the lonely man. Why is it I must always lose the ones who mean so much to me?"

"Am I lost? I will be with you always. We have become as one mind, even if one is old and the other is young. Where could either of us go without the other being there?" Her eyes traveled over him as if he was a memory stone and she did not want to forget any small detail about him.

"You must go and I must stay. We have both known this almost from the beginning. But we shall not be separated. Our minds will commune whenever we have the need, or desire, to do so," she told him, and though he was a man, his voice was filled with sadness when he replied.

"I know what you say is true and I shall treasure the time we spent together, always. But I was speaking of physical loss. I have had only one other friend before I knew you. Little Frog was the only friend of my boyhood and early manhood. She was all I had, and then she died. Now I have become very attached to you. You are more than a teacher to me. More than a mother. You are my friend. Now we must separate and our eyes may never rest on each other again. We may never hear each other's voice again. I know it must be this way, but I will miss you Wise One, there shall never be another to take your place."

Paataga patted his arm and bid him be seated, just as in the days when she had taught him. He sat cross-legged on the ground. Paataga took her place on the ancient log in front of her fire by the doorway.

"There is something I must tell you. I have waited to see for sure that you were going to leave before I spoke further on this subject. It has to do with my dream and you. I can only assume this is not part of your dream because you have not mentioned it to me."

"I have told you all of my dream, all that I can recall."

"Oh I am sure of that, but as I said, I have waited to be sure you were going to leave. I know now that this is your intention and I feel I should tell you this one little part that I have never mentioned before."

Kaoto waited patiently, not asking, knowing she would tell him when she was ready.

"In my dream I see you are not always alone. I see a comely woman at your side. She is not always at your side; sometimes your trails separate, but they always come back together again. In the end of my dream you are on the same path, side by side, walking into the sunset. I take this to mean you will not be separated again. This must mean she is your mate for the rest of your lives."

"I do not know, Paataga." Kaoto shook his head slowly. "I somehow do not see any place in my life for a mate. I have been so used to living alone and have planned to go on living alone. I do not know if I would be able to conduct myself like a man if I did have a mate."

"True, you are ancient, Kaoto." She smiled at him. "And I know you have never been with a maiden. Still, I think when the time comes and the maiden is the right one, you will not have any trouble conducting yourself as a man should."

"I do not think I want a mate. I seem to be destined to lead a lonely life, most of it on the trail. Where would I find a mate who could travel with me, or one who would be willing to wait for me?"

"Our plans are not always what happen. If it is to be so, then it shall be so," Paataga said.

"Well, at least tell me where I can find her, and what this paragon of women looks like so I will recognize her when I see her," Kaoto said with irony.

"Do not mock me," she scolded him as if he were a child again. "I cannot tell you where she is or what she looks like. I have never seen her and probably never will. But she somehow seemed familiar to me. Do not worry about knowing her. When you meet her, the sky will split open and the world will topple. Then you will know you have found her of whom I speak this day."

"I did not mean to mock you, old mother. I will remember what you have said and keep it in my memory also. Rising, he picked up his bundle of belongings. Looking long and hard at Paataga and her little home he said, "The time is now. I must leave or I will turn and hang on your dress like a baby and cry to be comforted. Farewell, Paataga. Be looking for your first pupil soon. I shall endeavor to find a likely person so your home will ring with joy and laughter. The thought of this makes my going a little easier." He wrapped his arms around the tiny woman and held her close for a moment before he let her go and stepped back. Swinging his bundle to his back and adjusting his gear, he loped down the trail without looking back.

Paataga watched with tear filled eyes as he hit the bottom of the valley and swung on to the main road. Here, only once, he stopped and looked back at her. He waved before he took off again. It was as if he wanted to memorize the valley and the side of the canyon where he had spent the last three summers. Then he was gone, out of sight.

Once on the road, he dropped into his own particular gait, a long loping step that would take him far down the trail before sundown. He had already said goodbye to Matuga and his parents. There was no one else to care or miss him. A few runner acquaintances were waiting on the trail and ran with him for a while before they began to peal off on their own missions. Then he was alone, as he had been most of his life. It almost seemed like a portent of his future.

Kaoto had no real destination. He had decided to go south rather than north for one simple reason: to the north were the high mountains and he longed to go to them, but this would be just for his own benefit and would not serve the People. His conscience had made him chose the opposite direction. It was his intention to make a circle, trying to cover as much of the borderland of the People as he possibly could. He wanted to stop at each village and visit with the People, just as he had said he would. He must get to know the People and understand them better before he could make any attempt to get them to move. There was no doubt in his mind that he must make them move even though he did not know why. So he must find out just what the threat was. Was it real or just a figment of his imagination?

He had no concern about where he might be at nightfall; the villages, large and small, were so close together that he would never be far from one of them when darkness approached. He was prepared to stay wherever he decided to stop. During his days as a runner he had learned every water hole and shady place along the road for several day's run in any direction.

Since it was still warm in the late summer, he wore only his breach cloth. He had his new cloak draped over his shoulders and caught in at the waist. It was pulled back so it did not hinder his running and it was so light that he was hardly aware of it being there. On his back he carried a light pack with a few essentials: extra sandals, leggings, and a pair of heavier boots for rough going. None of these were weighty and did not hold him back. On one side he carried a water skin and on the other side a packet of dried corn and a casing of dried meat that was mixed with sweet berries. These were emergency rations because food and water would not be a problem as long as he was in this part of the nation. As the Wise One he would be provided for all along his route by the villages on his path.

The only weapon he carried, if it could be called a weapon, was the long bow his father had made for him and a bundle of arrows, also made by his father. The bow was a new one, made this past summer and was made in accordance with his height. Bow and arrows hung down either side of his pack. He had no need of protection, there was no one in the nation who would try to harm him, and there were very few wild animals to worry about. Knowing this, he had left his short spear and larger knives with his father. He carried only a small flint knife in his pack.

To help overcome his depression of leaving Paataga, he ran at a brisk pace. He was happy to be on the trail again; it seemed like the only natural place for him. He loved the feel of his heaving breast as his lungs sucked in clean, fresh air. He reveled in the long strides he could make due to his great height. As a runner he had developed and perfected several different styles of running - some for speed, some for endurance and others just for the exhilaration and joy of running. One that he favored when the trail was clear and level, as it was here, gave him a sensation of floating. He would spring up using a thrust of his ankles and toes to lift him up and thrust him forward, then bring the other leg quickly forward to catch himself and repeat the same action. It was extremely hard on the muscles in the lower leg, but he had done it enough to be in good shape. The reason he particularly enjoyed this pace was because it reminded him of the end of his great run. When he had come in he had felt like he was flying, and this pace gave him a similar sensation.

He had just passed his eighteenth summer. Fall was already in the air even as he went south and east. Most of the men his age were already mated and had one or two children. They were settled and respected adult members of their villages. He was single and a wanderer but at each village he was greeted with the respect befitting his position. The People in the smallest village would beg him to tarry with them. They all longed for the honor of having hosted the Wise One. He often thought of how different their welcome would have been if he had just been Kaoto, the tall giant, of whom most were afraid.

He often longed to continue down the trail until dark, thinking about how much more distance he could cover. But he had promised, so he would stop and take a meal with the People and talk or listen. This was part of what was expected of him. They did not have any real problems that called for his attention but they were delighted just by his presence. It did not take long for him to see how out of place he was and how out of touch with them he had grown in his isolated life. Never having had a mate, or raised a family, he knew very little of the family life, or the ties between relatives. He could solve petty disputes over crops, water or lodgings, but when it came to real problems of in-laws or trouble between father and son, mother and daughter, he was lost.

His judgment seemed to satisfy them but he knew he was only making lucky guesses. It humbled him when he thought, I of all People, who know so little about them, have never been a part of them but rather one held apart from them, I am to be their Wise One? I am to lead them out of this country where they have lived longer than any of them can remember? Who am I to have such power? Who am I to persuade a People of whom I know nothing?

He stopped less after this and stayed only a short time when he did stop. He felt he must have time to reassess his own being. He must find himself, and then get to know himself before he could do anything for others. All that he was doing now was shallow and really useless. He was sure that Paataga would be disappointed in him.

His progress south and east was bringing him close to a range of mountains. They were not as impressive as those he had seen to the north, but they were still a formidable obstacle across his path. They called to him just as the other mountains did and he could not resist the temptation to enter them and see for himself what they were really like. He had a desire for solitude and serenity to purify his body and mind. Maybe on the top of one of these peaks that seemed as removed from the land as he was from the People, maybe there he could find the man he needed to be.

He entered the mountains from the west and at first was disappointed in them. They were drier and more hostile than he had pictured them in his mind's eye. It would take him much longer to attain the high country than he anticipated. Each day he noted changes. The valley he was following took him higher and higher. Here the villages were farther apart and the People lived a different kind of life, more of the hunter and less of the farmer. They explained to him that some crops could not grow well here, the season was too short and the air too thin. When he told them he intended to go to the top of the mountains, they cautioned him not to get caught up in the higher country when winter came. He would not be able to get back down and would never be found. He did not tell them he was already lost and the only one who could find him was himself.

He followed a stream, going deeper into the wild and challenging country. The scene continued to change with every turn he took. The pines were different; they were taller. The air became more crisp, especially at night when he had to hug his fire before retiring.

Soon he was beyond the last village. He was alone as he had never been before but loneliness held no fear for him. He was as entranced with the mountains as he was sure he would be. He could not turn back now even if he wanted to. He could not explain the fascination, but just accepted it and walked on.

For several days he followed game trails close to the stream that lead through meadows high with grass. Even this late in the season it was lush and green. The fragrance of the pine filling the air was heady and almost made him dizzy, but he loved it and pushed on. He begrudged the time it took to eat and soon was eating only after dark when he could no longer see to travel.

Kaoto lost track of time. He awoke each morning before the Spirit Watcher and impatiently waited for enough light to move on. The animals were unafraid of him; they had seldom seen men in this rugged retreat. They were mildly curious about him, but not frightened.

At last he climbed a lofty peak, he reached the top just as the Spirit Watcher was going to rest. His sister, Moon, was already on her way up and this night, as if she knew it was special to him, she shed her full light on the surrounding country. Going to the highest point possible, he sat on an outcropping of bare rock, taking little notice of the cold wind. He finally tugged his cloak free and pulled it around him. In the mellow glow of the moonlight he drank in the beauty of the land spreading out in all direction from him.

Weary and sore, he sat until Sister Moon deserted the sky, and only then did he succumb to sleep. He did not seek a bed, but just pulled his cloak closer to his body and leaned back against the cold rock and slept.

The Spirit Watcher found him thus seated in the morning. Sometime during the brief time of darkness, a light coating of snow had fallen silently over the land, dusting every limb, bush and crevasse with its whiteness. The wind had calmed and there was no sound in the land. The few venturesome birds that braved this high spot watched Kaoto in hushed silence. A mountain sheep eyed him suspiciously before it, too, went on its way, leaving the strange animal in peace and solitude.

The wise man awoke. He was startled. The Spirit Watcher was already high in the sky. His warm rays had melted some of the snow on the slopes exposed to his favor, leaving the shaded parts ghostly and white. Kaoto stood up and stretched the stiffness from his body. He had not realized how tired he was. The air was charged. Breathing deeply, Kaoto felt completely alive for the first time in his life. Like the air, his mind was sharp and clear.

From where he stood, he could see many days' run in every direction. It was not unlike his dream; he could not see the People but he could see the land. If there was this much land, how many People could there be? More than he could ever hope to visit in his lifetime. Even if he had as many summers as Paataga, he could never hope to talk to all of them. For a moment it seemed hopeless for him to even try. He knew he had to devise some other method of contacting them all.

Kaoto spent three days and nights on the mountaintop, living on his emergency rations and water he found in a hollow in the rocks. When he was ready to come down out of the mountains, he had resolved his own problems. He knew what he must do to serve the People. Yes, he would travel among them, stopping and listening whenever he was close. He would listen and give what comfort he could. But now he knew he must push on farther and faster to the outer limits of the nation. Here he would find the dark shadows and learn how they were a threat to the People and what he must do about them.

Once this was done, he would employ the runners to carry his words for him. They alone could cover this vast land. They could carry his words, and be accepted wherever they were heard. This was their office. His office was to find the real problem and deliver his People from it.

Greatly relieved, at peace with himself and refreshed in body and spirit beyond his wildest expectations, he set his pace to the steady stride he had come to know so well. Far south and east he would come to his first boundary. Here he would make his investigation and decide what must be done. Then he would know what to tell the runners he would send out to report to the People.

Back in the Chaco Canyon, Paataga smiled at the Spirit Watcher and her heart sang a song of gladness and thanks, which was pleasant to his ears. Her Kaoto had hit his stride; the little bird that ran with the wind had left his nest and was free at last. In all ways he was now a man, a man who had just discovered his full potential and was satisfied with his place in life.

Chapter Fourteen

Kaoto's path out of the mountains led him eastward. He traveled along ridges instead of valleys until he came out on a sheer drop down to the valley below. From the heights he could see the silvery ribbon of a wide river far below. He followed it with his eye as far north and south as he could see. It disappeared in the misty haze of distance as it wandered gracefully back and forth across the valley floor; sometimes disappearing in deep, narrow canyons only to reappear in wider areas of the valley. He knew this river even though he had never seen it before. He had never been this far east in his running days; most of his trips had taken him more to the north or west. He had made many trips to Mesa Verde, once as far as Hovenweep, and several trips west to Canyon de Chelly, but seldom to the east or south.

Following the rim southward he came to a village set against the rocks. The soft sandstone had made it possible to dig holes into the wall. Roof supports were anchored there and often, additional rooms had been added by tunneling back into the face of the rock. Kaoto was easily persuaded to stop here long enough to rebuild his strength, which had been worn down by his hard travel and scant rations. It was here, as he recuperated, that he had occasion to take notice of the creatures at the dumpsite.

There were several unfortunates here, and while that was not uncommon, he decided to see if he could not do something to improve their lot. His first thought was to ask the villagers if they would not take them in and care for them, but he knew this was not the proper way. The people of the village were not bad people; it was just their way. It had been so as long as any man could remember. People who could not care for themselves and had no family to look after them had nowhere to go but the dumpsite.

This was the first time since he had left the Chaco that he had seen anyone on the dumps. The sight of the dump with human garbage brought back memories of Little Frog and her plight before he had rescued her. He had helped her. Why then could he not do as much for the rest of them?

This was, as with his days with Paataga, a problem within a problem, one leading to another and another. How could he best solve the problem and make it a permanent solution, not something that would revert back just as soon as he was out of sight? He gave this much thought as he rested. It came to him that a working approach would be the most effective way. Deeds were what counted, not words. Not what he could command others to do, but what he could inspire them to do on their own.

The ruler of the village was thus dismayed one day to find the Wise One out at the dumpsite, sharing his meal with the creatures there. It was known, of course, that he made a habit of sharing his meals with them when he was a runner, but it was not fitting for a person of his position to sit at the dump heap and share their misery, not to mention the vermin. When he was reproached for his conduct, Kaoto protested.

"I realize you are in doubt of the wisdom of my action, and I suppose you might even suspect my intelligence or my motive, but you might as well get used to my eccentric ways. It is the way I am and it is the way I will always be. From now on, when anyone wishes to address me, they will find me here." He looked around to see just what he was letting himself in for. The prospect was bleak.

"But Wise One, how can we possibly let you stay here? What will the other villages say of us when they hear we let you sleep in the dump?" the ruler protested.

"They will have nothing to say because I will do the same in their village, or any village where there are these poor creatures to be provided for." His voice was calm and mild, and the ruler knew he could not argue with him.

"Then we will take them away." Seeing the Wise One's frown, the ruler hastily changed his plan. "We will take them in and feed them ourselves, anything you desire, just so you do not insist on staying here."

"No. That will not do. It is not the way of the People to take in outsiders, People not of their own family. I am not here to change the way. Besides, who among you could stand to have them around you? As soon as I am gone they will be back out here just as they are now. No. I will stay here with them." His answer was final, and to demonstrate his intentions, he started looking around the dumpsite for anything he might be able to use to make a shelter. There were a few stones scattered around. They were rough stones, uneven, not worthy of being dressed. Kaoto did not seem to notice their inferior condition as he began to gather them and stack them into a semblance of a wall.

"Wise One. What are you doing?" The shocked ruler asked.

Kaoto looked up with mild surprise. "Well, I thought I might pile up a few of these stones to make a wind break. Sometimes the wind becomes chilly of an evening as it comes down the valley. A low wall would offer some protection, do you not think?" He went on stacking the stones in a haphazard method, seemingly unaware of how crude and awkward his wall was.

The ruler threw up his hands in surrender. He hurried back to the village and consulted his elders about the Wise One, who was determined to sleep and eat at their dumpsite.

"What are we to do? We cannot let him stay there. Yet he is determined to do so. He is stacking up rough stones, trying to build a wall for a shelter." The elders talked among themselves. Each was as shocked as the ruler with this development, but none of them had any idea how to help the ruler in this dilemma.

"To make things even worse, we cannot ask the Wise One for help."

"Maybe we should at least offer to help him. Then we could make it look respectable and take some of the shame from us," one of them finally suggested.

After more consultation it was agreed that they all could contribute some decent stones and dress them for him. So it was done.

Kaoto worked slowly and clumsily at his project. He did not hurry and was therefore not very far advanced when the men of the village came carrying baskets of stones and jugs of water to mix mud to set the stones in.

The creatures of the dump watched in stoic wonder at the events transpiring in their domain. It soon became evident to them that while the Wise One might be wise in some matters, he was nearly helpless in the art of building. The men, one by one, came forward and offered to help him. Kaoto thanked them so profusely that they were embarrassed. They took down his pitiful wall and then decided it would be better built at a different location on the south end of the dump.

"During the summer it will be cooler this way and during the winter when the wind comes across the dump, at least the smell will be less," they explained.

"Ah, yes. And the sun will warm it in the winter. In the summer, the winds will come from the other direction and help cool it," Kaoto mused as if he had just discovered the ways of the wind.

What started as a simple project soon grew as more and more of the villagers came to help in the building.

"What a beautiful wall," Kaoto exclaimed as the first rows went up. "My, if I had a few more stones I would be tempted to put a short wall on each end, just in case the wind changes a little during the night."

The ends were added and went up with the back wall. Somehow it became longer and larger than they had first planned. But it was for the Wise One, so it should be a little larger. They all agreed on this, for he was a large man.

Before the walls were completed, Kaoto was seen dragging up a crooked, half-rotten log.

"What are you going to do with that Wise One?" The ruler asked him. "It is too wet and rotten for a fire."

"Oh, no. I was not going to burn it. I thought I might get some these men to help me lay it across the top, and then I could put some brush over it." He looked knowingly at the sky. "I thought it might rain tonight." He continued pulling on the log.

"But it is far too heavy for that. Besides, it is so crooked you could never make a decent roof with it. Let us get you some straight timbers." The ruler called to several men, knowing well that every man had an extra timber or two laid away for future use in their own building plans.

The timbers were produced and laid across the top with the last few rows of stones cemented between them to hold them in place. Swarms of children were sent to cut and carry willow wands and cedar bark to lay over the timbers. When this was completed it was a simple matter to cover this frame with fresh earth. It would soak with the first rain and become a hard-packed, water-resistant roof.

Kaoto thanked the people over and over. He was so grateful to them for helping him, he was so clumsy, and he could have never done such a fine job by himself. The villagers were inclined to agree with him, although they refrained from saying so.

"Is it not wonderful what can be done when enough of the People all work together on such a project?" he remarked as he picked up his bed roll and prepared to spread it inside the shelter, even though it was still mid-day.

The people watched him, wondering, until one of the women ran back to her room and returned with a fresh mat. After working with Kaoto and seeing him as less than perfect, as a builder anyway, they had lost some of their awe of him. The woman was the first to call him by his name.

"Here, Kaoto, lay this under your bed. It will keep you dry and clean."

Not to be outdone, other women also searched their rooms and came back with more mats and skins to cover the floor and serve as bedding.

At this point, Kaoto's clumsy, bumbling guise dropped away and he took on a dramatic change. He seemed to be transformed as he mixed a smooth paste from the adobe. He started covering the walls to seal them in a permanent fashion, just as the pueblos were sealed. Inside and out, his long arms spread the mud in long smooth arcs. With this done, he pulled a bundle from his pack and began to mix paints in a small bowl. With deft strokes he drew designs on the inner walls; bold reliefs of animals and men. Across the entire back wall he drew a mural depicting the villagers building the new shelter.

It was then that it dawned on them what he had done, or rather what he had made them do. Frowns soon turned into smiles. The people enjoyed a good joke, no matter who was the butt of it. They could see now that his clumsiness was just an act to get them to do what they should have done in the first place. They would not have to be ashamed of the shelter the Wise One slept in. It was as good as any building in the village, and why not? They had built it, had they not? They were not poor workmen; they were all skilled in their craft. The ruler came forth shamefaced, and approached Kaoto to speak for them all.

"You could have just asked us to build you a shelter here. You have the right to do so, and you would not have had to use all this pretense. We would have been glad to do it for you."

"I did not want you to build it for me. I wanted you to build it for yourselves. Oh, I know you do not think you needed it, and maybe you do not. But as you said, you built it for me. So it is mine now, is it not?"

"Yes, of course. It is yours," the ruler answered. "It will be yours forever if you wish it so."

"I do. And if it is mine, forever, then I can invite who ever I want to join me here, just as you can in your house." He turned his back to them and waved his hand to the startled creatures on the dump. "I would consider it an honor if you would share it with me. You could protect it for me while I am gone. The only way you can do a good job of this is to stay in it and live in it all the time. I ask this in the name of my little sister that has no other name. Come. I welcome you to our house. Come." He motioned to them because they sat in stone like silence. "Eat with me, sleep with me in this new shelter. My little sister will be insulted if you do not."

The ruler relaxed and gave a grudging smile to the wily young man of such great stature. It appeared his wisdom was equal to his size.

"I do not suppose you would object if we were to increase the amount of food you would set aside for your little sister, would you Kaoto? Or maybe a few extra cloaks"

Kaoto returned the smile, open, without guile. "You have learned your lesson fast and well. Yes, I would appreciate it very much if you would send some extra food and clothing. After I am gone, you will never know in advance when I may return, so maybe you could continue to set out extra, just in case I came in unexpectedly, so I would not go hungry."

"I can assure you it will be done just as you ask," the ruler said.

"I would not want to work a hardship on anyone in the village, and I do not want anyone to have to go on short rations just to supply me and my house. Anyone who is unable to provide for his family does not have to contribute anything. I will understand."

The ruler shook his head in respect for this young man who had so much wisdom. He knew that no one would admit to being unable to provide for his family. The donations would be ample. These poor creatures ate little; it would not put a hardship on anyone. But Kaoto was not through with them yet. He turned to the women and children and spoke to them.

"My little sister had a problem getting a drink, and she suffered much from lack of water. I do not suppose there is a large jug lying around that is not in use? Suppose a large jug was placed here in the corner, buried part way in the ground so the water would stay cool and be easy to reach. For those who have trouble walking, it would be handy if you would put a little water in it. You women, if each of you would put in a little gourd of water when you go to get your own water, it would soon fill the jug. You surely could spare one small gourd of water, could you not? Just a little each day would soon add up to enough for my home. And you children, you can be a big help, also. When you are playing, you could bring a little extra water and maybe a few twigs of firewood. If you would do this, my little sister and I would be very thankful to you for it."

"Consider it all done, Kaoto," the ruler said. "We can see your point now that you have forced us to look at it in your light." He turned away toward the village, confident that all was right again. "Now that this is settled, will you come join us in the kiva for a long overdue meal?"

Kaoto smiled wistfully at the expectant villagers and their ruler. He declined the invitation. Instead, he went to the dump and offered his hand to an ancient person. One by one he escorted them all to the accommodations of the new structure. He seated them as comfortably as he could, adjusting mats or folding skins to make seats and back rests for them. He tipped his water skin onto a clean deerskin patch and wiped the dust and grime from them. The villagers stood watching and waiting. Another delay before they could retire to the village for their meal. Finally, the Wise One addressed them again.

"I will be here if you have need of me. There is a storehouse of knowledge sitting here. Wisdom and knowledge locked up in these old bones. When I am gone, you could come here and ask for their help and advice. It might surprise you what these ancient ones know. I know I was amazed by such and old one when I was young. You do not throw away last summer's grain just because there is a new crop, so why do you throw away their summers of experience just because you are young and healthy? Think on my words and deeds, ask questions, and see for yourself if I am right. What have you to lose?"

He turned back to his guests and offered them food from his bowl and asked each one his name. Finally the villagers drifted away, perplexed with this new development. They soon returned with offerings of more food and water along with other useful items. Each person looked at the gathering with the Wise One and carried the picture away with them. These creatures were no longer non-persons, they were one of the People again because not only did the Wise One recognize them, but he had forced them to recognize them also.

It was always possible that in the future one of them might end up on the dumpsite, or someone they knew or loved. They would no longer face the fate of sitting and waiting for the refuse of the village, nor would they be forced to endure the shame of being a non-person. Things looked better today than they did yesterday, and it was all thanks to the tall, hairy young giant who came to them hungry and tired. But he also came to them as a Wise One and his wisdom had proven to be valid. They also understood that wisdom was not restricted to just one man, but anyone could be wise if they received a nudge in the right direction.

Chapter Fifteen

From this village Kaoto began his descent toward the shining river. At each village in which he stopped, he repeated his clumsy act at the dumpsite until word started to precede his visits. He was not surprised to fine a neat, tidy shelter with the creatures already housed there and being cared for. The word spread in all directions, carried by the runners who were as anxious to assist Kaoto, the runner, as they were to aid Kaoto, the Wise One. Soon most villages in the nation would provide for their unfortunates in this manner.

Kaoto still insisted on staying at the dump, and nothing could tempt him away. A few stubborn villages refused to build shelters. They discovered the Wise One would not set foot inside their villages. He would turn his back on them and refuse to speak with anyone from these villages or to help them in any way.

At one such village the People refused to recognize him as the Wise One. They said it was because of his youth. Kaoto sat on the dump and shouted to every runner who passed by.

"Look," he called to them. "See what has become of Kaoto in this village. They have cast out the Wise One. They are a fortunate People who need no help from anyone, nor do they need to give help to anyone either." The runners carried the story, and so much shame was brought on this village that the ruler, after pleading unsuccessfully for forgiveness, came and sat at the foot of the dump in abject misery. After the second day, with no response from the Wise One, the elders, came and when still the Wise One ignored them, the entire village came. They all sat at the foot of the dump in silence, awaiting his judgment. They sat through the night, and only in the morning when the little children came forth did he speak to them.

"Where is the shelter to honor my little sister?"

"We have none," one of the braver ones answered.

"And why do you not have one?" he asked.

The children puzzled over this between them until they came to an answer that to them made sense. "Because no one has built one, Wise One."

"Who do you suppose we could get to help me build one?" he asked of them, ignoring the abject elders.

"We will help you, Wise One. We can help you build a shelter. Just tell us what you want us to do."

When the elders tried to assure him that a shelter would be built, he turned around as if looking for it. When he saw nothing was being done, he turned his back on them again. He took neither food nor water, nor did he seek a bed or any comforts. He spoke only to the children.

At last the ruler, in fear of losing all his followers, as well as the respect of the entire nation, started to gather and dress stones with his own hands. The elders and the rest of the villagers quickly moved to help him. When the shelter

116 - Norman D. Messenger

was finished, the ruler asked Kaoto if it was satisfactory.

"Do not ask me. Ask them," he said, indicating the four creatures that inhabited the dump. "Ask them for forgiveness for being such stiff-necked fools with hearts like stones. Such a contrary People I have never known." The creatures were embarrassed by this exhibition and quickly accepted the ruler's apology. They entered the new shelter, assisted by the Wise One and the children, and were quick to praise the shelter and give thanks for it. When they offered thanks to the Wise One, he would not hear their words of praise.

"Thank the people of the village. They are the ones who built it, however it took them long enough. I did nothing but sit as you sit and do as you do, nothing. The People of this nation can do remarkable things when they cooperate with each other. But when they become stubborn they blind themselves. One person can only do so much; with help he can do much more. Everyone benefits from the combined actions and then they wonder why they did not work together sooner."

He spent a little time at most villages and tried to keep moving steadily down the shining river, always asking about the outer limits of the nation. Some knew very little, others a bit more.

He was told that the villages did not extend more than a few days run to the south. When he asked what lay beyond, he was met with ignorance; no one seemed to know.

When he reached the last outpost, it became evident. What lay beyond was the desert, hot, dry, silent, and hostile. It was cruel to the careless, ignorant or unwary. He recalled the history mentioning the evil in the darkness waiting to snare the unwary. The desert was not dark, nor was it evil, but the unwary would fall into its trap just the same. The desert was a problem, but Kaoto was sure this was not what he had seen in his dreams.

The river continued but the dry sand came to the edge of the water as if to lap it up before any plants could have a chance. The only plants to grow in this area seemed to be just as hard and hostile as the desert itself. Tough, hard, covered with spines, the entire area was devoid of any means to support human life.

There were signs that the ancient roadway had once continued on from here, but it was only a distant shadow and almost forgotten memory. No one could remember when it had been last used. Sand had drifted across it, obliterating much of it. In other places the sparse plant life had sprung up to reclaim it for the desert again.

He was told there were more of the People living east over a low range of dry, uninhabited mountains. He was warned that it was a long, difficult and dangerous journey, and that he should not make the trip alone. They told him of a place of such desolation that nothing lived there. He was mesmerized by their description of the burning white sands and knew he must go and see for himself. They said the sands were as white as fresh snow and shone in the sunlight so brightly that it hurt the eyes to look on it. In the light of the moon it caused one to see images that were not there. It was not like a mirage, for they all knew of them; these images were sinister and frightening.

Kaoto knew he must see this sight. It was too similar to his dream and he knew he must examine it to see if there was any connection between the sand of his dream and the ones they described. After checking his emergency rations and procuring extra water skins, he set his course to the east and the white sand.

From the top of the mountains he could see the gleaming white sands spread out before him. The sands were held captive in the valley below, much like water in a lake. At a distance they looked like fresh snow, even having drifts, but the land around them was dry and barren. His course brought him across the northern portion of the sands. When he reached them, he was slightly disappointed; they were not quite what he expected. There was nothing mysterious about the sand, other than it was white. Otherwise, it behaved and reacted just as any other sand would do. Still, he had to satisfy his curiosity by walking out a way and digging about in search of bones. He found none and was convinced that it was either not the right desert or it was not the right time. In his dream it had seemed the time was in the future. Possibly this would be the place for the fulfillment of his dream sometime in the future. He felt a chill down his spine and a sense of trepidation, along with a desire to leave this place far behind. Before he left, however, he made several more trips out into the sand to dig for possible clues. He found none. By mid-day he was away from the sand and moving more to the north again.

He had been told of another landmark. It was an area of black rocks not unlike the ones south and west of the Chaco, close to where the "Sky People" lived. The main difference was the sharp, defined line of the flow of black rock, like a black ribbon laying down the valley floor. He had been warned that he must decide on which side of it he wanted to travel, because once set on his course he would not be able to cross over to the other side until he reached the far end. There were no villages left on the south side of the barrier, but there were rumors of a strange and savage people roaming near the barrier. They were considered an inferior and barbaric people and no one wanted to associate with them.

The warning about the barrier being impassible was not exaggerated. While it was not very high, in many places he could look over the top and see the opposite side. Nor was it very wide; in most places it was not more than two arrow flights in width. But there was no way to cross over. He had tried several times, unwilling to believe that mere rocks could stop him. He soon gave up. Each time the black rock cut into his sandals after only a few steps and he left his blood on several rocks before he gained the safety of the plains. Not only did the black rocks cut his sandals and feet, they absorbed and radiated back the heat of the sun multiplied several times. His feet were uncomfortably hot after each venture. A man could become stranded out there in the middle if he was not careful. Heavy sandals might carry him a way, but soon even they would be cut into ribbons and he would then be forced to either continue or retreat without any protection at all. The black rock over in the land of the "Sky People" was much older and time had worn down some of the sharp edges. There a man could cross if he was careful and determined. These rocks were much younger, and time and wind had not yet taken the sharp edge off from them.

As he traveled along the wall of the barrier, he explored every crack and channel that led back into its heart. None of them gave him access to the other side. The wall did have the advantage of the warmth it retained after the Spirit Watcher had left the sky, and the cool nights of approaching fall made the Wise One search for such warmth. He could curl up with his back next to the wall and the radiant heat kept him comfortable all night long.

During his travels he kept an eye out for signs of anyone else that might be traversing this area, particularly the savages he had been told about. It was a strange experience for him. He had never had to be watchful among his own people. No one would harm him there. But here, well, here he was not so sure. Among his People warring was unknown. The most serious grievances were usually settled by the district ruler, or in some cases by the Wise One. The most serious confrontations ended up in shouting matches where insults were flung back and forth across a gauntlet. But this almost never led to bloodshed or even bodily harm. Man did not maliciously attack another man for any reason.

On the second day he found evidence of some other human occupancy. There were campsites left by a careless and indifferent people who had no pride. Their campsites were littered with bones and bits of skin. There was a blackened area where a fire had been left to burn out of control until it came to the black rock, which stopped the fire just as effectively as it did Kaoto. He also noticed that animals here were scarce, and those he did see were more anxious than the animals he was used to.

Later in the day he came upon a huge buffalo bull lying close to the black barrier. Protruding from the bull's shoulder was a long, heavy shaft of a spear. One quick glance told him it was not one of the People's spears. For the first time he hesitated and felt a twinge of anxiety, not really fear, but uneasiness. He knew he could not cross the barrier and he did not relish the idea of being forced to venture too far away into open country. He was uncertain as to whether he should try to squeeze in between the wall and the wounded animal or circle farther out so as not to arouse the bull. Either way he was risking his life, something he had never had to do before. The bull was a certain threat while the open land was a possible threat. He chose to circle out and avoid the bull.

The huge old bull was very still; only the waving of the shaft as he breathed indicated he was still alive. The Wise One did not feel at all wise as he left the doubtful security of the black barrier and glided out into the open. He moved as quickly as he could without running, hoping to slip by without bothering the wounded animal.

He was concentrating so hard on his footing and trying to watch in all directions at one time that his attention was temporarily diverted from the buf-

falo. His action proved to be nearly fatal. He had passed the bull and was beginning to make his way back to the barrier when he heard a drumming of feet
behind him. He turned to see the gigantic form of the bull bearing down on him.
The animal had its head down, swinging its horns from side to side like a double
scythe, ready to cut down anything in its path.

Kaoto had never raced a wild animal before and wounded or not he knew
a buffalo could outrun a man for a short distance. It was not as fast as a deer or
antelope, but it could nonetheless move amazingly fast for its immense size. In
spite of its bulk and short legs, it was closing the gap between them with alarming speed. The shaft of the embedded spear sticking up like a staff did nothing to
slow the bull down.

Kaoto had no choice but to run. His bow and arrows were on his back, but
even if he had them in hand he doubted he could have stopped this charge
before he was struck down himself. He had not carried his own heavy spear or
his long club that was normally used for hunting larger animals. He had not
intended to engage in this sort of game. So he sprinted toward the wall. It was
the only object around, and as his eyes swept over it, he could not find anything
in the way of encouragement. At this point it was nearly twice as high as he was
and appeared to be solid without a break, a crack or crease, nothing projecting
with which he could pull himself up. Farther down there seemed to be an opening.

He tried to increase his speed, as he knew the bull was still gaining on him.
The bull was so close he could hear his labored breathing and he could imagine
he could feel his hot breath on his back. He did not dare look back for fear of
losing his footing. The wall seemed so close, but it was just out of his reach. By
now he could actually feel the hot breath as the bull blew frothy saliva on the
back of his legs. At last, the wall. It was directly in front of him now. Where
could he go when he reached it? There were no handholds, no openings. Could
he jump high enough to catch the top? If he did, would he be able to hang on or
pull himself up without seriously cutting his hands? He surely did not want to
fall back down before this enraged beast.

With one vicious swipe of its giant head, swinging across and upward at
the same time, the bull hit Kaoto. One of its black, curled horns caught in the
flesh of his side just above the hipbone. He felt a searing pain, and then numbness as the horn tore through skin and flesh. Kaoto was lifted from his feet and
sent flying toward the wall in helpless flight. He fell to earth just short of the
barrier. As he hit the ground, he could see a place where the wall jutted out,
leaving a cave like opening at ground level. Hoping for enough time and strength
to make it, hoping the opening would be large enough for him to hide and not
room enough for the bull to be able to reach him, he rolled and clawed his way
toward the opening.

The bull gave him an assist as it butted him viciously once more, sending
him rolling deep into the aperture. Stunned and sick, with his wound bleeding
profusely, Kaoto crawled and dragged himself deeper into the darkness of the

cavity. The thought came to him that this would be a likely place for rattle-snakes to den up to escape the fierce sun and cold nights. But he did not have much choice and no time at all to consider it.

Just before the spirit of consciousness left the Wise One, he was sure he could see light at the other end of this tunnel. Gasping and panting from exertion and pain, he pulled himself into a small opening at the other end of the cave.

Lying on his back, facing the Spirit Watcher, Kaoto wavered on the border-line of consciousness for a few seconds. He could hear the bull's bellow a short distance away. He tried to turn to see if there was any way that the bull could get to him here. The effort and strain of this movement was the last straw. Kaoto passed out of the world of sunshine, black rocks and enraged buffaloes.

A pair of sharp brown eyes watched him suspiciously, but the owner of these eyes did not approach the giant who lay bleeding his life away on the sands of a strange world, far from the runners of Chaco, and the known world of the Wise One of the People.

Chapter Sixteen

The Spirit Watcher had traveled far to the west and the side of the narrow cleft cast a shadow near the wounded man on the sand. Nothing had changed while he lay there. The bull was still snorting at the outside entrance. Its limited mind was sure the creature that had escaped him would have to emerge from the same hole it had gone into.

At the first sign of Kaoto's arousal, a pair of silent feet came up to his side and the owner stood watching him impassively, waiting to see if this intruder would live or die, not caring, only watching.

Kaoto slowly awoke to a world of red haze and pain. The bright light hurt his eyes so he kept them closed. He could feel the pain in his side. It was not as fierce as he had expected. He could feel more pain in his back where the bull had hit him the last time. He did not know if there was any serious damage in this area or not. His knees throbbed from being battered as he scrambled through the hole in the black rocks. There was another, smaller pain, not serious, but annoying, in the center of his chest. It was between two ribs close to his heart. It felt like an ant bite. This made him think of the time he and Paataga had talked about the relationship of feelings between ant and man as compared to man and the Spirit Watcher. This time he would play the benevolent God to this ant even though its bite was irritating him. He would not kill it, he would pluck it off his chest and deposit it back on the ground and tell it to run along and not bother him. Then he would listen very carefully to see if he could hear the ant thank him for sparing his life.

With a trace of a smile, he raised his hand to find the offending ant. Moving his hand slowly and cautiously so he would not crush his little uninvited guest, he brought his hands over his chest. His hands stopped when they came in contact with a solid wooden object directly over the source of pain. He must have rolled under a tree. He let his hand slide down the object until it came to a binding, then a sharp stone point. His hands dropped on down the point to his chest. The pain was coming from the pressure of the stone. This needed some thinking over. Why would there be a stone on the end of a tree limb? And why was it hanging down on him so hard it brought pain? He opened his eyes again to the blinding glare of the light in the otherwise dark crevice where he lay. Indistinctly he could see the outline of something above him. It was not a tree. The pain became more intense as the pressure on the stone point bore down harder against him. When he tried to pull back from it, it increased significantly.

Kaoto lay very still; his mind was becoming clearer now and he could grasp the situation. Someone was standing over him with a spear held firmly against his heart. He could feel a trickle of blood running down his side from the small wound in his chest. His eyes focused until he could see a man, not unlike his father. He was short, stocky, and wide, his face was expressionless. That he had not already killed him seemed to be in his favor. Also, he could not see anyone else nearby. He must be waiting for some kind of an explanation before he decided what to do with him.

"Greetings, old father," Kaoto spoke without attempting to move. His hands still lay across his chest beside the offending spear point.

The spear jabbed him harder and he gasped from the pain.

"Hold, old one. I am not your enemy. I come in peace."

"Humph. Maybe. But where did you come from? How did you find your way in here?"

"I came from the far north, the land of the Chaco." The spear did not waver or relent. "As to how I found this place, I do not really know. You might ask the angry bull out there. He is the one responsible for my being here."

"I hear the buffalo. It seems he has a score to settle with you, too. But how did you get in here?"

"He was chasing me and would have killed me if I had not accidentally found the opening back there and crawled through it." The spear point still held him pinned to the ground in a helpless position.

"The old bull is harmless. He has been there for many summers and has never attempted to harm anyone. Why would he be chasing you?" the old man asked, still without showing any emotion.

"Have you seen him lately? Have you seen the spear in his shoulder?"

The spear jabbed again, biting deeper into his flesh, bringing a new flow of blood.

"So you tried to kill the old man with your spear and he was too tough for you. No wonder he turned on you. Too bad he did not finish the job and save me the trouble."

Kaoto's mind was returning to normal. He knew he was in grave danger and he knew he must convince this old man that he had not tried to kill the buffalo and he did not mean any harm to either of them.

"Old father. I did not try to kill the bull. What reason would I have to kill him? He is as old and tough as you are. I am not that hungry, there is food in my pack. Besides, I do not even carry a spear," Kaoto tried to explain.

"It is plain to see why you do not have a spear. It is still stuck in the bull."

"It is not my spear. I do not carry a spear in my travels," Kaoto tried once again to explain, but the old man cut him short.

"Humph. What man would travel in strange country without his spear? What kind of a fool do you think I am? I may be old, but my mind does not wander." He poked the wounded giant again with his own spear.

Kaoto closed his eyes and tried to think. He must convince this man somehow. The spear point in his chest did not relax its pressure. It was becoming difficult to breathe as the point came dangerously close to piercing him fatally.

"Well, you do have the advantage over me. I am at your mercy, yet you have not killed me while I lay here helpless. I can only assume that you are a fair-minded man and are willing to hear the truth before you make a decision. If I am wrong, then go ahead and kill me and get it over with. Either way, I will die soon if I cannot stop the bleeding in my side."

The point of the spear retracted a fraction and while it allowed Kaoto to draw a deep breath, it never wavered. The old man's hand was as steady as the rocks around them. Heartened by the lesser pressure, Kaoto decided he must keep talking until he could make his captor believe him.

"Are you not one of the People?" he asked the old one.

"Humph. What do you know of the People?" he asked, his voice indicating the scorn and contempt he felt for his victim.

"I too, am one of the People." The point came instantly back into his chest, driving the last breath from him in an explosive burst.

"Liar! Do you think I do not know my own People when I see them? Do you think I am blind? One of the People huh? Well, I have never seen one of our People that looked anything like you. You carry a long bow. Where did the long bow come from? And even lying down I can see you are not a short man. How do you explain that? All my People put together never had so much hair. One of the People you say. Bear, maybe, I say. Savage, more likely," the old man snorted in disgust.

Kaoto knew he would have a tough time making this old man believe him. What could he say? There was very little he could do to make this old one let him up before he bled to death.

"If you have seen my bow and arrows, you surely recognized the points as being made in fashions of the People. If you will pull back your spear, I could get something from my pack that might help explain to you that I am who I say I am."

"Arrow points can be found or stolen and fastened to anyone's shaft. It has been done before and will be done again. I have no intention of letting you live now that you have found my hiding place. You are not one of the People, you are one of them." His free hand indicated the area to the south and east of them.

Kaoto could see he was losing ground with this man. His time was running out with his blood, which soaked the sand at his side. He had to do something fast to save himself. If this man did not kill him, then nature would. He knew he did not look like the People; this was why he had always been an outcast. But at least in the world where he had grown up the word had spread about him until all the People knew who he was. His height had been one of the ways they had recognized him. He had been naive enough to think that all the People must know of him by now and he would be accepted everywhere he went. He had been very wrong in thinking this. Quite evidently this old man had never heard of the tall, hairy, Wise One who traveled the nation. The old man had not heard of him and cared even less to find out.

During his interrogation, Kaoto had lain very still with his hands on his stomach. Without giving his intentions away, he had gradually tensed his muscles in preparation until he was like a coiled snake about to strike. He knew his own strength; it was equal to his size, as was his speed and skill. The only deterrent to his plan was the ragged hole in his side and the pool of blood in the sand.

With all the speed he could muster, when the bellowing of the bull momentarily distracted the old man's attention, Kaoto made his move. He brought his hands up over the spear shaft and closed in a vise like grip. Once he had his grip, he held it steady, knowing the old man's next move would be the determining factor.

When the old man threw all his weight on the shaft, as Kaoto knew he would, the giant was able to hold the point so it did not sink any further. Then, with what must have seemed superhuman strength to the old man, Kaoto raised the point-spear, man and all - from his chest and carefully laid it to one side. Then he sat up and became even more aware of his pain. He also realized he was not out of danger yet, as the old man relinquished his hold on the spear and drew his knife, ready to spring to attack again.

"Hold, old father," Kaoto said mildly as he held up one bloody hand in the peace sign. "Do not make me hurt you. Give me a chance to prove to you that I am not what you think."

The old man remained still, but his mind was racing with new thoughts. If this man, wounded as he was, could do what he had just done, and seemingly without effort, what more could he do? He was not going to be easy to kill now. He should have killed him from the beginning and not waited. Now it might be too late.

"I am sure you have never heard the name Kaoto, or Sun Bear." The old man shook his head, but still did not move. "But maybe even this far away you have heard of Paataga, the Wise One of the nation?"

At the mention of Paataga's name, Kaoto could tell he had found someone the old man did know about. The knife did not lower, nor did his stance change, but his eyes grew shrewd and Kaoto could almost hear his thought flowing.

"So you know of Paataga do you? Well, every man knows of the pretty young woman who is said to be so wise."

Kaoto smiled a little, and relaxed for the first time. Negotiations were in progress and he was sure it was only a matter of time now until he could reach some sort of an agreement with the old one.

"I do not think we are talking about the same person. Unless, of course, you are remembering her in your youth, and I do not think that even you have enough summers to remember her as a young woman. She was an ancient crone when I saw her last, just this past summer."

"It was a test," the old one said belligerently. "It has been many summers since I have seen her, but I can remember how ugly she was. All covered with warts with long black hairs in them. She was so fat that she waddled like a toad. It's a wonder she could get around to the villages, the shape she was in."

"If you are still testing me, why do you not try asking me something that at least bears on the truth? Paataga is not fat, never has been. She has no warts or long hairs. Some might call her ugly, those who do not know her and her many summers, but to me she is not. She is old, and to some that might seem ugly, but I know her and to me she is like a great mother."

"All right. Maybe you have seen her, or heard of her. That does not prove you are one of the People," the old man persisted.

While they talked, Kaoto had pulled his pack from his back and pressed a piece of clean, soft deerskin against the wound in his side. It slowed the bleeding, but did not stop it. Now he laid the pack on the ground in front of him. The old one watched him with sharp eyes, never moving so much as an eyelid. His face never changed expression as the wounded giant pulled a small packet from deep inside. Unwrapping its contents carefully, he laid his necklace reverently before the old man. It was the necklace of the history.

"What is that?" the old man asked skeptically.

"If you knew Paataga, as you claim, then you must know this is the record of the history of the People," Kaoto said.

"Yes. I have seen one like it before. It could have been stolen. Paataga is old, as you say. She was old when I knew her. In fact, I doubt mightily that she still lives and that you ever saw her. You found her bones along the trail and took the necklace. Did you not?"

Kaoto shook his head. He had known a few stubborn people in his time spent with Paataga, and Paataga herself was stubborn, but none could equal this old man. He began to think the old man did not want to trust him, did not want to let him go. He must have some other reason, something he was trying to hide or protect besides his hiding place.

"I could recite some of the history, but I doubt that you would recognize it. Not many have heard it, and if you had you would not remember enough to know if I spoke the truth or not. But here is something no thief would take. Those who recognize it would never touch it, and those who do not, would not know its worth." While he spoke he pulled another packet from his pack and unwrapped it. "It is mine, I made it and I have the right to wear it. I won the right in such a way that I will not tell you now, because you would never believe that either."

He placed a stained piece of buffalo hide on the ground between them. It had been cut from the thickest part of the skin where it runs down the back. It was about half the size of the palm of a man's hand and had a rawhide thong running through it so it could be worn around the neck. The stains on both the patch and the thong were from several summers of wearing. Both dirt and sweat streaked it. A figure of a running man had been burned in the center of the patch. It was the badge of a runner.

"I was, for three summers, the runner of Matuga, ruler of the Chaco," Kaoto said with pride.

The old man picked it up and examined it carefully, turning it over and around in his hands several times. There was no denying it, it was the real thing and had seen several summers of use. It had been carefully oiled and wrapped to protect it, although this man had not worn it today. He handed it back to Kaoto.

"Perhaps you might be one of the northern tribes. That might account for all the hair, but not for your size. How do you account for your height?" The old man was still holding on to his stubbornness and doubts.

"I do not account for it. My father was the same size as you are and my mother was considered tiny. I do not know how I came to be this size, or where all the extra hair came from. I cannot take credit for either, and in truth it is more of a curse than a blessing. I can only accept what the Spirit Watcher gave me and use it to the best of my ability," Kaoto answered him.

The old man was still filled with questions; no more trick questions, but rather questions about news of some of the southern tribes that he had once been familiar with. If this tall young man really was a runner, and evidently he was, then he might know something of his relatives.

Kaoto answered his questions faithfully, volunteering as much as he could. He did not try to tell the old one that he knew these things because he had recently traveled this land as the Wise One, not as a runner. He thought it better to let the old one accept him as a runner than try to make him believe he was the new Wise One. At last he seemed to be reassured that the tall giant was not one of the savages.

The word of a runner was taken for truth without reservation. This was a custom that had not been broken for as long as anyone could remember and would not be broken by him now. The runner was trusted by everyone, so how could he doubt the word of a runner? Besides, there would not be any savages smart enough to know all the things this young giant knew. He relaxed his vigil by lowering his knife, but he did not put it away yet.

"I will let you live. You may leave. But you must never come this way again, or I will surely kill you the next time."

"What are you afraid of? What are you trying to hide from me that you would send me, a runner and wounded man, out into the wilderness to face a wounded bull and who knows what else? This is not the hospitality I have always known among the People."

"Then you are indeed a stranger to this area. The savages are out there. I wonder how you got this far without being spotted by them. They rummage all over this territory and it is not safe for anyone to travel in the daylight." the old man told him, still holding the knife at his side, still standing ready to resume battle.

"Yet you would send me back out there. I have been lucky so far, but I am in no shape to depend on luck now." Kaoto made no attempt to move. He was getting dizzy from loss of blood and was afraid any movement would send him back into darkness. He must keep talking. He must stay awake.

"If it is so dangerous, how do you manage?"

"I have my own ways. Do not worry about that, but they are my ways and I do not intend to share them with every stranger who blunders in here."

"I have no doubt about that. But how am I to manage? I do not know if I can even walk, let alone outrun a wounded buffalo. I am still losing blood while I am sitting here talking to you. So what difference does it make to me if you kill me here or send me out there to die? I am very disappointed in the way you would treat a runner who came to you in trouble." Kaoto was trying to shame the man into helping him. He was sure that he did not intend to kill him, but what he said was true. What difference how he died? If he did not get the wound tended to, and soon, he would be too weak to do anything else.

The old man was puzzled. What should he do? He was aware of the code of honor that offered hospitality to everyone, especially to a runner in trouble. This man was a runner, there was no doubt of that, and as a runner he had the right to demand all the old man could give him. He had the right to demand the last mouthful of food and the last drink of water. Yet he was demanding nothing, he was simply asking for the right to live. This was not much to ask. Under any other circumstances the old man would have been the first to help him, but he did not want to take him deeper into his retreat. Yet there was not much he could do for him in this place. What should he do?

The problem was taken from both their hands as they heard the approach of rapidly running feet. Before the old man could call out a command to stop, a pair of young maidens burst into view from around an outcropping of the black rocks, which concealed the rest of the narrow passage beyond. They stopped in their tracks, like startled deer, when they saw the stranger seated on the ground.

"What are you doing here?" the old one demanded.

"We came looking for you," one of them answered, never taking her eyes from the stranger.

"Is this what you are trying to protect, old father?" Kaoto asked.

Before the old man could speak, another clamor of approaching feet and voices announced the arrival of even more maidens. They nearly collided with the ones already there as they came running around the corner. Six in all came to stand in a semi circle around the wounded stranger seated in the sand with his life's blood seeping from his wounded side. Though the old one was stern, they did not seem to be frightened of him.

"Who is this?" the oldest one asked. "Will he be staying with us?" Kaoto thought he could detect a note of hopefulness in her voice.

"No. He is leaving. Get back where you belong and leave men's talk to men." The old one was quite obviously upset. This posed another problem for him. It was bad enough to have a stranger find his secret entrance, but now he had seen his six daughters, and his six daughters had seen him. This would never do.

"But, father," one of the six pouted. "We never see anyone anymore. Now there is a young man here and you want to run him away. How can we ever find mates if you will not let us go anywhere or see anyone?" It was a good question, and the old one was not prepared to answer.

The old one slumped. It seemed to him that all was lost. He had protected his daughters this long without incident. But now, due to an unforeseen accident, he was in a difficult situation. His daughters would never let him send the giant away. They could see the wound in his side and knew he needed help. What could he do? He could keep him here until he could decide what he should do with him. This, of course, was dangerous also, but what choice was left to him? He knew he should have killed him the instant he laid eyes on him. He should have driven the spear through him and dragged him back outside for the wolves to eat. But it was too late now. The girls would have to be trusted. He doubted if this was a practical idea. He was old, but he was not that old. He knew what it was like to be young. He also knew that his daughters had been denied the pleasure of knowing any young men. It was not altogether his fault; there were no young men available.

Many summers ago, when the People had moved out of the path of the invading savages, the girls had been very young and their mother had just died. It had seemed right to him then to bring them to this secret place, where he could raise them and protect them until they were old enough to get along in the world. All had been well; they had been easy to provide for and had been happy with life as it was in this secluded place. They had not asked many questions and were satisfied with his explanations.

The summers had slipped by so quickly and uneventfully that he had lost track of time. He knew, of course, they would grow up some day and be young women with women's needs, and he had been sure he would be prepared for that day when it came. He had expected a gradual change, and had never dreamed it would all come to happen so suddenly. He had put off moving because the savages were there and it was impossible to leave this hiding place while they were around, or at least that is what he had told himself. Now, in the blink of an eye, all that had changed. The danger was not the savages outside, but the young giant inside, right here on the ground in front of them all.

"Come," he snapped at Kaoto, who was the cause of all his troubles. "We will offer you our hospitality, but do not make the mistake of thinking it is over between me and you."

"I would never underestimate the rage of a jealous father, especially when he thinks his family is in danger." Kaoto tried to rise but found he was already too weak to move without help. "I can assure you, you have nothing to fear from me."

"Humph," the old one snorted.

Chapter Seventeen

Kaoto could not stand. He was sore all over and his side throbbed with wicked pain. The rest of his body was bruised, but apparently not seriously damaged. The wound in his side was deep, but he did not think it would have to be fatal if treated soon. The bull's horns had torn a deep path through skin and flesh, leaving a gruesome looking hole. The loss of blood was the worst part of it. The efforts he made trying to get up only aggravated the wound more and sent a fresh stream of blood onto the ground at his side.

"Father, we cannot leave his wound like this. It must be bound up before we move him," the eldest daughter said. Without waiting for her father's consent, she went to Kaoto's side and began to timidly minister to him. She wrapped and bound up his wound with strips from her own garments, which left her nearly naked, but this was normal among the People and did not embarrass anyone.

It was a temporary dressing, just enough to slow the flow of blood. The old man scowled at her but said nothing as she, with the help of another sister, drew the giant to his feet. He was weak and faint but was able to stand by himself and felt he could walk, if the distance was not to far and they started soon.

"I think it only fair to warn you, you might be wise to bind my eyes also. I seem to have the ability to find my way back to any place once I have seen the way," he told the old man.

"No need," the old man said sagely. "No one can find their way in here. It took me a lifetime to unravel all these cracks in this maze of rocks. I am not worried about you finding your way anywhere. There are so many twists and turns, with false leads, that I do not doubt you would be completely lost in just a few steps," the old one muttered as he led the way.

"All right. It is up to you. But do not say I did not warn you," Kaoto said through clenched teeth as he took his first feeble steps after the old man, who never looked back.

The girls fell in behind them. The youngest gathered up his pack, which she dragged along behind. She refused any offer of help with it. True to the old one's words, the path was constantly changing directions as they went up one crack and down another, with sudden turnoffs from the bigger cracks into some so narrow that Kaoto's shoulders scrapped on both sides. He began to believe the old one was right. No one could remember all these turns without many trips over them. At any one time there were several choices that all looked equally good, or better than the one they followed. However, even in his unstable condition, with all the pain, his mind was still registering each turn and every cross crevice, making mental notes of each change in direction and the approximate distance between them.

As he stumbled along behind the old man, he was pleased to discover he still had enough strength to keep up. Behind him he could hear the girls whispering back and forth among themselves. He was able to gather quite a little about them and their life here. Paataga had told him many times that a Wise One had to know when and how to listen. He was listening with all his senses.

In actual distance, they did not penetrate the barrier very far. By actual footsteps, it was a long and painful journey, which seemed endless to Kaoto. He was considering just how much longer he could stay on his feet when they came around a last curve and into a large opening. By some freak of nature, the black rock had separated and left a wide, circular tract in the center of the otherwise tangled mass of sharp rocks. Here the ground was level and free of the harsh rocks. He was led to a shelter built against the wall where it would catch most of the Spirit Watcher's rays.

Kaoto was helped to lie down near the shelter and the girls all came to tend his wounds. Each vied with the other to be the most helpful until Kaoto began to doubt they would ever be done with him. The old man sat to one side, watching but not offering to help. In truth, he was reluctant to get too close to the young giant again. Kaoto felt a need to explain who he was and began to talk while they worked on him. He was careful to address all his remarks to their father and ignore the girls. He was treating the old one as a ruler because that is what he considered him to be, no matter if his district was small.

"You have not asked but I will tell you anyway. My name is Kaoto."

The maidens all giggled, except the youngest one, who was not tending his wound but sitting on his pack listening to everything with wide-eyed awe. "I was given the name for my running ability." He ran one hand over his tousled hair, then down his prominent nose. "And for my physical attributes, I suspect."

This brought another round of giggles from the maidens. They had never seen any man but their father. They did not know if all men should look alike or if they should be strikingly different, as these two were.

"I am called Mula," the old one grudgingly offered, as the custom demanded. If a man gave you his name, he was being open and above suspicion. To withhold your name was to invite distrust and hostility. He did not bother to introduce his daughters, partly because they were only women, but mostly because he did not want this stranger to know. He was not sure what he was going to do with him, but he was sure he was not going to let him stay around long enough to get friendly with them.

Kaoto had managed to sit up unaided. He sat with his long legs crossed in front of him while Mula sat on the customary log outside the doorway. They were still on the same eye level this way.

He had been thinking as he walked here and as they had talked. He must do something to impress on Mula his true identity. He could not just suddenly claim to be the Wise One. Mula was having enough trouble accepting him as one of the People and a runner. This was quite a lot for someone cut off from the rest of the nation. He would have to do something out of the ordinary to impress the old one; the necklace had not been effective. Then it became clear to him what he must do and he started to perform. He became like one of those who put on the plays in the Great Kiva. He could hardly believe what he was doing and saying.

Crossing his arms across his chest, for showmanship, he began. He did not like to fool people but sometimes they expected something more than just every day incidents. They wanted something dramatic, some sort of action instead of just words. He threw his head back and stared off into the space above him. He tried to become as rigid as he possibly could, considering his condition. He slowly brought his arms up and extended them to the sky, assuming a near trance-like state similar to what he had seen Paataga do as she recited the history.

"Mula, Father of these six young maidens, hear the words of Kaoto." He paused a moment to make sure they were listening. They were all watching him expectantly. Even Mula was watching, although suspiciously.

"I have traveled many days to find this place. The Spirit Watcher has guided my steps and shown me the way to find you. Your wisdom and knowledge of this country are so great that the Spirit Watcher has sent me to listen to you." He let his eyes drop slightly to see the effect he was having. So far the girls were captivated, but Mula was no fool. It would take more than this to convince this tough old man.

"I must tell you that I am not just one of the People, nor am I just a runner. I am a special messenger sent here by Paataga to learn the truth about the savages who threaten all of us." Glancing quickly toward Mula, he could see the old one was still unmoved. Furthermore, he was becoming even more suspicious of the tall stranger who was having such a telling effect on his daughters. Of course they were impressed. They had never been out among the People and knew nothing of play-acting.

Kaoto knew he would have to take a risk and either make some good guesses or some bad mistakes. Either way he did not think he had much to lose. He was sure that Mula did not intend to let him walk out of here without some struggle. He took the plunge.

"The Spirit Watcher has told me many things about you, Mula. He has told me that your mate has been dead these many summers, and that you have had to raise your daughters alone." This was a safe guess. He did not know how long Mula's mate had been dead, but he had seen no evidence of the woman, nor had he heard any of them mention a mother. Now he would get into something more difficult. He had managed to pick up and remember their names as they walked talking behind him. As of yet he did not have all the names connected to the right girl, but this was no time to hesitate, so he continued.

"Your daughters Polla, Maken, Tola, Casen, Parna, and the little one Mateep, are all the products of a kind and loving father who has provided for them and protected them from strangers for all the days of their lives." Of Mateep he had been sure, she had made him think of Little Frog, not because of her looks but because she was the only other person he had ever seen with two different colored eyes. He placed Mateep as a little girl probably several summers from puberty. Otherwise, she was just a normal girl without a twisted deformed body.

There had been gasps from the girls as he had called out their names. As they looked at each other and pointed, he was able to place each girl with the proper name and now he would know how to call them in the future without any introduction. Once more he was thankful for his marvelous memory. But Mula was still skeptical. What a stubborn old man, but at least Kaoto had his attention now.

Kaoto dropped his hands and all pretense and acting. He looked Mula straight in the eye with an unwavering gaze. He did not smile, he did not frown, and he did not speak: he only held the old man's eyes with his own until the old man looked away. There was an uncomfortable silence that lasted an unbearably long time. The young maidens sat as though frozen, waiting to see what was going to happen next and who would be the first to speak. Mula finally broke the silence.

"Who are you, Kaoto?" he asked, almost in a whisper. This tall young man who seemed to know so much about him and his daughters genuinely puzzled him. No one knew of his presence here, yet this man had called them each by name and knew his mate had been dead these many summers. How had he known she had died in childbirth with Mateep? These things were not common knowledge. No one knew but himself and his daughters, and they had not had a chance to tell him anything. This giant was more than just a runner or a messenger from Paataga.

Cautiously Kaoto rose and stood to his full height before Mula. He smiled faintly as he looked at the fierce old man and his six daughters, who were ready to accept anything he said. Mula, on the other hand, was still puzzled. He seemed to think this man promised to be a threat to him and his little covey. He still needed more to convince him. Kaoto must make Mula believe him, and he knew he could not use any tricks or falsehoods. He must tell him the truth in such a way he would be believed. No more acting. Only straight talk would do now. Another risk.

"You must know I am a runner. Do you not?" Mula mutely nodded his head in acceptance of this as a fact. "And you know the word of a runner is to be trusted and never disputed. Do you not?" Again Mula nodded his head. "Then you must know I cannot lie to you, yet what I must tell you will be hard for you to believe. You must think about what I tell you and try to understand why I would say what I do, and why I could not say it if it were not true." Sinking back to the ground with his eyes on the same level with Mula, he still held his eye contact with the old one.

"As I have told you, I am Kaoto. I have studied at the feet of Paataga. This also I have already told you. Last summer, at the celebration in the Chaco Canyon, in the Great Kiva there, I received the office from Paataga. I am now the Wise One of the People." He heard the intake of breaths. Even as remote as they were here, the maidens had been told by their father of the Wise One.

"I travel for the People, to come to them in their time of need. The People of the nation are in great danger and I must find out what this danger is so I can help them. I have come to you Mula, but by accident not by plan. I have never heard of you or your daughters before and I had no idea anyone lived in here. But surely the Spirit Watcher must have guided my steps, because who else can tell me more about the threat from the savages than you, old father?"

Another long silence fell over the small glade in the black rocks. The girls were still quiet, waiting to see what their father would say or do. Mula stood up. He did not let his eyes meet those of the giant. They were focused on the small dark red spot on Kaoto's chest. The spot where his spear had pierced the skin over the young giant's heart and come so close to ending the life of the most revered person in their nation. He, Mula, an unknown recluse and widower, had almost been guilty of the most horrendous crime that could be committed. To make things even worse, he was guilty of the crime in his heart and mind. He had wanted to drive his spear home, but had withheld his hand because he, like most of the People, had never killed another man before, so the crime would have been double.

He rose and stepped forward and placed his hand over the wound on the giant's chest as if to hide it from his eyes, as if this act could make it disappear. As if it had never been inflicted. His normally strong voice trembled as he spoke.

"What is to become of me Wise One?" Kaoto noted this recognition and was relieved. "I would beg for mercy on behalf of my children. They know nothing of the world. I beg you, do not punish them for the stubborn stupidity of their foolish father."

Kaoto took the hand from his chest and gripped Mula's wrists in the formal greeting between friends. "Punish? Who would punish a father for trying to protect his children? Would any man worthy of being called a man do less in the same position?" Stiffly he rose again to stand before the old father. "I did not speak thus to humble you, but to inform you of what you were ignorant of. I do not wish to punish you Mula. I would honor you for your courage and your kind heart, a heart that would not let you kill a man, even one who posed a threat to your family, without first hearing him out." He placed his other hand on Mula's shoulder just as he would have to his own father. A man did not touch another man unless they were very good friends or relatives. Mula recognized this honor and was even more humbled by it.

"You could have killed me while I lay unconscious. You did not. This speaks well of you. I see your daughters. They are fine young maidens, strong and healthy. I see your camp is clean. To raise such daughters without the help of a mate has taken much time, love, patience and hard work. There is no one to condemn you for what you have done."

"But I almost killed you. I wanted to kill you. I wanted to keep you from seeing my daughters. I must have been weak not to have done it." He was suddenly inspired with a new thought. "It must have been the hand of the Spirit Watcher who stayed my hand when I wanted so desperately to plunge my spear into your heart before you woke up."

Kaoto thought again of his talks with Paataga about the ants, and how they had compared the ants to men and the men to the Spirit Watcher. He wanted to tell Mula that he did not think the Spirit Watcher was much concerned with men, not even the Wise One. But he decided he would hold his words for now.

"You can give credit to whoever you think deserves it, and I will do the same. I think the credit goes to the man, not the Spirit. The man is not evil. He did not need the Spirit to tell him what was right. It was in the heart of the man, it spoke for him."

Mula did not argue with him, but he still held his own opinion as to who had stayed his hand from killing the most powerful man in the world; powerful in more ways than one. When he remembered how the young giant had picked both himself and his spear up as if they were toys, he was not so sure just who was responsible. He was, however, thankful that the Wise One was not angry with him. Who could guess what he was capable of such strength that he possessed?

Now that Mula was satisfied with the giant's identity and there was no longer any doubt in his mind, there was nothing too good for Kaoto. His daughters must bring him freshly prepared food, hot broth and tender meats. They took his soiled clothing to be cleaned. They would prepare a shelter for him, because it was plain to see that he would never fit into their small rooms. But first a bed was prepared for him just outside the shelter and close to the black wall so he would benefit from the warmth it would radiate to him.

Mula took a personal interest in his wound now and treated it with his own brand of medicine. The opening was first covered with spider webs and the sides were drawn together with sinew. Fresh bindings were wrapped around his waist to hold everything in place. The wound was painful but the horns had not penetrated deeply enough to damage anything more than muscle and skin. The six maidens provided anything the Wise One wanted or needed, and he was assured he had nothing to fear.

Kaoto permitted them to wait on him more than was necessary, but made the excuse that it would make Mula feel better. The attention was not wasted; he was weak and sore and needed the rest. The good nourishing food prepared over their smokeless fire was a welcome change from the dry trail food he had been eating since leaving the shining river.

Sleep, like a drug, took its hold on him and soon he was resting peacefully. Although it was mid-winter, the temperature inside the enclosure of the black rock barrier was mild and pleasant.

Tomorrow he would have plenty of time to talk to Mula about the savages who roamed the countryside, forcing the People to leave. Tomorrow would suffice to take care of the questions both he and Mula had to ask of each other. But for now, blessed sleep would do more for him than anything else. His young body was strong and healthy, and he would mend rapidly without complications. Tomorrow was another day and he would arise early to greet the Spirit Watcher and offer his thanks for sparing his life, even if he was in doubt as to whether the Spirit Watcher was involved or not.

As the rest of the family drifted off to take care of household chores and evening needs, Mateep sat nearby keeping watch over this fascinating man who was so tall and covered with so much hair. She had not been impressed with his act or his knowing their names. Even she could figure that one out, and being a Wise One did not mean much to her either. But someone who could make her father, the greatest man in the world, back down and change, now this was a man to consider.

Sitting with her chin resting on one knee, the other foot idly tracing figures in the sand she fantasized what it would be like to live with such a man and how the hair on his body would feel next to hers. She giggled behind one hand. She was too young to know she should not even have such ideas. Her older sisters would never admit to such thoughts, but Mateep knew they had them.

Chapter Eighteen

Kaoto did not wake early to greet the Spirit Watcher as he had planned. He slept straight through the day, only rousing occasionally to turn or shift positions. The sun had nearly completed its traverse of the sky when he came fully awake. He sat up cautiously and was relieved to find that, while his side was stiff and painful, he was able to move without too much discomfort. There was a gourd filled with water at his side and a bowl of fresh corn cakes with meat close by. No one was in sight, nor could he hear their voices. He assumed they were engaged in their daily work somewhere outside the immediate area. The thought crossed his mind that they might have abandoned him while he slept, but somehow he could not believe this.

He drained the gourd in one single draft and quickly downed the corn cakes and meat. After stretching to test the soreness of his body, he used the wall for a support to pull himself upright. Standing with one hand on the wall, he experimented with a few steps and was pleased to find he could walk with only minimal pain. He was still tender in the region where the horn had torn its way through his side, but that was to be expected. His other bruises and scrapes were slight, but were as sore as his wound. He knew they would soon limber up with movement.

The spot on his chest where Mula's spear had come so close to ending his life was covered with a dry scab. He touched it gingerly and made a mental note to use it as a reminder in the future. All the People did not know of him. He would have to be more humble and not assume that everyone knew about him and his transfer from runner to Wise One.

He was still thirsty and began a search for more water. He located a large water jug just outside the door where it was customary to keep one. He filled the smaller gourd and drank this water a little more slowly and felt as good as he had any reason to expect. He found his water skin and filled it also and hung it at his side. He had found his clothing hanging on the limbs of an ancient cedar tree. His longbow and arrows lay beside his bed, along with his pack.

Favoring his wounded side, he wandered around the compound. It was neat and tidy, everything hung in its proper place. Mula and his daughters did not suffer from want of food in this isolated garden. The storage bins were filled to overflowing with all manner of foods, some fresh, some dried. Many were foreign to him.

Mula's spare weapons hung just outside his doorway, another sign he had not been abandoned. The tips of his arrows were made from the same black rocks as the barrier. He tested the cutting edge of a piece lying on the ground and discovered it was extremely sharp, but it appeared to be very brittle and would probably be good for only one use before it would break.

As he hobbled around limbering up his stiffness, he knew there was something he must do. He was not eager to attend this chore but for his own peace of mind he knew it must be done, and the sooner the better. It would be best to do it now while his host was not around because he was sure Mula would not allow it if he were here. He was confident his strength and agility were up to the task, but there was only one way to find out. He would be able to rest better once it was over.

The Spirit Watcher might not be directly concerned. On the other hand, all signs pointed to the fact that he might have been watching over this son of man more than the son of man had given him credit for. If so, he surely would not turn his back on him in his time of need.

He picked his way unerringly back along the trail Mula had brought him in on. As he had told Mula, once he had traveled a path, he could retrace it without any trouble. Landmarks made an automatic pattern in his mind and came back to guide him when he needed to go over the same terrain again.

The Spirit Watcher was just short of the horizon when Kaoto eased his way back through the opening leading to the plains beyond. His target, the wounded bull, was laying only a few short steps away. Kaoto did not know if he was waiting for him to return or if he had finally given up and lain down in the nearest place that appealed to him. Either way, it was as Kaoto had hoped it would be and the closer to the opening, the better for him.

Standing outside the barrier, he waited a moment to see if the bull was aware of his presence. The bull turned his head to see Kaoto but he did not attempt to rise. The spear shaft was still protruding from his shoulder, just as it had been yesterday. Kaoto walked slowly towards the wounded animal. His movements were orchestrated; each step was a continuation of the last. His movements were fluid, no jerking or halting motion, nothing to attract or irritate the already angry bull lying just ahead of him.

The buffalo never took his eyes from the hairy giant approaching him. Its heavy breathing made the shaft rise and fall in a rhythmical arch. Kaoto made no sound until he was standing beside the wounded bull, which seemed to accept this new tormentor with resignation. If he could have spoken, he might have said, "Do what you will with me; I am finished anyway."

"Brother, I do not come to harm you." Kaoto spoke in a quiet voice, hoping not to alarm the animal further, but he must speak. "I come to honor you and repay the debt I owe to you. Without you I would have passed by this place and never found Mula." He did not bother to mention the six maidens, but the thought surely was in the back of his mind.

"What I am going to do will pain you, but it will end soon. I will understand if you are angry with me. I will not hold it against you and in the end we will still be brothers under the fatherhood of the Spirit Watcher, who watches us both with equal concern."

As he spoke in a low, soothing voice he took the shaft in both hands, careful not to change its position so the point would not be moved inside the throbbing shoulder until he was ready. Looking around to make sure there were no obstacles in his path, in case this did not work as it should, he exerted all his strength on the shaft, and with one massive effort tore the point from the bull's shoulder. With it came a great clot of black blood and a stinking, infectious ooze.

Once the spear was free, Kaoto leaped backward and prepared to dash to the safety of the opening. The bull, however, did not seem to take notice of him. It gave a great sighing noise of relief as it got up with all the dignity of a reigning monarch. It stood watching the man a short distance from him, and then took several steps backward. Lowering its shaggy head, it snorted and raked the dust with its front hooves, sending a shower of dirt and sand high in the air to rain down over both of them. Kaoto remained poised to run at the first sign of hostility, but the bull only looked him over again before it turned its back on him and walked away with a magnificent pomp and stateliness. A short way out it lowered its head and commenced to graze contentedly as if nothing had ever happened.

Kaoto let out a pent up breath he had been holding ever since he had taken hold of the spear. Now he backed toward the opening, keeping an eye on the bull just in case he should change his mind. When his back came in contact with the barrier, he stopped and turned his eyes to the waning Spirit Watcher on the far horizon.

"I give thanks for all you have allowed me to do and see. I wish to tell you I have learned many lessons in the short time I have been here, and will faithfully look for more lessons each day. Teach me humility; I am sure I need this more than any other type of knowledge at this time."

While making this silent statement, he caught a movement out of the corner of his eye. There was something on the barrier wall just to one side of where he stood. Swinging around swiftly, he held the foreign spear at the ready. It could have been a bird or a small rodent but he did not think so and was not surprised to see a small head rise warily over the top of the wall. It was the youngest, Mateep. She stared down at him as he lowered his spear and warned her.

"You must be very careful who you sneak up on, it might be dangerous. If I had not known who you were I would have been up on the wall after you before you could have gotten away."

Mateep smiled innocently at him. Her two different colored eyes did not show any sign of fear. Kaoto heard her climbing down inside of the wall, and soon was peeking out of the opening and motioning for him to come back inside. Once inside, Kaoto looked her over and guessed her to be about ten summers. She was still a child, but nearing maturity. In a village her naked body would indicate she was under ten summers, but out here he was not sure; she might run naked most of the time. The lack of body development was not always a sign of age, either.

"You are strong; my father found that out. You are brave; I have just seen that for myself. But I do not think you are ever dangerous, Kaoto. I do not see danger in your eyes. You are like my father; you would not kill anyone without first finding out their intentions." Her low husky voice sounded so serious that Kaoto chuckled in spite of his chagrin at the situation.

"And you are a pretty shrewd judge of character for one so young. What you say about your father and me is true, little one, but according to your father there are others about who are not so selective as he and I might be. He says they have a reputation for killing without asking any questions at all, or even caring, for that matter."

"True. They are out there sometimes and it is dangerous for us to be seen coming and going in the daylight. You should have waited a little longer until it was dark. Of course, it would have been harder to find the bull and do what you did, so I guess it was all right. I was afraid you were going to kill him at first, and was glad when you did not. But if the savages ever find the opening, they will surely kill us all. The old bull has been our best protection. Father says he must be the spirit of someone we once knew who has come back to guard us."

"Your father is a very wise man in his own right. I have heard it said that the spirit of our ancestors may live in the bodies of animals. If this is true, then he surely must have been a good friend to your father while he was alive because he takes his job so seriously."

As can only happen on the open west land, total darkness descended very quickly as they were talking. They started back to the compound. Kaoto did not wait for the child to lead the way but struck off on his own, confident he could find his way back even in darkness. Mateep was full of questions as she followed along behind him but there was one question she did not ask. She did not think it was a woman's business so she would wait and see if this tall, hairy, stranger would answer it in his discussions with her father. Then they would all know it the Wise One had a mate.

Kaoto never hesitated or took a wrong turn as he walked back to the opening. When they came to the fire by the shelter, Mula was watching him and wondering what he had been up to. He knew Kaoto had not taken any supplies, nor his pack or weapons, so he assumed he planned to return.

"Did you get lost in your wanderings?" he asked with a smirk. "It is lucky for you that Mateep found you when she did, because after dark even I have trouble finding my way around in here."

"He was not lost. I did not have to show him the way back; he came back without making a mistake." She gave her father a smirk in return for his earlier statement. "I think he told you he could do it when you brought him in here and he did, did he not?"

Mula looked to Kaoto for further explanations of his actions. He did not ask in words, but the question was in his eyes. He felt himself in a unique position. This was his home and he should be master here. On the other hand, the Wise One was over all People and had to answer to no one. But he still felt he was due some sort of explanation as to why this man had wandered off when they had expressly warned him about the dangers of getting lost or being found out by the savages. Kaoto started to reply but was interrupted by Mateep's outburst. She was unable to hold back any longer and must tell what she had seen.

"You should have seen him, father," she said, the excitement ringing in her voice and dancing in her eyes. "He was so brave. He walked right up to the old bull and pulled that spear out of him." Her naked little body did an exaggerated re-enactment of Kaoto's movements. "And the bull did not seem to pay any attention to him." Again she mimicked the actions of the bull so well Kaoto could not help but laugh at her. "He just looked at Kaoto and turned his back and walked away, never offered to bother him." Her swift and short version of what happened prompted Kaoto to explain the best that he could.

"I do not know if you will understand what I did, but I felt it was something I must do. I owed it to him. It was not nearly as brave as Mateep makes it sound. I guess it really could be called stupid and not the proper action for a wise person."

Mula mulled this over before he spoke, and while the other daughters were pretending to be busy with their chores, they all remained close enough to hear every word that passed between them. Mateep would be wrung dry of all she knew as soon as they could get her off to one side.

"Yes. I think I can understand, although I agree it was not what I would call wise. Brave? Yes. Unselfish might be a better word for it. I am glad it is done. I too feel I owe him a debt. He has been watching over our path for so long it would not seem right not to have him there. I guess he has chosen this place to live out what is left of his life. He is too old and tough to eat, and even the savages give him a wide berth when they come this way. I suppose he must have charged them and that is how he came to have the spear in him. But as long as he lives, we are safe from the savages, unless they stumble in as you did. I am glad you did what you did for him. I am glad it is over; now I will not have to attempt it. It was a job I was not looking forward to."

"Mateep told me of your belief that animals may be the home of spirits. I am sure there is a spirit in the old bull or he would not have stayed here so long. I became more sure of it today when I pulled the spear from him. He seemed to understand what I was going to do and let me do it for him." Kaoto had seated himself on the ground, as was his custom. He had found that People did not think of him as being so tall or intimidating when he was seated, and the lower the better. Mula with his seat on the log could look him nearly in the eye. Mateep, standing beside him, still had to look up a little.

"It was the thought of the spirit in the animal that made me do what I did today. Otherwise, I would have probably tried to kill it to put it out of its misery. I do not know if the spirits can feel the pain of the animal, but even if they do not it still is their home and we should not disturb them if we can help it," Kaoto continued. "And if there is no spirit living in his body, he still deserved my respect. Anything I could do to ease his pain was little enough for what he has done for me."

"Not many men would admit to what might be called a weakness. I am glad you have told me how you feel. Even so, if you had told me what you planned to do I would have tried to stop you." Mula gave Kaoto a knowing look. "Perhaps that is why you went off without telling me. I was so sure you would be lost that the thought never entered my mind. That comes from living here alone too long, I guess. I have gotten so I judge everything by my own abilities." He wagged his head at his own ignorance. "Whatever the reasons, you have made a friend of Mula for as long as there is life in these bones, and after death, if I have a choice, I will come back in some animal and offer my help to you."

This was the highest compliment he could offer Kaoto, and the young giant accepted it as was fitting, by nodding his head and saying nothing. He had found a soft spot in this old man after all. He had appeared to be as solid as the barrier around them, but even rocks have their weak spots. Every stone knapper knows this.

"If you should return, father," Tola spoke shyly without raising her eyes from the cook fire, "it will surely be in the body of a bear." The other girls laughed at this reference to their beloved father. They all knew that in spite of his gruff words and actions, he was gentle and kind to his daughters, whom he loved fiercely.

"If I do not see food immediately for myself and our——my guest, you will find out what a bear is really like." He turned back to Kaoto and pretended to address him as if the girls were not around.

"Why do we have to sit here with empty stomachs while these worthless women talk when they have no right to talk, listen when they should not be listening and let the cook fire grow cold and the food burn?"

The girls had never stopped working even as they listened and talked. Their father did not frighten them. They knew him too well. The meal was soon served to the two men. Once they were sure that their father and Kaoto were properly served, they filled their own bowls. Instead of leaving the area, as was the custom of most women, they sat down in a semi circle at the men's feet.

"I have often thought I should have built a kiva," Mula offered by way of apology to Kaoto for his daughters' lack of manners. "But since their mother died and we have lived here alone, I have never found it necessary to bring them up right, so you will please forgive them for their brash and forward ways. It is my fault and I suppose it is too late to start now. I could ask them to leave." This was more of a question than a statement. It was plain to see, however, that he was not ashamed of his family.

Kaoto looked around at the eager young faces in the firelight and knew that Mula would not have wanted to retreat even if he had a kiva. Why would he want to leave them out of his life? They were his life. Without them he would be nothing. This started Kaoto to wondering about the wisdom of the People's custom of men cutting the women out of their lives at important times. They obviously enjoyed their families the rest of the time. Paataga certainly had every right to share whatever talks or decisions there were to be made. Yet she was not allowed to go to the kiva except on special occasions, and even then she could not enter through the main entrance, but had to creep in through the tunnel.

He had thought then it was wrong, and now he was sure of it. He knew he could not change all the customs of the People but he could make a few changes and suggestions, just as he had with the creatures on the dump, or as he had by asking Paataga to hold his position while he was away. These were small things, but important to him. After he had more time in his office and more experience and had gained some real wisdom, maybe then he could make even more changes, if he had the time. Mula had proven it was not necessary to run the women off to be able to enjoy life. No man Kaoto had ever known enjoyed life more than Mula and his six daughters.

"Mula is very fortunate in many ways and it is I who should ask forgiveness, for stumbling in here uninvited. I have made myself a burden on you and your family. I can see you were quite content here without me butting in."

"You are here. We should not question the wisdom of spirit or man. I will now extend an invitation to you to stay with us as long as you wish. You have brought honor on my home and my daughters. Who could ask for more than this?" Mula was sincere. This was not the ritual invitation extended without real desire. Mula meant what he said. He was glad now that this young man had come along, and if he had not been such a stubborn old fool he would have thought of it sooner. That this man was also the Wise One made it even better for his purpose. This would help him solve some of his problems, problems he had been putting off because he did not know what else to do.

Mula sat silently smiling into his fire. Life was good to him. He had been more fortunate than anyone he had ever known, and the Spirit Watcher surely was smiling with him now, since only he would know what he was thinking.

Chapter Nineteen

After the evening meal was over, Mula led Kaoto away from the cook fire back toward a low-lying formation of the black rocks, which was at the junction of two cracks leading back into the maze. Somewhere deep in the broken surface, a spring of clean water had burst forth and found its way to this island. Mula had been able to channel some of this water into a depression in the low-lying rock. Over the summers, with the help of his daughters, he had scoured the depression with hard round rocks until the basin was smooth. This depression held a considerable amount of water. The black rock soaked up the sun's heat and warmed the water to a very comfortable degree. The depth of the water was only to Kaoto's knees, but it was sufficient for a comfortable soak and bath. At first the water seemed uncomfortably hot, but in a moment Kaoto was stretched out full length, letting it leech the soreness from his body.

Sister Moon came out in full light this night and her light put the darkness of the rocks in sharp contrast to the open space. Mula's daughters came to join them as soon as they had cleaned up after the meal. Nudity held no mystery among the People and was considered nature's way. All children ran naked as long as the weather permitted; only the coldest part of the winter would induce them to wear cloaks.

When a child reached the age of puberty, both boys and girls wore breechcloths, but they still went bare above the waist. Older People were more inclined to be fully clothed. The very old wore full dress nearly all the time except to bathe. Paataga once mentioned that she was more inclined to feel the temperature changes and wore clothing for this reason rather than any notion of modesty. So Mula's daughters came to the pool as they had come into the world. The pool was large enough to accommodate them all in comfort, and left room for Mateep to splash and make a nuisance of herself. Being the youngest, with the least responsibilities, she spent a good part of her day here.

The hot water induced an attitude of euphoria and all the worries and miseries of the day seemed to wash away, leaving the body relaxed and the mind free to wander. Conversation was easy, and even Mateep became subdued after a short time. Mula and Kaoto exchanged periods of questions and answers. Once in a while one of the girls would timidly ask something of life outside the barrier. Kaoto noticed that whenever this happened Mula would watch him closely, and as quickly as possible he would change the subject and steer away from the outside world.

"You have many comforts here that the rest of us never dreamed of. I wish Paataga could afford herself the luxury of this pool."

"Yes. It does wonders for the body, young or old."

"You said yesterday that you knew Paataga. When did you know the Wise One?"

Mula got out of the pool and hurried to his shelter. He came back and handed a small packet to Kaoto with a certain amount of pride. By the light of the moon, Kaoto could easily identify the same kind of badge as he had shown Mula earlier. It was much older, but Mula had kept it soft by rubbing it down with grease so it would not fall apart. It had been many summers since he had worn it. Kaoto knew what it was even before his fingers traced the shallow groves depicting a running man. Mula had also served as a runner. This was why he had to believe Kaoto's words. He knew a runner was trusted.

"What district did you run in?" Kaoto asked him.

Mula waved his hand vaguely to the north and east. "I cannot say exactly where it is from here, but we were called the Gallins. I have heard of your Chaco Canyon, but I never have been there. I never got beyond the shining river. It was there that I first heard of Paataga, there near the river. She had come to the river country in search of a youngster who according to rumors was very wise, wise beyond his time."

"Did she find him?" Kaoto was interested. Paataga had never told him about this in all their time together.

"No. It was strange. She did not travel very fast, and before she arrived, the youth was stricken with a strange illness and never recovered. He died before she got there to help him. It is probably just as well for all of us."

"Why? I would have thought all would have been glad for Paataga that she had found a replacement when she was still young." Kaoto was puzzled.

"Perhaps. True, the lad was very smart in many things. But he had a strange perversion for cruelty. He was the kind who would torment animals and birds just for his own evil enjoyment. I have never known of anyone like him, before or since." Mula paused as if he were trying to recall all the people he had known back then and compare them with the boy in question.

"I do not think anyone would have liked to see him as Paataga's student, let alone as her successor. I think we are much more fortunate that she waited for you. You have already shown you have compassion with the old buffalo, and you have been kind to an old man who acted so foolishly. What might have happened to our nation if the cruel youth had taken the responsibility you now hold?"

"Only the Spirit Watcher knows," Kaoto said. He, too, was glad the youth had not become the Wise One. If this had happened he would never have known Paataga, and in turn would never have ventured down to this country and found this retreat and all its wonders.

Over the next few days Kaoto let his body rest and mend while Mula and his daughters waited on him. Each evening they would all converge on the pool where, after a couple days, the maidens were asking every conceivable question about the rest of the world and the People of the nation. Mula had to give up on trying to change the subject because they would not relent. He protested about their impudence, but Kaoto assured him he did not mind; in fact, he rather enjoyed all this attention. It was far different for the boy who had grown up so alone in a village filled with people.

It was perfectly normal for the young to enjoy each other's company, and Mula became resigned to losing control over his daughters for a time. Kaoto had told him of his mission and what he felt he must be doing soon. Mula knew this was just a temporary interlude for the Wise One and he would be moving on as soon as his wound had healed.

The sexual habits of the People contained few taboos. Once a man and woman were mated, formally announcing their intentions of remaining together for the rest of their lives, they were expected to be faithful to each other. Before they mated, the young were allowed to experiment with each other and to relieve themselves as they wished. Rape was unknown; no one would force a partner when there was plenty of willing ones available. Any child born to a young woman before she mated was considered her child alone. The child went with the bargain when she did mate for life. Her mate was not disappointed in her, just the opposite. It proved she was capable of bearing children and therefore a worthy mate to make a man proud.

Mula, who had tried so hard to protect his daughters up until now, began to entertain thoughts of what would be the outcome of coupling his daughters with this tall, hairy, young giant. He knew they would do the natural thing and he could see the advantages of having a Wise One be the father of their children. He had never had a son, and had hoped fervently that some day he would at least have one man-child to call him Great Father.

By the count of the fingers on one hand, Kaoto's wound was sealed. By the count of the fingers on both hands, they were red scars to remind him of what had happened. Kaoto relaxed and stayed another count of both hands. He told himself he needed to rest and be completely healed before he set out on his mission again. It was hard to think of problems when he was enclosed here, where there were no problems. He could readily understand why Mula had never gotten around to taking his daughters away from here.

During his recuperation, Mula found many excuses to be gone for long periods of time, allowing the young people to do what they enjoyed most and could tell by the new look in their eyes that what he expected was taking place. The girls in their turn wondered about their father's long absences, but were not concerned. They reveled in the festive atmosphere now that Kaoto was here.

Kaoto became well acquainted with all of them. He learned that Polla had twenty summers, two more than himself. Tola, the quiet one, had nineteen summers. Parna had the same summers as he did. Casen had seventeen summers, and Maken only sixteen. Casen was the liveliest of the all and did much of the talking for them; often asking questions the others wanted to know but were to shy to ask for themselves.

Mateep had ten summers and did not get to join in all their activities because of her youth. She did not resent being left out because she felt they were all being very silly. She made up by being twice as obnoxious whenever she had the chance. Her exuberance and never ending vitality won her a special place in the heart of the Wise One, and he knew that he would never forget her either.

From force of habit he had continued to set aside a small portion of his food, and since there were no creatures here, he shared with the small rodents. When Mateep asked him about this peculiar habit, he explained about his little sister. He did not tell of Little Frog's history because he did not think they would understand. Living here as they did, there was no need for anyone to live at the dump. He also did not mention her deformity, because in his eyes she was no longer the same creature he had rescued so long ago. He did, however, tell Mateep that his little sister had two different colored eyes just as she did, and the same eyes were the same color as Mateep's. This made a secret bond between Mateep and the Wise One, who she only thought of as the hairy giant.

During the meals and at night at the pool, Mula told Kaoto all he knew about the savages outside the barrier. He recalled that when he was a young man they had rarely been seen. But as the drought became more and more severe and the animals more scarce, the savages had become a real problem as they foraged further into the land of the People.

Originally they had lived far to the east on the plains. There they had followed the great herds of buffalo. When the spirit of rain forgot the land, or was driven from it by the constant attention of the Spirit Watcher, the grass withered and died. The buffalo had split into smaller herds to find new grazing lands. The savages had followed these smaller herds. Most had gone toward the rising sun, where the plains were fruitful and the buffalo flourished. Those who had worked westward had found a harsh land where the herds did not multiply as fast. It was this cruel land that made them a brutal People. Eventually they had come to the land of the People, where the land was not quite so barren yet, and where they found they could forage through the crops of the timid little farmers.

Mula told Kaoto that it was not just the men, but the women also, who were all called savages. The women were as cruel and barbaric as their mates. They carried weapons and joined in the hunt to kill. If anything, they were even more terrible than the men.

Being nomads, they did not stay in one central place as the People did. They did not raise crops, nor gather for the winter. They were not confined to one place and carried their tent-like homes with them wherever they went. A slovenly People, they took no pride in their homes, their campsites or their personal appearance. They were prone to paint their faces and bodies with hideous designs that made them even more frightful to see. They were taller than the People, though not as tall as the Wise One. Who was? Their hair was black and coarse, not soft and brown like the People's hair. They seemed to have no regard for human life, not even their own kind. They would leave their wounded to die untended. Their trail was littered with the old and the dying, and filthy campsites. He had never witnessed this but had heard horrible stories of what they did to their captives. Again, the women were supposed to be the worst.

The People, rather than fight these troublesome invaders, retreated farther and farther west, leaving a wide margin between themselves and the plains

Indians. The savages, however, did not recognize this boundary, and moved into it just as quickly as the People vacated it.

This had been a slow process at first, but over the summers they had become increasingly arrogant and aggressive, causing the People to move time and again in order to be free of their fierce neighbors. This was the reason Mula had been stranded here in the black rocks.

He had found this place quite by accident, much as Kaoto had, only he had been a runner at the time and had taken refuge in the rocks when pursued by a small band of the savages. Later he had brought his mate and first daughters here for protection. The savages had known he was in here, they knew there were People living behind the barrier and had tried for a long time to find a way in. In time they had tired of the game but occasionally still tried to find them.

On several occasions they had tried to navigate the top of the barrier and had been forced to give up when their footwear was cut and they were left with awful cuts on their feet, hands and legs. One had dropped down inside in one of the cracks. Fortunately it was not one of those that led back to Mula's retreat. He forged his way up and down the endless maze; often only a short distance separated him from Mula. In the end he had tried to crawl out over the top and had died a horrible death in the middle of the barrier. His body was food for carrion birds and his bleached bones lay there as a reminder for any who might attempt to cross here.

Mula felt safe inside the barrier and had never thought it necessary to take his family out. He was content here, his daughters were happy. Why should he leave?

Kaoto knew that he must leave soon. This was borrowed time but he would have to pay it back somewhere along the trail. He asked Mula when would be the best time for him to leave and where he should go once he was outside the barrier. Mula informed him he would show him a secret way out that would be less hazardous. It would bring him out on the opposite side of the barrier so he would not have to circle around in the hostile plains. He could make his way very quickly into the higher country where the savages did not like to go. It would not be easy and there would be risks, but the risks would be less than the other way.

The night of his departure was a sad time for all of them. Kaoto had tried to make excuses to stay and the maidens had tried equally hard to persuade him to stay. He knew that if he stayed any longer it would not be a sojourn but a permanent arrangement. It was not the worst possible scenario, and if he had not given his oath to Paataga and all the People present on the day he took office, he might have succumbed to the temptation. The wise man's word was sacred and could not be broken.

"I know," Mateep wept when he told here that he must go. "I have known all along you would not stay. The others said you would stay with them forever, but I knew you would not."

"Will you still feed the little ones for me, just as you have while we were together?" he asked of her because she had followed his habit of setting a small portion aside. She knew nothing of the creatures of the dump. All she knew was that they feed the little rodents. It had been her favorite time of the day because it was the only time he paid strict attention to her. It had become a special time for her, one she would always remember.

"I will remember, Kaoto," she sobbed as she tried to stop the flow of tears that betrayed her. "I will tell them it is for Kaoto's little sister who has no other name. But, will you ever come back to us?"

"I will come back. Someday. I am sure of it. I just do not know when. I hope I do not find you here when I come back. I hope your father will take you away from here to a village where you can live with the rest of the People."

He had never mentioned Little Frog to her by name, but now he thought he would tell Mateep about her to help her get over the loneliness of his leaving.

"Can I trust you to keep a big secret for me?" Kaoto asked her. "You seem like the kind of girl I could trust."

"Oh yes. I can keep a secret better than anyone. You just ask my sisters how well I can keep a secret."

"I do not have to ask them. I have asked you and you are the one who knows. Now I will tell you something about my little sister that know one else knows. It will be just between you and me." Mateep squirmed in nervous excitement. Something not even her sisters knew? This would be the best secret ever.

"You and my little sister share two things. She also had two different colored eyes, just like yours, the same color in the same eyes." Mateep beamed. Her smile seemed to spread across her face like the sun on a rock. "Second, she shared your name."

"Her name was Mateep? Then why do you say she had no other name?"

"No, her name was not Mateep, but I always called her Little Frog, just as your sisters do you for being in the water all the time, just like a little frog."

"Really? You really called her Little Frog? I thought I was the only one to be called that. I did not like it when they teased me all the time. Now I like it and will always remember when they try to tease me." Mateep was filled with pride in the confidence the Wise One had shared with her. This was a secret she would never reveal to any of her sisters. They thought they were so great spending all their time with him doing silly things, but he had not trusted them with his secret; he had trusted only her.

When Kaoto tried to reason with Mula about moving his daughters out of the barrier, he knew he was fighting a losing battle. He had nothing to offer them that was better than what they had here. If he had only been here for one turn of Sister Moon and had to force himself to leave, how could he expect them to leave when it was the only home and life they knew? He did get Mula to promise to think about it. He realized he would not live forever and someday he would not be here to look after them. Yes, he would think about it.

When the Spirit Watcher had gone to rest and Sister Moon did not show her face, Mula led Kaoto deeper into one of the cracks where he had never been in before. It came to a dead end as all the others did, but Kaoto knew they were deep inside the barrier, possibly closer to the opposite side now. Mula had carried a bundle in his hand that proved to be two pairs of sandals with heavy wooden soles. The thongs were affixed in such a way that they were not exposed on the lower side where the black rocks could cut them. His were old, but Kaoto's were freshly carved.

"You must follow in my footsteps so you will not slip or fall. I hate to have you make this trip in the dark, but it is the only safe way. If you should fall you will think the bull was kind to you, and there is nothing I could do to help you. You are too big for me to carry." As he talked, he had been securing his sandals. Then he checked the lacing on those of the Wise One. Satisfied, he climbed a set of crude steps carved into the wall.

"These rocks are mean and unforgiving to anyone who does not respect them." Mula pulled a huge pack from where it was wedged in the rocks. "It is filled with dried foods and our hopes of a safe journey. I do not know how far you will have to go on it. I have not been out this way in many summers, but I do know the savages are also on this side."

"Why did you not take your daughters out long ago when it was still safe? While you had a chance, while they were still children? They could have grown up with other children in a village and known a normal life. They would have been mated by now, with children to gladden your heart. You would have been a great father many times over by now."

"It is easy for you to tell me what to do now," Mula said sadly. "Perhaps you are right, but at the time this was the place of our happiness. Living was easy here. It was easy to look after my daughters and care for them properly without the sympathy and help of well meaning strangers. Anywhere I would have gone, it would have been the same. I have been here too long to know anyone outside any more." As he was talking, he was leading Kaoto steadily across the vast black expanse of wilderness in rocks.

"I have always found an excuse to put it off just a little longer. In my heart I did not want to leave this place, and now I fear it is too late."

"It is never too late to rectify a mistake as long as you have life in your bones, Mula. Think hard on what I say. I do not command it, but I do request it of you."

Suddenly a crack opened up at their feet. If Mula had not warned Kaoto he would never have seen it in the darkness. Without Mula's guidance, Kaoto had no doubt he would have fallen and been lost several times on this trip. They dropped down to the sandy bottom of the opening and removed their sandals. Kaoto offered his to Mula, who shook his head.

"Do you think you could find your way back across that path, even in daylight?" Mula asked.

"I am sure of it. Not only in daylight, but also in the dark, just as it is now. Even without light there is still a picture of the way in my head," Kaoto offered as an explanation.

"Then we will hide the sandals here where you can find them. If you ever come back this way, you must come on this side of the barrier and use these sandals to come across in safety."

"I hope to return someday, and when I do I hope to find no one here. I hope to find you have taken your daughters out to live with the People, where they belong."

"From here you must follow the stars, as I have shown you. They will lead you to the mountains where there is a trail that goes back to the shining river. I do not know how far you will have to go before you find a village with our people, so we have prepared a big enough pack of food to make you sweat carrying it."

Mula bid the Wise One goodbye without further comment on the subject of his leaving. In a moment the old one vanished in the darkness to return to his loved ones in the peaceful seclusion offered by the black lava rocks.

Mula was content. He had questioned his daughters a few nights earlier and they had told him they had all slept with the Wise One. All except Mateep, of course, who was too young. With this knowledge he awaited the arrival of the Spirit Watcher the next morning after Kaoto had left them.

He stood defiantly in the center of his clearing and shouted his challenge to the sun god as soon as he rose.

"I dare you to deny me at least one man child. He would spring from the seed of the Wise One, your favored son. You would not insult him by not leaving at least some sign of his being here in my home."

Mula chuckled to himself because he felt he shared a secret with the deity in the sky. Something they both knew if no one else did. He shook his fist at the Spirit Watcher and shouted:

"Even you cannot control all five of them. I, their father, know this to be true." He dropped his fist and his voice also dropped to what could almost be described as a plea.

"I deserve a man child for my old age." Once more his voice rose in a shout of defiance.

"And you will not deny me this child. I have outsmarted you at last, you old fraud." Again chuckling quietly to himself, Mula turned and walked back to where his daughters were just waking from their night's rest, disturbed by their father's shouting. Mula was not in the least afraid of what the Spirit Watcher might do to him or his daughters.

Chapter Twenty

Kaoto followed the winding path out of the black rocks. Once clear of the barrier, he took his bearings on the star cluster Mula had shown him. He could see the silhouette of the darker mountains framed against the night sky. Adjusting his pack, he followed the stars, which would lead him to the pass in those mountains. Mula had told him the savages were apparently frightened by the darkness and would not be a threat until after sunrise.

He moved as swiftly as the darkness would allow. The stars led him true and before the middle of the night he was over the top and down the other side. Descending in the darkness, he could hear the faint sound of a stream of running water close by and he knew this stream would eventually lead him back to the shining river. Traveling a strange trail in almost total darkness was almost impossible, so he left the faint trail and felt his way to the stream. It was a small trickle so he was able to cross over and work his way well back into a clump of brushes. Feeling as much as seeing, he found a tiny clearing at the foot of a large outcropping of rocks. Here he made a quick camp and waited for the light of day.

He would not be as careless as he had been previously. He would not make the mistake of assuming his identity would be known. There could well be many like Mula who had never heard of him and might mistake him for one of the savages instead of a Wise One.

His convalescence time with Mula and his daughters had been pleasant, but it had also been informative and he had learned a great deal about the eastern boundaries of the nation. What Mula had told him about the savages had an influence on his plans for the future. Up until now he had only a vague objective, but now time seemed suddenly more important to him. He knew he must travel far and fast if he was to circumnavigate the entire nation in order to ascertain what he should do to help his People.

First light found him jogging down the trail to the shinning river. He was grateful to Mula and his daughters for the extra food they had provided for him. Trail food was what he would need now, so he could travel fast without having to stop more often than necessary. His plan was to stay close to the southern boundary, stopping occasionally to ask questions and listen. He would restock his supplies whenever it was convenient.

Holding to a general westward direction, his path led him along the edge of a dry, desolate region. The villages were more scattered but he was able to establish that the savages in this area did not bother them. The threat here was the silent, shifting desert. His enemy was thirst and heat. At each stop he inquired, "How far does this desert extend to the south?" He received diverse answers, but the consensus was that no one knew for sure. They had hazy recollections of tales from the past that varied with every telling. Some claimed to remember when trade routes went south, others insisted it was long before any living man's time. The one thing they all agreed on was that no one crossed the desert these days, so no one knew what lay beyond.

Pushing ever westward, it felt good to be on the trail again. Most of his best memories were related to his time spent as a runner. He had enjoyed his time with Paataga and more recently his stop with Mula and his daughters. Still, he knew that these were only short interludes, never to be repeated. It was his only taste of true family life. From now on he would travel fast and not know the comforts of home or friends.

He was born to be a runner and he was in his element when he struck out each morning. He ran at his easy, ground-eating lope, and felt good as he became used to the trail again. He could allow his mind the freedom of thinking about what ever he pleased as he ran. Running did not take any concentration. His eyes read the path as it unfolded before him and transmitted the necessary information to his feet, leaving the rest of his mind free to wander where it pleased. Distance drifted out behind him like portions of a dream, half remembered, half forgotten.

The land was constantly changing under his gliding feet. The rock formations and soil varied from one day to the next. The plant life also underwent some changes as he forged west across the vast emptiness of the southwest. Here on the edge of the desert land every form of life had its own defense. Everything that grew in this hostile land was covered with sharp spines of thorns. He learned to watch his step more closely after having to stop several times to dig offending spikes from his feet and sandals. Some broke off below the skin and their nearly transparent tips made it almost impossible for him to find. Time alone would cause them to fester until he could squeeze them out, and until that happened he would have to put up with the pain.

Growing weary of the constant desert, he changed his course to go farther to the north where he would be at a higher elevation. Here the vegetation was more abundant and more kindly disposed to the bare skin of runners' legs. Villages were closer together here, and while the crops might be different to what he was used to, the village life was still the same.

At one desolated place, he came across the bones of ancient trees. They could be seen lying about on the ground. They had been dead so long that they had turned to stone - bright, shiny, beautiful, stones. Even though the ground here was barren, he still found a few hardy People living amongst them. They told him of more prosperous settlements farther to the west, close to the edge of the nation. Kaoto pressed on impatiently, striving to find the westernmost boundary of the nation.

He lost track of time and the turn of the moon as he ran. The weather could be temperate one day and bone chilling the next as he crossed ranges of mountains and dropped down into deep, dry valleys.

He eventually was running along the edge of a high rim. It was not a side of a valley with another range on the other side; there was no other side. The land beyond the rim ran endlessly south. This rim was a line separating two different worlds: the high country, and the low land. Above the rim the trees were tall and the land was good for farming, although the season was short. Below the rim there was a narrow stretch of land that was fertile and easily watered, but beyond this lay the desert for as far as his eye could see. The water, which ran down from the high country, was soon lost in the vastness of the dry land below.

He took a trail leading down the side of the rim to where a village was visible in this marginal land. The air grew noticeably warmer as he descended from the heights of the rim. The northerly wind diminished almost as soon as he dropped over the edge. As he neared the bottom, it was as though he had re-treated a season. It was not winter down here, it was more like early fall.

The People here were almost identical to those in Chaco Canyon and their homes were constructed along similar design. The building materials were different, however. There were no regular sandstone ledges here to contribute uniform building blocks. Instead they had to use various sizes of undressed stones, and an exterior frame of wood was used to define the outline of the building. These were covered with a coating of mud and grasses and willow twigs. The end result was nearly the same. The wattle walls were covered with the thin covering of adobe mud and adorned with the same drawings he was familiar with. Many of the smaller buildings were made entirely of wattle, but the hot dry sun made them as strong as stone.

He began to hear rumors of the savages again in these villages. They seemed to be a different species, but the story of their raids and destruction was the same. They were nomads who raised no crops, built no buildings, nor settled in any one place. Instead they roamed the land hunting and raiding the fields and storage bins of the People. These savages were also warriors who would rather fight than try to find a peaceful means of settling disagreements.

In one beautiful canyon, near a bountiful stream, he came upon a village. Actually, it was two villages serving one purpose. The People lived mostly in the small village, built close to the face of the cliff. Above this village, hanging from the cliff, they had built another dwelling under the overhanging rocks. It clung to the side of the cliff like some wasp's nest. This was their retreat during raids. They could scamper up the ladders to the safety of this dwelling whenever the other village was threatened. Once everyone was safely inside, they could pull up the ladders and seal off the openings. The place was kept well stocked with food and supplies in case of raids and the villagers could withstand a long siege. The nomadic savages seldom had the patience to stay put very long and would wander off after they had practically destroyed the lower village and dev-astated the outlying fields.

This was the home of Moot, the ruler of this district. He had been one of the few rulers from this far away who had been able to attend when Kaoto took his office. He had not made the long trip for this reason. He had been on other business when the runners came bearing the news and had decided to continue on to the Chaco for the occasion, since it was something that few men got to see.

Like most of the other visiting rulers, he had been surprised to find so much wisdom in such a young man, and his unique size made it difficult for Moot to forget. He had stood in awe of the hairy young giant who had overshadowed every man in the nation. He had heard Kaoto make his pledge to visit every village, but had taken it as a courtesy statement and never considered the possibility of seeing the Wise One again. When he saw the tall form bearing down on his village, he recognized him immediately and passed the word that he was the Wise One; a friend, not a member of the dreaded savage tribes.

The curious villagers gathered around Moot and his distinguished guest, marveling at his size and the covering of golden hair that glowed in the late afternoon sun. They had heard Moot's story of this young giant and his golden hair, but had found it hard to visualize. Now Kaoto stood before them and they could see that he truly did shine, as a representative of the Spirit Watcher should.

"We are glad to see you, Kaoto. You truly must be able to run like the bird whose name you carry."

"I have not run all the way. I sometimes walked a little so I would not miss anything." Kaoto answered the humor with his own humor.

Moot ushered Kaoto into the center of his village and sent the women scurrying to furnish fresh food and drink for the Wise One. Although his squat face registered his delight in this unexpected visit, Kaoto could detect worry on the faces of the People, and especially on Moot's.

"What troubles you Moot?" he asked, even before the women could return with refreshments.

"You have come at a bad time, Kaoto. There is much unrest in our area these days."

"Then it must be an opportune time for me. When could be a better time? Anyone can walk among you when the times are good, but it's not my office to just enjoy life when it is easy. I must learn to look for trouble and take joy in meeting it wherever I go. I fear I will find much of it in my life, if the past few moons are any indications of the future," Kaoto said as he seated himself on the ground in the plaza.

Moot could use the help of a wise person at this time. He was deeply troubled. The nomads had been around ever since he could remember, but they had not been a real threat until recently. Of late they had become increasingly bold and their harassment had increased over the past few summers.

When the women brought their food, Moot was silent for a while, letting the young man eat and enjoy his food. When the bowl was empty and Kaoto had licked his fingers clean, Moot spoke of what had been happening in his part of the nation.

"Things are so bad now that we keep a watch constantly from the top of the cliff house. That is how I knew you were coming long before I could see you. We keep some of the old and afflicted ones up there all the time. That way they can be of service and they are already out of harm's way when the savages do arrive. We need every able-bodied person to work in the fields and gather wild crops." He went on to explain how signals were sent with smoke and fire on the balcony at the top of the structure so the villagers could see them at a great distance as they tended their fields.

"We have to hide our fields in unlikely places in order to escape with enough food to take care of our own."

This was something new to Kaoto. Back in the canyon where he was raised, the only threat was the drought. Food had never been a problem. It was well known that one healthy man could raise enough to feed several families.

Moot took him up to the top of the cliff dwelling. Here there was a large area that served as an open sided kiva. He stood at the parapet and looked far to the south, toward the ever-present desert lurking just out of reach, waiting, waiting for the unwary.

"We once farmed and lived as far down the valley as you can see; but no longer. We do not dare get caught out in the open away from the protection of the cliff," Moot told him sadly.

It did make a good watchtower. No one could slip in on them unless they came from the top of the rim. So far, the savages had not climbed to the top of the rim; they seemed to prefer the lower lands. They were similar to the savages Mula had told him about in the land of the black rocks. They were dark-skinned people who were a definite threat to the People. The shadows of Kaoto's dreams were beginning to take shape. In the back recesses of his mind he felt a faint stirring, something in the past, something to do with the history of the People.

Kaoto stopped his journey at Moot's village and spent his days looking and his evenings listening. The People told him of the horrors of the savages who were victimizing them. Their stories sounded much the same as those told to him by Mula, and while they were a different tribe they all seemed bent on exterminating his People from the face of the earth. His dream was beginning to make sense to him at last. The pieces were fitting together and he was no longer haunted by doubts.

"Does Moot have any plans for the future?" the Wise One asked.

"I only have two choices," Moot said. "I either stay here and watch my People starve and be slaughtered, or I can lead them away to a different place. If I do this, we will still stand a chance of starving as we wander over a strange land in search of a dream."

Kaoto glanced quickly at him at the word dream. "A dream? What does Moot mean by a search for a dream?"

Moot hesitated. He wondered how much he could tell this strange young man. He thought of his dream and felt foolish, but something in the tone of the Wise One's voice and the intent look in his eyes made Moot decide to trust him. Who else did he have to turn to?

"I do not know if I can explain what I mean. It is not really a dream, such as we all have at night, nor can I call it a vision, although it could be one,

I guess. I do not know. Do people like me have visions, or is this reserved for wise men?"

"We all have dreams, some more that others. Dreams are not just for the Wise One."

"They come to me in the night, but they are hard to define." Moot said hesitantly, not sure if he could explain these strange dreams he had been having.

Kaoto nodded his head in understanding. He knew what Moot was trying to say. He had had the same feeling about his dreams when he tried to explain them to Paataga. It might help Moot if he let him know that he, too, had gone through these same feelings. There were moments when he had thoughts that were neither dream nor conscious thought. They were like uninvited guests who crept into his mind when he least expected them, and left him puzzled and almost frightened.

"I think I know what you mean, Moot. They come like a fly when you are nearly asleep. They are there, but you are not awake enough to drive them away or asleep enough to ignore them."

Moot accepted this comparison. It was very near what he had experienced. It was good to know that he was not alone, that someone else had these same feelings. He felt more at ease. He was not afraid to talk now to the Wise One.

"Yes, that is very close to how I feel. The dream, if that is what I should call it, comes when I sit alone and have been worrying about what to do." He paused and looked to Kaoto, a little self-conscious of how he might sound. But the Wise One was waiting for him to go on. Moot felt encouraged and continued, "Some would call it wishful thinking, hoping for something better, chasing patches of sunshine on a cloudy day. I know, we all think about a perfect place, a place where there are no problems. Where everything goes well and everyone is happy. I know this is so and often wonder if this is what I am doing to myself. But I do not think so. I do not think what I see is just an old man's dream of peace and prosperity. I feel it is real, as if someone is looking down from above and telling me something that I do not quite understand. I do not know where to look for what I have been shown, nor do I know what to do about what I think I am told to do."

"Tell me. What do you see?" Kaoto prompted him. "Some dreams are important. True, some dreams are just that and nothing more, but others are often something in our mind that we do not understand. Something that is trying to make itself known to us. We control our minds so strictly when we are awake that these dreams cannot speak, but when we are resting, relaxed and not yet asleep, they can talk to us."

Moot was feeling much better about his dreams now. Kaoto not only understood him but also seemed to accept his dreams as real, not just idle thoughts. Not just an old man's dreams for something better. The Wise One's belief in him made it possible to go on without fear of being laughed at. The hairy, giant youth was truly the Wise One to him now. His ability to understand made him ageless and timeless. He did not act as a green youth might be expected to act, nor did he flaunt his office as might be expected of one so young. He was not playing a part. His concern was real, as was his interest in Moot's thoughts and dreams. Paataga had told Kaoto once that listening to people helped them to help themselves. By letting them solve their own problems, it made the one listening seem wiser than he really was.

"I see my village moving to some place different, very different. The plants are different. There are more plants and they are greener than here. I am told it used to be that way here in the beginning. But my dream is not here, and it is not in the past. It seems to be in the future, as though I could see tomorrow. But that is foolish; no one can see ahead to what is going to happen, can they, Wise One?" Moot asked.

"I would not judge that yet. I sometimes think we do see little patches of the future sometimes. But tell me more. Tell me all of your dream."

"Everything is different there. The rocks, the trees, the soil, even the weather. I know my People can live there in peace. They do not have to fight or run in fear anymore. There are People there ahead of us, but they do not fight us. They make room for us and are not our enemies." Moot shook his head sorrowfully. "Oh, how I wish I could find this place for my People." His voice expressed his belief in the futility of this hope. Where could a man find all these things and not have to fight for them?

Kaoto sat silent. He was digesting what Moot had told him. Did it have some connection with his own dreams, and those of Paataga? There was so much about them that were similar. He was tempted to tell Moot of his own dreams and his quest to find the answers to them, but decided it would not be fair to burden this man with more problems when he was having enough trouble facing his own. Neither did he want to give Moot false hope nor misleading ideas. He decided he would wait until he had been here longer and had a chance to look over the country and listen to more from the surrounding villages. He needed to be sure of his own mind before he could make any recommendations to others. Still, he felt he must say something in answer to Moot, who was also silent now, waiting for some reply from the Wise One.

"Moot has seen something of importance, of this I am sure. I intend to do what I can to help you find this land. But before I do something that might be foolish, I will think on it. I will talk with the People." Seeing the look of concern on the other man's face, he hurried to reassure him. "I will not speak to them of your dream, not yet. What would be the purpose? Most would not understand, not yet anyway. I think we will keep this counsel to ourselves for now, until we are ready to act on it."

Moot breathed a sign of relief. He had been right to trust this young man. Paataga had chosen well when she placed so much trust in this hairy young giant.

Kaoto knew he would stay here for as long as it took for him to make up his mind. He was deeply troubled by the way in which this problem had presented itself so swiftly. He had hoped for more time, but now realized that he would never have been ready. He would always have wanted more time. This was the reason Paataga had trained him and sent him out into the world. She had foreseen this happenstance and had known she would not be in condition to handle it. That was why he was here. There would be no more time for running and talking; there would be no more frontiers to see before he made a decision. Up until now, all his decisions had been child's play. Now he would be called on to live up to the name of the Wise One.

There were savages on both sides of the nation. There would be only one path open for his People. He knew he could not wait until he had gone to the north; he must make up his mind now. If what he had heard so far was true, and he had no reason to believe otherwise, then these People were too hard-pressed to wait longer. Somehow he must get a first hand look at these savage men. Moot assured him he would not have long to wait. They were on the move already and reports of small bands were coming in every day.

Kaoto rose from the seat he had taken near the edge of the parapet. Unconsciously he ducked his head as he stood, for the roof of the overhanging cliff was perilously close to his head. His gaze swept the empty land that stretched southward and he felt a cold chill up his spine, an unspeakable dread of what lay ahead for Moot and his People.

"What you search for is possible. Rather it is something that must be very real or else you would not have such vivid recollections of the land of your dreams." He turned and started toward the shaft that would lead them down to the lower levels and thus back to the ground. "We will work together to find out more of this promised land before we make up our minds what to do, but I think it would be wise to be prepared for whatever might happen in the near future."

Moot's dream troubled the Wise One more than he cared to admit. It seemed to confirm his own fear for the future of all the People.

Chapter Twenty One

Kaoto stayed with Moot much longer than he had anticipated, but his time was not wasted. He visited as many People in the area as he could, often running far afield and risking the deep snow on the rim in order to complete his rounds. He asked questions concerning the savages who threatened them. He talked little and listened much as they told him of their experiences with the roaming nomads. He learned from the local people that the savages would usually migrate farther south during the winter moons, evidently looking for more temperate weather. But as soon as the days became warm and fair they would return like the mosquitoes, only far more dangerous. It would seem they were also afraid of the darkness when the Spirit Watcher was not present to comfort or aid them. They were the most troublesome during early spring and late fall: in the spring because of a long winter of lean food supplies, and in the fall when the fields would yield a plentiful supply for them. They also seemed to shun the high country and preferred the lower lands.

As he traveled among the People, Kaoto encouraged them to plant more crops than usual. He warned them they must spread them out even farther apart and take advantage of any small area that would produce food and be harder to find. They must not use the same trail each time so there would be no give-away path leading to these small fields. He urged the hunters to bring in all the game they could. Instead of just hunting for the immediate need, he ask them to dry much more and preserve it for future use, using dried fruit and berries and packing it in the gut casings normally used for trail provision.

Among themselves, the People discussed the possibility that the Wise One was preparing them for a siege. Kaoto did not bother to tell them any differently. He did not know his own mind yet and was not prepared to try to explain to them the things he was not sure of.

During his past travels he had, true to his word, searched for and found capable women to send back to Paataga to be trained. Here in this far country he hesitated to send anyone so far from their village when there was so much unrest and danger, so he began training them himself. He gathered them in from the nearby villages, women and their mates, and taught them the rudiments of the history and what he could about decision-making. As Paataga had done with him, he encouraged their natural tendencies, and cultivated the wisdom they already possessed, rather than trying to instill new doctrines or ideas. Using the same principles of Paataga he would get them to talk, to ask him questions, and he would subtly make them find their own truths that would satisfy them in the days ahead. As soon as he was convinced they were ready, he would return them to their village. He told them to act in his behalf, explaining that in the near future he might not be present and they would have to act without him.

He recited the history to them, and although he did not expect them to remember it all, he was content that they would remember the main theme and be able to pass it on to others that would follow them. The history of the People must not be lost; it could not be retained by just one man such as himself. Now that there was a danger from the savages, it was necessary for more People to know of it. Some were gifted rememberers and could repeat the history nearly perfectly. He spent more time with them, giving them all the help he could.

When his pupils were ready to return to their villages, he would call them aside and tell them of his dream. He did not mention Moot's dreams because he had promised the man to respect his wishes on this. He did not try to explain the dream because he was not certain of it himself, and because it was not necessary for it to be explained. What he was trying to accomplish was to establish the dream sequence ahead of time, so when events began to transpire, the select few would recognize what was happening and feel confident. By knowing the future, they could handle it.

When he was not teaching, the Wise One was traveling the trails up and down along the rim, spreading advice about crops and other supplies. The people were puzzled, but promised to comply with his wishes as soon as spring arrived.

Finally the winter passed and spring returned to the land below the rim and began its slow climb up the rim to the high country above. The incense of blossoms filled the air and insects hummed in the warm rays of the Spirit Watcher. Moot warned Kaoto that this was the time of the normal return of the savages. Their arrival would be reported any day now.

Kaoto did not have long to wait. He was on his way back from a far western village late one afternoon. He knew he must hurry if he was going to make it back to Moot's village in time for the evening meal. He was running easily along a well-marked trail that followed the base of the cliff leading back up to the rim. Even though he had been warned repeatedly to be on the lookout for the savages, and even though they were always first on his mind, a lifetime of living without fear of living things had made him careless in spite of his best intentions.

He was just rounding a point of a steep cliff wall that projected out into the valley causing the trail to detour off its nearly straight path. As he came around the point, he came face to face with a small band of strange looking men. They were on the same trail, heading in the opposite direction, and were apparently as startled as he was. For a moment there was a frozen scene with each one of them coming to an abrupt halt, uncertain of his next move.

Kaoto was the first to regain his composure, and while he was not frightened, he was still poised and ready for any action. He held out his hand in the universal peace sign and stood his ground. The strange Indians did not seem inclined to be friendly as they fingered their weapons and waited for a sign from their leader. Kaoto had a slight advantage; he at least had been warned about what to expect. The savages, however, had never encountered such a giant of a man, even among themselves, and most certainly not among the little People who inhabited this land.

Kaoto was standing in the middle of the trail with the afternoon sun striking his back and making the hair on his body shine like a golden aura about him. It had the effect of magnifying his size and making him seem even more imposing than he was. They had always considered themselves to be the largest of men, much taller than the little farmers around here. They quickly took in his stature and the two eagle feathers he wore. This marked him as a man of distinction and power, a man worthy of their time and effort to capture or kill. Nor did they fail to note his long bow, much longer and more powerful than their own. This promise of strength was the only thing they might find to respect about him.

"Peace, brothers." Kaoto spoke and signed at the same time.

The leader sneered at this declaration. This tall one might be of another tribe, but he seemed to posses the same timid heart of the little farmers.

The leader puffed out his chest and managed a swagger as he signed his own intentions of traveling this trail and killing anyone that crossed his path. While Kaoto did not understand the guttural words spoken, there was no way he could misunderstand the tones or the signs the man made.

With speed that comes from a lifetime of practice, Kaoto swung his long bow off his shoulder, and in one smooth continuous motion nocked an arrow, drew it back and trained the point on the other man's throat. He did not need to sign his intentions; they were plain enough for the arrogant savages to understand. He was telling them that the boastful man in the lead who seemed to be speaking for them all was in danger of forfeiting his life for his foolish beliefs and intents.

The fact that the giant did not loose his arrow told them he did not want to kill them, but the long arrow also announced he was not going to be frightened of them like the little farmers were.

As one man they scrambled off the trail into the bushes and rocks scattered along the base of the cliff. Howls of pain reverberated along the face of the cliff as thorns and spikes tore their bodies in their mad flight.

The young hairy giant stood quite still. His bow remained drawn and his arrow was weaving back and forth over the area as if in search of a target. But none was to be found as quiet settled back over the trail.

Deep in the brush the savages were scowling and waiting for their leader to make the first move. This was a new tactic for them. The small farmers never drew an arrow to bow against them, but instead fled before them. This bought Kaoto some time, if not respect.

As the evening breeze ruffled the eagle feathers in his hair, Kaoto decided on his next move. He knew it would only be a short time until they would spread out and try to surround him and attack him from all sides at once. He was not a warrior, but common sense told him this was how they would think. It was much the same way his father and his friends hunted buffalo. There was no advantage to his position here in the middle of the trail, but just a few steps behind him all this could be changed. He took those few steps quickly backward and disappeared behind the outcropping of rock, which had blocked the trail. As soon as he was out of sight, he could hear the cries of anger and frustration as the savages bound back on the trail and prepared to give chase. This was more to their liking; this was what they were used to. This tall strange man would no doubt be a fast runner, but maybe they could run a relay on him and wear him down.

Kaoto did not waste his time running; although he was sure he could easily out distance them with very little effort. Instead he took advantage of his memory. He knew the backside of the projection was steep, but not sheer like the front side. A determined man could climb it, and a determined man could easily defend the top of the projection from anyone below. This way he would have time to study his attackers without danger from them and their ineffectual short bows. The top of the rock would be a long shot for even his long bow. On the other hand, he could easily stop them from following him by simply rolling rocks at them. Their superior number would not help them now.

Slipping his bow back over his shoulder, he leaped up the face of the rock, catching hold of every handhold and piece of brush in his path, anything that would offer him purchase as he climbed rapidly to the top. The sharp turn in the trail temporarily hid his actions from the savages, who were cautiously approaching the turn. They wanted to be sure he was running down the trail, not standing back with his bow drawn waiting for them to come into sight. They were sure his long bow would carry far enough to kill at a long distance.

The first one leaped around the projection and crouched to one side of the trail. A look of disappointment crossed his face when he saw the trail was empty. The look changed to cunning as he realized the stranger might not have run; he might be hiding somewhere nearby and still be a threat. When he heard Kaoto's efforts as he climbed the bare face of the rock, he looked up and let loose a howl of glee. They had their victim trapped. There was no escape except back down the way he had gone up.

Kaoto, however, was not concerned about his position. They could not reach him in the daylight and he could easily defend himself. According to what he had heard, they would not linger to fight after dark. Kaoto did not know of their fear of being killed in the dark and being forced to wander the nether world in darkness forever. To the Wise One, it did not matter why. It was enough that after darkness he could safely continue on his way without fear of them. If they decided to camp nearby, he would worry about that when the time came.

The savages spread out at the base of the projection. They could see there was no other way down and it seemed impossible to continue upward. They soon worked themselves into a state of ecstatic frenzy over the prospect of the man trapped alone.

Seemingly unmindful of the howling savages below, the giant stood on a sharp point of rock overlooking them and with a cool, unconcerned detachment relieved his straining bladder downward toward them. He had not thought of it as an insult; it was just a call of nature that he felt needed attention now that he had time. The effect on the savages was more than he had expected as they went into a fit of rage, shooting arrow after arrow up at him.

He had been correct in his assumption that their short bows could not send an arrow this high, so he had nothing to worry about from this direction. When he had finished his nature call, he slipped his own bow from his shoulder and fitted an arrow to his string. Still as calm as if he were target practicing, he let the arrow fly. It landed almost between the feet of the leader of the pack.

The savage stared at the arrow with stoic detachment. Showing no sign of fear, he picked the arrow from the ground and, with a calm equal to his tall tormentor, held it over his head in both hands and broke the shaft in half. He threw the pieces from him in disdain.

Kaoto drew another arrow and let if fly. The Spirit Watcher must have been pleased with Kaoto this day. The second arrow hit in the same spot as his first, the point entering the same hole in the ground. This was too much for the savage leader. He could plainly see that the tall man could place his arrows where he wanted them. He could pick them off one at a time at his leisure with no danger to himself, and they were powerless to stop him. All they could do was retreat and make more noise.

The group pulled back and gathered out of range of the deadly shafts and entered into a heated argument with one another. Apparently the leader was in favor of moving on, while some of the others wanted to stay and attempt to dislodge the tall one. The tide of the argument went back and forth without their coming to any conclusion.

On an impulse, no doubt inspired by his youth and curiosity, Kaoto released one more arrow. He knew the range was extreme but it was downhill and the breeze had died. Hearing a high-pitched whine of the incoming arrow, the group scattered, with the exception of the leader. He stood staunchly and watched the arrow arch out over the treetops and fall nearly straight down. Once again, the arrow struck within a hand span of the leader's feet.

He did not touch the arrow this time. He raised his fist skyward in a threat to Kaoto, who understood the meaning well. The leader was looking forward to meeting the tall one again sometime, sometime when they would be on more equal terms. Turning without haste or a backward glance, he walked down the trail to the west and joined the rest of his small band. They soon vanished from sight, leaving the Wise One alone with his thoughts.

Darkness fell with Kaoto still standing on the projecting rock. He had come seeking an answer to his dream, especially the portion that dealt with the dark shadows that seem to offer a threat to his People. Now it was no longer a dream. The shadows were real and he had met the reality face to face this day.

Chapter Twenty Two

Kaoto stayed on through the summer with Moot. The savages became bolder than before and Moot and his People spent more of their time in the cliff house, not trusting to luck for protection any longer.

The Spirit of Rain was helpful and their crops were plentiful. Even with the savages raiding their fields they were able to produce a surplus from the hidden fields. The hunters brought in more meat. The women and the elderly kept fires going under the drying racks. When the meat was dried it was ground to powder and stored in gut casings. Some of their efforts were lost to raiding savages, but still they were able to build up a supply such as no living man could remember.

Kaoto continued to travel among the People, but he was much more cautious. He kept his eyes alert for invaders, knowing his luck would not always keep him safe as it had the first time he encountered them. Having at last confronted his enemies and finding them to be men, not shadows, had one advantage. They were real, they were something the People could see and understand. His task would not be easy, but at least it would be a positive action taken against men, not elusive shadows.

Summer passed and fall was rapidly drawing to an end when he once more summoned the local rulers to Moot's village. With the dawn of the new moon, a large gathering assembled during the night in the upper level of the cliff house. It consisted of rulers and their elders, and many runners. The rulers and their elders were seated in a semi-circle around the fire pit. The runners took any space left over. Kaoto wanted as many of them present as were able to be there because they were the ones who would carry his word to the rest of the villages.

The Wise One appeared before them dressed only in a breechcloth. He stood by the parapet wall, alone. He felt more alone than he ever had before in his life. Even the death of Little Frog paled with the prospects he faced here. On his young shoulders rested the lives of many of his People, possibly all of his People in time. He had sworn to help, serve, and protect them. Now he must do it.

He knew these men would not question his judgment. They knew the danger that faced them and would accept what he said as a revelation from the Spirit Watcher. They would follow his advice and counsel as if it had come from on high.

Aside from the runners, he was the youngest man present. All of the rulers and elders were his senior by many summers. Some could boast at least twice his twenty summers, yet they were waiting for the Wise One to speak to them. To advise them. They did not see a young man in front of them. Instead they saw a representative of the Spirit Watcher. They were sure when he opened his mouth the words he spoke would not be his own, but would come directly from the Spirit Watcher.

Kaoto knew this was not true. He had received no instructions from the spirits, although he had called on them to come to his aid. He was reminded again of Paataga's comparison of men and ants. Were the spirits aware of the problem facing him? Did they care about what was happening to the People? If they did, they had not given him any sign of their awareness.

While the group waited, Kaoto stood looking out across the vast expanse to the south. The Spirit Watcher had just started his walk across the sky, and although it was still early morning, the heat waves were shimmering over the desert, leaving a hazy, impenetrable curtain hanging in the air. Turning at last, he squared his shoulders and raised his head. He hoped to convey a confidence he did not feel and was sure he did not possess. From within the darkened space, the People could see him silhouetted against the morning light. His tall frame made a most impressive figure.

"Brothers. I would speak to you." Complete silence greeted him. He had their undivided attention. "I must tell you things which make my heart heavy, and I am sure they will sadden you also." He looked around at them, almost hoping for a scoffer or unbeliever, but there were none here. Every man was waiting for his words, words that would be a death sentence to most of them. Although his voice was low, it carried clearly to each one present.

"The time has come for you to take action. You cannot wait any longer." He paced back and forth in the narrow space left for him between the fire pit and the parapet. The silence hung heavily over the gathering as they waited for him to continue.

"Moot has told me of his dream. I suspect from visiting with the rest of you and listening to you talk that many, if not all, of you have also had similar dreams but have not felt free to discuss them with me or anyone else." The solemn nods from around the circle confirmed that his guess was accurate.

"I am here to tell you that what you dream is not a fantasy. It is real. I too have had a dream." He went on to tell them at least a portion of his dream. He told them of the part where he sat on high and called for the People to return to the land of little earth. He described the land they must search for, and again he saw recognition in more than one pair of eyes. He did not tell them about the burning sand or of the scattered bones. He did not think this would help them or make their decision to follow his plan any easier. He was still in great doubt of the meaning of this part of his dream. He could hardly expect them to understand what he did not.

"In spite of all the raids of the past summer, you have all been able to raise large crops. The hunter's success has made it possible for your women to lay by great stores of meat. Now the summer is over, the harvest is done, and winter is near to hand." They knew all of this, but still they listened as if it were part of a revelation. A good speaker was expected to build to a climax. They knew their Wise One was leading up to something. Most of them had been speculating all summer as to what his plan would be. Many thought they already knew, but they were wrong. They could not suspect how far they were from the truth.

"The savages are beginning to retreat to wherever they go in the winter, and we will be untroubled by them for a short time. Now we must watch for a sign from the weather." He directed their attention to a bank of dark clouds moving in from the west.

"Here is what you must do." Every man watched Kaoto's face in this moment of truth. They not only wanted to hear, they wanted to see and feel his decision. "You must leave this place and go in search of the place in your dreams. Each village must go on its own way, in small groups, so as not to attract too much attention, and to spread out the food supply in your paths." He paused to wipe the sweat from his brow. Even though the air under the overhang was cool, the Wise One was laboring heavily with his interpretation of what was expected of him and his People. His next words ended their suspense.

"You must leave your homes forever. You can never return."

A low sigh escaped each member of the gathering. This was far worse than they had thought. They were prepared for a long siege or maybe learning to do battle. At the worst they had thought they might be asked to move up on the rim until the threat had passed. Then they could return to their homes and live life as usual. But now he was telling even those who lived up on the rim that they, too, must go. Leave their homes forever, never to return. This was a lot to ask of them, but he was not really asking. It was more like he was telling them and they knew they must listen. The Spirit Watcher did not warn his People twice, nor did he bargain with men. He spoke, and they could ignore him at their peril. The Wise One spoke on.

"You will pack all the food you can carry, every man, woman and child. You will leave nothing behind to comfort the enemy. What you cannot take with you, you will burn or bury." Each word he spoke was more appalling than the one before. Even worse, there was no room for challenge or debate. This was reality being presented to them, and the faces around the fire pit became grim. A mistiness was evident in almost every eye.

"You will travel at night whenever you can and rest during the day. At first you must do this because of the threat of being discovered. Later you will do this because the heat of the day will become almost unendurable and the nights will be so cold you will be glad to be up and moving about. The days will be hot and will dry the moisture from your bodies, leaving your bones in the dust."

He stopped suddenly. Was this what he had seen in his dream? Was he sending them to certain death? He passed his hand in front of his eyes as if trying to recall what he had just said. He waited for his dream to make itself known, but the dream did not come and he had to go on. If this is what he saw, then it must happen, although he was still awash with doubts.

"The travel will be dangerous and difficult, but it is the only way to save our People. We cannot fight these men. We are not warriors. We cannot learn the art of war in a few days and win against those who have lived it since the day of their birth. If we stay and fight, we all die. If we go south, many of you will die on the trail, but some will live to reach the land beyond the desert which you have all dreamed of."

He stopped and waited to see if any man among them wished to speak. He almost would welcome their arguments, but none of them would contest the word of the Wise One. After all, the spirits inspired him, and they were simple men who had no connections with the spirit world. True, this was more serious than they had ever thought. They had thought their dreams were just old men's dreams of a promised land. None of them had been willing to pack up and leave their homes on the strength of these dreams. Yet Kaoto was talking about their dreams. It gave credence to what he said when they stopped to think about it. The spirits had tried to warn them in advance. They had just not listened. They should have known this was going to happen some day. Did any of them honestly think the savages would ever move on and leave them in peace?

They had the privilege to have the guidance of the Wise One and did not have to rely on their own judgment. They should be thankful for this, at least. Now they knew they were doing the right thing. But the Wise One was not through talking yet.

"The journey will be long. You will not make it in one summer, or in two summers. It will be many summers before the trip is done. Most of you seated here will not live long enough to see the end of it, but your children will." At last Kaoto's dream began to make sense to him. The old would die and vanish in the desert, but the children, bone of their bone, would survive and be reunited in the land of little earth. Not much comfort to those gathered before him.

"The first summer you must not stop to plant corn or squash. They take too long to grow. You must push on using what you carry sparingly and gathering as much along the way as possible. There will be strange plants and animals for you to learn to use and live on, but it is what you must do. The second summer you will be able to stop and plant to raise food. But come harvest time you must pack up and move on again, always heading as near south as the land will allow. In time you will meet more savages. They will not be friendly. They will be even more savage than the ones here. The land they live is narrow and you will soon pass through it and be free of them." Kaoto was amazed to hear himself speaking these words. He knew nothing of the land to the south or of the People who lived there. He had never traveled in that direction and in his travels he had never heard anyone speak of any tribes to the south. Perhaps the Spirit Watcher had heard his call for help, after all, and was actually speaking through him, just as these men believed. Whatever was happening, he felt compelled to go on.

"You will send out scouts by day to find a safe passage through this country. The rest of you will travel by night, following the trail marked by your scout. You must be very careful as you travel to leave no sign of your passage. Once through this land of the fierce People you will come to a barren land without any People and few animals. When you have given up hope of ever seeing man again, you will come to a land of a different People. These people will be very much like you are. They are not warriors, nor are they savages. They are relatives of our distant past. They will not welcome you. They will not be glad to see you, but they will not drive you away. When you reach this land you must break up your villages and each family must scatter in different directions and make your homes among them."

He waited as a low moan went up from around the fire. Family was of first importance to them, but second came their bond with the village. A village was made up of a close-knit family group. The daughters of a family, when they picked their mates, usually built an addition next to their parents' house. Young men would most often be from neighboring villages. To break up the village ties was to break up a large family. How much could be expected of them? But the Wise One spoke on.

"You will have to settle for poor sections of land. You will have to work harder to make a living for yourselves. You may have to eat weeds and bugs to stay alive, but you will not starve, and the children will live. They will mate with the children of this new land, and in time they will all be one People, as it should be." He had to give them some hope, something to cling to, some reason beyond just their own survival or fear.

"Remember," he told them, "all the time you are traveling and suffering, it is for the children. They are the ones who have a chance. We do not. If this was just for yourselves, you might be tempted to stop short of your goal. You might find a place where you could live out your life, but there would be nothing to protect your children." His eyes flashed. "They must live." When he stopped speaking, the silence lingered on. The only noise was the deep sighs escaping from the old men as they accepted his words. Moot was the first to break this silence.

"Doing something, even though it is hard and bitter, is better than doing nothing. We will go as you say. But you said we must watch for a sign from the weather. How will we know what to watch for?"

As if in answer to his question, the dark clouds were split with an enormous display of lightning followed by equally large rolls of thunder. Kaoto did not have to speak. He, like them, looked at the approaching cloudbank as it crossed the open sky and closed with the sun. Moot hung his head in sorrow as he again acted as spokesman for the gathering.

"It would seem the time is upon us. We must not delay. Return to your villages and do what you must do, as I will be doing the same here."

The group rose and each man in turn, according to his age, came to Kaoto to take his wrist in their hand, laying their other hand on his shoulder. It was a salute of a man to another man. Kaoto returned the warm salute with steady eyes, although his heart was breaking for them. Each ruler dropped his eye contact in recognition of Kaoto's rank as the Wise One. When the runners gathered around him, he prepared to give them his instructions.

"Travel the rim after dark. You must not fall to the enemy. The lives of many of our People depend on you. As for my words, do not try to remember them all. I am afraid I became quite long winded indeed, and forgot you would try to remember it all. I, too, was once a runner, and I always dreaded the wordy rulers who would weigh you down with their long speeches." This was met with smiles as they all could relate to his words. Among them they each knew of at least one ruler who was over fond of the sound of his own voice and could not resist the temptation to become an orator whenever he sent out a runner.

"Just carry the meat of my word, leave the hide and bones for the wind to carry. If any man doubts you, return to me and I will come to him personally." He released them and they filed out to leave him alone with Moot, who waited for a word in private with Kaoto.

"Will you be traveling with my village?" He asked hopefully.

"No. I will remain here. I will want to be here in case any of the runners return for me. I had also thought I would keep a fire going with much smoke to make the savages who still might be around think you were still living here. If they come and find you gone, they might try to follow you and you would be helpless. There is no way you could outrun them with the old, the children, and all with heavy packs. Besides, there are still many more People left for me to warn. I must spread the word of the coming savages. I fear they will sweep the land before them, leaving nothing or no one in their path. Sometime soon all the People will face the same decision you now face, and they must be prepared to make the same trip you are making." Moot's wrinkled face reflected his gloom over the prospects ahead of them all.

"Since I cannot be with you, you must learn to honor the women I have trained to take my place. Revere them as you do me. They will be the most valuable link with your past. It is only through them that our children will be able to remember our history and be able to remember who they are."

It saddened Moot's heart to leave the Wise One alone to face the enemy while they were in effect running south to hide. He had come to like this tall young man who was so covered with golden hair. He had begun to think of him as a son as well as a Wise One.

"I will miss you, my son, for you have been like a son to me. When you return to your own village, tell your father that Moot was pleased to have his son for a guest."

Kaoto was deeply moved by these words. After spending such a lonely boyhood and an even more lonely early manhood, it was a great tribute and comfort to be so received. His voice softened as he spoke to the old man who stood before him with his broken heart.

"If ever I see Maata again, I will tell him your words and of your kindness to his son. He will be very pleased to hear such words from such a man as Moot. But I do not have a village anymore. The entire nation is my village, and I must go to them all before I can even consider returning to the dwelling of my father. Go now, Moot, and know that the Spirit Watcher will be with you. Be of stout heart. Do not yield to the temptation to return here when things do not go well with you on your journey. Your dream is a true dream. You must follow it until you reach the land of your dream, or die trying. Prepare a young man to take your place. Do not count on your elders to replace you. They will die on the trail also. Be sure the young man is as loyal to the People as you have been all these summers. Be sure he will lead them on in your absence."

By late afternoon the storm had broken in full fury, heralding the start of winter. In the first darkness of night Moot led his People from their homes. They were almost staggering under their loads of supplies. Even the children were quiet and solemn as they shifted their heavy, unfamiliar packs, trying to find a comfortable spot for them. Many paused to look back with anguish at their homes of a lifetime. Moot, however, did not hesitate or falter as he set his face steadfastly to the south and began the journey to an unseen goal. The land of his dream.

Kaoto sat on the parapet and watched them leave. He was still seated in the same place to greet the Spirit Watcher when he arose the next morning. The storm had passed quickly and left the air cool and clear. Far to the south, Kaoto could see a tiny chain moving across the open wasteland. He knew it was Moot and his village. They were taking advantage of the cool morning air to make a little more distance before they would hole up for the day in some secluded wash or canyon.

They seemed so tiny, so little and defenseless out in the vast reaches of the dried waste. Kaoto felt a tug at his breast for the forlorn travelers, leaving everything they knew and loved behind them forever. He was a man, but he could weep for his People. He turned his eyes up towards the Spirit Watcher and asked of him, "Have I been in time? Tell me, Spirit Watcher. You do not have to care about them or me, but from where you sit, can you see as I did in my dream? Can you see the past and the future from there? Did I do the right thing? Did I come in time, or am I too late?" His voice dropped to a whisper. "I fear I have been too slow. I fear they will perish out there and it will be my fault. I fear I have sent them to a horrible death for no cause other than my pride."

There was no answer. He had not expected one. He had spoken to relieve his tortured soul of the pain he was feeling for the wandering People he had sentenced to a lifetime of searching for his elusive dream. They would roam for the rest of their lives over the vast stretch of land between here and the land of little earth. Had he done the right thing? Did he have the right to send them to their deaths just to save the children? It was a heavy weight for such a young man to carry, but in his heart he knew it was the only thing he could have done. The only decision left open to him. It had to be. The worst part was knowing he would never live long enough to know what the outcome would be. He would never know if they reached the land, or if in fact it even existed, as he believed it did.

An arrow struck the face of the cliff dwelling. The harmless missile left only a faint scratch where it hit. It did serve to bring the dreamer back to the present state of being. Looking down, he saw the face of the same savage who had taunted him previously on the trail. There was a gleam of satisfaction in the savage man's eyes as he surveyed the empty village at the base of the cliff. He had his victim trapped again and this time he would have the advantage. He could set up a camp here and wait for the tall one to come out. He would not let him get away as he had the last time. He withheld his desire to shout. Something about the quiet dignity of the tall one stopped him from making an empty threat.

The situation was more equal this time, although the tall one was still out of his reach and out of range of their arrows. He would take all the time that was necessary and enjoy every bit of it. He would let the tall one sweat and worry until hunger and thirst drove him out of his hole and into their hands.

He slapped one hand on his chest and then threw it out and up in the manner of a salute, but his jeering face belied the intent of the action.

Kaoto returned the salute, solemnly, with the same dignity he would show to any of his own People. His situation was hopeless. It was only a matter of time, but time was what he was here to buy. Time for the villagers to slip far enough away that the savages would not be able to follow them. He had asked the Spirit Watcher about time; maybe this was his answer. Anyway, he would use all the time he could to the best advantage. He was glad he had acted on Moot's last piece of advice to him.

"Pull up the ladder, Kaoto. You never know when you might have unexpected visitors."

Chapter Twenty Three

He counted the enemies who were camped below him. They numbered the same as his fingers on both hands. There were no women in this group and they all appeared to be very young men, not much older than himself.

The difference between the savages and the People was noticeable in several ways besides the obvious difference in their appearance. They had a completely different attitude. The People were happy by their very nature and wore their happiness on their faces for all to see. The savages, however, went about with perpetual scowls and did not appear to enjoy anything. They fought amongst themselves over trivial matters.

The first day they destroyed the village at the base of the cliff. They searched for food, but Moot had been thorough and they did not find anything of value. This made them angrier. Now they must send out hunters to provide for them all. This caused more dissension among them. None of them wanted to go away and risk missing the kill.

Kaoto could not understand their tongue, but he could understand their tones and actions. They made it plain with sign and gesture what they planned to do with him once he had been captured. None of it was pleasant, but he did not fear them; he had no intention of being captured. He had a good food supply and there was a tiny pool of water that seeped from the back wall of the cliff. It had been channeled into a large bowl. There was enough water to sustain him all winter if need be. He thought he would be able to live more comfortably than they would, which only added to their chagrin.

He spent most of the day on the parapet watching their activities and making mental notes on how they lived and how they apparently thought. He did not try to communicate with them, and though they were constantly taunting him and making obscene gestures, he chose to ignore them.

On the third morning he caught sight of a movement on the rim off to his left. Watching closely, he recognized one of the runners he had sent out earlier. He imagined the runner had returned so he could join Moot and the villagers.

"Go back," he called with his hands cupped to his mouth. The lone runner stood stone still looking over the situation below. "It is a trap," Kaoto called to him. "There are many savages here. Go, run, be free." He watched with satisfaction as the runner drew back before the savages could locate him. There was no reason to endanger another life needlessly.

His enemies had learned their lesson from their first encounter with the tall, hairy one and made their camp far back beyond the reach of the arrows from his long bow. He had already demonstrated his proficiency with the weapon. They tried to entice him into wasting some of his arrows, but he did not respond or even pick up his weapon.

At night, even though the savages feared death in the dark, they kept the fires going and took turns keeping watch. This caused more disagreement among, them and quarrels were frequent and often bloody.

They soon discovered that their taunts and insults were not going to dislodge Kaoto and they became weary of waiting for hunger and thirst to drive him out to them. They tried a new approach. Pulling all the timbers from the razed village and gathering as much wood as possible, they built and maintained a fire directly under him, risking his deadly arrows. The cliff house was encased in adobe so it would not burn, but they hoped to drive him out with either the intense heat or smoke. He would either come down to them or roast alive. Either way was all right with them.

Kaoto remained at his post on the parapet and watched them with interest. He did not attempt to shoot at them, although they were ridiculously easy targets. The fire raged up toward his level but the air current under the cliff carried the heat and smoke harmlessly past his position, and if anything it increased the flow of cool air. The heat became so great on the rocks below that he could hear them crack. He could see flakes pop from their surfaces. Soon the rocks were black and every hole or cave around the cliff was also covered with soot, a reminder for centuries to come of the infamy of their deed. All day and all night they kept the fire going without any noticeable effect on the prisoner at the top of the parapet. Seeing him watching them undisturbed only infuriated the savages more. They became desperate to take him captive and several of them took another course.

After the fire died down, they made a rush on the cliff house with an improvised ladder. It was too short to reach to the opening at the base of the cliff house, which was sealed from inside. They still tried to climb beyond the ladder, grappling around the side of the dwelling, finding hand holds here and there, which slowly brought them closer to where Kaoto stood watching. Something inside the Wise One snapped. His anger, which he had kept in check up to this point, burst forth in a scream that was equal to their savagery.

"Ayiee!" he screamed down at them as he broke off bits of the wall and hurled it down at them. It did very little to hamper them. In fact it encouraged them because he did not produce his fearful longbow and equally long arrows.

"Savage beasts. You think you can climb up and just take me?" he taunted them now. "Your minds must be made of clay. You think you can climb up and take me like a baby bird from the nest? Maybe it is time you learned what kind of bird you are trying to catch." He picked up his bow and leaned his arrows against the wall. "This bird eats snakes like you for his dinner. He has a sharp beak and talons. If you insist on bothering me, you will feel them." When he had first cried out, the climbers had stopped, but now they started up again, desperately trying to reach him.

Kaoto stopped shouting. He stopped throwing debris at the savage men. Instead, with cold, deliberate movements, he released an arrow, followed in quick succession by two more. At this range he did not even have to aim; it was impossible to miss such large targets. The top three men fell to the valley floor, each with a long arrow running length-wise of their bodies. They did not rise or cry out. Those left on the ladder jumped down and scurried away from the rain of death. No more arrows followed them. The tall hairy giant stood looking sky-ward as if they were no longer there.

For the first time in his life, Kaoto had taken the life of a human. His first reaction had been one of fierce elation; that was why he had sent down the last two arrows. He had felt a surge of power raging through his veins. He had taken their lives as easily as he could crush an ant. This feeling was immediately swept away and replaced with a feeling of revulsion and sickness, both of mind and body. He had dropped his weapons and looked to the sky.

"Spirit Watcher! Hear me!" he cried to the sun in his anguish. "I have killed men today. Are they also your creatures? Do you care that they died? Do you care about anything?" His voice lowered, but his eyes remain cast to the sky. "Can you see me down here as I can see you? Or am I so small and you are so big and so far away that you cannot see us at all? Surely you know what I have just done." His breath came in great racking sobs as he was overcome with emo-tions. His head drooped and his voice became even lower.

"Why have you forsaken me? Why have you made me take the life of other men?" His voice rose again as he looked once more at the sky. "It sickens me." He screamed once more. "This is not what I trained for at the feet of Paataga. I am not a warrior; I am a man, just as they are men. If you care for these men, and for me, then take them away from here, or I must kill them all."

He did not consider this a boast; it was a fact. He knew he could and would kill them if they did not leave him in peace. He had done what he had set out to do. He had bought Moot some time. Now he could not only give Moot time, he could give him security from these men, at least. With their deaths the route of Moot would be lost.

He stood near the edge of the parapet as he talked. His voice carried to the savages below. They could not understand his words, but they knew he was distraught. They pulled farther back from the swift and sure death of his long bow. They would wait a little longer. Time was on their side. To them it sounded as if he was going mad, and while this held them in awe, it was not enough to make them want to let him go free. They listened as he continued to talk to the sky.

"Spirit Watcher. We are not ants; we are men. We think like men, we are able to feel. We are able to talk and you can hear and understand us. Hear me then. Take these cursed People from me. You know I have a mission to com-plete. Did you not send me on this mission? I cannot sit here all winter. I must go on."

The savages were so engrossed with their prospective quarry they did not see the movement behind them. Even Kaoto did not see what transpired until it was almost over. The savage men had no enemy to fear; they were not watching their backs. They had seen no sign of the little men who lived here, and even if they had they would not have feared them.

The band of small men came running swiftly, approaching them from one side and to the rear. Each man carried a short but powerful bow and a handful of arrows. Around each man's neck hung a piece of buffalo hide with the symbol or a running man burned deep into it.

The runners gave a burst of speed as they came within range of the savage men. As one voice they gave a piercing cry, which caused the savages to turn to face them just in time to see the first man loose his arrow and speed on by out of range down the trail. He was closely followed by another, and yet another.

Seven men lay dead or dying in the dust in the same number of heart-beats. Not one of them had had time to draw a bow or loose and an arrow. Kaoto's brotherhood of the runners had returned to give aid to one of their own, not the Wise One, but to a fellow runner in trouble. Kaoto dropped down his ladder and was soon on the ground among them, speechless at what he had just witnessed. These men had killed just as he had killed.

"Brothers. I am glad to see you and thankful for your help, but I am sorry you had to taste the same bitterness that I did." He gripped each man by hand and shoulder. "You have done a brave thing and I thank you for the sacrifice."

"Could we do less?" one of the runners answered. Kaoto recognized him as one of the runners from this village. It was the same one he had warned earlier on the rim. He was called Mute.

"Are we not sworn to help a fellow runner whenever he needs us? Would you have done less for us?" he asked.

"We knew you stayed here and we know why you took the risk. What we have done is no more than what you have done for the People of the village. By staying here, you have given our village a chance to escape," said yet another.

Kaoto regarded his fellow runners with respect and pride. All were young men, and the tallest among them did not come to his shoulder. Yet they had proven their bravery and courage as well as their devotion to their brothers in the charge they had made in his defense. Size did not make a man; his actions were what counted.

"I owe you my life and for that I thank you, but I still am sorry that you had to kill to spare me."

"We heard you tell the Spirit Watcher of your grief. Is it true this is the first time you have had to kill a man?" Mute asked.

"Yes. I have never hurt another human before this," he answered in sorrow.

"Then we can understand your feelings," Mute told him. "We are not as fortunate as those deeper in the nation. We have had to kill before. It is not a new feeling to us. But we understand how it feels to kill a man for the first time, or any time after that. It causes a sickness in the heart and the belly. It is different than killing an animal for food, but it must be done. These men do not

176 - Norman D. Messenger

understand our ways or us, and they do not respect us. They scorn us for what they would call a weakness when we do not fight back."

"They have no regard for human life as we do. I have seen them kill their own kind," said yet another. They were trying to comfort him by revealing something they had not told most other men, only the new runners.

"Then maybe I was wrong to send our People away. Maybe they could have become warriors just as you have. I have not heard of the necessity of killing before. It is not spoken of by any of the rulers I have met since I came here."

"We do not speak of it to other men. Only those of us who have had to do it know of our killing. It is something we tell new runners before they go out. It is not something we are proud of, but it is something we must sometimes do," Mute told him.

The other runners nodded their heads in solemn agreement. They were an elite band; they fulfilled their obligations as runners without complaint. Somewhere along the line it had become necessary for them to defend themselves if they were to continue to dispatch the messages given them. In defending themselves, they had to kill. The word had been passed on to each new generation of runners and the secret was taken with them when they left the service. None of them knew when the first runner had had to kill. It was not recorded. But now they accepted it as a way of life. Kaoto could understand the need but was filled with sorrow for the carefree life of the runner that had to be cast aside in this land.

"You were not wrong, Wise One. Our People could never become the savages these men are nor would we want them to be so. We kill when we feel we have to, just as we did here today, but we could never attain their relish for killing and torture."

"Torture? You have seen this?" Kaoto asked.

"Yes. Let me tell you of things I have seen them do." Mute said. "Once, I saw them cut the heart and liver from a wounded man, while he yet lived. Then they ate these organs, raw, and became like wild animals, running and dancing in a frenzy."

Another runner picked up the tale with a recount of his own experiences with the savages. "Their women are probably worse than their men. I have seen women torture a man to death, then cut up his body like a butchered animal. They would run around screaming and carrying pieces they had hacked off, like they were a prize. Mothers would rub their breast with fresh blood before allowing the young to suckle. The babies are raised with the taste of blood mixed with mother's milk. No. Our People could never compete with them, and we are glad."

"But if you can learn to kill without turning into beasts, why could not the rest of our People do the same?" Kaoto asked. "At least they could learn to protect themselves and their families; they would not have to leave their homes."

Mute studied Kaoto's face for a moment before he spoke. As before, he was speaking for all of them.

"Will you ever be the same man you were before you killed? You have had the feeling, both the desire to kill again and the dread of the thought of it. Would you want our People to live like that? Would you have your father or mother go through what you have just suffered?"

"No. I can see what you are saying, but I do wish I could honor you among the People. They should know of your sacrifice."

"None of our People know. We have told no one but the other runners. It is a secret kept among us. We would rather it remained a secret. Someday maybe we will not have to kill and men can go back to being men again." Mute impressed Kaoto with his wisdom, and he wished he had time to train him, but thought he was probably of more value here than anywhere else.

"Your secret shall remain a secret with me. Perhaps it is best this way. But now what will you do? You have my permission to go join your villages on their trail south. They may have need of someone with your skills before their journey is over."

"No, Wise One. We will not join them. Once we have tasted the blood of our enemies we can never be one of the People again. We have forfeited the right to ever mate or raise children, lest they too should desire blood."

"Then what will you do?"

"We will stay in this area. Not every village will do as you ask. Not yet, at least. We will serve as runners for them and try to spare other young men of our plight." Once more, Mute spoke for them all as they nodded their heads in agreement. It was plain to Kaoto that this was not something they had just thought of. Evidently they had talked this over among themselves before. He could see the wisdom of Mute's words. They could still be a great service to the People who remained.

Looking over the wreckage of the village and the bodies of the slain savages, Kaoto now felt the uncleanness Mute spoke of, and while he was still sick at heart, he knew he must put his life back together and go on with his life and his mission. There was still much to do. Moot and the surrounding villages were only a small portion of the vast nation. He must continue on and do as he had sworn he would; that is to visit every village and warn them, even if the danger to them was not yet immediate. He knew now that it would only be a matter of time until everyone would be faced with the same situation as Moot and his People.

But first he would clean up this desecration. With disgust and revulsion he grasped one of the slain savages by a leg and proceeded to drag him away from the scene. He pulled the body over to a ravine deep enough to hide the body and rolled the dead man over the bank. The runners gathered the others and did the same. When the last trace of blood had been kicked into the dust, when all the tracks had been swept away, when all the weapons were broken and deposited with the late owners, only then did Kaoto turn to leave. The runners led him away from the once peaceful valley and headed up toward the rim and the more secure high country.

The Wise One was sure that Moot and his villagers were now out of danger from anyone from this tribe. What they might run into farther south was out of his hands. He had done all he could to buy them time. Only the Spirit Watcher would know their fate from here on out.

He had spent one whole summer with Moot and his People, and while he did not regret his time here, he knew he must not waste any more time in this area. Once safely back from the rim he stopped and gave the runners his final instructions.

"Spread out and cover as much territory as you can. Use your own judgment as to what you tell the rulers about what has happened here to day. Whatever you do, you must convince them that the danger is real and it will come to them soon. It is up to them whether they follow the path south, or retreat farther north into the forest. Either way, the time will come when they will have no choice other than going south. The sooner they get started, the more children they will save. I am sure the danger is on all sides of the nation and our world will get smaller with every passing day. Do the best you can. It is all that can be asked of you."

The Wise One left the runners with these words and started his own long journey. He would work his way to the north, with many stops in between.

Chapter Twenty Four

Kaoto moved steadily northward, visiting every village in his line of travel. This led him away from the desert and the low lands below the rim. The farther he went, the less he heard of the savages. The main concern here was the lack or rain and the poor crops that they could raise in this dry climate. It was the same everywhere he went. Each village had at least one elder who could tell him of the old days when it was green and fresh, when rains were to be depended on and a man could not help but raise a crop. But now the rains failed and the corn withered on the stock before it was mature enough to harvest. The pumpkins and squash shriveled on the vine, and the bugs ate them faster than they could grow. The animals were growing more scarce and harder to find. Life was not easy these days. The lament for the old days and the times of plenty was heard everywhere Kaoto went.

His counsel to these villages was the same as it had been to those in the south. "Go south to the land of little earth. Go, now, before it is too late." They would listen respectfully, but they remained noncommittal.

"There is a land a long journey to the south. Many have already left to go there. It is a land much as you remember. There is rain there, the plants grow well there; it is a land of plenty. You must make up your minds soon. If you wait, it will be too late."

"We know times are bad, but we will manage. There are better summers coming. We have not heard of these savages you talk about. Why should we leave out homes because of some rumors? We are sorry for the People to the south of us, but we do not have a problem such as you tell us they had." It was the same answer in every village. He tried to explain to them.

"I have seen these savages and tried to deal with them. They are not rumors. They are real. They will come to your village and when they do, you will not be able to stop them. They will not talk of trade with you. They will raid and kill to take what they want. Moot had some protection in his cliff house. You have none." The elders would listen and wag their heads and ask him when all this would happen.

"They may not come this summer or even the next, but believe me, they will come. The longer you wait, the worse it will become. Right now there are only a few scattered bands of them between you and the south land, but the same dry summers that you complain of are just as bad for them. They will push this way, looking for more fields to raid, more animals to hunt. By the time they get to you here, there will be many more of them for you to try get through. Do not wait until they are pounding on your door. By then it will be too late. Leave now. This afternoon, this season, do not wait for another summer."

Still they were not convinced. They could not believe there were people as violent and blood thirsty as the men he told of. No one in their village had seen such things. This man was young and inexperienced. He was exaggerating the danger. No one killed another man. It was not the way of the People. No animal killed one of its own. Men would shout insults across a gauntlet, and in extreme cases they would wrestle until one man had proven himself superior, but no one killed.

They had never heard Paataga speak. Many had never even heard her name. They had heard of a mythical person reported to be the Wise One of the nation, but no one had ever seen such a person or knew of anyone who had. It was a myth, a story told to entertain children.

Kaoto left in sorrow. He could not stay with them until the threat arrived. He must travel on. There were many of his People in the nation; surely all of them would not be so stubborn. He must carry his warning to all of them.

The villagers were polite and promised they would think about what he said, but he knew they would not move. They might think about it and talk about it. But each summer they would decide to wait and see what happened. They would put it off summer after summer until one day they would wake up to find the savages upon them, and then they would turn and run northward toward more populated regions. The only hope he could see for the future was the stories they took with them into the heart of the nation. These stories might substantiate what he had already told them. In time, drought, savage raids, and overcrowding of the People would force them to take some action. He hoped at that time they would remember his words and they would follow his advice and flee to the south.

As he pushed farther north, he remained mostly in the high country. It was not as mountainous as the first high country he had visited, but he could feel the coolness at night and knew that winter was in the air. Giant pines adorned the land, and his line of sight was limited to only an occasional glimpse ahead.

Once he thought he could see the beginning of a valley. He pushed on in hopes of finding lower land before nightfall. The feathered cloak his mother had made for him was not nearly warm enough for these cold nights. The Spirit Watcher had gone to bed and he was still on high ground. He pushed on, feeling sure the ground would soon drop and he would at least have the protection of a sun-warmed cliff to sleep against that night. It was a night when Sister Moon would not show her face, so he stumbled along in the darkness. A bank of clouds blocked out the feeble light of the stars.

Instinct told him to stop. Feeling the rush of warm air coming up in his face, he knew he was on the rim of a canyon. He was about to drop over the edge to try to find a way down. Pausing long enough to drop a rock first to check for distance, he was greeted by a long silence and then a feeble echo came up to him as the rock struck some other rocks very far below him. He could hardly believe his ears, but a second rock returned the same message.

He felt around until he found a secluded place at the base of a huge pine. Wedging himself between the bole of the tree and a large rock, he made himself as comfortable as possible and waited for morning.

A deep blanket of snow in the morning did not surprise him. It was not as cold as he had expected because the wind was not blowing. The Spirit Watcher was just now rising from his bed. Kaoto rose also and stretched the stiffness from his long frame. He took a couple of steps towards the cliff when his eyes beheld a sight he would never forget.

He caught his breath when he saw its beauty and majesty. He stood on the lip of a precipice of such magnitude that he could hardly believe his eyes. He had been told of this place, but no words could have prepared him for what he saw. This had to be the Great Father of all canyons. He could not even see the bottom. The ground dropped away from his feet like an abyss, leaving him dizzy. Far across to the other side he could see the snow mass, which continued on to the horizon, but down in the canyon the snow soon gave way to dry rocks. He could only estimate the distance down and across. Both had to be immense.

His experienced eye searched for the likelihood of a trail leading across this great expanse of canyon land. He could see none. No one made it a practice of crossing, not even the animals. This at least posed a natural barrier. There would be no threat of the savages from this direction.

The canyon ran in both directions as far as the eye could see. The Spirit Watcher's early rays marched down the canyon walls, tinting them with many colors, painting new scenes as they went. It defied description. One had to see it to believe it. Never could he tell others the true glory and splendor of this place. No wonder the elders could not prepare him for this view. He wondered, idly, if there were any of the People living down in the narrow valley at the bottom of the canyon, but decided there would not be because there was no way down. It would surely be a safe and pleasant place if there was some way to get there.

As he watched, far down the wall he saw a tiny speck separate itself from the wall and float in the air current. It was so small it looked to be a hummingbird, but he knew the distance was so great that it had to be something bigger. Possibly a hawk. It continued to float upwards in a lazy circle, increasing in size until he recognized it as a carrion bird. It proved to be the largest he had ever seen, with a wingspan over twice that of those in his native Chaco Canyon. As it came level and directly in front of him, he could see that each wing was nearly as long as he was tall.

The condor saw the man on the lip of the canyon and scornfully circled over him, unafraid of this puny animal. After a wide sweep over the plateau, it set its wings in a long glide, taking it away from the man and back down into the canyon. Its arrow-straight flight took it toward a point of rock protruding from the same wall on which Kaoto stood. The sun's rays made the bird's blackness stand out in contrast against the pink glow of the rocks. Kaoto watched in fascination as the giant bird became smaller and smaller until it disappeared, seemingly in mid flight, deep in the mysterious canyon. If a bird of this size could be lost in that much distance, then truly this was the Great Father of all canyons.

He could not help but draw a parallel between himself and the bird. Both of them were bigger than average, but both could be swallowed up in this land and become as insignificant as the ants. It was another lesson in humility for him. He thought it was the Spirit Watchers way of letting him know that his size did not make him important in his eyes. He could not help but wonder if his path across the nation would leave no more impression than the bird's flight across the sky. It made him feel small and helpless against the staggering chore facing him. For the first time since he had begun his mission, he felt inadequate to the task. He wondered if even Paataga had underestimated the immensity of this undertaking. His thinking brought him back to the bird and the part it played in life. The bird did not choose its way of life, yet it served a purpose without complaint. He was a man with freedom of choice but the task facing him had been offered to him and he could have refused. He had not. He had accepted, willingly.

The spectacular view soon washed away any vestige of depression he had felt earlier. He thought of Moot and the villagers and Mute and the other runners. If they were willing to accept their place in life, could he do less?

He followed the side of the canyon eastward until it made a wide swing to the north and disappeared into oblivion. It appeared to be getting much narrower and somewhat shallower, but it was still a formidable obstacle in the path of anyone or anything that wanted to cross it. He thought for a moment of how it would feel to be like the giant bird that could cross this crack in the earth with impunity. This type of thinking always confused him, and for now he had to keep his mind on his business. Someday, maybe, he would have time to contemplate such things at leisure.

For now his path led him away from the canyon as he followed a side canyon on to the east. His People were scattered far and wide to every horizon, with the exception of the canyon. Unknown to the Wise One, and to the rest of the People, there were forgotten tribes of the People living on the other side of the canyon. Time and distance had separated them until the memory of each other had been wiped from their minds. He did, however, know of the many who were out in front of him, waiting for his visit, needing his counsel and guidance.

In the impatience of his youth he had thought to cover the entire nation in a short time. He could see now that it was not possible to rush. He knew he could devote his entire life to travel and still not reach every village. He also could see that he was not doing justice to the People by rushing from one large village to another without taking time for the little villages scattered along the way. He was faced with a decision: was speed more important, or thoroughness? Either way, it was going to take much longer than he had anticipated.

When Paataga had first sent for him and told him she had chosen him to take her place as the Wise One, he had doubted her wisdom and his own ability. He was sure he could never replace her intelligence and patience. Time had shown him the wisdom of her choice. She had sensed the eminent changes moving across the nation. She had known of the need for a strong, young body, a runner of exception. Someone to move rapidly, as she never could. He had knowingly accepted this challenge, more on her assurance than on his own sense of ability or duty.

His days as a runner were of double value to him in his present office. First, he was a tireless runner and could run for days without rest. Second, his summers as a runner had given him validity and acceptance. No one would doubt the word of a runner. He had taken his runner's badge from his pack and wore it proudly once again. Lastly, both his time as a runner and the time he had spent talking to Little Frog and later to Paataga, had sharpened his perceptive memory. His long legs and strong body would carry him to every corner of the nation, and his mind would relate to the People all they should know. Paataga had been faithful to her office.

At Moot's village there had been no creatures on the dumpsite. They were all utilized for watch duty, and surprisingly there had been none so invalid that they had not been able to at least start the long trip. But here, in the heart of the nation, Kaoto once more renewed his custom of staying at the dumpsites with the poor creatures found there. Their accommodations had been greatly improved long before his arrival because of the word spread by the runners, so his thoughts of Little Frog were more pleasant.

Most of the problems brought to his attention were minor ones, much like the two men and the pumpkin, important only to those involved. His solutions were along the same lines. By listening to the complaints of each party, he accomplished half the battle without saying a word. Most people only wanted to be heard, to be allowed to express their thoughts or complaints. Once they had lodged their complaints, they were willing to accept his judgment without reservations.

Kaoto tried very hard to be fair and assuage both sides of a dispute without offending either one. Sometimes this would seem impossible. When this happened, and he was unable to arrive at a solution, he would invoke the aid of the elders because they were better advised on the source of the problem and local habits. He had learned another valuable lesson in diplomacy. Often the same message would be better received from different people. Sometimes it took an outsider to moderate, but quite often just his presence made the voice of the elders more official.

When he became completely perplexed, when there seemed no way to make anyone happy, he would call on the children of the village. He would seat them around him like a council meeting and explain the problem to them in detail, asking them to give their opinion on the matter. It would be a public meeting with everyone in attendance. The adults could listen in but were not asked to participate in the discussions. Kaoto would treat the children with adult respect. He would appear grave and serious as if he were soliciting the advice of the oldest members of the village. All the children, boys and girls, were encouraged to speak out with their thoughts on the problem. The Wise One would listen to them as religiously as he did the adults. Often the answers he received from the children were more precise and pertinent than the advice he had received from the elders.

Their little minds were not cluttered with preconceived notions and adult prejudices. They could see clearly what needed to be done, and were not concerned with false pride or sensitive feelings. Their solutions went straight to the truth, and the announcement coming from a bright eyed, sincere child would usually make the complaining parties see just how silly they were. The results would often be astonishing. Usually both sides would give in and concede to the other. Sometimes a new quarrel would break out over who owed whom an apology. No matter who gave the final answer, the Wise One received the credit for his wisdom.

He often wondered in his own mind just how important he really was. But in the end he decided this was not important, either. What was important was that someone had been able to come up with a solution. It did not matter who worked out the problem, as long as they were all satisfied with the end results. The credit belonged to the Spirit Watcher.

For two summers he roamed the land, looping north and south in an eastward trek. His destination would ultimately be the Hovenweep and Mesa Verde.

He had several strange adventures on this pilgrimage. He met people he would never have believed existed and seen sights that were strange and wonderful to his eyes. Perhaps the strangest of them all, and the one that would have the most far-reaching effects on the nation, happened when he sought shelter from a sandstorm.

He was on the edge of a small desert when the storm struck and led him to meet Kuat, the father of a speechless son, a son with no name until Kaoto named him Kalo.

Kalo, the quiet one.

Chapter Twenty Five

Kaoto's path led him to a part of the desert that crept into the heart of the land. Its withered arm lay across his chosen route. Rather than detour around it, he thought to cross it here and be done with it. On the shimmering distant horizon he thought he could see where the desert ended and more moderate plains continued.

By late afternoon he was still far from the opposite side, and the heat and thirst were becoming intense. There was a ridge of bare rocks to his left and he was bearing toward this with the hope of finding a water hole when he was caught in a sandstorm. The hot, stinging sand blinded him and attacked his exposed skin with a demon-like tenacity. He knew that if he did not find shelter very quickly, he would perish here. Squinting his eyes against the tiny particles of sand, he pushed on, trying to find the rocky ridge and get behind it to break the force of the howling winds. It was his only hope if the storm was to last any length of time. Otherwise, the Wise One would disappear and no one would know what became of him.

Keeping the wind to his back, he stumbled blindly until he felt the bare stone with his outstretched hands. He pulled himself up and over the ridge and dropped down into the calm on the leeward side. Here the wind did not strike, but the air was still filled with floating red dust that choked and irritated him. Offering a quick thanks to the Spirit Watcher for bringing him to this relatively safe place, he worked his way along the wall, searching for even more protection. The wall led him into a small neck where another wall closed in to make a narrow passageway into the stone. Here the storm was nullified, but it was still hard to breathe.

The farther he progressed, the more relief he got as the walls became higher and the wind howled over the top. Here the air was less dusty, and wiping the grit from his eyes, he could see where he was going. The storm blocked the sun and left the narrow alcove in a red, murky, haze. The crevice reminded him of the black rock country where Mula lived, so he was not surprised to see a small shelter along one side of the wall where the valley widened slightly. He had nearly missed it in the filter of red sand drifting down from above. The dark, regular shape of the doorway caught his eye. It was a single dwelling and in dilapidated condition but scattered bones and belongings led him to think some-one still lived there.

He approached it openly, not wishing to frighten anyone with his sudden appearance. On closer inspection, it seemed to be deserted at the present. Kaoto had seen some poorly constructed and ill kept dwellings in his travels, but by any standards this one was as crude and primitive as any he had ever seen. Wedged into a crack in the rocks as it was, he could have missed it altogether. If the storm had not driven him this way, he would have passed it by and never known it was here.

Settling down in a protected place beside one wall, he prepared to wait out the storm. It was drawing near to evening, and if the occupant should return he would ask permission to spend the night here. He drowsed in the heat of the late afternoon and was disturbed by the sound of a voice coming from deeper in the rocky valley. He listened closely but could only hear one person speaking. Unless he was talking to himself, which seemed unlikely, there must be at least one other person.

The voice was nasal, whining, and constantly complaining and belaboring someone else who, as far as Kaoto could determine, never answered back. As they came closer he could make out the word being spoken.

"Lazy, stupid, misbegotten son of a worthless woman who had no virtue. Why are you so clumsy? Can you not do anything right? Even carrying a gourd full of water is too much for you. You have spilled more than you saved. Well, I guess you know whose share you are spilling. Not mine. It will be you who goes thirsty tonight."

From behind a curve in the rock wall, which had hidden their approach, a small twisted man came, prodding a youngster before him. The lad could not have been more than ten or twelve summers. Both were ragged and unkempt, their hair matted and soiled, as were the shabby, undressed skins the man wore. The lad was naked. Giving the boy a final shove that nearly sent him sprawling, the man caught sight of the stranger seated between himself and his doorway.

He was so startled to see a visitor that probably for the first time in many summers he was speechless. He glanced around quickly to see if there were more present. When he was sure the stranger was alone, he made a blustering attempt to swagger.

"Ho, stranger. What brings you to the humble home of Kuat?" He stood with legs wide spread and arms across his chest, waiting for an explanation from this intruder in his home place.

"I was caught in the sand storm and came in here looking for shelter. I hope I did not frighten you."

"Frighten me? Not hardly. What have I to be frightened of?" The small man affected his swagger as he approached Kaoto. Seated, Kaoto did not look threatening. But Kuat drew back rather quickly when the young giant stood up, even though Kaoto extended his hand in friendship.

"I am called Kaoto. I hope I will be welcome to share your camp tonight." Kaoto held his voice low and tried to sound as pleasant as he could.

Kuat drew back even further. This was no ordinary man. He was far too big to one of the People. His hairy body coated with red dust was unfamiliar in a land where the People were normal sized and almost devoid of any body hair. His weapons, though larger, were of the People's design and the man spoke the language flawlessly.

"What do you want here?" Kuat demanded uneasily.

"I wish only for shelter from the storm, a place to sleep and directions out of here in the morning," Kaoto told him.

"You must be a stranger to this land. No one in their right mind would venture out in the desert in the middle of the day in this season. Any fool knows you have to travel at night or early in the morning to be safe from the storms. They can kill even a big man like you."

"Yes, I am a stranger to this part of the land," Kaoto spoke softly. He did not want to incite more fear than he already had. "Maybe I should go on my way. I did not mean to upset you, but it is the way of my People to offer hospitality to a stranger, especially a runner." He held out his skin badge for the little man to inspect. It usually worked to dispel suspicion among those who had never heard of him before.

Kuat eyed the running man burned into the hide. It was genuine and this man surely had the build of a runner.

"Who do you run for?" Kuat asked cautiously. It would not do to offend a neighboring ruler, although he recognized no man as his ruler. He lived alone in the desert by choice with his only son. No man ever came to visit him. No man came this way for any reason. As far as the rest of the nation was concerned he did not exist, and that was the way he preferred it.

"I run for Paataga," the giant said.

"I know of no one called Paataga," Kuat answered tersely.

"I am from the land of the Chaco. It lies far to the east of here, many days' run east."

"I have heard of Chaco, but what does the land of Chaco want of me and the desert?"

"The land of Chaco wants nothing of you. I told you, I was on my way back and took a short cut across the desert. I did not know of the danger. From back on the west ridge it looked only a short run to get across and there was no sign of a storm when I started," Kaoto told him patiently.

Kuat relaxed slightly as he edged close to his hut and his weapons just inside the doorway. He seldom carried his weapons unless he was on a hunt, and today he had only been up the canyon for water.

"They spring up out of nowhere. There is never any warning. Only the wise and crafty can live out here and get along with them," He bragged.

Kaoto could see there was no immediate danger from this man and was sure that Kuat would feel more secure once he was in possession of his weapons, so he made no effort to detain or stop him. In a similar circumstance, if he were unarmed, he might feel uneasy facing a stranger this much larger than himself.

He let his attention wander to the boy, who had remained motionless and silent during the conversation. He now placed the gourd carefully on the ground near the door and sprawled listlessly on the ground. He was seemingly uninterested in what was being said between his father and the strange looking man.

Kaoto could not help but notice that his lean, thin body was covered with scars and welts of many kinds. Every part of his body carried them. Many were easily recognized as insect bites; other represented cuts and burns, not uncommon among boys of his age. But Kaoto could not recall ever seeing any one lad with so many of every kind at one time. Even the bottom of his feet had not been spared. Noticing the stranger's gaze, Kuat was quick to explain.

"He is the most clumsy, stupid son any father has ever been forced to endure."

Kaoto returned his gaze to Kuat, but from the corner of his eyes he still watched the lad. Unaware of being watched, the boy showed the first signs of emotion. His eyes alone registered his feelings. They were two smoldering pits of hate, and Kaoto was not sure who was the recipient of this hate, himself or the boy's father. He turned his full attention to Kuat.

"You live here alone, just the two of you?" he asked.

"Yes. Alone. Even worse than alone, when you live with a son like this one. He will not even speak to me, his father."

"Will not? Or cannot?"

"Will not. He can speak if he wants to, this lazy worthless son. But he will not. Nothing can induce him to speak."

"Has he always been this way?" Kaoto could not believe a boy could remain silent for very long.

"Not always, although before, when he did try to talk, it was just as bad." Kuat threw a contemptuous glare at the silent boy.

"Oh. How could it be worse than not talking at all?" Kaoto was beginning to have some doubts about all of this.

"Up until his mother died in his fifth summer he would talk, if you could call it that. He stuttered and stammered so much that it was impossible to make any sense out of his gibberish. His mother babied him and would do nothing to correct him. After she died, he just quit talking altogether. The Spirit Watcher knows I tried to persuade him."

"Yes, it is a father's responsibility to help his son in every way he can. I remember my father was very patient with me."

"Yes. Mine also," Kuat said with a plea for sympathy. "I have tried everything in my power. Patience. You talk about patience. Why, this lad has sorely tried mine, let me tell you." Kuat rolled his eyes skyward as if asking confirmation from the Spirit Watcher.

In the course of their conversation, Kuat had kindled a small cook fire using the small, twisted, almost branchless limbs of the tough bushes that grew in these parts. These hardy plants seldom grew as big as a man's wrist. Many were as small as a man's thumb. Once the fire was going to his satisfaction, he called to his son.

"Bring me a piece of meat and put it in to soak with some beans." He spoke sharply and loudly as if the boy were not only speechless but also deaf.

The lad rose slowly and did as he was told. Kaoto could see no signs of clumsiness in the boy's movements, he seemed more like a sleep walker than a normal youth. His movements were slow and deliberate, but he did not falter or stumble.

In the back of his mind, Kaoto had a terrible suspicion growing. He wanted to reject it but it persisted and continued to nag at him. He must know the truth. He could not rest or leave this valley until he had put this evil shadow of doubt to rest.

"I suppose you have used the magic stick to try and persuade him, have you not?" he asked Kuat, seemingly interested.

Kuat laughed and shook his head. "Oh yes. Believe me, I have tried the magic stick, many times. I told you I have done everything I could think of to make him talk, and nothing works. He is a stubborn one, this misbegotten son of mine."

The magic stick contained no magic. It was a common willow switch used by mothers to dissuade naughty children before they became old enough to be adults. It was seldom used after the fifth summer, after a child received his pet name, and it was seldom use in anger or with a vengeance. It was referred to as magic because usually just the mention of it, or the sight of it, would work magic on a child's behavior. Any child of this age would be shamed beyond endurance if they were disciplined with physical force. So the mention of the magic stick was enough to get the desired results.

The more Kaoto looked at the scarred body of the boy, the more he was convinced there was more than gentle persuasion involved here. Many of the scars were fresh, and there were unhealed welts to be seen on the boy's back and lower legs. There was not a place left that did not bear the signs of some one's villainy.

"With your permission, I would like to try my magic stick. I have a reputation for persuasion that is well known in my part of the country. I would like to show you how it works."

"Welcome. I wish you more luck than I have had. You cannot know the shame he brings to me," Kuat said with relish as he settled down near the fire.

Under his breath Kaoto answered, "Oh yes. I know the shame. It is indeed very great." Out loud he said. "Ah, this one will do very well." He picked up one of the glowing limbs from the fire. Only one end of the stick burned. It was about the length of his arm and only half as big around. He watched the lad gather himself as if to flee. Then he slumped back in resignation. Kaoto remembered the bull buffalo's look when he had approached it to remove the spear from its shoulder. The boy might not talk, but there was no doubt that he understood what was being said.

Kuat watched both of them and leaned forward, licking his lips in anticipation of the treat he was about to witness. This would be a new thrill for him. He had grown weary of his own efforts.

Kaoto started to take a step toward the listless boy, only to turn in mid stride and suddenly leap at Kuat. Caught off guard, the man stumbled in his effort to get up or out of the way and fell flat on his back, unable to recover himself. He was the victim of Kaoto's charge. He found he was pinned forcefully by one strong, capable foot of the hairy young giant.

Kaoto placed his foot in the middle of Kuat's chest and crushed him mercilessly into the ground, where sharp rocks cut into his flesh and brought screams of pain from him. Swinging the fire brand over his head until all the ashes were gone and the end of the stick glowed cherry red, Kaoto spoke to Kuat in the quiet, gentle voice of a parent speaking to a baby.

"Would you like to tell me how hard you have tried to persuade him to speak?"

Kuat lay stunned, his breath driven from his lungs by the violence of the attack. He tried to wiggle loose from the weight of the foot holding him helpless in his own yard. It was futile. He was pinned as helplessly as a bug on a cactus spine. Looking up at the hairy giant over him, he was reminded of the look he had seen on an eagle perched on a stone clutching a writhing snake. The two feathers in Kaoto's hair and his long pointed nose resembling a cruel beak served to enhance the illusion. Great beads of sweat poured from Kuat's body as his whining voice began to bleat in its nasal way.

"I have done nothing to him," he cried in weak bluster and anger, but he was shaking with fear. The odor of fear reeked from him like the trapped animal he was. "I did only what any father would do to make him talk."

"Oh, come now." Kaoto's voice was still calm and quiet; no trace of his disgust came through. Anyone hearing him would assume he was having a normal conversation with a distraught man. "You must have tried some other kinds of persuasion besides the magic stick, have you not?" Slowly he lowered the firebrand close to Kuat's quivering flesh. "I mean, it would only be natural and the duty of a concerned father to try almost anything to make a son speak, and of course he would want him to speak clearly, not mumble a mouthful of gibberish."

"Yes. Yes. Of course. I told you I tried to get him to speak, but he would not." Kuat tried to keep his eyes on the tip of the glowing firebrand as it swung carelessly from Kaoto's hand, describing an arch that was creeping closer to the tender skin of his legs between knee and thigh. As the brand came closer he could begin to feel the singeing heat drying and tightening the skin under it.

"What is the matter with you? Are you crazy?" he cried in terror. "You cannot come in and threaten a man in his own home."

"Yes. I guess I am crazy. It is strange what the sight of human suffering does to me. It has a queer way of making me act thoughtlessly, even in a man's own home." The stick slipped a little lower. "I sometimes have trouble controlling myself. Talking sometimes quiets me down, so why do you not tell me more?"

"There is nothing more to tell. I do not know what you want of me. It is the boy you should be talking to, not me." Kuat was nearly squealing in his panic.

Kaoto struck down savagely with the glowing ember. Kuat screamed as the live coals seared his inner leg about half way up from the knee. The stench of burning flesh was carried to his nostrils by the evening breeze.

"Did that help you recall anything else?" Kaoto asked gently. "No? Well, maybe this will do better." Once more the magic stick came in contact with Kuat's unprotected skin. Higher this time, in an even more tender spot. Kuat screamed and thrashed in agony but he could not free himself from the foot of the mad man who stood on top of him. Kaoto brought the stick forward and gave his victim several hard raps on either side of his head before bringing it back to his groin.

Kuat could not get away from his tormentor and in slow, agonizing detail, Kaoto got the story from him. How he had, after his mate's death, started at first to frighten the boy into better speech. How gradually he had turned his well-intentioned efforts into a horror of torture. Over the period of five summers he had repeatedly beaten and burned his son. How he had tied him out in the burning sun and sand storms without food or water. How he had closed him in their tiny hut with angry hornets and wasps and any other kind of stinging, biting insects he could find. Kaoto felt a knot twisting in his stomach and the same sickness he had felt when he had killed the three men down south. He wished Kuat would stop his recital, but his whining went on.

Once the dam was broken, the words came out in a torrent and no more persuasion was needed. Kaoto learned the boy was a normal boy who stuttered. After his mother had died and his older sister had died in childbirth from his father's seed, he had refused to talk at all.

"It seems my magic stick is more powerful than yours. It only took one lesson from it to make you talk. Or, just maybe you are much weaker than your son." Turning to the boy, he asked, as kindly as he could under the circumstances, "What is your name, lad?"

The boy looked at him in stunned silence. Even this violent demonstration did not shake his resolve to remain speechless.

"He has no name. We never gave him one," Kuat screamed, in fear of more reprisal.

"No name? You did all this to him and never gave him the dignity of a name? You are the most despicable man under the Spirit Watcher's golden vessel." He threw the firebrand back into the flames and took his foot from Kuat's quaking chest. He held out his hand to the boy and said, "Come with me son. You will have a name; it will be Kalo. Do you know what Kalo means?"

The boy shook his head in the negative as he got up and stood ready for the fierce giant's next move.

"Kalo means 'quiet one'. Will you come with me and be my son?" he asked. The boy stepped forward and took the giant's hand without fear. Something in Kaoto's eyes reassured him that his life of terror was over now. They stepped over the cringing man who still lay on the ground by the fire, and prepared to leave the valley forever, never to return.

"What is to become of me?" Kuat called after them in despair. "You cannot take my only son and leave me here alone."

Kaoto turned and regarded the hopeless mass of quivering humanity with both pity and contempt.

"If you are lucky, you will die. The Spirit Watcher knows you deserve no better. He also knows you deserve much worse. I will not dirty my hands further with you." Turning back to the lad, he placed his hand on his thin shoulder and together they walked out into the quiet of the moonlit night, with deaf ears to the whining and begging man who used to be the boy's father.

Chapter Twenty Six

The Wise One and his new charge, Kalo, walked out of the valley without looking back. Kalo seemed content to be away from his prison. Any type of life with this tall, hairy stranger would be preferable to living with his father. He had seen Kaoto attack his father and witnessed the violent force he had used to make him talk. He had seen him as a ruthless giant, but he had also seen his eyes during the proceedings and knew that Kaoto did not enjoy what he did. He was not by nature cruel, as his father had been.

Sister Moon was out early tonight and her light, though pale, was sufficient for them to travel albeit, slowly, in the nearly barren wasteland.

The storm had gone on its scouring way and in its wake had left a blissful quiet over the exposed skeletons of the earth. The night air was cold and crisp and Kalo was soon shivering uncontrollably. Kaoto placed his feathered cloak around the boy's thin, naked shoulders to help protect him against the chill. His anger was enough to keep his blood pumping hotly through his veins. At dawn's first light he found a sheltered place just below the top of a ridge. It overlooked their back trail. He did not think Kuat was in any condition to follow them even if he dared, but he was not going to take any chances.

"Kalo will rest while I see if I can find a small rabbit that will make us a meal. We will have to live off the land for a few meals until we can find a village with more to offer." He used the new name to remind the boy he had one.

Kalo dropped to the ground and was almost instantly asleep, the feathered cloak clutched tightly around him. Kaoto slipped back down the trial they had just traveled. He thought he could hunt in that direction just as well as any other and it would serve as insurance that they would not be disturbed.

In a very short time he returned with two plump young rabbits and an armful of firewood. Using his fire drill, he soon had a crackling fire going with the two rabbits drawn and spitted, roasting at the edge of the flames.

Kalo was aroused by the smell of cooking meat, crackling and dripping fat into the fire. He sat up and rubbed his eyes as he looked around in surprise. He had never left the valley before, so everything was new to him in the light of day.

"Hungry enough to eat a half-cooked rabbit?" Kaoto asked as he turned the sizzling carcasses for a last bit of cooking.

Kalo looked at him sharply, as if expecting a rain of blows or worse if he did not speak up. Kaoto's eyes, twinkling with pleasure, reassured him and he nodded his head eagerly.

"Kalo must know this. I will never strike him or do anything to hurt him for not talking. It would be nice for him to be able to talk without fear. I think it would be all right if he wanted to try to speak, even if he did not speak clearly, even if he stuttered and had to try several times. It would be nice. But I do not insist on it." He took the roasted meat from the fire and handed one whole rabbit to the boy.

Kalo ate ravenously. It was evident he was not used to having enough to eat. His body was so emaciated and deprived that his bones were exposed. It would take a lot of good food and time to bring his body back to normal. He was surprised that the boy had been able to stay on the trail at all. Kaoto was sure time would cure most of his physical wounds; his mental scars would be another matter. A lifetime of torment would be hard to overcome.

"Kalo can have all the food he wants as long as we can find it, but I think he would be wise not to eat too much too fast. He is not use to it and it might make him sick."

Kalo stopped tearing at his food and looked at Kaoto. He held out the remains of the rabbit for Kaoto to take from him.

"No. I do not want it. You keep it. Eat as much as you feel comfortable with. Later today, on the trail, you will want a little more to chew on as we move. A little nibble here and another there and it will all be gone soon enough."

Kalo held the food closely to his body and stared at it thoughtfully as he weighted the words of the hairy giant, who was eating sparingly. After watching Kaoto for a while, Kalo pulled loose a small piece of meat and chewed it slowly, savoring every bit of flavor and every drop of juice in it. He smiled at Kaoto cautiously, and was rewarded with a genuine smile of pleasure in return. Kaoto was content to let him rest for a while longer and savor the meat, now that he had shown he could control himself.

Kalo was busy turning the events over in his mind. Everything had happened so fast and now things were definitely different. He knew nothing of the rest of the world. On rare occasions, when someone did happen to drop by, his father would push him back into their hut and bar the doorway. He would warn him to keep out of sight. He had been able to hear them talk sometimes and he could faintly remember his mother and sister when they had talked about other people and other places. So he knew there were other people, but he did not know if they were all like his father. If they were, he did not think he wanted to meet any of them. But if they were like the giant, then it would be different.

He finally stopped eating and passed the uneaten portion back to Kaoto, who wrapped it in a piece of inner deerskin he carried in his pack. He handed it back to Kalo and told him to carry it with him so he would have it when he wanted more. Kalo, meanwhile, sat frowning at the ground, evidently pondering on something of great importance to him. At last, with his face and courage both screwed up, he stammered.

"G-g-ggo-goo-ggoo-gooood-d-ddd." He waited to see what the reaction from the giant would be. Would he get a cuff, or would he find some other form of punishment?

Kaoto, in turn, was so surprised he nearly stopped packing his bag, but he caught himself in time and continued to work without even looking up. He answered the lad.

"Yes. It was pretty good. It always seems to take a long trek on the trail to make a meal taste good. Well— shall we be on our way?"

Kalo smiled his relief and nodded his head in agreement. He followed Kaoto as they topped the ridge and descended the other side on a faint game trail. Kaoto was looking for signs of the waterhole that were sometimes found in these barren lands. As they walked along, he began talking.

"I once had a friend like you. He could not talk easily, either." Kaoto was preparing to do something no runner would every think of doing. He was going to tell a lie. He only had two friends, Little Frog and Paataga. Neither of them had any trouble talking. He had known of a boy who stuttered, but no one thought anything about it. He hoped the Spirit Watcher would understand his motive and not punish him for this. He had to gain Kalo's trust somehow, so he was going to pretend he knew something about the lad's speech problem. He was going to treat it like it was a natural, normal thing and make light of it. After all, Kalo had just spoken one word on his own. It was not perfect, but he understood the word, so maybe he could get him to speak again.

"My friend, he overcame his problem long before he became a man. He just had to work on it a lot." He did not look back. He kept a steady pace on the trail as he went on talking.

"He would take one word, just as you did, and think about that word as hard as he could. Then he would try saying it to himself. He said it over and over until his tongue became familiar with it. When he could say the word to himself without stuttering, he would say it to me." He cast a quick glance back at Kalo, who was looking down at the trail. He could not tell what effect he was having, if any, on the boy.

"So he would think about it and practice it in his head until he was ready. Then he would say it to me and start on the next word. Oh, he would stumble around and stammer sometimes. But it did not make any difference. We were friends. Sometimes I would try to guess what he was going to say next, but this just made him mad. He wanted to say it all himself, and so he did." Kaoto stopped talking as they climbed a steep portion of the trail, and then took up where he had left off when the trail leveled out again.

"He never stopped trying, though, until he got it right and said it all. We used to laugh a lot at some of the funny things he would come up with while he was trying to say a word. Sometimes I made fun of him and stuttered along with him. It was really funny and we both laughed a lot. I did not laugh at him. I laughed with him. There is a big difference." He wondered to himself, does the boy even know how to laugh? What has he ever had to laugh about? Does he even understand what I am saying? "When you laugh with somebody, it is because you both think it is funny. When you laugh at somebody, it is because only you think it is funny."

As near as he could determine, Kalo's only concern was keeping pace with him and not losing his footing on the path. If he heard, and believed him, he gave no indication. Like his mythical friend he had to just keep trying.

"Yes. He just kept at it until he got the first word right. Then he would start working on the next one he wanted to say. Sometimes it took him most of a day to get out what he wanted to talk about. Of course, it was hard for me to remember what his first words were. On the other hand, he was not going to start all over, so I just had to do the best I could to make out what it was he had said. I sometimes think even he forgot what he started to say and finished up on something else altogether. But what I am trying to tell you is, it did not make any difference to either one of us because we were having fun and he was learning. That was what was important to us, not how often he messed up in his efforts."

They had come to the bottom of a long valley and had found no water. Kaoto swung up along the wash in hopes of finding a seep. Animals often knew to find moist places at the base of a rock ledge. The People knew if they dug a small hole in the ground at the base of the ledge, it would usually fill with water in a short time. The game trail still led this way.

"One time I remember very well. He nearly died of thirst just trying to tell me he had forgotten his water skin. He was so stubborn, he made up his mind he would not use signs, he would tell me in words or not at all, and go dry until he did." Without looking back, or breaking stride, he passed his water skin back to the lad, who took a small drink and passed it back. From this brief encounter, Kaoto could see a slight frown on the boy's face.

Kaoto had tried to keep his pace slow and easy, taking shorter steps so as not to tire the boy. He stopped talking and let Kalo think things through for himself. He sneaked a quick glance every once in a while as they twisted and turned up the wash. The pinched face of Kalo was furrowed in a frown. He was sure Kalo was working on something and he wished he could help, but he did not know how. Maybe his idea was working after all. He was not taken by surprise when he heard Kalo speaking his own name. "Kkalloo's." It came out almost perfectly the first time he tried and he repeated it over and over as they went up the dry wash. Much later he came up with another word.

"Le-le-leeegg-g-gs." He said it only once, and there followed another long silence. The Spirit Watcher was nearing the middle of his day's flight when they halted in the shade of a pine nut tree and ate the rest of the rabbit left from the morning meal. They had found a water hole and drank heartily after refilling Kaoto's water skin. When they had finished eating, he offered the skin to Kalo, who waved it aside as he sat stonily working on yet another word. Kaoto was delighted with his progress. His plan was actually working. He had not known if it would work or not. It just seemed like a good idea at the time, and he had not had anything better to offer. After what he considered a long rest, he suggested they move on. He was hoping to find a village as soon as possible to ease the strain of travel for the boy.

Kalo waved his hand again and frowned even more deeply. He pursed his lips for the next word and in desperation, he nearly shouted, "Sh-sssh-sssh-sshooo-sshooorttt-t-t-t." It exploded from him as he looked at Kaoto expectantly.

"Kalo's—Legs—Short?" Kaoto repeated the phrase several times, trying to make some sense of what he had said. Of course Kalo's legs were short; he was short, but that was hardly worth all the effort he had put into the sentence. He was proud of him for trying so hard, but he was a little disappointed in the text.

"Oh, ho, so now I get it. Fine Wise One I turn out to be. I cannot even understand a simple statement." Kaoto wagged his head in appreciation of the joke on himself.

Kalo sat dumbfounded. He had never heard anyone laugh like that, and he did not know whether he should be frightened or glad. The smile of the giant's face seemed to say it was something to be happy about. So he cocked his head and waited.

"Kalo's legs are short. So Kalo is getting tired trying to keep up with my long legs? I understand now." He reached down and gave the boy a gentle slap on the shoulder. "You spent all morning trying to tell me to slow down. Yes, and all the time I thought I was just crawling. Yes, Kalo, your legs are short compared to mine. You have been taking three steps to every one of mine and it is as if you have had to walk three times as far as I have. Well, little man, we will change all that now that I know." He looked down on the puzzled boy in admiration. Brave lad, he had spent all morning working on those three words. He could have used signs, or simply said "tired," but no. He had felt a need to explain why he was tired.

Kalo relaxed slightly. It was all right. The giant was smiling and the slap on his shoulder, while it had been pretty hard, was not meant as punishment, he could tell that. He was sure the giant could hit much harder than that. He smiled back up at Kaoto and shook his head vigorously. He was tired. He was nearly exhausted from the trek last night and this morning. He did not think he could possibly go another step.

"I could throw you over my shoulder like a bag of corn, or stick you in my pack and carry you on my back," Kaoto said in all seriousness. Then, seeing the shocked look on the boy's face, he knew instantly that Kalo did not understand he was joking. He had probably never heard anyone joke, except maybe the cruel jokes his father might have played on him. He squatted down beside Kalo and in a softer voice said, "I forget that you do not understand fun and jokes. I forget that your life has not had any jokes or tricks in it that were not cruel and mean. But it is all right. You will learn in time. You will learn to laugh and play tricks on me someday. Then we can both laugh." He gave Kalo another gentle push on the shoulder.

Kalo rocked from even this gentle push. The difference in their size made the push seem more like a shove, and it was much harder than Kaoto had thought. But it was all right. The giant was smiling and laughing. True, Kalo did not know about jokes. He did not even know for sure what Kaoto was talking about, but as long as they sat here and he did not have to get up and start walking again, he would accept almost anything.

"Kalo will rest. I will scout and be back. We will camp here for the rest of the day and, we may not move until tomorrow." He squeezed Kalo's shoulder and left. Watching him swinging down the trail in his long easy stride made Kalo gasp in wonder. He had thought they were traveling fast before, but this man truly did run with the wind. Kalo had never seen the bird Kaoto was named for, but he did know the words and he was amazed at how quickly the giant had gone down the slope and was disappearing over the next ridge.

Kalo sat under the pine nut tree watching the empty trail. He swallowed the lump in his throat. He should not have told him he was tired. He should have tried to keep up. Now the giant was gone. He knew the tall man would not be back. He was already sorry he had taken along such a weakling. Had not his father time and again told him how weak and useless he was? His father had been right. He could not blame the giant. Who wanted a weak little boy to hold them back when he could move so fast and freely as the giant did? He was a burden, and the tall man had left him with the pretense of scouting out the trail. He had even made fun of him about carrying him on his back. This brought a flush of shame across his pinched face. He was not a baby to be carried, but was not that what the giant had tried to tell him? He had just been too dumb to understand.

He looked back along the trail they had been following. It was too far to go back alone. He was not even sure he could find his way back. Besides, he did not want to ever go back. It would be better to die out here on the trail than go back to that place. He would rest here awhile, and then he would try to make it on his own. It should not take much. He had never had enough to eat or drink anyway. He would find a secluded place, just as his father had, and he would spend the rest of his life there. It would not be necessary for him to talk. He was free, at least; he could thank the giant for that much.

His rest soon turned into a deep sleep. The Spirit Watcher smiled down on him and kept watch over him all afternoon as he lay on the lonely ridge under a pine nut tree.

He awoke with a start to find it was nearly dark. He had not intended to sleep all day, only a little while, and then he would start looking for a place of his own. He sat up, and as his eyes cleared, he could tell it was not really dark. He was in some kind of a shelter, made of skins. How had he gotten here? Cautiously he pushed back the flap, and he could see it was nearing dusk outside. There was a small fire going and next to it sat the tall, hairy giant. He had returned just as he said he would. Kalo smothered a tear as he crept out of the tent and edged up close to Kaoto.

Kaoto had his back turned to the tent as he faced the setting sun. It was his custom to say farewell to the Spirit Watcher whenever he had the chance. He liked to watch the sky change colors as the Spirit Watcher dipped below the horizon. He did not turn as he heard the tent flap rustle. He knew Kalo was there beside him. He laid a protecting arm on the boy's thin shoulders and pulled him close to his side.

Kalo was unable to control the tears any longer. Tears his father had never been able to force from him now came unbidden in a great deluge. He clung to the giant's arm and let them run free and unashamed. The only tears he had ever shed were tears of anger and frustration. Now Kaoto was back and everything would be all right in his world. He had doubted the giant. He had thought himself abandoned. He felt a strange, new feeling come over him. He was fascinated with this strange feeling of gratitude and well being

After he had left Kalo, Kaoto had set a fast pace, even for him. He had located a small village, as he had hoped. Here he had requested the necessary items for himself and his charge. The kindly people had willingly furnished all. They had heard he was in their area and were expecting him to pay a visit. His request was unusual, but he was known to be an eccentric. He had promised to return soon to pay them a visit before the summer was over.

He had returned with the skins for a tent, which he had spread over the sleeping boy for shade. He had also brought a supply of staples such as corn, beans, squash, and some dried berries and pine nuts. The women had sent along a bowl for cooking and gourds for more water. Kaoto was sure that with what they had given him and what he could find, they would not be in want for at least a turn of the moon. He could always go back to this village, or another, for more supplies.

A turn of the moon, properly spent, would heal the boy's body. It would let him build a reserve of strength and courage to travel again. As for meeting people? This was something else. They would have to deal with that later when the time was right. What he needed right now was rest, good food, and the comfort of someone he could rely on, and Kaoto was going to see he had all these things in abundance.

"Did you think I had run out on you?" he asked. When the boy nodded, he said, "I asked you to be my son. Would I run off and leave my son?" He thought of how Kalo's father had treated him and realized this was probably an unfair question.

"I would not leave you. I went for food and other things we might need, but I came back, just as I said I would. You must learn to trust me, Kalo. I will always return for you. We may become separated on the trail for short times, but I will always come back for you." His arm tightened on the quaking boy, and again he was aware of the bones barely beneath the skin, with no meat to cover them. In the back of his mind he was thinking, "I should have killed that man. He got off too easy." But he knew he could not have killed the helpless man and only hoped he never had to hurt anyone else. One thing was certain: Kalo's father would never plant any more seed to raise any more children.

Kalo shuddered with a huge sob. The warmth from the fire and the body of the giant were seeping in on him. He felt a lassitude he had never known before. Added to this was the gentle voice of the giant. Both were new things to him, but he liked them. He did not worry about tomorrow. Whatever the giant had in mind would be all right with him. He had kept his word and he had promised never to leave him. What more could he ask?

Chapter Twenty Seven

Once again Kaoto was faced with the decision of whether or not he should take time from his travels to take care of a special project. The project being Kalo. The lad was in no condition to travel even a short distance, let alone to follow him about the nation. It seemed that his mission at this time was to care for this boy. The boy needed his help just as much as anyone did.

The next day was spent walking leisurely to a place Kaoto had seen on his search for food. It was a small, secluded area that offered many of the necessities of life. In many ways, it was like the place where he had taken his survival test for manhood. There was water and an abundance of small game. There were flinty rocks for making points, and more importantly it was not far from a village, where Kaoto could obtain more staples for their diet. He had spread the word of his location and requested that he be left in solitude, a request that would be honored without question. If the Wise One wished to be alone, who would dare to bother him?

The unlikely pair set about establishing a permanent camp on a tall red rock formation. The huge rock's sides were steep, but there was a cleft angling up one slope to a bench about halfway up the height of the rock. The bench was actually a small hollow that had been filled with blowing sand and dirt. Over the centuries it had produced some trees and brush. The natural bowl shape of the rock made it a basin to hold what little moisture fell. There was a seep spring along the face of the cliff. They had a grand view to east south and west with the rock at their back to the north. The days were hot but the elevation gave them the benefit of the breeze, and the nights were made pleasant by the radiated heat stored by the rock prominence at their back. Kaoto showed Kalo how to erect a shelter made of willows and brush. It would offer shade during the day and would turn rain away on the few days it might fall. Kaoto did not anticipate being here very long, not long enough to erect a solid structure. He found that his charge, while lacking in practical experience, compensated for this with his enthusiasm and eagerness. What he did not know, he was eager to learn, and was so excited with each new adventure that he was more often in the way than helpful.

Kaoto's patience was his most endearing quality during this time. He never corrected Kalo without explaining carefully and completely what was right or wrong. Kalo was a fast learner and seldom had to be told twice. His stubbornness won Kaoto's respect as he watched the boy struggle to become perfect in every chore he attempted.

Once the shelter was erected and they had settled their few belongings, Kaoto was ready to begin Kalo's long neglected education. Most boys of his summers had already taken their manhood rites and were well on their way to adult life. In many ways Kalo was more advanced than they were because he had never experienced the fun and frolic of the young, not unlike his new father.

All that he lacked was the opportunity to learn. Kuat had never taken the time or interest to show him anything except how to keep the fire going or to carry water and gather wood. Kaoto compared him to a newly constructed wall, freshly plastered with red clay: blank, open, and ready to be painted or decorated at the artist's will.

His first lesson was on flint knapping to make the necessary stone implements. Next he helped him select the proper wood to make a bow and several arrows, as well as one for a spear shaft. Kalo used a knife he had made with his own hands and felt a sense of pride and accomplishment he had never known before.

Kaoto rotated from one lesson to another to keep any one lesson from becoming monotonous. He taught him how to strip and spin the fibers of the various plants used to make cords and ropes. From these were woven sandals and coarse cloth. Their first project was a simple belt to hold up a loin cloth cut from the skins Kaoto had brought for the tent. Kalo's pride in this simple garment brought home to Kaoto the great gap in this boy's young life. He had never had anything to call his own. Kaoto had learned that whenever the boy had tried to do anything for himself, his father had destroyed his efforts. He had even killed a chipmunk he had tried to tame for a pet.

Pottery making was another project he had never learned, but Kaoto soon discovered that Kalo was a natural artist. The first bowls they made and fired had been plain, corrugated, cooking bowls. Kalo had been amazed that he, a worthless, misbegotten son, could actually perform such a miracle. When they made the next batch, Kaoto showed him how to mix plant juices and natural minerals to make dyes and paints. When he showed him how to apply these paints to the bowl, Kalo was fascinated and asked if he might try. His designs were nearly perfect and his imagination knew no bounds.

The spear shaft had been easy to select and shape, but the arrows took longer and the bow even longer than the arrows. Under Kaoto's tutelage, Kalo had found the proper wood for a bow, and with patience, it was taking shape. The arrows had been trimmed and straightened. Knapping points was another lesson and his first attempts were so crude that Kaoto made him his first set of arrows. The spear point Kalo had made himself.

The highlight of Kalo's day was when they went hunting, not just for meat, but also for roots and berries, herbs and tubers, anything they could use to supplement their diet. Here Kalo was most helpful. He was used to being starved by his father and had learned to scrounge for extra food whenever he had a spare, unguarded moment. He had learned to eat every manner of insect and plant. Kaoto tried to discourage this habit without directly telling him that the People did not eat this type of food. He did not want to make the lad feel inferior, so he invented the theory that eating insects weakened the brain, which made it harder to learn. He even hinted that it might make a person stutter and stammer when he tried to talk. Kaoto knew there was no truth in this and did not insist that it was so. He just suggested that it might be. Kalo quickly dropped the habit, partly because he wanted to get over his speech problem, and partly because the giant always prepared ample food for them so he no longer knew hunger.

The days flowed by lazily, but seemed to pass too quickly for Kalo. Each day they would take a short run, extending these runs gradually until Kalo could see the daily change in his skinny body. He would always be thin and slightly undersized, but at least he was filling out his gaunt frame. His face no longer looked like a tiny skull. It now looked like and eager youth's face should. His strength and stamina grew until he could spend a decent day on the trail without falling out or being left behind. Of course, Kaoto had to shorten his own steps to make it possible for Kalo's short legs to keep up. He would never forget Kalo's reproach: "Kalo's——Legs——Short"

His bodily improvement was remarkable. His speech, however, was still painfully slow and he stammered over almost every word. Kaoto encouraged him to talk even if it was difficult for both of them. Kalo never gave up trying to improve his speech, and would frown and concentrate on words almost constantly while they worked, ran, or rested. It seemed the harder he tried the more difficult it became, until he would often sit silently with tears in his eyes, hammering his fist against the side of his head in frustration

Unable to endure this demonstration of self-punishment any longer, Kaoto would take the boy in his arms and hold him tight, crushing him to his chest as if he could drain the poison from the boy into himself, where he felt he could better handle it.

Held in the giant bear hug, almost breathless, Kalo laid his head over the great man's shoulder with his lips close to his ear. On impulse he whispered, "I love you, Kaoto." The words were clear, not a hint of stammer, no faltering.

Kaoto held him even closer and pondered this. Kalo did not seem to realize that he had not stuttered and was lying quietly against Kaoto's chest, not feeling ashamed or unmanly. He had never realized what a great void there had been in his life that was created by his father. Kuat, who had never shown any signs of affection for the little boy who stuttered and stammered, had never accepted Kalo as a son. Kalo had never known the comfort and security that only a father can give to a child. Mothers were expected to love and comfort children; it was nature's way. But fathers were different. You had to earn their love and respect and he had never been able to do this. Until now he had thought he had nothing to offer, nothing to make him worthy of love. With Kaoto, it was altogether different. The hairy giant did not seem to care how he talked or how he looked. He seemed to like him just the way he was. Kaoto's patience and kindness and love were doing what all of Kuat's threats, beatings and punishment could never achieve.

Kalo never spoke of his father and Kaoto thought it best to leave the subject lie until the boy felt the need to talk about him. His speech was not perfect, but it was improving ever so slightly, and the fact that he tried without fear of reprisal made it even easier. Kalo discovered that often-spontaneous speech came more easily than studied speech. The fact that Kaoto was not ashamed to show his affection for the lad, coupled with his patience, had removed a large barrier and lifted a heavy weight from his thin shoulders.

Sister Moon had made one full turn and was well into the next cycle before Kaoto decided they should move on. Kalo was reluctant to leave his new home. He was looking forward to all the travel Kaoto had told him about, but he was still shy about meeting the People that their traveling would force them to come in contact with.

When they left the brush shelter, Kalo carried his new bow and a good supply of arrows. Some had plain wooden tips and some had fresh flint points. He was becoming very proficient with them and was able to bring down his share of the meat they ate. Around his waist, tied with a cord he had made with his own two hands, was a small knife. On his back was a pack made in part from fibers and in part from skins. It contained an extra pair of sandals and a few small items he had fashioned under Kaoto's direction. Over his shoulder was draped a cape cut from the remainder of the tent skin. All in all, he was as well equipped now, as any other young man of his age would be. Besides these items, he carried two other things no other boy could claim. First, he was a personal friend of the Wise One, who shared his trust. Kaoto had told him of his office and his need to be on the move. Secondly he carried an enormous load of pride, both in himself for his accomplishments, and for his friend. This load did not weigh him down. If anything, it made him so light he could almost float. He was still behind other boys his age, but in terms of education, Kaoto's teaching and his own determination to learn were narrowing this gap with each passing of the sun. Kaoto knew that before Sister Moon completed her next turn he would be caught up, and in some areas surpassing all his peers.

The next chore was to take Kalo to a village to see if he could mingle with the People. They had often seen runners and other travelers passing by, far enough away so they would not intrude on the Wise One. Kaoto, on several occasions, asked Kalo if he would like to call out to them and have them come up to their shelf to visit. But each time Kalo had declined, putting off the inevitable until a later date. Now the time had come when Kaoto knew he could not wait any longer. His own mission was starting to call to him. His dream had returned and he knew he must be on the trail again. When he talked of the upcoming meetings with other people, he could sense Kalo's apprehension.

"Will they like me?" he asked frequently.

"They will like you if you like yourself," Kaoto had replied to the question each time.

"I do not know if I like myself. How will I know when I like myself? How can you tell?"

"When you do something and are well pleased with the way it turned out, when you make something and you have done better than you expected. When you feel you could run all day without any reason other than you just feel happy, that is how you will know," the Wise One explained.

"I feel that way now. I like most of the things I do and I love to run. Oh, I know I can never run as fast or as far as you can, but I still love it. But I am still afraid of meeting strangers."

"What are you afraid of? They are no different than I am and you are not afraid of me," Kaoto said.

"I cannot believe there is anyone else like you in the whole nation," Kalo said.

"The People are almost all like me, Kalo. Of course, they are not nearly as tall, but they treat everyone as I treat you." Kalo shook his head but did not argue the point.

"I guess I am afraid they will look at me and see all my scars and wonder how I got them. What can I tell them if they start asking questions? What do I say if they want to know where I come from and where I have been living?" he finally stammered.

"Trust me, Kalo. They will look and they will see your scars, but they will not ask you any questions. The scars are nothing to be ashamed of. You did nothing to deserve them. Besides, many people carry similar scars."

"You mean other people have been treated like me?"

"Of course not. What I was talking about is natural scars. Sometimes men, or boys, will suffer a bad fall, leaving them with many cuts or bruises. Sometimes they get caught in a wild fire and are badly burned. Once in a great while, a man will tangle with an animal and get scratched up. No one asks them questions. They know if the person wants to talk about it, he will."

"But I did not get mine in any of those ways. Would it be right to let them think something different than the truth?"

"Do you want to tell them how you got them?" Kaoto asked.

"No. Not now, anyway. Maybe later, after I get to know them and they get to know me. But not now." Kalo hung his head, as if ashamed of a weakness.

"Then do not say anything about them and they will not ask. Let them think what they will. There is nothing wrong in that. It is sort of like them thinking I am really wise. I know I am not, but they still call me the Wise One because it is my office. Is this wrong?"

"Of course not. You are wise. You are the wisest person I know of." Kalo smiled at this statement and amended it. "I guess you are the only person I have ever known besides my father, so that is not a fair comparison. But I know you are wise."

"Then if you think I am so wise, why not believe me? Why not trust me? I have not done anything to hurt you or cause you shame yet, have I?"

"No. You have done nothing to me but good and you have never lied to me. Have you?" He stopped and looked at his giant friend.

Kaoto stood in the middle of the path and placed his hands on Kalo's shoulders. He could still feel the bones under his skin, but there was a solid feel to his frame now. He looked deep into the trusting eyes of the young man in the making. He could not lie to him this time.

"Yes, I have lied to you, but I did not lie to hurt you. I did it to help you. First, I never had a friend who stuttered. I made that part up. I never had any friends besides the two I told you about. I did it to help you gain confidence to speak. Second, eating insects does not affect either your brain or your speech. The People just do not eat them unless they are starving. I know you had to before I met you, but you do not have to any longer. Third, there are no other people like me. No two people are alike, just as you and I are different. Still we think the same and most of the People are kind and will treat you well. Even if you were not traveling with me, they would still welcome you and feed you. But since you are with me, you will share many of the privileges that come to me. You will always have enough to eat and a place to stay. You will be greeted as a friend, not as a stranger. Trust me. This time I am not lying to you. I am telling you the truth." He let his hands fall to his side and stepped back.

"I believe you. But why do we have to go to a village? Why not stay out here and live as we have been living? We do not need other people, do we?" Kalo pleaded.

"I cannot stay here any longer. I have told you of my mission and I must get on with it. You say we do not need other people but everyone needs other people to live a proper life. The People need me and I have given my word in front of them and the Spirit Watcher that I would go to them and do what I can to help them, just as I have done for you. If I had stayed away from people I would never have found you or been able to help you. Surely you can understand that."

"Yes. I guess so. But I still wish we did not have to go to a village right now. Later, maybe, I would feel better about it," He said wistfully.

"There is no more time. I must do my job and I do not want to leave you out here by yourself. If I did, you would never leave here and would die alone."

"Your job. Can I go with you and help?" Kalo asked. "You will not go off and leave me, will you?" There was real concern in his eyes and his voice and he stuttered hopelessly for the first time that day.

Kaoto knelt down so his eyes were on the same level as Kalo's. Looking him straight in the eyes he told him, "One day our paths must separate. We must go our separate ways. I have many things to do, much land to cover. Even a full-grown man would have trouble keeping up with me. You have to grow up and become a man. Some day you will want to settle down and find a mate so you can raise sons of your own."

"I do not ever want to leave you, Kaoto. You are my father now and I love you. I could not live without you. Who would teach me if you leave?" His eyes were filled with mist and his voice trembled with emotion.

"I said someday. I did not say tomorrow. I will teach you and you will go with me for a long time yet. But still, the day will come when you must go your way and I must go mine. I do not stay with my father. I have left his home. I still love my father and will all the days of my life. I promise you, when the time comes, it will be your decision and you will be ready and will understand why it must be so. I will not leave you until them."

Kalo did not argue this point either. He knew he would never be ready to leave the side of this hairy giant who had saved him from his horrible fate. Who had fed him? Who had given him his first clothes? Who had taught him everything he knew? Never, as long as he lived, would he willingly leave Kaoto's side to take another path. The only way he would do that is if Kaoto told him he must go, but never willingly. Never of his own free will.

Day by day they moved across the land. Each village they visited made Kalo feel uneasy. At first he was afraid this would be the time Kaoto would decide they must part. He stayed so close to the giant's side that the elders made jokes about the tiny shadow of such a tall man. Kaoto was quite content to have the lad at his side and to introduce him as his son. For two summers the lad faithfully paced with him. His body was fully developed now and his mind had seemed to reject all thoughts of his past. His life began when he woke up under the tent Kaoto had erected over him while he slept. It had been the day of his rebirth.

In one village Kaoto arranged for Kalo to take his manhood rites and saw him finish first in the final race. At the ceremonies afterward he announced his desire to formally adopt him as his son. No one opposed him. They were all sure the Wise One knew what was right and proper. The formal adoption had little effect on Kalo. However, he accepted with pride the eagle feather taken from Kaoto's own hair, but he had always been Kaoto's son and did not need this to make it so.

On the trail Kaoto used Kalo for an audience to recite the nation's history and was amazed to discover that Kalo had a remarkable memory also. He asked many questions about the history and could repeat long sections of it. It became a game to see how much he could remember until he knew it almost as well as Kaoto himself. He started collecting chips of bone and stone to make his own necklace.

Whenever Kaoto was called upon to settle a dispute, he would invite Kalo to sit in and listen. Kalo would sit in silence at his side, never missing a word. Afterwards he would often discuss the issue with his new father. Kaoto was impressed with the boy's gentle spirit. In spite of his own violent and unpleasant boyhood days, he seemed to have empathy for people and an understanding of their feelings. His knowledge was growing as fast as his vocabulary. He seemed to have a knack for putting his finger on the cause of dissension. With a little encouragement he would offer his own suggestion on how he would handle such a problem.

Kaoto listened. He never forgot what Paataga had told him about listening and making the People think he was wise. He began to ask questions, just as Paataga had done with him, leading his pupil to find new depths of understanding, and making him ask questions of himself. It was a game to Kalo, and he never tired of it. Often by the end of the day Kaoto would be mentally exhausted with all the questions, counter questions, and cross-examinations.

One evening, as they sat by the fire in the emptiness of the plains between villages, Kaoto asked Kalo how many summers he thought he had.

"I am not sure, but I think it will be fifteen this summer," Kalo replied after giving the matter much thought.

"Fifteen? So many? My how the time has flown. A man of fifteen summers should be thinking of taking a mate and settling down and raising a family." Kaoto told him.

Kalo remained quiet. The time he feared was approaching. Kaoto was thinking about leaving him. What could he do or say?

"I have not thought much of a mate father. Where would I find a mate who would be able to take to the trail as we must?"

"You do not have to find a mate to take to the trail. It is the custom for a young man to live near his mate's mother. Her father will help him find a field to farm. You would build a house next to theirs so they are close by to help when they are needed." Kaoto had told him of this custom before but felt the need to explain it once more.

"You have not taken a mate and you have many more summers than I do," Kalo said. He knew this would not change Kaoto's mind, but he had to say it anyway. "So why must I find a mate when I do not want to?"

"I did not say you must. I have told you many times you are a free man. No one will force you to do anything you do not want to do. I am not forcing you or even asking you to. I am just telling you what most young men are doing at your age. Besides, there are not that many summers between us. Just because I am big does not mean I am old." According to Kaoto's figures he was in his twenty-fifth summer.

Kalo became quiet and moody again. He was sure of what Kaoto wanted him to do so he said no more, hoping his father would forget it and they could go on just as they had before.

Kaoto let the matter drop, but he had seen the wistful longing in the young man's eyes when the young maidens trooped by on their way down to the local water hole to bathe, with the young men tagging along behind. The noise from the stream testified to the delight that they were experiencing in each other's company at this unguarded moment.

Kalo did not recognize the strange emptiness he was feeling at these times, but Kaoto did and he made up his mind that at the next large village they came to he would make it a point to introduce Kalo to the joys a young man should know. Remembering his own lonely life, he was determined his son would not face the same thing. He at least had had Little Frog for a companion. Kalo had only Kaoto and that was not right for man of his early age.

The villages of Keet Seel and Betatkin were up ahead of them. Both were large and prosperous, as well as being in good locations. They were not far apart, and surely there would be someone in one of them who could take Kalo's mind off the trail and his dependence on his adopted father. They would stay as long as it took. Kaoto did not doubt that Kalo would be settling in one of these villages with some bright-eyed young maiden of his choice. As much as he would miss Kalo, he knew he was traveling much to slowly. He had been using his desire to help Kalo as an excuse.

He would take as long as necessary to get Kalo settled, but he knew that he must get on with his mission. His thoughts were often on Moot and his village. He wondered if they still lived, if they had made much progress. But the north land was calling him now and he knew he must be going that way, and soon.

Chapter Twenty Eight

Keet Seel and Betatkin lived up to Kaoto's expectations. Even though he had never been there before he had heard much about them. While neither was overly large, they both were favorably located and were surrounded by many smaller villages. Like Bonito in the Chaco, they were the central gathering points of the People of this region.

Butan, the ruler of the Keet Seel region was a tough wiry little man much like Mula of the Black Rock. Butan had not been to Chaco to see Kaoto receive his office as Wise One, but he had been informed by the runners that the Wise One was coming his way.

The past summers had worked a change on the young giant who had left Chaco with such high hopes and noble ideals. His frame was more filled out and his face was no longer that of an eager youth. His eyes reflected the horrors he had seen, and done, along the trail. Always a quiet man, he now carried shades of sorrow in his eyes and it was also found in his voice.

Butan had expected him to be brisk and formal. He thought he would be talking with the elders and himself about problems of the village and territory. But Kaoto came as a man, not a Wise One. He made no demands, asked few questions and talked to anyone who approached him. He took great delight in the children and young people, and some thought he wasted too much time with them.

Butan had also heard from the runners about Kaoto's concern for those on the dumpsite and had acted on his own. Due to the location of the village, the dumpsite was below the cliff house and the refuse was literally thrown down. He did not think that Kaoto would accept this as a good location for himself or the creatures of the dump, so he had erected a small lodging closer to the village. He showed no surprise when Kaoto established his living quarters there.

Keet Seel was situated on a high shelf under a huge overhanging cliff. It was relatively new by the People's standards and had been built with care and designed for its purpose. There was room for more expansion here if it was ever considered necessary. The protection of the cliff held back the cold north wind in winter; still, the long rays of the Spirit Watcher warmed it. In the summer the overhanging cliff cut some of the Spirit Watcher's heat and, as it set so high, the air rose up the cliff face to create ventilation. Giant cotton wood trees shaded a portion of the valley in front of the pueblo. It was a very pleasant spot, a place blessed twice over, and Kaoto knew he would enjoy his brief stay here.

He and Kalo had arrived in the late fall when the leaves were golden and the days were lazy. The harvest was over and the grain was stored. Nothing in the world seemed to be able to threaten the peaceful, happy life led by these People. The stories of the savages were just that, stories.

The weather was drier here than in the Chaco, and the People had learned long ago to build dams and dikes to hold back and control the water.

Fields were well irrigated so their pumpkins and squash grew large and the corn did not burn and shrivel from lack of moisture. Life was good. They lacked for nothing and could ask for little more than what they had.

How could he convince them of the danger he knew would eventually reach them, even here? Would he believe such a story if he had not seen it first hand? The Wise One knew he would have to give much thought to how he would present the subject to Butan and the elders. As for the rest of the People, he did not think he would be able to tell them at all. But while he waited, he would take in the idyllic days of peace here.

In the stream close to the front of the village, there was an irrigation dam to hold back water. It formed a large pool, and now that it was not needed for the fields it was allowed to stand and be warmed by the Spirit Watcher during the long cloudless days. Besides household needs it served as a bathing pool. The upper end was shallow and had a sandy bottom. Here mothers could leave their little children to play while they ventured into the deeper water farther down. Near the dam the water was deep enough to be over the heads of most of the adults. It was here the young people gathered to frolic. Along one side a stone ledge protruded out just under the water level. The older people gathered here to soak up the kindly warmth without having to swim where they would stir up the cooler water underneath.

Any afternoon the entire population of the village could be found somewhere in the pool. Kaoto chose the ledge with the elders and Butan. Kalo also sat silently in the warm waters close to the Wise One.

"Kalo, why do you sit here with the elders? Why do you not join the young people down by the dam? I know you can swim. I taught you myself," Kaoto asked him one afternoon.

"I feel more at ease here with you. I have nothing to talk about with the young people," he answered truthfully.

"Talk? They do not talk. They scream and laugh and splash, but they do not waste their time with meaningless talk. That is for us older people. Go join them. I am sure you will find it more interesting than sitting here with all us old bones," Kaoto chided him.

"I will go if you tell me I must," Kalo replied. "But I would rather stay here."

Kaoto could tell that it would not take much to coax him to join the youngsters. All he needed was someone to invite him. He was too shy to go without being asked.

Butan, who had been listening, knew a part of Kalo's story and understood the problem facing the young man. He motioned for his young daughter to come to his side.

"Pala, will you take this young man down and introduce him to your friends? Make him feel welcome in the village. He is a little shy and does not feel he should intrude without being asked."

"We did not invite you because we thought you were already mated.

Are you?"

"N-nn-nnn-ooo—o," he stammered painfully. He would have gladly dropped out of sight in the stream if he could have.

"Well, we thought you might be mated in another village and preferred to stay away from us so you could remain faithful to someone," Pala explained, ignoring his stammering. She took him by the hand and led him, although he was reluctant, down the bank to the noisy group below, shouting introductions as she went. Kalo looked back to Kaoto, who waved him on with a smile as he lay back in the warm water, content with the progress of his adopted son.

In a short time Kalo had become one of the young people and he was never far from Pala's side. Even from a distance, the worship in his eyes was evident to both fathers. From that day he could always be found near her side, but always there was a backward glance to Kaoto to see if he approved. Butan also watched them with interest during the following days.

"Kalo seems quite taken with my daughter," he said to Kaoto one afternoon.

"It would seem that way, and why not? She is a comely maiden," Kaoto agreed.

"Has the lad ever been mated?" Butan asked.

"No."

"Why not? I mean he is sound, is he not? There is nothing wrong with him, is there?" Butan persisted. "He is surely old enough, is he not?"

Kaoto weighed his words carefully before he spoke. "Kalo is a normal, healthy, young man. He has had a terrible past, but that is all behind him now. As I told you, he has been traveling with me for the past several summers and has not had a chance to settle down and get acquainted with anyone. This is the first time we have stopped for any length of time. But I do not know if he is ready for a mate yet or not."

"Will he be going with you when you leave here?" Butan asked.

"He is free. He can go or stay. It is as he pleases."

"You are his father."

"Yes." The Wise One watched Kalo and Pala playing like otters in the deep water. "But he is his own man. He just has not had time to think about it until now." This was true and he did not feel obligated to explain further. He stretched in the warm water to his full length. "I have thought I might stay here a while longer, if I am welcome?"

Butan smiled. "That is hardly a question that needs to be asked." He let a long silence settle between them, as older men often do when they are thinking more than talking.

"My daughter is of an age to mate, but she has shown no signs of being interested in any of the young men here. She tells me they are all so young, meaning she does not think any of them are mature enough for her. This is partly my fault. She is my only daughter and she came late in our life. When my mate died a few summers back, Pala took her mother's place in my home, and this has aged her somewhat. Now she does not feel she should go off and leave me alone. All of this has made her older than most of the other youngsters here."

"Kalo is also old for his summers. His former life aged him when he was still a child. He has never known the normal life of a happy, carefree youth," Kaoto said.

"Yes, I have noticed that he seems quite different from the other young men. That is why I asked you about him. I did not want to embarrass him or my daughter," Butan explained. "He is not filled with so much air and idle chatter as most young men of his age, nor have I ever heard him boast, as most of them do, about all the things he has done or is about to do."

Kaoto smiled. He was sure he knew where Butan's talk was leading and he thought he would encourage him to continue talking. "Pala also shows much wisdom for a mere child. It must come from her father."

Butan watched the young couple for a while before he spoke again. Kaoto's words were reassuring. He now felt comfortable to speak what was on his mind.

"I would be pleased to accept Kalo as a mate for my daughter. If you think he would have her, of course," he added hastily. It was not every man who had a chance to mate his daughter with the son of the Wise One. He had done all he could. He had praised the son to his father and made the offer. Now it was up to the father to speak his mind.

"I would be very pleased if they should mate. Pala seems like a good choice for Kalo. They suit each other temperamentally, but as I have said before, Kalo is his own man. I have made it plain to him I would never force him to do anything he did not want to do, nor will I try to influence him to do anything just to please me."

At this moment Kalo and Pala were racing across the pond side by side in smooth even strokes. "It does not look like it would take too much to persuade him to stay here, but it is his decision. Unfortunately, he also feels obligated not to leave me, and try as I might, I cannot convince him that he does not owe me anything. Perhaps Pala will be more persuasive than I have been." Stretching once more lazily in the warmth of the water, he added, "I guess we will stay a little longer and hope for the best for both of them and try to forget our own desires."

Butan was content to let it rest this way. He would talk to his daughter. He would find out how she felt about this young man and push as much as he could, when he could.

Kaoto was satisfied to let nature take its course. He found excuses to prolong their stay in Keet Seel. Kalo was satisfied to stay without questioning the Wise One's motives. He was, however, surprised one evening to return to their shelter and find his father packing a light pack for a journey.

Silently, he too began to pack, and although he did not say anything, Kaoto could sense his disappointment. "There is no reason for you to go with me, Kalo," he told the young man.

"Where you go, I go. Where do we go from here?" Kalo asked without looking up from his chores.

"I am going to visit a few villages a short distance to the north. I will be coming back this way in a ten days."

Kalo stopped packing and looked searchingly at his adopted father. "What you are telling me is true? You are not making an excuse to leave me behind?"

Kaoto did not try to hide the hurt he felt at this accusation. He had always known that Kalo had this great fear of being deserted. Nothing he could say or do seemed to ease the fear. Still, he would try once more to assure him.

"Have I ever given you reason to think I would leave you? What makes you think I would try to sneak off on you? If I wanted you to stay behind, I would simply tell you to do so."

"You have said our paths must part someday and that we would go our separate ways. Is this the time you spoke of?" Kalo asked.

"If you will stop to think, you will also remember I said when the time came you would be ready. Did I not?"

"I am not ready," Kalo said slowly, reluctantly. He was torn between two desires. One to stay with Pala, the other to go on with his father.

"Then if you do not trust me, by all means pack and come with me. But you will find yourself back here in ten days and wonder why you left in the first place." Kaoto continued to finish his pack without looking again at Kalo.

Kalo was undecided. He knew he should trust Kaoto. He did trust him, but he could not get rid of the feeling of being deserted. He really had no desire to leave this pleasant place. He was very happy here. For the first time in his life, he felt that he could live with these people in comfort and trust. He had a peculiar feeling for Butan's daughter. Being with Pala was all the happiness he could ever want and at times there were deeper feelings that disturbed him. It was partly these feelings that made him decide to go. He needed to be away from here for a time and be able to talk with his father in private about these feelings and what he should do about them. He had lacked courage to bring them up before, but on the trail he would be able to voice his doubts.

"I do trust you, my father," he said finally, "but I will go with you anyway. There are things I need to say to you and it will be easier on the trail. It is where we have always talked."

They were up and preparing to leave early in the morning. Kaoto had already explained his plans to Butan. Kalo, on the other hand, had not told Pala of their departure. He cast several thoughtful glances over his shoulder as they left the village.

"I will wait if there is someone you wish to speak with before we go," Kaoto told him.

"No. No, I think it is best this way."

"Whatever you think."

Their trail led them up the canyon and then followed a small branch until they were soon on top of the rim. From here they set off in a northern direction across rough terrain which kept them busy watching their footing, leaving little time for talk.

Kaoto set his pace briskly on the trail and did not stop to eat or drink. Instead they chewed on dry rations, the first they had eaten in many days. The Wise One pushed on until, near dusk, they came to the first of several tiny pueblos. It was secreted away in the twisting formation of the rocks and it would have been nearly impossible to find without prior instructions from Butan. The People here had heard of him but never expected to see him, let alone have a visit in person from the Wise One.

He made it a point to not only talk to the elders in these tiny villages, but also took time to speak with every person, old and young. He told them of the possible threat of the savages, but he was sure they would never be bothered here, so he did not suggest they ever leave. Instead, he cautioned them about the time when they might become surrounded and isolated by this threat. It was mentioned that they might want to pull in closer to Keet Seel when this time came so they could be more secure in their numbers. They listened politely, but he knew they would never leave this hidden valley until perchance the savages stumbled on them and slaughtered them all in their homes. In their place, he supposed, he would make the same choice they were going to make.

Without deliberately avoiding Kalo, he made it impossible for them to have any time alone to speak. Each night he would sit up late with the elders and then go directly to sleep. Early in the morning he would be away on the trail, setting such a pace that Kalo was lucky just to keep up with him. Kalo knew that his father was still not hitting his top speed, and if he had done so he would never have been able to keep him in sight.

Kaoto was certain of what was on Kalo's mind and he wanted him to have ample time to think before he spoke. He also wanted this time away from Pala and Keet Seel to be a reminder of what he would be leaving behind if he continued on the trail with him. Up until now the trail had been the only real life Kalo had known and it had been enough. Now Kaoto wanted him to experience the loneliness of the trail, and the hectic pace that he must set from now on. He wanted Kalo to know that the Wise One could no longer linger at the villages or dally on the trail to make it easy for anyone who might be following him. He wanted to impress on Kalo the fact that if he had trouble keeping up, how would Pala be able to travel with them. He was sure this was what was bothering Kalo. This is what he wanted to talk to him about. Now that he had enjoyed Keet Seel, he might have a different opinion than he had before.

During the first few days it was evident that Kalo resented Kaoto's enigmatic behavior. Later he seemed to accept it and waited patiently for the time when he would be able to speak to his father. His time came as they were on the last leg of their trip, which would bring them back to Keet Seel and all that he had left there. True to Kaoto's word, it was the tenth day since they had left, but to Kalo it seemed like a lifetime. Kaoto had stopped abruptly on a long ridge that overlooked a vast sea of rocks and sandy plains. Kalo had noticed in their travels together that his father almost always stopped on a high point where he could see as far as the geography would allow. He was sure it was due to the dreams of the Wise One.

There was a brisk breeze sweeping over the top to the ridge, making it a pleasant place to rest. He sat silent, waiting for Kalo to speak. He did not have long to wait.

"When you made to leave without me, I was a little angry. And when you deliberately made it impossible for me to speak with you the first day, I was even angrier. What I would have said would have been said in anger. It would have been hasty and ill planned. Now that you have so wisely let me think and cool off without distractions for the past ten days, I can see where I was wrong. What I have to say now is more carefully thought out."

"It must be as you say. I notice you have not stuttered on yours words. You often do when you are angry or excited."

"That is true. Something has happened to change all that. I no longer stutter because I am no longer a boy. I am a man now, a man with a purpose and a reason."

"And what does the man with a purpose and reason propose to say?" There was no trace of humor in his voice or on his face as he spoke to his son.

Kalo had been standing off to one side of his father as he spoke, looking at the horizon, trying to see what the Wise One saw. He now turned and placed himself in front of the seated giant. He was short, even for one of the People, and still did not come much above Kaoto's head. He tried several times before he could look his father in the eye and speak without faltering.

"With your permission, and assistance, I would take the one called Pala for my mate." He held his breath, waiting for Kaoto's reply. Kaoto's quick smile let him know this came as no surprise to the Wise One.

"You do not need my permission and I doubt very much you need my assistance, either."

"Your permission is very essential to me and always shall be. As for assistance, there is much both Pala and I are ignorant of and need instructions in. Who better to advise us than the Wise One?"

"Almost anyone would be better equipped to answer your questions than I am. I may be a Wise One, but I know nothing of mating or home life."

"But you always have answers for everyone else, no matter what the nature of their questions. Surely you can help us."

"If you have been listening as closely in the past as I believe you have, then you will know I do not have all the answers. I only help people find the answer within themselves."

"Yes. I have noticed that. So, if we already have the answers within ourselves, then can you not make us see them just as you do everyone else? Being your son does not exclude me from the benefit of your counsel, does it?"

216 - Norman D. Messenger

Kaoto was made aware again, as he had been so many times in the past, of his power over people simply because of the office he held. The great responsibilities that were placed on his shoulders were there because of his office, not because of himself. Everyone thought him capable of whatever they imagined a Wise One should be able to do. Of all the people he dealt with, he knew he could not disappoint his son.

"We will return to the village and I will think on it. Tomorrow you and Pala will come to me and we will talk on this matter. I already can tell you Butan favors this union, if that will ease your mind any." Kalo's long sigh and smile was an answer to this statement.

"But remember," he told Kalo as the youth started to take the trail back to Keet Seel to speak with Pala. "When you come to me tomorrow you must have all your questions ready so we may proceed without delay." Kalo nodded and started to again. "But," Kaoto's words halted him. "More important, and probably much harder to do, you must remember you will be talking to the Wise One, not your father." He had Kalo's full attention now and he waited patiently on the path, his head down, no longer thinking about Keet Seel or Pala.

"I must treat you as if you were both strangers to me. I must act as if I had never seen either one of you before this time and know nothing of your past or your plans for the future. The lad I have traveled with no longer exists; he is gone. In his place is the new man." Kaoto gave Kalo a long steady look, measuring him as if, in truth, he was a new man he had never seen before. "If you wish to ask the advice of the Wise One, you must come that way. No other way will do."

Kalo was silent for a long moment. He had not thought of this. He had thought he would be talking to his father, asking him for advice as someone he knew and trusted. Now he was being told this was not so. He must approach the Wise One just as any other man, with no special privilege. He should have known this. If he had given it any thought, he would have known Kaoto had to treat him the same as he treated the rest of the People. There was a moment of sadness in his heart when he realized he had crossed a canyon that he could never return from. His life had changed in the few moments they had talked here.

"It shall be as you say. It will be most difficult, but I can see the wisdom of your choice. If you are to help us, we must not be different from all the People. This does not pose a problem to us because I know you love all your People equally."

This last statement touched Kaoto. He had never thought of himself as being particularly loving toward the People. Maybe Kalo could see something he could not. He remembered his words to Paataga about how she loved her People, and the old crone had been equally surprised. It was a compliment he had not expected, and if anything, it would make his chore tomorrow even more difficult. He watched Kalo, who was now hurrying down the trail, in a hurry to get back to Pala and tell her the news.

Chapter Twenty Nine

As they came near to the village of Keet Seel, Kaoto called to Kalo, who was far ahead already. "I will wait and watch the Spirit Watcher goes to rest. I will see you both tomorrow. Until then I do not wish to be disturbed."

Kalo was so excited to be getting back to Pala that he hurried on without asking questions. He lengthened his stride and rushed on down the trail without a backward glance. Kalo did not see the sadness in the Wise One's eyes as he stood watching his son dash down to the valley floor, calling Pala's name as he ran.

Kaoto left the trail and walked along the rim to a point of rocks overlooking the valley. From this point above the canyon he could see the village nestled in against the opposite face of rock. He sat alone with his thoughts, thoughts he could not share with his son, or with anyone in the village. There was only one person with whom he could share his inner most feelings, and she was far away in the Chaco Canyon.

At first he had trouble controlling his emotions. His mind regressed back over the past summers of wandering with Kalo at his side. They had been good times. Times he would always treasure. But he had known they must come to an end. He himself had told Kalo as much. Now the time had come. Their paths were about to separate and go in different directions. Kalo would not be forced, at least not by the Wise One, but he would make a choice on his own that would lead him to his own life and destiny.

Now that the time was here, Kaoto did not know if he himself was ready. He had never guessed it would be this hard. Still, it was what he had planned. It was what he had hoped to accomplish when he lingered here at this pleasant village. He had wanted the lad to have a chance to get acquainted with other young people, especially young maidens he might choose for a mate, and he had done so. As a Wise One, he should be pleased. He was pleased, but still there was room for this nostalgic moment of precious memories.

The next morning, when Kalo rose from his sleeping mats, he could see Kaoto had not returned during the night. His mat was still rolled up against the wall in its usual place and his pack was not there. A flash of fear rushed over him, causing him to dart from the shelter and out into the open as if he expected someone to come tell him his father was gone. His fear was replaced by a wave of shame as he looked to the rim and saw the Wise One sitting on the same point of rock that he had been sitting on last night. He was a lonely looking profile against the rising sun. Kalo started to raise his hand and call, but something about the stalwart, solitary figure stopped him. It was then that he recalled his father's words. Today he was the Wise One.

Kaoto sat with his face toward the rising of the Spirit Watcher. He did not expect any consolation from his deity, but it always seemed to give him strength to face trying times. After his speech at Moot's cliff house he was never sure again just how much influence the Spirit Watcher might have on his life, but he was willing to give him all the credit, whether he deserved it or not.

Kalo lowered his hand and cleared his throat to dislodge the lump caught there. Today he was just another man, one of the People. He felt a shiver pass over him, a loneliness he had never known before. It took possession of him and left him cold and frightened. He realized he had severed the cord that had bound him to the tall, hairy giant. It would never be the same between them again. He had taken one of the many steps forward toward manhood, and he paused for a moment to mourn his lost boyhood.

His face was furrowed with thought when he arrived at Pala's lodgings. He had told her all that had transpired yesterday, and they must begin making preparations for their meeting with the Wise One tonight.

They spent much of the day discussing what, and how, they would ask the Wise One to grant their wish. Kalo soon knew that most of what they were talking about was just a sham, a stall, an evasion of the true reason for their meeting. He knew most of it was made up to impress the Wise One. No, not the Wise One, to impress his father, Kaoto. But was he his father anymore?

"Pala—how are we ever going to convince him to let us follow along? Can we make him believe that we will be no bother? And we both know we will slow him down. You should have seen him the last few days. An antelope would have had trouble keeping up with him. I have never seen him move like that and I know it was still not his top speed. He could go much faster and much longer. It made me feel like an infant again, and then I stood there and told him I was a man." In spite of his self-incrimination, he could not conceal his pride in his father.

"What if he does not want us with him?" Pala asked.

"I do not know." Kalo sat looking a Pala. He was dejected and confused. This was a real problem to him. He could not visualize living without his father around. It had never occurred to him that Kaoto might turn them down. Now he was beginning to have serious doubts. They would have to do everything they could to convince him. But how?

"He is the Wise One, he will know it is right for us to mate and it would be wrong for you not to go with him. He will have the answer. What else can he do?" Pala said as she tried to reassure him.

"I do not know." He repeated more to himself than to her. "But he can always find the truth and make it come to the surface where it is more evident than anyone wants it to be. He makes the truth seem more important than wishes or demands," Kalo said as he recalled many past meetings he had sat in on with the Wise One.

All through the day they watched the figure on the point of rocks. It never seemed to move, yet it was always facing the Spirit Watcher. Never had Kalo seen his father act this way. Nothing had ever disturbed him this much before. He had always been ready for a meeting without all this preparation. This indeed must be a serious situation to cause him to sit all day without food or water. The later in the day it became, the more nervous Kalo grew.

Just before the time of the meeting, Kalo looked up and was startled to see the point of rock was vacant. Kaoto was no longer there. Looking quickly around, he saw his father was rising from the waters of the pool. The late rays of sun, coming in on a long angle, shone on the droplets of water trapped in the hairs on his body, enhancing the golden hue of his mane and torso. Walking up from the water and shaking himself dry like a great golden lion, he donned his feathered cloak and his single eagle feather.

Kalo had always been impressed with his father's great height. In fact, he had thought he was quite used to it, but now he could not help but be amazed at how such a big man could present such a noble and yet humble appearance at the same time. In spite of his size, Kaoto had a way of making the People feel comfortable around him, but Kalo did not have that feeling now. He felt little and frightened, like a little boy hiding from his father in fear, although he knew he had nothing to fear from this man. In his heart he wished he could retreat back to the first summer this man had come to him and saved him. He wished he would live in that summer forever.

Would the Wise One know they were trying to fool him? Kalo felt not only small and alone, but physically ill. He wished he had not planned it this way. He wished he could do it differently, but now it was too late. The time of the meeting had arrived and the Wise One was seated with the elders, waiting for them.

Kaoto saw them approaching him and could not help but see what a pleasant looking couple they made. Even though they were both distressed, it was still plain to see that they were very much in love with one another. This was what was important at this meeting, how they felt about each other and nothing else.

Although it was a warm evening, a fire had been laid in front of the Wise One. A fire made the meeting official. Without a fire it would just have been a family gathering, a social event. Since these meetings were open to the public, most of the village had gathered here. They had never seen the Wise One act in his official capacity, and this would be something to tell their children's children about.

The young couple stood before him, not looking up until he spoke to them. Not calling them by name, he bid them to be seated in the place reserved for them, across the fire, directly in front of him. The gathering became ghostly quiet. Even the children seem to recognize the import of this occasion.

Kalo was the first to speak. He had sat in on enough of these sessions to know the procedure, but this was the first time he had been on the opposite side of the fire. Always before he had been seated beside the Wise One, not opposite him. Breathing deeply, he spoke without rising. This was the custom.

"Wise One. We have come to ask your help."

"Who asks for my help?" Kalo had forgotten this. Kaoto always asked those before him to identify themselves so everyone would know who they were.

"Kalo, son of——Kaoto, and Pala, daughter of Butan, ruler of the People," he answered, feeling strange in this position.

"And how may I help Kalo and Pala?" Kaoto asked in the same even tone of voice, no trace of emotion showing.

"This maiden and I have found pleasure in each other and feel we are well matched to mate." Pala nodded her head in agreement. "We would mate if it is agreeable to both our parents." This was another formality, but it was the necessary opening he needed to get to what they must discuss.

"This is a natural thing. It needs no discussion with me."

"True, but this is only part of the question." Kalo tried to remain calm and meet his father's eyes, but he could feel his control slipping away and panic beginning to set in its place.

"So then, what is this other question?" Kaoto was not making it any easier for him.

"The question is—where are we going to live, after we mate?"

Kaoto studied them both closely until first Pala, then Kalo, dropped their eyes, unable to meet his steady scrutiny.

"It is the custom, I believe, for a couple to build their shelter next to the maiden's mother's home so she may still be instructed by her honored mother at times of need," Kaoto said.

"Yes. We know this is the custom, but Pala has no mother, no aunts, no close family other than her father."

"Then where do you wish to build your shelter?" Kaoto asked, still not releasing them from his steadfast gaze.

This was the moment he and Pala had both dreaded. Somehow all their carefully planned questions leading up to this point had been done away with. Kaoto, in his usual fashion, had cut through the fat and came directly to the meat, nay, to the bone of the problem. They both were secretly relieved that it had happened this way. Neither of them could have sat there and looked the Wise One in the face and tried to make a fool of him as they had planned.

Yes, this was the question Kalo had known the Wise One would ask. Would he be able to tell him what he really wanted? Would Kaoto, or the Wise One, understand? The time had come. Now they would find out if they had the courage to say what they wanted.

"We had thought we would not build a shelter at this time. We thought we would live on the trail." Kalo started off bravely enough, but finished weakly.

"On the trail?" Kaoto's voice spoke of his doubts about this decision. "The trail is no place for a young couple to start a life together. They cannot have a home on the trail. They cannot have a family on the trail. How are they to tend to crops, raise food? Are they to become like the savages of the south land? How could they live? Begging off the villages they pass through? Have you thought about this seriously? What kind of a life is this to offer to your mate? She has always lived in a home, had food ready for her. Would you ask her to share the trail with you?" Kaoto asked these questions with such intensity that

Kalo knew he was serious. Kaoto, the Wise One, really did wonder how they were going to live. He evidently did not think they were intending to live with him, off his bounty.

Kalo could not raise his eyes above his feet. He was unable to look the Wise One in the eye. Yet he knew he must answer or be disgraced in front of the People and his proposed mate. Not only that, but he would disgrace his father, the Wise One.

"My father lives on the trail. We would travel with him so we could benefit from his wisdom. My mate is agreeable to this."

"But what does your father think about this? It is unusual for a mated man to go with his father. What kind of father would allow such a thing? Have you asked him how he would feel about having you and your mate along on the trail with him?"

"I—I—I——II—do—do—n—nottttt—kn—oooo—w." Kalo stammered, as he had not done in several summers. He felt tiny and helpless, wishing he could recant from this mockery.

"Have you not discussed this with him? It is an important decision to both of you and your father. Surely you have talked with him about it. Is it possible your father is not open to you, so that you do not feel you can talk with him? If this is so, then how could you possibly travel the trail with him?"

Kalo's spirits sank. He felt weak and foolish. This was not what he had expected. He had not thought Kaoto would question him in this manner. He had expected formal questions and answers, with his father announcing they would be welcome to go with him. He had honestly thought his father would be pleased that Pala had consented to take a chance living on the trail with them.

"Y—o-u knn—oo—w—I-I—ha—ve—n—ooo—ot——F-aa-th—er," Kalo sobbed in despair and anguish.

Kaoto ignored this outburst, and although he longed to reach out to his son, he had to put aside his fatherly instincts and act strictly as the Wise One rendering his judgment just as he would for any other young couple who might come with a similar problem. He would ask them the same questions and give them the same counsel as he did anyone else.

"Surely over the past summers with your father you must have talked over such a possibility. I cannot believe your father would neglect such an important matter as this. I am sure he did not intend for you to live with him forever, did he? He must have made some mention to you, at some time, the possibility of you and him becoming separated in the future. Did he do this?"

Kalo sagged at these words as if they were a physical blow to his body. He who had suffered immeasurably under his real father now cringed at words from his adopted father. Yes. Kaoto had told him that one day their paths would separate. "I have many things to do, much land to cover, land that a small boy might not be able to travel over. You have to grow up to become a man. Someday you will want to mate and raise sons of your own." And Kalo remembered his answer. "I do not want to leave you, Kaoto. You are my father. I could not live without you." And Kaoto had answered him, "I said some day, I did not say tomorrow. I have left my father's home. I still love my father and will all the days of my life. I promise you, when the time comes, you will be ready and willing." Yes, Kalo remembered their conversation very well.

"Y-Y-Y—esss w-w-is-e o-o-ne H-H-e—d-d-did d-d-is—cussss the po-po-poss—ss-i-bil-bil-ity w—ith m-m-me-me."

"And what was it he told you?"

"T-th-at some—dda-a-y ouu—r p-pp-ath-s-s must se-se-epar-rate, wh—en I wa-wa-was read—dy."

"Are you not ready to do so now?"

"B-b-b-ut yo—yo—ou said I—I—I w-w-w—ould b-b-b-be read—dy." Another long shudder passed over his body, leaving him even weaker than before. "But I—I—I am n-n-n—o-t w—w-ill—ling. This is-is-is th—the har—rdest th—ing I—I—I—have ev—ever h-h-had to-ooo fffa-ce, W-W-Wise O-O-On-ne."

Kalo's eyes were pleading for understanding, and Kaoto thought that if this was the hardest thing he had ever faced, knowing as he did about his earlier days with his real father, then this indeed must be terrible for him. But he must go on.

"Should not a man consider his mate first? Should not a mate come before all others, even a father? I think they should make their plans together. Their plans should be for themselves and their children and no one else."

Kalo resigned himself to the Wise One's counsel and found his voice became more steady and his body was more under his control. He forced his voice to become steady as he answered.

"As always, you are right, Wise One. I have been a fool."

"A father must surely love his son. He will enjoy his company. He may even be extremely proud of him, but this does not mean he wants him to follow him all his days, even if it would make them both happy. He loves him, so he wants him to find happiness for himself. With this happiness, the father can be happy for him, wherever he may go. Does this not sound reasonable?"

Kalo knew what his father was doing. The same thing he had always done. He was making him answer his own questions by asking more questions in return. He realized for the first time that Kaoto had always been the Wise One, even when he was being his father. The two were inseparable. He could not be one without being the other.

Only yesterday he had told him that he had the answers within himself. He knew his love for Pala was too strong for him to relinquish. Kaoto had known this and he guessed he had known it would happen from the first moment that he had met Pala. He knew that one day he would have to choose between her and life on the trail with his father.

He had tried to fool himself into believing his father would welcome them and take them along with him, but all the time he knew it would not work. He knew they could not follow.

He felt his heart throbbing like a foot drum in the Great Kiva. He wished he were a small boy again so he could throw himself on his father and sob out his grief. But he was a man; he had said so himself. More, he was the son of the Wise One. He could not shame him anymore. He must be a man and act like a man. He must make a man's choice.

"I understand, Wise One. I know now what I must do. There is still one question I would ask of you." Kalo was in complete control of himself again and Kaoto was proud of his son.

"You have but to ask. If it is within my knowledge, I shall answer you."

"After today, will you still be my father, or will you always be the Wise One who has no son?"

Kaoto rose and stretched out his arms to the young man and his waiting mate. After only a brief pause they flew into his embrace, where he enfolded them with his arms, his cloak and his love. Turning slowly so he could look out over their heads to the waiting people, Kaoto spoke to them all.

"This is my son. Should a father ever renounce his son? What kind of a father would turn his back on his son? Even wise men can be fools." Holding Kalo on one side and Pala on his other, he looked to the setting sun and made this promise to his deity.

"Until the sands cover my bones. Until the Spirit Watcher forsakes the skies. Until there are no People left on earth, and even after that, you will always be my son."

Turning his back on the gathering, he called to them.

"Go now. Go to your homes. I would talk with my son and his mate. Butan, come with us. This concerns you, also."

Kaoto drew Kalo and Pala along with him, Butan following a short distance behind. Kaoto led them to the water's edge where they could watch the sunset reflected in the pool. After a time of silence, Kaoto spoke to them again. He was a father now, but always he was the Wise One.

"You asked me where you should build your shelter. I know the reason for your question, now I will give you an answer, a real answer." Pala and Kalo both smiled at their feeble attempt at subterfuge. "I would ask you to build your first shelter next to that of Maata and Keenwah, parents of Kaoto. This will be a long journey, so you will get the taste of living on the trail. I am sure you will soon tire of it. As you travel across the land toward Chaco, I would ask you to spread my words for me as you go."

"We will do as you ask, Father," Kalo answered without hesitation. "But there is more, is there not?"

"Yes, my son, there is much more. You have heard me talk of studying at the feet of Paataga. Last night I spoke to her, never mind how. She and I are never very far apart. She has known about you ever since I found you. It is at her suggestion that I propose to send you to her. She is expecting you. I would ask you both to study at her feet and when she thinks you are ready and dismisses you, I want you to return here and be a counselor for Butan's People. In the future there will be more of the People moving into this district as they flee from the savages I have told you about. They will have need of a strong mind and sound counsel when this time comes. You know the history, but you must repeat it often so they will know who you are." With these last words, he hugged them both to him in a fierce clench that left them breathless when he released them.

"I may not be back this way for many summers, if ever. Kalo, you and Pala can be my eyes, ears, and voice, because you know my mission and what I have been telling everyone along our trail. This would make both of your parents proud."

Kalo took Pala's hand in his own and squeezed it gently in reassurance. She returned the pressure in agreement and acceptance of the Wise One's will.

Pala loved this strange young man she was taking for a mate. This morning he had told her his entire history and how he had come to live with the Wise One as his son. She had shed a tear for the poor tormented boy who had been rescued by the Wise One. She now owed a debt of love and allegiance to the giant who had saved this man and brought him to her. Whatever he asked of them, she would gladly do, all that she could do, just to repay this debt.

"You will lose a daughter, Butan, for a short time, but she shall return and gladden your heart. Accept this temporary separation and know it will be short compared to my separation from my son." He reached out and took Kalo's hand and placed it in Butan's.

"Kalo shall be to you as the son you never had." He took one of Pala's small hands in his own large hand. "And Pala shall be to me as the daughter I shall never have. By this sharing I can accept the loss and be at ease while I am on the trail, knowing they lack for nothing."

Butan took the Wise One's wrist in his hand and by stretching a bit, placed the other on the tall man's shoulder.

"It shall be as you say, wise Kaoto. All that you have said shall be done."

Chapter Thirty

The distance stretched out as Kaoto left Keet Seel behind him. He unleashed the power in his long legs. It felt good to really run again. It would take a few days to accustom himself to full stride after several summers of holding back for Kalo. Kalo had become a good runner, and under his training he had done exceptionally well, but no amount of training or determination could offset the difference in their sizes. His stunted early development had deprived him the endurance to ever be a great runner.

Kaoto reveled in his new freedom and it helped to take his mind off his loss. Not only did he run farther and faster each day, he soon found he was not stopping as often or as long in the villages he encountered. Here, in the heart of the nation, the threat was unknown. When he tried to tell the People about it, they could not comprehend what it was he was warning them of. It was beyond their imagination. Could there really be such people as the ones Kaoto described to them? He finally decided to rely on his runners to spread the word. He purposely sent some of them to contact Mute and his little band, to impress upon them the reality of what he was saying.

Day after day his path led almost straight east, sometimes bearing to the north. He was soon back in familiar territory as the towers of Hovenweep came into view. After a brief visit there, he went on to the green topped mountain with its hundreds of villages, both large and small. This was also a central gathering place where the trade routes stopped to dispense much of their goods.

Here again the peaceful serenity of his surroundings made it almost impossible to broach the subject of the invading savages. While they were not all close friends, still many were men he knew from his days as a runner, men who had known of him since childhood. Here in the peace and tranquility of the mesa, it was hard for him to recall all that he had seen and done. How, then, was he to convince them?

His long hard run and meager rations had trimmed his body of any excess and he partook, with relish, of the rich foods available here. Among them, meats, which was a rare treat. Seated out on the rim of the canyon one day, he saw two men carrying the cut up carcass of a large animal similar to a deer, but much larger. It was so large it took many men to carry it.

"What have you got there?" he called to them.

"Ho, Wise One. Do you not know an elk when you see one?" they taunted him. It was not often they knew something that the Wise One did not.

"I guess not. Maybe I would if I had ever hunted them. Where do you go to find such magnificent beasts?"

"Oh, we do not hunt them ourselves. We trade for them with the hunters who live over in the high mountains," they told him.

"Trade? What do you have to trade for one of these animals? Your mate? Many mates? Surely a man who killed this beast would not part with it easily.

Would he?"

The hunters laughed at Kaoto's expense. Apparently he had never been around high country where the elk abound.

"No, Kaoto, nothing as drastic as that. The men of the mountain hunt them all the time. They live over there and never come out of the mountains. But in the high valleys where they live, they cannot raise crops. So they are willing to trade meat for grain, or squash and pumpkins."

Kaoto walked over to them and admired the size of the animal. Even fully dressed out, it was still an impressive beast. Not as large as a buffalo, but much larger than the deer and antelope he was used to.

"I have seen a few of these animals from a distance, but never close enough to shoot. Besides, I seldom hunt for more than I can eat in one day. I would love to see them close up. I would like to hunt them. It would be a story worth telling to the rest of the People. Why, the skin of one of these animals would make a winter suit for a little person like myself."

"Hmmmm. Maybe, Kaoto, but it would surely take two to cover your legs and those feet." The men laughed at their joke. Kaoto might be the Wise One to most of the People, but these two men were once runners. They remembered him from the past, when he also was just a runner like themselves. They were not in awe of his office, although they respected it. They could joke with him as an equal and not feel self conscious about it. The brotherhood of the runners was a special, unique, group who never forgot their old ties to each other.

Kaoto laughed with them, feeling a warmth he had not known since he had left Matuga's service to study with Paataga. He had almost forgotten the rough humor of the runners. Mute and his followers were devoid of this humor because of the life they were forced to live.

"How do I find these men, these hunters of elk? I must see them. I want to hunt the elk and see snow so deep a man cannot walk thorough it. I have known some streams so cold a man cannot stand in them, but I would see valleys filled with green grass even under the snow. I have heard there is so much game up there that a blind man could throw a stone and not go hungry. Is this true?"

"Most of what you have heard is true, but it takes a special breed of people to live there. It is not the life for most of us." One of the men turned and pointed to the sharp mountain peaks, which seemed to be very close. "From here you can see the valley where they live. It is just below the snow-covered tops. The winter camp is farther down."

Kaoto stood beside him and sighted along his pointing arm. He could see a valley leading up into the high country to what appeared to be a huge bowl in the side of the mountains.

"See where the stream comes out of the hills? It is the same stream that runs just below us. All you have to do is cut across until you hit it over there and follow it until you come to the winter camp. There are always a few women and little children there, and a few old ones. They will tell you how to find the hunter's summer camp farther up. It is easy to find. Just look for the smoke of their drying fires."

Looking across the wide-open valley below, Kaoto could pick out countless small villages and single-family dwellings scattered all over. For every one he saw, he knew there were two more tucked into the landscape that he could not see. Could this many of the People be talked into leaving? Of course not. Could they be banded together to withstand the force of the savages? There were a superior number of the People here, but he doubted they would unite to fight and kill. Not as long as they thought there were any other alternatives, No one could conceive of such ruthless butchery as that of the savages who had tried to trap him at Moot's cliff house.

He needed more time to find a way to make them understand. He needed more time to convince them of the danger. He would visit the hunters. He would hunt with them if they would let him. He would see these people and how they lived, so differently from the valley farmers. Maybe he would get some ideas from them. Besides, he had long promised himself the luxury of a visit to the high mountain country someday, and what better time than now? It would still be within his promise. These men were of the People also, and he had promised to visit them all.

He did not have any trouble finding the winter camp. He was amazed at the difference in their living structures. Instead of stone and mortar they consisted mostly of large logs and huge stones covered with earth. They made him think of the little prairie dog houses on the open plains. They were dug into the side of the hills in such a way as to offer the most protection from the deep snows and cold winters.

A few elderly People maintained this camp, raising a few simple short term crops, and seeing to the general upkeep of the camp itself to keep the small varmints from taking over. They also told him they had to drive away the bears in the fall to keep them from hibernating in the inviting cave-like structures they called home. From here they directed Kaoto on up to the summer camp, farther into the hills.

At the summer camp he was met with a bustling community that lived mostly in huts constructed of animal skins stretched over poles. They were easily taken down and moved down to winter camp. This was the center of the village life. Here the animals were dressed out and the skins were tanned. The meat was cut and dried for winter consumption and for trade to districts farther away.

His welcome here was different, also. These people were mostly elders who were still active and women. The elders were too old to run in the hunts, but were too independent to stay down below in winter camp. Here they worked and supervised with the wisdom that comes with age. There was a definite difference between these people and the slow, contented farmers of the lower lands that Kaoto had grown used to. The farmers always had time to visit. Here, everyone was bustling about with their specific chores.

He introduced himself using only his adult name, Kaoto. The obvious spokesman for the camp looked him over thoroughly before he spoke.

"Kaoto? The name has little meaning to me. We do not have any birds around here that run with the wind, unless it is the quail, but they would still rather fly." He was a wizen old man of many summers, but showing little signs of the deterioration or decay that one might normally expect. His muscled arms and legs were firm and steady. He never stopped work, which consisted of cutting a carcass into long narrow strips and hanging them with hundreds of others to dry in the sun. The women and children tended small fires under the racks. A hazy smoke filled the air, discouraging flies and other insects from spoiling the meat before it was dried and taken in to be either ground or wrapped for the future. The entire valley was wrapped in the smoke, giving it a perpetual twilight glow.

"It is a common bird farther south where I lived as a boy. It would rather run than fly. It is quite a fast runner. I, too, have somewhat of a reputation for running fast." Kaoto's eyes crinkled with amusement.

"I would not doubt it. You have the build for it, with those long legs. I would imagine you could really run, with the proper training," the old one said without pausing in his work.

Kaoto was amused with the old one's candid remarks. He was sure that the past many summers had kept his body in pretty good shape. Admittedly, he had not been pushing as hard with Kalo along, but still his many side trips and the past turn of the moon had toned him up again. No matter how good you were, there were those who thought you could do better. Compared to this old one, he supposed he did look soft and out of shape.

"No doubt, old father. I admit I have been living an easy life too long. That is why I have sought out the mountains. Perhaps if I stick around here for a while you could give me some helpful hints to get me back in shape."

"I do not have the time. I have all I can do the way it is. All the young men are up in the hills killing meat. They never leave anyone down here to help us out," the old one complained as he hoisted a brimming basket filled with cut meat strips to his shoulder and headed out to the racks. "The young men have no respect for the elders these days," he grumbled over his shoulder as he strode swiftly away.

Kaoto knew the weight of the basket was considerable, but the old one seemed to handle it with ease. Kaoto doubted that he needed any help, and if the truth were known, would probably refuse any if offered. So he did not offer. Instead, he followed meekly along.

"When do you expect the young hunters back?" Kaoto asked.

The old one paused for a brief moment while he scanned the skies for his answer.

"Maybe one full turn of the moon, maybe a little longer." His statement led Kaoto to believe that the weather alone was the determining factor with regard to the hunters' return.

"Do you suppose I could find them? I mean, I would not expect anyone to take time to show me the way, what with everyone being so busy and all." Kaoto was enjoying this conversation with the old father. It had been a long time since he had been able to visit without being treated as the Wise One. This always changed the mood. All normal jest was suspended and everyone deferred to his judgment. This casual banter was a refreshing change.

"What do you want to go up there for? There is plenty of fresh meat down here. The young men training to be hunters bring it down every evening. Humph. As if they needed training. They could use some training down here."

"I was not looking for fresh meat," Kaoto answered.

"Then what are you looking for? Not hard work, I would wager my spent youth on that," the old father insisted as he deftly laid the strips of meat over the racks with precise movements, leaving them in neat rows with exact spacing.

"I thought I would visit the camp and talk with the hunters, maybe join in on one hunt if they would allow it. Do you suppose they would?" Kaoto asked. The old one snorted in disgust.

"I have already told you, they do not need more hunters. There are too many already if you asked me, which no one ever does." The old one's hands never slowed as he talked, and he was already on his way back to the trimming tables to strip more meat. "If they kill any more, we will have spoiled meat lying around rotting and stinking up the place. Smells bad enough as it is." The flint knife was making swift slices, showing a lifetime of practice. This old one must have already outlasted many of his old hunting companions.

"Let's just say I am curious. I have never been on an elk hunt. I have never been in the mountains. There is much I would like to know about and much I would like to see with my own eyes, instead of just hearing about it from others."

"Humph." The old one had already finished an impressive pile of meat and was looking around for more.

"You young men are all alike. None of you want to work your way up anymore. All of you want to start at the top. Just run around watching other people work. Is this the way your father taught you down in that south land you talk about? They must train their young men differently these days. Why, I can remember when I was a lad, I was glad to work for the right to go join the hunt. I never thought of walking up to the leader and saying, 'I want to join in one of your hunts.' He would have sent me back to my mother if I had."

Kaoto was still amused by this vocal rebuke, but his summers as both a runner and as the Wise One had not prepared him for such a cold reception. He could not resist dropping a small hint.

"Have you ever heard of Paataga?" The old one's head jerked around to peer at him. "I was trained by her."

"Paataga? That old woman who is supposed to be the Wise One? Every-

230 - Norman D. Messenger

one has heard of her. We may live up in the mountains, but we are not ignorant, young man. Only I heard she has turned over her office to some youngster who took off, and no one has heard of him since. It was said he was a great big hairy fellow."

The old one's hands fell idle for the first time in many summers. He studied Kaoto closely. His eyes were not as sharp as they had been back when he was a hunter, but there was a gnawing suspicion growing behind his dim sight. He had heard somewhere about a certain young man; he would be about the same age as this tall, hairy, giant. It had been said he was intelligent beyond his time. That he had served as a runner for several summers before he was chosen to train as a Wise One. It was said, by those who had seen him, that he was different from any of the People. He was very tall and covered with golden hair.

The old one made up his mind to say no more other than to direct Kaoto on his way up to the hunters. Whatever he was here for, let Forb deal with him. He was the ruler of this district. That was his job, not the job of an old man who had outlived his time.

"Follow the stream. You will come to one of the smaller camps. They can tell you where the rest of the hunters are. They move around so much, nobody knows where to find them. They are somewhere up behind that bare ridge sticking out like a finger." The old one waved his bloody knife toward a bare rock formation. He did not look up again and went on busily cutting meat.

Kaoto knew he had been dismissed. The old one was through talking and expected to be left in peace.

"Thank you, old father. I probably will see you again on my way back down." Kaoto was still smiling.

"Humph. Do not bother. I may not be here. Do not waste time looking for me." He picked up his basket and marched down to the drying racks, his back as straight and stiff as a new arrow.

"I have time, old father. I always have time to talk to those who will listen." He adjusted his pack again and took off up a well-defined trail along the bank of the stream, heading in the general direction of the barren ridge.

The old one's eyes turned to follow the young giant's progress until he was out of sight. Dropping his basket, he sat down and held his head in his hands and bemoaned his fate.

"Old fool. Talking when you should have been listening again, were you not? Serves you right if he is the one. You have lived all these summers only to meet the Wise One, and your stupid tongue has run him off with insults." He looked blankly at the meat spilled out on the ground in front of him.

"Maybe they are right. I have been here too long. My brains are addled. I guess I should be down in winter camp where I will not hurt anybody. Where they can keep an eye on me with the rest of the old fools down there." He dropped his knife and turned to his meager shelter, where he packed a few possessions, and without a word of explanation, walked down the path toward the winter camp.

Kaoto had no trouble finding the hunters' camp in the high country. The late fall had tinted the leaves of the aspen tree from yellow to bright gold. They outlined the dark blue of the spruce clinging higher up the slopes. Nature had hollowed out a huge basin on the western slope of the mountain range, creased with streams and strewn with meadows and low hummocks. He was presented with a pleasant vista up through the trees to the snow capped peaks in the background. It was a picture he would treasure in the hard times to come.

He first encountered a small band of hunters coming across one of the smaller streams. While they were evidently surprised to see a man of his stature up here in their domain, they asked no questions and willingly offered to show him on into their base camp. He followed them to an open meadow surrounded by dark pines and dotted with beaver dams.

While they all demonstration the same independence as the old one, they did seem to defer to one man as their leader. He introduced himself as Forb. He was of average height, but much more slender and lean than most of his farming cousins in the lower land. Like the old one, Forb, and all the hunters, were well muscled, springy, and yet as taut as a dried rawhide. His eyes were clear and bright, with a far-seeing gaze that took in everything and missed nothing. One sweep of his eyes over Kaoto told him this was no ordinary man, nor was he a freak of nature. This man's carriage and equipment spoke of someone with authority and purpose. Forb was slow to speak, and slower to ask questions.

"Welcome to our camp. You are just in time to eat," Forb addressed Kaoto. If he was surprised to see a giant in his camp, he did not let it show.

"I would welcome a meal. This tramp up here made me hungry."

"For one of your size, we might have to kill another elk."

"I feel I could eat a whole one, hide, horn, and all. I do not know why I feel so weak in the knees and out of breath. I feel like I have run for two days without stopping. I guess the old one down at summer camp must be right about my being out of shape." Kaoto panted a little as he sank down by the fire.

"It is not the walking," Forb told him with a slow smile. "Nor are you sick. It is the air up here. There is something different about it. When you first come up, it makes you weak and it is hard to get your breath, but after a little while it goes away and you will feel better than you ever have in your whole life." It was easy to tell that Forb loved his mountains.

"Whatever it is, it has not affected my appetite. I thought the old one was just being querulous, but I guess he was right."

All the hunters started to laugh at this report. "So you met the old guardian of the summer camp? You are lucky he did not put you to work for a summer before he would let you come up here. That is what he has done to all of us."

"He might have if I had stuck around much longer," Kaoto agreed.

Forb continued to laugh as he seated himself next to Kaoto.

"Do not let him, or your condition, worry you. This must be your first time up in the mountains?"

"Yes, it is. Oh, I was up in some mountains farther south many summers ago, but they did not make me feel this way," Kaoto confessed.

"You will get over it. Just hang around camp a few days and you will feel much better."

"I hope so. If not I will have a couple of you carry me back down." This brought another round of good-natured chuckles from the young hunters.

Over the fire, great pieces of meat were roasting. The newest members of the hunters' party were spending their apprenticeship tending the camp and cooking the meals. Later they would carry the day's kill down to summer camp. There they would sleep and then hurry back up in the morning to start another day. It was a strenuous life, but none of them would complain or trade it for any other life. If runners were the elite in the lowlands, hunters were equally envied here in the high country.

The aroma of the roasting meat drifted across to Kaoto, making his stomach grumble with anticipation as one of the youngsters raked baked mud balls from the edge of the fire and cracked them open to reveal baked tubers. To complete the meal, a large earthen jug sat in the coals emitting the promise of hot herbal tea, of an unfamiliar fragrance to Kaoto.

Kaoto gorged himself until he was ashamed, but he could not resist going back for a few more morsels of the succulent elk meat.

Forb and the hunters seemed to enjoy his ravenous appetite and plied him with more tubers and more tea until he groaned in contentment. The youngsters hurriedly put more meat on to cook for their own meal.

After the meal, everyone fell silent around the fire. There was little talk and none about the day's hunt, or the one coming up tomorrow. Each man was content to relive his day in privacy and let the others do the same.

Kaoto knew they were filled with questions about him and what he was doing here, but no one broke the silence. No one asked him anything. They were content to wait until he felt ready to talk; until then, they let it go. This was another big difference between them and their cousin farmers. The villagers below were polite and would not ask direct questions, but they would keep the conversation going, trying to worm their way around to finding out your reason for being there without being rude.

Here in the silence of the mountains, with only the whispering of the pines in the falling darkness, no small talk was made to pry into his reason. When he was ready to explain his presence, he would.

Kaoto gave a big sigh of contentment and settled down to an undisturbed slumber, pulling his feathered cloak up around him as the fire died down.

Chapter Thirty One

Time flew by swiftly in the high mountain camp. Kaoto kept himself busy at first with camp chores, bringing in wood, and going out with the youngsters to find a new and wide variety of plants to supplement their diet of mostly meat. Kaoto had always eaten some meat, but in the lower lands the diet had been mostly provided from the fields. Forb informed him that a diet of elk meat made them as strong as the animals they hunted. "I guess in the lowlands that would make a corn eater as strong as his corn."

The rest of the hunters laughed at Forb's humor and were delighted when Kaoto added, rubbing his stomach. "And a pumpkin eater as strong as his pumpkin?"

After a few days he could tell a difference. He was becoming used to the thinner air and no longer felt weak. He pushed himself to the limits of his endurance daily and was soon able to keep pace with Forb and the rest of the hunters.

He went with them on the hunt but did not participate in the kill, content to study their methods before he tried.

Word had come up from the lower camp that the old one suspected Kaoto of being the Wise One, but no mention of this was made. Forb and the hunters had their own code of ethics. When Kaoto was ready to tell them about himself, he would. Until then, they accepted him as a traveler who had expressed a desire to live and hunt with them.

Sitting at the fire one evening, he noticed the rising moon and was amazed that she had made almost a full turn while he had been here. Time always went by quickly for him whenever he stopped to rest or enjoy a different type of life than running. The night was clear and cold. Forb said they would see snow before long.

"I came to the mountains to see snow and hunt elk. It seems I shall see snow, at least," Kaoto said.

"That you will," Forb replied. "As for hunting elk, I think it is time for you to do more than follow along and watch."

"I have not wanted to hold you back or hinder your hunt," Kaoto said, but Forb could see the excitement building in the tall giant. He had admired his restraint and control. If this was the Wise One, he could have made almost any demand of them, but he had not.

"Yes, if I am to hunt, I should do it now. I must not stay much longer. I have already spent more time here than I had intended to. It is borrowed time. I will have to pay back somewhere along the line."

Forb studied the dwindling flames for many moments before he spoke, and even as he spoke, he kept his eyes on the fire, not looking at the tall hairy giant beside him.

"Since you have been with us, you have spoken little, and what you have said has told us nothing about you. The old one sent word up by the young men that he suspected you were the one called the Wise One. Even up here in this remote region, we still have heard of the Wise One and his mission. You seem to fit the description we have had of him."

"It is true. I am the one trained by Paataga. As for being a Wise One, I have my doubts of my wisdom. Still, what you say is true. I have undertaken a mission which I feel I must follow until it is completed," Kaoto explained, also keeping his eyes trained on the fire.

"I have heard that you are telling the People they should move, leave their homes and go somewhere far to the south. You have not yet said anything to us about moving." It was both a statement and a question.

Kaoto roused himself and stood up stretching full length as he stepped around the fire and looked far out over the night-shrouded valley to the west. Here, in the moonlight, he could see the lonely sentinels of the far west desert he had crossed to reach this place. Farther north, he could see the lone blue mountain sitting like an island in the vast expanse of wilderness. He was reminded once again of his dream, when he stood on an elevated plane and looked down on the People. It renewed the urgency of his mission. Turning back to Forb and the fire, he said, "From what I have observed since I came up here, you are as safe from the savages here as any place in the land. If anyone would be capable of dealing with them, it would be you and your hunters. Besides, I do not think I could convince you to move, even if I tried." He went on to relate to Forb the incident that had taken place at Moot's village, even of his part in the killings that took place there.

Forb was silent for a long while. He sat, still studying the fire as if he sought some sign from the feeble flames.

"We would be very reluctant to leave this land. I cannot imagine what it would be like to live some other place. A place where we could never hunt elk again, feel the crispness of the mornings, or see the Spirit Watcher rise over the peaks. The smell of pine is in our blood; the sound of running water is our heart beat. We could never live without it."

Kaoto could understand Forb's feelings. He himself was reluctant to leave the mountains, and he had only been here a short time. These hunters had lived here all their lives and knew no other way. He wished he could forget his obligations and live out the rest of his days here with them.

"I will not advise you. It is something you and your men must decide for yourselves. The time may come when you will wish you had gone. The time when you find yourselves surrounded by the savages and none of the People are left in the valley. But it is not for me to tell you; it is something each must decide for himself. As for me, I must soon be moving on to the north."

"We will watch and we will decide on what to do when the time comes. If necessary, we could kill these men just as easily as we kill an animal. From what you have told me, they are less than animals and do not deserve to live as men.

"Only the Spirit Watcher can say. They may be his People, just as we are."

"We will watch. But for now, we will hunt. There is a small herd in a distant part of this basin that we have never hunted. There is a great bull with them that is equal to you in size and strength. It is my thought that he might be worthy of such a hunter as yourself." Forb had put the question of the savages from his mind and returned to the business he knew best.

"Do you really think I could keep up with your men and not hold them back?" Kaoto could not contain the excitement in his voice. It made Forb think of his own first hunt, many summers ago. He smiled in the darkness as he spoke.

"They would crawl on their bellies all the way if it was necessary, just to make the hunt with you. Do you think they would consider it less than an honor to be able to tell their children that they once hunted with the Wise One?"

"There is little honor in traveling at the pace of a turtle when they can run like the deer, but if they are willing to make the sacrifice for me, then I will make every effort to hold their pace, for just this one hunt." Kaoto could feel the hunter's fever rising in his blood at the prospect of the long awaited hunt for such a noble beast.

Forb raised his head and emitted a long keening wail, which brought every hunter to his feet to assemble around him and Kaoto.

"On the morrow, Kaoto would join us in a hunt. Who among you would like to be in our group?"

Every man voiced his intention of going with them. No one would be left out of this great moment. This was the making of history; no one would miss it. Their children's children would tell the tale. Forb was even considerate enough to let the young men go along. This day they would do without someone to tend camp. They could cook their own meat when they returned. This was a day to be remembered, and he did not have the heart to make them miss it.

In spite of Kaoto's modest claim of a turtle's pace, he was soon running easily, following Forb's lead in the early dawn of the next day. His blood was hot with excitement, and the cold of the early morning did nothing to cool him. Like the rest of the hunters, he was stripped down to only his breechcloth and light moccasins made especially for him from the skins of the animal he now hunted. His single eagle feather floated back over his shock of hair like a ghost of the bird it had come from.

Over the tops of the ragged peaks the Spirit Watcher greeted them just as they approached a sheltered meadow far back in a narrow canyon. Forb was sure the herd would be feeding here. Kaoto's spirit sang a song of joy in time with his long strides as they came to the edge of the clearing. All was right in his world today. He was going to hunt the great beast.

They had traveled higher than he had ever been before. There were patches of old snow. Some were deep and hard packed in the shaded portions of the canyon, snow deeper than he was tall. The game was abundant in spite of the hunters. This was the place he had always hoped to find, even as a young boy looking at the mountains from as far away as the Chaco.

The group had remained silent all the way. They remained silent as Forb held up his hand in a signal to them. They were in a dense growth of blue spruce. Just ahead, Kaoto could see the open meadow. It was scarcely an arrow's shot across. On the opposite side, just out from the brush, stood the elk.

Even though they had come silently as shadows and there was no wind to carry their scent, the elk were standing with heads up, uneasy, testing the air for the hidden danger they could sense, even though they could not see it.

Forb drew Kaoto's attention far up toward the head of the valley to a slight rise above the herd. There, standing alone, like a statue, was the monarch of the forest. He was the greatest bull elk ever seen by man. His noble head was held high as he shifted his gaze over the valley to take in the entire scene below him.

Kaoto knew this animal had lived by his cunning and wits. It was not just a fluke of luck that he had gained this size and age. His antlers spread like a huge tree, studded with more prongs and spikes than he would have believed possible. Surely the Spirit Watcher must have protected him to allow him to grow to such superb proportions. A moment of doubt swept over him. Should he kill this one that was obviously protected by his deity? He must ask permission of the Spirit Watcher before he could kill such a magnificent specimen.

Taking slow, cautious steps backward, he carefully withdrew from the presence of the herd. The other hunters followed him, still silent, although they were puzzled by his actions. When he had withdrawn sufficiently to assure the herd and the bull would not detect him, he told Forb his intentions.

"I must ask permission of the Spirit Watcher before I can loose an arrow. Do you understand? I cannot just walk out there and shoot this animal, which has lived so many summers. It would be against all I have learned and been taught."

Forb nodded his head in understanding and waited for the Wise One to make his request.

"If you hear me, if you care for this animal's life, then answer me with the arrow I would use to kill this animal. Take my arrow and hide it from me, and I will know you want to protect him. If, on the other hand, you wish him to be mine, then bring my arrow back to me."

He pulled out his arrow, the one he had picked last night as being the most perfect, the most straight, the best balanced, and having the strongest point. Nocking the arrow, he drew it back to its full length. Without a pause he let it fly straight up over his head. As he released it he dropped his eyes to the ground in front of him and refused to try to follow the arrow's flight.

He knew the chances of ever seeing the arrow again were next to impossible. The dense growth and the unevenness of the ground would make it easy to lose even if it came to earth only a short distance from him. It was the only fair way he knew to ask the question. He waited for his answer.

The arrow climbed swiftly to the open sky to catch the Spirit Watcher's attention. While Kaoto had not tried to follow its flight, the other waiting hunters had. There was a unanimous gasp when the slender shaft continued to climb far beyond their expectations and disappeared from even the keenest eagle eye among them. They all stood like stones as they waited for it to return. They each tried to judge where it might fall, given the slight air current in the narrow canyon. After what seemed like an impossible time, a time in which they were wondering if the Spirit Watcher had indeed taken the arrow and would never bring it back, they heard the whispering hiss of the falling arrow.

Kaoto had stood quietly as the arrow sped away into the sky. He had mixed feelings about the outcome. He wanted to continue the hunt, and this animal was all that Forb had said it would be. But if the Spirit Watcher refused his request, he would not be disappointed. He admired this fine bull, and if he should be protected, then Kaoto would abide by that decision.

With a swift downward sound, the arrow came to rest with a hollow thud in a rotten log not over one long pace in front of the Wise One. Buried deep in the soft wood, the arrow stood erect and steady, not a hint of a quiver in its long shaft. The answer was clear to all who saw it.

Without a word, Kaoto claimed his arrow and wiped it clean. He tested the freshly knapped point for sharpness and was rewarded with a trickle of blood on his forefinger. He turned to Forb for instructions on how to best approach the bull.

With a few quick motions of his hand, Forb dispersed the hunters. They all seemed to know exactly what to do, and were soon invisible as if the mountain valley had swallowed them up.

Kaoto followed Forb as he led the way up the canyon. They were careful to stay close to the canyon wall and at no time exposed themselves to the sharp eyes of the skittish elk herd. Creeping slowly upward, they came at last to the upper end of the valley. Contrary to its appearance, the upper end was not blocked, as it had seemed. At closer range, Kaoto could see a twisting, steep trail leading up the side of the canyon wall. It was a well-used trail showing many fresh hoof marks.

Here beside the trail Forb signaled Kaoto to take his stand. When he was satisfied with every aspect of the location, he threw back his head and sent the clear, clucking sound of a contented crow, echoing down the valley. He repeated the call three times. Then he also disappeared, like a shadow among the pines.

From down the valley came an answering call, also emitted by a man's throat, but only an expert could have told the difference. This time it was not the crow but the snarling hiss of a mountain lion on the prowl. The elks turned as one to face this threat. There, in the deep grass, could be seen a brown body creeping toward them. With heads held high, the elk turned their backs on the menace and trotted up the valley toward Kaoto's position. The bull was no longer in sight.

Kaoto felt his chest tighten with disappointment when he saw he had lost the bull. He had no heart to kill any of the cows and was ready to call it off, when to his surprise the bull came out of the bushes behind the herd and stood staring at the creeping figure in the tall grass. He pawed the ground and sent several warning snorts in that direction before he trotted away.

As the bull came closer to his stand, Kaoto could see the hunters emerging from the dense spruce growth and forming a line behind the herd. The creeping figure stood upright and joined the rest of the hunters.

The regal bull looked at the men with scorn as he continued to make his way up behind his herd, looking back over his shoulder to keep a safe distance between himself and these puny men.

Kaoto was torn with doubt. He hated to kill this animal, but the hunters would be disappointed in him if he did not. As he stood weighing the consequences, a new threat made itself know. It was a real cat this time, and it was racing out from just below Kaoto's stand. It hurled itself through the herd of cows and aimed its attack at the bull.

The cows split and ran wide to either side, leaving a clear path for the mountain cat. The bull seemed to recognize his adversary and without hesitation launched his own attack. Head down, great antlers inviting the cat to impale itself, he plowed forward.

The cat would not yield to this maneuver and began to circle, trying to get to its favorite target. It wanted either a clean pass at the throat, or would settle for the hindquarters. Either one would be far safer than the direct approach.

Kaoto had his arrow drawn back and was wavering between the two. As the bull turned sideways to him, the cat leaped for the shoulder and ultimately the jugular vein.

Kaoto chose this moment to release his arrow. The shot was long but it was also downhill. He did not know just what he hoped to accomplish. Afterward, he admitted he secretly thought to kill the cat and spare the bull.

The long shaft with its freshly sharpened point pierced the lion through the chest cavity and continued deep into the bull elk. Here it found the heart. The thrashing of the cat made the point slash viciously in the great animal's surging heart. The shaft snapped and the cat fell to the ground, clawing and screaming, to die in a few moments. The bull stood dead still. To all appearances, it was untouched, unhurt. Then in slow, majestic dignity, it kneeled as if paying homage to the Wise One. Just as slowly, it settled down on it haunches as though it was lying down to rest.

As the hunters drew near they could see that both animals were dead. But the bull elk had retained his dignity and regal bearing even in death.

Chapter Thirty Two

An early snowstorm swept down on the hunter's camp in the high mountain basin. It came in gentle waves, each wave dropping its load before it could rise over the top of the range. The depth of the snow increased steadily and Kaoto became concerned when it showed no signs of stopping. Already it was well up to his knees and was reaching the thighs of the shorter members of the camp. Forb's calmness led Kaoto to believe this was not an uncommon occurrence in the high country.

"Should we not be getting down to the winter camp?"

"For a little storm like this?" Forb chided him. He had forgotten his guest did not know the high country winters.

"A little storm? I should hate to see a big storm, then."

Forb explained to Kaoto that this was an early storm and would not last very long. They would have more warm days and more hunting time. For now, they were safe here with plenty of food and a good shelter.

"We do not go down to winter camp until it begins to snow in earnest. First we go back to the main summer camp, then on down to winter camp. Once we go down, there will be no coming back until late spring. It is nearly summer before we can get back up to our regular hunting camp. Winter camp becomes like a cage to us. So we do not rush to it until we have to."

"I am terribly ignorant of this high country. I had planned to keep traveling into the north, but if an early storm, a little storm is like this, then when a real storm hits, I would be in serious trouble."

Forb considered Kaoto's statement. True, he was the Wise One, but he was not prepared for the snow that would come. He did not know how to prepare to live out the winter in the mountainous country. He had no idea what it was like in the middle of the winter, when a man could not leave his camp in safety. The Wise One needed instructions, but true to the code of the mountain tribes, he would not offer to tell any man what to do unless they should ask first. He spoke in a general way.

"I expect the winters are different here than down in the valley where you lived."

"I am beginning to suspect they are much different," Kaoto agreed as he settled down on a large green log that had been pulled up close to the fire. He watched the large snowflakes as they evaporated before they fell into the flames.

"You would be welcome to stay with us now, and later when we do go down to winter camp," Forb offered.

"I thank you for the offer, but I really must be moving on," Kaoto answered, his voice lacking conviction. Forb felt it would take very little to persuade him to stay with them.

"I know you have a mission, but it is my thought that you would not be able to carry it out if you were lying dead."

Forb was correct on both counts. It would not take much to induce him to stay, and he could see the wisdom in what Forb had said. He could not serve his People if he were lying dead somewhere in the mountains. In spite of his best intentions, his plans were always being altered, causing him to be delayed. It seemed time was his enemy.

He had always thought that life in the mountains would be easier than down in the valleys and the dry lands. Here there was an abundance of game and water, with many types of plants. There was no reason for a man to go hungry or thirsty. In many ways this was true, but he had not taken into consideration the depth of the snow or the length of the winters. It would be impossible for a man to travel any distance in the dead of winter.

All of his young life had been in preparation for living in the dry, milder, south land. If he was to survive in the mountains, he would have to gather new information. He would need to learn all over again, and what better teachers than the men who lived here by their wits? These wild, independent men, who took everything in their stride. They did not try to outwit the land but used all it could give them and accepted the winters as part of their life. After thinking on it, Kaoto told Forb, "There is much I would know."

"There is much to be learned," Forb agreed.

"Will you teach me?"

Forb studied long before he answered. He poked the fire and watched the sparks spiral up in the night sky. He gazed far out over the western horizon into the emptiness of the land beyond. He looked at the night sky as if checking the stars before he committed himself. Finally he answered the Wise One.

"I will share with you all that I know if that will help. But there is much to learn. It will take time. I have lived here some thirty summers and I do not know it all yet."

"I can see now that I must take the time. My only worry is getting in your way or holding you up from what you must do," Kaoto answered after a short pause. He knew he was committing himself to at least the rest of the winter and some of the early spring, but he must learn to survive in this new environment. "I learn fast. Once is enough."

"I am sure of it. You could not attain the office of Wise One at such an early age if you did not, and you will not get in our way. Most of the learning up here is in doing. Experience teaches faster than words. Stay with us until the storms drive us down. Hunt with us, live with us as you have been. Already you have gained much knowledge. The fact that you admit you are ignorant tells me how much you already have learned. Admitting to what we do not know makes it easier to learn what we need."

"I sometimes think my ignorance is my best asset. Paataga told me that a wise person listens and makes people think they are smarter than they are," Kaoto told Forb, a little sheepishly.

"You will get plenty of time for that when we get down to winter camp. Everyone there will share with you some of their experience. There is little else to do but eat, sleep, and swap stories, until spring thaw. You will not be able to travel until then anyway," Forb informed him.

Kaoto agreed. Once he made up his mind to this course, he put all thought of his future travels out of his mind and concentrated on learning as much as he could, as fast as he could. He asked questions constantly and listened to every word given him. When he did feel a tinge of guilt, he reminded himself it was necessary. He was not neglecting his duty; he was preparing himself to complete it.

Life in the high camp was what his body needed. He understood what the old one had meant when he hinted that the Wise One was not in top condition. His already lean body trimmed down even more, and every muscle became toned to perfection.

He learned to take readings from the prominent landmarks so he could travel a circular path to reach his destination. Unlike the open prairie land where he could see several day's run ahead of him, in the folds of the mountains, one had to have an understanding of where to go without being able to see the end of the trail.

One afternoon, Forb read the sky and announced it was time to retreat down to the lower park where the drying camp was set up. The next several days were spent in helping dry the last of the meat and gathering and curing the last of the skins. Each day the snow passed over them, leaving only a dusting of fresh white, but the high country was steadily being entombed in the deep, protecting blanket of winter snow.

With the advent of deep snow at this camp, they retreated once more to the lower camp, the permanent winter camp. As Forb had said, there was very little to do. The same snow that had driven them down also pushed the herds of elk down in search of new feeding grounds. What hunting there was to be done now was performed by the young men who had not yet served their apprenticeship in the camp and had not proven themselves worthy of the upper meadows. The elders, who observed and instructed, accompanied them. They never had to go far from camp to find fresh meat, but the winter snow prohibited trade, so they hunted for only what they needed to eat. Dry meat would sustain them in an emergency, but a hunter preferred fresh meat.

The summers' trading had furnished them with an ample supply of corn, squash, and pumpkin, along with dried berries and pinion nuts. The long winter months held no threat of hunger to them, only boredom. During the earlier months, the hunters would often visit friends or relatives in the valley. But they soon came drifting back, preferring the winter camp to the valley farmer life.

At the first camp, Kaoto had inquired about the old one and was told he had gone to winter camp. Once in winter camp, Kaoto made it a point of looking him up. The old one was reluctant to be drawn into conversation, feeling he had disgraced himself on their first encounter. Kaoto ignored this and refused to mention their first conversation. He would sit and talk with the old one whom he had renamed Old Bones, a name that was adopted by everyone in the camp.

Old Bones was a veritable fountain of information that Kaoto intended to draw on as much as possible. He had learned along the trail that people enjoyed being asked questions about things they knew about. Old Bones was no exception, and once he knew that Kaoto was sincerely interested and had a real desire to learn, he poured forth all he knew. He still had not changed his character and was still considered to be a cantankerous old man; feared, respected, and loved by all.

Winter camp was a communal affair. Everything was shared. The fire was a long narrow hearth in front of the great open-faced lodge. Long logs were added to the fire to keep it going and everyone used it for a cook fire. Several huge pots were kept boiling at its edge and served as a common kitchen for all that wished to contribute or partake. Large portions of meat were roasted daily to serve for the entire camp.

Kaoto had always known the People worked well together, but he had never seen it better demonstrated than at winter camp. During his stay he was never once called on to settle a dispute because there were none. He believed it was their very independence that accounted for this. They respected each person's individuality. They were in favor of everyone doing as they pleased, just as long as it did not infringe on the rights of others. He wondered if this was the way ants lived, remembering his talks with Paataga on this subject. He honestly believed these hunters could have lived just as harmoniously without the benefit of speech.

The village consisted of one structure, but unlike any he had ever seen before. The great room served as a kiva and gathering place when the weather was too cruel for them to be outside. The great room was really an open-faced shed with curtains of skins that could be lowered if the wind blew from the wrong direction. Its roof was supported by using the trunks of existing trees. Cross members were fastened to them with rawhide thongs and then covered with smaller branches and brush, and finally, with a layer of packed dirt. The back wall was the mountain itself. The long fire in front warmed the interior and was helped during the day by the long southern rays of the sun. The floor was covered with fresh rushes.

Extending from either side of the great room was a long, narrow wing, built in the same manner, only much smaller. This housed the sleeping rooms. Each was one long room. The back section was elevated and was actually a long trough filled with fragrantly scented pine and sage. This was covered with rushes and ferns to serve as a mattress. Each party had its own sleeping skin, usually two elk skins sewn together to form a tight bag. Over this was thrown an assortment of loose skins.

They all slept in these two rooms. A man and his mate would share one bag; sometimes several children would share one large bag. Those who were not mated could double up whenever they felt the desire to share each other's company.

It had been late evening when the hunting party had come into winter camp and the long fire was burning gaily, warming and lighting the great room. It seemed to beckon the cold and weary travelers to stop and rest and share in the fellowship it offered.

One of the first things that Forb had Kaoto do was go to the stream and pick out a smooth boulder about the size of his head. When he had found the rock, he was instructed to place it near the fire, along with a neat row of stones already placed there. As the evening progressed, the stones were turned until they were too hot to be handled with the bare hands. Just before they retired for the night, he was given a pouch made from the skin of a beaver. The hot rocks were rolled into the pouch and carried into the sleeping rooms.

Kaoto soon learned the art of crouching at the head of his bed and slowly working the hot rock down in his bag. When he had reached as far down as was convenient by hand, he slipped his feet in and continued the process until the rock rested in the bottom of the sack and the inner skin was warm to his body. The rock could, with a little skill, be brought back up and transferred around the body to where it might be needed most.

The front of the sleeping area was sealed off by skins pegged to the log at the roof, letting them drop beyond the platform. These could be raised or lowered according to the sleeper's desire.

This sleeping arrangement was close and the air became heavy with the musky, but not unpleasant, body odors. The hunters were a clean people, just as were all the People. They bathed daily in the stream despite the weather. They rubbed down with crushed herbs. This plus the aromatic mattress gave the bed area a pleasant smell, lasting almost until spring. By this time everything was beginning to smell musty and was ready to be aired.

Bathing was also a communal effort, with the people scrubbing each other's backs and drying around the fire, the braver youngsters leaping back and forth over the flames. Kaoto delighted them when he demonstrated his ability to straddle the fire with one foot on either side of the flames.

Old Bones warned him that he must be careful. "It is well known that too big of a fire will burn off the thatch of even a high tree." This was accompanied by much laughter and story telling of some similar adventure.

Standing naked by the fire, Kaoto was just a man they all knew and were learning to respect for his own merits, not his office.

One thing Kaoto immediately noticed was that there were no creatures at the dumpsite. In the winter camp everyone looked after everyone else, with no exceptions. The very young, the very old, and the afflicted were all taken care of without discrimination. It was as if they were all one family, which in a sense they were. The young men picked their mates from either friends in the valley or more often from other hunter camps much like theirs. This, and the large single dwelling lodge, made them all one family.

Early on Kaoto could see that Old Bones suffered much from the cold and was seldom outside except for his bath and meals, which he hurried through and got back inside the shelter. He wished he could do something to help him, but knew he was a proud and sensitive man who would reject any offer of assistance.

On one of his frequent trips out with the young hunters, Kaoto had found the den of a large bear that had unwisely chosen to hibernate this close to the winter camp. On the first warm day the Wise One went out alone and roused the bear. He killed it with a heavy spear he had borrowed from Forb. Since he had done this alone, it called for a celebration. Any excuse gave rise to a celebration, and killing a bear single-handed was no small thing. The carcass, after it was skinned and dressed out, was hung over the long fire and roasted the rest of the day and through the long night. The next day it was eaten, and the eating conjured up stories of great hunts. Stories were told not only of brave deeds, but foolish and humorous deeds as well.

Forb insisted on placing another eagle feather in the Wise One's hair. This replaced the one he had given Kalo at his adoption. When Kaoto protested, he was informed he would dishonor them if he did not accept it, so what could he do? Once more, his head of unruly hair boasted two eagle feathers. It is odd, he thought, I never seek them as other men do, but somehow they keep coming to me.

While the meat was cooking, Kaoto had stretched out the bearskin and pegged it down. He had started scrapping the inner skin when he discovered he had more help than he knew what to do with. He was pushed out of the way by the numerous young girls who all vied with each other to be the most helpful. It made him think of the daughters of Mula when he had been wounded by the buffalo. He was thankful for their help because it was a big job and he wanted to preserve the skin with all the hair intact. Laughing at him, they assured him that not one hair would be lost. If so, they would replace it with their own. The process of cleaning and curing the hide took many days and much hard work, but nothing was too good for the Wise One, especially since he was still young and without a mate.

When all were satisfied with the condition of the skin, a robe was made from it, and the collective bevy of young maidens brought it into camp and presented it to him with great pride. Kaoto in turn accepted it with humble grace and many thanks for their kindness. They were all so pleased with themselves and the job they had done that they were hardly ready for his next act.

Kaoto took the new robe and placed it over the stooped, shaking shoulders of Old Bones. A startled silence fell over the village. This would cause trouble. They all knew Old Bone's fierce pride and they trembled at the outcome.

Old Bones stood up and removed the robe, controlling his temper as he handed it back to the Wise One, saying, "I cannot accept such a valuable gift. I have nothing of equal value to return." Old customs had to be observed. A gift must always be returned in equal or greater value.

"The wisdom you have shared with me and will continue to share is worth far more than this small token," Kaoto told him, trying to place the robe back in his hands.

"What I share with you is nothing but the bragging of an old man. You could learn as much from any other man here. If anyone deserves this gift, it would be Forb. He has given you far more than I have," Old Bones insisted.

Kaoto knew the old man needed the robe. In fact, he wanted it very badly. He had not missed the gleam in the old one's eyes when he first saw and felt the robe. He would have to try some other way to get him to accept it without insulting him or the customs.

"Yes, I agree. It is far too valuable to be given or taken lightly. It is only the kind of a gift a son could give to his father without causing him shame." He paused as if to try to think, but he already knew what he would say. He had known all along that Old Bones would not accept it easily, but he thought he knew of a way that the old one could not refuse without bringing shame to both of them.

"But my father is far away in the Chaco and he does not need such a heavy robe down there." Once more he paused as if in deep thought. Then his face lit up with inspiration.

"Old Bones, you do not have a son, do you?" he asked.

"You know I do not. You have heard the story of how my only son was killed by a bear, probably this same creature," Old Bones told him sadly.

"Then could you not accept this in the name of your son who is no longer here, and my father who is so far away? I am sure they would both be pleased if you did. It would honor them both. Do you not think this is right? Besides, who has a better right to it than the man who lost his son to the animal who used to wear it? I think the son would be proud to know it now warmed his old father in his absence." Kaoto held out the robe with both hands, ready to lay it back on the old shoulders. Old Bones was shaking when he allowed it to be settled on him. How could he dispute the option of the Wise One?

"I would be happy to pay honor to the father of the Wise One. He should be very proud of his son." Choking a little on the lump forming in his throat, he said. "The spirit of my dead son would bid me accept it in his name."

He looked around belligerently as if he dared anyone to object or say anything, for or against his accepting the gift.

"I have insulted the Wise One once already. Do you want me to do so again? As well as add an insult to his father and the spirit of my dead son?" His old eyes were misty, but they still covered every man, woman and child to see if any would speak.

No one spoke. All were content for him to have the robe. They had their first opportunity to see the Wise One in action as such. Up until now he had only acted as a guest and a hunter, but now they could see why he had been chosen for this office. As always, Kaoto was the Wise One first and a man last. They were all pleased. This gift would add another five winters to Old Bone's life, not to mention the comfort and pride he would derive from it. Cantankerous as he was, everyone still loved and respected him for his long and active life. The story of Kaoto's gift would long live in this camp.

All winter Old Bones was never seen outside without his new robe. He was able to enjoy the days more now that he could be out and not feel the cold so much.

Once more he could sit with the hunters and relate his old, familiar tales of the hunt and dangers. Even when he squatted before the fire, he did not drop it, but let it shield his thin backside while the fire warmed his front.

There was no favor Kaoto could ask that was too great for Old Bones. He shared every experience he could bring to mind, and they were numerous. Kaoto retained each bit of information and treasured them. It was a fair exchange, and both were happy.

Chapter Thirty Three

Kaoto ran easily along the narrow trail. His eyes were on the break in the mountains ahead of him. He was going south again and hoped to be over the top before darkness set in. The pass was a sharp defile in the range. He had been told there was no easy passage. The going would soon become steep and more difficult.

It had been two summers since he had left Forb and his People in the echoing basin of the southern mountain. He had covered a great deal of the north and west country since then. He had ranged west to the canyon land that no one could cross and the mountains on the east where the only people were more hunters like Forb. He had crossed the mighty river where it came out of the deep canyons for a brief journey through a pleasant open valley where it was joined by another, lesser river. The confluence of the two streams had been the home of countless numbers of the People. Their homes were constructed mainly of willows and plastered with mud. They were scattered haphazardly forming a loose community along the streams with no central village. When the People chose to get together, they would pick an open area and erect temporary shelters. He had been surprised to hear rumors of trouble here. They had not seen anyone, but had heard rumors from beyond the next range of mountains.

He had not lingered long here but hurried on north to where they told him these savages seemed to originate. He had promised to return soon and spend more time with them. He was on his way to keep this promise now. Once again, the summer sun was gone and the season of harvest was over. Winter would soon grip the land again, and he wanted to be in the great valley, where they assured him the winters were mild.

His travel had taken him to a land where the bleached bones of giants could be found lying embedded in the rocks. Here they had told him the new savages were frequently seen. They were less violent than the southern tribe, but they still were making inroads into the heart of the People's nation. Heavy set and short, they followed the herds of buffalo, which made up their main diet. The skins of these animals were used to make tents for their home, homes that could be taken down easily and transported to a new location and erected again. They also were nomads who claimed large areas as their home.

They did not go out of their way to harass the People, but they would raid their fields and harvest their crops whenever they came across them. They would fight the small farmers if they were annoyed. They were just now beginning to claim this land as their own. Kaoto had not seen them but had found evidence of their camps in some areas farther north.

He had another problem on his mind now. He was puzzling over a report of another strange animal. At the last village he had visited, Gart, the ruler of this district, had been hesitant to talk about them, but felt the Wise One should know.

"We have seen a strange animal in our valley this last season. Something we have never seen before," Gart had said, keeping his eyes on his feet as he spoke, not daring to see what the Wise One's reaction would be.

"What kind of animal was it?" Kaoto had asked. He had seen many new types on his travels, and was always interested in the new and different.

"They are hard to describe," Gart said as he fidgeted, feeling very uncomfortable in his role as spokesman.

"Well, do the best you can," Kaoto told him.

"None of us has ever seen them up close. I, uh, I know you will not believe me when I tell you, but, well, I can only tell you what I have seen with my own eyes," Gart said defensively.

"Tell me anyway. I will not laugh or scoff at you. I have learned that there are many strange and different things to be seen in the land. I could tell you things you would have trouble believing, also."

"Well, they are big, and they sometimes walk like men, on two legs. Other times they seem to go on all fours." Gart leaned forward with arms dangling to demonstrate.

"Bears walk that way," Kaoto offered.

"I know a bear when I see one." Gart was insulted. "But these are not bears, or if they are, they are different from any bears we have ever seen before."

"Tell me what they do look like then." Kaoto continued to prompt his host for a more definite description.

Gart finally raised his eyes to look straight into those of the Wise One, who was seated as usual to make his height less intimidating. Eye contact was necessary to encourage the truth. He knew Kaoto had been a runner, and runners always delivered their messages by looking the listener in the eyes so they would know he did not lie.

"To my eyes they look like a cross between a man, a bear, and maybe a buffalo. If such is possible."

"I do not know. That would indeed be a different type of animal than I have ever seen or heard of," Kaoto admitted. "How do they resemble these animals?" He urged Gart to keep talking.

"Well, as I said, they sometimes stand up like a man, a big man, as big almost as you, not as tall, but heavier, and they look to be covered with hair." He quickly amended this statement, taking in to consideration the fact that the man he was speaking to was also covered with hair.

"Not soft, short hair like yours, but longer, coarse hair, and much darker. One I have seen with my own eyes has a pelt of hair that looks like flames in the sun."

"But how do they look like the buffalo? Buffalo do not walk upright like a man, and I have never seen one with red hair," Kaoto said.

"They have horns on their heads like a buffalo and great humps on their backs. Kind of like the buffalo, but much larger."

"What do they eat?"

"It seems to me they eat everything. They eat all the time. They eat meat, they eat out of our fields, they eat as they walk, and they eat when they camp. They never seem to stop eating." Gart shook his head as if he, too, were having trouble believing what he was saying.

Kaoto considered what he had just heard. This was something different than he had ever run into before. Gart was a respected man, a man whose word could not be doubted. Yet he was having trouble accepting these words. There had to be some explanation, something they were overlooking. He would just have to keep asking Gart questions until he discovered the truth.

"Do they threaten the People?"

"I cannot answer that. I have forbidden my people from going close to them. They look so frightening that I have had little trouble keeping my people far from them. Whenever they are spotted, the People move out of their way. They have raided our fields and homes, but they do not destroy everything. They just take what they want and move on. But they take much."

As he was talking, Gart had picked up a stick and had been sketching a rough picture in the dust between them. What Kaoto saw was something like a man stooped over with a great hump on his back. The creature's strangest attribute was its head. Here Gart had defined two large, curled horns, which seemed to stem from a bald plate that was fringed with more hair.

"They are the most ugly beasts I have ever seen. They look like something my mother would have made up to scare me with when I was yet a child," Gart confided.

Kaoto studied the picture intently, trying to bring to mind anything it might resemble, knowing that all men were not artists. Pointing to the hump, he said, "This could be a pack on their back, much like mine."

"If it is a pack," Gart said doubtfully, "Then it is much larger than any pack you could carry." He traced the hump again, showing Kaoto how it ran down from their shoulders nearly to their buttocks.

"Yes, that would be a very large pack," Kaoto scratched his head in puzzlement. "You said they camp. Most animals do not camp. They simply bed down. Do they camp as we do? Do they build any type of shelter? Do they make fire?"

"We have seen no shelter, but they carry a pot with fire. I do not think they can make fire, but they seem to know how to use it. Oh yes, and one of them carries a magic stick, not the kind my mother used, although it looks much the same. He holds it to his mouth and makes strange noises. I know, every boy knows how to make a whistle, but his is nothing like a whistle. He makes sounds like wind, and water, and birds, all mixed together. It is the strangest noise I have ever heard. It makes my hair feel funny and it makes me feel sad at the same time." Gart stopped talking. He knew he sounded ridiculous. "I cannot say what I really mean, but it is different. You have to see and hear them to believe," he finished lamely.

Kaoto laid one hand on the man's shoulder and told him, "I believe you

Gart. Why would you tell me something that is not true? No man in this valley would question your word, so why should I? I know you have seen something you cannot identify, and it is something I do not recognize, but that does not mean it is not out there. I hope to find it and maybe I can figure out just what it is."

"Thank you, Wise One," Gart said. The relief in his voice was evident. He had not expected the Wise One to believe him. He had thought he would be told he was getting too old to rule, that he was wandering in his mind. Maybe he was.

"Do they speak? Have you heard them talk?"

"They make grunting noises. Maybe it is speech to them; to us it is nothing. But they do carry weapons. They do not carry bows or spears, but odd sticks. They are gray in color like stones, only they shine like wet stones."

"How do they use these weapons?" Kaoto was finding something he could understand now. The animals he knew about did not carry weapons or use fire. Only men did these things.

"They use them like long knives, very long knives. No man could find the type of stone for a knife that would be this long or strong enough to do what they can do with them."

"How are they different from our knives?"

"Well, first, as I have said, they are long, longer than one of your arrows. Then, they can cut a small tree down with one swing, and even a larger tree only takes two cuts, one on each side. The cut is as smooth as if it had been polished. I have seen them cut down a tree as big as your leg with only two cuts. They slice a pumpkin in half like it was nothing. You know a dry pumpkin has to be chopped and broken, but not for them. One slice and it lies in two pieces."

Kaoto was impressed. It took a lot of work to cut a small tree, and it often looked more like a beaver had cut it down. As for the pumpkin, everyone knew they were hard to cut. As a small boy he had watched his mother break them over a rock and then cut up the pieces with a knife.

"I must see them and their magic sticks and weapons." Kaoto was determined to find these animals, or men, as he suspected them to be. After all, the savages were hardly more than animals by the standards of the People. He could not see how they could possibly fit into the dark shadows of his dream, but until he knew for sure he would not rule them out.

"Where would I have to go to find them?" Kaoto asked.

"We have only seen three of them so far. They were last seen heading up the valley toward the pass. I would advise you not to follow them very closely. They might turn on you." Gart was worried.

"If they are as you have told me, I think I could easily outrun them or outsmart them, whichever seemed the best. But I must go that way, and if I can find them I might be able to relieve the fear they have brought to this valley."

"I do not care what they are. All I care is that they leave and do not come back," Gart said.

"Yes, but they are heading down into the heart of the country where there are many more of the People. I must do what I can to protect them. I am sure they will be as afraid of them as you were."

"Go, then. The Spirit Watcher might protect you from them," Gart conceded.

"I do not think the Spirit Watcher is much concerned with my safety, but thanks for the information, and I shall send a runner to tell you what I find."

Kaoto had stood up and swung on his pack. It was early morning and he wanted to get a good start. He was determined to find these strange animal men. Somewhere up ahead of him he would surely see signs of them. The valley was narrow and the path led toward the only pass. If they were ahead of him, they should be easy to spot.

He did not have far to go before he found their tracks, or what he assumed must be their tracks. It was impossible to make anything out of them. They had walked upright like men, but the tracks were not those of barefoot men or sandals such as he wore. Even the moccasins worn by the savages would leave distinct markings.

What he found were shapeless blots with no distinction between heel and toe. All he could tell from them was that they were large. The length of the stride was almost equal to his own. Also, they indicated that whoever had made them was far heavier than he was.

The narrow, open valley came to an abrupt end as the mountains reared up in front of him. The trail disappeared around a jutting point of rock and was hidden from sight for a short way before it led up a steep incline toward the pass.

He had stopped short of the rocky point when he heard a hoarse, bellowing sound mixed with guttural gibberish. Concealing himself above the trail near the rocky point, he soon heard the pounding of footsteps on the trail close to his hiding place.

He caught sight of the three strange animal men Gart had told him about. At first glance, they looked just as Gart had described them. Looking closer, Kaoto could see they were definitely men of some sort. His attention was first drawn to their heads. There were two horns protruding from their heads, much like those of a buffalo. The morning was warm and they had pulled back their robes of crudely cured hides, revealing an upper torso which was covered with a thick matting of coarse, dark colored hair. The one bringing up the rear was the one Gart had spoken of. His hair was as red as the flames, and the glistening of sweat made the illusion even more believable.

Short skirts of hairless rawhide was bound around their mid-sections, but below this the red hair continued down over the legs, ending in crude boots made from skins tied around their ankles to serve as footwear. This explained the blotted tracks they made. Each man had a tangle of long hair growing from his face. The Red One looked like a flame running in the shape of a man.

On their backs were the huge humps Gart had seen. They were indeed large, and made to seem even larger when the loose robes were thrown back over them. The flapping skins of the robe made the packs look like part of the men. The weight of the packs must have been immense, because the men were leaning far forward to balance the weight, and each man carried a short heavy stick to help support him as he walked. This would explain why Gart thought they walked on all fours sometimes.

The muscles on the arms, legs, and torsos were thick, much larger than any Kaoto had ever seen before. They carried their packs tirelessly, and while they were not built for speed like runners, they seemed durable for the long run.

The reason for their retreat was soon evident, as a small group of the northern savages rounded the bend in pursuit of the animal men. They were not as tall as the southern savages, but were wider and showed the signs of endurance runners. They were not as fast as his own runners, but they looked to be able to run for great distances without tiring. It was plain they were chasing the animal men with a vengeance. He had no doubt they meant to kill the animal men without hesitation. They only lacked the opportunity.

The three animal men stopped near the rocky point and took a defensive position with their backs to the wall. They prepared to fight the savages with the strange gray sticks they had pulled from cords around their waists. They were long, slender sticks with tightly wrapped handles that seem to fit their hands and made them like an extension of their arms. These weapons made the air whistle as they swung them in vicious arches at the advancing savages. They cut a clean, deep gash in whatever they connected with, be it tree or man. They gave off a strange ringing sound when they hit rock or ground.

The savages fought with spears and did not seem to have any bows or arrows with which they could stand back and deal deathblows. Both savages and animal men used shields made from buffalo hides to deflect their enemy's blows. The gray sticks, however, cut through the shields with ease, while their own shields turned the spear points. Undaunted, the savages pressed the attack, not hesitating as their numbers diminished under the vicious gray sticks.

From where Kaoto lay he could almost have touched the animal men, and he could see their packs were hampering their efforts to fight. But they had been too hard pressed to drop them. One at a time each man got in between the other two and shed his pack so he could be free to move about and better defend himself.

All three animal men fought well, but the one with the flaming hair fought fearlessly. He possessed more courage and daring than the other two. He parried with his shield the spears of two men while he lunged at another with his magic gray stick. His weapon cut through the shaft of a spear with apparent ease. His next lunge brought the weapon whistling through the air in a flashing arch. It connected with one of the savages, decapitating the man in an instant. The head sprang from the body as if it had never been fastened. The body stood rigidly upright with a fountain of blood spurting from the severed neck. The head came to a stop in the trail with the neck stump in the dirt, the eyes on the head blinked slowly as if in disbelief as it watched its body crumpling to the ground nearby.

The Red One's lunge had left him momentarily off balance with his guard down. Two more savages took advantage of this to leap in close to him. One spear caught him in the side, ripping a ghastly wound just below his ribs. The other pierced the fleshy portion of his thigh, being deflected downward by the swing of his shield. Otherwise it would have gone through his stomach, where it had been intended to go. The two savages paid with their lives when the red animal man hacked them mercilessly with his weapon.

The two remaining animal men decided discretion was the better part of valor. They seemed to think their companion was no longer of any value to them. They pulled on their own packs and took his between them. They fled up the trail toward the pass, evidently hoping to find a better place to fight, or maybe to escape in the rugged, wild country ahead of them. The Red One shouted something after them, which Kaoto thought was probably more of a protest, because they were taking his pack than because they were deserting him.

The savages let them go without a struggle. It seemed they were waiting for some of their companions to join them, and as they waited for their friends, they prodded the Red One to see how badly he was wounded. The Red One tried to raise himself up to fight again, but was unable to make it all the way and slid back down the rock to the ground. One of the savages looked around until he found a large rock. He picked it up and slammed it down with considerable force on the Red One's already wounded leg. Kaoto could hear the sickening crack of breaking bones. It appeared they were in no hurry to kill him. But they did not want him to get up and wander away. After having broken his leg, they trotted off leisurely up the trail taken by the two retreating animal men.

Kaoto watched the next group of savages trot past without halting to even look at the wounded Red One. Kaoto remained concealed as he listened to the pursuers and pursued climbing up the steep mountainside. Long after all was silent, he still sat quietly, unmoving, watching the Red One with detached indifference. He was curious as to what would be the outcome of this foray.

The Red One was not about to admit to defeat and after a short period pulled himself away from the rock. He was trying to get to the little stream, and although it was close, it seemed a long distance down the slope and across an open meadow. His teeth were set and he uttered not a sound as he pushed through the thick brush along the side of the trail. Twice he tried to pull himself up using a small tree, but each time his mangled leg stopped him. Once he looked back at his weapon leaning against the rock. He must have decided it was too far to go back after it. He made no attempt to cover his trail. It would have been impossible, as he left a red bloodstain behind him on every blade of grass and bush he passed over.

Kaoto could not help but admire his stubborn determination and courage. The spear wounds were severe enough, but the broken leg made it hopeless, which is what the savages had intended. He was not surprised to see the animal man stop a short way out in the meadow. With a low moan, he lay his head down and did not move again. Still Kaoto waited with the patience he had learned over the summers on the trail. He listened for any sign of the returning savages. He watched the birds all around him for a sign of anything else strange.

The Spirit Watcher had just made his way down in the steep valley when the fight had begun. It was well past the halfway mark now and there was still no sign of the savages. The chase must have taken longer than they had expected.

The Red One had not moved again. A black and white bird swooped down to the silent, motionless figure and began to peck at the dry and clotting blood. Kaoto decided the Red One must be dead.

Slipping cautiously from his place of concealment, Kaoto scanned the trail in both directions. Satisfied he was alone, and in no danger at the moment, he retrieved the fallen weapon. He had been examining it all morning. He could tell it was a long knife made from some mysterious, unknown stone. With the weapon in his hand, he walked slowly down toward the crumpled figure in the meadow. The magpie relinquished its claim on its gristly prize at the approach of the tall man. Flitting to a tree branch, it proceeded to scold Kaoto for poaching on its territory.

Kaoto found the Red One was still alive after all. He was breathing heavily, but when Kaoto approached his eyelids fluttered open and a deep growl arose from his throat as he focused on the advancing man carrying his abandoned sword.

On an unbidden impulse, Kaoto dropped the weapon and grasped the Red One by the shoulders and pulled him down through the meadow to the stream. What he would do with the beast he did not know, but he thought he deserved better than to die out here, or to be captured by the savages. The Spirit Watcher seemed to be dictating his movements; he only followed the commands. For now he would see if he could revive the creature and hide it from the savages if they should return before dark. After that it would be up to the Spirit Watcher to decide the Red One's fate.

The wounded man made no protest at being pulled toward the stream. What might have been in his mind was a mystery to Kaoto. Besides, he was too busy trying to drag the heavy burden out of sight before the savages should return.

Chapter Thirty Four

His name was Torjan. It was a Viking name, but Torjan was not a Viking. Long before he was born, the bold and daring Vikings had raided up and down the coast of Europe and the islands of the Britons. They were the most dreaded of men, causing the inhabitants of the coastline to run in fear whenever a Viking ship was sighted. Running did not always mean safety. Shrewd, crafty men have always made money on other's suffering. Often these people were sold into slavery by their own countrymen for the protection of the rest of the community. Slaves were used to pull the oars when the wind did not favor the Viking ships. Women could pull on an oar as well as men, but the more favored of the women were taken for the entertainment of the captain and his crew on long voyages. When the slaves became too old or weak to be of any use, they were discarded and replaced with new members from whatever part of the coastline the ship happened to be near.

On one such raid, a fearless leader of men had taken slaves from a small island, part of the Emerald Isle. This ship then dashed across the cold northern seas to the last outpost of the Vikings; a place covered with ice and snow. But it did hold a few hot springs, which made it desirable to them. After a brief pause at Iceland where they loaded all the provisions the ships could safely carry, and recruited more ships to join in the venture, this leader of men struck out again.

He was headed due west into new and strange waters to search for the fabled land of plenty. No one in his generation had gone on such a search, but it was spoken of often. At every gathering of men, there would be someone who knew of someone who knew of someone else who had known a man whose father or grandfather had been there and seen it. They would swear by the beard of Woden, father of Thor, that it was true.

Their course took them through fields of floating ice and violent storms. Many vessels were lost, as well as many slaves, but the leader would not turn back. He was determined to find this land of plenty, a land just waiting for someone to develop it and claim it for their own. He planned to carve out his own kingdom and rule over this new land.

His search was rewarded at last when they came to the shores of a new land. First there were islands, then a large land. It was a land populated by ignorant savages, but truly a land of plenty. It had been late in the short summer. The coastline was covered with lush vegetation. Inland the ground was covered with thick trees and brush. Growing over all these were thousands of grapevines burdened with ripe fruit. A base was set up and the slaves were set to gathering the grapes and brewing a heady, potent wine. So thick were the vines that a man could hardly walk through them, so it was called Vine Land.

At first the natives of this land tried to ignore the invaders. The Vikings would not be ignored, so the natives moved farther away from these roving sea bandits. The Vikings settled at the mouths of streams, and fields were

256 - Norman D. Messenger

cleared and the next spring, crops were planted. The Vikings became lords of the land. While the slaves worked, the Vikings spent their time exploring, hunting, and siring children of the slave women, whom they never claimed. It was a good life and easy to adjust to. The older Vikings lost their desire to roam the seas and were content to sit by and watch their empire grow.

The new generation became restless, as youth usually does, and started pushing farther from the base, looking for new lands of their own. They explored the next land to the west and found it was not an island like Vine Land. It was a whole new continent, and it was theirs for the taking.

Being from the cold north land, they did not prefer the warm, temperate climate they found to the south. So they sailed up a mighty river, which led deep into the heart of this new country. They were sure they would find the fabled kingdoms, where it was reported riches such as no man had ever seen before could be found. There were rumored to be women of such beauty that men would gladly die just for one look at them. All they found were more ignorant savages whose women, while willing, were far from beautiful.

At last they came to a huge waterfall that blocked further passage, but the stories continued to come from the savages. They reported the river led to another ocean and a different land.

The ships were taken apart by the slaves and carried around the falls to be reassembled above it. One ship was left intact below to be used to take news back to the base when they found the next ocean.

The natives were more curious than fearful, and with signs and pictures directed the Vikings deeper and deeper into the heart of this great new land. When the river opened into a series of large lakes, the Vikings first thought they had found the ocean again. Closer investigation proved it to be only giant lakes. When they got over their disappointment, they looked over the ground and found it fertile and the climate was not too different from their homeland. They established villages on the lakes and began to trade with the local natives, clear the land, and plant their own crops. Not least among these were native children with Viking blood.

Still there was the lure of fabled kingdoms somewhere in this land, and scouting parties went out to discover what this land had to offer. They found a treasure, but it was not gold or jewels, nor beautiful women, but to the new colonists it was worth much more. They found a deposit of iron so near the surface that it required little work to mine. They also found copper. These two minerals were so important that they forgot their search for lost kingdoms, and began to develop their own empire.

On the farthest western lake, on its western shore, in a small village, Torjan had been born to a second generation of slaves. Unlike most of his friends, his blood was still pure. There was no taint of the Viking's blood in his veins. His parents were descendants of the slaves from the Emerald Isle. From the Irish he had inherited his flaming red hair. Though they were slaves, they still clung to their Irish heritage and passed it along to their children.

Torjan's father had been a worker of metal, as had his father, and his father's father before him. Torjan was gifted and trained in the art of metalworking. In spite of his great size, his fingers were skillful and patient, making delicate items that were dwarfed by his huge hands.

Hard times befell the Vikings. They fought among themselves, the weather was unstable and crops failed. The natives tired of their oppression and rebelled against them. They pushed the herds of buffalo away from them. Using fire and hunting parties, they caused the herds to migrate. Terrible storms shook the lakes and many ships were lost and broken beyond repair.

While the Vikings were diminishing, the slaves were increasing until the Vikings, fearing for their lives, fled the lakes, leaving many slaves behind. They took only the strongest and prettiest, leaving the old or young behind to fare for themselves until such time as the Vikings would return to reclaim them.

Most ships went back down the river to the falls. A few were carried over land to yet another river that led off to the south. None of these ships or their crews were ever heard from again.

Torjan had been young and strong, too strong. The Viking lords feared he would be more trouble than he was worth to them. His father was too old and his mother not comely enough. The Vikings cared nothing for them and so left them.

The slaves had manned the oars and even helped construct the ships, but they were not sailors. They did not possess the skills to navigate the uncharted oceans. Most would not have had any idea how to find their homeland. Torjan's generation knew only this land. It was home to them. They had no desire to leave for a land they knew nothing of. Torjan was consumed with a driving desire to know more of this land. He wanted to see how far he could go before he had to turn back. He wanted freedom.

After both of his parents died, he felt free to roam to his heart's desire. He organized a party of thirty young men with similar interests and set out on an extended expedition of their own. Torjan had also heard the rumors of lost kingdoms and cities of gold, and the lure was too much for a young man to resist. They did not know if the Vikings would ever return and if they did, he, for one, did not plan to be waiting around to be made a slave again.

For six summers the group had followed his lead, roaming the fertile lands of the Great Plains. Their path had always led westward, although they might detour north or south as the notion hit them.

Torjan saw a mountain of black glass that the savages used to trade with their eastern brothers. Ceremonial knives and points were made from this black rock. It was beautiful, but not very practical. He had led them through a place where there were hot water springs. The steam rose in the winter sky and beckoned them to discover it. He had heard the old ones talk of the springs in Iceland but had thought it was just another story for the children. They had suffered through hot summers, terrible storms, and winters pass believing.

At first they had little trouble with the natives, but the farther from the lakes they traveled the more trouble they got into. Mostly it involved the local women of the tribes. Torjan followed his Viking lord's rule. If they were not willing, use force. This added spice to the game. The natives did not accept the young men's role as lords and resented the abuse of their women.

They had stood up to most of the tribes without much difficulty. Their number was impressive. This, combined with their iron swords and heavy shields, made them seem invincible, but they lost a man here and another there; sometimes to the natives, sometimes to accidents, crossing swollen rivers, or clinging to the side of a precipice. Some were carried away in avalanches or mudslides. Now they had dwindled to the present three.

They had discussed the advisability of returning before they were all killed. They had agreed to swing to the south and cross over the mountains. They wanted to return over a new trail, partly out of the need for adventure, partly because their back trail was so strewn with ill will toward them.

Recently they had aroused a fierce tribe and had run before them into this valley. They had been pushed further west up the valley until they had crossed over a low range and came into the land of the gentle little farmers. They thought they had left their troubles behind them, but they had underestimated the tenacious vengeance the customs of the tribe demanded.

For several days they had been walking along a valley populated with the farming people, who ran at the sight of them. They offered no resistance to Torjan and his friends. The women of this tribe were fast runners, and he and his men could never catch any of them. Besides, they were so tiny they would not have been able to satisfy real men such as themselves.

For the first time Torjan began to believe they just might find one of the lost kingdoms he had heard of. These people were not like the ignorant savages they had been used to. They were not nomads, wanderers with no real homes. They had neat little dwellings and well-tended fields. With this much organization and population, Torjan reasoned there had to be a central government some place up ahead. Where there were rulers, there should be riches and splendid homes. They congratulated each other on their good fortune to survive over all the others. Now there would only be three of them to split the glory and wealth.

With their last enemies behind them and their heads filled with the prospects of wealth, they became careless. The living was better than at any other time since they had left the lakes. The crops were ripe and ready for harvest, and while meat was not as plentiful, other commodities were easily available to them. This bit of carelessness caused them to be caught in this trap.

Being more familiar with the surrounding country, the savages had sent out several separate parties, each intent on circling ahead of Torjan and his companions. They each had a path they would try to cut off so no matter what trail the three took, they would be turned back and detained until the main party could catch up with them and finish the job they had set out to accomplish.

Torjan had gone down fighting. That was as much as any man could hope for. He had not gone down alone. He knew at least three had gone down at his hand alone, probably more. That he had not been killed outright in the fight was regrettable. It would have been far better for him if he had died. Now he must face the humiliation of being taken prisoner. He had vowed he would never be taken by anyone. He had made his brag that he would never be the slave of another, as his forefathers had been. But now he was helpless, wounded, abandoned by his friends. Worst of all, he was weaponless in the hands of his enemy. There was no hope of help from his comrades. They had taken his pack. This let him know they considered him dead already, and would not be coming back to look for him. Chances are they would not fare any better than he had. The numbers of the savages were too great to be overcome by their swords and shield this time. It looked like the end of the trail for Torjan's expedition. No one would ever know what happened to them. There would be no trip to Valhalla for him.

He would not be a slave; of this he was sure. The savages were more intent on killing him, and in the most inglorious fashion they could conceive. His only hope was that he would die first. Failing that, he hoped to make them so angry they would kill him immediately, rather than the slow, lingering death some of his fellow adventurers had suffered. Torjan was not afraid to die, nor was he afraid of torture. Fear was not part of his makeup. But he did not relish the thought of providing them with any entertainment at his expense.

He resigned himself to whatever the tall, strange looking savage would do with him for now, but at the first opportunity, he would get his hands on him, and then they would see who had whom.

Chapter Thirty Five

Kaoto dragged the wounded man across the meadow and down into the stream. It had been a little easier to manage him in the water. Here he could half carry and half float him downstream. They crossed over several beaver dams before he found what he was looking for. On the opposite side of the stream was a small grove that nearly concealed an overhanging rock shelf. There were enough rocks to conceal their tracks when they left the water.

Torjan was nearly as tall as Kaoto, but at least a third broader in all his body proportions. Kaoto was able to pull his body but only with great difficulty. Once inside the grove of young aspens he had to wend his way among the trees wherever he could find passage. At the overhang, as carefully as he could, he pushed Torjan back out of sight. He then covered the front of the overhang with some dead branches, just enough to break up the contour, and hoped he would not be noticed there if the savages should return to look for him. He had removed all trace of blood from the rocks and sand where they had left the stream.

He retraced his steps and obliterated as much of his footprints and blood smears as possible. He made no attempt to alter the signs in the meadow other than to hide his own footprints. Let the savages think the Red One was still alone and trying to make his way upstream to join his companions. He picked up the fallen weapon and took a wide detour before he again approached the grove that concealed the wounded man.

He was surprised to see the man had aroused and pulled himself out of the shelter and back into the trees. It appeared he was preparing to try to set broken bones in his own fashion.

Kaoto watched in silence as the man lifted his mangled leg up with the aid of a long stick and draped the foot in a low fork of a tree. He eased back until he had taken all the slack out of his leg. Resting a moment, he gathered his strength and courage for what he must do next. Taking a deep breath and clenching his teeth in expectation, he threw himself backward with all his considerable strength and weight. He wanted the first time to be the last for this painful ordeal.

Kaoto could see and hear the bones snap back into position. Great beads of sweat broke out all over the wounded man's body, but he did not lose consciousness. He lay still, flat on his back, his leg held taunt by the fork of the tree. The first attempt had been successful. Now he was trying to think of what he should do next when he became aware of the tall stranger watching him.

Kaoto stepped closer to inspect the leg and could see everything seemed to be back in place. What was needed now was a good firm splint to keep the bones secure until they could mend.

Torjan glared at him in defiance, not moving, not sure what he could do, trussed up the way he was. If he had been helpless before, he was in even worse shape now. He had counted on getting his leg set and free before anyone returned for him. There was a stout limb he had intended to use for a club, but it was out of his reach as long as his foot remained caught up the way it was now. He lay thinking of what to do next when the strange one spoke to him for the first time.

"Do you speak?" Kaoto asked him.

Torjan continued to glare at him in confusion. He had picked up some Indian dialects in his travels but these words were strange to him. Unlike the guttural grunts of the Plains savages, this man's words flowed smoothly, almost melodiously, like the sound of a songbird. In spite of himself, Torjan's body relaxed a fraction of its tension.

"Surely you must speak? After all, you are a man. I will have to admit, you are the most fierce looking man I have ever seen, but still you are not an animal." His tones did not suggest either hostility or fear.

The red-haired man shifted his elbows back under his body and pushed himself up to a sitting position, never taking his eyes from Kaoto in the process. Then his glance shifted briefly from Kaoto's face to the weapon dangling from his hand. His weapon.

Kaoto caught the glance and understood the man's feelings. He was reluctant to part with the weapon. It was not out of fear; he could easily stay out of its reach. But he liked the feel of it in his hand. It had a balance that was new to him. It felt like an extension of his arm. He had not thought to keep it for himself. One did not use another's weapons, but he had not thought to return it just yet, either. Their eyes locked for a long moment until Kaoto let a slight hint of a smile flicker over his face. Once more, on impulse alone, he acted against his better judgment. He reversed the weapon and offered it to the man on the ground.

He had expected the Red One to accept it with dignity and grace. He was not prepared for the swiftness with which it was snatched from his hand and came whistling back at him in the ready position. Torjan gripped it in both hands and held it across his body in such a way that showed he was ready to die before he would relinquish it to anyone again.

"It takes a lot to stop you, does it not?" Kaoto said as he quickly stepped back out of possible reach of the flashing sword. "Now I have to somehow convince you that I want to help you. This is going to be difficult if I have to crack you over the head every time I want to do something for you." His voice was still soothing. The Red One did not find a threat in his words, but Torjan was not used to trusting anyone, especially strange savages who had so far proven quite hostile.

Torjan watched his imagined adversary closely as he lowered his sword and placed it under his extended leg. It was clear he intended to extract his foot from the fork of the tree. This would not do.

"Hold." Kaoto shouted as he started to step forward. "Do not move it yet. Leave it there. It will be much easier to bind up while you have it stretched out and everything is in place."

At his shout and movement, Torjan whipped the sword back up to the defensive position, his teeth flashed in an angry snarl through the tangle of red hair covering his face.

Kaoto just as quickly jumped back. He extended his open, empty hand outward in the generally accepted peace signal. He had to get past this man's suspicion if he was ever going to be able to help him. Somehow he had to make him understand that he was not his enemy, at least not yet. What more could he do? He had carried the man away from danger. He had returned his weapon. Now he was offering to help. What else could he possibly do? What had he learned from Paataga that he could use at a time like this? He stood staring off between the trees. Torjan turned a quick glance that way, and seeing no one, brought his eyes back to bear on the tall stranger. Kaoto saw what Torjan could not. Between two trees, seated on a dead log, was a blurred figure. Ignoring the wounded man, he concentrated on the seated figure and listened to what it was saying to him.

"You are mocking him with your words. He does not understand them. He thinks you are making sport of him, tormenting him before you kill him. Stop your senseless talking and do what you must do. Your actions will speak for you, not your mouth." The figure was gone just as swiftly as it had come. The rotten log was empty, but in his heart Kaoto knew that Paataga was still with him. She had told him on the day they had parted that he would never be really separated from her, and true to her words, in his time of need, she was there.

Torjan was still watching him ready for some sort of trickery, his sword still at the ready. When the tall stranger repeated the peace sign, he released the sword with one hand and returned the sign, but immediately his hand was back on the hilt of his sword, his only hope.

Kaoto smiled. "Yes, you are ready for peace but you will fight for it, will you?"

Then remembering Paataga's advice, he stopped speaking and went to his pack to remove his own stone knife and a strip of tanned leather used for mending or tying miscellaneous items to his pack. He looked around as Torjan stiffened at the sight of the knife. Kaoto held it up and looked from it to the sword and back again. He shook his head and smiled again as he made a false fencing motion. The ridiculousness of this situation even brought a faint smile to the lips of the wounded man with the sword. The point of the sword wavered and lowered, but only a bit.

Kaoto turned to the trees and began an inspection to find what he wanted. Satisfied with a tree of nearly the same size as the Red One's leg, he made quick work of stripping a piece of bark off and trimming it to the shape and size he desired. When he was satisfied with it he held it up for Torjan to see. He held it to his own leg in the same place that Torjan's was broken and made motions of tying it in place with the leather thongs he had cut.

Torjan had watched his movements closely, not missing anything, not willing to be taken off guard. He was trying to decide what to make of this strange young man who seemed bent on befriending him. He knew Kaoto could have killed him several times, up in the meadow and down here, and with his own weapon if he had wanted to. So could the first savages, who had broken his leg instead. This man had gone to a lot of trouble to bring him down here and hide him. He had gone back to cover their trail. He had even given him back his weapon. Now he seemed to be offering to bind up his broken leg. Why? What was his motive? No one went out of their way to help another man without some reason. What was his? Was he ashamed to kill a wounded, unarmed man? Maybe he wanted to get him back in shape before he offered to fight him. This Torjan could understand. He might do the same thing if the circumstances were in his favor. He had offered the peace sign. Was this some new trick, or was he really offering Torjan peace?

In the meantime, Kaoto had taken his long bow and arrows and placed them out of reach of either one of them. He made a show of placing his knife on top of his pack and then held out his arms to show that there were no more knives concealed on his person. With slow, deliberate steps, he came toward Torjan, keeping the tree holding the broken leg between them.

For what seemed an eternity they looked into each other's eyes. Neither man moved or blinked. Finally, Torjan let the point of his sword drop slowly to the ground. He kept both hands on the hilt and his grip tightened, ready for instant action.

Kaoto remained motionless looking at the sword and the hand that held it so fiercely. He was weighing the risk he would be taking if he came around the tree to place the splint on the broken leg. He would be very vulnerable. His neck would be exposed to a possible chop from that wicked weapon still held at the ready. While he hesitated, Torjan gave a great sigh of resignation and let the hilt of the sword slide from his grasp and come to rest on the ground at his side. It was still only a short distance away, but in an awkward position for quick use.

Kaoto was reminded of the ancient buffalo from which he had removed the spear struck by similar savages several summers ago. The Red One was giving permission, but he was not surrendering.

Working swiftly, Kaoto positioned the strip of bark around the broken leg and bound it securely with the strips of skin he had cut. He wished he had had time to kill and skin a rabbit to place next to the leg, but he would do the best he could for now. Later, he would see what happened.

Torjan made no move or sound, although Kaoto could hear the sharp intake of his breath whistling between his clenched teeth as he drew the bind-ings tight. When he was finished, he gently lifted the foot from the fork and lowered it onto a piece of rotten wood to leave it elevated slightly. He offered his water skin, which was accepted and nearly drained.

"I have known some brave men, but few could come close to you," he said.

Torjan drank the water and it helped to ease the queasiness in his stomach, but his leg throbbed painfully. Of course this was no more than he had expected from the beginning. The binding on his leg was a bonus he had not counted on. This was painful, but the wound in his side was troubling him the most. It felt as if a thousand red ants were feasting on his insides. The one on his thigh was superficial and would heal on its own without any trouble.

Kaoto stood off to one side and looked at the wound. He pointed to the similar scar on his side where the buffalo had gored him.

"I know it looks bad but I do not think it hit anything important. I do not see the seeping of body fluids which would indicate your guts were torn, and there are no bubbles to make me think they hit your lung."

Torjan could not understand the words, but he could understand the tone. It was somehow reassuring to hear the easy flow of words coming from the tall stranger. When Kaoto pulled a pouch of bear grease from his pack and tossed it across to Torjan, it fell to the ground at his side, next to his sword. This was the best medicine available for the gash in his side, but he could not readily see the wound and was not sure how to go about cleaning it before he applied the grease. So he let the pouch lie and looked at Kaoto.

Drawing a deep breath, Kaoto decided to take the risk. He had two choices; he could help this man or he could go off and leave him to his fate. If it had only been the broken leg he would have probably chosen the latter, but he knew the wound on his side needed attention, and it was something the man could not do for himself. He needed help, and Kaoto was the only chance he had.

He repeated his sign for peace, which Torjan returned. Kaoto stood looking thoughtfully at the weapon at Torjan's side. It still posed a threat that could not be dismissed. Torjan could read his thoughts and knew what the other was thinking. He had his own problem about the sword. It was a big problem for both of them. The tall stranger feared the weapon. Torjan feared to part with it again. However, he stood to gain the most and the tall stranger stood to lose the most. A weapon was useless to a dead man.

Torjan closed his hand over the hilt of his sword. He brought it up in front of him in a salute. He was puzzled with what he should do with it. To give it up to the stranger seemed like consigning himself to being Kaoto's slave. When a man surrendered his sword he is somehow less than a man. Yet to keep it was a threat for his chance to live. Neither choice was to Torjan's liking. He would not turn over his sword to anyone willingly, nor would he hold it as a threat to the life of the only one who could help him. His life was in the balance either way.

Shifting his grip on the sword, he threw it with considerable force at the tree that had held his foot. It stuck quivering in the soft flesh of the tree. He had not surrendered it. If the stranger chose to take it there was nothing he could do about it. It was as much as he knew how to do. He hoped the stranger recognized the gesture and honored it.

The meaning was clear to Kaoto and he turned his back on the useless sword and ignored it as his face lit up with a pleasant smile.

"I honor you and your wish. What an enemy you must be, and equally, what a friend you could be. With one such as you at my side we could drive every savage from our land."

His hands were not idle as he talked. He cleaned the wound, probed and checked it for dirt or any foreign matter. The wound was deep, but as he had suspected the spear point had not hit anything vital. It would be sore and take a while to heal, but with luck the Red One would carry a mean looking spear wound for many summers.

When it was cleaned, he spread the bear grease liberally over it and closed the sides of the wound with wood splinters and strands of his own hair, drawing the edges tight together. He did the same for the lesser gash in Torjan's thigh.

Torjan remained impassive, immobile and silent during this process. The stranger seemed to know what he was doing and already the red ants were subsiding from his body. He still could not imagine why he was being helped, but for now he would accept it. As soon as he was strong enough to defend himself, he would fight this man, if that was his desire. But he hoped he would not have to kill him. He would just have to keep a close watch and do what he had to do when the time came. As for now, he was ravenously hungry and his throat was already parched again. He had suffered worse before and he would survive this.

Kaoto did not try to move the Red One back into the overhang. Instead he tried to make him as comfortable as possible where he lay. The Spirit Watcher was just leaving the sky for his own bed and the night would be on them soon, bringing with it the cold of the evening

Kaoto's pack was light. He never carried any surplus, so they would have to chew on his emergency rations tonight. He did not want to risk a fire. He pulled both his elk robe and his feathered robe over the Red One to keep him from chilling. Together they munched on dried meat and drank from the refilled water skin.

Kaoto settled himself against the trunk of the tree just below the swaying sword and prepared for a long and cold night. Tomorrow he would have to make better arrangements. Tonight he was young and healthy and would live.

Torjan, in spite of the incessant throbbing in his side and his leg, fell asleep almost immediately after he had consumed the last of the dried rations. His thunderous snoring gave Kaoto great concern for their safety. His only hope was that these savages were also afraid to travel after dark. If not, they would surely hear the noise and come to investigate.

The Spirit Watcher sank from sight, leaving his favorite son cold and cheerless, in a strange country with an even stranger companion.

Chapter Thirty Six

Torjan's recovery was swift. However, the combination of the wounds in his side along with the broken leg were more than enough to keep down even such a man as this misplaced Viking slave.

Kaoto was concerned about the return of the warriors of the savage tribe. He had not strayed far from the camp and had taken the precaution of building a fire only during midday when the flames would not be easily seen. He had used dead aspen so the smoke would be almost nonexistent. After five days without sign of them, he had ventured back down to the nearest village to make inquiries. No on had seen any further sign of either the savages or the animal men. Kaoto told them he had seen the animal men and they were just men, not animals. He did not explain yet about Torjan or the other two. He felt he needed time to understand his reason before he tried to tell anyone else. He took back some fresh supplies to supplement their diet, although Torjan seemed to be content with a steady diet of rich, red meat, and only altered this to please his host.

The trail was cold but Kaoto's trail-wise eyes were able to follow the muffled tracks made by Torjan's companions as they had hurried up the trail for the pass. They had crossed over the top and were a short way down the other side when the trail was lost. He had to double back several times before he found where they had left the trail to make their way along the face of a ragged cliff. Here he found the scene of their last battle and the reason the savages had not come back looking for Torjan. His two companions had sold their lives dearly. The battle had lasted a long time. Kneeling beside the bodies of the two men, Kaoto was able to piece the story together as if he had been a witness to the final moments.

Once more the savages had anticipated their enemy's direction and had sent part of their force to circle around and get ahead of them. On the face of the cliff they had trapped the two. Unable to go either forward or backward, the men had taken a defensive position near the center of the cliff, making it as difficult to approach them as was possible. Their position was ideal for defending but impossible for retreat. They had no choice. The cliff behind them was not climbable, the savages were blocking to the right and left, and a perilous drop in front of them. They stood back to back and waited for the savages to attack.

The savages, not eager to face the cold steel of the long knives, had held them trapped until another group appeared. This group carried bows both for themselves and the others. They had expended their arrows over most of the long day. These had proven futile against the shields of the two, trapped men. They either turned the arrows aside or let them strike harmlessly on the rocks surrounding them. When the last arrow had flown the enemy still stood, unscathed and waiting for the next attack.

The savages could not wait for nature to weaken the animal men, so in desperation they had mounted an attack from both sides simultaneously. Armed with their short heavy spears they had come at the two, screaming their heathen war cries as they went. The two met the charge in silence.

The last stand had been short and violent. The bodies of the dead savages were piled one on top of another as they had scrambled to reach the dreaded foe. Below, Kaoto could see several broken bodies lying where they had fallen. The two animal men were still together, their backs braced against each other. Numerous wounds covered their hairy frames and several spears were still embedded deeply in them. They had died as they had lived, violently and without apologies.

Beside one of the larger rocks Kaoto found three packs, one of which he was sure belonged to Torjan. Tied along the side of this pack was the magic stick Gart had referred to. He opened them all and took only things he thought to be useful. There were many items he did not recognize and had no idea what they might be used for. He made up one pack from the one he had selected. The other two he covered with rocks near the site of the battle so he could return for them at a later time. They were extremely heavy compared to his own, and he marveled that they could carry such packs all day and still have enough strength left to fight.

During Torjan's convalescence they began the arduous chore of communicating with each other. With the help of signs and common objects, they rapidly broke down the barrier. Kaoto learned fast but Torjan seemed to have a linguist's tongue and was soon far more proficient in Kaoto's language than Kaoto was in his.

To Kaoto, it was humorous to hear his own language, which was soft and mellow compared to Torjan's harsh language, coming from the Red One. It seemed impossible for such a fierce looking face to pronounce the smooth, flowing vowels of the People's language. Sometimes in desperation, when he found the words hard, he would almost spit them out, bearing his own fiery temperament, which seemed to convert them into altogether different meanings.

On the other hand, Viking words coming from Kaoto's tongue seemed to lose their combative spirit and fall harmlessly. This caused Torjan to shake his shaggy head in frustration. If anyone had ventured close to them, they would have beaten a hasty retreat at the sounds that came from their camp. However, in time, they began to iron out the difficulties and establish a language of there own using some of the words of the People and a few of Torjan's language. He told Kaoto, "Your language just does not have some of the words I need to express myself."

To which Kaoto had replied, "And yours has too many words that I have no need for. It seems to me, all your words are either threats, or promises of threats. You are always going to kill or hurt someone. Why talk so much if that is what you are going to do? Among the People, we do not do most of these things, and the rest we do instead of wasting time talking about it."

If not a true friendship, at least a truce, which developed into mutual

268 - Norman D. Messenger

respect, grew between them. Torjan accepted the death of his companions as easily as he accepted his own fate. There had been too many deaths on their journey; two more did not surprise him. With some difficulty, Kaoto asked Torjan, "What are your plans when you are well enough to get around?"

Torjan looked at him closely, trying to read his captor's mind.

"I will fight you to the death, if that is what you want," he had said with all seriousness. Kaoto burst into a peel of laughter.

"Death may be honorable to you, but why the hurry?" He shook his head at the thought. "As for myself, I have too much to do to die just to please you."

For the first time Kaoto heard Torjan's booming laugh. It came from deep within the cavernous chest and rumbled out to fill the small grove and roll up the sides of the canyon. It was so loud and unexpected that everything in nature became silent and waited to see if there was a storm following it.

"Your death would not please me. Why should it? But from what I have seen of your People, the only things that seem to please you are our deaths. The slower and more painful the better. I guess it is the only way you can prove yourselves men, by killing someone bigger and better than you are."

Although Torjan had been laughing, Kaoto knew he was not joking. He was serious. He honestly believed they would have to fight in order to satisfy some sense of twisted honor.

"The savages with whom you fought are not my People. My People are the peaceful little farmers you have been stealing from. They do not fight. They do not kill over a mouthful of food. They prove their manhood by being men, not animals." Kaoto had been stung by Torjan's description of his People.

"Your People are the little People? How was I to know that? You are not little like them, and besides, what other reason did you have to keep me alive other than to fight me in the end?" Torjan was puzzled.

"I do not really know why I helped you. I guess you put up a good fight and I thought you deserved better than to die at the hands of the savages. They are the enemy of my People as well. Other than that, I had no plans for you. You are free to go your way whenever you are already. I and my People will not hinder you. I only hope you will not bother my People further."

Their respect for each other grew with each passing day. Kaoto respected Torjan for his tremendous strength and fierce pride and courage. Torjan on his part respected Kaoto for his peaceful intent and help. He had seldom met a young man who did not boast and threaten what he planned to do. Kaoto made simple statements and lived up to his word. He was able to accept Torjan and his views without asking endless questions and demanding explanations. By the time Torjan was able to hobble about with the use of a stout limb for a crutch, they had formed a bond between them; a mutual trust to replace the mistrust they had started with.

"I have been thinking," Torjan said one evening as they sat before the open fire they dared to have now that the danger was gone. "There is still much land ahead of me that I have not seen. If it would be agreeable to you, I would follow along and travel with you for awhile." He did not look at Kaoto but kept his eyes on the flickering flames. "There is much I would know of you and your People. Who better to teach and show me?"

"I would not object. However, I fear you will frighten my People so much that you will not see much of them," Kaoto told him truthfully. Torjan was a frightening sight to behold. Kaoto was still a little awed by the great mass of curly red hair which abounded all over the man's body. "They have never seen such a man as you. Even my hairy body and great height makes them uneasy at first. They are slow to accept anything so different from themselves, and you, well . . . " He left the sentence unfinished.

"Surely you, as a Wise One to them, could explain me to them so they would understand and not be afraid. I solemnly promise not to harm a hair on their heads. I give you my hand on it." He extended one huge paw to prove his honesty.

Kaoto looked at the hand and wondered if it could crush his own. He was no weakling, but again he was not built like Torjan, either. He ignored the hand and grasped the wrist, as was the custom of his People. For an instant, Torjan tensed as if he expected to have to wrestle with Kaoto. Then he relaxed and accepted the grip.

"I am not sure about explaining you to them. I have trouble accepting your explanation myself, and after all I am supposed to be wiser than they are. Besides that, do you not want to return to your own People in the land by the lakes you have told me about?"

"My home and my People are so far away in both time and distance that I do not think I could ever find my way back. Even if I did, there is nothing for me there. I fear the bottom of my feet will itch if I stay too long in one place. I need the feel of the trail under them to relieve the itching."

Each day, as Torjan was able to move farther from the camp, Kaoto pondered what he should do about him. The Spirit Watcher had wanted him to save this man for some reason other than to satisfy his curiosity. Soon they would be able to take to the trail. Kaoto doubted Torjan would ever be able to keep the pace he usually set, but what he lacked in speed, he more than made up in endurance. He would like to have this man at his side as he went about his work. Surely he could justify it somehow. There was still a little time before he must be on the move again.

The strange wood stick had proven to be almost magic. Torjan, for all his fierce appearance and nature, had a soul that loved beauty. When he had discovered the flute in his pack, he had been delighted, and proceeded to give Kaoto a demonstration of its abilities. He had spent most of his time in enforced confinement, blowing softly on the flute, producing wondrous sounds that Kaoto had never heard before outside of nature itself. Torjan could capture the sounds of the turtledoves, of the wind in the spruce trees, of water splashing happily over the rocks and the sound of calling birds.

He had let Kaoto try his hand at it, and with practice he too could produce some of the sounds, but never as easily and truly as the master. They satisfied him as nothing else had ever done. He was profoundly moved to discover the deep sense of both contentment and nostalgic loneliness he felt when he blew soft notes from the flute. Under Torjan's patient tutelage, he began to construct a flute of his own. The task began with the complicated task of finding the proper kind of wood to make the instrument.

"You cannot just use any stick you pick up," Torjan told him. "It has to be a special piece of wood. It must have a soul of its own. The sound must be in the wood first."

He went on to explain how long it had taken him to find the right one. It had to be straight grained without any knots or swirls, and it must be very old. Old wood held true sounds much better than young wood. The wood must be very hard. Only hard wood could hold the sounds they wanted. Wood that was soft would do for a child's whistle, but its soft grain would soon lose the sounds of nature and pick up inferior sounds from the camp, and thus be useless.

"And where will I find this kind of wood?" Kaoto asked, fearing Torjan might tell him that he could not find it in this area.

"The best place would be near a waterfall, but it should be high up in the mountains. Up where the wind blows free and the birds sing uninterrupted. If possible, it should be far from any place where man has ever been, so the sounds of man are not embedded in its grain," Torjan told him. His fierce countenance temporarily softened as he searched for the words to convey his meaning.

"I think you would have liked my great mother Paataga," Kaoto told him. "She understood the spirits of all things."

"Sounds like a smart woman, but she would have to be young and pretty to interest me for very long," Torjan had snorted, embarrassed by his lapse of character. Most would have considered it a weakness to speak of such things, but Kaoto did not feel that way.

Kaoto smiled at the thought of Paataga as young and beautiful. Maybe in her younger days, many summers before their time, but not in any living man's memory.

"She was neither young nor pretty in the ways of women, but you would have found her interesting. Maybe yet you will have a chance to meet and talk with her."

The search for the proper wood had taken several days. Each time Kaoto brought a piece to Torjan for inspection, it would be rejected because of a fault or flaw in it to make it unworthy.

"Even when you find one you think is just right, we will not know until we split it open and look at its heart," Torjan had warned him as he rejected the last specimen Kaoto had brought him.

Kaoto returned one afternoon after being gone for much of the day. He carried a small, straight piece of ancient wood in his hand. It had been many summers dead. One end showed the marks of a beaver's teeth, but he had found it high above anyplace a beaver would normally go. He thought it was possible a large bird intent on using it in its nest had carried it. There was no bark on it and there were no knots showing on its perfectly smooth surface. He handed it to Torjan.

Torjan took it with almost a reverence and turned it slowly in his huge hands.

"I have passed by this stick several times in the last few days. Each time I left it because I thought it was too small and probably rotten, but somehow I always came back to it," Kaoto said apologetically as he waited for Torjan to pass judgment on it. If this one was not right, he was ready to give up hope of ever finding one in this area.

Torjan remained silent as he turned the stick, noting every mark on it searching for the hidden flaw. Kaoto also became silent, afraid of casting a spell on his selection.

"We will know soon enough," Torjan said as he picked up his sword and placed the blade on one end of the piece. Without hesitation, he sliced the stick neatly in two halves, exposing the heart to the afternoon sun. He began his in-spection again just as thoroughly as before. At last, he nodded his head and ex-pressed his opinion.

"I think it has the soul you are looking for. It is thinner than mine, but so are you thinner than me. It may have a slightly higher pitch. No two are ever exactly the same, but I think it will have the sound that will suit you."

Kaoto worked patiently on shaping the new flute. Torjan showed him how to carve a straight groove down each half and then how to polish those grooves with tiny pebbles until they were smooth and free of any distortions.

"One little piece of loose wood or uncarved section can ruin the whole flute," Torjan explained.

The two pieces were glued together in their original position. The glue was made from boiling down the hooves of a recently killed deer. The pieces were bound together with a piece of raw, wet hide, which would tighten as it dried. For three days it was left to hang from a tree branch in the bright sunlight until it was bonded firmly forever. Torjan then cut the bindings and handed it to Kaoto saying, it was ready to be worked on, on the outside now.

"How thin shall I make it?" Kaoto asked as he gently scraped the sides of the flute with a splinter of broken stone.

"That is the hardest part. No one can tell you that," Torjan said as he took the flute and ran his fingers over the smooth surface. "It is something you just have to do by feel. Not just with your fingers, but here." He tapped his hairy chest with one blunt finger. "Inside of you, you have to know when it is right." He handed the flute back to Kaoto and picked up his own flute, caressing it as gently as if it were a baby.

Kaoto continued to scrape at the flute in his free time, never rushing it, running his fingers over the surface, feeling for any irregularities. When at last he felt sure he could do no more, he once more held it out for Torjan's inspection. The last step Torjan performed for him. He seemed to sense just where each hole should be drilled, each in its own place and of its own size. After this he showed Kaoto how to rub it up along the side of his nose. When Kaoto looked at him skeptically, he explained.

"The oil in your skin is good for the wood. There is more of this oil on either side of your nose than any place on your body. You have an ample nose, so you should be able to keep it in good shape."

"I have noticed you doing that, but I just thought it was a habit. I did not know you were doing it for a reason," Kaoto said.

"The wood soaks up your body oil. This way it becomes a part of you."

Finally he pronounced it finished and handed it back to Kaoto, who insisted Torjan give it its first test.

"No. You must take this instrument out in the woods by yourself. You must take it to as high and lonely a place as you can find, away from the ears of other men. There you must offer it to whatever god you serve. You must ask him to instruct this flute to play just for you. If he is pleased with it, and you, and your effort, he will let the flute sing. If not, it will only squawk and make horrible noises."

Kaoto watched Torjan's face intently for a sign of humor. He had found Torjan had a great sense of humor and would often tease him, but not this time. Today his ugly face was serious. There was a serenity about the look in his eyes that laid to rest any doubts Kaoto might have had about him. He began to rub it along the side of his nose and could see immediately that Torjan had been right about the oil in his skin. The wood soon took on a soft, mellow hue that would darken over the long summers ahead until it became as dark as the one Torjan carried.

Carrying the flute wrapped in a special piece of deerskin, Kaoto climbed back up the mountain, heading away from the pass and the trail leading that way. He could see a point of rock sticking out from the forest like an exposed finger. He was sure no man had ever been there before him. Here in the early morning light of the Spirit Watcher, he opened the skin wrapper containing the flute and tenderly laid the instrument out for the Spirit Watcher's inspection.

Seated cross-legged with the flute lying on a flat stone in front of him, he let the rays of the Spirit Watcher play over its finely polished, hand rubbed exterior. After a time, he turned it over so the other side could be seen. He waited for a sign of approval or disapproval. Kaoto had learned patience. He knew the Spirit Watcher did not respect time as man did. Sometimes the Spirit Watcher took longer to decide than man. He would wait, forever if necessary, before he would precede fate or risk profaning the instrument before him.

A long passage of time ensued in silence. Nothing in his world moved, not even a bird or the ever-present chipmunks. The Spirit Watcher beat down on Kaoto and his flute. His heat could be felt because there was no breeze to fan the air.

His first sign came when a bird of blue feathers flew in a straight line from far down the ridge. Straight as an arrow's flight, it flew to land in the topmost branch of a tree in front of Kaoto, on the same level as the Wise One's eyes. Throwing back its head, it gave forth a burst of melodious song. Only once did it sing; then it flew out of sight. It was a good sign, but still Kaoto waited. Then, from far down the same ridge as the bird had come from, he could see the stirring of a breeze as the trees began to sway. The breeze rushed toward him, strengthening as it came. With it came the sound of the tree branches rubbing together and the needles as they sang their joyful song. It was an isolated breeze and came only up the ridge to Kaoto. The rest of the world in his sight was still and calm. The breeze wafted over the point of rock and gently swayed the flute. Then, with a final motion, it nudged the flute off the stone and rolled it over to Kaoto's waiting hand.

The Spirit Watcher was pleased.

Chapter Thirty Seven

Kaoto stood back to admire his work as he wiped the red paint from his fingers on some dried grass at the base of the flat rock. Before him, on the face of a rock facing the trail, was an imposing figure. All in red, the figure was hard to describe. It depicted a hump-backed creature that supported two oversized, prominent horns on its head. It appeared to hold a stick to its mouth.

"That is supposed to represent me?" Torjan snorted in disgust.

"Did I claim to be an artist?" Kaoto smiled ruefully at his companion as he continued to inspect his work. "Besides, it tells everyone what they need to know."

"All I can see is that someone made a bad drawing of some misshapen creature," Torjan insisted.

"Well, to my People it says that the man beast with the red hair - that is you, there with the flute, has gone south over the mountain with me. It also lets them know there is nothing to fear. That you mean them no harm," Kaoto explained as he pointed to various aspects of the drawing.

"What about the rest of the pictures, those funny lines over there, and up here?" Torjan asked doubtfully.

"Those funny lines, as you put it, tell them the time we were here and where we are going in case someone wants to find me." Kaoto was busy putting the last of the paints back in his pack, preparing to move out on the trail.

Torjan was completely recovered now, and although he walked with a noticeable limp, he was as strong as ever. His pack was not as heavy as before. Kaoto had not brought back nearly all of his equipment, but had assured him the other two packs would still be where he had left them. When they crossed over the pass, they could stop and pick up whatever he wanted from them.

They had to move on because there was already a light snow on the top of the mountain, and if they did not cross over soon they would be forced to stay on this side until spring. Kaoto wanted to be over in the next valley for the winter, where the weather was milder and he would be free to travel among the People all winter. There were many for him to see and they must be told of the impending threat of the northern savages.

After they had crossed the pass, Kaoto turned off to the side and led Torjan to the site of his companion's last battle. Nothing had changed since he had been here. No one had come close to the battleground.

Torjan callously threw the bodies of his comrades over the edge of the cliff without showing any concern for them. With Kaoto's, help he dislodged several large stones and sent them tumbling down after the bodies. These stones dislodged others until a full-scale landslide occurred, entombing friend and foe alike for all eternity.

"It is the best I can do for them," Torjan said by way of explanation. "I did not want them to be eaten by wolves or other animals. The birds of carrion have already feasted on them enough as it is."

"If you had asked me, we could have made other arrangements for them. It would have been a small task to bury them in the custom of my People."

"Not necessary. This is good enough, more than a lot of the others got, although we did try to leave some sort of a marker for them." Torjan looked around for something to mark this place. His gaze came to rest on the face of the cliff.

"Have you enough of that paint left to make a picture of them here?" He pointed to the bald face of the cliff.

Kaoto produced his supply of paint. There was very little left, especially of the precious red paint that Paataga had given him, but he decided to use it. It was a small thing to do for this man's friends. When he was through, he explained the picture to Torjan, although Torjan had already made out most of it for himself. It depicted two men fighting, holding shields out in front of them. This told how they had died and where they had come to their final rest. It was simple, but enough.

Torjan had sorted through their packs and taken a few items he wanted. The rest he had thrown over the cliff with their bodies. One sword was not to be found, the other was broken in two pieces. Torjan tucked the pieces in his pack for future use. Iron was not to be found in this country.

Even though Kaoto had sent a runner ahead of him to announce his arrival and the guest he would be bringing with him, the People were not prepared for the huge, red-haired giant with his barbaric appearance and his outlandish costume. His helmet of buffalo hide with the buffalo horns attached was sufficient to cause quite a stir among the villagers. He had taken it off to show them it was just a covering for his head and not actually a part of his body, but they still were mistrustful of him. His flaming red beard, among a people who had little or no facial hair, was also quite alarming, not to mention the coarse red hair covering the rest of his enormous body. They had grown accustomed to Kaoto's height and his soft downy covering of golden hair, but this was a different kind of man. They still referred to him as the man beast.

Kaoto had pleaded with him, but Torjan could not or would not drop his fierce scowl. This was enough to keep everyone at a distance.

"How can you expect to make friends with anyone when you insist on scaring them to death?" Kaoto had asked him repeatedly.

Torjan had only deepened his scowl and mumbled heathen phrases under his breath, which came out in a low rumbling, like an afternoon storm in the mountaintops.

Kaoto observed the first sign of human weakness in his friend at one of the larger villages where they had stopped. It was nearly evening and the Spirit Watcher was well on his way to rest when they had entered the village. As usual, Kaoto had made his way to the dumpsite to take up his temporary residence with the human refuse. The elders had learned, as all the rest before them, that if they wished to speak with the Wise One, they must meet him there. They had compromised by building an open courtyard and meeting place between their village and the dump. It was a pleasant place and was frequented by the children. When Kaoto spoke with the elders, Torjan would sit off to one side, listening without comment, content to hear and observe these quaint little People.

Two small children were playing tag, chasing each other around in circles, squealing and laughing. They were so engrossed in their play they did not notice Torjan, who they normally would have avoided at all cost.

They ran straight into him. One child fell down at his feet, the other backed away in awe and terror. Torjan scooped up the fallen youngster and balanced it on his broad knee while he checked it over to see if it was hurt. The little one shivered when it discovered it was being held captive by the fearsome man beast, but made no outcry, it seemed to be resigned to its fate.

All around a silence fell as the villagers watched to see what Torjan intended to do. Satisfied the little one had not suffered any harm, Torjan set it on its feet and gave it a gentle swap on its bare bottom to send it on to play again. Aware of the silence around him, Torjan's scowl deepened as he voiced his anger at them in his deep, hoarse voice, speaking their words in such a way as they had never heard before.

"What? Did you think I was going to eat it? Bah. You make me sick. I fight men, not children. You think I am not human? We have children too. We did not hatch from eggs or crawl out from under a rock." He continued to scowl around him, causing the People to take several steps backward away from the threat. Torjan stood up, looking for something to vent his anger on.

"Take it easy my big friend," Kaoto cautioned him. "So far you have not given them a chance to know you as I do. I have tried to tell you that you were frightening them, but you would not listen to me. What do you expect from them?"

"You are always telling me how I scare people." Torjan looked around him. He threw up his hands in disgust and resignation. "I cannot help what they think. This is my face. I cannot change it. I would not if I could. This is me. This is the way I look. But I have not hurt them, have I? So why do they fear me so?"

"People always fear what they do not understand, and they do not understand you as I do. You will have to admit you are both new and strange to them. Give them a chance. Show them the softer side of yourself. Do not hide behind that perpetual scowl. Even when you are not scowling, that beard and your eyes are enough to give them pause." Kaoto tried to explain once again to his friend that his fearsome appearance was hard to accept.

"I have already said I cannot change my looks. I will not cut off my beard. It is a part of me. Do you put on a new face at each village? No. Yet you are accepted, even though you are as strange to them as I am. But they are not afraid of you. So why do they fear me?" Torjan was puzzled by their reaction to him at each new camp.

Kaoto crossed over to Torjan and laid one hand on the Red One's wide shoulder. It was one of the few times he had touched Torjan since he had tended his wounds. Touching was an intimate thing, something that held special meaning. Not a thing to be done lightly. To his surprise he felt a warm surge of latent power spring from Torjan to himself, an understanding between the two of them, a warm feeling of brotherhood that had not existed previously. Torjan was aware of it also and his expression softened, albeit ever so slightly.

"I noticed when we were in camp together while your leg was mending that when you play your flute, your eyes lose some of their fierce looks. In fact, your whole face changes and you look like a different person. Perhaps this is the way to show the People what you are really like. Why do you not get out your flute and play some for them?" As Torjan began to shake his huge head, Kaoto insisted.

"What have you got to lose? What could it hurt? Besides, they have never heard anything like it. You play so much better than I do. I am sure it will fascinate them as it does me, and just maybe they will see you are really a man after all."

Doubtfully, Torjan removed his flute from his pack leaning beside him. Tapping it gently in his hand before he placed it to his lips, he began to blow, ever so softly at first. So softly did the sound come that it could hardly be heard by those closest to him. As Kaoto had said, his face melted, the scowl dissolved in a relaxed, if yet somewhat bestial, countenance. His eyes lost their habitual glare and became mellow and glazed with the dreamy softness Kaoto had seen so often before when they were alone together. Kaoto returned to his seat with the elders and all were respectfully silent.

Torjan played on now, separated from all those around him, lost in his own world, unaware of the ensuing silence that fell over the village. The volume grew until the sound of the flute filled the village and overflowed to the outlying fields. Not loud, not shrill or piercing, but commanding everyone to stop whatever they were doing and listen. Even the birds were hushed with the new, unexpected rival. Like water, the sound flowed out to fill every nook and corner, leaving no vacant spot behind.

Torjan's eyes were closed and he became immersed in his music. He was no longer aware of anyone. The sound came from the depth of his soul and was emitted from the flute in long, liquid, melodious notes. The mellowness of the sounds gripped the People in a stone-like trance. The only sound of music they had ever known came from the beating of log drums and the chanting of the singers in the kivas at religious ceremonies or festive occasions. None had heard such sounds coming from a man. Only nature herself could produce these wondrous sounds. Yet the man-beast held them in the palm of his hand and released them at his will.

The sound of Torjan's flute was having the desired result on the villagers. As they stopped whatever they were doing and came closer to see the source of this new sound, they became aware of the change passing over the man making them. Just as Kaoto had predicted, Torjan's face had softened, and although he was still as large as ever and still covered with the coarse red hair, it was plain for all to see that he was a man, a man with a soul. They need not fear him anymore. The wisdom of the Wise One was made clear to them.

Slowly, one by one at first, many of the children came forward to be closer to the sound. They sat in a semi-circle at Torjan's feet in rapt wonder. They would never fear this man again. Any person who could command the doves to sing, who could make the water and wind talk at his will, could not be an evil person.

The spell was broken when Torjan ceased to blow his flute and all sound faded away. The silence wore on unbroken. Everyone feared to speak. No one had words to express their feelings. At last a scolding squirrel barked in a nearby tree and everyone laughed in nervous release.

Timidly, the mother of the child Torjan had picked up came forward with an offering of food. It was in the largest bowl she could find and was heaped full. She held it out to Torjan with a gentle smile. He accepted it in embarrassment, not daring to speak for fear he would frighten the little woman away.

With this offering and his acceptance, everyone started to breathe freely again. Torjan was accepted. He would be welcome to stay as long as he liked in this village. Soon word would spread of his magic and other villages would be looking forward to his visit with excitement instead of the fear they had been experiencing at the prospect of his visit with the Wise One.

In this village everyone felt they had witnessed something special. They had all been touched by a great event. This moment would live in their hearts forever, and it would become part of their history. They surely had heard the spirits speak through this coarse looking brute of a man who had commanded the slender stick to speak when it was held in his hands. Torjan was no longer referred to as the man-beast. He would become a legend in the land of the People. He was most often called the Great Red One. Over the passing season, long after he had departed with the Wise One, they would refer to the winter they were privileged to have received a visit from the Horned Humpback who played the Magic Flute.

Chapter Thirty Eight

The winter passed quickly. Sometimes Torjan accompanied Kaoto on his rounds. More often he would choose to stay at one of the larger villages near the junction of the two rivers, awaiting Kaoto's return. He ran daily. His wounded leg developed strength, and his limp was soon a thing of the past. His endurance was matchless, but his speed was slow in comparison to that of Kaoto or any of the runners. Even the women could outrun him for a short distance. With continuous training he was able to increase his speed. It would never equal Kaoto's tireless strides, but he was determined to travel with his new brother and would not hold him back. The young men coached him, and he paid special attention to the runners. His open admiration of their fleetness won him new friends wherever he went. Soon he was as much at ease with these little people as Kaoto himself. He found that the ability to laugh at one's own expense was necessary in this new life, and his bellowing laughter could be heard ringing over the valley many times during the winter. He even found there were young maidens willing to accommodate him on the long winter nights. Life had never been better for him. He hated to think of leaving.

He had other chores to tend to which kept him from being idle or bored. He constructed a forge using stones for framework and mud for mortar. After this was completed, he made a simple bellows from deer skins and the willow wands that grew in abundance near the water's edge. There were plenty of volunteers to operate the bellows. It was considered an honor to work the bellows and be able to watch Torjan perform miracles with the strange metals he had brought with him.

At the death site of his former companions Torjan had salvaged one broken sword. The other had never been found. The sword had been broken close to the handle, but iron was not to be found in this country and it was the last Torjan had to work with. Heating the iron and forging it with crude stone hammers, he reshaped the iron into a pair of shorter, slender knives and two hatchet heads. Each was then fitted with serviceable wooden handles. He tempered them and sharpened them. Last, he blued them with the aid of animal fats. He presented one set to Kaoto and kept the other for himself.

Kaoto was impressed with both implements and their usefulness. His own flint knife was sharper than the iron one, but its edge was quickly broken and had to be chipped regularly to form a new edge. This constant chipping soon wore the knife down until it was no longer useful as a knife. He had never had a knife with a separate wooden handle, which improved its use. The new hatchet was light and versatile, capable of doing many simple camp chores.

From deep in his pack, Torjan had produced a lump of bluish green stone. There was one large piece and several smaller ones, all wrapped in a pouch to keep them from getting lost. The villagers watched in fascination as he commenced to pound the stone. They expected it to fly apart, but instead the stone was mashed down into a flat mass. Repeated heating and hammering removed many impurities from the stone until the end result was a soft, malleable piece of metal with a dull reddish hue. It was raw copper from near the great lakes that Torjan had carried with him on his long journey.

Selecting a smaller piece to his liking, Torjan flattened it until it was as thin as a leaf from the oak tree. He took another small pouch from his pack and laid out a small iron hammer, a chisel, a tiny punch and a crude shear. Laying the piece of copper on a large flat rock, he took the small tools, which were dwarfed in his huge hands, and began to cut and trim the copper in a curious, intricate design. It looked like a flower with four identical pedals. With the tiny punch, he pressed two holes near the center of the flower.

Taking one of the smaller pieces he had trimmed off, he began to hammer again, tapping the flat sheet back into a small ball with a slight projection on one side. Once more using the tiny punch, he made a hole in this projection. The children were crowded around him to see what he would do next. Torjan pulled a long strand from his beard and with fingers and thumb too large and too rough for the task, tried to thread the hair through the last hole he had made. After several futile attempts he enlisted the aid of a little child pressing to the front. The child, a girl child of less than ten summers, was always close by. She had an injured foot that left her permanently crippled so she could not run and frolic with the others. Uncomplaining, she had elected to oversee the Red One's daily work.

Torjan showed her what he wanted done and she nimbly drew the strand of hair through the small lump and then up through the two holes in the center of the flower and tied them loosely, leaving the clump dangling.

Torjan took the metal back and with thumb and forefinger he curled each petal of the flower up over the clump in a circular fashion until all four met at the center, forming a little open ball. Now the flower looked like a bud about to open. Holding the object up by the threads of hair, Torjan gently shook it next to the little girl's ear. A clear, tinkling bell note pealed out, to the merriment and delight of the child. She timidly took the bell when Torjan offered it to her and shook it herself. Her eyes sparkled with wonderment when she discovered she could produce the same tones with the little copper rose bud. When she offered it back to Torjan he smiled, a feat that seemed impossible when she looked at his otherwise terrible face. He told her it was to be hers. She could keep it all for her own. Boldly she hobbled over to the seated giant and placed her arms around his neck and gave him a hug, giggling when his beard tickled her nose.

Gingerly returning the hug, afraid he might crush her, Torjan said, "With your help, we will make a necklace from your hair and then we will hang this around your neck. That way, I will never lose you. I will be able to listen and hear the bell and know just where to look for you. That way I will not step on you."

"You will never have to look very far. I will never get very far away with this foot," she said as she held up the injured member. "Besides, I like being here with you."

"Are you not afraid of me?" he asked.

"No." Another giggle. "Should I be?" She asked, the innocence of a child in her eyes.

"No reason, little one. No reason at all. But some are, you know. Some are still frightened when they look at me with all this red hair."

The little girl giggled again with mischief. Surely Torjan was making a joke. Who could be afraid of him? Her child's heart could see what grownup hearts could not. Inside this big hairy body was a gentle person. The outward appearance and loud sounds of the man-beast did not fool her.

The necklace was made, and she wore the tiny copper bell for thirty summers before she wore it to her grave for all eternity so Torjan, the Red One, would always know where to find her.

Torjan helped the People create crude boats, more raft-like than a boat. With these they could cross the river more easily than before. The rafts were large enough to carry several People and supplies, keeping all high and dry. He cautioned them about using the rafts during the flood season when the current was so strong that they would not be able to manage them and would be drawn down into the forbidden canyon, from which no one ever returned.

With the coming of the spring thaw, Kaoto bid farewell to the valley and pushed south at an even pace. Runners had gone out ahead of him, so the People were not surprised to see him accompanied by the Red One and his magic flute. Torjan was widely accepted now as the traveling companion of the Wise One. His strength had become legendary. Even the Wise One could not compete with him in lifting logs and stones. Their combined efforts made impossible jobs seem like child's play. They often assisted in the building of new structures, especially when timbers were to be raised to upper levels.

Kaoto tried to instruct Torjan in the use of the long bow. Torjan could pull it back with ease and send an arrow out of sight, but he could never attain any accuracy. He referred to it as a toy and much preferred a dependable sword. On the few occasions when they encountered some of the roving savages, they were soon sent on their way. Kaoto's long bow could send arrows far out to threaten them, and the sight of Torjan standing in their path, wielding his terrible sword and shouting Viking curses at them, was more than they wanted to face.

They left Hovenweep behind. And after a short stay at Mesa Verde and Aztec, they headed south again. Kaoto was going to return to his home in the Chaco. He was anxious to show his new brother to his parents. The runners said they still lived. Just as important, he wanted to introduce him to Paataga.

Torjan had no argument with this arrangement. He was resigned to living out the rest of his days with Kaoto. He had no desire to return to the land of lakes, although he missed the lush green growth and plentiful water supply. He had the distinction of being introduced as the brother of the Wise One. He would travel with him and lend him his arm and sword whenever needed. He would serve him in any way he could. Contrary to his former belief, he had become a slave. He had never surrendered his sword, but he was nevertheless a willing slave who could not do enough for his new master, and would have thrashed anyone who might have suggested this was the case.

Little by little, over the back trail, Kaoto had told Torjan of the nature of his travels, the reason he must be continually on the move, the mission he felt compelled to complete. Torjan did not understand it but he would do what he could to help his brother.

"This is the trail I followed on my manhood run," Kaoto told him as they ran smoothly along the wide road from Aztec to the Chaco canyon.

"I remember on the way back when I came to this rise and could see that landmark over there. I could not believe I had really come this far. I could not remember the rest of the path behind me. It was like someone had picked me up back there and set me down up here. I guess I had run over it without seeing it. Near to exhaustion, probably."

"You ran up this road and back, in one day?" Torjan asked in disbelief.

"Yes. Well, it was a long day. I started early in the morning and it was getting late when I got back."

"The way you run now I suspect you could do it much faster and easier. Could you not? If you did not have someone like me along to slow you down?"

Kaoto smiled at the sweating man at his side. True, Torjan did hold him back, but he would not have parted with him for any reason. The slower pace was worth the trouble of having him.

"It seems like a short run to me now, but over the past summers I have often kept track of my runs when I could see long distances ahead. I have often run much further in shorter times without near the effort. But it was a good run for a boy, even a long-legged boy such as I was. I only had twelve summers at the time."

Torjan shook his head. "It is a good run for a full-grown man like my-self." He knew he would be worn out when they finally stopped for the evening. Kaoto did not realize it, but he had steadily increased his pace the nearer they came to the canyon.

When they topped the canyon wall where the steps led down to the valley, Kaoto stopped and told him about his friend, Little Frog, and how she had crawled all the way up here just to shout encouragement to him. He was still amazed at her blind faith that he would make it when he had had grave doubts about his own ability. There was no way to account for the loyalty of a friend. Memories flooded over him, leaving him silent and melancholy as they descended the steps to the valley floor.

Although Matuga had been informed of Kaoto's return, there was no one out to greet them. As the Wise One, he would be greeted with dignity of his office at the front of the pueblo just as any other dignitary would. There was no shelter at the dumpsite. In honor of the Wise One and Little Frog, the village took care of the unfortunates by command of Matuga. So the Wise One would not have to sit at the dump to hold an audience.

Today he was not Sun Bear returning from his long run, nor was he Kaoto, prized runner of the Chaco, coming back from a distant village. Today he was the Wise One, coming to visit, just as he had visited so many other villages over the intervening summers. The People knew he was not coming home to stay. This was just another of his visits, and then he would be on his way again. No one knew how long he would stay or whom he would want to speak with. Time had a way of changing people, and they did not know this man who came to them in the guise of Kaoto.

Once again he was reminded just how lonely his life had become, and now he understood how lonely Paataga had been while she lived here with, yet apart from, her People. It was the way it had to be and would always remain, but he still had his moments of regret.

"I cannot help but wish sometimes that I was still just a runner for Matuga," Kaoto confided to Torjan. "As a runner there was always someone waiting for you. There were usually some boys to pace you on your final lap home, boys in training for their manhood rites who were proud to be able to run with one of the runners. I know. I have done it many times myself. But now I return as a stranger."

"That is as it should be. You are a stranger. Certainly you are not the same young man they knew. You have told me it was many summers since you left. When you were here, they knew you as a funny looking boy, then as a great runner. They did not have a chance to know you when you studied with the old woman, and did you not say you left shortly after you took her place? And you have never returned since then either, have you?"

"No. Many times I have longed to come back but I just could not take the time. There were so many places I had to go and so many of the People I needed to see." Kaoto felt a need to explain his actions.

"Has it occurred to you that these people might resent your being gone so long?"

"Resent my being gone? Why should they? They knew I had a job to do. It is what I trained for. It is my obligation to visit all of the People," Kaoto said defensively.

"That may all be true, but in doing this have you not neglected these people? I mean, do they not have the same right of seeing the Wise One as all the rest of the People? After all, they probably feel a certain amount of responsibility for helping produce you and making you the Wise One."

"I guess. I never thought of it that way. I was raised here and I know all these people. It seemed to me the rest of the nation was where I was needed the most."

"That may also be true. Perhaps it is necessary for you to go all over as you have. I do not know, but I would guess your Spirit Watcher you speak of must have directed your steps. But still, you say you know these people, but do they know you? You did not give them much of a chance to get to know you as a Wise One if you left so quickly. They knew the boy and then the runner, but did they ever get to know the Wise One? You yourself have told me how lonely the old woman was and she has lived here all her life. You are set apart from the People, and that makes it harder to get to know you," Torjan insisted.

"What you say is true. It gives me new areas for thought."

"You say you know these people," Torjan repeated. "But stop and think. Since you have left, there have no doubt been many that have died. There have been some that have moved in from other districts. And what of the youngsters? How many have grown up and reached maturity while you were gone? There are probably many men and women who have never seen you and only know you by the stories told to them by elders."

Kaoto smiled at his giant friend. "As usual, you are right my brother. I sometimes think your People must be missing a great deal by not having the benefits of your counsel."

"We did not have anyone to act in this capacity among my People. The strongest and the smartest ended up being the leader. Then he must constantly be on guard against someone else trying to unseat him and take over his power. Fighting and killing was our strongest point. There was little time for wisdom."

"It sounds like a cruel world you lived in. I am surprised that you turned out as gentle as you did."

"It is hard for me to believe that your rulers are chosen by the People for their kindness and wisdom. He never has to fight anyone to gain or keep his position. Such a man would not have lasted one day in my land. And you may think me gentle, but scratch me and you will find that under my skin I am just like my sword," Torjan declared loudly.

"Yes, I know what is under your skin. I have seen under your skin and there is red blood and torn meat just like any other animal. There are many children back up the line who would argue with you about how tough and mean you are." Kaoto laughed as he slapped Torjan on the back, making the trail dust fly.

As they talked, their path had brought them down the heart of the canyon. To their left Kaoto could see his old home in Bonito. Raising his eyes to the lip of the canyon on his right, he sought out the home of his great mother, Paataga. He was surprised to see several new buildings near her humble home. These would no doubt be the homes of the students he had sent her. Well, she would not be lonely anymore.

He was able to pick out Paataga's house above the others. Still aloft and lonely. Paataga might appreciate the company, but she insisted on her privacy. Lifting his eyes still higher, he could distinguish a tiny figure on the top of the canyon above her home. As still as the rocks around her, Paataga stood watching the return of her prodigy, her student, her son.

Kaoto raised his hand in salute to the lone figure and saw the feeble return from the slight figure on the butte. This was his welcoming committee. After all, this was the one person he wanted most to see. His parents were secondary, as were his friends and former runners. Paataga was the one his heart went out to. Paataga was the one who had come to him time after time all across the nation. She had come to his side in his time of need. Only she could bridge time and distance to advise and counsel him when he needed her. Now he was home and it seemed he had never really left. All that had happened over the past ten summers was like a dream, something that he had heard about but could not possibly have ever done.

Chapter Thirty Nine

"You have learned much, my son," Paataga spoke at last. She had been listening to Kaoto's account of the past summers. "Now tell me what you think it all means. What do you make of what you have learned?"

Kaoto sat, as he had sat before, cross-legged on the ground at Paataga's feet. He was no longer the thin young man who had come to her so belligerently and reluctantly after Little Frog's death. Time had increased his height as it had diminished Paataga's. His shoulders had broadened and his whole body was more muscled. There was a certain pain in his eyes that had been brought on by all the suffering he had witnessed, but there was a sense of authority in his voice that had not been there when he left.

"What I have learned makes me believe my original plan was correct. I think it was necessary for Moot and his People to move south. By this time they should be well on their way. They should be out of the land of the savages by now. I am sorry to say that I feel in time that we will all have to make the trip. Whether we want to or not. It will become a choice of moving or dying. Of this I am sure."

Paataga nodded her ancient head in agreement as she said, "I at least will be spared the journey. My bones shall never leave this valley. But what you say is probably true. While you were gone, rumors have been coming in about the savages. They are coming closer. Some of our runners have encountered them. Only their fleetness of foot has spared them so far."

"Yes, Matuga mentioned these rumors to me and I am convinced they are not rumors, but fact," Kaoto said.

"They have come up the shining river and made raids out in the land on either side. Our People are getting uneasy, but instead of going south as you suggested, they have pulled in closer to us here in the canyon and other larger villages."

"That explains why there seems to be more people here than when I left."

"And more coming every day." Paataga confirmed his suspicion. "Some good, some bad."

"That is why I have advised Matuga to have the People build a new wall around the village, so they can at least find some protection from the savages when they do get here."

"You travel with a companion. This is not the one I had visions of you traveling with. What of her? Have you not found a mate yet?"

"Mate? Paataga, when would I have time to find a mate? Who would travel the lonely trail to be the mate of a fool like me? Oh, I know, they think me wise. But you and I know just how little wisdom I really have. If I were truly wise, I would have never left this valley. I would have stayed here and found a mate and raised a family instead of roaming over the face of our world to become discouraged, discontented, and disillusioned." He could not keep the bitterness from creeping into his voice.

"Hush, Kaoto. I know you get discouraged. I know you suffer loneliness. But you are no fool. You could never have stayed here, not after your dreams. You had to go. You had to find out what was happening in our world. I know of no one else who could have done what you have done. Who could have made the decisions you have had to make? It took a man, a strong man and a wise man."

"I suppose what you say is true. You are always right but I do not feel strong, brave, or wise anymore. The more I travel and learn, the more I suspect I am really quite ignorant."

"And I would have been disappointed in you if you had felt any different. Wisdom is an odd thing. Often those who claim to have it are only fooling themselves and those who choose to believe them. We have some of those here. It takes someone on the outside to see another's wisdom, or lack of it." Paataga's wizen faced smiled. She was proud of this young man who still seemed like a child to her summers.

"From the runners and the students you have sent me, I have been able to keep track of your travels. You have gone farther than I could imagine even in a lifetime." Paataga changed the subject temporarily.

"Yes." Kaoto shook his head. "I have trouble believing that I have actually been all the places I remember but it seems like a life time to me already."

"Kalo has told me much about you. There is a boy, or man, you can be proud of. He learned almost as fast as you did. Of course he had a head start with your training."

"Tell me about him and Pala. I have had no word of them since I left them." Kaoto was anxious to hear of his adopted son.

"He and Pala had two fine sons before I was willing to see them go. I miss him almost as much as I did you."

"I have great hopes for him," Kaoto said proudly. "I hope he went back to Pala's people and will serve them in their time of need. I feel that they are going to have a rough time of it out there. I know they will not want to move either, until it is too late. By that time, they will be over-crowded in their valley, just as we will be here."

"I am sure you can count on him. He is faithful to you beyond a doubt. He told me how it broke his heart to leave you, but he has come to understand it had to be. He knows now that he could not have run with you forever. He does not have the same drive that you and I do. He needed his mate and family to make up for the loss in his childhood."

Kaoto and Paataga had covered many topics in their first visit, a visit he had to delay for three days after his return. Protocol insisted he visit Matuga first, because he was the ruler of the district, and because he was Kaoto's adopted father. Matuga had made the meeting brief, knowing there would be time for personal talks later. He had then gone to see his parents. He had silently mourned for them. Time had been unkind to them, but more so to Maata. His health was poor. His time was limited, so much so that Kaoto feared he would be gone any day now.

One full day had been spent with the elders. They met in the common kiva, since there was no one at the dumpsite. Little Frog's memory lived on long after her death. Then he had to conduct an open meeting with some of the People who brought him their problems. Most of these were imaginary, used as an excuse to see him once more. He listened and dispensed his wisdom on them solemnly, just as he had all across the land. Finally, he had made his way up to see his old mentor. Now he had returned for an extended visit.

"I knew you would understand the delay," Kaoto told Paataga.

"Yes, they have to be served also. After all, that was what you promised when you took office. Private time is very precious when your life belongs to the People."

"Well, I have stolen this time in spite of my obligations. I feel this is just as necessary as anything else. This is the main reason I came home. This is part of my duty also."

"It is easy to convince oneself when duty happens to coincide with our own desires," Paataga chided him. "But you are right. This time is necessary for both of us and I have longed to speak with you again."

"Tell me more about the stories from the south. That is where I first heard about the savages that I have been telling you about. I am sure they represent the dark shadows in our dreams."

"They tell me they have been moving deeper into our land with the beginning of each summer. They come in the warm weather and pull back when it becomes colder. But each spring they are back, just like mosquitoes, bringing more with them each time."

"Have you ever heard of the land of black shining rocks?" Kaoto asked, trying to seem casual.

"I have heard of different places called that. There is one not too far south of here. Is that the one you mean?"

"No, those are black rocks but they do not really shine. I am talking about another one. Far south and east of here. Beyond the shining river and over a range of mountains. It is at the limits of our nation. There is an area of white sand there, as white as the snow. It was so much like the one in my dreams that I had to go out and search for the bones." Kaoto told her about his visit to the white sands.

"And did you find them?" she asked.

"No. Either it was not the place or it was not the time." Kaoto hesitated a moment before he went on. Paataga did not miss his hesitation. "Have you heard if they have been overrun by the savages yet?"

"Not specifically, but I am sure they would have been if the savages are already at the shining river and coming this way. Why? Is there someone there that concerns you?" Paataga asked, studying Kaoto's face intently.

"There was a man and his daughters living there when I first went that way. I tried to persuade him to leave, but like everyone else he was reluctant to go. He was sure he would be all right where he was."

"In all the nation, one man and his daughters interest you? They must have been special to you to make you remember them after all this time," Paataga said with a quizzical look on her face. "Were they pretty?"

"I have not thought of them for many summers, but the mention of the savages coming from that direction brought them back to mind."

Kaoto went on to tell Paataga more of the particulars of his visit with Mula and his six daughters and the possible seed he had planted there.

"It comes to my mind that by now I could be a father several times over. I might have children of my own out there, in danger," he told her.

"I am sure that if they had children they would have moved out to find proper mates of their own. If they did, then you do not have children. They would belong to their mother's mates." Paataga reminded him."

"That is true but there was the younger one. Mateep, she was called. I remember her because she had the two colored eyes like Little Frog. She was too young to be included in our frolics but she could still be living there with her stubborn father and the venerable old buffalo bull."

"If the rock barrier was as formidable as you have said, then I would think they would still be safe."

"The savages might find a way in just as I did, and Mula before me. It is only a matter of time before they are found out. They already knew they were hiding in there; they just could not find a way in."

"I do not see what you have to worry about. In this length of time they have either moved, or they are all dead. Either way, there is nothing you can do about it now."

Kaoto flinched at Paataga's cruel, matter of fact words. In his mind's eye, he could see the lovely daughters strewn over the enclosed area, ravaged by the savages before they were killed. He knew Mula was too stubborn to ever leave the barrier. He only hoped the savages had tired of trying to find them and had moved on, leaving them in peace. A slim hope, but the only one he had.

"That may be true, but I would feel better if I knew for sure one way or the other," he said. It was obvious to Paataga that Kaoto was worried, more than he wanted to admit.

Torjan had not been present at their first meeting. He had respected their privacy and left them to be together without interruption. Today, when Kaoto had left, he had asked Torjan to join them later when he had eaten his fill and felt like coming up. They could see him making his final ascent toward them.

"I know you have heard of Torjan. Now I want you to meet him." He was relieved to change the subject and get away from Paataga's prying interest in the daughters of Mula.

"I want the two of you to become acquainted," he said as Torjan came to stand at his side.

Paataga stood up but still could not see his face. "Sit down!" Paataga struck the ground in front of her log seat with her ever-present walking stick. "I will not get a crick in my neck looking up at you. Sit!" She took her place back on the log as Torjan lowered himself beside Kaoto. They looked like two giant children at her feet.

"Even with you two down there and me up here, you are still taller than I am. Why did the Spirit Watcher see fit to make men so tall? What purpose could be foreseen in such height?"

"A tall man can see farther than a short one," Kaoto answered formally, as he had in his youth as a student. "I can see also where a tall man can cover more distance each day than a short man. Without his size, I doubt if Torjan could have made it to this country. Then I would not have had him for a brother and you would never have seen such as he, nor would he have been able to tell you of the strange places he has been or tell you of the wonders he has seen." Kaoto's humor was not lost on Paataga, although she chose to ignore his banter. Looking at the huge man-beast seated at her feet she said, "Torjan? That has a harsh sound to it. It does not have the smooth roll on the tongue like the names of our People."

"I fear we are a harsh people, old mother," Torjan spoke for the first time in Paataga's hearing. His voice, even when he tried to hold it down, had an angry sound to it.

Paataga studied him closely. Time, even though it had bent her body, had not been able to dim her eyes or disable her mind. Both were as sharp as ever.

"I can believe you. Your voice sounds like thunder in the mountains. If you were as angry as you sound I think you would be more dangerous than a wounded buffalo. Yet in your eyes, I see a gentleness, maybe even kindness. If you are a friend and brother to Kaoto, then you must have some good qualities, even if they are well hidden."

"I think, old mother, your eyes see more clearly than most. So far it has only been little children who have seen so deep and have been so quick to accept me. But looks can be deceiving. To look at you I would never have judged you to be wise or kind. Your eyes have a way of looking right through me, making me feel uneasy, like a little boy again."

"Humph. You speak you mind frankly enough. I suppose being so big makes you feel brave?" Paataga shot back at him.

"Ho! You think me brave? I do not think so. If a tiny woman such as you can make me shake, then brave is not a good word for me." Torjan laughed, but he was serious in what he said. Paataga did make him feel ill at ease.

Paataga's eyes sparkled deep in their withered sockets. Her mouth lost some of its grim lines to be replaced with what could have been a smile. "We will get along, you and I. We do not believe in mincing words. We say what we think and let the others think what they please about it. Yes, we will get along just fine."

Kaoto had been watching them, amused at his big friend's uneasiness. He had once felt the same way in this old one's presence. He knew both of them well and was not disappointed with either of them. He had known all along that Torjan's bluff about Paataga having to be young and pretty was just that, a bluff. He knew Torjan would take immediately to this old mother. Somewhere inside they had the same material; Torjan just had more of it because of his size.

"Great mother, it occurred to me when I first met Torjan that you might like to meet him. That is why I bothered with him and nursed him along and wasted so much time getting here. He has been long on the trail, away from his home; he needs a mother to look after him out here in the wild."

"Oh, yes. I can see he needs looking after, like a bear in the woods he does. I think maybe he could look after himself."

"Mostly I do, old mother," Torjan thundered. Then looking at Kaoto he said. "Once, though, I did need someone to look after me, and he was there when I had the need."

"Still I did think you might want to meet someone who has traveled as far as he has and has seen as many wonderful things as he has told me about," Kaoto said quickly to cover any emotion displayed by Torjan. "He can tell you much and in turn you can tell him much about the People and our ways."

"We will talk much, of that I am sure. That is if he is going to be around here very long. Or is he going with you soon?"

"I can never hide anything from you, can I? Yes, I would like to leave Torjan here with you while I make a quick trip. I will be traveling far and fast. Torjan is big and he is strong but he is not fast. He could never keep up with me this trip because I am in a hurry."

"Would it be south you will be going? South and east, across the shining river? Maybe even to a land of black rocks?" Paataga said without hesitation or doubt.

"Yes, great mother. I have not fooled you. I wonder sometimes why I ever try." He smiled at the old crone with wonder and adoration. "I must go back to find Mula and his daughters, if they are still there. I had another dream last night. Someone was calling to me for help. I did not recognize the person but I did recognize the black rocks where she lived," he said.

"She?"

"Yes. She. Surely you must know as I do that one cannot always explain how or why you know something. You just know it and that is all, and it is impossible to explain with mere words. I will never rest until I have made this trip and satisfied myself with their safety."

"I know. I know. It is only for such as you and I to understand. To try to explain in words paints such a dull picture that it loses all importance. Go, Kaoto. If you are not gone too long, I will be here when you return."

"I will go like my namesake, great mother. It is only the dream that makes me leave you after such a long absence. That is why I must leave Torjan with you, so I can run at my speed, not his."

"Yes. I understand. You must go. Besides, I would like to see my vision come true. I would like to see this woman who seemed somewhat familiar to me but was not any woman I have known. She is the one who travels at your side part of the time," Paataga told him.

Torjan listened to the two talk in fragmented, unfinished sentences. He was baffled by their conversation.

"Woman? Black rock country? What are you two talking about? If you suspect trouble, I should go with you, brother." Torjan started to get up in preparation of leaving at once.

"Sit down, Torjan. You are not going any place. No offense, but as I have just said, you cannot keep up with me when I am in a hurry. You would be a day or more behind me by the time I got there. I can run much faster than you have ever seen me run. I do not boast. I can run all day and all night at a pace that you would not believe." He could tell that Torjan was still not satisfied. If there was any kind of trouble he felt he should be there to do his part.

"I do not foresee any trouble," Kaoto assured him. "All I know is I must go to a far place and see for myself that all is well with some people I know. As for women, well that is something Paataga has dreamed up. Like all old women she wants to see me tied down with a mate to make me be good and live right. I think she wants me to settle down and raise corn and pumpkins and children and stay in this valley where she can bully me." His smile slipped from his face and he finished with, "but she knows this cannot be."

"No, Kaoto. You do me an injustice. I do not ever see you staying in this valley and raising corn, children or pumpkins. Someday, somewhere maybe, but not here. Just remember that I did see you walking into the sunset with a woman at your side. Do not disappoint me in this, my son." While she was talking, Paataga was stirring her fire and looking about expectantly. "Now where am I supposed to find enough food to feed this great beast you would settle on me? Even Matuga's granaries do not hold enough to fill him."

"Do not worry about that. Torjan is an adequate provider. He will see to it there is enough for both of you. I admit he does eat a great amount, but one jar of corn and one deer a day is enough for him if you keep him quiet and do not let him free to run with the women. That always works up a terrible appetite in him the next day."

"We will manage, old mother. I will starve if necessary, so do not worry about me," Torjan told her, trying to capture their mood of humor.

"I will worry about it. It is my business to worry if I want to. That is all that is left for me to do," she snapped. "Besides, a man cannot think and talk right on an empty stomach. He spends all his time thinking about his meal"

Torjan was beginning to understand Paataga and he could see he was going to like this little dried up woman. She was not to be feared, she was just another version of Kaoto, and so he would like her if for no other reason than this.

Vikings had lacked much in the way of humor. They laughed, but it was usually when someone was defeated, humiliated, or killed. They never laughed at subtle jokes or innuendoes. They never made impossible or impractical suggestions just for a joke. With these people, he had come to understand a good joke was more important than a great physical feat or a daring deed. The sound of laughter could be heard almost any time of the day and much of the night throughout the land. This little woman had fooled him at first with her stern appearance and sharp tongue. She was no different than the rest of the People in this respect; she liked a good joke. You just had to be quicker with her to catch her meaning.

Yes, he would be comfortable here after all. He had had his misgivings at first, but it would be pleasant to sit here by her fire and relax. It would be nice to get up and hunt and then return, knowing he did not have to take off and run farther than he could see before he could rest again. She was so tiny and frail looking that he started to feel protective toward her, although he doubted seriously that she would ever need protection. "Yes, Kaoto. Go. Find this woman or whatever it is you want to find. Paataga and I will be fine without you. Maybe we can talk without you always butting in and interrupting us." Torjan grinned at his own attempt at humor, well satisfied with himself when they both joined him in a good laugh.

Kaoto got up and stretched his long frame. He was planning to leave soon and needed to make some preparations. He looked out over the valley floor and could see a strange procession of figures. They were walking in a single file and all were dressed in the same manner. The leader and a few behind him were dressed in white while the rest were all in dark colors. The leader had some sort of a strange headdress on and each figure carried a short lender staff over his right shoulder and held some small object in his other hand.

"What is that supposed to be?" he asked Paataga.

"Those? Oh, never mind about them. I will tell you all about them when you get back." Paataga stared at the line in disgust. Then she spat a mouthful of phlegm in their general direction. This was something Kaoto could not remember having seen her do before. "Bunch of fools, that is what they are." She continued to stare after them. "Grown men acting up worse than spoiled children. Humph." She turned her back on them as if to make them disappear at her dismissal.

Kaoto knew there was a story behind all this but as usual she would tell him in her own time. All he knew for sure was that she did not approve of them, so automatically he did not like them. Something about them sent a shiver down his spine and a heavy feeling of apprehension settled on him. Deep down inside he knew that somehow they would be associated with his future and this association would be unpleasant to either him or them.

Paataga was busy with her fire and refused to look up or take any further notice of them. Torjan watched the strange procession with the same feeling of trepidation as Kaoto had. Their solemn procession in this land of happiness and laughter was almost profane.

Chapter Forty

Kaoto did not get to leave as soon as he expected. His father was lying on his sleeping mat, near to death's door. He had been failing rapidly, and now that his son had returned, he seemed content to let go and drift effortlessly away. Keenwah accepted his impending death with stoic endurance. By the People's standards they were both past an average life span. She knew she would soon be following him and was content to wait for her turn.

The night before his death, Maata had called his son to his side. He talked very little but asked his son to tell him of his travels, and lay quietly listening to the wonders his son had seen and heard.

Later he pulled a small packet from the edge of his sleeping pad and unfolded it. He held a single eagle feather in his hand. "I want you to have this eagle feather. It is the one I received the day of your run, the one Toolke gave to me."

"I do not really need another feather," Kaoto told him. "I seem to always come up with another whenever I give one away." He told him of the one he had given to Kalo, only to have it replaced by Forb while he was up in the mountains with the hunters.

"So I still have two. That is as many as any man needs."

"I want you to have it, son. I have never worn it. I have kept it wrapped in skin to protect it."

"Then why do not you keep it until your time here is over? You might want to take it with you to the next world," Kaoto suggested.

"I will have no need for it, son." He laid the feather in Kaoto's hand as he went on to explain.
"I have never talked about religion with you, or anyone else, but I have my own belief. When I go I will not be taking this body with me, so I will not be needing all the things of this world that are customarily sent with the dead. Oh, your mother and my friends will insist on the containers of corn and beans, my bow and spear and a few other personal belongings. Let them, it will make them feel better, but you and I know I will not be taking them with me."

"How can you be sure? No one has ever come back to tell us one way or the other," Kaoto asked his father.

"Do you think your friend Little Frog took her twisted body with her? Did she not tell you she would be strong, tall and beautiful? Then how could she be that way with her old body?"

"I do not know, Father. I guess I have never given it any thought. I guess I was content to find out when my own time comes."

There is another reason I know," Maata said, his strength failing him and his hands falling beside him. "Once, long ago, I dug a grave for a friend. Someone had been careless with marker stones so I dug into another man's grave. Even though he had been many summers dead, his body was still there.

His bow was still there, the food in the pots was still there, molded and unfit to eat, but still there. The man had gone but his body did not go with him. This is how I know." Maata closed his eyes, exhausted. He lay for a long time, regaining enough strength to speak again.

"I leave this world tonight, son. I have nothing to give you. No wisdom, no parting words to make your life easier. At least let me give you the feather. It has always been yours. It was your deed that won it, not anything that I did."

"Nothing? You did nothing?" Kaoto shook his head sadly looking at the wasted man he knew as Father. "You say you have given me nothing. Who planted the seed that grew into this body that sits before you? Who encouraged a lonely boy to run as no one has ever run before? Who taught him everything he needed to know to stay alive on the lonely trail? Wisdom? Someone had to give me wisdom. It did not grow by itself. Paataga helped me develop my wisdom, but even she admits it was already there before she sent for me." Kaoto laid his hand on his father's cold hands and smiled at him.

"I would say you have already given me much more than any other boy has ever received." Maata opened his eyes and his face answered Kaoto's smile.

"You are a good son. You have made your parents proud. Who could ask for anything more?" he whispered.

Kaoto did not question his father's belief that he would die that night. It was not uncommon for a man to know when the time of his death was approaching. If his father said he was leaving tonight, then it was probably so. Little Frog had tried to tell him when she was leaving, but he had been too busy with his own schemes and plans to listen to her. He had learned much since then. He had learned to listen and not to argue when there was no point to be gained in an argument.

He sat the long night with his father, hearing his shallow breathing. In the early morning, when the land was silently waiting for the Spirit Watcher, Maata gave his last sigh and was silent also.

Maata's body was buried in the age-old custom of the People. It was not until the last few summers, when the savages had closed in on them, that they changed their customs. Unable to go out as they pleased, the remaining people started burying their dead in the floors of their homes or in empty rooms. These they filled in and sealed off in hopes the savages would not find them and desecrate their bodies.

Alongside of Maata's assigned plot of land was a row of flat stones set at regular intervals. Each stone marked the grave of a former tiller of the soil. There were no marks on the stones to distinguish the occupant, only a plain stone to indicate the site of the last grave.

Maata's grave was dug in its turn and Maata's body was lowered into the ground unadorned. It was the way of the people to return to the earth all the things they had taken from it during their lives. His body would eventually feed the plants that would feed the next generation of the people. His possessions were laid beside him and Kaoto recalled his words of the night before about not needing them any longer.

"You are probably right, Father, but it will not hurt just in case you are wrong. I would hate to have you show up in the next world and be the only one there without the necessary equipment. It would be embarrassing to Mother and me if your friends found you empty handed and asked what kind of a son did you have who would send you off without anything, like a newborn baby."

Torjan was given responsibility for looking after Keenwah as well as Paataga until Kaoto returned. This was only a formality. Matuga would see that she did not lack for all she needed. Torjan had been impressed by this tiny woman and marveled at how such a small body could have produced such a large son. He assured Kaoto he would be glad to look in on her and help out when needed while Kaoto was away.

Free to travel again, Kaoto took to the trail, knowing the two women he honored most were in the hands of his trusted friend. He could delegate all his senses to running.

He did not make any stops to visit on this trip. His trail led as nearly straight as the terrain would allow, often leaving the beaten path for barren fields and washes. When Sister Moon shone he would continue running long into the night. He ate sparingly and rested only briefly.

Near the shining river he encountered a band of savages who immediately gave chase. Kaoto had been running hard all day when he met them in a willow thicket just after he had crossed the waters. He held his pace to match theirs and resisted the temptation to give a burst of speed and outrun them. He knew they could not catch him in an open race, but feared he might run into more ahead of him. In this willow-covered section of the bank he could not see far in any direction. Nor could they, but their screams could be a signal to others.

He had left the wide path quite some way back and had crossed where there was no marked trail. If there was one band here, there could well be others scattered around him. If he ran headlong into them, sheer numbers could overpower him. After hearing the horror stories over the past summers of what they did to their captives, he did not want to take that risk.

His luck held until he hit the main road again and broke free of the willows into the open land where he could see and be seen. Directly ahead of him he spotted another band at the same time as they saw him. They had picked up the hooting calls of the first band and were watching expectantly for their quarry to emerge. They were already dispersed in a wide semi-circle, shouting to those behind them in their harsh tongue, urging them to spread out also making retreat impossible.

Kaoto took this all in with one quick glance and without breaking his stride. He could see it would be folly to stop and offer them a fight. His bow was superior to theirs, but their greater number would eventually wear him down. He could drop many of them, but their number was far greater than the number of arrows he carried. His best hope lay in his long legs, not his long bow.

To the north he noticed the savages had neglected to join together, leaving a wide, inviting gap. Several of the savages were making an effort to call attention to this miscalculation on their part as they waved and shouted for someone to close it.

Kaoto swung toward the opening and was about to put on his burst of speed when he thought he could see a blurred figure standing in the center of the gap. The figure was small and bent, ancient and withered. It was too far away to be sure who it was, but a voice came to him clearly.

"Go back, Kaoto. Turn around and go south." Paataga's unmistakable voice came to him. "Do not try to run through here. Can you not see it is too easy? It is what they want you to do. It is a trap. There are more you cannot see just over the rise. If you come through here, they will have twenty arrows in you in one heartbeat."

The figure vanished as quickly as it had appeared, so quickly that Kaoto was never sure he had actually seen it. But he had heard the voice and chose to heed the advice the apparition had given him.

Feinting a quick burst of speed toward the opening, Kaoto could hear the shouts of glee from those behind him as they began to run parallel to his course, no longer worried about him turning back. They knew they had him now.

Kaoto slowed his pace to let them catch up with him as he approached the inviting opening. At the last moment he suddenly veered off and changed directions. His long legs flashed in a blur of speed and motion. With each bound, he was gathering speed. There was no holding back now. He would show them what a real runner could do. Behind him he could hear the victory shouts turning to wails of anger and frustration as they saw their intended victim racing away from the jaws of the trap. True, they still had men all around him, but they had scattered carelessly when Kaoto had turned toward the opening. Those along either side did not have time to string an arrow before he shot by them and was out of range. The only hope they had, was the ragged line bringing up the rear. They tried to regroup as soon as they realized what was happening, but the line was not as solid as it had been before. There was more space between the savages.

Kaoto was tempted to swing back into the cover of the willows along the river bank, but he knew he ran the risk of running into more of them and he would not be able to see them until it was too late.

He decided the best chance was in front of him to the south as the voice had instructed. He could see open ground beyond them and there was no place for another trap. Once clear, he would be free. Once clear, there was no man alive who could keep up with him, even though he had been running all day. His adrenaline was being pumped into his body to bring it to peak performance. He set his course over the clearest path he could select and ran as he had never run before. He did not feel fear; instead he felt his heart surging with elation at the challenge.

"Ayeiee!" He screamed at the struggling savages. "Have you ever tried to kill a kaoto? I think not or you would know it is impossible." His voice rang out over them, a new war cry they had never heard from the little farmers. Surely this was an enemy worthy of the chase. They gave renewed effort to outrun him and close the gap before he escaped.

When he came within range of their short but powerful bows, he began to weave like a rabbit, changing course almost in mid-step. Arrows that were loosed at him went wide of their mark as he charged first right and then left. He never paused or looked back, confident that those behind him were not gaining any ground on him. He concentrated all his energy on breaking through the human barrier that blocked his way to freedom.

As he ran, he slipped his bow from his shoulder and drew three arrows from their nesting place at his back next to his pack. He was sure he could get off at least two shots, maybe a third. He was also sure of placing his shots where he wanted them to go. For many summers now he had practiced shooting small game as he ran. He had never tried while running as fast and hard as he was running now, but still he felt he could hit a target as large as these men.

Three men. If he could drop three men he would have a wide avenue to escape, although he would still be close enough to be in danger from those on either side. But it would be an enormous advantage over what he had now.

His first shot arched high out to this right. The arrow flew straight and true and found its mark in one of the dark savage's throat, strangling his angry cry in mid-note. The second arrow was in flight before the first had found its target. Straight ahead it flew, like an angry wasp. Its target was a savage in the act of pulling his own bow back. Kaoto's arrow took him squarely in the chest. The surprised savage sank to his knees, unable to believe what had happened to him. As he fell face forward, he released his own arrow only to have it strike the ground a scant body's length in front of his prone figure.

The increase of the screaming and howling of the savages told Kaoto they were aware of what had happened. His next target drew back swiftly, tripping and falling in his haste to get out of reach of the deadly long arrows. Kaoto held his last arrow and ran swiftly through the open gap he had created. He replaced his unused arrow as casually as he would have if he had been hunting small game. His bow went back over his shoulder from force of habit.

Several arrows fell to earth beside him and in front of him as he ran across the open land and up a gentle slope. It was the first of many slopes leading up to the higher ground and safety. The sound behind him reminded him of the mosquitoes in the river bottom when he had made his first run to Aztec. This was rapidly diminishing behind him and would soon be locked out by the crest of the high ridge he was climbing. As long as there were no more savages in front of him, he would be safe. Night would soon be falling, and if these men were as concerned with the dark as the others he had met, they would not follow him very far. Not that they had a chance of catching him anyway.

The higher ground was bathed in the last rays of the Spirit Watcher, but the low lands were already fading into gloom of darkness. The savages turned back toward their camp. They did not want to risk dying in the dark and roaming the after world in darkness forever. They would tell many tales about the hairy giant that they could not stop. His legend would grow among them until they would one day claim he was one of their own founding fathers, and future generations would draw on his strength and speed as part of their own folklore.

Chapter Forty One

Silence prevailed over all the land. It was empty, void. It was as if there was no other life besides the lonely runner. Not even the customary birds of carrion were to be seen. Here and there Kaoto came across signs of a struggle. Small villages had been laid to waste. Individual dwellings had been deserted for several summers. There was a smell of death in the air, although he had seen no bodies or fresh graves.

Keeping to the high ground slowed his pace, but he felt it was necessary for his own safety. He did not want to run the risk of being surprised again as he had down on the river. The next time he might not be so lucky. Several times, as he had to cross open valleys to gain another ridge line, he came across abandoned campsites, which were definitely those of the savages, and each time he experienced a feeling of apprehension. In the ten summers since he had been this way, the savages had made many inroads into the land of the People. The farther he went, the more he was sure he would not find Mula and his daughters alive. However, he pushed on, driven by an inner force he could not explain.

At last he approached the valley of black rocks. He was coming in on the same trail he had used to leave the valley many summers ago. The Spirit Watcher had dropped low in search of his nightly bed when Kaoto came to the top of the last hill, allowing him to look down on the barrier. It was much too far away to be able to make out Mula's hidden home site but he knew approximately where it was. He would not attempt to cross tonight. He wanted daylight to announce his arrival just in case Mula was still there. He would find the niche where Mula had buried the wooden sandals and there he would spend the night. Keeping a close watch to make sure he was not being observed, Kaoto ran the final lap across to the barrier. He had never questioned his ability to retrace his steps. It was just a talent he had and used it to his advantage.

Unerringly, he found the cleft that would lead him back in the general direction of Mula's retreat. With certainty, he knelt at the end of the defile and using his iron knife, dug in the ground beside a prominent rock. He soon turned out his sandals, just as he had left them. The wood still showed the scars left by the sharp black rocks just as if they had been used yesterday. The tongs, however, were badly decayed and of no use. Having foreseeing such a possibility, Kaoto was prepared with new strips of woven fibers to replace them. He tied them securely to his feet as a precaution in case he was discovered here. He wanted to be able to use the black rocks for a retreat if necessary.

Finding a dark chamber in the rocks, he settled down for a restless night. He did not go to sleep immediately, but lay with his mind exploring the possible reception awaiting him on the morrow. He tried to picture each of the daughters as they might look after ten summers. He was sure he would still recognize them. Mateep would have changed the most. She would be a young maiden by now. Still, he was sure he would know her.

The wind had been blowing strong all afternoon and well into the evening, moaning among the cracks and crevices, whistling and sighing as it went. Suddenly it dropped, leaving an enveloping silence lying like a blanket over the barrier. Then the silence was broken by a shrill cry. Any number of small animals or night birds could have made it, but it haunted Kaoto. He sat listening for it to be repeated so he could satisfy himself as to its identity. His patience was rewarded after a short time when the cry rang out again. This time he was sure it was not a night animal. It came from the throat of a human, a human in distress or pain. It came from the direction of Mula's valley. It almost sounded like someone was calling his name. The dream he had told to Paataga flashed across his mind. Someone was calling him for help. He did not hesitate.

In the dark he climbed to the top of the barrier and launched himself out into the vacant blackness of the black rocks. He had told Mula he could find his way across in the middle of the night; now he would have a chance to prove it.

Finding his way was not difficult, although Sister Moon had not risen yet to shed her feeble light. His feet could sense the roughness of the rock even in the darkness and he made his way without incident. He listened, but the cry was not repeated. He began to think his imagination had run away with him until through one of the many breaks in the rocks he thought he could see the reflection of a fire ahead. Someone was there; whether it was Mula or not, he did not venture to guess. The closer he drew, the more certain he was of the fire. Soon he could detect the smell of smoke drifting toward him.

When he reached the niche where he could have gone down, he hesitated and decided not to. Instead he continued on, feeling his way over the top. He could see the fire and it temporarily blinded him, making him rely entirely on his sense of feel. He could faintly hear the sound of guttural voices and smell the faint musky odor he had learned to associate with the savages. He moved forward cautiously, on guard, bow and arrows in hand.

He had already recalled the location and how Mula's camp would lay. He pictured the scene he might see. The sight he did see made him freeze on the lip of the rock overlooking the bathing pool.

He stood for a brief moment while he made a count of the enemy in sight below. He nocked his arrow. Once more he was ready to kill men. For the first time, he would be killing men who were not directly threatening him, but they were threatening someone else, some of his defenseless People. He had no twinge of conscience this time. He might have regrets afterward but he knew what he had to do now.

It was as he had feared. The savages had finally found their way into Mula's stronghold. They must have surprised Mula and his daughters. Mula lay face up on the sand with many arrows prickling his body. He lay where he had died. In his outstretched hand was his short heavy spear, held in a death grip. There were no other bodies around him, which led Kaoto to believe he had never had a chance to defend his family.

Close to the fire was the figure of a woman. The flickering light of the fire was not enough for him to identify who it was, but he was sure it was one of Mula's daughters. Her arms were extended and he could see they had been bound to a cedar tree. Her arms supported her weight as she hung limply, apparently unconscious.

Out of the darkness near the pool one of the savages came carrying a pot filled with water, which he flung into the woman's face in an attempt to revive her. This was the one whose cries he had heard, so there was a chance she still lived.

From where he stood, undetected, Kaoto could see two men standing across the fire watching the first man in his efforts. Three more were lying in sleeping skins beside the fire, also watching with anticipation. Another figure lay off to one side, not moving. Kaoto did not know if he was dead or just asleep.

While Kaoto watched, the savage with the water pot drew back his hand and slapped the woman viciously across the face. The sound carried to Kaoto with a sharp report. His first arrow dropped this savage as he drew his hand back to deliver another slap at his helpless victim.

Before the two standing beyond the fire knew what had transpired, two more arrows were embedded in their bodies. One dropped without a sound. The other, impaled on the arrow shaft, which had penetrated him and stuck deep into the tree behind him, stood transfixed, his eyes wide in terror. He did not die silently as the first two had. His screams brought the three who had been lounging near the fire to their feet, casting searching glances about them as they scrambled for their weapons, which they had carelessly laid aside. They had apparently thought themselves safe now that Mula was dead.

Kaoto had kicked off his sandals and leaped across the pool, landing close to the woman suspended from the tree. The iron knife flashed in the firelight as the woman's arms were cut free and she slumped to sit on the ground. The three savages spread out to meet this new and deadly foe. They could see he was just a man after all, not some demon of the night as they had first feared. They could fight a man. A spirit could not be harmed by them, but a man could be killed just as any other man. Only this was not any other man.

Kaoto did not wait for their attack. He used his momentum to carry him over the fire into their midst. His knife sliced a wicked path around him as the stunned savages fell back before his vicious advance. He caught the first savage with a slice across his abdomen, spilling his intestines as it went. The savage dropped his own weapon and tried to stem the flow with his hands, loops of intestines dropping over his hands and between his fingers.

The second savage fell backward, tripping over his sleeping skins. Before he could recover, he found himself pinned by a huge foot placed with crushing force across his windpipe. He kicked and pawed as he thrashed about trying to free himself from the strangling weight of the crazed giant on top of him.

The third picked this time to launch his own attack, hoping his downed companion would offer a distraction to the enemy. His guess was wrong. Kaoto's eye never left the last standing savage. He met his onslaught with cool deliberation, one foot on solid ground, the other crushing the neck of the downed savage.

The attacking savage had picked up his short spear. Holding it with both hands in front of him, he aimed it at Kaoto's chest. His spear was swept aside as if it were a blade of grass. Then it was gripped just behind the point and yanked forward. Unable to release his own grip soon enough, the savage's weight carried him onto the extended knifepoint. The knife entered just below his ribs and was pushed upward to find his heart and grant him instant death. It was a quicker death than Kaoto would have wished.

Disengaging the blade, Kaoto stepped back from the fallen man under his foot and swept the sharp blade down across the bruised throat. The only sound left was the bubbling noise of the wounded savage as he tried to draw a breath through his slit gullet.

Crouching low, Kaoto turned to face the last savage, who had lain quietly on the farther side of the fire. There was no movement from the wrapped figure. Delivering a swift kick, Kaoto discovered the savage was already dead. Mula must have accounted for at least this one before he went down. This made Kaoto feel a little better.

He grasped the young woman around the waist and drew her back into the dark shadows away from the faint light of the dying fire. He waited for a short time to see if there would be others coming to investigate the sounds of their battle. When time passed and no one showed, he carried her to the edge of the pool where he would bathe her injuries and administer what aid he could.

Sister Moon was just making her belated appearance from behind a cloudbank and shone full on the badly bruised face of the maiden in his arms. She had a cruel gash through her hair on the side of her head above her ear. Her face was mottled with welts from the slaps she had just received, and the blood from the open wound covered her face. Even with all these conspicuous disfigurements, Kaoto recognized Mateep, the child from his past: the happy, carefree child with all the questions, the one with the two colored eyes like Little Frog. The thought of anyone harming her in this way made Kaoto's flesh crawl. A low, unbidden animal like growl rose from his throat as he lowered her to the pool's edge and began to wash away the blood to see just how badly she had suffered.

The scalp wound had been made by a glancing blow from a spear or stone ax. It left a long, ugly tear from her temple back around her head. Kaoto had no way of telling how hard the blow had been so he did not know how serious it might be. It was the only wound he could find other than the bruises from the vicious beating she had received.

The water partially revived Mateep and she began to make a feeble attempt to disengage herself from his hold. Making a mewing sound like a wounded animal, she placed her hands against his chest and tried to push him away. Kaoto held her loosely. His long arms still encircled her as he spoke to her softly.

"Easy, little one. You are in no danger now. Your enemies are all dead."

Mateep relaxed at these reassuring words spoken to her in her own language.

"Father?" She whispered.

"No, not your father. It is a friend. You probably do not remember me but I have come back to help you." Kaoto continued to bathe the gash, washing gently to remove the dirt encrusted in the blood.

The maiden mercifully lapsed back into unconsciousness as Kaoto gathered her up and carried her back to the fire, which he built up to make more light so he could see the extent of the gash. He secured the sides of the wound with spines from a cactus. Later he would do a better job, but this was the best he could do in a short time. He wanted to get her out of here before other savages discovered them.

He retrieved his wooden sandals where he had left them above the pool. Her small body offered no hindrance to Kaoto as he moved back over the rocks. At mid-point of the crossing, he remembered a small opening. With Sister Moon's light he was able to find it. A quick survey proved it to be an ideal spot for them to rest. It was so small that there was barely room for both of them, but it offered almost perfect protection. No one could reach them without heavy sandals. Nor could they come without making noise to warn Kaoto of their approach. While he and Mateep would be hidden in the blackness of the hole, any intruder would be silhouetted against Sister Moon's mellow glow.

The bottom of the niche was covered with loose blow sand. Removing any loose chips of rocks, Kaoto lay his burden down and covered her with his feathered cloak. The warmth the rocks had soaked up during the day was radiated back to them, making it warm, and the walls would protect them from the winds that would spring up at first light. There was no water, but Kaoto's water skin had enough to moisten her lips and cool her fevered face throughout the long night.

Mateep lay very still and quiet. Whether she was asleep or unconscious, Kaoto did not know. He was, however, reassured by her deep, regular breathing and the near normal temperature of her body. If the spear point had not broken any bones, she would easily survive the gash it had left. The bruises would be painful and unsightly for a time, but not serious. Mateep was young and healthy. Her physical recovery would be fast. The mental shock of what had happened to her and her father was a different story. It might leave scars she could never shed. Only time would tell, but for now he would do all he could to relieve the tension and protect her until he could decide where he should take her.

He leaned back against the wall. He was glad he had come when he had; he only wished he had come sooner. At least he had been able to save one of Mula's daughters. Tomorrow, maybe Mateep could tell him what had happened to the others. He hoped they had moved out as Paataga had suggested they would.

Kaoto drifted off in a fitful sleep, filled with dreams of dark savages leaping and howling around him as he carried Mateep toward Chaco.

Chapter Forty Two

Kaoto awoke with a start. He remained motionless, his eyes sweeping the top of the rock wall surrounding them. He did not know just how long he had been asleep but the Spirit Watcher was just sending his first pink rays over the horizon. Something had reached Kaoto's subconscious and brought him fully awake. It had been a sense of being watched.

"You did come back." Mateep's simple statement snapped his eyes to her. She lay as he had placed her the night before. Her face was covered with splotches of purple mingled with greenish and yellow tints, the marks from her beating. Her hair was tangled and matted in places with the blood he had missed in his hurried clean up of her.

"I thought it was just a dream last night. I was afraid to open my eyes at first, afraid you would not be here and I would still be with those awful men."

Kaoto's stern features broke in a smile, a mixture of relief and pleasure. "I did not expect you to remember anything about my being there last night."

"I remember." She frowned a little as she tried to get a clear picture of what happened. "It is kind of like looking through a fog, but I remember you coming out of the night, off the top of the rocks. You were wonderful and terrible at the same time. I knew they did not have a chance against you, even though there were so many of them." Mateep's voice came softly in the early dawn light. Her two colored eyes were alert although they were dimmed with pain.

"It is not the way of our People to kill other men," Kaoto said. "But my anger over what I saw was so great I could not stop myself."

"They killed my father. Did they not? They would have killed me and they most surely would have killed you," she replied.

"Maybe, but I could have tried to talk to them," Kaoto said doubtfully.

"They would not have listened to talk, even if you had known their language. They do not talk. They just kill."

"That is probably true but I am not proud this morning of what I did last night. A few times I have been forced to kill, and it still leaves me with an empty feeling, as though I had failed." Kaoto leaned close to inspect her face to see how effective his treatment of last night had been.

"How could you recognize me? It has been many summers since I left here and we have both changed since then." he said.

"Oh, I knew you were coming, so I was looking for you. I have been expecting you for several days now." Her childlike faith stirred something deep inside him.

"You knew I was coming? That is odd. I have only known myself in the last few days that I was going to come back here. So how could you know?"

Mateep hesitated, her eyes searching his face as if for a clue. "You will make fun of me when I tell you."

"Try me. I do not laugh at people or strange ideas. I have had enough strange things happen to make me believe many things that I would have laughed at when I was younger," Kaoto told her.

"Well, back when the savages first began to look for us in earnest, the past moon, I was worried because I knew Father would never leave here. One night I was sitting by the fire, long after everyone else was asleep. I was remembering you and your promise to return someday. I have thought of you often, ever since you left." She still had a childlike innocence.

"I am flattered to think you would remember me. You were only a child when I was here before."

"I am not a child now."

"No. I guess you are not," Kaoto admitted as he looked at her slender form. She had filled out as a woman should, but she still seemed very small and young to him.

"When I was a child, I had many childhood dreams and fantasies. Many about you. But as I grew up, I began to have different feelings and see things others could not see."

Kaoto nodded his head in understanding. Somehow it did not surprise him that this child of his youth should have special talents.

"One night, as I sat looking into the fire, the flames flared up as they sometimes do without any particular reason. For a few moments I thought I could see this little old woman in the flames. She was so old, no one has ever been this old before, and she was all wrinkled and stooped over. She sat on a log and held a crooked stick in her hand. She wore a necklace made of queer beads, like the ones you showed my father when you first came here."

"Paataga," Kaoto breathed, almost to himself.

"Yes, that was what she said her name was. How did you know that?" Mateep asked in wonder.

"Paataga and I are old friends, but I did not think she knew about you. I guess I should never be surprised at anything coming from her," Kaoto told her.

"I did not know her but she seemed to know me. She told me to be brave and strong, that you were coming to save me. So that is how I knew. I never doubted her. She had no reason to lie to me."

"No. Paataga would never lie, not even to save her own life. Rest assured, you can always count on Paataga. She comes to me at times when I need her most. She has never failed me." Kaoto was convinced that Mateep had actually received a visit from his great mother.

"Even when the savages found their way in here and killed father, I still did not doubt that you would be here in time to save me."

"Tell me about it, if you can." Kaoto prompted her.

"They found their way through the hole just as you did. They had been exploring every opening for days. It was just a matter of time until they found the right one, but Father was sure they still could not find us through all the mazes. But he was wrong this time."

"I tried to tell him that when I was here but, he would not listen," Kaoto said in sorrow.

"Yes, I remember you telling him that. When they came in on us last night, Father tried to stop them. He killed one with his spear but the rest would not come in close and fight. They just stood back in a circle around him and filled him with arrows. Even after he was down, they still shot more arrows into him. When I ran to try to stop them, one of them hit me on the side of the head with his spear. When I came to again I was tied to the tree. They seemed to like to hear me make noise, and when I was not noisy enough to satisfy them, they knocked me around some more. And then I heard you coming out of the night off the top of the rocks, like a storm breaking over the top of them. And you killed all of them, did you not?" she asked.

"Yes. I killed them all. I am glad I got here as soon as I did. I only wish I could have gotten here sooner. I might have been able to save your father," Kaoto said, thinking of the brave old man dying alone, not knowing the fate of his daughters.

"Father would never have changed his mind, not as long as he thought there was still a chance we could hide from them. You know how stubborn he could be. Right up to the last moment he was sure they would never find their way in to us."

"What about your sisters? I did not see any sign of them," Kaoto asked.

"They ran and hid before they were seen. They took the children and ran for cover. I think they all escaped. I guess Father at least bought them enough time to get away and find a safe place. The savages probably thought they were going to have plenty of time today to search them out after they got through with me."

"Children? Your sisters had children?" Kaoto asked haltingly, almost afraid to hear her answer.

"Yes. Children." Mateep smiled. "You were quite busy when you were here. Remember? All five of my sisters now have fine sons who show every sign of being tall like their father. Not as tall, maybe, and not covered with hair, but all are tall like their father."

Kaoto was silent. This was just what he had feared. He had children here. Children he should have been here looking after instead of running all over the nation. Who had taught them? Did they know enough to live in the world? They would soon be old enough for their manhood rites, and had no father to help them get ready.

"You are sure they are my sons?" he asked at last.

"Who else? There has been no other man here, only you. We may be cut off from the rest of the People here, but Father at least taught us that babies do not grow without someone planting their seed." She looked at Kaoto to see if he was listening and believing her. Sensing his concern, she told him, "Father taught them and taught them well, all he knew. They are really quite clever. Of course, they should be with a Wise One for a father. Do you not think?" She could not resist teasing him a little.

Kaoto nodded numbly, not ready to trust his voice to make a comment.

"We did not have lots of room in here and we did not dare go outside, so Father made them run the paths in here every day until they could satisfy him. This was no small thing. Father was a runner himself in his younger days."

"Yes, I remember him showing me his runner's badge and I should have known he would not neglect them, even if they were not his own sons."

"My father could not have been more proud if they had been his own. When they were born, he told us how he had tricked the Spirit Watcher at last. He said there was no way he could be robbed of at least one man-child. When all five turned out to be man-children he was so proud we could hardly live with him and his boasting. I was only sorry I could not present him with a man-child too, but that was your fault. You never looked at me as you did my sisters." Her look accused him of neglect.

"You were only a child yourself when I was here," Kaoto defended himself.

"Not as much a child as you thought. Anyway, Father was so proud. He acted like he had planned it all himself."

"I am not so sure he did not," Kaoto reflected, remembering how Mula was always finding some chore to take him away from the pool. He had always insisted he did not need help. What he needed to do could be better done alone. He must have been right, and knew what would happen.

"I am glad he was pleased. He deserved some comfort and joy in his old age, but if you think they are still in there alive, I had better get back and try to find them."

"We will both go." As Kaoto started to protest, she hurried on before he could speak.

"You could never find them without my help. I know all the places they would hide. I do not think they would come out even if you called to them. They have been badly frightened and they did not have the vision I had of your return." Mateep had sat up and was holding her head gingerly in her hands, feeling to find the extent of the damage she had sustained from the savages.

"You will not move from here. I will not have you going back and exposing yourself to more danger now that I have pulled you out of there," Kaoto insisted.

"I will not be in danger as long as I stay beside you. Paataga told me that, too," Mateep said with a confidence she did readily share.

"Paataga is a very wise old woman but she does not know everything," Kaoto argued.

"But you told me she would never lie to me. Is that not what you said? That I could always count on her to tell me the truth?" Mateep's two colored eyes searched his face for confirmation.

"Yes," Kaoto admitted. "I told you that and it is true. But can you be sure you understood her right? How could anyone tell if you were going to be safe? Even I do not know that much." Kaoto knew he was talking himself into a corner but he could not back out now.

"I understood her just as if she has been across the fire from me. I do not know how she knows such things. After all, you said she was your friend; you studied with her, so you should know. Besides, you are the Wise One, not me." Kaoto did not believe she was being disrespectful, but he was not sure. He did not know much about young women.

"Then I will go with you. I will be safer beside you than I will be here alone. Come." She held out her hand for him to help her stand up and climb out of the pit they were in.

"I still do like the idea of you going with me," Kaoto doggedly protested, although he knew he would not succeed.

"You might as well get used to it," Mateep informed him. "I will be going with you most of the time from now on."

"Did Paataga tell you this also?" He asked this time without being skeptical.

"Yes, she told me that. Of course I already knew it. I have known from the first time you were here. I knew that I would be going with you someday."

"As long ago as that?" Kaoto would have been amused if she had not been so serious.

"Ever since you told me about Little Frog and her two colored eyes like mine. Somehow this bound me to you. It was meant to be. I do not know why, I just knew it was so."

"I am supposed to be the Wise One, but between you and Paataga, you make me feel quite foolish," Kaoto said as he stood up and dusted himself off.

"You are not foolish, Kaoto. You just did not know because no one told you," Mateep replied, still waiting for him to help her out of the pit.

Without sandals Mateep could not walk over the black rocks. Kaoto carried her back to where the narrow cleft began. His sandals were showing signs of wear. After a few more trips they would have to be replaced.

"Put me down in the path and you can stay on top," Mateep suggested. This seemed like a good idea. From this vantage point he could keep a close lookout just in case there might be someone else below.

The precaution proved unnecessary, however. Other than the dead savages and Mula, there was no sign of anyone else in the stronghold. Kaoto dropped down with Mateep when he came to the pool. He made a quick search of the ground for fresh tracks that might indicate someone had been there since last night. Satisfied they were alone, he led Mateep to the edge of the pool.

"Before you go any farther let me wash the blood from your hair and take another look at that wound. I did not have a chance to close it properly last night."

Mateep clenched her teeth and made no outcry as Kaoto pulled the cactus spines from the edges of the grisly looking gash across the side of her head. Carefully, he washed it again, making sure it was completely clean before he covered it with bear grease and closed it once more, this time using strands of her hair to lace the sides together. It would heal, but for a time it would leave an awful looking spot and she would carry a scar for the rest of her days.

"It should heal all right now. It will be sore for quite a while but in time you will not even know it is there."

Mateep smiled a thank you, but she knew he was just trying to make her feel good. A wound of this size would always be noticeable.

"I will be fine now. I will go find my sisters and your sons. Why do you not see if you can get rid of the savages before I bring them back? It is not a pleasant sight."

"I will not feel easy with you out of my sight. I think I should go with you," Kaoto said, knowing she would argue.

"I will be all right. I will not be taken by surprise again. I will be on familiar ground, and I will check for tracks before I go anywhere. I will call you again if I need help."

Kaoto watched Mateep disappear down one of the many branches leading away from the central opening. He tried to assure himself that she would be all right, and as she said, she would call him if she needed him.

He retrieved his arrows from the bodies of the men he had shot last night. Two were as they had fallen. The third, the one he had pinned to the tree, had slid down, snapping the shaft as he went. He had died slowly and painfully during the night. Kaoto carried their bodies to a vacant storage bin and deposited them out of sight. He then turned to Mula's perforated form.

"Old friend, your stubborn ways cost you your life. That was your business. Are you satisfied? It almost cost your daughters and my children their lives. This you had no right to do. Now I will take them away from here to some of our People."

He removed all the arrows from the old man and wiped away as much of his blood as he could before he laid him out to wait for the return of Mateep. While he waited he scooped out a shallow grave next to the pool where the overflow kept the ground soft and easier to dig. While he worked, his mind was still with Mateep. He looked up often and listened intently for any sound but heard nothing until he saw her leading a small group back to where Mula lay.

"Everyone is safe," she called to him. "I have found them all."

Mateep's sisters came slowly across to the gravesite. Each gave Kaoto a shy greeting. Behind them ranged five young boys walking silently and fugitively eyeing the tall man who had stepped up out of the grave. He was much taller than they had expected him to be. Their mother and great father had not exaggerated.

One glance was all Kaoto needed to know they were indeed his sons. Each was taller than his mother and they had not reached their tenth summer yet. Besides their height, each had his long nose and a shock of unruly hair. None of them carried the downy hair on their bodies as he did but unmistakably they were sprouts of his seed, planted so many summers ago.

The boys did not speak and Kaoto was unsure of what he should say to them. Casen broke the silence as she introduced them.

"This is your father. He is the Wise One we have all told you about, the one Mula bragged on all the time to you and used to compare you to." She turned to Kaoto. "They have not yet been given their names. Now that you are here, you can do that for them."

"I shall see to it. They will soon be ready for their manhood rites. When that time comes, I will have their names ready for them to wear. Now let us lay your great father to his final rest and think about how we are going to get out of here."

The grave was filled and covered with large stones to insure no animal would disturb Mula's sleep. Then Kaoto began to look about for wood to make more sandals.

Mateep went to their sleeping rooms and pulled aside Mula's sleeping mat. Beneath it, she disclosed a small bin. In it were stacked several sandals. There was a pair for each member of the family, including a pair for himself.

"He never told the rest of you about these," Mateep said. "He would not admit to any of you that you might have to leave someday. Still he had them ready just in case. If he had more time, he might have led you out himself, although I doubt it. Now Kaoto will lead us all out." Turning to Kaoto she asked, "Where will you take us?"

Kaoto looked over the gathering and wondered just where he should take them. He wanted to find someplace where they would be safe. A place where his sons could take their manhood rights and where the women could find proper mates.

"I have not thought of that yet. I just want to get you away from here first. Then I will think about where to go."

They had all put on the sandals and gathered a few possessions to make up a pack so they would not go empty handed like beggars to a village. They would not embarrass the Wise One.

"I will find a place for you so you can find mates. Soon you will all have to go south, but I do not want you to go alone. I want you to go with a village, as a family."

"All but me," Mateep said. "I will be going with you, remember?"

Kaoto did not answer her. He turned and led the way up the niche to where they could mount the top of the rocks and cross over to the other side. This did not necessarily mean safety, but it was the first step in the direction of joining the People.

Chapter Forty Three

Staying to the higher ground as much as possible and crossing the lower regions after dark, they ran less risk of meeting with the savages. They had crossed the shining river with the aid of Sister Moon's light and now stood once more on the higher hills. Kaoto announced his intentions to the waiting women and boys.

"I have two choices," He told them. "I can take you back to my home or I can take you over there." He pointed west toward more mountainous country.

"It is up to you. We know nothing of this world outside the barrier." This came from Casen, now at twenty-and-six summers. She was plump and by far still the most talkative of them all. The rest remained silent, only speaking when he directed a question at them individually. They talked quietly among themselves, but only Casen addressed, him aside from Mateep, who alone felt completely at ease with him.

"I want to find a place among the People where you will feel at ease. I am sure it will only take a short time for all of you to find mates and settle down to village life," Kaoto told them.

"Maybe we do not want mates. We might be happy with the one man we have known and not want to risk disappointment with another man who could never live up to this one." Casen said.

"Casen, you are shameless." Mateep scolded her older sister while the others smothered a giggle behind their hands.

"We may be shameless, Mateep, but at least we do not have to be stupid. Besides, we know what we are speaking of. You can only guess," Casen cut back at her.

Mateep, undaunted by her sister's remark, smiled so sweetly that Kaoto was fooled. Her sisters, however, knew her better and understood the battle was on in earnest.

"I might be guessing now but I will have all the rest of my life to know the truth, while some of the older People will just have to live in their memories of what used to be," Mateep answered.

"Hush," Kaoto commanded. "I have traveled all over the nation and everywhere I go there is peace among the People. Now in a few short days, with only the six of you women, I have heard more arguing and fighting over nothing than I have all my days. Did not Mula teach you anything of courtesy and manners?"

Mateep took his large hand in her tiny one. Her strength had not come back to her as fast as he had hoped, and she suffered from occasional dizzy spells, but her humor bore her up so she could keep up her end of the endless banter.

"Do not worry about us, Kaoto. I am sure my sisters will not fight once they get to a village. It is just that we have all lived together so long with no one else to talk to, so, we fight. But it does not mean we do not like each other. We love and respect each other very much."

"Among the People, do not men ever fight each other?" Tola, the shy one, asked.

"Children sometimes fight or argue, scream, call names. But men talk," Kaoto said curtly to end the discussion.

His five sons looked at each other and smiled. Kaoto was not so much different than their old great father. Bigger, yes, but his manner with the women was very much the same and with even better results. To them Kaoto was more than father. He was a legend they had grown up with, someone to look up to and respect. Someone their mothers had told stories about in the late evening around the fire while they were growing up. They admired him and respected him as much as they had Mula, but Mula would always fill their father image. Kaoto was more like one of the gods their great father had told them about. No boy could have such a man for a father. It was too much to comprehend.

Behind Kaoto's back the women smiled secretly between themselves. They too thought he was not so much different than their stern old father with whom they knew they could only go so far before arousing his anger. Mateep, with her face solemn, asked, "Where do you think is the best place for my sisters and their sons, Wise One?"

Kaoto looked at her sharply, trying to decide if she was making fun of him again.

"And what of you, little mite? Do not tell me you will not stay with your sisters in the same village. Do I have to find a separate place just for you?"

"No. I will be content to go wherever you go," she said, looking up into his face as she spoke. Her eyes were still clouded with pain, but he could tell she was telling what she considered to be the truth.

"There is no room on the trail for anyone to keep me company. I travel alone and fast. You could never keep up with me. Besides, I do not remember asking you to come with me."

"I do not need an invitation. The one called Paataga told me I would be traveling with you and I believe her. You told me she never lies."

Kaoto shook his head. He did not want to get back into this discussion. He felt he would only lose again.

"If you are so fond of the old mother, then maybe I should take you to live with her. It might be good for both of you meddling women to have to live with each other for awhile."

He was just now seriously considering sending Mateep to Paataga as a student. She had the sharp wits and keen insight to make a good student, and the discipline of Paataga did not hurt anyone. It would solve his problem and keep her out of his way.

When Mateep became strangely silent on the trail, Kaoto began to watch her more closely. She had managed to keep to the trail but was traveling more slowly as the day progressed. She never complained, but she stumbled often and seemed to be disoriented much of the time. Whenever he would ask, she would assure him she was fine.

"I will be all right as soon as we stop and I can get a little rest. I am so tired that I guess I do not know what I am doing." She laughed, but her eyes did not laugh with her.

When Kaoto found a narrow canyon that seemed to offer a good camp-site, he led them in and sent the boys back to obliterate their tracks so any passing savages would not follow them. Mateep slumped down immediately and did not arouse when she was offered food and water. Kaoto shook her gently and found she was unconscious and he could not revive her.

He left her with her sisters and set off with a great burst of speed toward a nearby village. He knew there was an old mother with healing powers living there. He returned in a very short time and scooped Mateep up in his arms.

"Stay here until I return for you." He cautioned them about leaving the valley. "I will be back as soon as I find out what is wrong with her. If she can be helped, I will bring her back. If not, we will go to this village and stay until she is better."

Mateep was so tiny in his arms that he could not help but compare her with Little Frog when he had carried her down the steps on his long run.

The old mother instructed Kaoto to lay his frail charge down on a fragrant bed of fresh sage she had gathered in his absence. She shooed Kaoto from the room, and when he tried to protest, she scolded him for being selfish and anything but wise.

"Go, you big clumsy buffalo. There is no room for you in here. You breathe all the air and leave none for her. You get in my way so I cannot do my work. Go! Get out! Go away. Come back later."

"Later? How much later?" he asked anxiously.

"Much later. Days later. How should I know? She needs rest. She cannot get it with you stomping around and bellowing like a wounded bull, asking me stupid questions. Go. Quit making so much noise."

Protesting but unable to change the old mother's mind, he backed away from the tiny room and stood feeling useless in the opening in front of the little home. The Wise One had no wisdom for himself. It seemed his wisdom was only for others, never for himself in his time of need.

"I have five women and children waiting for me out in the canyon," he said at last.

"Five women and children? Fine, then what do you need with this one? Are not five enough for you? Must you hang around here like a love stricken bull, mourning over the one you cannot have? Go! Leave me alone. Go to your five women."

"They are not my five women. They are her sisters and I am leading them to a new home. A place where they will be safe and the children can grow up without the threat of the savages."

Kaoto tried to explain but could see the old mother was not listening to him and would not understand even if she did. She had turned back to Mateep and had excluded him from their world. At last he turned and started to leave, when the old mother relented a little and came to the doorway to speak to him.

"Take them. Do what you must do. There is nothing you can do here. Time is the only sure thing. Sometimes they come around very soon, other times it takes longer. Sometimes they never fully recover. If she is your woman, surely the Spirit Watcher will do what he can for her to please the Wise One. It is in his hands now, not ours."

Kaoto was not reassured by these words. They were platitudes often offered by the well meaning but ignorant People. He recalled again his conversation with Paataga about men and ants. He did not think the Spirit Watcher cared whether Mateep lived or died. Either way, he still had a responsibility to Mateep's sisters and his sons. He would not bring them here. He would take them to the destination he had decided on earlier. While he was doing this, he would hope for the best, but deep down he could only feel the worst.

He took the daughters of Mula up the river and then back up side streams until they were far from the shining river, deep in the heart of the mountains, close to another field of black rocks.

There was a high bluff of white rocks, and on top of it was a village that had recently been built to escape the encroaching savages. Here he was sure his family would be as safe as any place in the nation. Except perhaps with Forb and the hunters. But Forb's camp was too far away for the women to make the trip. Also, he did not want to be gone from Mateep that long. Here the boys could train and take their manhood rites and become respected members of a community. Being the sons of the Wise One would be considered a bonus. If they had to move south, they would go with a considerable number of the People well versed in survival.

As soon as they were settled and his last farewells were made, he hurried back to the village where he had left Mateep. The old mother informed him that Mateep had roused enough to eat and take water, but never seemed to come around enough to know who she was or where she came from.

"Do not despair, Wise One. Time is the only medicine I can give her. Time is the only thing that will give you the answer. At least she lives, she eats, and will regain her strength. This alone is good. I will tend her as long as it takes. She will not be cast out on the dump heap as many others would have been."

"I would like to stay here with her but I should not. My life is not my own. My time is not my own, either. There is so much I have to do, so many places I must go. What shall I do, old mother?" He pleaded with her for some sign of reassurance.

The old mother shook her head sadly. She could not give the Wise One comfort as he hoped. She could not lie to him. She could only repeat what she had said before.

"Go about your business. You are less than useless here. There is nothing you can do for her. If you have things to do, then go do them. At least that will keep your mind occupied. If there are those who need your help, then you must go to them and do what you can. That is what I must do here. Meanwhile, the time will pass more quickly for you if you stay busy, and time is all we have to hope for now."

Reluctantly, Kaoto accepted the old mother's advice. What she said was true. Staying busy would make the time go faster and time was all he could give her. He could not sit here and do nothing, so he left, heavy hearted, and if possible, more lonely than ever.

He started by making a few short trips to nearby villages and quickly returned. Each time, he was met with the same words.

"Time, Wise One, give her time. Can you not see she is getting better?"

Mateep could stand up and walk about but she did not know him. She looked at him as if trying to place him but somehow could not fit the name and the face together. Otherwise, her young body was rapidly mending and the cut on her head was closed and healing, as he had expected.

After several such trips, Kaoto decided to take an extended run and check on the progress of the savages. He found that the gap between the People and the savages was narrowing with alarming speed. The same drought that was diminishing the People's food supplies was making it more difficult for the savages also. This resulted in their making more raids to steal more from the little farmers. It was proving easier to raid them than to hunt for themselves. They lacked the intelligence to see they were driving their source of food from the land.

So far they had not come close to the village where he had left Mateep, but he still felt uncomfortable about being absent for such a long period time. As he turned his steps once more back to Mateep and the old mother who looked after her, he found he was running at top speed. He could not rest until he could see for himself that she was still safe. She had been in the hands of the savages once already. His thoughts of foreboding increased as he approached the village. When it came in sight, his worst fears were confirmed. The village had been raided and sacked.

With his heart in his throat, he searched for any sign of a struggle. There were no signs that the People had put up a fight. There were no bodies of either party in evidence. Apparently they had fled before the savages had struck. The savages, in turn, had taken what they wanted, and in their customary fashion tried to destroy all they could not carry.

He circled far out, searching for some clue as to where his People might have gone. All he found were scattered tracks where individuals had run in separate directions. It was their only means of defense, to try and confuse the savages by leaving numerous tracks leading to many false trails. Their tactics had worked. There were tracks of the savages going a short distance after the false trails, only to turn back to the village in a few steps.

Kaoto tried to decide which set might belong to Mateep and the old mother, but there were so many tracks and nothing to guide him. He did not even know if she was alone or with someone. Had she been able to run? Had she been carried, or had she been left for the savages to take again? His People were not warriors, but neither were they cowards. They would surely have helped her even if she was not of their village, but where would they have taken her? Did they have a chance to get her out before the savages struck them?

If she had been left on her own, with no one to guide her, where would she have gone? With her memory clouded, would she remember she was going toward safety? Or would she follow the back trail to the black rock country, the only home she had ever known? These and many more questions poured through his mind as he circled around the abandoned village in search of any trace of the tiny maiden who had laid a claim to him.

He thought of the surrounding villages and tried to imagine which one the old mother might try to lead Mateep to. The selection was staggering. They could have gone in any direction. He cast his eyes to the sky and was not surprised when the Spirit Watcher returned his gaze without offering to help. In the back of his mind he had a recurring picture of a tiny figure stumbling back down the trail toward the river. He took that trail and ran with all his strength and speed in hopes of finding her before she stumbled into the hands of the savages again.

Chapter Forty Four

Early in the morning, word of the approaching savages reached the tiny village where Mateep lived with the old mother. A runner brought word that a band had been spotted heading in their direction.

Mateep was stronger now and could get up and walk without help, but she still could not quite remember where she was. The old mother told her daily and often repeated her name to her. Mateep. It sounded vaguely familiar and it was a good name, but somehow it did not seem like it belonged to her. It was more like the name of someone she had once known.

When news of the savages came, the old mother had hurriedly packed a few provisions, and taking Mateep by the hand, led her away from the village and, she hoped, far from the suspected path of the savages.

All day, they had pushed as fast as the old mother could walk. Her running days were long past. They did not go to another village but stayed clear of them all out of fear that they might still run into the savages. The old mother later regretted she had not told anyone of her plans so at least someone could have told Kaoto where they were going. At the time, all she could think of was getting her charge away from danger. She knew Kaoto came from the land of the Chaco and though she had never been there, she thought she knew the general direction she should take to reach it. It never occurred to the old one that she was in no condition to make this long trip.

The first night they lay hidden in a sparsely covered ditch on the side of the hill. The next day she hurried Mateep further from her village, deeper into unknown country. They ran out of water, and the heat of the day became extremely hard on the old mother. Soon it was Mateep who was helping the elderly woman traverse the rugged terrain. In the afternoon, they took shelter from the beating rays of the Spirit Watcher by crouching in the shade of a large rock. From this point they saw a small band of the savages loping along on the trail below them. Mateep's memory registered fear of these men. She did not know why, but she knew they were a threat to her. She sank back against the rock and held the old mother in her arms until the men were out of sight.

The old mother was unable to move any further. Her heart could not take the strain of the prolonged flight. The heat was oppressive and beat down on her relentlessly, draining her last reserve of strength, leaving her exhausted and worn. She tried to get Mateep to leave her and go without her. She gave her instructions on how to find the land of the Chaco, but Mateep refused to leave her and sat with her until her final breath had escaped her weary body. The only thing Mateep held in her memory was that the savage men were her enemy and that she should try to find a way to Chaco. There were some vague shadows in the back of her mind that surfaced momentarily, only to disappear before she could capture them. There was someone she had to find, but she could not remember who, or why.

She decided to move after dark when it was cooler, not realizing it was the safest time for her to travel. Traveling at night, she was able to cover a vast stretch of ground without being seen by anyone, friend or foe.

Her food supply ran out and her sandals were wearing thin. She found water occasionally and refilled her water skin. She dug roots and chewed grass stems and small twigs to quiet her hunger and to get what small nourishment she could from them.

Quite by accident she stumbled into a village of the People and sensed they were not to be feared as the savages were. All she could manage to say was "Chaco?" She repeated this single word at several small villages and was always asked the same question. "Chaco? You want to go to Chaco?" When she nodded in the affirmative, they would point the way. Sometimes she was offered food and once she was given a pair of old sandals that were still better than the ones she wore.

At one larger village she stumbled into the structure at the dumpsite. The creatures here were kindly toward her and shared their meager supplies with her, telling her it was given in the name of Kaoto's little sister, who had no other name.

The name "Kaoto" stirred something in her scattered memory, but she could not connect it to anyone or any place. She stored it away and clung to it like a precious possession. The creatures of the dump told her the way to the next village, which was large enough to support a building at the dump such as theirs. They told her she would be welcomed at any of these places.

So it was that Mateep traveled in a haphazard manner, mostly to the northwest, always asking for directions to the mysterious Chaco. She no longer tried to communicate with the villagers, but instead hunted out the dumps. Her hair became tangled and her clothing torn. She had to accept rags from the poor creatures in order to cover herself at all.

Her journey was often interrupted by delays. She would sometimes become discouraged and linger on for a few days with the creatures, but always something would come up to remind her that she should be moving, and she would once more take to the lonely trail. She hid from sight whenever a runner approached, fearful he might be an enemy. She was so successful that no one saw her. Nothing ever changed for her. One day was much the same as the last and the next. It was a succession of short trips from one dumpsite to the next, always the same question, "Chaco?" and a wave of the hand in the northwestern direction.

Once, while visiting a dump, a tall man ran past the village. He did not stop and Mateep did not see him until he was almost out of sight. Something strange whirled in her head and she tried to call out to him but could not. She watched as his long strides took him around a curve in the trail and he vanished. She wanted to follow him, to find out why she felt she should know him but she knew she could never catch up with him; he was running much to fast.

"Who was that?" she asked one of her companions.

"Do you not know him? He is the one responsible for the place we stay and the food we eat. He is the Wise One, but surely you have heard of him. We honor his little sister. His name is Kaoto."

"Kaoto? The name does sound familiar. I feel I should know him, but I just cannot remember anything anymore. Where would I find him? Where does he live?" she asked.

"It is hard to say. He lives on the run, mostly. He usually stops for a visit with us when he comes by. He must be in an awful hurry today," one of the ancients answered her.

"But does he not have a home? A place where he stays when he is not running?"

"They say he used to live up north somewhere. It is the place where he took his training with Paataga."

"Paataga. Yes, I know that name, too. I talked with her once, I think. Where would I find her?" Mateep's eyes were shining for the first time in many days. There was a glint of intelligence that had not been there before the runner went past.

"We do not really know. It is up north. That is all we know. It may be in the Chaco you keep asking about. It seems that is what he said one time when he did stop here." The ancient one was puzzled by this wild looking young woman who claimed to know Kaoto and Paataga but did not know where to find them.

"Why do you want to find Chaco? Does it have something to do with the Wise One?"

"I do not know. Oh, there is so much I do not know, but I do know I must go there, and now I am more sure than ever." Mateep stood weeping, looking after the tall runner who had passed. "If only he had stopped I could have asked him. He might have been able to tell me what to do. If he is the Wise One, as you say, he should be able to tell me who I am and why I should go there."

"That is possible. He is very wise," the ancient one told her. He hesitated to give advice but finally offered some.

"Why do you not wait here a little longer? He may come this way again. He often does, and all we have is time, anyway."

"No. I cannot wait. I must go. I must go now."

Filling her water skin and accepting a few scraps of food, she set off up the same trail the tall man had taken. She was determined to follow him until she could either catch up with him or until she found the Chaco. The ancient one had told her that he might stop at the next village.

On the trail, up near the bend where the tall man had disappeared, she found a single eagle feather lying in the trail. She remembered a man with two feathers in his hair. She picked up the feather. It was a link between the present and her forgotten past. She tucked it in the front of her ragged clothing and carried it with her. Each night she slept with it clutched in her hand. It was a comfort to her. It was the only possession she had. She did not know that only distinguished persons with honored positions rightfully possessed a feather of this kind. In the valley of the black rocks there had never been any eagle feathers, and Mula had never thought it necessary to inform his daughters of this custom. Mateep traveled in ignorance of the customs of the People, not knowing she was violating the time-honored right of the rulers and their chosen few.

She stopped and made inquiries at each village, large or small, and was always told she was far behind the tall runner. But at least she knew she was on the same path as he had traveled. At one village she was told to follow a path that would lead her to the main road. This would take her to Chaco. They told her that once on this road, she could not become lost because it led straight to the canyon.

After this she did not stop to ask questions or for food, but continued doggedly on her way, thinking that once she reached the Chaco she would find all her answers. Haggard, lame, and weary, she pushed on, still hiding at the approach of any stranger on the road. Afraid, afraid of the unknown, and she knew so little.

Darkness had descended and Sister Moon had just begun to show her feeble light when Mateep stumbled into the Chaco canyon. In the moonlight she could make out many villages. Which one should she go to? She had not been told there were so many different villages. She had thought there would be one large village. It was late. All the villages were quiet. There were no fires to invite her in. She limped along the main road in indecision. The road led her close to one large village. Lacking any better choice, she turned off the road and took the path that led over into its courtyard. Across the front of the village stood a low wall. Every fire was out. There was no one stirring. She could hear the sounds made by sleeping people coming from various parts of the village, mostly from the small kivas.

What to do? Should she wait here until morning? There did not seem to be any structures at the dumpsite, even though this was a very large village. Was everyone so healthy and prosperous that there were no unfortunate creatures to inhabit the dump? Then this must surely be the home of the Wise One.

She sank down beside the wall to rest and think. It seemed easier to just sit here than to get back up and find another place. Weariness overcame her and she dozed off as she leaned back against the warmth of the wall.

Much later, when Sister Moon was almost out of sight, Mateep was aroused by the sound of someone's persistent coughing. The rest of the pueblo was entombed in silence. Even the snoring had subsided, but from one room the coughing continued. It sounded like someone was having trouble breathing and each breath came in long, suffering gasps in between the coughs.

Mateep got up and slowly walked toward the sound until she found the doorway from which the coughing issued. Since she had not been raised in a village and had never been instructed on the proper etiquette of pueblo life, she did not know she should never cross a threshold without first being invited.

There were no doors to close, but the doorway was considered a solid barrier. Even a friend coming to visit would stop at the doorway and speak, waiting for the occupant to acknowledge their presence and either ask them in or, more likely the occupant would come out in the courtyard. A person's sleeping room was as private as their thoughts, and no one would intrude on either.

Ignorant of this custom, Mateep crept silently into the tiny room and found an old woman lying half off her sleeping mat. She was trying to reach the water jug near her door. In the faint light of Sister Moon she looked somewhat like the old mother who had tended her. Mateep remembered her with tenderness, so she helped the old woman get back on her mat and looked around for something in which to bring water. Finding a small gourd cut for a drinking dipper, she filled it with water and brought it to the old woman's lips.

"Bless you, my child," Keenwah muttered through toothless gums. She tried to raise herself to a sitting position, but fell back again.

Mateep put an arm around her and raised her enough to drink without choking. The water gave Keenwah temporary relief, and as she rested in the young woman's arms, she tried to see who it was who had come to her help.

"Who are you, child? Do I know you?"

Mateep tried to pull a name from her memory but came up blank. Far back in the distance, when she was a little girl in the pool, they had told her she was a little frog. It was the only name she could think of.

"Once, long ago, someone called me a little frog. I think that is my name," She said haltingly, not sure this was right.

"Little Frog?" Keenwah's old mind tried to make sense out of this. "But you left us many summers ago. I did not think you would ever come back to us."

"I have been gone a long time." Mateep strained to find something in her mind that would help her, but it was all so vague, so scattered. There was nothing solid she could hold on to, so she said the first thing that came to her.

"I do not know where I have been. I have been lost, and now I am looking for the Wise One. Maybe he can help me."

"He will be glad to see you again, Little Frog. He missed you so much when you went away without him. He will be so happy you have come back."

Keenwah did not try to understand how a deformed girl rescued from the dump, who had died so long ago, could be back in the body of this naturally shaped young person. It was too hard to think about anything but getting her breath and not coughing. All she was sure of was that this girl had come and given her water when she needed help, and now sat beside her. It was a comfort to not be alone. Maybe Torjan could make it out in the morning when he came by, or Kaoto might come back any day now. He could surely tell her what it all meant.

Mateep lowered Keenwah back to her sleeping mat and sat dripping a little water from her fingers on the parched lips.

"Why are you alone, old mother? Do not you have anyone to look after you?" she asked.

"Oh, yes. I have two fine young men who care for me, but they cannot sit with me constantly." She felt it necessary to defend Torjan in his absence. Kaoto's absence needed no explanation. Everyone knew he must travel a lot.

"I felt just a little tired when I came to my mat last night. Torjan told me he would be back at first light. He was going to see Paataga, you know. He has his hands full looking after two old women who live so far apart." She smiled a little at this, thinking of Torjan running back and forth between her home and Paataga's hut on the side of the canyon.

"He thought Paataga might be able to tell him when Kaoto might come back. Kaoto is my son. Did you know that? Yes, he is my son. Kaoto, the Wise One." This long speech drained her strength. She closed her eyes and lapsed into a long silence interrupted by her coughing. Once she opened her eyes and looked at the tangled mass of hair on the young woman. She fumbled her hand beside her mat and came up with her old headband. She offered it to the young woman, saying, "Here, take this. It will help keep the hair out of your eyes." Mateep took the headband in her hand and looked at it in wonder. Another possession. It was hers. The old mother had given it to her. Had she not?

Mateep continued to moisten the dry lips and let a little water trickle down the old mother's throat without choking her. Her actions were instinctive. Her mind was still wandering through a maze, trying to put some of the scattered pieces together. The old one had used the name Kaoto and said he was the Wise One. Were they the same people? She did not know. She thought she should know but she could not connect the name with a face.

And Paataga? The old mother had mentioned Paataga. This brought a misty picture of a tiny figure seated on a log looking at her through the flames of a fire. This tiny figure had spoken to her. What had she said? It was important. She had known it was important and had made a promise to remember it always. But now she could not remember. What had she said? If she could just remember one thing, just one little thing, it would be such a help.

Mateep knew little of death. She had seen her father die, but did not remember her mother's death. The old mother who had helped her had died on the trail. Did she not? She sat beside Keenwah when the old one drew her last breath and coughed no more. Mateep laid the old one's hand over her breast and covered her with a light robe she had found next to her.

She discovered the headband she still clutched in her hand. It was set with some heavy stones and was so old that it was very dark and nearly dried out. That must have been why the old mother had given it to her. Absently, she pushed back her hair and pulled the band down to keep her tangled hair out of her eyes. She leaned back in the doorway, wondering what she should do now. The old one was dead so she would not mind if she rested here for a while. She had seemed like a kind person. She had given her a gift and she had talked to her. She had told her about her son, Kaoto, and the one called Paataga. Surely she would let her rest a few moments in her door. She should get up soon and see if she could find someone who could tell her where to find Kaoto or Paataga. She smiled as she recalled two names. This was better than she had done for a

324 - Norman D. Messenger

long time.

Her fingers went to the front of her clothing to find the feather she had carried and cherished since she had found it on the trail. She turned it in her hands and studied it as if it could render up some image of the man who had worn it, some clue to her identity, but it had nothing to offer. It never did. She did not know why she even kept it. It was a bother to carry in her clothes. It was always getting rumpled and messed up. She pushed the quill of it up under the headband and used it to scratch absently at an uninvited guest in her hair. She left it there, hanging down over her left cheek, once again ignorant of the customs.

She drifted off into a troubled sleep and was awaken violently by a pair of huge hair-covered hands belonging to a giant whose thundering voice boomed, "What's this?"

Chapter Forty Five

Sister moon beheld a sight that made her blush with shame. Never before in the history of the People had she been forced to witness such abnormal practices. There was not even a cloudbank for her to hide behind. She must look on and wonder at what transpired in her pale light.

On the flat land above the canyon lay a gentle swell in the land, and on top of this swell was located the ruins of what was once reported to be the trade center of the nation. From this building, the roads that led all over the nation had their beginning. They radiated out from here like girders from a spider web, leading to long forgotten destinations.

To the east, it was told by the elders, the road led to a land so flat that there were almost no hills. It was a land where the People had to build mounds of dirt to protect them from the wandering rivers that flooded their land each spring. The rulers lived on these mounds so they could look over their territory and see the lands of the next ruler.

To the north, the road led over mountains and valleys until it came to a great circle of stones on the top of a mountain. The circle was older than the People. No one knew who built it or why it was built there. The road terminated at the circle, but no one went there anymore.

To the west, the road crossed endless runs of barren land until it came to a great water, a water so wide no one could cross it. Stories about this west road told of great fish and strange animals. But no one alive had ever been there, so it was not known if these stories were true or just the wanderings of the old ones' minds.

To the south, the road led so far that it was beyond the imagination. The road to the south was the last road to die. Originally, the People of the nation had come up it. They had brought corn, and squash, pumpkins and beans. Later came the traders, bringing new foods for the People. These traders had brought the cotton plant that made the soft, beautiful cloth that the People treasured. From the south had come the shells of strange water life and exotic fruits and birds. But they no longer came. The People had all they needed; there was no need to bring more of what they already had. Slowly the trade route had disappeared.

Paataga, the oldest living person in the nation, had once worked on the road. She would say that traders from distant lands did not use it, but rather by men of local villages, who brought crops from where they were plentiful to locations that were suffering from a drought or some other disaster. Now the runners or visitors used the trade routes. So the People had been surprised when a strange procession was seen marching up the road from the south the past summer. There were no women among them, only men. Mostly young men. They had carried no trade goods, but they claimed to have come from a distant land of myth and legend that was linked to the history of the People. This is what had confused Paataga at first. They wore strange attire, and on several of the men's shoulders were perched brilliantly colored birds, the likes of which no man had ever seen. They were colored like the arch in the sky after the rains. They were magical birds. They could say the words of men and could shout strange phrases at the command of the men who carried them.

The men claimed to be magicians, and the People were inclined to believe them. They could perform feats that the People could not explain. Further, they were thought to be wise men. They had a physical resemblance to their own wise man. While they were not covered with downy hair, they were still tall, although not as tall as their own Wise One. Each man had a large, prominent nose, not unlike Kaoto's. Their hair was black but it was trimmed and trained to stand out from their heads instead of lying down, like the hair of the villagers. They had boasted of what they could do and of the powers they possessed. They made promises that appealed to all the People, and mostly to Matuga.

They claimed to be so powerful that they could keep the savages from them. They apparently had come through the land of the savages and had not been harmed. They claimed they could protect the villages from the invading savages by using their powers. To their credit, the villagers had to admit they had been successful. No savages had set a foot in the Chaco canyon, although they were reported to be moving this way. The crucial test would come this summer.

Their arrival had created quite a stir among the People. They walked in a single file and never varied their speed or the distance between individuals. The leader wore a sparkling white robe woven from the cotton plant. On his head he wore a headpiece made from brilliant red feathers. Several of the men directly behind him were also dressed in white. They wore plain headdresses that were also white but had no adornment. After them came their followers, dressed in dark, nearly black robes with similar black headbands.

Each man carried a long slender staff. It was straight and polished until it gleamed in the rays of the Spirit Watcher. It was used as a walking stick, a pointer, and it was said it was used in their rituals. Lastly, they each carried a strange piece of pottery. Unlike the pots of the People, which were gracefully curved to be pleasing to the eye, these pots were straight sided. It was not certain what purpose they served but they were also part of their rituals.

Paataga had shunned them like a pestilence. They, in turn, had stayed well away from the sharp tongued old woman and were content to leave her and her handful of students on the far side of the canyon alone, while they took up residence in the ruins of the old trade buildings up above the canyon.

In Kaoto's absence, the People had been easily impressed by anyone who would offer some diversion to their everyday lives. These men did. While there were rumors of their odd behavior and even more odd choice of sexual partners, as long as they did not try to force their ways on the People, the People were content to leave them alone.

The leader of this foreign group of travelers, Kiel, did all the talking for them. He strutted about the canyon speaking haughtily to the rulers, never passing words with the farmers or their families. His manner was considered more amusing by the People than offensive. Kiel was unaware of this factor or he might have been even harsher with them than he was. His ignorance left him blissfully unaware of how the People really felt about him and his followers.

At first they had made no demands other than to be left alone. Kiel and his followers had taken up residence in the vicinity of the trade building and only occasionally came down to the valley floor. As time passed, they began to make more trips down, always to demand food, or other items, the villagers could furnish easily. The People resented their arrogant demands but when Matuga backed the men, the villagers grudgingly contributed what was asked of them. Matuga explained his actions to them in an almost apologetic tone of voice.

"These men are capable of saving you from the invading savages. They have magic, which will keep the savages from the Chaco. It will only cost you a small tribute of common things you can easily provide."

This seemed simple enough, but over time they had come to demand more and more until they were a sore burden to the food supplies of the drought stricken Chaco Canyon. If anyone complained, they were reminded of the horror stories coming up from the land to the south. Matuga would ask them, "Do you want to suffer the same fate? No? Then provide for Kiel and his band."

Perhaps the hardest things to provide for them were the animals. They wanted all types of animals, but they wanted them alive. They explained it was necessary to have live animals to use as sacrifices in their moon worship rituals.

To show their good intentions, they offered to look after the orphans and anyone unable to look after themselves, but after several such people disappeared, no more were sent up to them.

Some of the young men had crept up on the rituals one night and had been found out by Kiel and his followers. The ritual was brought to a hurried end and the young men were driven from the area. The next day Kiel made a statement in the village courtyard that startled the People. He strutted up and down the open space, swinging his highly polished walking stick. Prodding with it at offending youths, he had berated them and made accusations. Then he had said words that had been hard for the People to understand, let alone believe.

"In the future, anyone found sneaking around our camp will be put to death. We will not stand for any interference. If this should happen again, we will no longer be responsible for the fate of the Chaco. For all we care, the savages will be welcome to come in and do whatever they wanted to the women and children in Matuga's domain."

The elders drew together and talked long about what should be done. They did not like to be threatened, but they did not like to think of what might happen to them if they no longer had Kiel's protection. It was decided they would warn the young men to never go near the camp of the magicians again.

But young men are a curious lot and it was impossible to police all the area, especially after dark, so more stories drifted back to the pueblo. These were stories that were disturbing to the serious minded People who had lived here all their lives without the benefit of Kiel's protection.

Kiel and his band of mystics had just descended on the quiet village when they heard the thunderous voice of Torjan. Kiel quickly brought his band in a circle around the red-haired giant and his trembling victim.

"What seems to be the trouble here?" demanded the leader of the group. His cynical smile irritated Torjan, as usual.

"Nothing I cannot handle without any help from the likes of you, Kiel." He barked at the appointed leader of the group.

"Handle, yes, but what is the trouble?" he insisted.

At this time Matuga came stumbling out of his sleeping room, rubbing his eyes to discover what all the shouting was about. Every able-bodied person in the pueblo soon joined him. All were milling around, trying to get a closer look at the strange looking creature that Torjan held captive.

"Torjan, what is all this about?" Matuga asked, looking closer at Mateep as she tried to shrink from sight.

"I just came down to check on Keenwah when I found this creature in the doorway," Torjan explained as he turned Mateep around for Matuga to see. He bent down to look in the doorway.

"Keenwah? Are you awake, little mother?" he asked as softly as his gruff voice would allow. "Surely all this noise has awakened you, but you do not have to be afraid." he continued.

Mateep spoke. Apparently the red-haired giant did not know that the woman inside had died during the night.

"She is dead," Mateep said flatly.

"Dead? What have you done to Keenwah?" Torjan's voice boomed out, filling the courtyard like a flood. Still holding his victim by one hand, he pushed his head and shoulders through the small, keyhole-shaped doorway and, with his free hand, shook the tiny figure gently to rouse her from sleep. He soon knew the girl told the truth.

"She is dead, Matuga. And I was supposed to be looking after her while Kaoto was gone. Fine friend I turn out to be." He shook Mateep violently. "What have you done to her?" he demanded again.

"Nothing. I did nothing to her but give her a little water and sit by her side until she passed from this life," Mateep tried to explain. "She did not die alone. I was with her all night."

"All night? When did you get here? Where did you come from? Who are you, anyway?" Torjan's barrage of questions slammed against Mateep, leaving her even more confused than before. She did not know the answers to any of his questions.

"I do not know. I cannot remember anything."

Torjan took a good look at the wretched creature in his grip. He spotted the headband with the feather drooping down over one cheek. His anger grew like a storm within him.

"Why have you taken her headband? And where did you get the feather? This is Keenwah's most prized possession. You stole it from her, did you not? You little thief!"

"No. I —She—Oh, I do not know. I think she gave it to me last night, I cannot remember." Mateep hung her head again, trying to make some sense out of all that was going on.

"Gave it to you?" Kiel broke in. "Yes, I am sure that is just what the mother of the Wise One would do. Give away her prized possessions to the first thief who entered her door." He attempted to take a hold of Mateep's other hand.

Torjan pulled his catch back and stood between her and the leader of the mystics. He had only met Kiel on two occasions, both of which were after Kaoto had left. He did not like this man or any of his following. They were detestable specimens of men as far as he was concerned. While he had no feelings for his captive, he had no intentions, of turning her over to Kiel.

"What is to be done with her, Matuga?" Torjan asked, ignoring Kiel's menacing looks.

"Well, I—I do not really know. We have never had anything like this to deal with before." He looked around for confirmation from his elders, who were all nodding their heads in agreement. This was unheard of. No one stole, and to steal from the dead was beyond belief.

"It is simple," Kiel offered, speaking directly to Matuga and making it a point to ignore Torjan.

"What is simple about it?" Matuga asked, hopeful of a suggestion he could act on without having to make any decision himself. Lately it had been easier for him not to have to think too much. Let others do the thinking and then act on what they said.

"You do not seem to understand what a thief is. I have had more experience with them, it seems." Kiel's voice became as smooth as grease.

"I can just bet you have," Torjan snorted, even thought Matuga was holding up his hand to order silence and peace.

"A thief does not deserve to live. It is as simple as that." Kiel continued to speak to Matuga. He knew the old man's weakness and intended to take advantage of it now that it suited his purpose.

"That may be true, Kiel, but we do not kill people for any reason, especially for such a small matter," Matuga resisted.

"Small matter!" Torjan roared. "This is no small matter. This is the mother of my friend, your Wise One. How can you call it a small matter?"

"I mean no disrespect to either Keenwah or her son, but the headband was old, as she was old. It was of no value to anyone but her and she no longer cares. It was not like she was stealing food or something necessary to life, Torjan." Matuga tried to explain.

"Where I come from, we knew how to take care of thieves so they would not steal again. The first time they were caught we cut off their hand. If this did not stop them, the next time we cut off their head. This worked every time," Torjan said as he eyed the terrified girl in his clutches. He did not know if he could carry out his threat on this little thing, but nevertheless it was the law he had been raised to respect. To steal was not the crime, but to get caught was unforgivable.

"Oh, I do not think we could do that." Matuga did not like the suggestions coming from the great Red One. They were against all his peaceful beliefs and upbringing.

"I think maybe our big friend is a bit too eager," Kiel said. Again his voice was soothing to Matuga's frayed nerves. It was plain for all to see that Matuga was willing to listen to Kiel rather than Torjan.

"Do you have some idea that might be better? Less harsh? Something we could live with?" Matuga asked hopefully.

"Why, yes. As a matter of fact I do." Kiel smiled at Matuga but his eyes challenged those of Torjan. "I have already thought that we, my men and I, could take her off your hands. We could see that she was properly punished and sent on her way. I can tell you for sure she will not steal from this village again." Kiel's eyes wandered over the trembling girl. His tongue flicked across his lips, leaving them moist and shining in the early morning sun. To Torjan, he looked like a snake just before it swallowed its helpless victim.

"No. She is not going to be turned over to you so you can do to her what you do with those animals you are always wanting." Torjan's grip tightened on Mateep's wrists so sharply that she cried out in pain.

"And what are you doing to her? With us at least she would not have to suffer the torture she is getting from you. Matuga, this is your decision. I mean, you are still the ruler here, are you not?" Kiel looked from the tired old man to the Red One, and in the back of his mind he wondered just who did rule the People.

Apparently the same question crossed Matuga's mind and he straightened himself up and looked defiantly at Torjan. Squaring his shoulders, he let his eyes go from one man to the other. He feared them both; it was just a matter of whom he feared the most. Torjan could no doubt tear him apart with his bare hands, but he was all physical strength. He possessed no magic. Kiel was something different. He was no match for Torjan in strength but he did have mystic powers on his side. Besides his talk, of punishment for the girl instead of killing her appealed to Matuga much more than Torjan's threat of cutting off her hand and then her head.

"Torjan, I command you to release this creature into Kiel's custody." Kiel's faint sarcastic smile enraged Torjan all the more but he did not want to argue with Matuga. He was a guest in this village and did not want to embarrass his friend Kaoto by being rude and disrespectful to the old man. He really did not have any idea what he should do with her anyway. It was their problem. Let them handle it in their own way.

He let go of Mateep's wrist as Kiel grasped the other hand and pulled the girl swiftly away. Kiel was quickly surrounded by his faithful band and they swept up the valley and ascended the stairs. A deep humming noise accompanied them. It was the only sound that most of the villagers had heard issue from the throats of the black robed followers. It left an uneasy feeling with everyone present. It was like the low rumble of thunder before the storm broke. While they had no sympathy for the girl, each person was glad it was not him that was being herded away to an unknown fate at the hands of the mystics.

Torjan stood silently looking after the departing group. He felt that somehow he had failed. He was sure that Kaoto would have handled this differently if he had been here. Even Paataga would have surely had a different suggestion than this. He thought it was probably his own fault. That talk of cutting off a hand and then the head was a little strong for these timid little People. True, it is how they had dealt with hardened criminals in his world, but when he thought of the terrified little maiden he had held in his hands, he was not so sure she could be called a criminal.

He watched as the women of the village entered Keenwah's room and prepared her for her final trip. He felt completely useless, which he was. Turning his back on the village, he retraced his steps back up to Paataga's retreat. Perhaps she would have an answer for all this.

Why did not Kaoto come back? If they ever needed a Wise One, they most surely needed one now. He looked back to see Matuga talking with his elders.

"A bunch of old men, long past their time. What they need is a young man with some guts to take over now and let that old fool get some rest."

It never occurred to him that the one he was going to for advice had twice the summers of any man down there. To him, Paataga was ageless. She was just Paataga.

Chapter Forty Six

Mateep looked dubiously at the tall man who had taken her hand and pulled her away from the Red One. Was he the Wise One she was looking for? He was tall, but not as tall as she thought he should be. He had feathers in his hair, but not like the one she had picked up beside the trail. She did not feel the security in his presence she had hoped for.

Kiel was pulling her along at a rapid pace, looking back over his shoulder often as if he expected someone to come in pursuit. When Mateep stumbled, he yanked her painfully back to her feet and used strange, harsh words that she was sure were not complimentary.

"Are you the one they call the Wise One?" she asked timidly.

"Wise One?" Kiel looked at her curiously. "Oh yes, I am wise, but I am not the one the fools down in the valley call their Wise One. He is a fool also," Kiel spoke sharply, and there was nothing encouraging about his tone or his words.

"Will you take me to see Paataga?" Mateep ask, feeling sure all her troubles would be over if she could only speak to Paataga or the tall man who haunted her.

"Hardly. What do you want to see that old crone for? She cannot help you now." They had gained the top of the steps and were headed for the ruins of the trade buildings. Kiel seemed to feel more sure of himself now that they were away from the valley and slowed the pace slightly.

"Not that it matters, but did you really think you could get away with stealing the old woman's headband? It was not worth much, but after all they do have rights, you know."

"I did not steal it." Mateep put her free hand to her head trying to think. "I am sure she gave it too me last night. Yes. I remember now. She told me to use it to keep my hair out of my eyes." The frightened maiden tried to smile as she remembered the little woman who had spoken so kindly to her. "She was a nice woman and I did not hurt her." Mateep was still confused but she instinctively knew these men were not friends. They were not going to do anything to help her and it was too late to resist now. Not that she could have done anything against all of them.

She became silent, offering no resistance to Kiel. What was the use? No one believed her. No one knew who she was and no one seemed to care what became of her. Why could she not remember? Why could she not tell them who she was and where she came from? She had clung to the hope that the Chaco would be her salvation. She thought that once here Kaoto and Paataga, whoever they were, would come to her rescue and all would be right with her world. Now it was all a jumbled nightmare of confusion and pain

The single file of mystics marched straight across the open landscape leading toward the skeletal remains of the bleak buildings. The only sound was the continuous deep humming sound emanating from the dark robed men. It set an ominous mood of foreboding, and her skin crawled in spite of herself.

Kiel steered her inside the outer wall of the structure and guided her to a small room that still remained intact. Mateep was shoved roughly inside and a crude stone slab was put in place to act as a door, leaving her in semi-darkness.

She settled to the floor, all thought of escape washing from her. It seemed futile to even try to think, let alone take any action when she knew nothing of her surroundings. Where could she go? This had been her only hope. Now that hope was gone.

As she sat with her feet tucked under her, her hands resting in her lap, her attention was drawn to the darkest corner of the little room she was in. Blinking her eyes she continued to stare at the vacant corner. Something had caused her to focus her attention there, but what? There was nothing there. She studied the vacant wall intensely. Something was moving. It was nothing tangible, but there was a blurred spot where the walls met that did not look like the rest of the wall.

"Child? Why are you here?" The voice was familiar. Where had she heard it before?

"Who are you?" she asked softly, afraid of being heard by those outside.

"It is me, child. Do you not remember me?" The blurred portion of the wall was slowly forming into a slight figure seated on a log in front of a fire.

"I should know you but I cannot remember. I cannot remember anything. Help me. Please." Mateep held out her hands in supplication toward the figure.

"Patience, child. Help is on the way. There is nothing I can do by myself, but Kaoto will come soon. He will know what to do."

The figure began to grow more faint until Mateep was not sure she had ever seen anything in the first place.

"Please. Do not leave me here alone. I am afraid. I am afraid of these men. Help me. Please." Her voice raised as the figure vanished.

"Who are you talking to?" Kiel's voice came from the other side of the door. "She must be completely out of her mind. She is in there talking to herself and begging for help. Well, begging will not do her any good now. Matuga has washed his hands of her and the Red One has gone off to talk to the old crone."

"What are you going to do with her?" his lieutenants asked.

Kiel's grim face was emotionless, registering nothing. He had long prided himself on removing any trace of emotion from his countenance. It served him well. No one could find a weakness in him if he expressed nothing for them to judge him by.

"We have long hoped to have a celebration of the virgin. This seemed like too good a chance to miss," he said as he held his lieutenant's eyes until the underling dropped his gaze, as they always did when looking into the cold bleak stare of Kiel.

"But do you know she is a virgin? From what I have seen of the practice of these people, being a virgin is nothing to be proud of. They start pretty young and she is not a child."

"It does not really matter, but I suppose we could find out if you think it is necessary. I will leave that up to you. You can check her out if you want to." Kiel smiled an evil smile, knowing none of his men had an interest in women, and the thought of checking this one for virginity was repugnant to them.

"No. I guess we can assume she is. As filthy and dirty as she is, I cannot imagine anyone wanting to touch her."

"Right, Doss. She will do just fine for the ritual. The fact that she is so filthy will only enhance the proceedings." Kiel rubbed his hands together as if washing them in fantasy. "We will cleanse her with our sacred rites." Doss felt an involuntary shiver crawl up his back. He had never participated in the ritual before and, frankly, had never expected too. Only Kiel seemed to know what it consisted of and he had told them how it would be conducted. In spite of himself, Doss was somewhat sorry for the tiny maiden, whoever she was.

"There is no time to spare. There is no telling when someone down in the village will become curious as to how we intend to punish her and come snooping around again. You know the young men are still sneaking around out there at night, do you not?"

"I have suspected as much, but what can we do? There is too much open ground out there, and if we put all our men to guard against them there will be no one left to perform the rites."

"It does not matter," Kiel said, a note of satisfaction in his voice. "Let them snoop around. The more wild tales they tell, the less they will be believed. I think my speech the first time was enough to scare them. They may think they are safe, but they will not openly brag about being up here, for fear that Matuga and the elders will punish them. Matuga's incompetence has been our best ally." Again his cruel smile made even his closest associate feel uncomfortable.

Doss was a devoted man. He believed in their cause and their ability to do magic, but even he did not pretend to understand what motivated their leader. Kiel was as much a mystery to him as he was to the People in the village. Doss had witnessed some unusually cruel and perverted people in his life, but nothing to compare to Kiel.

Kiel not only hated females, as did they all, but he went further to show his hatred than was necessary for the cause. When he stopped to think about it, Doss did not know of anyone who could say they liked Kiel. On the other hand, he did not know of anyone for whom Kiel showed any respect or fondness.

Kiel was a strange person. He had founded their organization several summers ago and they had never been popular with the People of their country. Their perverted ways had attracted too much attention. On several occasions, Doss had tried to warn Kiel. He had tried to persuade him to be less obvious, less intimidating, but Kiel had refused to listen.

Their bizarre behavior had been the reason they had come up the trail to Chaco. They had been forcefully evicted from their former home. No magic could save them from the whip that had been used to drive them up the road like dogs.

It was true that the savages had not bothered them. Kiel claimed it was due to his magic. Doss had his reservations about this claim. It seemed more likely that they had been spared because they had traveled only at night when the savages were more inclined to stay in their camps.

"When do you want to hold the ceremony?" he asked at last, feeling that the sooner the better. He was already getting an uncomfortable itch between his shoulder blades, a feeling that in the past had always proved to be a prediction of prevailing disaster.

"Tonight," Kiel answered. He looked toward the sky as if he expected a conformation of this decision from an unknown, unseen God that only he knew about.

"Tonight? It will be more difficult on such short notice. You know that for an action such as this it is better for the men to have a chance to work themselves up to a state of ecstasy."

"They can work themselves up at a moment's notice. Especially the younger ones, and their enthusiasm will be contagious enough to get the few older ones all excited just watching them. Besides, you know that most of the justification and satisfaction comes after the ritual of the virgin, so what is the problem?" Kiel did not brook any interference or questioning, from even his most trusted men.

"It will be as you say, Kiel. But I think it is time to begin looking for a new place to set up. I think we are about to wear out our welcome here. Just as we did the last time." It was a gentle reminder of the unpleasant results of their last ceremony.

"Yes, yes. Of course we will move soon. This is just a temporary stopping place. I have already had a man out scouting for the ideal place, and I think he may have just found it. He was telling me last night about this place far north of here, up against the base of the mountains. From what he told me, it sounds almost perfect for our needs."

"I hope you are right. I grow tired of being driven from one village to another. One day these People may become angry enough to do more than just run us out. I have seen the desire to kill in more than one young man's eye since we came here. The runners from the west are the worst. Have you ever paid any attention to them?" Doss asked, hopeful that Kiel had seen the same message in their eyes as he had.

"Oh, timid man. You are always afraid of shadows. That is why you will never be a leader such as I am. I do not know what you would do if you did not have me to make these decisions for you." Kiel's smile could almost have been considered kindly until Doss looked close enough to see the brittle coldness in his eyes.

"Now go spread the word. Even if the time is short, I am sure they can do all that is necessary to make this a worthy celebration. Tell the men to pound up plenty of clay. I do not want to run short like we did the last time," Kiel told Doss.

"Yes, Kiel. I will tell them."

"I want to be certain. That is what got us in to trouble the last time. If we had had enough clay there would not have been any trouble. Lack of planning and proper preparations is what makes things to go wrong, not accidents or any power of the Gods."

"Yes, Kiel. That is why I wonder at you proceeding with this in such a hurry. Proper preparation is hard to maintain on such short notice," Doss tried to explain, but it was obvious he was frightened of his commander, as were all the men.

"Just see to it. I cannot do everything myself, unfortunately. If I could there would be no limit to what I could accomplish."

From the dark room Mateep could hear the flurry of activity but had no way of knowing what was being done. She pressed her face to the rock slab serving as a door but the narrow crack around one edge gave her a limited view directly in front of the cubical in which she was being held captive.

She could see them cross back and forth frequently, but other than carrying lumps of dry adobe clay, she could not make out anything they might be planning to do. She soon gave up trying and lay down on the bare floor, giving in to the exhaustion that had plagued her. She could not remember a time when she was not tired.

Several times she roused up during the day, hot and thirsty. She called out for water but her cries were either unheard or, she suspected, ignored. The Spirit Watcher beat down relentlessly on her prison, turning it into an oven. She slipped into oblivion and only awoke when the temporary door was pulled open and a rush of cool night air bathed her dirt-encrusted body. Kiel pulled her to her feet and hauled her out into the waiting night.

Stumbling in the darkness she felt herself being pushed and pulled to an open space on the south side of the ruins of the trade building. Here several fires made enough illumination for her to see that the entire band of Kiel's followers surrounded her. They sat about in a great circle. All were silent except for the low humming sound she had remembered when they had taken her from the village.

"What are you going to do with me?" she asked pathetically. "Why will you not take me to Kaoto? Why will you not help me?"

"Oh, we are going to help you. We do not need the Wise One's help to know what needs to be done with someone like you." Kiel's tone was made even more menacing by the dancing flames and the drone of the voices, which never varied in pitch or volume.

Strong hands tore her filthy rags from her. She thought they were going to give her clean clothes but her hopes were short lived. Instead she was pulled into the center of the circle where a large flat piece of sandstone had been placed on several other stones, making a low platform. Her nakedness did not bother her, although she did feel out of place since all the men were dressed in their long robes with cowls up over their heads, making it impossible to see their faces.

"Bind the virgin," Kiel instructed Doss and two other white robed men.

"It shall be done," they answered in unison, their voices sounding hollow, oddly dead and emotionless.

Mateep was placed on the flat stone and forced to sit cross-legged. Her ankles were bound together and the end of the rope was passed under her body and tied to an upright that had been placed at her back. The post had been placed in a hole in the flat stone and extended up to the level of the back of her head. A crosspiece was bound to this to correspond to the height of her shoulders.

A wide band was placed around her waist and another over her breasts. These were drawn painfully tight and secured to the same upright. Her arms were pulled out along the crosspiece, which was curved enough to bring her hands back out in front of her. Her arms and hands were bound securely to this crosspiece. She found she could not move and even breathing was difficult with the wide bands holding her so tightly. When she tried to complain, another band was tied over her mouth and nose. She thought she would suffocate, but they made arrangements for this by slicing holes in the band and placing a large section of hollow reed in her mouth. Thus trussed up she must sit up and look straight ahead. Her first fear had been put to rest. In this position they could not force her to have any sexual relations with them. But her heart still beat furiously in her tightly bound chest. They had said they would punish her and then send her on her way. What did they have in mind?

Kiel approached her. He stalked around her in a peculiar, stiff-legged gait that made her think of a giant bird that had occasionally visited the bathing pool. She realized she had just remembered something from her past. Why now? What else could she remember? She was brought back to the present as Kiel took his polished walking stick and traced curious designs over her body. She had thought he intended to whip her with it, but its touch was as light as a feather. All the time he chanted in a strange tongue. The words were not familiar to her, although she continued to listen, hoping for some clue as to what they had planned for her. When Kiel had made a circle around her, tracing imaginary designs over every exposed portion of her body, he stepped back as if to inspect his artistic work. Apparently satisfied he turned to his lieutenants and spoke a simple command to them that did nothing to relieve Mateep's apprehension.

"Let the ceremony begin."

Doss bowed his head in recognition. Then, turning to face out toward the circle of waiting men, he clapped his hands twice and pointed to a spot directly in front of the bound captive. The low humming sound ceased, leaving an eerie silence in its wake. The men formed a single file and the first approached the spot Doss had indicated.

For the first time, Mateep took notice of the ground surrounding her.

The adobe clay the men had been carrying all day had apparently been brought here and pounded into a fine powder. It had been spread evenly in a circle around her raised platform and formed a thick blanket, which was ringed with a row of stones to hold it in place.

All kinds of terrifying thoughts flashed through Mateep's mind as the man walked up to the designated point just in front of the row of holding stones, but her wildest idea did not prepare her for what happened next. The man carefully raised his robe to above his waist, and while she watched in disgust, the man relieved the entire contents of his bladder full in her face. When he had completed this action, he lowered his robe and took a step backward, and bowing to her, he turned and strode away out of sight behind her.

Mateep felt her senses reel as the reeking urine cascaded down over her body, insulting her sense of smell as well as stinging her eyes. She shuddered inside of her bindings but could not move or do anything to protect herself from the next assault coming from the second man in line, who had now assumed the same position as relinquished by the first man.

Mateep lost count of the line of men. She held her eyes tightly shut, and though she tried to cry out the reed in her mouth made her sounds all come out as a hooting cry, which only seem to stimulate the men more. For what seemed an eternity she endured this shame and degradation. When the last man had finally unburdened himself on her, she cautiously opened her eyes to see if this could possibly be the end of her humiliation. Her hopes rose again as she saw the men assembled once more in a circle around her. This time each man held the strange looking cylindrical piece of pottery in his hands.

Once more Doss indicated the spot directly in front of her. She looked down at the spot and could see the powder had soaked up all the offending urine leaving a dark stain in the flickering light of the fires. Again the first man approached and stood on the designated spot. He held out the pottery cylinder at arm's length and dumped its contents over the top of the bound captive's head.

Mateep had been expecting cool, refreshing water to rinse and cleanse her of the previous flood. Once again, her hopes were shattered as the descending liquid proved to be only more urine, which the men had obviously been saving up all day for this ritual. Jar after jar was emptied over her head, running down her front and back in streams, irritating the skin, especially under the binding straps which held her for this unprecedented treatment.

Time became meaningless to the captive girl. She had tried to imagine what they could do to punish her; now she knew. There could not have been anything more degrading, humiliating, and completely devastating to a person than to have to endure what she had endured here in the moonlight.

Finally it came to an end. What else could they do? She hung limply against her bindings and did not even try to think. Whatever came now, it could not be worse than what she had already endured. She fervently hoped they would end it all by mercifully killing her. Again she was doomed to disappointment.

The lieutenants, with their white robes carefully pulled up from the danger of stains, were stamping the clay and urine into a muddy mixture around the base of the platform where Mateep sat bound to the upright post. She was no longer curious. She no longer cared what they did to her. There was nothing left. There was nothing they could do to her now. She had abandon her body, left it far behind. She found herself standing out in a dark plain looking toward a dim light on the horizon. She thought if she could walk to the light she would find herself and everything would be all right again. She tried to move her feet but they refused to follow her command to move. She strained toward the dim point of light. It was like a dream in which she was half-awake and half-asleep. If she could only wake up, she could move.

She was yanked back to reality when Doss scooped up a double handful of the smooth plaster and flung it with considerable force into her face. This was followed by more from each of the white robed men who stood around her in the mud. As if they were in a hurry to finish, the mud was flung at her and spread to cover her from the flat rock to the crown of her head. As ridiculous as it seemed, her last conscious thought was worrying about the headband and the feather it held. They were going to be ruined by the red mud. The stains would never come out.

Chapter Forty Seven

Kaoto covered every possible route leading back to the shining river. He had even crossed the river and circled wide. When he found no sign of Mateep, he worked his way back to the destroyed village and again began to circle in ever widening sweeps, asking everywhere about the missing girl. He had not stopped to analyze his feelings toward her; he simply told himself he was responsible for her, that she was just another one of the People. She was one he had personally agreed to look after, just as he had Kalo.

Not having any experience with matters of the heart, he did not understand the deep sinking feeling in the pit of his stomach as his search kept turning up blank. No one could remember seeing the strange girl he described. It would seem that such a striking difference in the two colored eyes would have attracted attention among these People, who were all so nearly alike.

In one village he found refugees from the raided village. They recalled Mateep but could not tell him what had become of her. They tried to be helpful, but none of them had any real idea of where she might be. They knew she had left with the old mother, but no one knew where they had planned to go, and no one had seen them since.

As he went from one village to another, he continued to ask but always received the same answer. No one associated the girl he described with the wandering creature who had come and gone at their dumpsite. No one ever looked at the creatures at the dump. Of course, they put out food for them and clothing sometimes, but still they did not see them. To do so would be to recognize them as people. Everyone knew they were non-persons.

He knew he was neglecting his duty by lingering on this personal search, but he could not bring himself to abandon her or accept the fact that she might have fallen into the hands of the savages again. Each time this thought crossed his mind, he would see a red haze and would push himself harder, if that were possible.

Sometime in his hurried pace he lost one of his eagle feathers. The loss meant nothing to him other than to drive home the fact that he was becoming careless, both in his duties and his personal habits. He stopped to take stock of himself and discovered he could not remember when he had last bathed, or cleaned his clothing. Stopping at a small stream, he washed his body and his loincloth. He forced himself to take time to sort out his tangled hair, which was always a problem, but now was in such a state of disarray he seriously considered cutting it off. Ten days had passed and he had to admit that he was no closer to finding Mateep than the first day of his search. He also knew that his chances of finding her now were futile, and each passing day reduced any chances he might have had. He would have to do something different.

The only thing left for him to do was to rely on the runners to spread the word in their travels. They would bring him word if she should be found in some remote village that he had missed. In the meantime he had his own work to perform. There were still the advancing savages to be concerned with. There were more of the People to see. There were more villages to be checked, most of which were outside the perimeter of his search for Mateep. With a heavy heart, he realized his search must become secondary. In each village he visited he still asked about Mateep, and each passing of the sun brought his hopes lower, as no one knew anything about the maiden he sought.

His words were being more readily accepted these days. The same story was coming in quite frequently from the runners and refugees of raided villages. His worst fears were being realized. The dark shadows were closing in on the People and he had not been able to convince enough of them to make the trip south. Like frightened children, they had flocked together in the vain hope of finding protection in numbers. This would have been the right thing to do if they had been warriors, but they were not. They were simple farming people who knew nothing of the science of war.

There was still time. He must get back to his mission. He had to keep trying. With persistent and weary determination, he began to make his swing back and forth across the country. He was working his way gradually back toward the Chaco, where he knew he could receive Paataga's advice and where he could draw on the warm friendship he shared with Torjan.

He could have made it on into the pueblo Bonito even though it was after dark, but he wanted to see Paataga first and did not want to disturb her late at night. He made a hasty camp beside the trail and after a meager meal of dry rations, he dropped off to sleep with only his feathered robe for a cover against the slight chill of the night. Early in the morning, before the Spirit Watcher had made his presence known, Kaoto was running easily down the trail leading to the Chaco. His sleep had been troubled by wild dreams; dreams he could not recall but somehow made him feel he was needed in his old home.

His urgency made him push until he was running at full speed, bringing him to Paataga's doorway in the first light of day. In spite of the early time, Paataga was already up and had stirred the ashes of her fire, finding a few embers to start the morning cook fire without having to use a fire drill.

She had observed Kaoto from far down the road but had continued with her fire preparations and had it burning merrily when he arrived. She placed her cooking pot over the flames and added water and corn meal before she looked up at him.

"I have been expecting you, and none too soon," she snapped at him as if he had been a tardy pupil.

"I have come, old mother, but with nothing but bad tidings," Kaoto exclaimed as he dropped to the ground in his usual place near the fire in front of the log Paataga habitually sat on.

"Tell me all your news, and quickly. Then I shall tell you what I think has been happening here while you were gone." She entered her small room and returned with a parcel of herbs to make a stimulating tea.

Kaoto recounted all that had happened since he had left nearly a turn of the moon ago. He told of his adventures at the river, of finding Mula killed by the savages and his daughters with their sons, his sons, scattered among the crevasses of the black rocks. He told of his rescue of them and Mateep, and of her serious injuries.

"I have placed the other daughters and their sons with the People of the white rock, the sky People. I feel they will be safe there until they have a chance to grow up and get used to living with our People."

Paataga nodded her head but remained silent, sensing there was much more of his story yet to be told.

"The little one, Mateep, insisted she was going to come with me. She said she had been told by you that she was the one to travel at my side." He looked up from the corner of his eye to see what her reaction to this statement would be. Paataga's old wrinkled face remained impassive as she waited for him to go on.

"That is why I left her with an old one who said she could look after her while I settled the others down with the sky People. When I returned to the village, the savages had raided it and destroyed most of the buildings and crops. The villagers had left before the raid. Mateep and the old one had left together, but no one knew where they were going and no one has seen or had any word of them since. I looked everywhere for her but I did not find her," Kaoto ended, giving a long sigh and looking down at the ground in front of him.

"This girl, Mateep, you say she had a head injury which affected her memory?" Paataga asked as she stirred the corn meal to keep it from forming lumps.

"Yes. It did not seem very bad. It was a long wound just above her ear. I cleaned it and closed it as well as I could and it seemed to be healing well. It left a scar, but in time her hair will cover it, and with a headband over it, no one would ever notice it."

"Hmmmm. But she was able to travel, walk around without help when you left her?" Paataga was satisfied with the progress of the meal and had now placed a smaller pot of water near the edge of the fire to heat for tea.

"Yes. Her physical condition was improving rapidly but she just could not seem to remember what had happened to her, or for that matter, even who she was. We had to tell her over and over, every day, what her name was and what had happened to her. Still she could not remember. That is why I am so worried about her. She could not look after herself and could not tell anyone who she was or where she came from. She would be completely helpless without someone to look after her."

Paataga seated herself on the log that was close enough to the fire so she could stir the meal and keep a watch on the tea water without getting up. She studied the fire intently for quite some time before she spoke.

"There was a strange occurrence at the village while you were gone. First I should tell you about your mother. She has left for the next world. This, I am sure, does not come as a surprise to you. She was only passing time, waiting until she could go join your father."

"And I was not here. A son who is so busy with his own personal life that he does not have time for his mother is no son at all."

"Oh, do not be so hard on yourself, son. She knew when you came to study with me that you would never be like other sons. But she was proud of you, and there is nothing you could have done to make her going easier. Besides, she did not die alone."

"I am glad to hear that. Was Torjan with her? By the way, where is Torjan?" Kaoto looked around as if he expected to see the Red One standing there waiting for him.

"No. Torjan was with me that night. It keeps him hopping like a toad on a hot rock to try to look after two old women so far apart. No, it was someone else. A stranger. No one knew who she was or where she came from. She did not seem to know any of the answers to the questions put to her by Torjan the next morning when he found her sitting in your mother's doorway. He accused her of stealing your mother's favorite headband, the one Toolke's wife gave to you for her so long ago. They said she had it on but claimed your mother had given it to her. She also had a single eagle feather in it, draped down over her cheek just as Little Frog used to wear hers."

Kaoto looked up sharply at Paataga as she was speaking. He felt a surge of hope welling up inside of him.

"What did this girl look like?" he asked.

"I did not see her. I only know what Torjan told me. She was small, much like your mother. She was clothed in filthy rags and her hair was a tangled mess. She said Keenwah had told her to put the headband on to keep her hair out of her eyes. This sounds like what your mother would do, and if she had lived through the night she would have probably done much more. Unfortunately, the girl said, your mother died sometime during the night. She did not know just when but she thought it was close to morning."

"What became of this girl? Where is she now? I would like to speak to her. If nothing else I would like to thank her for being with my mother on her last journey." Kaoto said.

"That is the bad part. I do not know just where she might be now. There is much I need to tell you about what has been going on the last summer. Matuga has grown old. He is not the man he used to be. He should have been replaced but there has been no real crisis for him to deal with, so the People have been content to let him hold his position, but it is long past his time."

Paataga started from the beginning with the arrival of Kiel and his followers, of their demands and claims. She tried to explain how Matuga had grasped at the promise of Kiel to protect the village from savage attacks by using his magic. She ended with telling how Matuga had let Kiel and his followers take the girl to be punished and sent on her way.

Kaoto sat silently in deep thought. Could there be any connection between this strange girl who could not tell them who she was or where she came from and his beloved Mateep? It was a long chance, but was it possible that somewhere in Mateep's mind was buried the notion that she should come to Chaco in search of him. Long chance or not he was going to have to find her and see for himself.

"I know what you are thinking, Kaoto, and I too have had the same thought. Yesterday I had the strange feeling that someone was calling for me. I think it was her. I tried to communicate with her, to tell her you were on your way back and you would be able to help her, but I do not know if she heard me. I hope we are not too late."

Kaoto sprang to his feet, making ready to leave. Paataga motioned for him to sit back down and dipped up a bowl of cooked meal and a small mug of tea.

"Eat first. You have not been eating well; I can see it has drained your strength. You will need all your strength and wits if you are going to go up against Kiel. He has the villagers all frightened of him. Can you believe it? He told the young men of the valley that if he caught any of them snooping around their camp he would kill them. Imagine the nerve of the man, if he really is a man, and Matuga backed him. The old fool is so afraid of every shadow that he lets Kiel do anything he wants."

It was obvious that Paataga was not impressed with Kiel or his promise of magic. Neither of them believed in magic. They knew it was only tricks and illusions. Man did not posses the power to perform magic. Only the spirits could do this, and they had to be powerful spirits to do more than control the winds and rain or to bring snow or warmth. No man could control the weather or influence the savages to stay away from here. Kaoto would rather trust the magic of Torjan's mighty arm and sword than the mumbling and jar rubbing of some outlandish horde of intruders who claimed to be magicians.

"Where is Torjan? I want him with me when I go to confront this magician and his fellow mystics. I find it hard to believe that Matuga would stoop so low as to let men like them make their home here and actually side with them against his People."

Kaoto had taken the food and tea and consumed them mechanically. He even went back for another bowl. He had not realized how hungry he was until Paataga had insisted he sit and eat. The herbal tea flowed along his veins, warming him and giving him much needed stamina.

"Torjan said he was going up to the ruins the first thing this morning to see if he could discover what they had done to the girl. He is traveling under a triple load of guilt. First, because he was not there when your mother needed him. Second, because this strange girl had crept in to rob her. And third, as big and tough as he pretends to be, he is as soft as a baby when it comes to people who are little and defenseless. He knows he should not have let Kiel have her, but he was so distraught by your mother's death and his feeling of guilt that he did not put up a fight to protect her. So he is probably over there now, looking around and spoiling for a fight. You should go join him now."

Kaoto agreed heartily with his old mother and dropped down the trail to the valley floor, proceeding up to the ruins of the trade building as the Spirit Watcher spread his first rays of light over the unholy site of last night's debauchery.

Torjan, armed with his terrible sword, his metal knife, and hatchet hanging near his fingertips, stood taking in the same sight the Spirit Watcher had just seen. Naked male bodies were strewn about like the aftermath of a battle, only there was no sign of a fight. The bodies were intertwined in various sexual embraces. Apparently there had been some sort of a celebration last night that had lasted all night long, and only now had they collapsed in exhaustion from their perverted bliss.

Revulsion rippled over Torjan's face as he stood looking at the scene. At the approach of running feet he turned to see his friend coming at a rapid pace.

"What is this?" Kaoto asked, unable to believe what he was seeing.

"I do not know. I just got here myself, and I have not gone any farther." Torjan stood facing his friend. "You have talked to Paataga this morning?" When Kaoto nodded his head, he went on. "Then you know of your mother's death and my miserable failure to look after her as I had promised you."

"You have not failed me or her. There was nothing you could have done for her. Time was running out for her, just as the sand in the jug runs out for the runners. She will be glad to join my father and start a new life in the next world. Besides, I am the last man to judge anyone a failure. Come, let us look around and see what we can find out about this mess and what they might have done to the girl. I have hopes that she is the one I am looking for."

Kaoto told Torjan his story as they walked carefully among the prostrate bodies. They found no trace of the missing girl. Even a search of the abandoned buildings did not turn up any clues, although in one of them, Kaoto thought he could discern the shadow of what might have been a track of a small foot. But it was too indistinct for him to be sure.

Their tour brought them around to the south side of the building, where the Spirit Watcher was bearing down with full force. They saw a strange collection of outlandish figures that had been formed from wet clay. All bore some slight resemblance to animals or birds. Most were old enough to have been dried out by the heat until they were as solid as stone. Some even presumably represented human forms. The latest sculpture was a huge reptilian image. Its grotesque form resembled some sort of a toad-like figure with slightly human features. It was squatted on a base of flat rock and sat with its arms extended out in front of a great rounded belly, which supported two large pendulous breasts. Its face was even more toad-like in that the huge mouth was open, exposing a long dangling tongue that looked more like the male sex organ than a tongue. The eyes were protruding on stems unlike anything either of them had ever seen before.

A cold chill crept up Kaoto's back as he looked at the repulsive creatures depicted in fresh adobe clay. The sun was already starting to dry it into stone-like hardness. As large as it was, it would take quite some time for it to cure out rock hard all the way through.

"No sign of her anywhere. Whatever they were going to do with her, they must have already done," Torjan said. "Kiel told Matuga they would punish her and send her on her way, but which way? Where?" Torjan's face was a picture of torment and anguish.

"Why do we not wake up some of these sleeping masters of magic and see if they cannot conjure up a vision for us that will tell us which way she was sent and in what condition?" There was no humor in Kaoto's voice as he spoke.

"Fine with me. Let me wake up the leader of this pack of fools," Torjan roared as he started looking for Kiel.

He found his victim nestled in the arms of two of his lieutenants. Kiel lay with his mouth open, jaw slack, and his smooth face revealed the first sign of human weakness that Torjan had ever seen. Raising his sword, he brought the flat side down on the exposed posterior of one of the sleeping attendants of the mystic leader.

A howl of pain brought the man out of his stupor and he rolled away from Kiel, screaming, "Why punish me, Kiel? I have not forsaken you." The man sat up and rubbed his eyes. He had only assumed Kiel had struck him with his long stick as he often did. The last thing any of them expected were intruders from the timid valley farmers.

Torjan's sword descended again, this time on the thigh of Kiel, who was just starting to rouse after Doss' screams of pain and indignation.

He sprang to his feet to be confronted by two giants, either of which could have crushed him with one hand. He looked about to see if his followers were going to be of any help, but one look was enough to tell him they were not. Last night's fermented meal, made from fungus growth, had put all of them in a stupor. Even Doss' shouting had not brought them around. His own head was throbbing like a drum and felt just as empty. He tried to focus his eyes on his adversary and in the blur of morning light he made out the faintly familiar face of the Red One. The other man he had not seen before, but he did not have to be told he was the one they called the Wise One.

His bluster slowly returned to him as he recognized Kaoto for who he was. He had heard stories about this man, how kind and compassionate he was. Kiel was sure he had nothing to fear from this man. He was just a large form of the valley farmers who were afraid to fight anyone. He only hoped the Wise One could control the red giant, who was not as disposed to peace as the rest.

He brought his hands up in front of his eyes with fingers extended. He made several mystical gestures, which normally impressed the locals. His eyes began to harden into his infamous stare of expulsion, the stare that his lieutenants could not stand. He filled his lungs in preparation for a great vocal sound that would wake all his men and serve to emphasize his signs.

Before he could complete his magic rites, he was caught off guard by the Wise One. Contrary to his belief, Kaoto was not a mild farmer. His vicious slap across Kiel's face forced arms and hands down. The first was followed by a second and a third. The hail of open-handed slaps rained over his face with such rapidity and force that he was driven to his knees with blood flowing copiously from his nose and mouth. His ears were ringing and burned with the repeated stinging slaps that were delivered to them. Kiel's world had taken a definite twist for the worst.

He remained on his knees, trembling with fear for the first time in many summers. Usually he was in control of the situation and it was someone else who was waiting for his decision. There was no hope of help from any of his band of followers. He had been so sure of himself and the villagers that he had let all of his men participate in last night's ceremony. He had not placed anyone on guard. A bad mistake, he realized now that it was too late.

A quick glance at the adobe figure assured him they had not discovered anything there. Good. He had that much left to bargain with, but it would be the last piece he would use. He would try every other contingency before he revealed the presence of the girl. He would have his revenge one way or another.

Chapter Forty Eight

Seeing Kiel writhing at his feet only infuriated Kaoto more. He pulled back his arm for yet another vicious blow, only to find his wrist caught in an unrelenting grip. There had never been a contest of strength between these two giants before, and now Kaoto knew that Torjan had the greater strength. If Torjan had never known the limits of Kaoto's running ability, then Kaoto had never known the limits of his friend's terrible strength. For a moment he had struggled to free himself from the formidable grip, but it was useless. He was like a child in the hands of this displaced son of Ireland. He relaxed and ceased his struggle.

"No, my friend. This is not the way of the Wise One. This is the way of a savage. I understand how you feel. It is the way I would have handled it before I met you and your People." Torjan's gentle admonishment brought Kaoto back to his senses.

"You are right. I am behaving like a spoiled child and deserve to be treated like one," Kaoto told his friend, but he looked down on Kiel and felt a shudder of revulsion run through his body. He could not believe he had soiled his hands with the likes of this vermin. He realized that in another place and time, he would have been just as Torjan said. A savage. He had already learned to kill and now he had been prepared to beat a man to death with his bare hands. He remembered the words of Mute, down in the land of Moot.

"We have tasted blood and are no longer fit to live with the People. We would not raise children for fear they too might have a taste for blood."

At the time Kaoto had not understood what Mute had meant, but now he was beginning to see. Once you have killed another human, the death of the next was not so hard, and after a while it was less than killing an animal. He had looked forward to beating Kiel into a senseless pulp. He had felt a fierce joy in the sting in his hands as they came in contact with Kiel's smooth, beardless face. He dropped his hands and stepped back from the bloodied man at his feet.

"That is better. After all, this is my kind of job," Torjan grinned at him. He never failed to amaze Kaoto. When he tried to compare the vicious, blood-thirsty, red bearded giant he had seen fighting in the north mountains with this overgrown boy who joked and laughed with him and the People now, there was no comparison. The children had started the transformation but his old mother, Paataga, had completed it. He did not doubt that Torjan could and would still put up a terrible fight but now he weighed the reasons for the fight first and then decided whether it was worth it or not.

The Red One reached down and pulled Kiel to his feet. Holding him with one hand, he made a ceremony of dusting him off with the other, turning him around to inspect his body for damage. It seemed that his face was the only thing to receive any serious damage, but that had been considerable.

Kiel's cheeks were bruised and turning a dark purple. Both ears were swelling and were glowing crimson red. One had been nearly torn from his head and blood flowed down the side of his face in a stream. His nose, already large, was puffed up until it had a comic look about it, and while it had stopped bleeding it, was still dark red in color. His mouth hung slackly and his lips were battered and torn. The lower lip, badly swollen, gave him the look of a pouting child.

"I have to apologize for my friend," Torjan said as gently as his deep gruff voice would allow. "He has never been used to bad boys like you and your little band of merry makers."

Kiel eyed the giant through swollen eyes. He did not know which one he was more afraid of. He had felt the fury of Kaoto's wrath but he had also seen how Torjan had stopped the Wise One's swings with the use of only one hand. Even now he could feel the latent strength in the hand that held him by the scruff of the neck. He did not doubt that Torjan could break his neck with as little effort as he would break a piece of firewood.

"Now, why do you not just tell us what you did with that little girl you took away from me? My friend here is interested in her. He is afraid you might have hurt her. You did not do that, did you?" Although his tone was kind and friendly, Kiel did not for one instant doubt the deadly seriousness of the man's intention.

"She is gone," Kiel mumbled through his battered lips.

"Gone? Gone where?" Torjan gently shook Kiel as if to prompt his memory.

"I do not know where. We brought her here and punished her, just as I told Matuga we would do. Then we sent her on her way. I would presume she has enough sense not to come back to this village and try to rob the dead again." Kiel held his voice down to meek subservience. He wanted them to believe him. He did not want to taste any more of the Wise One's persuasion and he did not want them to ever suspect what had really happened to the maiden.

"Just like that, she is gone? No one saw her go? No one knows which way she went? My, you must really posses magic to make this happen." While his voice remained calm, the hand on the back of Kiel's neck had gradually tightened until he could feel his skin stretch to near breaking, and the fingers thrust deep into his neck were causing numbness to spread down his arms as nerves there were being crushed.

"She went that way." Kiel pointed clumsily with his numb arm toward a rock point in the south. "She said she was going back home. She said she would never come this way again and hoped no one would follow her to tell of her shame."

Under different circumstances this might have been a perfect story, but Kaoto did not believe it. If this had indeed been Mateep, she would not have known which way her home was. And if she had known where her home was, she would have known she could never return there. No. All of this rang false to him.

"I think maybe Kiel needs more time to think. I believe his mind is muddled from too much celebration last night. Why do we not wake up some of his friends and see if they can remember any more than he does?"

"No. Do not wake them. They cannot tell you anything." Kiel registered real distress at the prospect of his men being questioned by these two giants. It was not that he cared for their safety, but he did not think they could hold out against such threats and he feared they would tell the truth. And he did not want his followers to see him in the giant's power.

"Look, I will take you out the way she went. I will show you the direction she took. If you hurry, you could probably catch her. She was not going very fast. I would not be surprised if she did not hole up somewhere down in one of the side canyons. She might be hard to find if she really wants to stay hidden, and I think she does. She was very shamed by being caught like that by Torjan. She seemed really frightened by him and begged us not to send her back to him. I think she just wants to be left alone for a while until things cool down." This was pure inspiration and he was satisfied to see Torjan flinch at his words.

Kiel's rapid speech had an effect. What he was saying was probably partially true. Mateep would be shamed if she had been accused of stealing and she might well want to hide. The trouble with this was that she was in no condition to make such a decision, and she definitely was in no shape to look after herself. She could become lost in those canyons and die of thirst and hunger before she could be found.

"What do you think?" Torjan asked Kaoto, who was looking off in the southeasterly direction Kiel had pointed. Was he telling the truth? That was the general direction of Mateep's former home. Had she gone that way, or had Kiel just made a lucky guess?

"I do not know what to think. I only know we must find her, and soon. I have lost her once and I do not want to lose her again." Turning to Kiel, he told the trembling man, "If you have lied to us, I will come back and twist off your head like a woman dressing a rabbit."

Kiel shuddered with fear as he contemplated his death. He did not doubt that they could do just what they said, and after the rage of the Wise One, he did not doubt that he would enjoy doing it.

"No lie. I am telling you the truth. See that place in the rim of the canyon down there? That is the spot she headed for." The path Kiel marked out was the main road leading south. Its hard-packed surface would leave no tracks for them to follow. They would just have to go along it and hope they could find any place where she might have turned off.

"We will go look for her." Torjan gave him one last shake before he released his prisoner. Kiel slumped to the ground. He looked about to see if any of his men had witnessed his shame. They were all blissfully still asleep; even Doss had gone back into oblivion after Torjan had so rudely awakened him earlier. Not one of his men had seen what had happened to him. He would have to make up some convincing story to account for his bruised and swollen face.

They were naive. They would believe almost anything he told them. Maybe he had wrestled with a demon spirit during the night. Yes. He had made the supreme sacrifice of fighting this spirit to protect them from its terrible power. This would not be a complete fabrication. Could anyone who had seen these two giants have doubted that they were demon spirits? And he had struggled with them, to save his men. Of course, he had used his wits and his mind, not his muscle, but the end results were the same.

"I do not ever want to see you or your followers around here again." Kaoto delivered this ultimatum before he turned his back on Kiel and started off in the direction indicated by the fallen mystic. He paused beside the grotesque statue and looked back at Kiel.

"I suggest you use your magic and fly away from here, and take this abomination with you."

As he let his eyes drift over the clay figure, he was once more revolted by the grotesque figure. When he returned he would have Torjan help him destroy these offending pieces of artwork. Looking about, he thought it would be easy to tip them over and roll them over to the edge of the cliff, where they would shatter beyond recognition at the base of the sandstone prominence.

His eye was caught by a tiny fleck of white standing out against the red of the drying clay. Reaching out, he brushed his finger against this one piece of white. To his surprise the white fleck turned out to be a piece of feather. It must have gotten mixed up in their clay and they had not bothered to take it out. It seemed oddly out of place against the background of the red clay.

"Are you coming with me?" Kaoto called back to Torjan, who stood surveying the scattered figures about him.

"Yes. I might as well. If I stay here, I might get in more trouble. Besides, we have not had a chance to talk since you came back and I have a feeling this may be a long trip." Torjan turned his back on Kiel and strode after Kaoto's rapidly retreating figure.

"Hold up a little, friend. You know I cannot keep up with you when you take a notion to run, and if I am going to travel by myself then there is no reason for both of us going."

Kaoto slowed his pace until Torjan caught up with him and then set the pace at an easy run that he knew Torjan could match.

"Do you believe him?" he asked of Torjan as they ran.

"I do not know. Why would he lie? What would he have to gain? That is something you have to keep in mind all the time when you are dealing with trash like him. They always have something to gain out of every move they make. Sure, he was scared to death, after the way you were beating him senseless, and he would say anything to get you to stop. He also knew that I did not have any love for him either. So he would want to get us both off his back. But why would he lie to us about where she was going? If we do not find her, he knows we will be back and I might not be able to stop you the next time. You might hurt him if you got real mad. So I guess this time what he had to gain was his freedom from us. So maybe he is telling the truth."

Torjan looked back once to see Kiel frantically running from man to man, trying to wake them. He was screaming and beating at them with his walking stick. Slowly they began to respond to his demands and stood shakily to their feet and listened to his tale of a battle with spirits, while they had peacefully slept and left him alone to defend them. He had made sure that Torjan and Kaoto were well out of hearing before he started this story. It was hard enough to make them believe it without those two still around.

"I have won a vision from the spirits in this battle. Even though the spirit marked me, I still won, and the spirit had to forfeit to me one demand. I asked that I might see the intended land. The place where we will make our permanent home."

He paused to let this sink in. Kiel was a natural performer and knew how to get the desired effects. He knew when to perform to satisfy, as he had with the giants, and when to elucidate, as he did now with his men.

"And where is this promised land?" Doss asked, rubbing his bruised hind side, wondering how it came to have such a big, wide red welt. This was not caused by Kiel's stick. Maybe he had been engaged in combat with the spirits too, although he could not remember, but it would have been nice if he had been the only one to help Kiel in this deadly fight.

"It is the place I told you about yesterday. It is the place that one of our men has scouted out." He turned and pointed north toward the distant mountains. Swinging a little to the east, his walking stick stretched out like a magic wand and quivered as if being pulled by some invisible force until it pointed directly in the direction Kiel wanted to go.

"In my vision I saw mountains, but they were too high for what I wanted, and then I saw this smaller mountain sitting out from the rest of the mountains. I knew the instant it was revealed to me that it was the place I have dreamed of and searched for all these summers. On the top of this mountain was a long narrow ridge that would be ideal for a pueblo. It would be easy to keep snooping villagers away. They could not come up the side of the mountain without making noise and we could see them coming from a great distance. The place looked almost perfect but it lacked one thing." Kiel stopped and looked around like a teacher, waiting to see if any of his pupils could fill in the gap.

"What does it lack?" Doss asked obediently. He was used to Kiel's habits and knew what he wanted.

"Did lack. It lacks nothing now," Kiel said with a certain smugness.

"The top of the ridge was bare. It needed something to mark it so all men would know it was ours and they should not trespass on it." Once more he paused for effect, making sure that every man was listening, every man but the one who had scouted out the area and brought back his report to Kiel. He had carefully described the place and just a short time ago this man had mysteriously died in his sleep. No one had noticed yet. No one except Kiel, and it was to his advantage.

"Since I defeated the spirit, it had to grant me whatever I asked of if. So I told this spirit I wanted our mountain marked in a special way. I told him I want a tall growth of rock to point to the stars, and while he was at it he could make the rock look like our manhood. Of course rocks are hard and the spirit was in a hurry, but he did a fair job of making what I asked for. It will be easy to recognize from far away. All you have to do is look for the hardened member thrust up into the sky, with the seed pods nestled at its base just as they should be."

He could see they were impressed. He had led them before and he would lead them again, but they must hurry. He did not know how long they would have before Torjan and Kaoto discovered they were following a blind trail. He did not know to what length they would go to follow them, but he did not intend to wait around to find out. He would break his men up into small groups and they would dress as the local People. They would travel in small groups and on different paths, all of which would eventually lead them to the rock he had told them about. As for himself, he would travel alone and fast. He would be invisible until they reached the mountain and until he was sure he was not being pursued. Quickly the men gathered their few belongings and made ready to depart. Kiel looked at the wand-like sticks they all carried and the special cylindrical jars. They were a dead give away to anyone who would see them and they could not all pass unobserved through the land. He must make another decision, and quickly.

"Leave your wands and jars here." He heard the mutter of protest from the men and knew he had to allay their suspicions before they openly revolted on him.

"They are no longer necessary. Besides, we must change our image. You will not wear your dark robes, as we will not wear our white ones, until we get to where we are going. You will make a pack of your robes and headbands. You will smear your hair with mud to make it lie down and appear lighter in color. We will leave our staffs and jars sitting here in a big circle. It will make them think we used them to disappear, because they will never see us again."

"What of the figure?" Doss asked, pointing to the drying clay figure squatted on the flat rock.

Kiel's face broke into a smile that was made even more evil by its disfigurement.

"We will leave it as a memento for the Wise One. It will bake to such hardness in the next few days that they will never be able to break it up. It will be a constant reminder to them that they were once graced with the presence of greatness."

Doss pushed the men for a hurried departure without more talk or argument. The sooner he was off this plateau, the better he would like it. In the hustle of leaving he had failed to note Kiel's disappearance. One moment he was walking among them, urging them to hurry. The next he was gone, vanished from the face of the earth. Where could he have gone? There was wide-open space in all directions but no one had seen him cross this space. Sometimes Doss had his doubts about Kiel, and then other times he was sure that the man could perform magic just as he claimed. What else but magic could explain his quick disappearance?

There was no mystery to Kiel's feat. He had simply slipped around the side of the ruined building and ran without looking back until he was over the side of the rim and out of sight. He intended to become invisible, and he had. If they did not know where he was, they could not be forced to tell anything even if the giants decided to beat them as they had him.

He would circle wide in a direction far away from the path his men would be following. He would raid some village to replace the clothing he had left behind. Food and water were no problem. He could pick up what he needed as he traveled. He already had a plan for this. He prided himself on being prepared. In a small, secluded niche in the rocks was a cache he had put there days ago. In fact, as soon as the Wise One had returned, he knew their days were numbered and had started making plans for their departure. Of course he had not foreseen such a violent reaction to their punishment of the girl. What would have it been like if they had known the truth about what they had done to her?

In the niche was a water skin, a packet of dried meat, a simple loin cloth, and a pair of sandals such as those worn by the local People. These had been easy to come by, but one item he had had to make for himself and it had been harder to do. It had to look old. It could not look new. He was proud of his efforts as he took the palm-sized piece of buffalo skin from its oiled skin covering and hung the prized runner's emblem around his sore and swollen neck. He could pass as a runner from some out flung area that was little known. He knew the customs of the runners and how they could demand food and water of anyone at anytime. He would travel as a runner and not suffer from want. He could explain his battered face by saying he had suffered a bad fall.

From a vantage point he watched his faithful followers disband and take off in different directions in groups of two or three. He was sure they would pass without comment. Everyone was used to seeing them in their dark robes and walking in single file. Now, from a distance, they did not look so much different than any other group of travelers. There were many strangers on the trail now, what with the raids of the savages getting closer every day. They would pass unnoticed, of this he was sure.

He chuckled without mirth as he complimented himself on his superior intelligence. They called Kaoto a Wise One, but the Wise One had been easily fooled by a superior intelligence such as he, Kiel, possessed. He slipped down the side of the cliff to the trail below where he would assume his new identity as a runner, and no one would ever see Kiel the mystic again until he was ready.

Far to the south, two tall men had stopped to inspect the trail. Here in a section of low land, where the trail crossed a sandy wash, they stooped and inspected the sand closely, looking for the tracks of a tiny maiden.

All they found were various animal tracks, numerous distinct tracks of lizards, but no human had crossed this section of loose sand for many days.

Puzzled, Kaoto studied the surrounding countryside. Where could she have gone? He and Torjan had watched both sides of the trail, looking for any sign, no matter how small, that she might have left the trail. They had seen nothing. They would return and watch even more closely, but he had a feeling they would not find anything. Deep down in the pit of his stomach the sinking feeling of failure was starting to grow again. Once more he had arrived too late to help the one person he wanted most to help.

Torjan was strangely silent. He was suffering his own brand of guilt. If he had stayed with Keenwah this would never have happened. If he had not let Kiel have the frightened little maiden, she would have been safe when Kaoto had come looking for her. He had no comfort to give to his friend. He had no comfort to give himself.

It was near to the middle of the day when they turned back and started to search the ground on both sides of the trail for tracks they both secretly knew they would never find. Still, they walked slowly, checking every possible sign, looking diligently wherever there were hard places, places where a track could be hidden. They would search far out on the off chance the maiden had made some attempt to hide her tracks.

It was slow work and the Spirit Watcher beat down on them relent-lessly, making the sweat pour from their bodies in little rivulets, streaking the dust on their torsos.

"We are wasting our time here," Kaoto finally spoke.

"I fear you are right but I keep hoping we are both wrong." Torjan responded, even as he continued to search.

"I am going back to get Kiel, and this time I will not stop until he has given us the complete truth." Kaoto started back up the trail at a brisk trot with Torjan at his side.

Chapter Forty Nine

Torjan walked around the ring of cylindrical jars. Each had been placed in position with care and all of the polished wooden sticks were inserted into each jar in such a way that the ends leaned toward the center of the circle. They created a mystical array, just as they were intended to do; however, they had no effect on him. The young men who had managed to get close enough to witness the strange proceedings taking place on top of the mesa had reported that Kiel's men had used the jars in their rituals. With the jars in front of them and clamped between their bare feet, they had placed the large end of their wands down in the jars and rubbed the lip of the jars while they intoned their mystical incantations. The friction between the two created an accompaniment that blended well with their own voices.

Torjan picked up one of the cylindrical jars and the stick protruding from it. He held it in his hands and puzzled over how anyone could possibly believe they possessed magical forces. They were, after all, only ordinary crockery and the stick was nothing more than wood. He tapped the stick in the bottom of the jars as he stood thinking. After several sharp raps the bottom of the jar cracked and he pushed the stick through the bottom and let it fall to the ground. He dropped the jar beside it and went on.

It seemed odd that they would leave such unique equipment behind. Surely they did not intend to return. All indications pointed to a hurried leave taking. All their other possessions had been cleared out and taken with them, but the mysterious jars and wands sat in this stark circle as if they were some sort of a message.

Kaoto stood looking at the statues. His attention was drawn to the fresh one they apparently had made last night. The long day in the burning sun had dried its outer shell, although there were still dark spots showing where the moisture still had not been drawn out.

"What do you think this is supposed to represent? I know you have never been impressed with my art work, but this is ridiculous." Kaoto reached out and touched the piece of exposed feather again. Looking closely he decided it was the tip of an eagle feather.

"They do not even recognize the value of this feather or they would not have buried it in this mess." He turned away from the disgusting figurine, only glancing at the others before he started to search the surrounding area for a hint as to where Kiel had gone.

"I guess we must have made a believer of him this morning. You told him you did not want to see them around here anymore, and apparently they took you at your word, because they are most surely gone. All except this one. He must have died of fright." Torjan still studied the circle as he stood by the man who had died so mysteriously during the night.

"Well, I meant it but I did not think they would leave this quickly Makes me even more suspicious of Kiel. He knew we would be back after we found out he was lying and he did not want to be around for any more questions. Not that I blame him." Kaoto started walking around the circle of jars, searching the ground for signs of their passage. As the circle widened he became convinced they had broken up their customary single file column and had left in small groups.

"They have split up," he told Torjan. "See, a few went this way, a few left off that direction. It seems like they are using our trick to confuse any effort to follow them. I care not where they went, I just wish I knew which tracks belong to Kiel."

"I am willing to bet that his tracks will not be mingled with any of the others. He is the type who looks after himself first. Wherever he went, he went alone. Find a single set of tracks and they will be his," Torjan said.

"I found a drop of blood over here and it looks like one man had been running straight across the top toward the cliff over there."

"That would most likely be his," Torjan stated as he went on with his own search.

Kaoto bent nearly double as he walked along beside a set of tracks. The way the toes and fore foot had been dug in told him the man had taken off in a sprint. He followed the tracks to the edge of the cliff, where he dropped down to a small ledge. Here he found a few more drops of blood and a small skin packet. It was empty, but the inside of it had been oiled and it was new. There was nothing else of interest here so Kaoto climbed down the cliff to the trail below. Here he found where someone had come out of the brush and stepped out onto the trail. The tracks were those of new sandals. The impression they left in the fresh dust was too perfect to have been made by older sandals. The tracks turned to the east and after a short stint, Kaoto decided the man making them was not trying to hide his tracks but he was pushing at a hard pace. He had no doubt as to who had made them. He was tempted to follow them but knew they were made this morning and whoever made them would have a considerable lead on him.

Torjan had followed to the edge of the cliff but had not climbed down. He stood watching Kaoto, waiting to see what he planned to do. He called down to his friend.

"Well? What do you think?"

"I think you were right. Kiel slipped away from his followers and ran away as fast as he could. Too bad we did not break his leg. It worked on you, so I guess it would have worked on him." Kaoto stood in the middle of the trail, pointing in the direction of the receding tracks.

"What are you going to do? Go after him or go back to the village and start all over?"

"I think it would be a waste of time for me to try to catch him now. I will send out word with the runners to be on the lookout for him and to let me know where he is going. But for now I guess I will go back and ask some questions.

Someone had to see them. Maybe I can get a lead on them that way."

"What do you want me to do?" Torjan called down to him.

"Why not stay there and look around some more? We might have missed something. I will send up some young men to gather up their toys and bring them back down. It might serve as a lesson in the future for all to remember. They can see for themselves there is no magic in the sticks and jars."

Torjan started to turn back, but then he thought of something else. "What about these statues? What do you want me to do with them? Leave them so the People can see how foolish they were, or do you want me to smash them?"

"We will dump them over the cliff later, but for now I think you have a good idea. Let everyone come up and look at them so they can see just what was going to protect them from the savages."

Torjan turned and started back to the site of the ritual as Kaoto circled around the cliff and went back to the Pueblo Bonito.

By evening, everyone in the surrounding communities had made the pilgrimage to the ruins to see for themselves the clay idols and the circle of jars. They had to admit it was not a very impressive show for all the tribute they had been forced to give to Kiel and his followers.

Matuga walked around, shamefaced. He tried repeatedly to apologize to Kaoto.

"All right, so I was wrong. A man can make a mistake, can he not? I was only doing everything I could to insure the safety of the People. You were not here. We did not know where you were or when you would be back." His tone held an accusation in it.

"I know, Matuga, and I do not hold you at fault. We all make mistakes. I of all the People can attest to that. Let us forget about it now and make new plans for the safety of our People." He laid one hand on the old man's shoulder and led him back toward the trail descending to the pueblo. He did not want to witness the old man's shame. The last thing he felt he could do now was to find fault with others for their shortcomings when he was so overcome with his own feelings of failure.

"Go home, Matuga. Leave this to Torjan and I. Tomorrow we will talk and it will be like old times." Matuga nodded his head in gratitude as he walked stiffly down the trail, refusing help from anyone as he descended. Tomorrow he would appoint a successor to take his place until the People could find another man to be their ruler. His time was over. Why had he held on so long? He was so tired. It would be a welcome relief to let some young man take over and he would sit back and rest. Besides, he would not have to face Paataga anymore. He could avoid her now without feeling guilty.

The jars and wands had all been picked up and carried down the face of the cliff to be put on display in the courtyard. Later they would be stored away in a vacant room of the pueblo. All that was left to remind them of Kiel were the clay figures. The most prominent was the fresh one that squatted on the flat rock. It had a high odor and it had not taken much to decide what had moistened the clay.

"These people were in worse shape than I thought. What kind of people would play in their own waste? The smell alone is enough to drive most sane people away from it." Torjan stood surveying the figure. It did not disturb him as much as it did Kaoto. Torjan had been used to seeing strange Gods depicted on the figureheads of the Viking ships and carved into their shields. So the looks of this clay figure did not offend him as it did Kaoto, but the smell did. He pulled his sword and advanced on the figure.

"I think if we cut off these arms the rest will roll easily enough and like you said, with the center still wet, it will smash to pieces if we drop it over the edge of the cliff." He stepped in close and prepared to hack of the offending arms.

"I do not think I would use my sword on it. You never know what they might have inside. They probably filled it with rocks to make up the bulk of the figure, so it would not take so much clay. Even their bladders can only produce so much," Kaoto cautioned him.

"You are probably right, but I hate to touch it with my hands." Torjan put his sword away and pulled out his small hatchet instead.

Kaoto had also stepped close and once again was inspecting the feather. It bothered him that they should be so careless with such a valuable item.

"I wonder what else they have mixed up in this mess?" He brought up the iron knife Torjan had made for him. Trying to follow the line of the feather with the point of it he delicately carved away a portion of the figure's head. He did not know why. He would never claim the feather after what it had been through. But he was curious as to why a feather would be used in the first place, and secondly, why in this particular place. It was roughly in the same place that one of Matuga's adopted children would wear it. Could there be significance to this fact? He had uncovered about half the length of the feather and tried to pull the rest of it free. It seemed to be stuck or fastened to something inside. He continued to dig.

The point of his knife hit something hard. He scraped the mud away and a slight tint of blue showed. This was no ordinary stone. It looked like turquoise. He increased the size of the hole and continued to scrape away at the stone. He discovered it was fastened to a piece of leather. More investigation proved it to be a headband.

Kaoto felt a strange tinkling sensation in the pit of his stomach. In nervous haste he cleaned more of the area. He thought he recognized the headband as the one he had given his mother.

"Torjan, did you not say this girl had my mother's head band on when you found her?"

"Yes she did. She claimed your mother gave it to her but I did not believe her."

"What happened to it? Did you take it, or did she still have it on when Kiel took her?"

"I do not remember. I guess she must have still had it on. I know I did not take it from her and I do not remember if anyone else did. Why? Did you want it back? I should have taken it but I just was not thinking right."

"No. I was not thinking about that, but if she was still wearing it I think I have just found it." His voice was rising with excitement." And did you not say she had a feather hanging down from it?"

"Yes. She said she had found it on the trail. For someone who had no memory she seemed to have a ready answer for the head band and the feather." Torjan had leaned over to see what Kaoto was so excited about.

"I have found them both. But what are they doing buried in this statue?" Kaoto and Torjan were hit with the same idea at once and began to tear at the face of the statue. They used their bare hands, no longer concerned with touching the disgusting mixture.

A couple moments confirmed their fear. Kiel had used something to fill the center of the statue. He had used the maiden.

It was impossible to identify her because of the consistency of the mud. It clung to her tenaciously, but careful scraping revealed the bindings. First the tube was removed from her mouth. Kaoto held his ear close to her open lips and could feel the faint moist breath.

"She is still alive," he said as he began to tear at the offending clay with wild abandon.

"Easy. Easy. Do not hurt her any more," Torjan cautioned, but he too was removing the clay as fast as hand and knife would permit.

It took only a short time to uncover the maiden and slash her bonds. She slumped limply forward and made no sound or movement when her last restraint was cut from her.

When Kaoto started to pick her up, Torjan pushed him aside and clasped the tiny, muddy figure in his arms. Before Kaoto could offer protest, Torjan told him, "You run faster than I do. Go find Paataga. Bring her and all the clean clothing you need. I will meet you down at the irrigation pond at the foot of the cliff. Go. Hurry, we do not have all day." He shoved the stunned wise man ahead of him as he started toward the steps leading down the cliff.

Kaoto quickly regained his senses and knew Torjan spoke the truth. He dashed off at a reckless speed, remembering how once before he had come down into the valley with the same reckless speed. His feelings were much different today, but his speed was increased by his concern.

By chance or by intent, he never knew for sure, Paataga was in the courtyard of the Pueblo Bonito when he got there. He called to some women who were close by and asked for clean cloth and blankets. Holding Paataga by the arm, he escorted her to the pond designated by Torjan, to find the Red One had already arrived and was in the process of submerging the maiden in the tepid waters, which had been warmed by the afternoon sun.

With such gentleness as seemed impossible from one of his size, Torjan was soaking and washing the foul smelling clay from her face and neck. As he pulled the old headband from her, it revealed an angry red scar extending from above her ear back through her hair to the back of her head.

"Mateep!" Kaoto cried. There could be no doubt as who this little maiden was now. There could be only one with such a scar. A weakness, almost giddiness, swept over the Wise One and he settled down in the water at the edge of the pond.

At first only weakly, then with more strength, Mateep began to struggle in Torjan's arms. He held her loosely so she would not slip beneath the water. Crooning softly to her, he carefully cleared the mud from her face and eyes, trying to keep as much as possible out of her mouth. Her eyelids fluttered open and she looked up into his great, red bearded, face. She put her arms against his chest and tried to push herself away from him.

"Easy, little one. I will not hurt you. Never again. I swear by the beard of Thor."

At the sound of Torjan's voice, Kaoto snapped back to life. He pushed himself across to Torjan and took the frightened girl in his own arms and spoke her name softly.

"Mateep. It's all right, Mateep. You are safe now." He looked to Paataga for assistance. The old mother had dropped her shawl and waded into the water beside him. She held the girl's face in her hands so Mateep had to look directly at her.

"You know me. We have talked before." Paataga spoke to Mateep, blocking out all the rest of the world.

"You are safe now. You will be coming to live with me for a while until you are strong again. No one will harm you. No one will take you away from me." As she spoke, she continued to wash the little body until most of the offensive mixture was gone.

"Bring her to my place," she told Kaoto. "We can always finish cleaning up later. Right now she needs warmth and something inside her. I just happen to have a rich broth made up that should do her some good."

Kaoto rose from the water, the dripping girl held tightly to his chest. She had stopped fighting. Paataga's soothing voice had seemed to calm her more than Kaoto had.

Torjan rinsed himself and followed far behind them. He intended to stay out of Mateep's sigh, at least until she had a chance to collect herself. Later he would offer his apology. He only hoped she would accept it. He could not blame her if she did not.

The curious crowd parted before Paataga's waving stick. They had learned long ago that she did not care who she struck. And while her blows were not hard enough to cause serious damage, no one wanted to stand in her way.

The strange procession made its way across the valley floor and up the steep slope leading to Paataga's home. Paataga was in the lead, with Kaoto directly behind her, carrying the strange girl who had broke into Keenwah's room and stolen her head band. Behind them came Torjan, bringing up the rear and making sure no one got too close. This was an unnecessary precaution. No one followed Paataga. No one went to her home unless there was a dire necessity. Paataga's privacy was honored by all.

Later investigation revealed that all the clay figures had been built around the remains of birds, animals, and even the unfortunates who had been turned over to Kiel for his protection. Of course none were still alive. The rage at Kiel and his band was of such magnitude that it was well none of them were around to be found.

Far to the east, Kiel ran lightly down the trail. He had not seen anyone all day. This seemed strange; there had been people on the trail all the time recently, and runners were being kept busy constantly. Kiel had gone over his story several times until he had what he believed would be a reasonable explanation for himself and his condition, but he had no occasion to use it.

He paused on the top of a slope that led down to a wide valley. He was not familiar with this country, but he believed this valley led to the north and in the general direction of the rocky ridge he wanted to reach.

He ran easily down to the valley floor and crossed to the streambed in hopes of finding water there. His water skin had been dry for too long already. He needed fresh water. Food was no problem. He was used to fasting before big events so his stomach did not complain, but his throat was dry and parched.

The stream had dried up but there were several stagnate pools of water. He could not be choosy. There was a long crack in the stone floor of the stream and the water there appeared to be the cleanest and probably the coolest he would find. He dropped down to his stomach and stretched out on the rock bottom. The crack was just wide enough for him to put his face in and get his dry lips down to the waters below. He could have filled his skin first and drank from it, but the water looked too inviting to resist.

He took one long swallow and had just pulled in the second mouthful when he thought he heard a noise. As he started to raise his face out of the crack, he felt a foot stomping down on the back of his neck, forcing his head back into the water. He struggled, but his awkward position made him helpless. He felt rough hands pull his arms and bind them behind his back. His lungs were nearly bursting before he was hauled unceremoniously out of the crack and thrown on his back beside the opening.

He looked up into the face of six strange creatures he knew must be the savages who so frightened the villagers. Their eyes were dark and hostile. They showed no respect for his magic. He tried to sit up but was kicked violently back flat on his back, and a spear point held him there.

There was much shouting and gesturing between the six men. It seemed they had a difference of opinion as to what the fate of the magician should be. They made signs of cutting the throat and slashing his body. This appalled Kiel. He had always been proud of his body. It was perfectly formed and he bore no scars to disfigure it as so many men did. His men had feared him but they had loved his body and had begged for a chance to caress it. Now these men threatened to mar this perfect body. His face carried scars but nothing had touched his beautiful body.

He tried to scream his protest but received a sound knock on the side of his head with a stone hammer that sent sparks flying above his face. He decided to remain quiet until he knew what their plans for him were.

After considerable discussion they reached some sort of an agreement. To Kiel's relief they apparently did not have anything planned for him right at this moment. They were going to hold him prisoner while they made up their minds. Good. He could use the time. They were spreading him out on a sandy section of ground where they could drive stakes easily. The cords that held him were tight and caused great pain, but he could endure this.

It did not register at first that the cords that bound him were wet. They were soaked rawhide. Slowly it all became apparent to Kiel. The rawhide was stretched to its limit when they tied him. Now it would begin to dry, and as it dried, the cords would become shorter as they shrank. In order for them to become shorter, his arms and legs would be slowly pulled from their sockets and they would never return. If this were not enough, he felt the stinging bite of the first red ant to find a tender spot between his buttocks. The first was followed by many more and a burning sensation was rapidly spreading over his entire body. While his face was nearly numb from the beating he had received this morning, he could still feel the crawling insects as they invaded his nose and began to crawl around his eyes.

In the shade of a willow tree the six savages sat and watched their victim struggle in his hopeless position. He promised to be good entertainment to them. He was healthy and strong; he would last a long time. The ants would stop tonight because it would be dark soon. The savages would soak the cords of rawhide tonight so they would not pull anymore. But in the morning, the sun would strike the cords again and the ants would return. It promised to be a good show. The six men debated the advisability of sending someone to the main camp so the rest could come up and join them in the fun. Maybe before the ants ate all of him, they would cut off a few choice pieces for the ritual feast.

Chapter Fifty

Paataga settled Mateep on her own sleeping mat just inside her doorway. Dipping a little broth from the steaming pot over her fire, she brought it to the girl and forced her to swallow a few spoons full. She wrapped her in blankets and placed a heavy robe over her to insure she would be warm.

"Torjan, take Kaoto with you and gather me fresh boughs to make a bed for her. As soon as I get her warm and comfortable, I will want to put her outside where she can get fresh air. I have a feeling she will be more comfortable out there than she will in my house. We can spread a shelter over her, with sides that can be rolled up or down, according to the weather."

Kaoto was reluctant to leave Mateep's side, but Paataga responded much as the old mother where he had left Mateep before.

"Get out. She has managed to live this long without you hanging over her all the time. She will manage a while longer." When Kaoto still did not move, she scolded him more.

"What? You do not trust me? What can you do for her? Nothing. That is what you can do. You can sit there like a moon-struck lover, but can you nurse her back to life? No, you cannot. So get out of my way and let me do what I can."

Kaoto realized Paataga was right, as always, but he hated to leave Mateep. Every time he did, something terrible happened to her. He wanted to stay by her side and make sure she was never bothered again. Rational thinking precluded this action. He knew that Mateep would receive the best possible treatment at the hands of his old great mother. It was also true that he did not know what to do. He followed Torjan up the trail to the top of the canyon wall, where they gathered the materials to make a couch for the maiden.

Mateep ate a little and slept a great deal for the first two days. Her mind had miraculously returned to her. She could recall all that had happened. She remembered her rescue in the black rocks. She told them of her flight with the old mother after word of the impending raid. Some of her memory was still a little sketchy about her wandering from one village dump to the next, but she recalled going to Kaoto's mother's doorway and sitting with her until she left on her last journey.

While her mind seemed to be mending, her physical condition remained in jeopardy. She would seem to be getting better for a short time, but would relapse quickly. She remained weak and unable to get out of her bed.

"What is wrong with her?" Kaoto repeatedly ask Paataga.

"What's wrong with her?" Paataga snapped at him. "What would you expect?" She shook her head and muttered beneath her breath.

"I thank the Spirit Watcher she lives and you are not satisfied. You want her to dance and sing. How long has it taken for her to get into this condition? Huh? And now you want her to get up in one day."

"I know, great mother, but it seems to me she is not gaining at all. I thought we should be able to see some improvement."

Paataga pounded her walking stick against the hard ground in her yard. She, too, was concerned about the girl's slow recovery, but she would not admit it to anyone. Her inability to discover the source of Mateep's illness made her short tempered and hard to talk to.

"I tell you this. If you do not quit pestering me with all these childish questions I will never be able to heal her. Why do you not take Torjan, he is just as big a nuisance as you are, take him with you and go some place and do what you do best. Then I can do what I have to do without having to stop and explain each move to the two of you."

"I will not leave her again," Kaoto insisted stubbornly.

"You will." Paataga became very angry. She was not used to having anyone question her or refuse to do as she said. Kaoto might be the new Wise One, but she was still Paataga, and Paataga would not tolerate any more nonsense from him. Swinging her stick, she struck him about the knees and waist.

"Go. Get out. Leave us alone. If we have need of you we will call for you, but until we do, I do not want to see either of you hanging around here anymore."

She turned her back on Kaoto, who knew he had been dismissed like a child. What Paataga said was true. He was less than useless here. He had no idea what he could do to help Mateep, and there were still many things to be done. Time hung heavy on his hands as he sat here waiting, but he knew that time flew when he was busy. Yes, Paataga was right, as usual. He must get on with his mission and he must trust her to do what she could for Mateep. There was no one who could do more for her and he knew there was already a bond between the two, although they had only just met.

"You are right as usual, great mother. We will go, but let me know as soon as anything changes. Will you?" Kaoto stood ready to leave but his face still looked like a little boy. As far as Paataga was concerned, he would always be a child to her.

She relented a little and tapped him on the chest with her walking stick, gently this time.

"Go. Give us time. She will be all right. I know she will. This is the one I have seen walking at your side, so she has to be all right or this could not happen. I must have some time to work with her, to discover what the trouble is, and you know I think and work better when I am alone. So leave and trust me. Have I ever failed you so far?"

"No, great mother. You have never failed me. I owe my life to you on several occasions. I am sorry if I have offended you. It is just that I worry so much about her. I do not understand this feeling. I have never had feelings like this about anyone before."

Paataga smiled. Her eyes crinkled deep within her withered face. Her lips arched and there was a far away look on her face.

366 - Norman D. Messenger

"It is love, my son. Oh, I know, you love everyone, but this is different. You have never known love, unless it might have been the feeling you had for Little Frog. Trust me, you will not die from it. You will live but you may never be the same again."

"Yes. That is what it is like. I had nearly forgotten. I do feel much the same for Mateep as I did for Little Frog. But Little Frog was so helpless and she needed me. When I first knew Mateep she was so strong and independent she did not need anyone. How could I feel the same about them when they are so different?"

"If I did not know better, I would think you were trying to turn things around on me. Asking all those questions. But I know you are just a love struck young man and your mind is muddled. Go. Think about it while you are gone. Maybe you will find your own answers."

"You never change, do you? Still making me find the answers to my own questions. All right, I will go. But I shall return, and when I do you had better be able to tell me what I do not know about this love you speak of." Kaoto turned and motioned for Torjan to follow him as he trotted down the path, not looking back.

Paataga shaded her eyes and watched him go. Love? Did she still re-member love? What could she tell him of love? She had loved once, so long ago, but now she could not recreate the feeling. She had lived so long alone that she did not feel like one of the People. Did she have the same feelings as the rest of them did? Love? Yes, she could remember it. She loved yet today. She loved this tall man and she loved the frail maiden in her care, but did this count as the same type of love he was experiencing? She doubted it. Oh well, time would take care of everything, just as it always did. When Mateep was well and able to get about they would know what to do and they would go off and leave her alone. They would not be bothering her with all these silly questions. Alone? Had she said she would be alone? How could she ever be alone? This little home and the small clearing around it was filled with memories. She could conjure up many happy days spent here. First with Kaoto, then later, with his pupils. No, she would never be alone. She had a family surrounding her. Kaoto had seen to that and he would never be separated from her until death closed her eyes.

"Pafffh!" she snorted to herself. "Getting old when you start to talk to yourself. Getting soft in the head like a frost bitten pumpkin. You have work to do. You cannot be standing around here talking to yourself." She smiled in spite of her self-abuse. How life had changed for her in the past summers since she had taken Kaoto in for her prodigy. Now he was in love and she would live to see him take a mate after all.

Kaoto began by taking stock of what was going on in the Chaco Can-yon. The valley was crowded with the influx of refugees from the outlying dis-tricts. The savages were closing in on the land of the People. It was too late now for the mass exodus he had hoped to accomplish.

True to his word, Matuga had resigned from his post as ruler. A younger man had been chosen, who now stood facing Kaoto, ready to accept the advice and counsel of the Wise One.

He had been chosen as all rulers were chosen; not for his strength or cunning, but for his ability to think and act in the best interest of the People he served. He was younger than Matuga but not an unseasoned youth, either. He had thirty summers to his credit. He was called Seit.

Seit listened as Kaoto outlined a plan, seconded by the giant Red One. Since the People had not left and the savages were already getting closer, it was Kaoto's plan to start fortifications of their pueblos. In the dry ground at his feet he had drawn a rough sketch of what he thought should be done to make them less vulnerable to the raids of the savages.

Towers should be built at vantage points to give the People ample warning of the savages' approach. Walls should be built around the large villages so they could be enclosed when they were threatened. New storerooms were to be built and stocked with the surplus crops from all the surrounding area. If a siege were undertaken, the People could fall back to the large, walled, villages and live off the produce stored there. Large cisterns were dug and walled, the inner walls sealed with adobe clay to hold the precious water. Channels were cut from the rooftops and led to these cisterns. In smaller villages, especially those built up in the over hanging cliffs, large jugs were buried in the floor. These were filled with water during the wet season and were to be used only in times of emergency.

The People readily followed this advice. It was easier than pulling up and leaving the area for some unknown promise in the south. With Torjan's strength to help them, the walls were completed in record time. The People began to feel secure in their newly walled villages. Kaoto knew this security was unfounded. They would be able to withstand enemy attacks for a while, but in the summers to come much would depend on their ability to raise crops and harvest them without interruption. This also depended on more rainfall to compensate for the heavy population now converging on the Chaco Canyon.

This same advice was repeated all across the land. Wherever there were cliffs and canyons, the People were encouraged to build in secluded niches that were hard to see and harder to climb to. They would also be easier to defend.

With some misgivings, at first, the young men had started taking training from Torjan in the ways of war. They practiced daily on life-sized targets, and while they proved to be accurate bowmen he did not know if they could ever kill other men, even in battle. Perhaps when the savages pushed them hard enough and threatened their families, maybe then they would be able to fight back. They needed to learn anger, but this was hard to teach to a people who had lived all their lives in peace.

Even with all this activity directed toward defense, Kaoto still urged the People to make the trip south. A few followed. Often younger people would heed his advice, and not being as attached as the older ones, and having a spirit of adventure, they welcomed the change. Periodically small groups would slip away in the night and wend their way south through the land now overrun by the savages.

"There was no magic in Kiel's method of getting through the land of the savages," Kaoto told them. "You must travel at night and rest by day. Make sure you leave no sign of your passing. The savages do not relish making war at night, so you will be safe then. During the day, if you can find a safe place to hide, they will not find you and you can make it to safer lands to the south."

When a small village knew they were in the line of the savages' march, they would often choose to pack up and go south, beyond the reach of the savages. They were willing to risk the hunger and privation of the march rather than face the threat of the savages or the humiliation of having to move in with strangers and beg for food.

Over the next few summers the population of their nation dwindled. The People left behind were mostly the elderly or those physically unable to travel. The sound of children became scarce in the land of the People who loved children so much. The sound of laughter, which had always marked them, was heard less often now, and the friendly, easy manner of living became more con-strained. No one traveled without constantly looking over his shoulder. Fear, which had hitherto been virtually unknown, now made its home in the land of the People. Fear hung like a cloud over every village and each secluded single-family dwelling nestled up under the cliffs, like the homes of the wasps.

Mateep's recovery was slow. She suffered from long bouts of fever and chills. When her physical condition was stable, her mind was sharp and keen, but when her body was racked with fever her mind would wander and she would talk incoherently about things that had happened to her on the trail. It was in this way that much of her story was unraveled. Many things she did not choose to tell in her more lucid moments were readily revealed when the fever held her in its grip.

"It is odd how things work out, is it not?" Torjan said to Kaoto one evening as they rested by the trail.

"How are things working out?" Kaoto asked, puzzled by this turn in the conversation.

"I was just thinking. You started the custom of feeding those at the dump to satisfy your little friend who died, the one you called your little sister. Then, much later, this same custom is what undoubtedly saved Mateep from dying on the trail before she found her way here."

"I had not thought of it that way, but I guess it is true."

"I was thinking that if this one little thing you did so long ago could have such an influence on later times, what might some of the other things we do accomplish?"

"This is deep thinking for a Viking, is it not?" Kaoto asked amused at the twisted brow of his friend.

"You use the term Viking to make me angry, but it does not work any more. Maybe I am a Viking, not by blood, but by nature. I was wondering about my travel to this distant world from the lakes. Just what difference I might have made in the history of the People, or the whole world for that matter."

"I am sure we will never be the same as we would have been without your timely arrival." Kaoto laughed again at Torjan's sober face.

"You laugh at me and make fun, but you know what I mean. If our paths had not crossed I definitely would not have been here today. But what about you? Would you have been here today? Has not your life been changed by my appearance?"

"I know what you mean. Yes, it has no doubt been changed. Just the fact that I spent the extra time while your leg mended made a difference in my travel and where I would have been at different times. If I had not met you I might not have come back home when I did, and I might not have gone south and found Mateep. Yes, many things might have been different. But we will never know, will we?"

"It could work both ways. You might have come home sooner and you might have been able to save Mateep and her stubborn old father without all the trouble that has come to her, much of it because of me and the way I treated her when I found her."

Kaoto knew the cause of Torjan's serious talk. He had never forgiven himself for his mistreatment of Mateep. And Mateep had never completely trusted him in return. She always seemed uneasy when ever he was around. In the times of her fever, she was very frightened by the sight of him. She pretended to accept him for Kaoto's sake, but they all knew the barrier was still there between them.

"Paataga says time. Time is the only healing medicine there is now. She should know, she has seen more time than any two people put together. I trust her even though I become impatient with her at times. Give her time, my friend; she will come to know you just as the little children do. She is more a child than an adult, and I am sure that time will solve the problem."

"What worries me is, how much time do we have?"

"As long as it takes, I guess." Kaoto answered absently without thinking about the full content of Torjan's words.

"No. What I mean is, how much time do you and your People have? This cannot go on for much longer. The savages will become impatient with your walls and your hiding. They will force you to fight or die. As for myself, I will welcome the fight, even death, in preference to this constant running and hiding. I was not made for running I was made to stand and fight. I will never go south with you or your People. I will die here in this strange land, fighting for these little People who will not fight for themselves. This is not the way of a Viking. A Viking glories in a good fight, even death, but he never fights for those too weak and frightened to fight for themselves. This is a sure way of getting killed. This is just another of those changes I was thinking about."

After this long speech Torjan became strangely silent and Kaoto could not get a rise out him, even when he teased him about the young women in the village who showed a preference for the Red One.

Back at Paataga's dwelling, Mateep suddenly shed all of her problems. Her fever left her as mysteriously as it had come, and while her body was weak from the long battle, her mind was completely clear.

"I am hungry," she said to Paataga, who was seated at her customary place by the fire.

Paataga turned and looked at her. Her face crackled into a wrinkled smile. This was good news. She had about given up hope that Mateep would ever be well and strong again. But when a young person's first waking words were a request for food, well, that was a good sign. They usually got better fast after this happened.

"Well, there is food by the fire; get up and get it. I am through waiting on you as if you were a baby. It is about time you got up and started looking after yourself, maybe even help look after me." Paataga's harsh words did not fool Mateep. She knew Paataga used her hard manner and harsh words to guard her secret softness.

"Yes, great mother," she said meekly as if she did believe. "I am sorry for being such a burden to you. You must be very tired. Maybe you should come and rest and let me look after you."

Paataga did not wait to see if Mateep could rise on her own but hurried to assist her to a sitting position and brought food and water to her. Tomorrow would be soon enough, or the day after that. Now that she showed signs of recovery, time no longer meant anything to her.

"I have been a great bother, have I not?" Mateep asked between sips of broth and spoons full of soft mush.

"Hummmph."

Chapter Fifty One

A runner with a strange story was brought to Kaoto's attention, along with a badge that had belonged to an unfortunate runner.

"I was coming back over the old long trail when I found this," the runner told Kaoto as he handed him the unmistakable badge of a runner.

"That is the trail that runs almost straight east to the shining river, is it not? It has been many summers since I was a runner, but I seemed to remember that route." Kaoto was absently turning the badge over in his hands while the runner told his story.

"Yes, that is the one." He was pleased that Kaoto remembered his days as a runner even though he was now the Wise One. "We seldom use it anymore because of the raiders. They have found it convenient to use. I only use it when I am in a hurry, and even then I keep a close eye out for them. It was deserted this time so I was making good time." The runner was from one of the far eastern districts and knew the habits of the savages better than most.

"As you probably remember, it is terribly dry across there during this season, so I stopped at the water hole in the dry creek bed, the one with the stone bottom that holds water all summer long."

"Oh yes. I remember it now. There is a long crack in the stone floor where the water is deep and cold. I used that route a few times and remember looking forward to getting a good drink there." Kaoto recalled the days of his youth. How many summers ago? It must have been close to twelve or more.

"That is the place, all right. I found the remains of this man there. He had been staked out over an anthill, and if that were not enough, they had used wet rawhide to tie him. They were gone when I got there so I took time to study things out as best I could." The runner waited for an approval from the Wise One. He knew it was not enough to carry messages from one man to another. A good runner also could report any new happenings along the trail. Runners were the newsmen of their time. Much of what was known about the nation was carried by these runners.

"You did well." Kaoto's simple statement was all the praise the runner asked for.

"As near as I could figure out, he must have lived several days in spite of all this. There were signs that they had poured water over him every so often to wash away the ants and to give new life to the rawhide. Toward the last it looked like they had cut pieces from his legs. I hear that they sometimes eat the flesh of their enemies, so I guess this is what they did to him." The runner's face registered his disgust with this custom.

"Did you recognize him, or was there enough left of him for you to tell?" Kaoto asked.

"His face looked pretty horrible, as though they had beat him in the face before they started. One ear was nearly gone. His hair had been cut in a strange fashion and was a little darker than most men's. No, I did not recognize him. I think even in his condition I would have been able to recognize him if I had ever seen him before." The ability of a runner to remember extended to the ability to remember people as well as messages.

At the mention of his beaten appearance and dangling ear, Kaoto looked more closely at the badge he held in his hand. At first glance it looked genuine, but on closer inspection he could see that it was a new piece of leather, which had been treated to appear old. The cracks on its surface were not cracks, after all, but tiny lines etched in with the sharp edge of a chip of flint. Dirt and grime had been rubbed into these cuts to make them appear as though they had been there for a long time, but the one thing it lacked that any good runner's badge was sure to have was sweat. A runner's badge was practically cured in its owner's sweat. This badge did not look like it had been so cured. Kaoto cut a small slice across the edge of the badge. The inner portion was still fresh and clean. He tossed the badge in the fire.

"This man was not a runner. He was not one of the People. He deserved to die, but not like this. No man deserves to die in this manner no matter how bad he is." He turned back to the runner with one final question. "What did you do about his body?"

"The time was short and I did not want to run the risk of being discovered, so I left it as it was. I figured someone could go back to bury it if they wanted to," the runner reported.

"Good. We will leave it there as a warning to any that see it. It seems Kiel's magic was not strong enough to protect him after all. At least no one will have to worry about him. As for his followers, I have been keeping close track of them and they are all heading toward the same place. Some of them have already started building there."

Kaoto drew a map in the dust at his feet. He indicated the place where the men were congregating. Not all of the People knew the place, but most knew the general area. The runners among them knew the place with a certainty.

"Tell the People of this district to stay away from them. They are to give them nothing, nor are they to go near them. As long as they stay on their ridge they will be tolerated, but that is all. Now that their leader is gone, they will probably not be as much of a problem as they have been here. Time will eliminate them because they do not take mates among the women, and unless they posses more magic than I have seen, I do not think they can produce children among themselves."

There was a hearty laugh forthcoming from the crowd at his suggestion. It was the first good laugh they had been able to indulge in at the expense of the mystics.

"If they did produce children, it would serve them right," chuckled one old mother, and the other women joined her in laughter about such an event.

In one of the spare rooms of the pueblo, the collection of jars and wands used by the former mystics was carefully stacked. Later the room was sealed off. The days of the mystics were soon forgotten and the People went about, facing the threat of the advancing raiders in their own way.

The story of Kiel's death was passed on to each runner, not as a piece of gossip, but as an object lesson on what could and did happen to those who were careless enough to be caught by the savages.

Mateep's recovery had been rapid after her fever had finally broken and left her. She ate, Kaoto said, like a runner, meaning she ate more than an ordinary person should. Her strength had returned as it can do only in young people and before another turn of the moon she was able to run well enough to satisfy Paataga, who pronounced her cured.

She still stayed close to Paataga and helped her around the camp, doing the extra cooking for Torjan and Kaoto, but she set aside a time each day to run and build up her long-range ability.

At night, when Kaoto and Torjan were present, they spent much time sitting before the fire, talking of the day's events and the general situation concerning the advancing savages.

Mateep noticed that during these conversations, when she sat on the ground close to Kaoto and Paataga on her usual log, Torjan would step back and stay well behind them. He never entered into the conversation and never under any circumstance spoke directly to her.

At first this pleased her. Although he had once apologized to her, she could not accept him as easily as the others did. After having time to think, she could see that he was just a hurt human. In spite of his great size, he was no different on the inside than she or anyone else she knew.

One evening, as Kaoto and Paataga were in deep discussion on a subject that was close to both of them, Mateep slipped away from Kaoto's side and approached Torjan. Her heart was in her throat and she did not know if she could follow through with her plan. It had seemed easy when she thought of it, but now, standing and looking up at this huge hairy giant, she had to admit he just plain frightened her. But reasoning told her that this was not necessary. After all, he was a friend of Kaoto's. He could not be bad or Kaoto would never have brought him here. She pumped up her courage, remembering Kaoto and the wounded bull buffalo. He had been able to do what he knew had to be done. He had weighed the danger and taken the risk. She could do no less, and the comparison of Torjan to the wounded buffalo brought a smile to her face in spite of her misgivings and doubts. She took Torjan's huge hand in both of her tiny ones and pulled him after her down the trail, away from the fire and the two talking there.

"Torjan, you and I have to talk." She waited for his reaction.

The Red One hung his head and looked down at the ground. Slowly he raised his eyes to meet hers, but he did not offer to speak.

"Torjan, I mean it. We have to talk. You never speak to me and when I try to talk to you, you always avoid me." This was not as hard as she had imagined. Somehow Torjan's great size made him seem even more vulnerable. Oddly enough she felt she had the advantage over him because she knew she belonged here and he was still feeling like an outsider, a stranger in a strange land.

"This has not all been your fault, Torjan. In fact I guess none of it has been your fault. I have treated you so badly. I do not blame you for not talking to me, but we are both friends of Kaoto, and so if nothing else we owe it to him to try to get along with each other." This did not sound as she had meant it. It sounded like she was saying that she wanted them to be friends just to please Kaoto.

"You do not have to explain it to me, little one," Torjan mumbled as quietly as he could.

"I was not trying to explain it to you, Torjan. I messed it up. I think I am trying to apologize to you for being the way I have been lately."

"You do not owe me any apology, little one. It is I who have been wrong. Wrong from the very first moment I set eyes on you and accused you of harming Keenwah. And then not believing you when you said she gave you the headband. And I was wrong to let Kiel and his men have you. For the other things you might forgive me, or even make excuses, but for the last there is no excuse."

Torjan was not given too long speeches and Mateep realized this was the most he had ever said to her at one time since they had met. All this time she had feared him because of his anger. Now she saw it was not anger, at least not at her, but shame that dictated his actions and lack of words.

"Sit, Torjan. I want to talk to you, to your face, not your belly." Mateep tugged at his hand until he relented and seated himself at her feet.

"That is better. Now I can see your eyes. Almost, anyway. Between your beard and those shaggy eyebrows, even your eyes are almost lost."

"I am what you see, little one. Kaoto has always told me I frighten the People with my looks, but this is how I look." Torjan ran a huge hand through his red hair under the helmet with the buffalo horns. "He said if I would cut off my hair I might not be as frightening, but I do not think that would make any difference. I might look even worse without my hair."

"I will admit you did frighten me that first morning. I can remember you pulling me out and bellowing at me. But you did not hurt me. You could have easy enough. You could have crushed me with one hand, and I think you wanted to. But you did not."

"I have learned to be careful with you little People. I am more used to people much like myself, who take a lot more to hurt. Even Kaoto has told me he can understand this because he has the same feelings. Of course, he is much more gentle than I am to begin with."

"I do know about that. I saw him kill those men down in the black rocks. There was nothing gentle about him them. He was terrible. I would have been frightened of him, too, if I had not known him before and seen him do some things which no cruel or mean man would have done."

"I know he has killed men, but he does not do it the way I would do it.

He takes no joy in it. Killing a man who is a good enemy or a man who needs it, is a satisfaction in its self. But Kaoto, and all of your People, they cannot see it that way."

"A good enemy? How can that be?" Mateep was puzzled.

"Yes, a good enemy. A man who puts up a good fight. One worthy of your effort to fight. One you do not have to be ashamed of killing. If a man comes at you one on one, with equal weapons, and offers to fight you on equal terms, this is a good enemy," Torjan tried to explain, but knew the little maiden did not understand.

"It seems that this type of a man would be a better friend than an enemy."

"Sometimes he would be if you were fighting on the same side. That is the way it was with Kaoto. When I had regained my strength after my broken leg had healed enough I could stand well on it, I offered to fight him. I thought I was honoring him by making this offer. Do you know what he did?"

"Well, he quite evidently did not fight you or else one of you would not be here." Mateep was interested. She had never heard Torjan tell his side of this story.

"He laughed at me. Yes, he stood there and laughed at me. He said he had better things to do than stand around and let me kill him. I did not know what to make of that, but for the first time in my life it struck me as funny that two men who were equally good fighters should want to kill each other. I told Kaoto it would not please me to kill him, but I thought I owed him the opportunity. He refused my offer and we have been good friends ever since." Torjan shook his great hairy head. He still did not understand the working of Kaoto's mind, but as long as Kaoto needed a friend, he was going to be there.

Mateep stood looking at Torjan. She understood him a little bit better now, although he would always be somewhat of a mystery to her. But at least she knew what had formed the bond between him and Kaoto. It was mutual respect. Two colossuses in a land of midgets. To fight each other would indeed be foolish.

"I will make you the same offer, then. If it worked for you two, then why will it not work for me and you?" Mateep backed off a little ways to give Torjan room to stand.

"What are you talking about, little one?" Torjan made no effort to move.

"Come on. Get up and fight me." Mateep motioned with her hands.

It started as a low rumble somewhere deep inside the Red One. Gradually it built until he began to shake. Then everything around him began to shake. His ruby complexion became even redder as his mirth shook him. He drew his great sword and saluted the tiny maiden. Then he threw it to the ground at her feet.

Mateep did not know what he was doing and jumped back as the iron weapon hit the ground and rang off a protruding stone.

"Here, take my weapon. It will not be a fair fight unless you are properly armed." Torjan was nearly choking with his fit of laughter.

"I am serious, Torjan." Mateep tried to keep her face straight but found it difficult in light of Torjan's booming laughter.

"So am I, little one. Take my weapon. I surrender to the better man. Like Kaoto said, I have more things to do than offer you the pleasure of killing me." Torjan's face suddenly became grave and the banter dropped from his voice.

"It is within your rights to kill me with my own weapon. When a man throws down his weapon without striking a blow, it proves he is no man at all."

"Oh, Torjan. I do not want to hurt you. I have already hurt you enough over the last few days. I do not wish to hurt you anymore. I can never think of you as less than a man. You have to be a man or Kaoto would not have you as a friend."

"In the land of my People," Torjan spoke softly, "there is a saying. Let me see if I can translate if from my tongue to the language of the People. A friend is something you are lucky to have even once in a lifetime. To have two is to flaunt fate."

"I am not sure I understand what you mean. I was raised away from the People so I never had any friends until Kaoto came along, and I have not had much chance to make more since I came here, other than Paataga. But she is more than just a friend, she is—well—she is Paataga. Great Mother of the world."

"What it means is that you may know many people and you may like many of them. But only for a friend would you lay down your life. Only to a friend would you willingly offer your weapon."

"Oh. You mean as you just did to me? You are saying this is your way of showing you trust me? That you are offering me your life? Why, Torjan, who would have ever thought there was such a big soft spot inside all the hair and noise?" Mateep laughed at this statement. To be sure, Torjan did not look like anything soft, but now that she had talked with him she knew there was nothing about him for her to fear.

She reached down to pick up the sword in the trail. She found it took both hands to raise it from the ground and it was still awkward in her hands. Just to be safe, she set the point back on the ground and held to the handle.

"Here, you had better take this back. I do not think it would be a fair fight if I could not even pick up the weapon. Why not keep it until I am strong enough to handle it? Then maybe I can give you a fair fight. Until then, can we not just be friends?" She let go of the sword with one hand and offered it to Torjan.

The Red One took the offered hand as delicately as if it were a piece of fragile pottery. Mateep was surprised that such huge hands could be so dainty and sensitive. She had never seen him work with the tiny pieces of copper, as some had.

"If you can forgive me for all I have done to you, then I guess I must forgive myself. It would not be right of me to be angry with one of your friends. Would it?"

"No. It surely would not. That is something I could never forgive. Now come, let us go join the two masters. I doubt they have missed us. They never know there is anyone else around when they get to talking. Have you ever noticed, that for two people who are renowned for their wisdom, they talk about some odd things? I heard then talking about ants the other day. Comparing them to the People. What could they possibly have in common with the People?"

Torjan stood up and followed the little maiden back up to where Kaoto and Paataga sat talking. As Mateep said, they did not appear to have missed them; they were so busy talking about things only they could understand. Mateep seated herself beside Paataga on the log and motioned for Torjan to join them.

As the Red One lowered himself to the ground beside Kaoto, a quick wink and just a hint of a smile passed between the Wise One and his great mother. Very little happened in their world that they were not aware of, even if they did not make a show of it.

From that night on Torjan focused much of his attention on Mateep. Whenever they ran he would watch to see if she was becoming tired. The first time she stumbled or misplaced a foot, he would scoop her up and carry her, regardless of her protests. He would carry her as long as he could get her to let him.

His pack was much lighter now than when Kaoto had first returned it to him long ago up in the mountains. In an effort to keep up with Kaoto, he had begun to discard some of the heavier items along the trail. He soon discovered he was carrying more things than he would ever need now that he had decided he would live out the rest of his days here with Kaoto. His pack was still heavy by the People's standards, but to him it felt as light as an empty sack. The difference made it much easier for him to carry her extra weight.

It was not long until she was traveling with Kaoto. At first he had protested, but when Torjan and Paataga teamed up with Mateep, he realized it was useless to argue with them. He felt she would soon tire of the trail and would be content to stay home with Paataga, but he had underestimated Mateep's determination to be with him. She remembered Paataga's words from before he had rescued her. She was destined to be the companion of the Wise One. She was not going to let his objections upset her plans.

Chapter Fifty Two

The seasons changed, one following another in the regular pattern of centuries. This was the only thing the People could depend on; everything else in their world was changing. The changes were taking place so fast it was almost impossible to keep up with them.

The savages were growing bolder with each passing day. They invaded the little villages with impunity, not bothering to carry out their normal destructive pattern. They grew weary of destroying buildings and tearing up fields. The People were keeping a closer watch than before and were seldom caught without warning. They fled their homes at the approach of the savages and did not return until it was considered safe, if ever. A few had been discovered sneaking south, trying to escape from the threat in their homeland. Some of these were captured. Some escaped.

The droughts became even more severe, causing great suffering among all the People and savages alike. Even the animals were driven from the land, searching for new, greener, pastures.

Kaoto did not relent on his continuous travel. He was known in every village and small gathering point across the land. He seemed tireless in his ability to run, stopping to speak a few words, eating a hurried bite of food, and leaving again to run over the trails once more. His message was the same every place he went. It was often heard, but seldom heeded.

"My first recommendation is to take your families and go south. Go now, before it is too late. To those of you who I know will not heed my words, let me then urge you to at least fortify your village. If your village is too small for this, then join with others until you form a large enough group to be able to protect yourselves a little.

"Build new homes. Build them on places where it is hard for anyone to sneak up on you without your being able to see them. Keep a watch always. Build towers for this purpose. Whenever possible, build your homes up under the rocks on the side of the canyons. Here it is easier to hide yourselves and your families and it will be harder for them to destroy you than if you are sitting out in the open on the land as you have always done.

"Plant your fields far away from your homes. Spread them out so they are not close together. This way some of them may escape the notice of the savages. Gather your foods on the very first day they are ready. Do not wait for any sign or special time for harvest. Harvest every day so that you may save as much as you can. If the savages should find your field, you will have at least salvaged as much as possible before they get to it.

"Do not store all your food in one place. Bury some in the floor of your home so it will be easy to get to in case you are surrounded. Bury some outside so if they do invade your home and dig up your stores, you will still have some left. Hide some up under the cliffs where they will be safe and dry; anywhere that you think the savages might not look.

"And always be prepared; be prepared to run, prepared to hide, and last, be prepared to die, because this is what will happen to all of you in time if you do not leave here and go south."

Kaoto's words were harsh but he would not spare them the brutal truth. He felt they should all know the inevitable outcome of their stubbornness. They should all know what they were bringing, not only on themselves, but also on their mates and their children. No one was spared when a raid caught the People off guard; they all had seen or heard of the fate of the captives.

The People listened. They knew he spoke the truth and they wished they had the strength and courage to go south as he admonished them to do. But they were weak. They loved their homes. They did not want to give up their way of life. They did not want to abandon their fields. Their fathers and mothers were buried there. Their families had lived here since the beginning of time. There had been bad times before and sometimes many had died. But things had always come back to normal. Would not this also pass? Would not the savages leave eventually? Would not the rains come again so the crops would grow in abundance? Surely the Spirit Watcher would not forget them for all times.

So stubbornly they hung on. They stayed on the land. And one by one, they died. Some were buried in their fields in the age-old custom, so their bodies could feed the land and thus feed the future generations. Others were buried in the floors of their homes so they would not be discovered by the savages and desecrated. Some were sealed up in spare rooms that were no longer used for storage or visiting families, who no longer came.

The numbers of the People in the homeland were dwindling so rapidly it was impossible to believe that only a few short summers back they had numbered like the blades of grass. A great sorrow hung over the land like a dark cloud; it was like a threatening storm. The People were no longer happy. They were frightened, and their fright was communicated to every living thing in the land. Even the savages were not immune to this prevalent doom. They, too, became frightened, not just of dying in the dark, but also of all the signs of the weather and nature.

Among some of the savages there was a new belief, a new feeling being experienced. They no longer thought of the little People as a fail-proof method of providing food. They could see that the dry weather was making it impossible for any of them to live. The savages, who had been nomads for hundreds of summers now, began to think like the People. They began to make homes and tried to tend fields left vacant by the retreating farmers. They tried to raise their own crops. They lacked the skills and knowledge to accomplish this, so they had to find a new system, a new method of providing food.

They no longer killed and tortured the People when they were able to capture them. Instead, they took them prisoners and made them slaves. They forced them to give of their knowledge. They made them build new homes. Bigger, more commodious, to suit the needs of the large bodies of the savages.

They used them to plant and tend crops, and in the process the savages started to learn to do these things for themselves. The wandering savages became pueblo builders. The nomads stayed close to one place so they could raise and reap the harvest of the fields. Necessity made them do these things. It was not something they would have been willing to accept if nature had not forced it upon them.

In a very short time a great change had swept across the land. The runners were no longer free to run as they pleased and were obligated to run at night, or not run at all. There were few demands for the runners' service. The villages no longer communicated with each other. There were no celebrations to be called to. There were no festivities to bring the People together. News of each other became less important as they struggled to survive in this time of crisis.

Families retreated into the canyon lands and drew up under the cliffs. A few here, a few there. They discovered their chances of escaping notice were increased as their numbers decreased.

There were no new Grand Kivas. The old established pueblos were abandoned, vacated to sit in the sun and grow silent as the sands, driven by the ever-present winds, drifted over them, filling the front rooms and breaking down the roofs to fill some of the others. The only inhabitants of these once grand villages were the lizards and sidewinders. Spiders spun webs over the doorways and were undisturbed by any man.

The savages shunned these former residences. Once they would have torn them down and destroyed them. They could have lived in them, but they did not. They told themselves they were too small for them, and this might have been true. Even if they had been spacious mansions, they would still not have lived in them. They not only feared dying in the dark, they feared the spirits who might inhabit these homes. They feared the Gods of the People. While their Gods had not protected the People, they might still deal out retribution against those who would be foolish enough to enter and thus tempt them. The homes of the People were sacred. When the People had lived in them, the savages did not fear to enter them. But now they were deserted, they were an evil omen.

Far to the west, in the land of Keet Seel, Kalo had grown in stature and esteem in the hearts of the People. In the absence of the Wise One, who had never returned to them, the People had accepted Kalo as his representative without question. His wisdom was evident to all who had dealings with him. None could doubt he had trained at the feet of Paataga, and few could believe that the one called Kaoto could equal him in handling their affairs.

Kalo and his mate Pala were known in every village. Even the smallest, most humble, dwelling was known to them. Doing his best to emulate his foster father, Kalo dispensed his wisdom and knowledge in the best manner he knew. He was sure his father would have been proud of him and would have sanctioned his decisions without question.

But there was one field in which they had different opinions. This one field would make a great difference in the eventual outcome of the history of the People.

Kalo had had his dreams also and they were nearly the same as those of Kaoto and Paataga. The difference was in the interpretation of these dreams. Kalo had also heard the voice telling him the People must return to the land of little earth. He was sure the dream was accurate because Kaoto had once told him of his dream, and Kalo's dream matched it almost word for word.

To Kalo, raised in this land remote from the Chaco, it seemed clear to him what the meaning of the message was. There was no secret to him as to what the term "land of little earth" could mean. There were many such areas surrounding them. He as a child had been raised in just such an area. A land of little earth could only mean the barren, wind swept rock formations. It was just as clear that the message meant for the People to return to these barren places where they would be safe from the invading savages, who as of yet had not drifted this far.

The drought was felt here as it was elsewhere in the land of the People, but the difference was not as great as in some other places. This land had always been drier and more hostile than the land of Kaoto back at Chaco. Here the People had always had to struggle with the elements to make a crop grow, and they had used more extensive irrigation means than in other parts of the nation. So Kalo had traveled among the People, just as Kaoto would have him do. He had spread his own warning and advice based on his interpretation of the message from the dream.

"Now, before the time of danger arrives, you should all go out and find a place of your own. A place hidden away from the rest of the world. Build a home there and mark out your fields, and begin to plan for your irrigation lines to furnish them."

This part of his instructions was the same as those of Kaoto, but he did not urge them to leave the land and journey south. So it was that no one from his area made the trip to safety in the south land that Kaoto had envisioned.

"Are you telling us to move out of this pleasant valley, to abandon our homes and flee to the rocks?" he was asked repeatedly.

"No. What I am telling you is to plan for the future. Go find a place now in your leisure time. Take plenty of time to find a suitable place to build. Think it over; talk it over with your mate. If it pleases you both, then start to build on it. You have ample time to build a second home and furnish it. But do it now. Do not wait until the savages are at your door, when you will have to sneak off in the middle of the night and be able to take only what you can carry. Go now and prepare for that time so when it does come, which I am sure it will, you will have a place to go and provisions to sustain you and your family. This way there will not be an over crowding of the People all trying to flee to the same place at the same time."

"When do you think the savages will come? Do you really think they will come this far? None have been seen yet. Are we not safe here as we have always been?"

"The time is known only to the Spirit Watcher. He has given us a warning of their coming but he has not chosen to tell us the exact day. A wise man does not have to be told twice. When thunder and lightening march across the sky, do you come asking when will it rain? No. You know it is coming and make preparations for it," Kalo told them patiently.

"But what if they never come? What then? Every thunderstorm does not bring rain. We will have wasted much of our time and energy building a home for the animals and insects. They do not need such a home. If they do, let them provide their own."

"But what if they do come? What then? You can always come out of a shelter if it does not rain. But if you do not have a place to go, will the animals welcome you into their homes? I think not. They will say just what you have said to me. If they need homes, let them build their own."

Kalo's reasoning won out over time, and although they did not really believe they would ever need them, the People humored their Wise One and searched until they found suitable locations. They built homes, hiding them up under overhanging rocks, or in deep niches in the rocks where they were almost impossible to see or find. It was not easy but it was better than thinking of leaving the home land forever and going to a mysterious land in the south, as had been advised by the first Wise One.

In time they began to live in their new homes part of the summer, tending an extra crop and planning new fields and their water management. As reports of the savages began to come in, along with the stories of the atrocities being committed on some of the People who were captured by them, the People were glad of their foresight. They were glad they had homes to go to, and many did not wait for the threat to arrive on their doorstep, but moved permanently into these hidden homes.

Like the Chaco, runners became less necessary. News was not spread from the far lands as it had been in the past. Each home or tiny village became a world of its own, like a little island in the great sea of doubt and fear that was rapidly moving across the nation. Here, as everywhere else in the land, large pueblos were being left vacant as the families slipped away and hid themselves in the land of little earth. Here, as elsewhere, fear took its toll on the People. They became shy, hiding even from each other. There was virtually no travel between them now. No one wanted to be caught out in the open when the savages came by. No one wanted to leave a plainly marked trail leading to their hidden homes in the rocks. If no one knew where they were, no one could be tortured into revealing their presence.

Fear, almost unknown previous to this time, became an unwelcome visitor in every dwelling place. Silence reigned over the land that once rang with laughter. The sense and smell of fear was carried on the wind. It was absorbed by the very rocks around them to be radiated back to anyone who came near. The feeling is still there today. The great villages give off a feeling of peace and prosperity, but the little homes up under the rocks still project the feeling of fear and despair.

Kaoto finally convinced Mateep that she could no longer travel with him. She could see the danger she faced concerned not only herself, but him also. There was no danger on the trail he could not outwit or outrun, but she held him back and he would be bound to protect her. In the event of danger, he would be forced to stop and fight, thus endangering them both. Torjan even admitted he was more of hindrance than help and reluctantly agreed to stay with Mateep and keep an eye on Paataga during Kaoto's absence.

Returning from one of his countless trips, Kaoto found Paataga seated by her fire pit late one evening. She sat stirring the ashes in an idle fashion, spreading them out evenly over the small fire pit area. She separated the few glowing coals that were left so they would burn themselves out, leaving a cold fire pit in the morning. This was an action Kaoto had not seen her perform before. A cold chill sent an involuntary shudder up his back and caused a tingling sensation in the hair on the back of his neck, but he remained silent, sensing his old great mother had things to say to him. Paataga, satisfied at last with her chore, brought the walking stick up and laid the tip of it across her other hand. A heavy knot rested in the crook of her little finger, the tip of the stick protruding only a small way out into the palm of her hand. A trace of a smile crossed her face and was lost almost before it began.

"It is odd, the way things work out. When I first picked up this stick, it was just the right length for me. But I noticed that the end of it was wearing, ever so slowly, on the sand and stones as I used it to walk about. I thought then, one of these days it will be worn off so much it will be too short to use any more, and I hated to think of that day, because I was partial to this particular stick." She studied it as if to renew her convictions about it.

"I placed it in my hand, just as I hold it now, and with the knot resting on my little finger like this, the tip reached out to the end of my thumb. Over the summers I have occasionally measured it like this and the tip has slowly retreated down across my palm. When I was through measuring it in my hand, I would let it rest back against my shoulder, like this." The old woman placed the tip of the stick between her feet and let the other end rest on her shoulder. It came just to the top of her shoulder.

"It has always been so. It has always managed to reach the top of my shoulder. I wondered about this. How could this be? Was there something I was missing? Then the truth came to me. As the stick was shrinking, getting shorter, so was I. Over the summers I have slowly drooped until the stick and I remain equal. Odd, is it not?" She asked, looking up at Kaoto for the first time since she had started talking.

Kaoto was deeply troubled by her words. This was not the way Paataga usually spoke. He knew she never wasted words on trivial things. There was a deeper meaning, something he had not caught as of yet.

"Yes. It is odd, I guess. But, old mother, why are you talking of sticks?

This is not what you wish to say. This is the first time I have known you to stall, to evade speaking out about what is on your mind. Is it so bad? Are you afraid to tell me? What can be so bad that it can not be spoken of between us?" In spite of his words, Kaoto knew deep in his being what Paataga would say next.

"I am tired, my son. Very tired. For the first time in all my summers here, I did not walk on the top of the cliff today. My heart wanted to go, but my legs did not want to make the journey. For the first time I have not put my bedding out to air. And tonight I have spread my fire. I will not need it anymore." The finality of her words fell like darkness between them. A great shuddering sob escaped the Wise One. Then it was gone. He was in control of himself again and the curtain that had descended between them was lifted; he could see plainly once more.

"You deserve your rest, old mother. You have served long past the time anyone could have reasonably asked of you. I have been selfish in keeping you this long."

"Selfish? No. Not selfish. The feeling has been mutual. I have lingered on because it pleased me. I have enjoyed these last summers more than all the others put together. But now I am tired. I am glad you understand. I hate to leave you and the valley, but I must. The time is short now. The savages will soon be here, as they are everywhere else in the land. I am a coward. I do not wish to see them. I do not want to see them lay waste to this land that has been my home. So I will rest now, with your permission."

"Granted, old mother. It is with great sorrow that I let you go. I know the sorrow I feel is for myself, not for you. It is I who will miss you, and in missing you, I will mourn for me, not for you. You will be at rest in the next world. Go in peace, old mother, but always remember me. Do not completely forsake me even in the next world. Can you do that?"

"I am sure of it. I could not forget you and I told you once before, not even death shall separate us. I ask one last favor of you."

"Anything within my power is yours to command, great mother."

"When you bury me, put me in the little crack in the rocks over there." She pointed with her worn walking stick at a tiny dark mark on the face of the cliff. As a boy he had explored it and knew it was exceedingly small, but large enough to conceal the body of this frail little woman.

"If you cover the opening with adobe and mix it with sand, it will stand undisturbed and the savages will never find my bones to decorate themselves with."

"It shall be as you ask, old mother. I will make sure that your resting-place is never found. It is the least I can do for one who has done so much for me. Is it not?"

"Then leave me now, son. I wish to sit here alone until the last breath has gone. Come back in the morning. I will be waiting for you here." Paataga's tired countenance held a look of peace and tranquility that he had seldom seen before.

Kaoto rose and stepped close to her slight figure. He rested a hand on her frail shoulder and was amazed to find so little there. He had seldom touched his old teacher. Out of respect and love, he had honored her wish not to be touched. The tiny bones were scarcely covered by her dry, parched skin. She felt like a tiny owl, all feathers and bone with no substance, a shadow without substance. He hated to leave her but respected her wish to be left alone. After all she had done for him, could he do less than honor this last wish?

In the morning he brought Torjan and Mateep with him. Just as she had promised, Paataga was waiting for him. She was still seated on the log. The walking stick propped against her shoulder kept her from falling forward. Kaoto had warned his friends of her death, but Mateep rushed forward to comfort the old one, only to find Kaoto had told the truth. Paataga, great mother of the world, Wise One of the nation, was no more. She was only a husk that had housed the great person they had known.

She was buried without ceremony in the tiny crack. Torjan carried mud mixture and stones while Kaoto carefully filled the niche until it was no longer there. Even a close inspection made it impossible to find the opening hidden under the adobe mixture.

Paataga's rest would not be interrupted now or for all time. No man would ever lay eyes on the bones of the great mother. Paataga, and the others who rested in death, were the only ones to find peace in this land. They slept undisturbed by the tumult that swung back and forth across the land.

The living had to face the threat. Sometimes daily, sometime intermittently, but whether or not the savages were in sight, they were still a constant threat to everything that drew breath in the land, man or animal.

Chapter Fifty Three

"Put me down, you big bear," Mateep cried as Torjan held her and ran down the trail with her cradled in his arms as if she were a child.

"Not until we catch up with Kaoto," he informed her without altering his pace or his hold on her.

"That may not be until we stop for the night then, because you surely can never catch him," Mateep told Torjan.

"And I suppose you think you could? Why, you can not even keep up with me, so how are you going to catch him?"

"I do not have to catch him. I already have. All I have to do is stop and wait. He will come back for me."

"That is true, but then you would be holding him back, something you promised you would never do."

"I was just teasing, Torjan. You know I would never pull that kind of a trick on him. But I do feel much rested now, so I could run again for awhile and give you a rest."

"When I need rest, I will tell you. Until then, be still and be quiet or you might make me loose my step. If I fell down on top of you there would not be enough left for him to come back after."

It was one of the rare times that Kaoto had consented for his two companions to take the trail with him. Now that Paataga was gone, he felt no permanent ties to the land of Chaco. Torjan and Mateep shared this feeling with him and were anxious to take up residence somewhere far away from the valley that held so much sorrow for all of them.

Torjan had expressed a desire to return to the Mesa Verde area. He had spent only a short time there with Kaoto on the way down from the north land. But he had been able to stand on the brink of the cliffs and look far away in several directions. It seemed to him that this was the safest place he had seen in this threatened land.

Fall was settling over the land and the harvest, such as it was, had been completed. The villages were walled up or left vacant. All had been done to prepare for the long winter and the invasion of the savages.

There was nothing left for them to do in this land. The People had made their choices; now they would live with, and die with, them.

There had been a greater number stay than leave. Still, there had been enough make the trip south to insure the history of the People would be preserved. Those who were left were the old, those who would never have lived out the trip anyway. They probably were doing the younger ones a favor. Those who chose to make the long, uncertain trek to the south had to be able to travel swiftly. They needed to be strong enough to stand the rigors of the long trail. Many of those left behind would have held them back, impeding their drive for safety.

Kaoto decided it was for the Spirit Watcher to judge what was best. It was beyond his capacity to understand what made some of the People stay and some go. As for himself and his companions, he would go to the Mesa and try to make some sort of order out of the chaos that reigned over the surrounding country.

The People here were being threatened from three directions and by three different types of savages, all equally vicious. The People had a respite sometimes when the various factions would war among themselves, leaving the country laid waste, but each side would retreat temporarily to lick their wounds and regroup. This was one of those times, and Kaoto felt it was safe to travel if they moved quickly and did not linger anywhere. They would not take the risk of being caught out in the open when the next round of attacks took place.

As they approached the Mesa from the south, Kaoto was once again impressed with the impregnability of this place. No matter what direction he came from, the Mesa reared up as a barrier, a barrier that encouraged a traveler to detour around it rather than to try to travel the ragged terrain. The only open path led around the west end of the Mesa before it opened back into the pleasant valley nestled between the high mountains and the Mesa.

Mateep was enthralled with the mountains and was thrilled when Kaoto promised to take her up to the elk hunters' camp sometime. It was due to her love for the mountains that she and Torjan were seated under an ancient cedar tree near the lip of the cliff. From here they could see both to the east and south, and the east held the mountains. They had been left behind once again while Kaoto had taken a quick run over to the Hovenweep country. The view here belied the turmoil that terrorized the gentle farmers of the valley land below them.

"Why did they have to come? Why could they not have stayed away from us and our lands?" Mateep voiced the same question that Kaoto had heard ever since the invasion had begun.

"Kaoto says that only the Spirit Watcher knows, and he has not seen fit to inform him as to why," Torjan answered her absently, without thought. It is the only answer he had heard, and so repeated it to her. He did not feel wise. He felt ignorant.

"The Spirit Watcher does not care. Kaoto says we give the Spirit Watcher too much credit. That he does not care what happens to the People. He says even the savages are his People."

"I know." Torjan shook his head. "I have heard him and Paataga discuss it at length and I have to admit, they went way over my head. I could not understand what they were saying. The Gods of the Vikings were easier to understand. If you put up a good fight, they would reward you in the next life. If not, well, I do not know what was supposed to happen. No one ever talked about that."

"But why here?"

"It is just the nature of people," Torjan informed her. "Oh, I know it is not the nature of your People, but you are a minority in this world. I am surprised you have remained so long without someone coming and taking this land away from you."

"But why?" Mateep insisted. "There is land where they came from. They did not just spring up from the desert like a cactus. They had to have homes some place. So why did they come here? And why do they have to fight and kill? Why can they not just pass through the land and leave it as they found it?"

"That is hard to answer for you," Torjan said as he stroked the edge of his sword with a gray stone he carried for sharpening purposes.

"All people do not feel the same about the land as you do. Take me, for instance. I never had a feeling of belonging anyplace. Wherever I went, the land was mine as long as I stayed there, but I always had an itch on the bottom of my feet to see what was over the next hill and around the next bend in the river."

"Is it so much different here than where you have been before?" Mateep asked in wonder.

"Every place is different, even if it looks the same. If you have not been there before, then how do you know what you will find there? In many ways I am more like these savages than I am like your People. I took what I wanted and if anyone objected, I fought them and killed them. It never seemed wrong to me. It just seemed like the natural thing to do, until I met Kaoto. He has shown me a different side of life. If he had time, he could probably persuade the savages to change, too. But there are too many of them and not enough time for him to do it."

"Do you think they will ever go away? Do you think they will get an itch in their feet and move on someday and leave us in peace?" Mateep asked, hopeful for the future.

"Oh, I'm sure of it. But I do not think it will do you any good. By that time there will be none of your People left, and even if there were, there would be someone else to come in after the savages. No, in the long run Kaoto is right. The only chance the People have is to go somewhere else and start a new life under different circumstances. Chances are, in doing this they will be shoving other people out of their homes just as they are being shoved out of theirs here."

In an open space below, Torjan could see a file of men moving along a narrow trail. Their stealthy movements told him they were not of the People. They were savages on the prowl for some unaware prey. Watching them closely, he thought he could see their intended victims in a little group of structures nestled in the fold of a canyon that opened up on the main stream, which lead through the heart of the Mesa Verde.

"I'm going to go down there and stir up some action," Torjan stated as he rose to his feet and dropped his sword into the leather sheath secured at his waist. He loosened his knife and drew his hatchet to test its edge.

"Torjan. Do not go. I know you are spoiling for a fight, but could we not just call down and warn the People without you having to go down?"

"We could, and if I do not get down there in time to stop them you do just that. But I think I can cut them off before they can cause any trouble."

Before she could protest more, the Red One dropped over the edge of the cliff and began picking his way down to intercept the savages before they reached their quarry. For such a large man, he moved with such caution and silence that he did not betray his presence until he jumped out into the trail directly in front of the approaching file of men.

Mateep watched in wonder as Torjan drew his sword and advanced on the leader of the group with deadly intentions. His confidence in his ability to outfight ten men, armed with bows and spears, made Mateep proud of him in spite of her concern for his safety.

Torjan's buffalo hide shield turned away the first flight of arrows with ease. His bestial appearance had upset the savages and their aim had been hasty and poorly placed. Before they could loose a second round, he was upon them, slashing with his terrible sword. The freshly sharpened edge, flashing in the noon sun, left a silver arch each time he swung it. The leader crumpled and fell as Torjan sprang over him to disembowel the next two men as they stood abreast of each other, vying for a shot at the red-haired terror in their path.

Mateep gave a gasp as she saw tiny arrows that seemed to spring from Torjan's arms and legs. His shield could not stop all of them, but they seemed puny to the massive giant and he did not falter as he charged on down the trail at the remaining men. One by one they fell, their spears swept aside and their bodies hacked to pieces and left bleeding on the ground, as if laid out by an untidy butcher.

Eight of the ten fell before the last two turned and fled down the trail in a desperate flight for their lives. Torjan tried to lumber after them but the offending arrows made running painful and he soon gave up the chase. Disdainful of his wounds and the arrows still clinging to him, he carefully wiped the edge of his sword, removing any trace of blood that would stain the bright weapon.

When the last two turned tail and ran, Mateep dropped over the edge and descended on Torjan, screaming as she ran, all caution thrown to the wind. Next to Kaoto, Torjan meant more to her than anyone else in the world. To see her giant friend bleeding and trying to pull out the arrows made her run at a dangerous speed nearly straight down the hill.

Torjan heard and saw her coming. He tried to wave her back but she did not pay any attention to him. All she could see was that he was hurt and needed someone to assist him.

The two fleeing savages had also seen her, and at the same time saw a second party of savages that had been following some distance behind the first party. With reinforcements, their courage returned and they urged the second party forward to continue the attack, now that the Red One was wounded and distracted by the tiny maiden who had dropped out of the clouds.

Mateep attacked the arrows that seemed to be everywhere in Torjan's great body. He had not lost a great amount of blood yet and surprisingly did not seem to feel very much pain. Most of the arrows had either hit fleshy parts of his frame or had not penetrated enough to do him great injury. They were more bothersome than serious.

Grasping one after another, Mateep pulled them from him as though she was pulling cactus stickers from a child. She wiped away the blood and inspected each wound to see how much damage he had sustained.

"You great fool!" she shouted at him. "You could have been killed! Why? Why did you think you were the only one to fight them?" Tears streamed down her cheeks as she ministered to him. She was so relieved to find him still alive that she released her pent up emotions by expressing her anger at him. Torjan in turn took it like a small boy caught in some mischief by his mother.

"These are nothing, little one. Mosquitoes cause me more pain than this. But you should not have come down here. Kaoto would not forgive me if anything should happen to you. Go, get back up the hill before anyone sees you."

Even as he spoke, urging her to go, the savages returned. They made the mistake of announcing their presence with their chilling war cries. Torjan roared a challenge as he turned to face them. He was trying to put his large body between them and Mateep, but she would have none of it. She slipped by him and raced to the nearest downed man and grasped his weapons. The bow was large for her, but she was strong and desperation lent strength so that she pulled the bow back and sent an arrow into the midst of the running men. One man fell, pinned through with one of his comrade's arrows sent by a tiny maiden who should have been no threat to them at all.

Torjan followed suit by picking up a fallen spear and hurling it with such violence that it passed completely through its target and fell on the trail behind him. Without hesitation, he followed the spear, charging into them, bellowing like the wounded animal he was. Once more his sword was flashing, dealing grievous wounds everywhere it went. His charge, backed by Mateep's rain of arrows, was too much for the savages and once again they fell back to regroup.

In their haste they failed to notice a third person coming down the hillside in long strides. Even as he ran, his bow was up and arrows came like sudden death, felling men right and left. Kaoto came into the trail behind them. Now they were caught between two mad men and an avenging girl.

"None of them must leave here alive," Kaoto called over to Torjan. "If they do, they might figure out where we came from and start looking up on the side of the canyon for others."

Between the two giants the savages had no chance. Even those who tried to flee in the brush at the side of the trail were cut down until the last man died, taking the secret of the Mesa with him into the next world, but not back to his tribe.

After inspecting each fallen man to ascertain he was truly dead, Kaoto steered his companions back up the steep slope, helping Torjan when the going got rough.

"You great idiot," Kaoto accused his friend, once they were back safely on the top of the canyon. "What were you doing? Did you think you could fight the whole world by yourself? Probably so. It is the way you would think." Kaoto was torn between relief and anger.

"There were just a few in the first group. I did not see the second batch until they came running back. Besides, someone has to fight them or they will kill everyone in the nation." Torjan had never seen Kaoto this angry and he tried to defend his actions.

"And you!" Kaoto took Mateep by the shoulders and shook her as he would a small child. "Who told you that you were a warrior? What got into you to come down here like that?"

Mateep was still shaking from fear, and Kaoto's scolding made her shake even more. Her stomach was just now feeling the effect of the killing she had participated in. She fought to keep from becoming violently ill. She hung her head and tried to explain.

"I only did what you would have done, what you did do when you saw the danger. I could not leave him down here alone to face them all. He needed help. You were not here, so I helped him."

"Give me a couple more like her and we would not have to run from these savages. We could wipe them off the land." Torjan was looking at Mateep with pride and wonder.

Kaoto looked from one to the other. He was gaining his composure now that they were out of harm's way and apparently not seriously wounded. He wanted to laugh and cry at the same time. He could not explain his feelings when he had returned from Hovenweep just in time to see Mateep join in the battle. To keep from saying any more, he inspected Torjan's numerous wounds. None of them posed a threat to the red giant's life, but there was one arrow point still buried deep in the Red One's side. It had entered from the side and penetrated deep in the muscle along his spine. The shaft had come out, but the point was still embedded in the soft flesh. He did not know if he would be able to dig it out without causing more danger.

Torjan tried to ignore the irritation and made light of it, but it bothered him more than he wanted to let on. The pain had been excruciating as they climbed and now it throbbed with each step. He had weathered many wounds in the past and he would overcome this one in time, just like the others.

Kaoto watched him intently as he squared his shoulders and limped slowly back to the village they were living in while they were up on the Mesa. Mateep followed meekly along behind them, but she also had noticed Torjan's painful steps and wondered if even a giant such as he was could overcome this obstacle.

Chapter Fifty Four

Kaoto made the green tabletop mountain his headquarters. Here he felt safe in leaving Mateep and Torjan while he continued his travels about the land. From this point Kaoto could move out to a troubled area in the shortest possible time. His duties kept him almost constantly on the move, leaving him little time to spend with his companions. He established his own corps of runners to keep him posted on the activities of the invading savages, who were now filtering deeper into the heart of the nation. The runners brought discouraging news with each passing day.

Torjan's wounds healed rapidly and soon all that was left to remind him of his adventure were numerous small scars, which were hard to differentiate from those he had collected over his wild and adventurous life.

The arrow point lodged near his spine had been removed by applications of hot poultices and time. When the point had finally popped from the dark opening in his side he had felt relieved and expected to be back to normal in a short time. However, when Kaoto inspected the offending stone point he discovered it was not complete. A small portion of the tip was missing. It was possible it could have been broken before it had been shot at Torjan, but it was also possible the missing piece was still embedded in his body. As time passed and Torjan still limped and complained of the pain in his back, Kaoto suspected the broken point was the cause of this trouble.

The Red One could walk, and did most of the things he had always done before, but running was a thing of the past for him. Whenever he attempted to run, he was soon forced to slow his pace until he was back to walking again. The jolt of his feet hitting the path was transmitted up the trunk of his legs and registered as a pain in the small of his back.

"I have always told you I was not made for running anyway," he told Kaoto. "So it is no great loss to me, other than it keeps me from accompanying you. Which, if the truth were known, is a great relief to you."

Kaoto smiled at his big friend but did not deny the accusation. He was relieved. While he hated to see Torjan restricted in his travels and the pain made him feel guilty, he no longer had to leave Mateep alone. She had accepted the Red One as her brother and Kaoto used the excuse that she was needed to look after him as a means of getting her to consent to stay when he left on one of his many trips. All in all it was a good working relationship for all of them. But in time, when Torjan had recovered sufficiently to wander about without worry or aid, Mateep again became restless with staying at home while Kaoto was gone. Soon she was able to get him to consent to let her go with him on short runs when he considered the risk to be minimal.

They took the long promised and often postponed trip to the high country elk hunters' camp. It was still early fall and the activities of the savages had somewhat diminished with the approach of winter. There had been fresh snow at the high camps, but the lower camps were still relaxed in the fall sun and temperate weather.

"Why do you not set up your headquarters here?" Mateep asked Kaoto one afternoon as they sat on a rocky point overlooking the land to the west. From here she could see the tall sentinels of the wasteland far west of the mountains. Kaoto pointed out to her the location of Kalo's home, which was still farther west than these tall, bleak, landmarks.

"It is tempting. I have always longed to stay here and just be a hunter. I think it would be too easy for me to slack off my duties if I stayed here." Kaoto let his eyes drift over the vast landscape that unfolded before him. From here he could see the floating mountain, which looked like an island in the blue haze. He could see the sharp, up-pointed rock that stood alone in the near desert just beyond the Mesa. And far south, even though he could not see it, he knew lay his homeland in the Chaco.

"Sometimes when I am up here I am overwhelmed by the size of the land and the distances I have traveled and must travel again. It does not seem possible for one man to do all that I have done and must continue to do. There are times when I want to ask the Spirit Watcher why he did not send someone to help me."

"Why did he not? If he is so powerful, why did he not give you help? It seems to me that he is being unfair to demand so much of you and nothing of anyone else." Mateep, like all women, was not frightened of talking about the Spirit Watcher. In fact sometimes her irreverence made Kaoto uneasy.

"Perhaps he did not think it was such a big job from where he sits and the speed in which he travels. Or perhaps he did know the suffering that would be required of me and decided he would not inflict it on any more of the People than he had too. I do not know what he thinks. All I do know is that the job fell to me and I accepted it with my eyes open, knowing fully what my life would entail."

"Did you? I mean when you were a young man, studying with Paataga, did you really know just what you were letting yourself in for? I talked much with Paataga and I managed to get her to tell me about you and what you were like as a young man. She told me of how you were literally an outcast among the young people. She told me of your lonely life with only Little Frog for a companion. How could you have known what it would be like to live alone and travel alone for all this time?"

"The very fact of my lonely life as a child is what prepared me for this job. If I had been accepted and honored in my home, by the people of my village, I probably could never have been able to do what I have done. Little Frog was my only contact with People, and for all of her infirmities she had a wisdom of her own that never failed to amaze me. Between her and Paataga I was taught to look at things from a different perspective than the farmers of the land."

"It still is not fair. I have a need for you and there is no reason why you should have to give up everything, including a normal life with me, just to instruct the People about something they do not want to hear and do not want to do."

"Perhaps not. But it has been and shall be my responsibility until such a day as the Spirit Watcher informs me it is over. Until then I will have to keep doing what I know I must do."

Mateep wanted to continue arguing with him. She wanted desperately to influence him to stay here, to give up his lonely life. She felt they could live here among the hunters in the land he obviously loved more than any other place in the land. She wanted to, but she did not. She knew that if she did this, in time she would loose him just as surely as she occasionally did now. The difference would be that if he stayed here to please her, in time he would grow to resent her, even hate her for what she had made him do. Would he blame her for his captivity, for his desertion of what he felt was his life? Paataga's long talks had prepared her for this and now she drew on the wisdom of the ancient Wise One to instruct her. She remembered Paataga's words:

"If you love him, which I know you do, then you must love him on his own terms. You must be prepared for much sorrow and heartache. You, too, must know loneliness, just as he does. While the People may surround you, if he is not with you, you will be alone. He is a tall man, a big man, and you are a little tiny woman, but you must give him strength. I know this sounds silly, looking at the two of you standing side by side. It would seem more likely that he would be lending you his strength, but strength comes in different packages, for different reasons. He needs someone like you to lean on. Someone to talk to. He spends so much time listening to others and trying to advise them, that I fear he does not ever have the time to be heard himself. We all have our doubts and fears. Yes, even Wise One's." Paataga had seen the look of disbelief crossing Mateep's features. "You think we are mountains of strength having all the answers, knowing the past and the future. Well you, like all the others, are wrong.

"We do not have all the answers. We do not know much more than you or they do. The difference is what we do with what we know. Our memories enable us to put things together, much as you did as a child when you pieced together the pieces of a broken jug. You did it for entertainment, not to use the jug again, but just something to do to pass time. We do it to preserve the People. We are attempting to save a lifestyle that is being threatened. The pieces we try to put together can make the difference in whether the People continue or are lost for all time."

"You make me feel like a small, ignorant child when you talk that way," Mateep had told her. "How can I help him? How can I give him strength? He should search the land to find someone with your wisdom to be his mate, not an untutored child from the black rocks who does not even know what the life of the People is about."

"You are wrong again. Your background, raised alone as you were, gives you an advantage over anyone else. You are not filled with customs and beliefs of the People. You are open to the new and the different. You have no established belief in how a man and woman should live. You are not tied down with family and a home that would bind you to one place and thus make him feel obligated to stay at your side as normal mates do. No, you have a great advantage over them all, even me. You can do for him what no other woman can do. You can be his companion wherever he must go. You can follow him. You can be close to him when he needs you. How could he go away for summer after summer if you were in one place and could not, or would not, move? Your strength is in your ability to understand him and you can help him by not standing between his love for you and his responsibility."

At the time Mateep had not understood what Paataga was telling her, but over the past few turns of the moon she had come to realize that, as usual, the old great mother had been right. This was one of those times when she must choose between what she desired for herself and what she knew was right for him. If it was right for him, then it would have to be right for her. If he could make all the sacrifices as he had, then could she do less? Could she not sacrifice a little for him?

On another occasion Paataga had told her, "You must accept what is offered when it is available. It is like eating berries in the summer. If you do not eat them when they are ripe, you do not eat them at all. You enjoy them in their season knowing they will soon be gone, but come another summer they will be back and you look forward to their return."

Life was already like that. She enjoyed Kaoto when he was here and when he left, even before he was out of sight, she was looking forward to the time when he returned. The old mother had truly been a Wise One. She too had lived a lonesome life, but she could look into the hearts of others and know how they would feel and what they should do. Mateep would always revere the time spent with the old one who had been far more than a mother to her. She had been as always, Paataga, the Wise One.

With Paataga's words still fresh in her mind, Mateep refrained from saying more. She put aside her desire for his safety. She hid her longing for a permanent home where they could live out their days in peace and contentment. Kaoto's life precluded such a thing ever happening as long as he felt the Spirit Watcher had a need for him.

After a short time, a brief vacation, they had returned to the top of the Mesa and life had continued for them much as it had in the past. Kaoto went on long, extended trips while Mateep and Torjan took turns looking after each other.

It was at Mateep's insistence and urging that the Red One finally consented to taking a mate among the available women of the Mesa.

Weepena had shown a great interest in the Red One from the first moment she had laid eyes on him. This had occurred during their first stop here before going on down to the Chaco canyon. Weepena was not a young maiden anymore, not by the standards of the People. She had seen twenty-and-five summers and had already known one mate. Her mate had fallen from one of the cliffs, and while he did not die of the fall, he had been a hopeless cripple. She had tended to him as best as she could with the assistance of her aging father and mother.

Weepena was a lively person and the restrictions put on her by tending a crippled mate had troubled her deeply. She did not want to be unfaithful to her man, but she did not want to have to sleep alone for the rest of her life, either. When she had seen the great Red One, she had fantasized what life would be like with such a man for a mate.

Weepena's mate had lingered on for several turns of the moon, but when his condition did not improve, he did what he considered best for all concerned. He had ended his own life in his own way. He had opened his veins one evening and quietly let his life's blood flow in the darkness, so that morning found him departed on his journey into the next land.

Weepena had mourned his death as any good and devoted mate should and none could fault her on her behavior. But now she was free, and unless she took another mate, she would have to live with her parents until their death. Then she would be forced to take herself to the dumpsite to live out the remainder of her life there as a non-person.

When Torjan had returned with Kaoto, Weepena had taken this as a sign from the Spirit Watcher that she would be spared this humiliation. While not brazen or forward, she had hovered near the Red One and had been the one to assist Mateep when the arrows had been pulled from his great frame. Mateep could not help but notice how her touch was longer than necessary whenever she placed her hands on the huge hairy body. The look in Weepena's eyes was no mystery to another woman who was equally in love.

When Mateep confronted her with the truth, Weepena did not deny her longing to be the Red One's mate. Together they planned a carefully laid strategy that they hoped would lead to the capitulation of the seemingly insurmountable Irish slave.

Torjan had taken longer to tumble than they had expected, but in the end he had made the first open move of announcing his desire to live with her. In true maiden fashion, Weepena had acted surprised at such an offer and had told him she must think on it. She advised him to consult the Wise One for his consent. Mateep and Weepena retired to a vacant part of the building and hugged each other in their shared happiness.

"How could you do it?" Mateep had whispered as soon as they were out of hearing of the Red One.

"Do what?" Weepena asked in mocked innocence.

"You know what I mean. How could you possibly act like you were surprised, and on top of that you have the nerve to say you had to think about it, as if you had thought of anything else ever since we came here?" Mateep laughed with her hand over her mouth to muffle the sound.

"Well, I do need to think about it. I mean, is it really fair to trap a man just as you would a rabbit?"

"Fool. Since when have you slept with a rabbit?" They both broke into gales of laughter that drifted into Torjan's earshot, but he mistakenly thought it was the sound of crying. Women. They cried when they were happy and cried when they were sad. How was a man supposed to figure them out?

Torjan had approached the Wise One with the idea, which by now he was sure had been his own all along. Kaoto had suppressed a smile while he listened with straight-faced concern to his friend's request, wondering why the Red One felt any need of his permission to do anything he chose to do. Looking away, pretending to study nature for signs, he passed a quick look to Mateep, who had come around the corner of the building as they talked. He called her over to consult her on such a grave matter.

"What do you think about Torjan's proposal?" he asked her.

"Oh, what does he propose to do now? Go out single handedly and remove all the savages from our land? I think he has tried that before, and so far it has not worked out very well. So I guess I will have to vote against it." Mateep tried desperately to match Kaoto's blank expression, but she was unable and gave up the farce.

"I think it is a wonderful idea, Torjan. Weepena is a good woman and she will make you a wonderful mate. I have talked with her and I am sure between the both of you, you can persuade her to accept. She is only holding back because she does not know if it is proper for her to behave in this manner." This was at least the truth. Weepena had asked if it was right to trap him this way. Mateep did not feel it was necessary to add the details of Weepena's thinking.

So it had been done. With Kaoto acting in his capacity as both Wise One and friend, he sanctioned the union of the Red One with Weepena, honorable and respected woman of the People. In the custom of the People, Torjan had erected a room connecting with Weepena's mother's building. The room was considerably larger than any other room outside of the kivas, but it was still small and cramped to him and he spent most of his time outside. The nights when the weather was disagreeable, they could snuggle in the close quarters of the room and neither complained about the closeness.

Mated for the first time in his life, Torjan underwent another transformation, much as he had when he had decided to be a friend to the Wise One. Just as most of the People already knew, there was a very gentle and kind man buried in the mountain of red hair and giant sized body of Torjan. Now he let that man out to be dominant. The Viking was laid to rest, not for all time, but for most of the time. The Viking only appeared when something disastrous happened, or when new stories of the savages came pouring in. Then his anger vented itself in true Viking expression. He roared and strutted about, waving his sword, and making threats; threats he would have gladly carried out except for the gentling effect of Weepena, who calmed him and brought him back to her hearth fire.

Weepena's parents had mixed emotions at first, but soon grew to accept the Red One as a son. He proved to be a good provider and shared his bounty with them, as a good son should. It was a good match, and being a friend of the Wise One was an extra bonus.

Kaoto was also relieved for Torjan. Now he felt his problem had been permanently solved. Torjan would have an excuse to stay here. He would no longer have to feel badly about not going with Kaoto or Mateep when they left. Kaoto knew the time was coming when they would have to leave even these peaceful surroundings. He did not know when or where they would go, but deep inside he knew their days here were limited. He only hoped he would be allowed to finish out the winter before he must move on. Already this place was beginning to feel like home to him, a feeling he must not allow to grow. A feeling he must suppress before he was tempted beyond his endurance to stay.

Several times of late he had found himself asking the Spirit Watcher to release him from his duty if it were possible without breaking his promise to the People. He had requested the right to make a home and live a life of his own. He had been humble in his request but deep down in his inner being he knew what he wanted. He also knew the Spirit Watcher knew the hearts of all men. His only fear was that he would be tempting fate to even make such a request. He remembered his parents' warning that to even mention some things might attract the attention of the deity and cause him to become angry and retaliate against the offending person or persons. He did not really believe this, but still he did not want to cause harm to come to Mateep.

Chapter Fifty Five

The winter held off until late, giving a false sense of security to the farmers of the valleys. Their crops had not been as plentiful as sometimes, but the long fall and temperate early winter led them to believe they would have ample supplies to last until another crop could be raised. But when the real winter came, it came with a vengeance.

The second moon of winter had just passed when the storms began to build and angry, cold clouds blocked the Spirit Watcher's warming rays from the People. Snow fell almost continuously, piling high and staying on the ground. Opening paths became increasingly difficult. Firewood supplies dwindled until the People crouched in their small compartments and huddled together to keep warm. Many of the old and weak could not endure the cold and expired in silence to a cold and miserable death. Most of these were interned in the floors of their homes because it was too miserable to dig graves out in the winter weather. Many of these homes were abandoned, never to know life again.

The violence of the weather was suffered by the herds of deer and elk also, and the wolves and coyotes feasted on the frozen carcasses, ensuring an ever-increasing number of these predators the next spring. Their large numbers would be faced with far less food in the coming summer, and they would overcome their fear of man and prey on him as another means of food.

The savages were also severely crippled by this coldest of winters, so the People were spared their threats during the winter. They could not traverse the deep snow any more than others, beasts or men.

Kaoto was forced to stay in one place, seldom venturing outside the village where he now lived with Mateep. He and Torjan managed to keep a path open between their two homes and they spent more time together than they had in several moons.

When the first moon of spring came, they looked longingly at the skies for relief, but found no comfort there as the snows continued to build up. The death toll was staggering to the mind. Over half of the population of the nation lay dead or dying. The weather had proven a worse enemy than the savages, and had shown no mercy on any living thing.

On occasions, the stronger members braved the snow and winds to salvage the carcasses of frozen animals, but these starved bodies offered little nourishment to the People. Kaoto began to spend long periods of time in isolation, pleading with the Spirit Watcher for solace.

"These are your People. Why do you punish them this way?" he cried at the angry, dark skies. "Is it because they did not leave as you requested them to do? If that is so, then punish me and leave them in peace. It is I who have failed you, not them. They never received word from you as I did. I failed to convince them they were in so much danger. You did not tell me of this threat, only of the savages."

He wondered if this were the truth. Had he been wrong interpreting the signs? Had the dark shadows also included these dark clouds? There was so much to know and so much to learn. Had he failed in his mission because he had not been thorough enough? Should he have searched deeper for the meanings? It would seem so. Now that the terrible winter had descended on them, he could see the possibility of it being part of the dark shadows circling the People.

Torjan and Mateep could not lift this deep depression from him, and his load of guilt bore down on him as no other responsibility had in the past. When the spring finally arrived he was quickly out of his home and on the trail, often suffering the cold and sweeping wind when no man should have been out.

"Kaoto you have to stop this," Mateep cried out to him when he came limping back one evening nearly frozen, drenched with cold rain and exhausted from long periods of exposure.

"I cannot rest. I have to be out and see to the People," he tried to explain to her. "Oh, little one, it breaks my heart to see what has happened this winter. You would not believe the number of dead I have found. Whole families lying dead in their homes, clutching to each other in their last moments. It tears my heart from me and my eyes are sore with weeping for them. There are no more tears left for me to shed for them and it is all my fault. I have failed them. I failed them in the time when they needed me the most. I am only glad that Paataga did not live to witness my shame."

"How can you be to blame? Do you control the wind and the snow? No. No more than you could stem the flow of the savages. If the People had listened to you, they would not have been here to face this winter. It was their choice, not yours, my beloved. Please, if not for your sake, then for mine, stop this senseless wandering. What can you do for them now? Learn as I have, the dead are dead. There is nothing you can do for the dead and very little you can do for the living. You have to think about yourself for a change." Mateep's tiny body was wasted to skin and bone from the long winter of privation. What little food they had they had insisted on sharing with those who had less.

"My brother," Torjan said as he laid his hand on his wasted friend's shoulder, shocked to feel so little flesh and so much bone under his hand. "Mateep is right. You cannot take all this blame on yourself. I must remind you of what Paataga said about the importance of men and ants. At the time I could not see the comparison, but now I think I understand what she was saying. Even the insects have suffered from this winter, and according to you and your old mother, the ants are just as important to your God as you are. Is there one ant out there somewhere, shouting to your Spirit Watcher that he is to blame for all the misfortune that has fallen on all the ant population of the nation? Think about this, my friend. Think of what Paataga would say to you if she were here."

This long, extended speech from the normally taciturn man gave Kaoto pause to think. How long had it been since he had talked to his old teacher, or even thought about her and what she would have had to say about this turn of events? He hung his head in sorrow and shame. He had failed in this also. He had asked her never to forget him, even in death, but he had so easily forgotten her. He knew that if he had listened she would have spoken to him from the grave if she had to, or from the next world. If he had only taken the time to listen. But no, he had been so puffed up with his own importance that he had neglected to seek the help that was available to him.

He dropped to the floor and sat leaning against the wall. He remained silent, refusing to answer either their questions or accusations. They were right. He knew that now. Who was he to think he was so important that the world would bow to his requests? He was nothing. One, lone man in a world of men. His claim to wisdom did not make him special to the Spirit Watcher. What did he have to offer to make him a mediator for his People? He had been given one task and he had failed in it, so why should anyone pay any attention to him now?

Tired beyond his memory, exhausted and weak, he toppled over onto the floor, sound asleep. Mateep covered him with as many robes as she could find and curled up next to him to add what little body heat she had to help warm his chilled body. As she lay awake, because sleep would not come to her, she thought of her conversations with Paataga about her giving him strength. As she lay, a misted vision formed before her eyes. She blinked, but the vision remained. There, against the opposite wall, in the gloom of the dark room, she could see a tiny fire flickering. Across the fire, seated on her log, Paataga gazed at her through the smoke.

"Why do you weep, little one?" She asked gently.

"Oh, old mother. The world is so sad since you have gone."

"The world has always been sad, little one. What is so different now?" The wraith-like apparition asked.

"Kaoto thinks he has failed, and if he has it is because I failed him. You told me he would need my strength and I have none to give to him." Mateep realized she was speaking out loud and hearing Paataga's words in her ears, not her mind.

"Little one, little one. Why are the young always so impatient, and so full of doubts? You have not failed him. You are there. You have always been there when he needed you. Strength? What do you think he draws from you? There are maidens all over the nation who would gladly sleep with him, give of their bodies to him, but that is not what he has need of. What he has need of is someone to listen to him when he talks. Someone who cares what he feels and thinks. Someone who does not have a demand to make on his time and energies. No, you have not failed him, little one."

"But our world is coming to an end. No one can survive this winter and have strength enough left to raise food and hide from the savages. Kaoto fears all will be lost this summer, and he takes all the blame on his own shoulders. Oh, Paataga, he is growing so weak himself that he cannot keep up like this. He has to have rest and find peace, peace of mind. If he does not, then I will lose him. We will all lose him, for all time."

"Listen to me, little one. Kaoto has more strength than you give him credit for. He will bow and he will bend, but he will not break. His heart is as large as the rest of him and though it seems to break now, it will carry him on for many more summers. It is his mind that is suffering the most, and his mind is like a delicate flower that is beaten and torn by the winds. But in the long run that flower will still bear fruit. Some things are made stronger by the beatings they have to take. Look at the little trees that grow on the crest of a high ridge. They are beaten and twisted by the winds, but they survive and they live. They have to become stronger to be able to survive the next wind. Kaoto will survive and he will be stronger than ever."

The vision faded and was gone, but the words of the old mother remained fresh and clear in Mateep's mind. She did not know just what she should do, but she felt hope again for the first time since the long winter had set in. Paataga had spoken of the flower bearing fruit. Did she know what Mateep suspected? Did she know about the tiny seed, taking root deep within her? She smiled to herself. Of course she would. She was a Wise One and she was a woman. No woman could hide this fact from another woman. They seemed to sense it long before anyone else could know.

Kaoto's sleep was long and troubled. He had dreams as he had not had since he was a child. His old familiar dream sped by without change, but then a new dream came into focus.

He could see himself standing, looking up at a high cliff, so high he had to tip his head far back in order to see the top. At the top was a sliver of open sky, and in this open sky he could see what he knew was an eagle. The eagle had its wings spread as if to soar away, but it did not move. It hung in the sky like a painting on a rock. How long he stood looking at the bird he did not know, but he did know that he felt good. Slowly he realized it was night; there was no sun, no stars, no moon, but it was night. How then could he see so plainly? How could he know the bird was an eagle? It was much too far away to identify, yet he knew it was so and seemed to take comfort from the sighting.

When he awoke late the next day, the sun was shining clearly for the first time in many days. He could not remember when he had last seen a completely clear day such as this. With the sun came warmth, real warmth for the first time, and there was a promise of another season on the winds, which blew from a different direction now, carrying the sweet scent of spring and the promise of new life.

He rose and stretched, forgetting he was in a small room, and he laughed as he brushed his arms against the wall and bumped his head on the ceiling.

Mateep entered the room at the sound of his laughter. It was a foreign sound, long forgotten. She carried a steaming bowl of mush with a few scraps of meat on top. Handing him the bowl, she said, "Here, eat this. You need some food to fill out that big shell of yours."

"What about you?" he asked as he stepped outside into the glorious sunlight.

"I ate earlier, while you were still asleep," she told him. But he noticed she did not look at him when she spoke.

"Come here," he said as he seated himself on a rock near the door and leaned back against the wall, which was already radiating back the heat given off by the Spirit Watcher. Mateep came forward slowly. Her face carried a smile, but it was as shallow as the face it tried to cover. Kaoto encircled her tiny waist with one long arm and pulled her down on his knee. Filling the wooden ladle, he offered her food. Mateep shook her head and said, "That is for you. I have already eaten my share this morning early, while my lazy man slept."

"There are many things you do very well, my little cactus flower, but lying to me is not one of them. You have not eaten. This is all there is. You are trying to make me think you have already taken your share, but you have not. Now we will share this." He held the spoon close to her, coaxing her to eat.

"But I do not need much. You are the one who has been out all the time and you are so much bigger. You need food to run. I do not," she argued. But her eyes stayed on the ladle of mush.

"Equally, one bite for you, one bite for me. I will not take a bite until you have taken one." Kaoto held the food closer. The smell rose and tickled her nose.

"All right. I will eat a little, just to make you happy, but really I am not very hungry." Mateep took the mouthful of food and fought back the urge to swallow it without chewing.

"Equally, one bite for you, one for me, until the bowl is empty." He looked about quickly as a thought crossed his mind. There it was, a small bowl of food next to the fire. It was not saved back for her meal, it was the bowl of food they always set aside to be taken to the creatures of the dump. There were few of them left this spring, but surprisingly enough a few had managed to hang on in spite of the shortage of food and the severity of the winter. Not even extreme hunger could make either of them forget the pledge Kaoto had made so long ago.

Mateep ceased to argue and took her share of the food, and even though she felt guilty for taking so much when she was so little she could not help but enjoy it and think of the small person growing inside her. This person was like those on the dump. It was a non-person now and must depend on her to feed it so someday it could come out into the light and be one of the real People.

Torjan had managed better than some of the others during the winter. He had been able to breast the snowdrifts and gather meat. He had shared with all he could reach, but the People were more vegetarians and did not eat a steady diet of meat. Torjan, on the other hand, had been weaned on red meat and even old, tough, stringy, half-starved meat filled his gut and gave him strength.

He was considerably leaner than Kaoto had ever seen him before, but he was still a mountain of strength in the slowly dwindling pack of starved and frozen People who represented all that was left of a once proud nation.

As the warm weather held on and the promise of spring became a reality, Kaoto knew his time here was over. It was with great sadness he called Torjan to his hearth fire and told him.

"I must leave soon. Mateep and I will be going and I do not think we will ever be back. It makes my heart sore to leave you, my old friend, but it must be. You have a woman here and you could never stay on the trail, even if she wanted to travel with you."

Torjan nodded his head. He, too, had known that Kaoto would someday be leaving. He also knew he would have to stay here. He did not mind living out whatever days he had left here, but he did not like to see Kaoto leave. He did not argue, knowing how futile his words would be.

"It is as you say. I could not travel very far now even at a slow walk. I could never keep up with you on the trail when I was in good shape. Now it would not even be good for a laugh. I guess this is what you would call the fate of the Gods, yours or mine or both. I will make this my home as long as there is life in my bones. If you should ever return this way, you will find me here, surrounded by as many red-haired People as you can count."

Weepena had slipped under his arm as he spoke and smiled happily at her man, her red mountain of love and kindness. She did not say a word, but her eyes spoke for her. If she worshiped anything in this world, it was the man whose arm she stood under. He was the symbol of strength to her and all that knew him. Kaoto was sure he would be as good a representative as he could leave here in his place.

It was just as well that Kaoto and Mateep would never know the end of the Red One. Long after they had left, a band of the savages worked their way up on the northwestern slopes of the Mesa. They came upon a group of the little farmers who were searching for a cache of food supplies they had been unable to reach during the winter of the deep snows. Torjan was with them in the capacity of a human pack animal. He was capable of carrying more than several of the smaller men. Weepena had come along because she too was strong and could carry her share. Let it be known that Torjan died a fitting death for a Viking. His iron sword and knife exacted a high price before they were stilled. Standing over his fallen companions, the great Red One roared his defiance to anyone who could hear. Weepena stood at his side in spite of his attempts to shield her. She died fighting beside the Red One. What more could she ask for? Unable to run, and without his shield, he was at the mercy of the savages as they ringed him in and took their time driving arrow after arrow into his still gaunt body. Even in death he was fearsome as he sank to his knees, but his body refused to bow or fall before his enemies. The effect was so great that the savages pulled back and left him and his fallen comrades and Weepena. And so it was that he was found later by another group from the Mesa.

Torjan and his mate were buried near where they fell. It took a long grave to accommodate the Red One, but it was done. No one wanted the Red One to be cramped on his way to the next world. His iron sword was driven into the ground over his grave and his helmet set atop for all to see. The story passed among the savages about the man who refused to die, and they walked far to avoid setting foot on the ground where he lay. His only regret was that he failed to leave even one red-haired person to the People to mark his passing.

With a small pack for each of them, Kaoto and Mateep left the Mesa and headed south. Kaoto did not have a real destination. He was following the instinctive urge he had always counted on in the past, and it told him to go south. He might be longing to return to the Chaco but he did not think so. There was something else calling him, and as he had so often in the past, when the call came, he packed his few belongings and went in search of whoever or whatever had expressed a need for him. Mateep followed Kaoto without question. Wherever he went was where she must go. Paataga had renewed her hope and revived her belief that her place was at his side.

Their path led them south to the river flowing west. From here they moved steadily eastward toward the Pueblo at Aztec, although Kaoto did not feel this was the place he would be going. It was in the direction he felt he must travel, but somewhere between here and the pueblo there was a need that called to him in a voice only he could hear and understand. Mateep had long ago given up trying to hear or understand. It was her place to follow and be his companion. This was enough for her.

Spring blessed the land with rains; more rain than the sandy soil could hold, and the rivers were rising. The balmy weather had started the deep snow to melt in the high country, and this added to the river's volume. It was higher than Kaoto had ever seen it before, and showed every sign of rising higher.

Wherever he was going, he decided it was not across the river. Not right away, at least. It would be impossible to cross, it even using logs for a raft. The current was too swift and dangerous to risk.

He pulled back to the higher ground where the footing was better and the side streams were easier to cross. He had to carry Mateep across most of these to keep her from being swept away. At the mouth of a second river, a smaller one coming straight down from the mountains, they discovered a log jam which afforded them a crossing, and from here they climbed a steep bluff which overlooked the confluence of yet a third river that joined the first two.

Just above the joining of the three rivers, there was a conflict being acted out below them like players on a stage. Kaoto quickly made out the principal players. A small family group of the People was trapped on the central fork of the two larger rivers. They had taken refuge in the willows near the river. The other players were the savages, who were waiting for the rising water to flush the victims out in the open so they could take them without any danger to themselves.

Mateep felt Kaoto's muscles tense and saw the hard line of his chin. He would not pass this family by. Somehow he intended to assist them, although she could not see how he could do this from where they were. The raging river separated them. Still, she knew he would find a way. He did not admit defeat easily and when others were in danger he went far out of his way to help. It was odd; she did not feel fear, only excitement. She had confidence in his ability and knew that whatever he planned, she would be a part of it, because he would not leave here alone with the savages about.

Chapter Fifty Six

Kaoto stood on the top of the high bank overlooking the scene below. He said nothing but his mind was working at top speed. Satisfied at last with what he saw, he took Mateep by the hand and started to run at a brisk pace, staying on the high ground but moving steadily upstream.

Mateep could sense his urgency and did the best she could to hold a fast pace, painfully slow compared to what he could accomplish by himself. But he did not complain, only held firmly to her hand and exerted a steady pressure.

They had to cross several more swollen side streams before they again came to a stop on a steep bluff overlooking the middle river. They were beyond the camp of the savages now and again Kaoto studied the river below them. The sun was dropping far to the west. It would soon be dark. Darkness was going to be their ally. With the darkness, the savages would pull back to their camp. They might well leave guards out to keep the family from slipping by them, but they would be looking toward the trapped victims down in the willows, not behind them.

Kaoto led the way down the bluff, heading for the river where the last small stream had entered it. From his high perch he had been able to see that the force of the secondary stream pushed out into the current of the central river, making a cross current that swept close to the opposite bank. A quick search along the bank unearthed a dead cottonwood log. Not overly large, it was light enough to be moved and still large enough to hold them afloat.

Pushing the log out into the current, Kaoto held Mateep between himself and the log. She did not need to be told to hold on with all her strength. Soon the current was buffeting them about, swinging them wildly end for end in the turbulence caused by the merging streams.

Mateep found herself holding her breath as the current pushed them closer to the far bank, but before they could reach it they were swirled back toward the center of the stream. The log bobbed and twisted as if trying to dislodge the unwelcome riders who were frantically trying to push it back to the shore.

Over his many summers, Kaoto had learned patience, and he applied that trait now. Steadily he kicked and pushed at the log and was able to slowly guide it toward the far bank. They were already even with the savages and were soon swept on past them. They were not noticed until they were beyond the savages and were rapidly approaching the willows. Here the waters were spread out and some of the velocity was lost. Kaoto dropped his feet and discovered he could touch the bottom. He lunged with all his strength against the log and managed to push it over into the restraining growth on the fork of the rivers.

Taking Mateep on his shoulders, he waded into the willow screen, moving around other logs trapped in this maze. He gave a soft call to alert the family of his identity and was met by them in the shallow waters where they had taken refuge.

"Wise One, what are you doing here?" The man asked when he recognized Kaoto in the settling gloom.

"I have come to help you." Kaoto's simple statement was somehow reassuring to the man, who had considered himself and his family already lost.

"We welcome your help, but what can we do? There are too many for even you to fight, and the water is going to keep rising until we must either drown or go out in the open." The wiry little man stood waist deep in the calm waters, holding a child up with each hand. His mate clung to his side for support.

"Corb. What are you doing so far from your home?" Kaoto recalled this man who lived up stream at one of the small villages located there.

"They came, just as you said they would, and we were not ready, just as you said we would not be. I do not know if anyone else escaped or not. We were a ways downstream from the village when they struck. We had all been down to the river, checking on traps I had set for rabbits. I am glad Tulla and the children were with me, or else they would all be dead by now. Of course, it looks like we will all die anyway." Corb seemed to accept their fate with stoic resignation. This was something Kaoto, for all his summers and supposed wisdom, could not understand or accept.

"We will not die here. This I know. The Spirit Watcher has not led me here to die. If he wanted my life he could have taken it many times in the past. No Corb, we do not die here. Not tonight. How much rope do you have on you?" he asked, noting the coil of woven rope looped over the man's shoulder.

"I am not sure; several lengths. It was something I was working on and have been carrying it around with me the past few days. There is some more in a basket. It should be floating around here someplace. Why? How much do you need?"

"As much as you have and probably more, but maybe between us we will have enough. There are any number of dead logs floating around us. We will pull them together and make a raft. Torjan taught me how to make a raft that will carry us and not break up in the rough current."

As he spoke, Kaoto was already pulling up the log that had carried them over. Old cotton wood logs were light and buoyant until they became thoroughly soaked, which would take many days. They were usually straight and devoid of smaller limbs. Searching about before complete darkness set in, he was able to find a few more that were about equal in size and length to the one he already had. He ducked under the logs, carrying the rope with him, and soon had them tied securely into a long, if somewhat narrow, raft.

Instructing Corb and Tulla to place the children on top he began to slash the little willows and throw them on top of the raft. The children quickly spread them out, filling the gaps between the logs and then laying them crosswise over all to make a crude, but usable flooring.

Even as they worked, Kaoto could feel the water rising rapidly and knew they would soon be pulled out of the protection of the willows and thrust into the main stream. He double checked his bindings, hoping they would prove strong enough to hold the logs together until they could reach a safe spot farther downstream where they could escape. They would make more plans then.

With everyone aboard, Kaoto selected a pair of long slender sticks to use for poles to help guide them. He pushed the raft ahead of him until it burst free of the willows. He pulled himself up on the raft as the current grasped it and flung it wildly down the river. Complete darkness had descended while they worked, and this allowed them to slip unnoticed by the confident savages waiting for them to be flushed out to them.

Kaoto knew they had to trust to luck. He had lashed a short piece of the rope to the end of the logs and tried to use one of the poles as a crude rudder, the way Torjan had shown him. But it had little effect in the darkness on the roaring current. Still, he struggled through the night. Once they were tossed up on an island that was still above the raging waters. They rested as best they could, but just before daylight they were lifted free and sent careening down the stream in a mad race with the muddy waters.

Kaoto was kept busy just trying to keep the raft headed straight and had little time to consider where they were going. By late morning they had drifted far from their starting point and the canyon was beginning to close in around them. He searched for an opportunity to beach the unruly craft and deposit his passengers on solid ground again. Finally, on a wide bend of the river, the raft was abruptly grounded on a long sloping beach.

With everyone helping, they pulled the raft out of the water and left it lying high, if not dry, above the lapping river. There was a small, deserted village farther up the slope. They went there in search of relief from the steady downpour that had come with the morning. The air was hot and humid, unusual for this part of the country. Far up in the mountains, the snow was rapidly melting, adding to the volume of the river with alarming speed.

The village showed all the evidence of an attack by the savages and there was no sign of inhabitants. When the rain ceased momentarily, they searched about and found scattered utensils and possessions left where they had been thrown or dropped. In one building they found several bedraggled turkeys roosting out the storm.

"We might as well gather what we can use. I do not think anyone will be coming back here soon," Kaoto told them as he salvaged several small gourds filled with seed for the spring crop.

"Is it right to do this?" Corb asked, looking about in dismay at the ravished village.

"You were forced from your home. Do you think you could go back now? Even if the savages left, could you go back and sleep there, knowing they might return?"

"No. I could never rest there or anywhere else as long as they are still in our land," Corb answered him, a slight chill passing over him when he considered his narrow escape.

"But if I or someone else came along and found your home, would you mind if we used what you had left behind, especially if it meant it would save our lives?"

"No, of course not. Anyone would be welcome to use what we left, anyone but the savages that is. I hope they choke on any food they take from my door."

"Then do you not think these people, if they still live, would feel the same way about us? Do you not think they would rather that some of the People in need would use their possessions rather than leaving them lay to rot or to support the enemy?"

"I suppose you are right, but it just seems against the way we live to take things from someone without their consent. What if they should return? What if they come back and have need of the things left here?" Corb was still not completely satisfied.

"We will take only part of what is here. If they return, they will find some if they return in time. With weather like this things will rot and decay very soon, especially when they are left scattered out in the open as they are." Kaoto continued to search about, picking up a bowl and sleeping mats, which were strewn about everywhere.

"What are we going to do with all these things? We cannot carry very much. Besides, where will we go now?"

"In my travels over this land I have become quite well versed in the lay of it. This river flows westward for a long run before it joins with an even bigger and mightier river. I plan to improve on our raft, make it larger and stronger. I think we can even erect a shelter on it to protect us, and our supplies, from the weather. If we ride this river to the west, it will take us close to the land where I left Kalo. I think you might find safety there for a time at least. Then maybe you will be ready to go south, as I have advised all along. Maybe you can convince others to go with you." This had not been Kaoto's original plan, but now it seemed to be the best thing to do.

Working together they salvaged a sizable pile of miscellaneous items: clothing, skins, bowls and gourds for storage. And among the most important were the gourds filled with various seeds for spring planting. More logs were added to the raft, making it quite large. Smaller logs were tied crosswise over the larger ones to make a stable flooring on which they fashioned a shelter to cover not only themselves but also the precious seeds. As a last thought the turkeys were also tied by one leg and then to the upright supports of the shelter.

The weather was intermittently dry and then dark and rainy. The river continued to rise until Kaoto was beginning to have second thoughts about risking the trip. Maybe they should make up light packs and try traveling over land. They might meet more savages, but they also might have a better chance of survival than they would on the dubious river ride.

The decision was taken out of his hands when one of the children, who had been set as watchman, came running down the hillside calling out a warning to them.

"They are coming again. More than before. They are coming down both sides of the river on a fast run."

"How far away are they?" Kaoto shouted.

"Not far, they will be in sight any time now," the child answered as he ran up to them breathlessly.

On the rim of the hill overlooking the village they could see the dark forms of moving men. Turning to the other side of the river, they could see more coming into sight. Those on the far side did not offer any threat to them because the river would hold them back, but those on this side were definitely a threat, a threat which had to be taken care of immediately.

"All right. Quickly, everyone get on the raft," Kaoto said as he picked up the child and hurried the others toward the waiting raft. The water level had risen until the raft was floating nearly free again. Their combined effort pushed it off into the swirling current. They leaped aboard as the angry savages swarmed down toward them, coming through the village.

While the current was swift, it seemed it took an eternity for them to gain enough space to make Kaoto breath easier. He knew their bows would not cast an arrow this far with any accuracy, while his own long bow could reach them with ease. He pulled his weapon from the shelter and notched an arrow as the savages pulled up at the water's edge and began to follow down along the river, trying to get close enough to shoot at them. Mateep laid a hand on Kaoto's arm as he pulled back on his bow.

"Do not waste your arrow on them. What good to kill one or two? There are always more to take their place. They cannot harm us now so let them be. I do not wish to see you add more blood to the marks you already carry."

Kaoto let his bowstring go slack and he put his arrow back in the pouch, hanging it on the side of the crude shelter. It was true; he did not have a great supply of arrows. And as Mateep had said, "What good is it to kill one or two when there were so many ready to take their place?" It would be better to save his arrows for a time when they might have a greater need for them than now.

The raft shot around the bend and the savages were lost from sight. The speed of the river made it impossible for them to keep up by running along the banks, but they could cut across some of the wide bends and come out in front of them. They might be waiting on the next high bank or the next after that. Better to wait until he knew he must shoot.

He picked up the long pole he had used for a rudder and sweep on the back of the raft. He had added another much like it and was showing Corb how to help him maneuver the ungainly craft, trying to keep it as near the center of the river as was possible. On occasions the current would pull them in close to one bank or another and they spent many uncomfortable moments hoping the savages had not gotten ahead of them and were lying in wait for just such a time.

Either the savages did not know the lay of the land and the river or they had lost interest, because they were not seen again that day. The raft leaped and bounced down the river, which seemed to be gaining momentum with every passing second. Frothing rapids tossed and buffeted them until they were all drenched and near to dropping from exhaustion. At last a long stretch of the river afforded them an opportunity to relax. The current was still strong, but the river was straighter here and slightly wider, and their speed was not as fast. Kaoto found he could steer the raft by himself and relieved Corb so that he could eat and get some restless sleep.

As the Sister Moon rose over the river, she found one lone man awake on a strange craft floating down a wild river. His companions were sleeping wearily wherever they could find a place to lie down and be dry. The clouds had passed away leaving a clear night, but the wind from the southwest was still almost uncomfortably hot for this early in the spring. Its hot breath raced across the desert country and lapped up the sides of the mountains, rushing over the snow fields, sending them racing back down to the river to feed it and others like it in a flood like no other in the memory of the People.

The river ran straight and then twisted and turned back on itself until Kaoto was completely lost. He knew its general direction but he had no idea how far they had gone. He only hoped they could ride out the night. In the morning he would have to try to land this crude craft some place. Some place where they could get safely to solid ground. They would leave it, because he could see it was not safe for them to travel any farther this way.

As the night wore on, the banks rose higher and higher until the night sky had become a narrow strip overhead, making him uneasy. In the uncertain light of Sister Moon he could not make out any place where they might land. Possibly they would have to take a chance on getting as close as they could and make a jump for it. He did not like this. He might make it, and maybe Corb, but what of the women and children?

Corb woke somewhat refreshed and rested. He came back and relieved Kaoto at the sweep. Finding Mateep, Kaoto lay down beside her, trying not to disturb her as he rested with his eyes wide open. A tiny hand found his and gave him a gentle squeeze.

"Do not worry, Wise One," Mateep whispered. "We will be all right. Remember? Paataga told of seeing us standing on a ridge against the sunset. She has never been wrong before, so I believe in her now."

"Faith is wonderful, little one. I sometimes envy those who do not have so much knowledge and imagination. Faith is easier for them than those of us with too much. But wherever we are going or what ever happens to us, at least we are together. I am no longer alone in this world." With this Kaoto slipped off in to a deep, dreamless sleep. Mateep nestled at his side. She could not help but marvel at his strength and endurance. No other man, besides possibly Torjan, could have done what he had done in the past two days and nights. He had saved them. He had kept the raft in the middle of the river, and to the best of her knowledge he had not eaten or rested once in this time until now. Mateep was happy she had a man to be proud of above all men. She was made humble just to think she was to share her life with such a man.

Chapter Fifty Seven

Far north in the land that one day would carry the names of Wyoming and Colorado, two mighty rivers were being fed by the runoff caused by freak winds that raised the temperature rapidly and caused the winter snows to melt in record time. To the east, in the heart of the Rocky Mountains, the Colorado River roared and rumbled as it filled to overflowing and cascaded down across the land. The Green River, farther north, heard the challenge and rushed to meet its competitor to see who would claim the riverbed, downstream. They met in what would be known as Utah. Here they clashed and wrestled with each other for the right of way in the canyon encased within red stones. Lesser rivers and small streams joined the titans along the way. Their identities were soon lost as they became one and raced on toward their destiny with the great ocean to the west.

Over many centuries they had carved this passageway to the sea. They had fought with the earth itself to keep this passageway open. The crust of the earth kept pushing its way upward as the mighty river fought to cut its channel deeper. The rise of the earth's surface and the erosion of the river maintained a balance, neither gaining on the other. The end result was a fantastic canyon carved out of red and yellow sandstone.

Twisting and turning, the river made its torturous way across the land, becoming a natural barrier that separated both men and animals. Men on one side could see the men on the other side, but they could not communicate over the noise and distance. Although they were once brothers they lost contact with each other and went about their separate ways.

In the time of the dying nation of the Anasazi, the combinations of these two rivers, aided by their many smaller tributaries, were in an unequaled flood stage. The high water lines left on the canyon walls would remain untouched for many more centuries. The tremendous energy of the racing waters tore huge boulders from their seats and flung them down the streambeds. Their rumbling could be heard even over the noise of the turbulent waters.

Many humble homes were inundated by the angry waters, which had no respect for the puny men who dared to live near their enforced channels. Animals, large and small, were swept away if they ventured to near the edge. The river became a flotsam of dead and dying animals and plants. The walls on either side rose higher as if to block the terrible sight from the eyes of the Spirit Watcher, who could only see directly down on the river at different times of the day, from different angles, as the river twisted back and forth, trying to hide itself in the bowels of Mother Earth.

It was on this awesome display of strength and cruelty that Kaoto and his companions were thrust as the river they rode, later to be known as the San Juan river, joined the other two, almost unnoticed. Kaoto had thought the first to be a wild river until he looked upon the force of the gargantuan Colorado

River.

He had not been able to find a place to beach their raft and had been forced to continue on through the day. He was still hoping for some sign or clue as to what he should do. All he could do was lash everyone to the raft and hold on. It was no longer in his hands. The Spirit Watcher looked down on them sometimes and other times ignored them, leaving them to their fate. If they lived or died the Spirit Watcher showed no signs of caring.

If Kaoto's faith had ever suffered before it was sorely tried now. Surely the Spirit Watcher knew of their plight down here. Did he care? Kaoto had seen numerous small animals struggling in the flood. Some made it to shore, others did not. It seemed to him that the animals that struggled the hardest were often swept away, while those who seemed to give up were carried to safety.

He decided to give up struggling. Perhaps Corb had been right earlier when he had accepted their fate without a struggle. Maybe all of the People had been right. Perhaps this is what the Spirit Watcher had planned for them. Perhaps he no longer favored the People. It would seem he now had turned his face from them to smile on the encroaching savages.

Kaoto still stood at the rear of the craft, clinging to the pole he had designed for a sweep and rudder. He owed it to those who trusted him to try to keep them alive, but he no longer tried to find a place to beach their craft. Wherever they went was where they would go. Live or die, it was no longer his responsibility. Was this the Spirit Watcher's answer to his request to be released from his mission? Was he being dismissed and set to drift on his own?

Whatever was happening, he was powerless to change it now. Not that he knew if he wanted to. Even death here on the river would be preferable to a life of constant roaming and near death. He had done all he could to spread the word. Some had listened, as Moot and his village. Others had turned a deaf ear to him, and in turn had paid the consequences.

He tried to think of what more he could have done. What else could he have said or added that might have made a difference? He could think of nothing. Perhaps the deafening noise of the river was addling his mind. It seemed impossible to think in this din. They could not even communicate with each other, except by hand signals. It did not matter. What was there to say? What could he tell them and what did they have to say to him? Nothing. There were no words to express the fear and despair they were feeling now, and words would not stop the flow of the river or reverse the direction of the plummeting raft. No, he was resigned to whatever their fate was to be.

He looked longingly at his beloved mate as she held one of the terrified children close to her, burying its head on her shoulder so it would not have to see the speeding walls as they flashed by in a blur. What had he given her? How was her life improved by his interference? Would she not have been better off dead, buried with her father down in the black rock country? At least she would have been spared the horror of this trip.

He had always done what he thought was right, what was best for all the People but what had it mattered? What had he accomplished in the long run? He had spread fear and confusion, but had he done any of the People any good? What of Moot and his village? They had gone south as he had instructed them. Did they still live? Had they survived the rigors of the trail? Had they escaped the fury of the savages they met in the land farther south? Would Moot thank him now if they could meet face to face? He doubted it. Never in his life had he felt so completely lost and helpless. Even as a young man serving under Paataga, he had always been able to find some redeeming factor to make his life worthwhile. Now? He found nothing. The Spirit Watcher was forcing him to look at himself as he really was, not as he had always thought himself to be. Humility had always seemed important to him to keep him from looking down on those he served. However, he had never been forced to look as closely and as keenly at himself as he was now, and he did not like what he saw.

Time became meaningless. They ate from the large jars of dried grains they had stored aboard and drank from another large jar, which they had surrounded with mud to hold it upright and in one place. The stopper was wedged firmly in place to preserve the precious liquid inside. Corb took his place at the sweep from time to time and spent the rest of his time holding on to his mate and their children. If he had any resentment toward the Wise One, he never let it show in his face or his actions.

Of all of them, only Mateep seemed to be untouched by their ordeal, and although she could not speak out, she showed her faith and belief with open smiles and touches of encouragement. She alone believed they would survive, just because an old woman had told her she would stand on a ridge in the sunset with the Wise One. What he would have given for such faith.

The raft, surprisingly, held together in spite of all the harsh treatment that it was forced to endure. The only real danger came from its brushes with the sides of the canyon. The rocks in the streambed that normally would have torn it to pieces were buried so deep under the water that the raft floated over them in relative safety.

The walls reared up higher over them, blocking out all of the sky except for a narrow strip directly above them. It looked as if the river was destined to go so deep that eventually it would go underground. Perhaps this was their ultimate goal. Would they be returned to the place under the ground where the People had first come from? Too many questions and no answers. Kaoto tried to stop the thinking process but was powerless to do so. His mind continued to grind the meal of his discontent exceedingly fine.

The stages of the trip were smoother and easier where the channel was straight and the top of the water less roiled. On these occasions they built a fire, using some of the clay around the water jar to make a fire pit. They pulled a struggling deer from the water and butchered it. They feasted on hot, half raw meat while they had the chance, before the next turn of the river plunged them down the next steep descent of rapids. They preserved some of the cooked meat for the next day when they might not be so fortunate as to have a smooth place to rest.

Once they were swept into a side canyon where they twisted in the arms of a whirlpool. Kaoto searched the surrounding rock walls for a possible place to get away. The sides were sheer, without handholds or any place of purchase. Eventually they were jettisoned back out into the main current and swept away again.

Quick showers drenched them periodically so they were never quite dry, even when the river spray did not hit them. Kaoto's arms ached with pulling on the sweep. Even when Corb helped, the strain was exhausting and demanding. His shoulder blades ached with the constant tension, the inability to relax even for a moment. How long could he go on this way? How long could any of them continue? Did this angry river never end? And if it did, where would they find themselves? He had never heard anyone claim to know where this river went.

On one particularly difficult portion of the river, where the rapids seemed more violent than all the rest, the sweep pole snapped and Kaoto fell before he could regain his balance. He plunged headlong into the foaming waters and was swept past the raft before they could throw him a rope. Mateep stood at the front of the raft, wringing her hands in despair as she watched her mate dashed about. She soon lost sight of him in the rough waves. She did not know if he was even trying to swim. She thought of throwing herself in after him, but Tulla, sensing her grief, held her tight until she no longer struggled.

Mateep could not control her grief. She who had cheered them all in the troubled times before, now lay on the flooring and did not move. She had lost all interest in life. She remembered the days when she was wandering from one dump to another in search of the Wise One. Then it had seemed hopeless, but there was at least a chance, no matter how slim. Now there was no chance. No hope. All was gone. Why? She had believed Paataga. Trusted her completely. But Kaoto was no longer at her side. While he was here, nothing had frightened her. Now, everything frightened her.

She was so immersed in her grief she did not even notice when the current shoved them into a side canyon where the water was green and clear, not muddy like the river. The raft rocked gently in this backwater as if it could not stop after the violent trip it had just endured.

She only aroused when she heard someone shouting her name. Looking up, she could see someone swimming in the green water, coming toward the raft. Unbelieving, she shaded her eyes to get a better look. Could it be? Had the same force that pushed the raft in here done the same for her beloved? It had indeed. There he was, swimming toward her. His long arms were flashing in the light as they cut the water and pulled him closer to her. She hung her head in spite of her joy. She made a silent apology to Paataga for doubting her.

With all of them working together, they managed to pull and push the ungainly craft deep into the side canyon until they were safe from the uncertain current of the flood. The stream they were on was not fed by giant snowfields. It started only a short distance away and the water it carried was clear and refreshing.

They did not progress very far up the new stream before they found their way was blocked by a high fall where the stream almost literally burst from the side of the mountain and fell in a beautiful arch down to the streambed where they now lay.

Kaoto secured the raft to a large boulder and let what little current there was swing it broadside against the bank. It rested here easily and it was safe for all to disembark, taking all their possessions with them, including the turkeys.

There was a bench beyond the beach large enough to give them all room to stretch out, and the children quickly began investigating. The walls did not hold out any promise of easy ascent, but Kaoto could not discover any high water marks here that indicated the water ever rose any higher than it was now.

Having nothing to judge by, Kaoto could not determine what time of day it might be. He could not even see the sun from here, and until one day had passed, he would not have known the time. As he stood looking up the steep walls, his head thrown back as far as it would go so he could see the top, he suddenly realized that this was a familiar place to him. But how? He had never been down this river before. How could he know this place? But he did. Then the memory came back. While he was still in the green mesa country, before they had started on this ill-fated trip, he had had a new dream. He had stood looking up these very same walls at the same sliver of sky. It had been nighttime in his dream, and an eagle had floated above him, but this was the same place.

Deep down inside, he heaved a sigh of relief. Everything was as it should be. In spite of his doubts and self-incrimination, he was just where he was supposed to be. This was all part of the master plan and once more it had come about without his aid or hindrance. Nothing he had done or could have done would have changed anything. He was in the hands of a superior being who directed his footsteps and took him where it wanted him to go in spite of himself.

Seeing the look of peace and acceptance on his face, Mateep also relaxed. All was right with the world once more. She did not disturb him as she began to set up camp, knowing instinctively that this was where they would stay. They would not risk the river again, ever. She had Kaoto to herself. Of course there were Corb and Tulla, and the two children, but the world was locked out from them and could not touch them here. No one could come making demands on Kaoto's time and energy and he could not run away, because there was nowhere to run.

At that moment the Spirit Watcher sent down a few rays as if to check on his son. The rays did not reach them, but it spread loving warm beams over a small ridge just before them. Kaoto took Mateep's hand and together they walked up the crest of the ridge and stood looking into the sunset.

"It is just as Paataga said, is it not?" Mateep asked.

"Yes. It is just as she said. And to think I doubted her. It seems I will never learn to trust her completely."

"When you were swept over the edge and into the water, I also doubted her. I could not see how we would ever be together again. But here we are, just as she saw us in her dream."

Kaoto remained silent. His eyes were searching, just as they had all of his life. They were searching the canyon walls as far as he could see, looking for a possible avenue of escape. He would have to give the walls a closer look. For now he could not see any place where a man might climb above the falls, and the river effectively blocked them from the other direction. Of course, they still had the raft, but he did not think he would ever be so desperate as to try the raft on that river again, even when it was not flooding.

Mateep saw his eyes sweeping the sides of the canyon and knew what he was thinking.

"Why can you not accept things the way they are? Why are you always trying to make things more difficult? The Spirit Watcher has given you a sign. He has granted you your wish. You asked to be relieved of your responsibility. It has happened. So why fight it? Why not just accept it and enjoy it?"

"I'm sorry, little one, but nothing is as simple and easy as it seems. I have to test and try everything before I can accept it. It would be too easy to stay here and pretend it was meant to be. It would be easy to stay here and not even look for a way out. But it is not my nature to take anything the easy way. I must know for sure that this is true; then I can relax and enjoy."

"I somehow doubt you will ever relax and enjoy, but I do feel you will be forced to stay here, just as I was forced to stay in the black rocks."

She took Kaoto's large hand and placed it on her small stomach. He looked at her, waiting for some explanation. It was too early to show or for him to feel, but Mateep knew now it was true. She carried the seed of the Wise One. She would present him with a son who might make him want to stay home when nothing else would.

"The seed you planted has sprouted and taken root." Mateep told him. "This fall you shall harvest your crop. It will not be a large crop, but I am sure it will satisfy you."

Kaoto gathered her up in his arms and held her tightly, so tightly she could hardly breathe, but she did not complain. She was too happy to complain.

Chapter Fifty Eight

In time the waters receded, leaving the survivors in a side canyon cut off by the waterfalls at one end and the angry river at the other. Even in late summer, the Colorado was not a river to take lightly and they all agreed they did not want to risk traveling it any farther. They did not know they were almost out of the canyon. They could have continued and been free.

Deep in the heart of each one of them was a common feeling, although none of them spoke of it. They did not want to be free of this peaceful side canyon. While it was small and confining, it offered them protection such as they had not known since the advent of the savages in their land.

Checking daily with the Spirit Watcher's course, they discovered level places where he spread his life-giving rays the most during the days. Here they planted the seeds they had carried with them. Corn and beans, squash and pumpkins did well enough here to ensure they would not go hungry. The turkeys were released to fend for themselves; soon they would increase their numbers and contribute to the meals. Small game abounded down in the temperate climate at the bottom of the canyon. Larger game sometimes dropped in unexpectedly. The sheer walls of the canyon proved treacherous footing and a careless deer, or even a mountain goat, would occasionally loose its footing and plunge down. Often they would land in the water and survive the fall; these were left alone to propagate with others of their kind that joined them. The ones that did not survive the fall were quickly butchered and added to the larder of smoke-dried meat.

Life began to settle into a daily routine of peace and tranquility. Kaoto built a shelter for Mateep, and Corb and Tulla added their structure to a common back wall. After all, they were all a family now, and this was the family custom. Corb's children, a man-child and a woman child, were a delight to them all, filling the narrow confines with the sound of their shouts and laughter.

In late fall, Mateep presented her mate with the promised harvest; a small, squirming son, covered with light downy hair. He soon developed a prominent nose, setting aside any doubts as to who his father was. He was followed the next fall by another harvest, a woman-child this time. In the following summers, Corb and Tulla contributed their share of the new offspring, and soon the canyon was becoming populated.

The river below them contributed its share to them also. An occasional animal was deposited in the lagoon-like pool that formed where the side stream tried to force its way out into the main channel. Besides animals, there was a never ending supply of driftwood and anything else that would float.

Since time was of no importance to them, they often spent much of their time at this junction, watching for anything of interest that might be brought to them. On one such occasion, the river brought them two more human animals.

"Father! Look!" Shouted Kula, Kaoto and Mateep's first born. "There is someone like us, they are hanging onto that log. See them?" Kula jumped up and down in his excitement, waking his little sister, which had been sleeping on the sand bar at her mother's side.

"I think you are right," Kaoto said as he stood up to see better. "Yes, there is someone out there." He ran to pick up the long pole they often used to help salvage objects from the river.

With the aid of the pole and the current, the log was pulled gently into the green lagoon, along with its two nearly drowned passengers, who clung to the log in desperation.

They proved to be from one of the long-hated and feared savage tribes. The woman was great with child, and her mate tried valiantly to defend her. But, exhausted as he was, he was no match for Kaoto, who quickly defeated him and then forcibly restrained him when he would not surrender.

Mateep and Tulla carried the woman back to their camp and settled her as comfortably as possible on clean fresh ferns in the open air, where the Spirit Watcher sent down his rays for the longest part of their otherwise short day. Worn and frightened, the woman gave birth to a howling, red-faced infant.

When Mateep took the squirming bundle and headed for the water, the woman's mate struggled against his bonds, shouting in his guttural gibberish. He had fully expected to see his child picked up by the heels and dashed against a rock. That was what would have happened to any enemy child born in his camp. When that did not happen, he resigned himself to having to watch his child drowned in the green waters of the peaceful stream.

Mateep lowered the child to the water and carefully cleansed it before returning it to its waiting mother, where she nestled it against her ample breast. The woman could only express her thanks with her looks. Her words were of no use to her. Her face did not know how to register a smile, but her dark eyes were very expressive.

Mateep and Tulla tried to reassure her with their smiles and cooing sounds made only for babies and small animals. Their message was received and the woman relaxed and lay back, holding her child so it could nurse if it so chose.

It would take time to settle their differences. But they had plenty of time. The savage man was released when he ceased to struggle. He was apprehensive for many days before he was convinced he and his family were in no danger. Then the long process of learning each other's languages began.

"Wise One, these are our enemies, are they not?" Corb asked.

"Enemy? Yes. I suppose they would have been out in the land. But here we are all the same. We are all in the hands of the Spirit Watcher. He sent them here, just as he sent us. I do not think we are enemies here." It had been a puzzle to Kaoto, how they should treat these newcomers. True, they were of the hated savage tribes, but they could do them no harm now. If the Spirit Watcher had sent them here, then there must have been a reason.

"I do not wish to harm them, but it is hard not to remember that they, or others just like them, have killed and tortured our People. They might have been the same ones who drove us from our home," Corb continued.

"This is also true, but they cannot frighten you now. Can they?"

"As long as you are here, no. But if you were not here, then I think things would be different. He is bigger than I am and more used to fighting and killing. If it had happened the other way around, if he had been here and Tulla and I had been pulled in, what then? What do you think they would have done to us?"

"I do not know. I do not think we will ever be able to find out. And since it did not happen that way, it is up to us to decide what will happen. What do you want to do about them?"

Corb mulled this over. He had never considered being asked what he would do. He had assumed the Wise One would make the decisions for them all. After all, he was the Wise One. He was supposed to make decisions, was he not?

"I cannot honestly say. I wish they had not come here. I wish they had been taken some place else," he finally answered.

"But they were not. They were brought here to us. Now what do you want to do about them?" Kaoto insisted. He was following the example of his old teacher, doing what he himself had done over the past summers: answering questions by asking questions, making Corb express his desires to find out what he really thought.

"Well, I do not wish to harm them. I certainly do not want to kill them, especially the little one, but its father makes me uneasy. I do not know if I could ever trust him. I do not know if I could ever turn my back on him or leave him here alone with my family. What if he should become hungry and decide to eat them?"

Kaoto smiled at Corb. The man's fears were simple and to the point. He could understand this and thought he could overcome them in time.

"Then we must see that he never becomes hungry." He laughed as Corb weighed this advice as if taking it seriously, then grinning sheepishly when he realized the Wise One was making a joke. Still, he listened intently when Kaoto continued. "I do not think they ever ate their enemies out of hunger. I think it was more of a ritual. I do not understand it, but I think it was done to capture the strength and spirit of the man, not to feed their stomachs."

The first turn of the moon was the worst. Distrust on both sides made it difficult for them to live together without someone being on constant watch. Kaoto's patience paid off in the long run as he spent much of the day trying to communicate. At first, simple signs were all they had, but in time he began to understand some of the savages' simple words. The savages, in turn, began to pick up some of their words. In trying to discover where they had come from, Kaoto had little success. The savage did not know how to describe where his tribe lived or how he and his mate had been trapped in a flash flood.

The savage child was a woman child. The savage man seemed to be disgusted with this outcome and paid no attention to her once he discovered her sex. Mateep and Tulla, however, were delighted, and the child was seldom left unattended; one of them would pick her up and carry her about. Even Kaoto and Corb showed interest in her and were not ashamed to be seen with her. They even performed some of the simple chores that come with a baby, even in the wilds.

Slowly the savage, whom Kaoto had tagged with the name of Buit, came to accept his daughter as a person, just as the others did. He came to understand that it was no shame to have a woman child. It was not unmanly to hold or like his daughter. His mate, who they had affectionately named Tuba, responded quickly to their tenderness and show of love. She was happy that her first offspring had been accepted, even though it was not a man-child.

Summers passed in slow, easy successions of moons. The family in the canyon grew and became a close-knit unit. The children grew to adults. While they could not compete in the games of the People's manhood rites, they were still trained and tested in skills and endurance. Both boys and girls were expected to be responsible young people. They were assigned tasks for which they alone were responsible and were praised whenever they succeeded in these tasks.

Slowly Buit and Tuba joined into the family activities, adding from their own experiences and accepting the new. They built their home up against the same wall as the others. Trust was imperative here, and trust was rewarded. Any display of anger or hostility was dealt with immediately. Kaoto acted in turn as judge, jury, and the executioner. He listened and observed. When a complaint was brought to him, he listened to both sides and then passed down his sentence. He then saw to it that this sentence was carried out.

The most serious crimes were personal insults or invasion of personal space and possessions. For this he handed down the stiffest punishment: he personally took the offending party up to the water falls and held the person under it until he was satisfied he or she had been washed clean of their guilt. One trip to the falls was usually enough. Lesser crimes were punished by work details, or sometimes a sincere apology would be all that was demanded.

The first summer saw a few crimes punished in this manner. But by the second summer, crime was something they joked and laughed about when they were recalling their turn at the falls. They especially liked to tell of the time when Kaoto himself had felt guilty of a crime and stood under the waterfalls until they all begged him to come out. Could any man be more fair than this?

Life in the canyon was good. They grew sufficient crops to feed themselves. The winter moons were never severe. The only bad times were when the spring thaw sent the Colorado into spasms of anger and contortion. They waited out each flood season in fear that the flood might become even higher than the one that had carried them here. They were trapped here, and if the water rose higher than before, there was no place for them to go.

But this fear passed as many summers came and went without the high waters ever coming close to that level. The remains of their raft lay on the sand where it had been left by the first flood. The floodwaters never came close to it again.

More children were born, and an occasional person was pulled from the river, just as Buit and Tuba had been. The children grew up and took mates from among their playmates, and had children of their own. Kaoto had taken to making marks on a particular stretch of the canyon wall where the Spirit Watcher struck each day. From the marks he was able to determine the farthest swing north and south so he could predict the seasons. The summers were marked so they would know how long they had been here.

When fifteen marks had been made, Buit was buried in the custom of the People. His body would nourish the tiny field he had tended. The next summer, Tuba's body was laid next to his. At twenty long marks on the wall, Mateep was laid to rest in Kaoto's field. Kaoto was ancient now. His time was long passed. He hoped he would not attain the summers of Paataga. He had grown used to having someone with him, but now, even with the children around, he was alone again. He spent much of his time sitting on the ridge looking into the sunset. Waiting, waiting for his turn to make the journey to the next land.

The first summer he had scoured the walls, searching diligently for a means of scaling the walls and gaining freedom, freedom none of them really wanted. His search had proved futile. He had managed to climb quite high in several places, but they always ran into a dead end where he could climb no higher.

One such place was a long, if not too difficult, climb to a projection of rock that overlooked the canyon. From this position he could look both ways in the canyon. It afforded the longest view of the canyon that he could attain. He spent much time there in silence, alone with his thoughts. He usually held his beads in his hand, running his fingers over them idly.

The children had asked him what they were and he had told them they held the secret of all the past history of the People. They could not understand this. Of what People? Were they not the only People there were?

Of course, the elders had told them stories about what it was like where they had come from, but the children had no way of comparing this with the way they lived now. So while they listened, Kaoto could tell they did not really believe. He had thought he should train some of them to know the history as he did. His first son would have been a natural choice, but what was the use? What good would this long litany do them? So he told them only short stories, weaving some of the history into a short version that they could all remember. He added the story of their incredible journey down the river so they would remember how they came to be here, and that there were other People like them somewhere.

The long version that only he knew remained locked inside him and the twenty-and-four beads of stone, bone, and shells. He started once to recite it to the stone wall across from him just to see if he could still remember it all.

He knew he could. He could never forget it. It was too much a part of him. But the wall did not want to listen, and neither did he. Now he told the story with his fingers as he traced the designs he had carved on the beads so long ago. So many summers ago that the sharp edges were now worn smooth with the constant touch of his fingers.

One thing that continued to bother Kaoto was his dream, the last dream he had had of standing in this place and looking up at an eagle. Everyday he had stood and looked up, but never had he seen an eagle. He had seen the great birds of carrion glide by, looking down to see if he still lived. He had seen song birds of all kinds, and once or twice an owl, but never an eagle. Why? He had seen it plainly in his dream. There must have been some reason. Why had he never seen the eagle since he had arrived here?

He sat now, as so often of late, on this point of rocks. It was getting more difficult to make the climb as each summer passed. Every passing day seemed to make the trail steeper and more arduous. He remembered Paataga taking her daily walk on the top of the cliff behind her home, until that final day when she told him she had not gone up. For the first time since she had lived there, she had not walked to the rim above her home. Was that day coming soon for him? He honestly was looking forward to that day. He, too, was growing tired.

The Spirit Watcher had gone to rest and Sister Moon had come up to show her full face on this night. He had not gone back down when his oldest son called him to his evening meal. His son's mate, who ironically was the first daughter of Buit and Tuba the savages, had called to him several times since. She had offered to bring his meal up to him, but he had told her not to bother, he would come down later.

Food did not interest him much anymore, especially since it could not be shared with Mateep. He still set aside a small amount to be shared with the little animals. It was all he had left of his past.

Leaning back against the rock wall, he let his gaze drift up the wall to the narrow strip of sky above.

"Old mother," he said to the empty space above him. " I, too, am growing tired. When do I get to leave this world? When do I get to join you and the others in the next world? There is no reason for me to stay here any longer. No one has a need of me now. I am just an old man who gets in the way. I am a chore, someone to look after. A burden to even the children."

In the slice of open night sky, a shadow drifted into view. His tired old eyes tried to focus on the shape silhouetted against the faint glow of the moon, which had moved away in search of a new place. With trembling hands, he pulled himself erect, his beads forgotten, still clutched in one hand. He took hold of a scraggly bush growing from a crack in the wall beside him. He steadied himself and raised his other hand to the sky.

"Old mother, is that you?" he said softly. He did not want to attract the attention of those below. They would know he had lost his mind if they heard him talking to the sky.

The dark shadow slowly took form and he recognized the eagle of his dream. It was coming lower, as if searching for him in the darkness. He leaned out further and called softly again.

"I am here. I am waiting for you." He rubbed his eyes as the eagle started to change shape as it drew closer, until it was no longer a bird, but a person. A woman. It was Paataga, but not Paataga. She was young and strong, and tall, not bent. There was no mistake. It was Paataga. She held out her hand to him.

"Come, my son. It is time. Your days here are over. You have earned the right to cross over to the next land."

Her hand was close to his now. He could almost reach it. He knew if he once touched her he would be transported with her to the next world, the next world where all his friends and family would be waiting for him. He had no doubt of Paataga now. He would never doubt her again. She had come for him. She remembered him in the next world, just as she had promised.

As he let go of the bush, the string of beads caught in the branches. The string broke and one bead dropped at his feet and rolled into a crack. The others clung together on the broken string and swung gently in the evening breeze. He was turning to try to retrieve them when the shadow spoke to him again.

"Leave them, Kaoto. You will not need them where you are going now. Forget them. Just take my hand and follow me."

Kaoto, the once tall, hairy, fabled runner and Wise One, released his hold on the bush and stepped out to clasp the hand of his old mother. He felt her touch, he felt the strength of her hand on his and his worries and troubles dropped away from him, leaving him feeling young and strong again. Together they drifted up out of the canyon, far up above the land. Together they looked down on the world below and he could see, just as in his dream, all the land stretched out below them. He could see far into the past and equally far into the future. He could see little bands of the People moving across the land, going to the south to a new home in a new land. He could see other little family groups, hiding in the rocks, frightened and alone. He watched them wither and die like flowers picked and left in the sun.

He looked to the future, but the horizon was hazy and he could not see clearly. He knew he would see two People standing before him who were both strange and familiar at the same time. He wanted to stay here and look some more. He wanted to ask questions, but Paataga gently but firmly urged him to follow her.

"Time, my son, time. There is no end to the sand in the jug. You have all the time you need now, and all the questions you can ask will be answered. Come. They are waiting for you."

"Who, old mother? Who is waiting for me?"

"Oh, everyone. Little Frog, Matuga, Moot, your mother and father, Mateep, and the little girl you lost many summers ago. Sons you do not remember. Those who you left with the Sky People in the land of the white rocks.

Torjan, and many, many more. Come."

"Torjan?" Yes, he wanted to see his old friend again. How many times had he thought of the Red One and wondered what had ever become of him. Now Paataga told him he would see him and be able to ask him about what had happened after he left him.

They floated away. It was so easy that Kaoto wondered why he had never tried it before. He recalled his long run when he had thought he was floating. It had been very much like this. This was so much better than running. He did not get tired and he did not fall. The land drifted by below him without effort.

In the morning, Kula was the first one to find the broken body of his father lying at the base of the cliff. He could not be sure, but he thought he could almost see a ghost of a smile on the tired old man's face.

Each in their turn tried to take the blame for his death. Everyone thought they should have been up there looking after him, helping him. Or they should not have let him go in the first place, knowing he was old, and tired, and weak. But each in turn knew there was nothing that could have been done to change things.

Kaoto, great runner, Wise One, father, friend to all, was laid to rest in his field beside the bones of his mate. There were few belongings to be placed with him. His long bow. His feathers. A pot of food and a smaller pot for those less fortunate. His beads were not placed with him. Kula had climbed up to the point where his father had fallen and found the broken string on the branch. He looked for the lost bead, but could not find it and had given up. He had found something else of interest, though. Lying on the stones where his father had apparently slipped and fallen to his death, was a new fresh eagle feather. He had heard of eagles and had seen the old feathers his father wore in his hair, but he had never seen the bird they came from. Now, here on the rock, lay a feather from the fabled bird of wealth and wisdom. He picked up the feather and placed it with the beads in a special pouch he made for them.

Over the summers, the pouch was passed from father to son, or grandson if no son appeared in that generation. It always passed in direct lineage with the wise old man who had brought them here and told them all the history they knew of their origin and the People from whom they had sprung. It was all that was left of Kaoto, the little bird who ran with the wind.

Chapter Fifty Nine

"John."

"Hummm?"

"John! Look at me."

The young man turned slowly from his desk where he had been sitting starring out over the southwestern landscape. Though his eyes were trained on the young woman, they were still seeing the great desert stretched out below him.

"What were you saying, Tina?" he asked.

"John, look at me. Your body might be here, but your mind is somewhere a thousand miles from here."

"Thousand? No. Maybe a hundred, but not a thousand. I'm sorry, Tina. I kind of get lost sometimes. Be patient. It will all go away. I think." He rubbed his hands over his face, making an honest attempt to bring himself back to the room in which they were both seated.

"I have said I would marry you, and I want to. Really I do." Tina sat in a comfortable old chair not far from the desk. It blended in well with the room. Everything in here was old and worn, but comfortable. Everything except John, of course. He was young and definitely not worn, and sometimes not very comfortable.

"So? What's the problem, then?"

"The problem is what you have to tell me." At his blank, innocent stare she hurried on.

"Ever since I have known you there has been something you have held back. Something you will not tell me. John, if I am going to share your life, you have to let me in. Don't leave me out here like this."

"What do you mean, leave you out? I'm not leaving you out of anything. I'm an open book." John looked at Tina, puzzled by her words.

"Like a book all right, but some of the pages are glued together. You can see them, but nobody else can."

She had his full attention now. She was serious. Something was bothering her and he needed to find out what it was.

"I'm sorry. I guess I missed out on something. Let's start all over again from the beginning. Now, what is this all about? What is it that I am doing that has you so upset?"

"That is what I am talking about. I have been here for several minutes talking to you and it's like I had never came into the room in the first place. You sit there staring out the window, lost in some personal world of your own. A world I can't seem to penetrate, no matter how hard I try. What do you see out there that I can't see? What are you thinking about that takes you completely away from me?"

John studied the young woman before him as if he had just now seen her for the first time. She was very small and slender; petite would probably the word to best describe her, but she was even small for petite. Her long hair was the same color as honey and hung down her back like a golden fall. She was a very striking woman, pleasant to look at. Most striking of all, and what had attracted his attention in the first place, were her two different colored eyes.

In her turn, Tina was looking at the man she intended to spend the rest of her life with. Young, good looking in his own way. She had to make an exception for his rather unruly hair, which never seemed to want to stay in place, and his rather large nose. But all in all these features did not look bad on a man.

"You always have that bunch of loose beads lying out in front of you and that old eagle feather. You said there was a story behind them and that you would tell me about them someday, but you never have. What have they to do with us?"

John turned back to his desk and gathered the collection of bones and stones in his hand, holding them as if they were precious gems. Slowly he turned back to face the woman who had promised to become his wife. Yes, he had a story, but not all of it. He had hoped to get it altogether before he tried to explain it to anyone. How could he tell her what he did not know himself? She did deserve some sort of an explanation. But where to start?

"You know, of course that I am part Indian. If the facts are right, I should be half Indian and half white."

"Yes, you have told me that much. So what? So am I, or so they tell me. I don't know for sure how much of which blood is which, but there is some of both. My friends would never believe it when I tried to tell them. They said my hair and eyes made me more Scandinavian than anything else. But, so the story goes, my forefathers lived somewhere in southern New Mexico. Grandpa supposedly found my grandmother in a Pueblo down along the Rio Grande somewhere and married her. After that he set about educating her in the ways of the white men. He was a school teacher, you know?"

"It's odd, isn't it? We are both cross breeds but neither of us show any traits of the Indian side of our families. People have told me the same thing. They said if I shut up, no one would know and I could pass. Pass? Pass for what? A white man, I guess. But I am both, so I will pass on passing."

"This is nothing new, John. We've been over this before, many times. What does it have to do with your wandering mind?"

"Okay. I'll tell you my story, not very interesting or original, but it's all the truth and nothing but the truth, so help me whoever." He held his right hand in the air and clutched the beads in his left.

"Drop the theatrics. All I want is to know where you go when you take off and leave me sitting here babysitting your body?"

"Is it that bad?"

"Worse. If it was just a body, I could leave it. I could forget it, and I definitely would not marry it."

John got up, took her hand, and pulled her up and led her out of the room and down the hall to a spacious living room. It was decorated with Indian artifacts, both old and new. He ushered her to another equally old and comfortable leather chair and sat her down. He pulled up the footstool and sat facing her, keeping hold of her hand. He thought for a few moments and then cleared his throat and started his story.

"After the Second World War, the helicopter came into its own. It was a very useful tool in more ways than just warfare. It was also used in exploration. The Grand Canyon had long beckoned to men. Powell, of course, made it down the canyon in a wooden boat, supposedly the first man to ever navigate the length of the canyon. Maybe so, maybe no. Anyway, with the advent of the helicopter it was easier to fly up and down the canyon than to run the rapids. Airplanes, of course, had been flying all over, but they could not get down in the little narrow places, the side canyons and such.

"One day a helicopter came into a little lost and forgotten canyon. They discovered a tribe of Indians living there below the falls. It turned out they were trapped there, brought in over the years by the floods, and trapped by the falls. They lived out their lives there in isolation.

"They were not all Indians. Some white men, trappers, traders, even a cowboy or two, had been swept down and pulled out here. But, so the story goes, there was one line of Indians that went back to some old wise Shaman, or whatever they called them back then. Seems he and his wife and a few other people had been caught in a flood and had managed to get out of the river. They had lived there for the rest of their days.

"The story was passed down from one generation to another, and like all good stories it got better with each telling.

"This old wise man, it is said his name was something like Ka Oto Ah. Some say it was Coyote and that's where the Indians came up with all their coyote stories, but this doesn't hold water. Coyote is a fractured Spanish word, and according to the story, this old man was down there long before the Spanish ever came to this country.

"Anyway, whatever his name was, he always carried these beads, only then they were on a string. The string has long since been lost and they are now loose, as you see. The story says that he used these beads in some sort of ceremony. Like everything else they can't identify, they say they were used for religious purposes." John paused in his story and looked at the beads lying in the palm of his hand.

"But they are wrong. These were more than some religious symbol, much more. They took time to find and make. Too much time to be just a religious symbol."

Tina held out her hand and John grudgingly handed them to her. He watched closely as she spread them out in her lap, picking up each one separately for closer inspection. She looked up, waiting expectantly for him to continue with his story.

"Yes. Where was I? Oh yes. When the helicopter came out of the canyon with the story, it made the newspapers for a while but was soon forgotten. Not so for the pilot. He went back as often as he could and got as much of the story from them as he could. They spoke a strange mixture of many Indian tongues, but used enough white man's words to express themselves pretty well. The pilot offered to fly them out, but they weren't interested. Seems they were perfectly happy where they were. Smart people. Can't say as I blame them. Anyway, he did manage to get them to let him take out one little boy who expressed an interest in seeing the outside world. He was very young, probably about eight or nine by their record keeping.

"The pilot took him home with him and ended up keeping him, like a son of his own. No one paid any attention. No questions were asked. After a year or so of home teaching, the little boy was ready to go to white man's school and learn all about the strange, new world outside of the canyon. He grew up and went to college. He married and had a son of his own.

"That little boy was my father." John let his hands drop into his lap and waited for some reply from Tina.

"That's it? That's all? Oh, come on now there's more to it than that. Now that you have started, why don't you tell me the rest of it? It can't make any difference between us now, can it?"

"No. I guess not. And even if it did, you still have a right to know." He sat back and picked up the story once more.

"Before my father came out with the pilot, his mother took him aside and gave him the pouch with these beads and the old eagle feather, and told him they were a link with the past. He had to promise her he would continue the custom and see they were passed on and not lost or turned over to anyone who did not have the right to hold them.

"Last year, when my father passed them on to me, he made me make the same promise. And he added another promise of his own. He made me promise to keep trying to solve the riddle locked up inside them. You see, my father felt just as I do about them. He spent much of his life trying to decipher the meaning of it all."

"Does there have to be some special meaning in those stones and bones? Couldn't they have been just what they seem, just beads for decoration, nothing else?"

"No. Here. Look at them more closely." He got up and went back to his desk and returned carrying a magnifying glass with a light attached.

Holding the beads one at a time under the light, Tina studied them. They were uneven, marred and scratched. At first glance, that was all she saw. Then she drew in her breath and held it. These were not random marks. They were carefully laid out so they did not cross or interfere with each other. Someone had spent a lot of time and effort to make these marks, and the smoothness of the top of them showed they had been handled for many years.

"I guess you're right. They can't be just decorations. But if not, then what are they?"

"That is the question. That is what takes me away from you and the whole world. That is the question my father tried to find the answer to, and what he made me promise to keep looking for. Now do you see what I mean? It's not easy to explain this to someone else when I don't really understand it myself.

"Father was sure that somewhere down the line there would be a son who could make sense out of them. He, of course, hoped it would be himself, but when that didn't happen, he turned this worry and trust over to me. Now I am stuck with it, only I don't consider it being stuck. It's more like an honor, or let's say an obligation, which has been passed on to me. Now it's my turn."

He picked up the beads and laid them out on the arm of the chair, each one in a special order. One stone, one bone, one seashell. Then he repeated this pattern until all the beads lay in a row.

"This is the order in which they belong, but there is one missing."

"How can you tell?"

"I just know. Don't ask me how I know, but I do. They belong in just this order. Not just stone, bone, shell, but each one is in its proper place. Except for the one that is missing. It would have been the first one on the string. Without it, I can't begin. I have to find the missing bead. See, there are only twenty-three of them. No one would have twenty-three, they would have an even number. The first one should have been a stone. Then it would have come out right." He stopped talking and looked at the row of beads.

"It was supposedly lost on the night the old man died. They claimed he took it with him, but that's a bunch of bunk. He didn't take anything else with him, and if he were going to take one, why wouldn't he take them all? Huh? Answer me that one?"

"Hey, wait a minute. This is your question, not mine. Remember, I just came in here. I don't know anything about this."

"I know. I get so wrapped up in this I forget where I am sometimes. Besides, you wanted to know all about it. So now you know as much as I do. Not much, is it?"

"No, not much. But at least I can understand why you are so pre-occupied sometimes. This is enough to try the patience of a saint, as my old grandfather used to say. But if it was lost that far back, how are you ever going to find it?"

"That is another good question without an answer. If I knew for sure where to look, I would go back there and look for myself. But no one seems to know just which canyon it was. There are so many and there are tribes living in most all of them now. This is going to be the crazy part, but you asked for it, so here it comes.

"Lately I've been having these strange dreams, wild dreams like nothing I have ever had before."

"Are they about the beads?" Tina asked, her eyes intent on his.

"I don't know, but I think so. See, it's like this. I go to sleep, only it's like I'm not really asleep, just lying there looking at the ceiling. Then I start to see things, things that aren't there." He stopped, searching for words, when Tina interrupted him.

"Things like a little old woman so old and ancient she looks like one of those mummies they have down at the museum at the ruins by Camp Verde?"

"Yes." John was astonished. "How did you know?"

"Because you are not the only one to have weird dreams."

"You have seen her too, then?"

"Oh yes, I not only seen her, but she has talked to me. I can tell you, it scared the hell out of me. Here I am lying down, minding my own business, when this little old crone appears and starts talking to me. You don't know how relieved I am to find out you have seen her too. I was afraid I was going out of my mind. I didn't tell anyone. You know how people are today. With all the channeling and mind swapping. One wrong word and they all go to making funny noises."

"Yes. I sure know what you mean. That's why I haven't wanted to say anything about this, even to you. But you said she talked to you. What did she say?"

"Not a lot really, just said I needed to talk to you. I guess she was right about that part, anyway."

"Think hard. Was there anything else, anything at all?"

"Well, yes. She said for me to tell you to stop fighting her, whatever that means. Does than mean anything to you?"

John got up and put his hands to his temples and walked about the room.

"Oh, my God. I can't believe this is really happening, and to us of all people. Boy, what would our friends make of this? They would have a field day, wouldn't they?"

"I guess they probably would, if we told them. But we are not going to tell them. Are we?"

"No. Not now, anyway. Someday when we have all of it maybe, but not now. So she said I should stop fighting her, did she? Well, I guess she is right about that, too. I have been resisting her. I didn't want to believe it was anything more than a dream." He stopped walking and sat down again, facing Tina.

"Listen. There is still a little more. I didn't think it was important, but now I know it is. In the story passed down from one family to another, there is the mention of an old wise woman. She was reputed to be the oldest person in the Anasazi nation. She was supposed to have been the one who taught old Ka Oto Ah, or whatever, when he was just a youngster. So the story goes she often showed up when he was in trouble, even after she had died. Strange, isn't it? I mean, how the pieces fit together when you have them all.

"I've been fighting her, and I guess she has been trying to talk to me, too, only I would not listen. Thank God you did and had the courage to tell me. Now maybe I can find out what she wants."

John pulled Tina up and held her in his embrace. He stood looking over the top of her head, out the window, out into the desert land beyond them.

"I don't know who to thank, the white man's God I have been brought up to know, or the ancient God of my Indian heritage. But whoever; I thank one and all for bringing you into my life."

"I feel the same way, John, but what brought this on?"

"Don't you see? Without you I might have gone all my life without finding this out. I might have resisted the ole girl and never let her communicate with me. Now I will be waiting for her the next time she tries to come through. Maybe she can give me some help in all this."

He picked the little maiden up and swung her around, knocking over a small table and lamp in his enthusiasm. Neither seemed to notice or care.

Tina, for her part, was content to be included in his inner most secret. She truly felt she was a part of his life, now and for all times. She had unknowingly contributed to his happiness, and he was sure she had helped him unlock a door that he did not even know was there. Tomorrow would surely be easier and more productive because of her.

But tomorrow and the days to follow were a bitter disappointment, as nothing happened. No matter how he tried, he could not conjure up the little old woman that had been pestering him of late. Now that he was ready, it seemed she had disappeared.

Chapter Sixty

"Hello. Tina?" John's voice sounded breathless, urgent.

"John? John, what's the matter?" Tina's voice was muffled, sleepy. She had been roused from a sound sleep by the insistent ringing of her bedside phone.

"Tina. I have to talk to you, now."

"All right, John, I'm sort of awake now. What's the matter?"

"Can you come over? I need to talk to you, not to a telephone with an abstract voice on the other end."

"Do you know what time it is? It's nearly midnight." Tina sat up in bed and looked at the clock on the nightstand.

"I know it's late, but please. Tina — It's happened."

Tina was wide-awake now. Her voice came back expectantly.

"You mean you have made contact?"

"Yes, Oh, I just have to talk to you. I have to tell somebody just to make sure it's real. And who else could I talk to?"

"All right, dear. I'll be there in, oh, say a half-hour. Okay?"

"Great. Look, I'll make a pot of coffee and dig up a little snack. We can have a midnight supper. How's that sound?"

"Fine, John. Just try to contain yourself until I get there. Promise me you won't go running off someplace half cocked?"

"Promise, but hurry."

Tina arrived, her hair tousled and her eyes still a little bleary. She didn't have on any make-up, but John thought she had never looked lovelier, and told her so.

"It must be love. If you can say that at this time of night and mean it, then it has to be love."

"Oh, I mean it all right. Come and sit down. I have coffee poured and some cheese and crackers and pickles. Not much of a supper, but I'm too excited to do any better."

"That will be fine. I think you are too excited to eat, anyway. So? Tell me all about it."

Tina took the big soft leather chair and picked up her cup of coffee while John paced back and forth.

"It's been three weeks. Every night I lie down and wait and nothing happens. I had about given up hope. Tonight was the first time that I went to bed without thinking about her. I was so tired I just dropped in bed and was about two thirds asleep when there she was. Right up there in the middle of the air, just floating there. But listen to this: she wasn't alone. She had someone with her."

Tina leaned forward, her cup of coffee forgotten, as was the bit of cheese in her other hand.

"Who?"

436 - Norman D. Messenger

"It was the ole boy himself. Yeah. He told me his name. It's Kaoto. It has nothing to do with a coyote. It has something to do with the bird we call the Roadrunner. And the old woman is Paataga." He stopped pacing and looked searchingly at the young woman's face to see if she would believe him. Satisfied, he went on.

"Boy, it's been quite a night. I wasn't prepared for all that happened after that. Tina, I know where the missing bead is. They showed me how to find it."

"Showed you? How did they show you?"

"Are you ready for this? They took me by the hand and they just lifted me up out of myself. Yeah, I could see me still lying in bed, asleep no less, but there I was up in the air with them, looking down on me. Then we were away up in the air, looking down on my house and all the countryside around. It was fantastic, just like being up in a balloon."

Tina raised one eyebrow skeptically. "Are you sure you are all right, dear? Your face is flushed. Do you have a fever?"

"Don't do that, hon'. You have to believe me. I have told you my story and I thought you would understand. After all, you were the one who told me you had seen this old woman Paataga."

"I'm sorry, John. Yes, of course I believe you, but this is kind of — different. I mean, I saw a misty vision of an old woman telling me to talk to you, but no names, no drifting off into space. I just don't want you to let your imagination get away with your enthusiasm."

"Trust me, hon'. This is not my imagination. I couldn't possibly have imagined all this. It's too wild, even for me. It had to be real. How else can I explain it?"

"Sorry. Go ahead. Tell me about it."

"Well, we were up in the air, and the next thing I know we are over the Grand Canyon. Way up high, like an aerial photo. Then we let down slow-like so I could identify each landmark, until we came down in this little canyon just off the main river. There was this waterfall and pretty green water. There were some people living there, but they were all asleep. They took me over to the base of the cliff and just sort of drifted up the path to the point of rock. When we got there this old man, only he did not seem old, sort of ageless, he could have been old or young - I can't seem to recall now - anyway he pointed to a crack in the rock at my feet, and said dig.

"The crack was filled in with dirt and old leaves until it was hard to dig, but I know the bead is down there. I could see it down under all that junk. I tried to pick it up, but my fingers seemed to just pass right through it.

"Then Kaoto told me I would have to return in my own body. Yeah, that's what he said. Come back in my own body and dig it up. He said when I had the bead I would understand.

I asked him what I would understand, but he just kept repeating 'You will understand,' and the old woman, Paataga, kept smiling and nodding her head. They faded away and I was frightened to be left there by myself. I was thinking, 'How am I going to get out of here?' Then I woke up here in my bed." He stopped, breathless from his long, hurried speech. He waited for a reaction from Tina.

The young woman put down her cup and brushed the crumbs from her fingers. She did not look at him for a few moments. Finally she spoke.

"What are you going to do about it?"

"I'm going to look for it." Seeing the young woman's slight frown, he added, "I want you to come with me. No more going off alone. No more leaving you out. I want you with me. Partly to prove to you that it was real. So you will know, without a shadow of a doubt, that I do find the bead in the crack in the rock, that it's not something I make up or pretend to find."

"John, I do believe you. I would never accuse you of making up a story like this."

"I know, but if you are there with me when I dig it up, well, maybe I will know it's true, too. Otherwise, there would always be a little doubt hanging over it. Don't you see what I mean?"

"Yes, I do. And I will go with you. When are we going? How are we going to get there? Are you sure you can find it again? After all, as you told me earlier, there are hundreds of little canyons down there. How will you know where to look?"

John went to the coffee table beside the chair and picked up a folded piece of paper. Unfolding it, he spread it out on Tina's lap. It was a photo taken from high above the canyon. He carefully placed his finger at the lower end of the canyon where a little stream made its way down to join the Colorado River.

"Right there, that's the place. I've been looking over this photo for a year now. After I called you I got it out again, and there it was, just like I had seen it from the air with them."

Tina looked at the place he had indicated. Then sweeping her eyes over the entire area, she said, "It's going to be hard to get to, isn't it? I mean, there are no roads, not even any trails showing up. Even a little trail would show up on something like this. But that's about as remote as you could find."

"Helicopter. Just like the pilot who found my father. We'll go to the canyon and rent a 'copter. I'll show the pilot where I want him to take us on the map. After that it's up to him to get us there. Once there, we land and I will climb — we will climb up to the point, and I will find the bead."

"You make it sound simple."

"Really it is, that's the easy part. It's after I find it that worries me. What will I do with it then?"

"Didn't you say this Kaoto, or whoever, said you would understand?"

"That's what he said."

"Well? If you're willing to believe him enough to go looking for this lost bead, why don't you believe enough to think you'll understand?"

"Now you're the one making it sound simple."

"There's only one way to find out. When do we go?"

"I'm ready to leave right now. I couldn't go back to sleep. I'd be afraid I'd wake up in the morning and not be able to remember it, or think it was just a dream. That's why I wanted you to come over and talk to me now instead of waiting until morning. How about you? Can you go now?"

"Sure. Why not? Only let me run back home and pack a few things while you get dressed and pack your shaving gear and toothbrush. I don't think anything else would matter to you."

John seemed to realize for the first time that he was still in his robe and slippers. He had been so excited he had not taken time to get dressed, or even to try to calm down his wild hair.

The 'copter settled easily onto a narrow strip of sandy soil beside an emerald green piece of water. Up ahead, waterfalls fell gracefully into the stream. In the pool, at the base of the falls, several children splashed and frolicked. The thunder of the falls had drowned out the sound of the 'copter. Higher up on the bank, close to their landing spot, a small cluster of clay huts and branch covered patios sat silently in the afternoon sun. A few adults had wandered out at the sound of the machine, and now stood watching John and Tina as they climbed out.

"I guess we'd better go introduce ourselves. In my dream they were all asleep."

"What a place. It's like those movies about those places lost and cut off from the rest of the world. I wouldn't be surprised to see a dinosaur come walking up out of the water."

Taking Tina by the hand, John led her up to an elderly man who sat in the sun. He had not gotten up at their landing, and did not bother to get up as they approached on foot.

"Hello."

"Hmmmm." The elderly man raised one hand in greeting.

"My name is John. This is my wife to be, Tina."

"Hmmmm." Again the wave of the hand in greeting.

John shifted from one foot to the other nervously, not knowing just what to say, or how to explain his reason for being here. These people were evidently used to an occasional tourist dropping, in but would they allow him to wander about and dig up artifacts?

"My father grew up here. As a small boy he flew out of here on one of these machines. Maybe you remember him. His name was, —" John had to stop and think for a moment to recall the name his father had used down here. "He was called Muat."

The elderly man's eyes showed interest for the first time.

"Muat? I grew up with Muat. He left before we reached our manhood. How is my old friend Muat? I had hoped he would come back and visit us some-time."

"I'm sorry to say he died last summer. He talked of coming back, but never seemed to find time."

"Time? We have lots of time here. He should have come back. We would have given him all the time he needed." There was a faint twinkle in the old man's eyes, making John think he was not as ignorant as he had first believed.

"What can we do for the son of Muat? You have not come just to tell me of your father's death."

"No." How much should he tell this old man? Would these people understand and believe him if he told them the whole story? Why not? They were closer to the truth here than he was. After all weren't their lives tied up in this mixture of legend and myths?

He squatted down before the old one and told him all he knew, including the visit from Paataga and Kaoto and their instructions about finding the bead.

"Hmmmm." The old one seemed to be in deep thought. After a prolonged silence he spoke again.

"It is good. The story needs to be told. One has only to look at you to know you are of the line of Kaoto. Tell me, are you a good runner, also?"

"Well, yes, as a matter of fact, I am. I don't mean to brag, but no one could catch me in track. But why do you ask? Is it important?"

"Important? No, I just wondered. According to the old stories, Kaoto was the greatest runner of the nation. That is where he got his name, you know."

"Yes, it was mentioned to me, something about a bird."

"Yes, it is a shorter version for the little desert bird who runs rather than flies. Oh, yes I know about such things. I, too, have been out of the canyon, but I chose to come back. I like it better here." His smile was real now. It was as if he were enjoying a private joke at John's expense.

"What I need to know is if it's all right for me to go up to the ledge and try to find the bead. I don't want to impose on anything that is sacred to you and the people."

"No problem. Go. Dig. Find it if you can. You have as much right as anyone else, maybe more. They were your people, also. No one else has every really looked for it. After your father left, taking the beads with him, no one cared to find just one. It is probably up there. Otherwise, they would not have bothered to tell you so."

The bead was exactly where he had been shown it would be. Tina watched him as he dug it up and held it in his hands with such reverence it could have been a piece of Christ's own garment.

He showed it to the old one, who was only mildly interested, and then hurried to the copter. He could not wait to get back home and put it with the others.

"There. How's that for blending the old with the new? Seven hundred year old beads on a nylon fish string?"

The beads were all strung now in the order in which John knew they should be. But what now? What was he going to do with them? The old man had told him he would understand. Understand what? What had he hoped they would tell him? Somehow he was disappointed. Perhaps he had expected too much. What did he expect? A clap of thunder, a bolt of lighting, then an old Indian Shaman descending from the clouds to hand him a scroll with all the hidden secrets of the Anasazi written on it? That would have been impossible. They did not have a written language.

He placed them back in a new leather pouch, pulled the drawstring, and dropped it back into his desk drawer. Patience, that was what he needed, and time. Maybe he should go back to the canyon and get some of the time they had so much of, or maybe, just maybe, he needed to go back there to be able to understand.

No, that did not make sense. Kaoto and his people had not started there. He needed to go to where it all began. But where was that?"

"What a place to spend your honeymoon. Are you sorry you came?" John sat at a portable table. A compact portable typewriter sat in front of him, waiting.

"I agree, it is different, but, no, I am not sorry. I asked to be let into your life. Well, I'm in, aren't I?"

"As far in as anyone can be. This will make our friends really go nuts when they find out we came down here to Chaco Canyon and lived in a tent on the bluff for a honeymoon."

"To each his own. This is where you would have to come anyway some time. So why not now? After all, people supposedly go away on a honeymoon to get away from their friends and family and work. Well, who would look for us here?"

"Right. It was nice of the park people to let us set our tent up here. They said it was late enough in the season that summer tourists wouldn't bother us very much. They also said that most of the people who come down here to walk around are the type of people who respect others and will leave them alone unless they're invited."

"Hmmmm. Well, lets not invite anyone just yet. What do you say?"

"Right. We can divide the days for work and the nights for-"

"Nights for visions? I hope those old folks understand about honeymoons and newlyweds. I mean, I like them and all, but not just now. If you know what I mean." Tina pinched his cheek as she turned to check on the dinner she was cooking over a Coleman.

"Who do you suppose would be the most embarrassed? Us or them? Relax, hon'. I'm sure they knew about love just as we do, and from all I can understand about their way of life, they respected each person's privacy as much or more than we do."

Tina went on with her meal as John draped the string of ancient beads around his neck. He leaned back and thoughtfully ran his fingers over them. Suddenly he felt a faint tinkling in his hand as his fingers caressed the lost bead, the one he had just recovered and strung at the beginning of the string. The sensation grew as he carefully traced the time-worn designs etched on its surface.

Although the sky was clear, he felt like darkness was descending over him. He wiped his eyes but the darkness continued. He became frightened and was about to call to Tina when a blinding flash of light appeared for a second.

High up in the fall sky, the Spirit Watcher was roused from his long sleep. What had disturbed his sleep? He had thought he had heard someone call for him. But who? His people were all gone from the land. They were scattered to the winds. They were dead and buried over a vast stretch of desert and mountains. Who? Who had dared to blaspheme his sleep by calling him in the name of the People?

Looking down, the Spirit Watcher saw two people on a bluff overlooking his favorite valley. They were strangers to him, but somehow they did seem familiar, and they were calling for him in the name of the People. The man, tall, covered with soft downy hair, long nose, built like a runner even if he was sitting at a table with a foreign machine. And the young woman? Where had he seen that face before? She did not look like an Anasazi, yet there was some resemblance. And those eyes. Yes. He knew those eyes.

A great tear rolled from the corner of his eye and splashed down his cheek, scattering into a shower of tiny droplets as it fell down through the cloudless sky.

A sense of peace and serenity settled over the young man on the top of the bluff looking down on the ruined remains of Pueblo Bonito. He saw a young man running down the roadway, little puffs of dust churning up at each step. He was carrying some small person on his back. Off across the road an old woman was walking, swinging a stick, and knocking people out of her way as she went.

The young man's hands were flying over the keyboard of his typewriter and each page, as it came out, was handed to a tiny young woman with two colored eyes. She was quietly reading, unmindful of their dinner growing cold on the table between them.

"In the beginning, the Spirit Watcher was asleep. He didn't travel the sky each day and then go to sleep at night. Instead, he was so sound asleep that nothing seemed to wake him. The world was dark; there was nothing living on the face of the earth. The people existed, but they all moved deep in the ground and were afraid to come out into the darkness.

"Then something happened to the earth. It was shaken by some sleeping giant."

"What did you say dear? I wasn't listening." John looked up from his typing.

"Oh. Nothing." Tina looked up from the page she was reading, wiping a few sprinkles of moisture from the paper. "I was just thinking how in a dry land like this, and on a clear day, still there are times when you feel a few drops of water, like it was starting to rain."

THE END

Epilogue

No one knows for a certainty what really happened to The People, the Anasazi. We have very little to go on, but as I said at the beginning of this book, Kaoto and Paataga were apparently pleased with what I wrote about them, so I will let the book speak for them.

The Hopi claim the Anasazi were a part of their ancestors. This is probably true. Still there was a large population that literally disappeared from the face of the earth without leaving a clue. I am sure that some of the population was the "Weed-Eaters" the Aztec spoke of. They spoke of "small people" who came from the north and lived on bugs and weeds around the edge of the lakes because there was no land for them to claim. They reckoned their time of arrival at about the same time the Anasazi were disappearing from their homes in the north.

Slaves were common among the Indian tribes and it is quite probable that some of the Anasazi were taken prisoners and the savages learned from them the ways of farming and pueblo building that still exists in the southwest. The successful farming practice followed in the southwest was different than those in any other part of the world.

There has been speculation recently about the signs of cannibalism found at some of the Anasazi building sites. It has been said that maybe cannibalism was used as a method to control The People. I find this objectionable.

The People were peaceful, farming people. They were not skilled in the arts of war. And being raised as a farmer myself, I doubt that they ever considered cannibalism. There is no denying the signs of flesh eating and the breaking of the bones to get to the marrow. The signs are there and they are true. My contention however, remains that the cannibalism was practiced by the savage, nomadic, Plains-Indians who oppressed the Anasazi and drove them from their homes. It was these nomadic Indians that resorted to eating their enemies. The nomads were primarily meat eaters in the first place, while the Anasazi diet consisted mostly of grains, berries and roots with a small amount of meat to complete their diet.

The savages were in the habit of eating meat; so eating a portion of their enemy after a battle would be acceptable. They did not eat the Anasazi out of hunger, nor as a method of control. They ate their enemy because they thought they could gain the knowledge, skills, and bravery possessed by them. Just as with other animals, the heart and brain was considered the prime portion. But since there was not enough to go around for everyone, only the leaders, the brave and the best were entitled to these. The rest of the body was parceled out to the remaining people, so that they too could feel they were participating in the ritual. Women and children were probably given the lesser pieces and quite possible they were the ones who broke the bones open for the marrow inside to feed to the babies.

Still, to the Anasazi, this practice must have been considered horribly barbaric and disgusting. It was most likely the reason they took to hiding the burial places of their dead, so the enemy could not find the bodies and desecrate them.

To the best of our knowledge, there are no true Anasazi left. All that could possibly remain would be the descendants of cross breeding between the slaves and their captors. The bloodline would be so diluted by now that it would be almost impossible to trace. DNA testing might someday prove more about where they went and what happened to them but it would still not account for all of them.

From the publisher...

I hope you enjoyed this story as much as I did. If you didn't, please tell me. If you did, please tell others.

Soon, you'll be able to find this book in other formats including hardback and other eBook formats. Please check with us frequently at our website.

Thank you.
Kokopelli Publishing, L.L.C.

www.kokopellipublishing.com

Kokopelli Publishing.com

JUST WHAT YOU'VE BEEN WAITING FOR...

Order Form

Postal Orders:
Kokopelli Publishing, L.L.C.
3236 Foxridge Dr.
Colorado Springs, CO 80916 - USA

Please send me a copy of KAOTO in the following formats:

TITLE	QTY	PRICE	TOTAL
PDF on CDROM	____	$14.95	_____
6x9 Paperback	____	$15.95	_____
6x9 Hardback	____	$25.95	_____

Subtotal _____

(Colorado Residents) TAX 6.1% _____

Shipping by UPS/USPS:
$5.00 for the first book/CD and   Shipping _____
$1.00 for each additional product.

TOTAL _____

Name: _____

Address: _____

City: _____ State: ____ Zip: _____

Telephone: _____

email address: _____

Or you can order online at:

www.kokopellipublishing.com

Order Form

Postal Orders:

Kokopelli Publishing, L.L.C.
3236 Foxridge Dr.
Colorado Springs, CO 80916 - USA

Please send me a copy of KAOTO in the following formats:

TITLE	QTY	PRICE	TOTAL
PDF on CDROM	____	$14.95	_____
6x9 Paperback	____	$15.95	_____
6x9 Hardback	____	$25.95	_____

Subtotal _____

(Colorado Residents) TAX 6.1% _____

Shipping by UPS/USPS:

$5.00 for the first book/CD and   Shipping _____
$1.00 for each additional product.

TOTAL _____

Name: _____

Address: _____

City: _____ State: ___ Zip: _____

Telephone: _____

email address: _____

Or you can order online at:

www.kokopellipublishing.com